THE WALKING DEAD

BOOK THIRTEEN

a continuing story of survival horror.

created by Robert Kirkman

image comics presents

The Walking Dead

book thirteen

ROBERT KIRKMAN
creator, writer

CHARLIE ADLARD
penciler, cover

STEFANO GAUDIANO
inker

CLIFF RATHBURN
gray tones

RUS WOOTON
letterer

SEAN MACKIEWICZ
editor

Original series covers by
CHARLIE ADLARD & DAVE STEWART

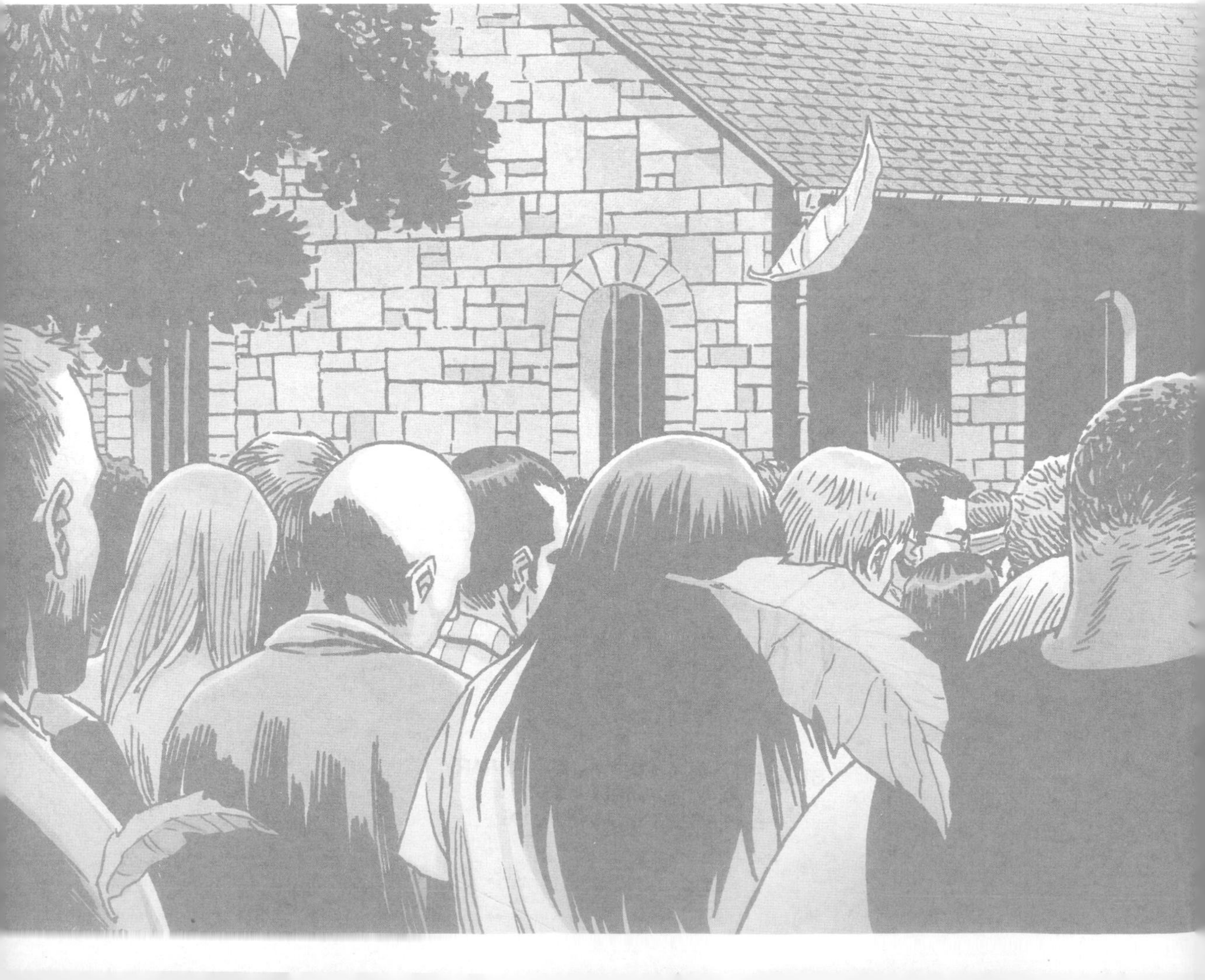

THE WALKING DEAD, BOOK THIRTEEN. First Printing. Published by Image Comics, Inc., Office of publication: 2001 Center Street, 6th Floor, Berkeley, California 94704. PRINTED IN CANADA. ISBN: 978-1-63215-916-8

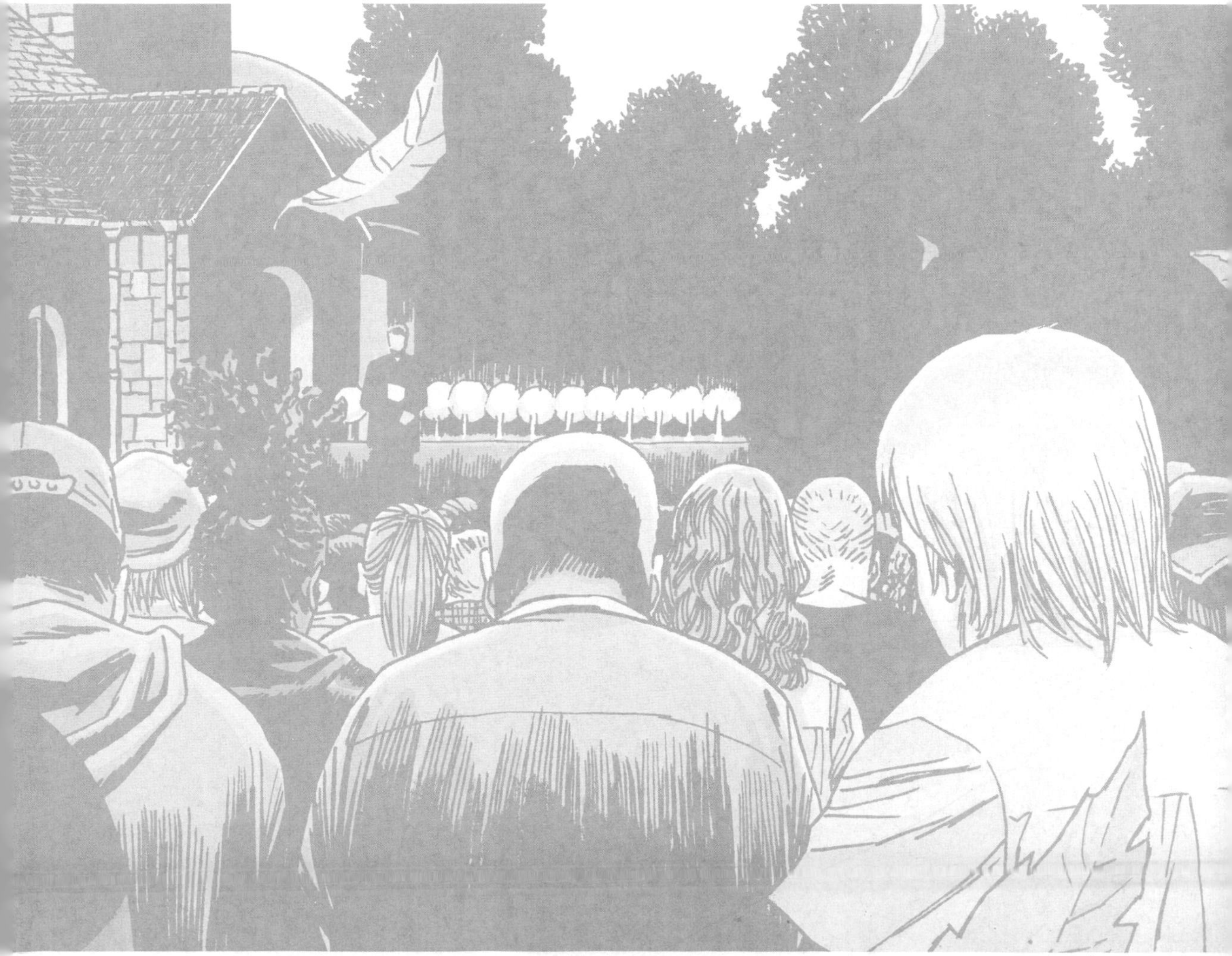

Chapter Twenty-Five:
No Turning Back

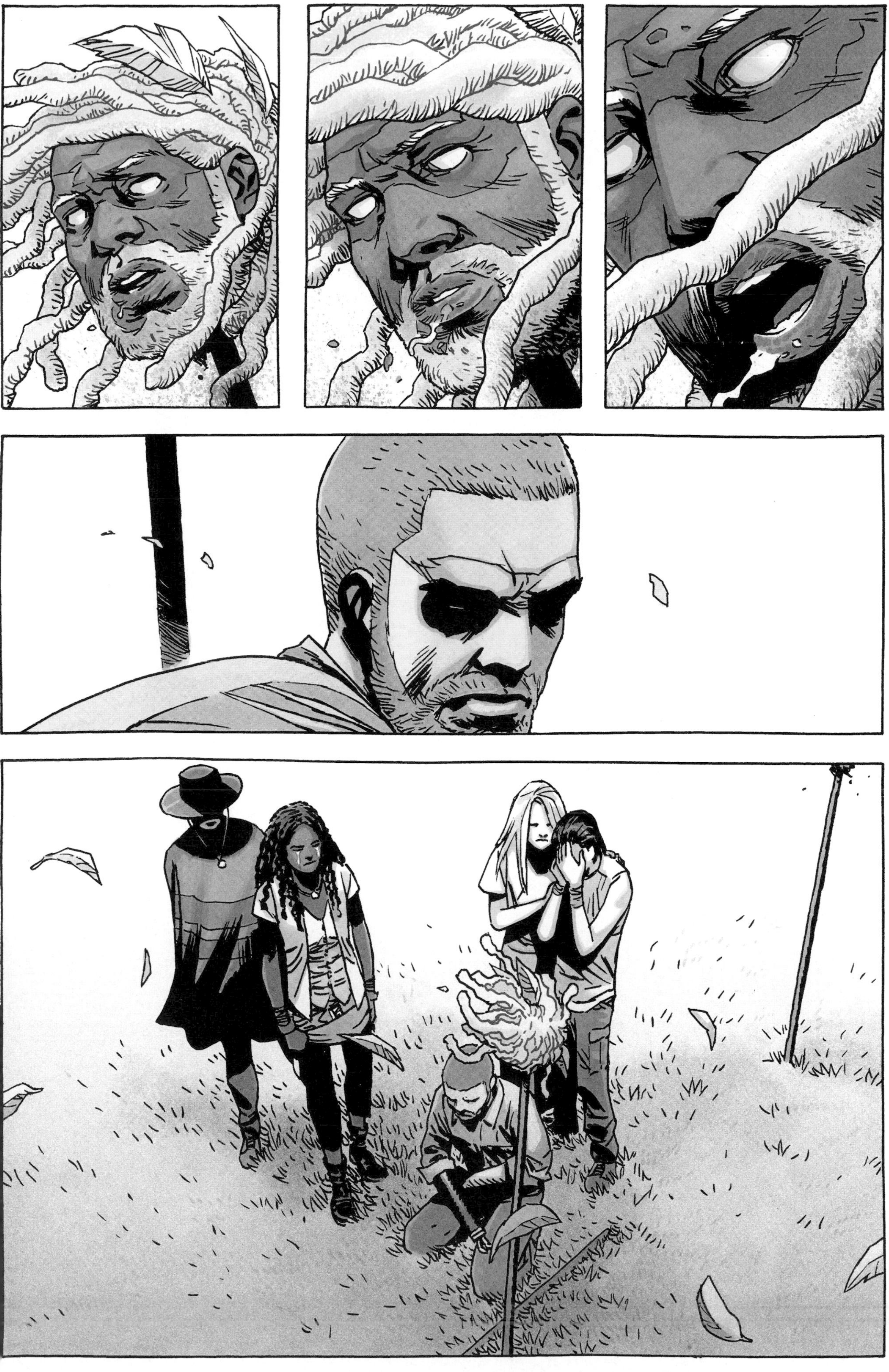

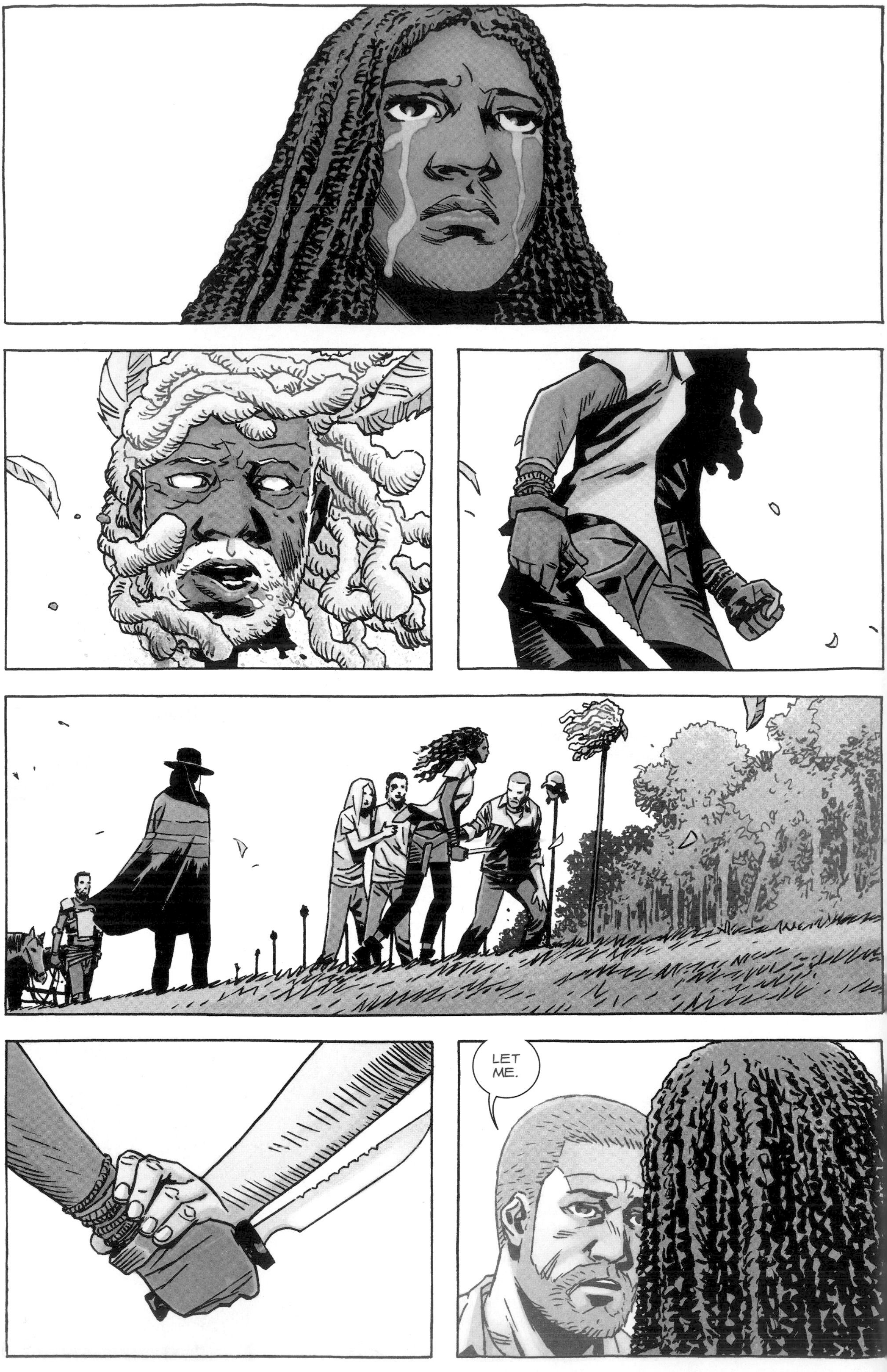
LET ME.

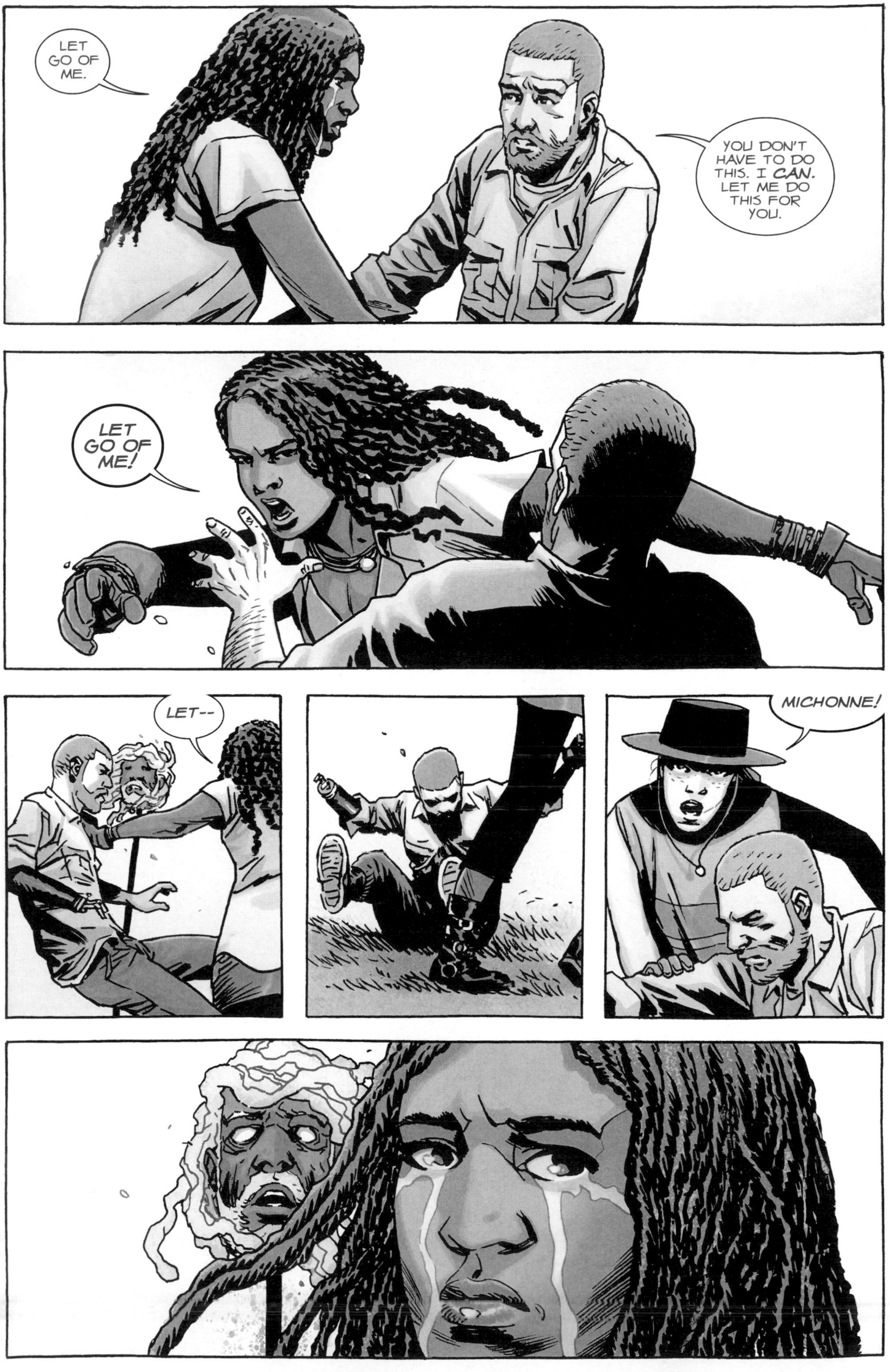
LET GO OF ME.
YOU DON'T HAVE TO DO THIS. I CAN. LET ME DO THIS FOR YOU.
LET GO OF ME!
LET--
MICHONNE!

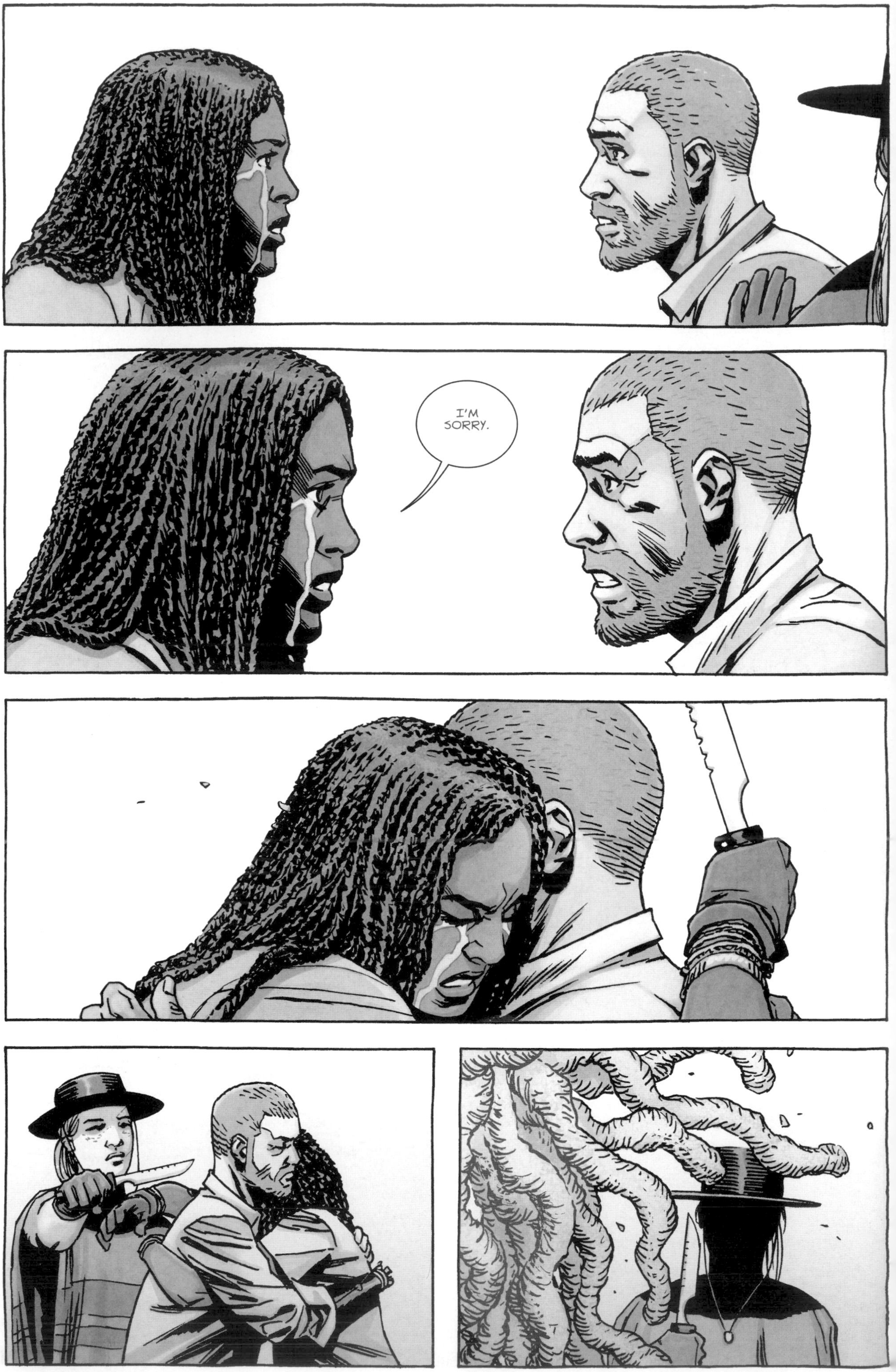
I'M SORRY.

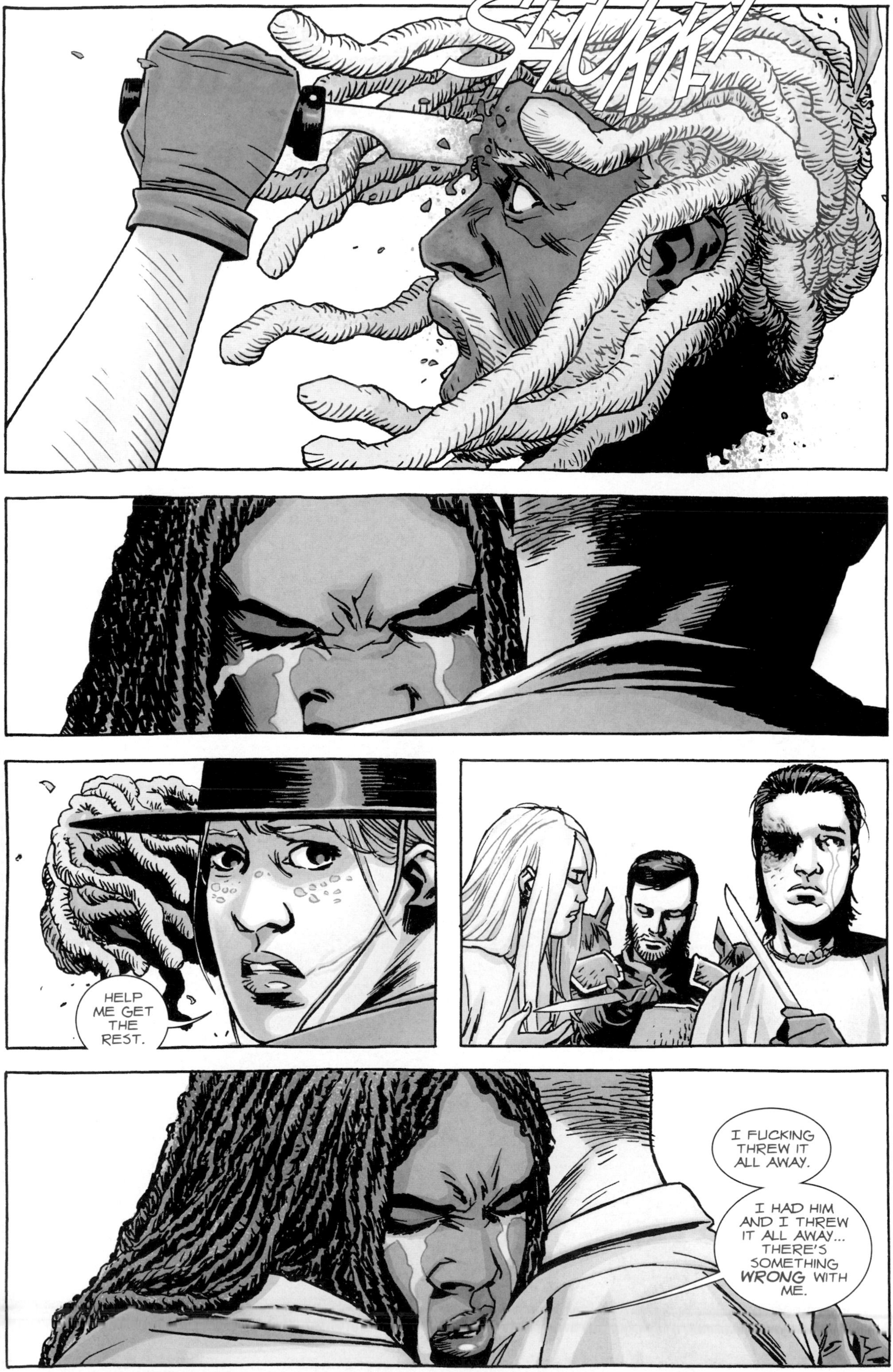

SHUKK!
HELP ME GET THE REST.
I FUCKING THREW IT ALL AWAY.
I HAD HIM AND I THREW IT ALL AWAY... THERE'S SOMETHING WRONG WITH ME.

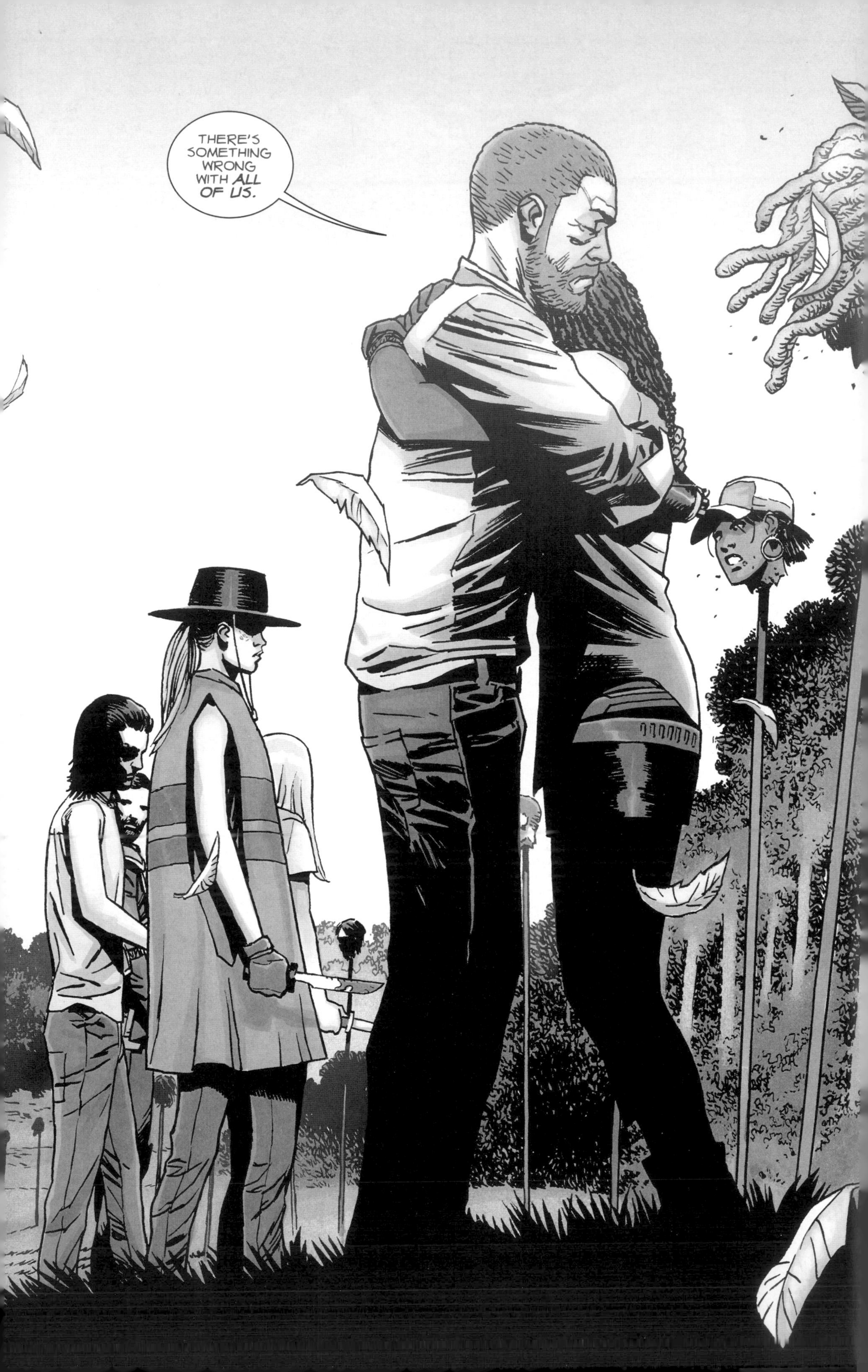
THERE'S SOMETHING WRONG WITH ALL OF US.

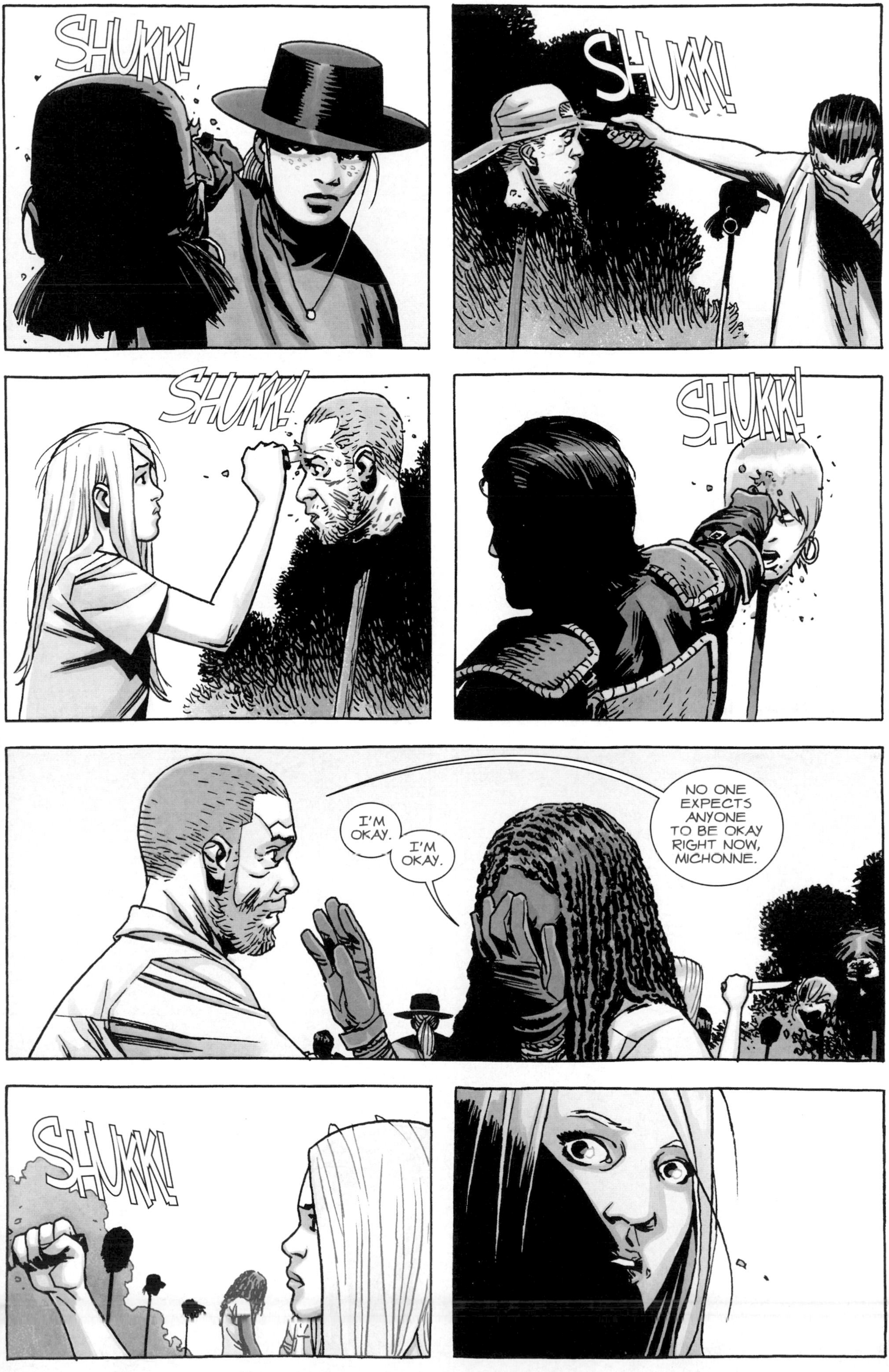
SHUKK!
SHUKK!
SHUKK!
SHUKK!
I'M OKAY.
I'M OKAY.
NO ONE EXPECTS ANYONE TO BE OKAY RIGHT NOW, MICHONNE.
SHUKK!

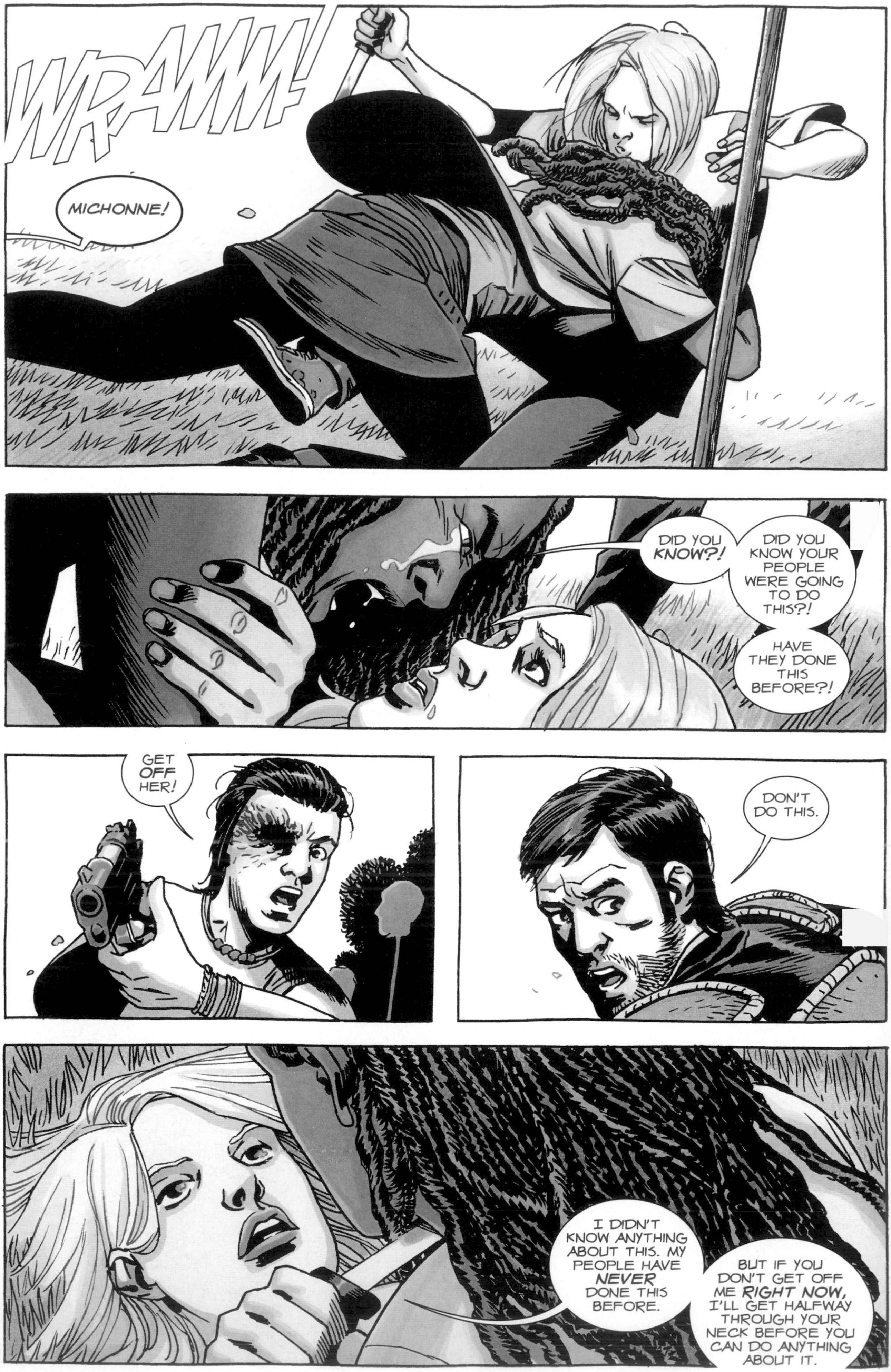
WRAMM!
MICHONNE!
DID YOU KNOW?!
DID YOU KNOW YOUR PEOPLE WERE GOING TO DO THIS?!
HAVE THEY DONE THIS BEFORE?!
GET OFF HER!
DON'T DO THIS.
I DIDN'T KNOW ANYTHING ABOUT THIS. MY PEOPLE HAVE NEVER DONE THIS BEFORE.
BUT IF YOU DON'T GET OFF ME RIGHT NOW, I'LL GET HALFWAY THROUGH YOUR NECK BEFORE YOU CAN DO ANYTHING ABOUT IT.

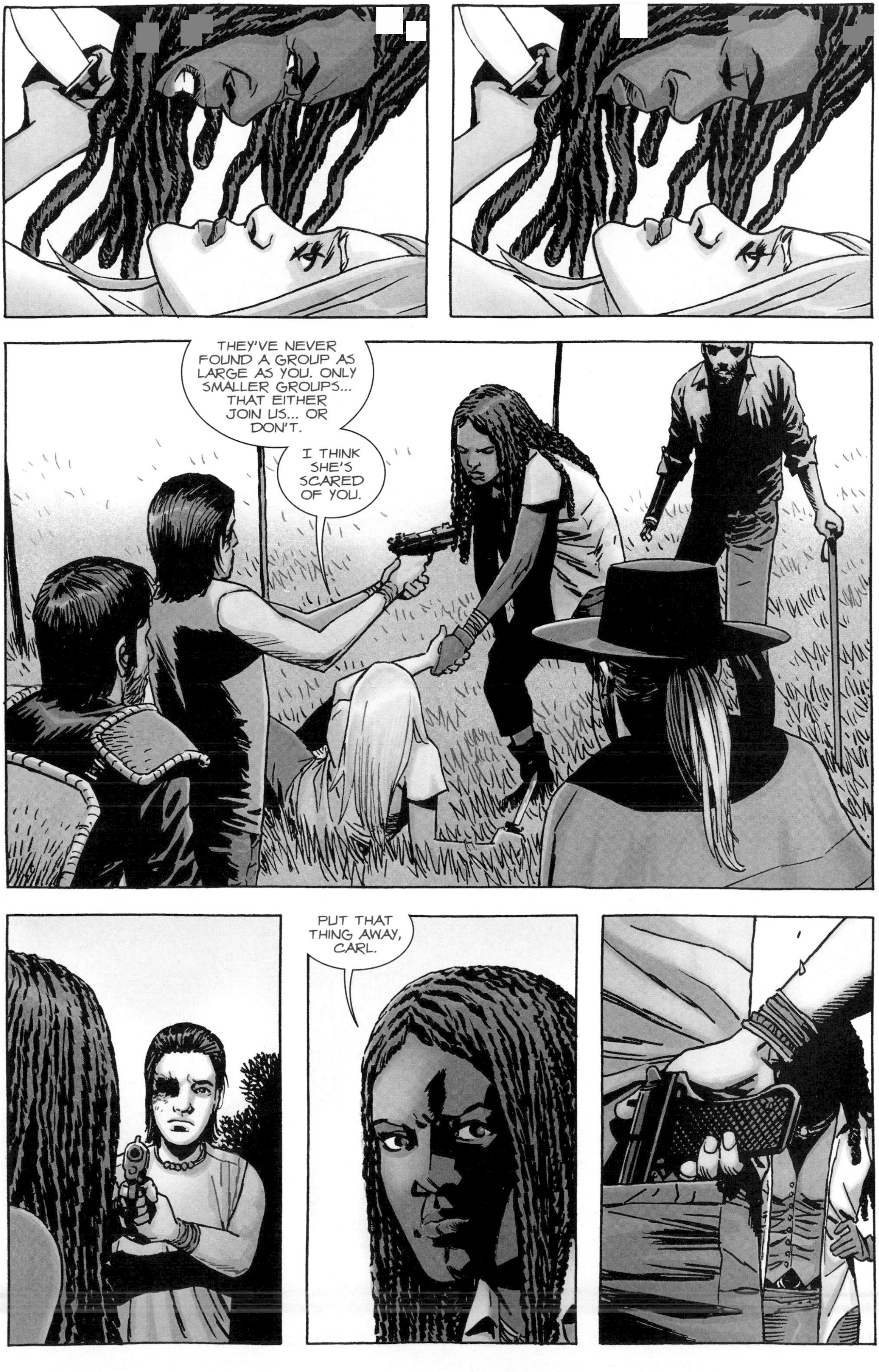
THEY'VE NEVER FOUND A GROUP AS LARGE AS YOU. ONLY SMALLER GROUPS... THAT EITHER JOIN US... OR DON'T.
I THINK SHE'S SCARED OF YOU.
PUT THAT THING AWAY, CARL.

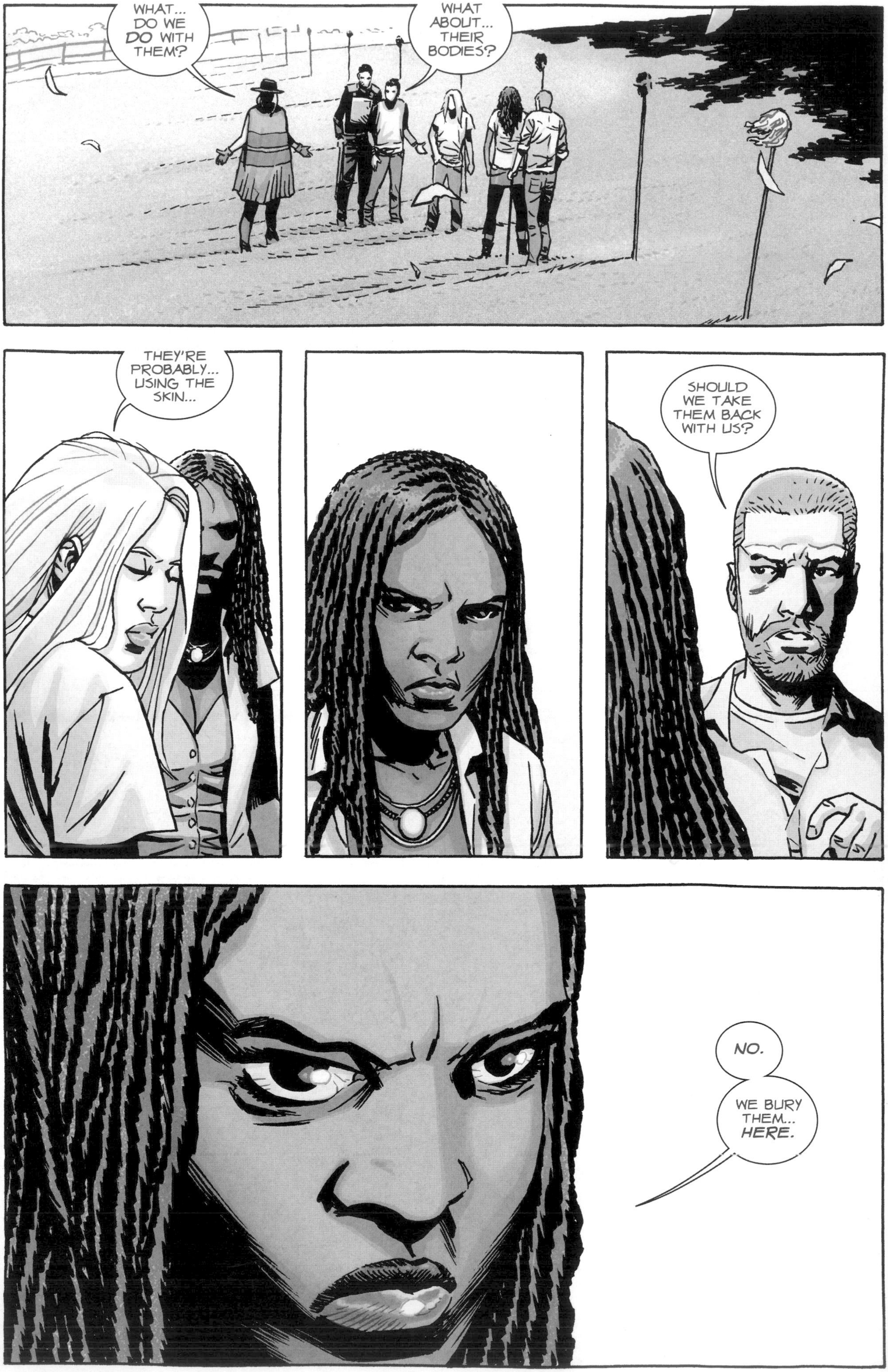
WHAT... DO WE *DO* WITH THEM?
WHAT ABOUT... THEIR BODIES?
THEY'RE PROBABLY... USING THE SKIN...
SHOULD WE TAKE THEM BACK WITH US?
NO.
WE BURY THEM... *HERE.*

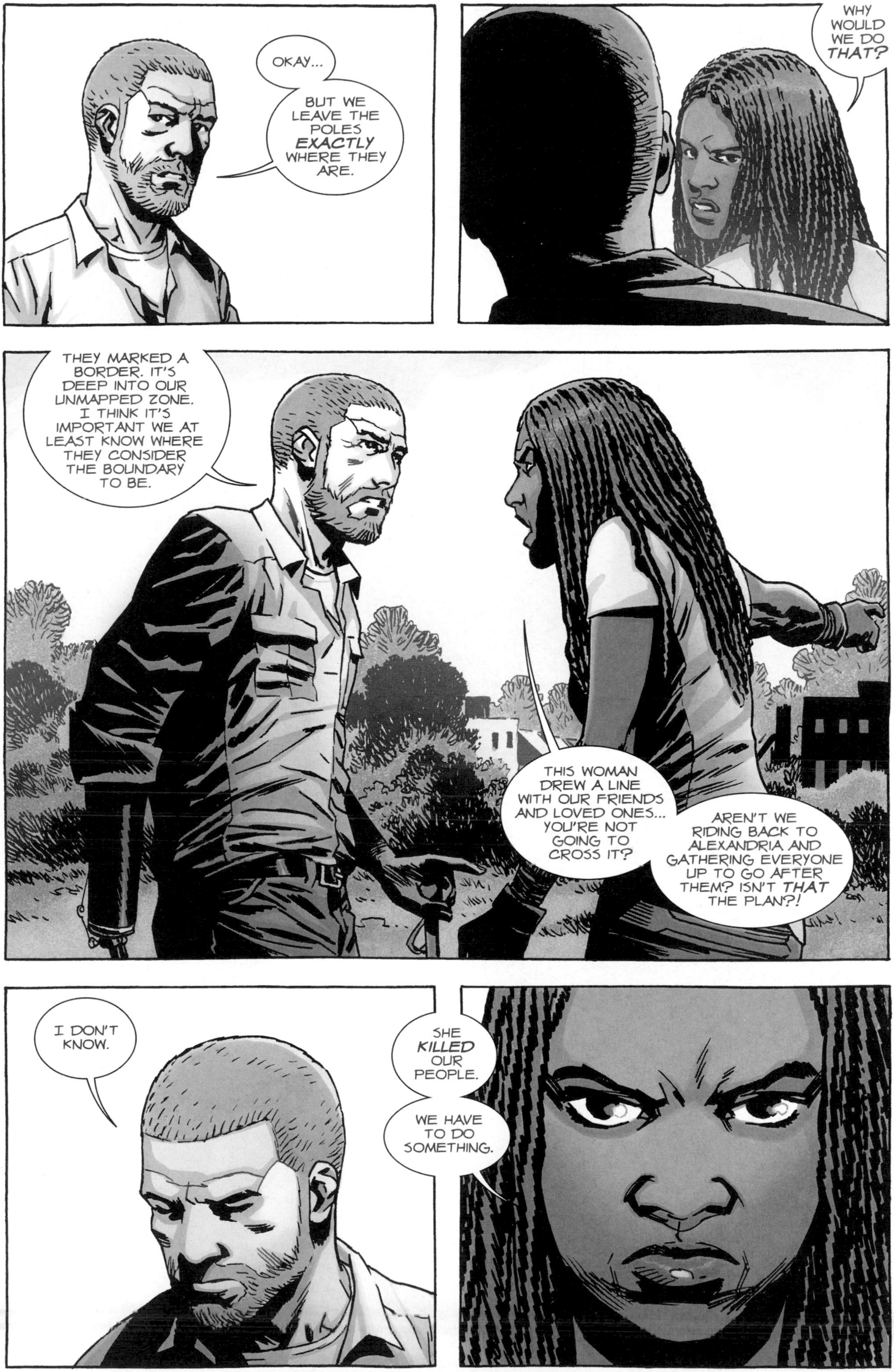
OKAY...
BUT WE LEAVE THE POLES EXACTLY WHERE THEY ARE.
WHY WOULD WE DO THAT?
THEY MARKED A BORDER. IT'S DEEP INTO OUR UNMAPPED ZONE. I THINK IT'S IMPORTANT WE AT LEAST KNOW WHERE THEY CONSIDER THE BOUNDARY TO BE.
THIS WOMAN DREW A LINE WITH OUR FRIENDS AND LOVED ONES... YOU'RE NOT GOING TO CROSS IT?
AREN'T WE RIDING BACK TO ALEXANDRIA AND GATHERING EVERYONE UP TO GO AFTER THEM? ISN'T THAT THE PLAN?!
I DON'T KNOW.
SHE KILLED OUR PEOPLE.
WE HAVE TO DO SOMETHING.

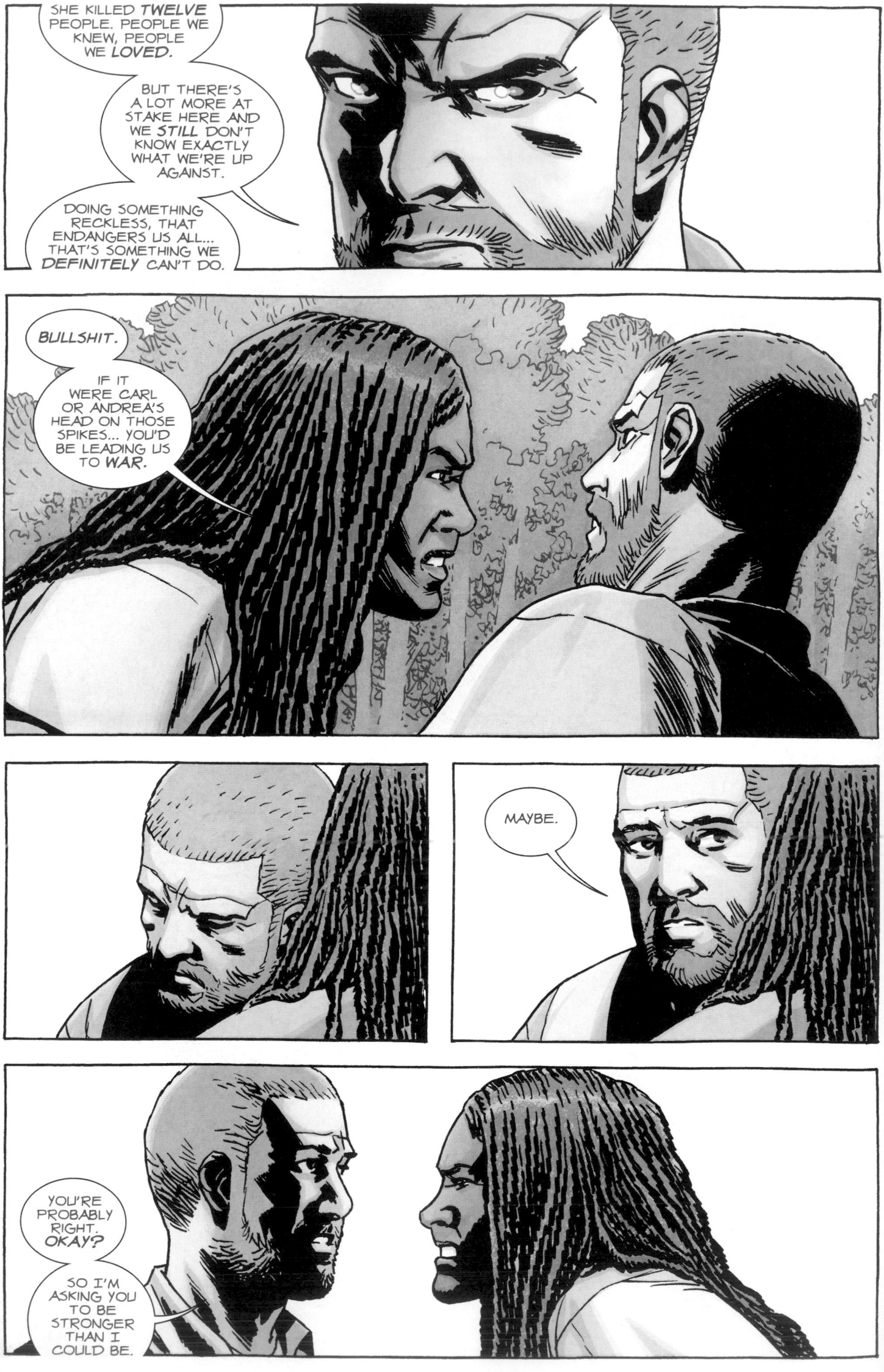
SHE KILLED TWELVE PEOPLE. PEOPLE WE KNEW, PEOPLE WE LOVED.
BUT THERE'S A LOT MORE AT STAKE HERE AND WE STILL DON'T KNOW EXACTLY WHAT WE'RE UP AGAINST.
DOING SOMETHING RECKLESS, THAT ENDANGERS US ALL... THAT'S SOMETHING WE DEFINITELY CAN'T DO.
BULLSHIT.
IF IT WERE CARL OR ANDREA'S HEAD ON THOSE SPIKES... YOU'D BE LEADING US TO WAR.
MAYBE.
YOU'RE PROBABLY RIGHT. OKAY?
SO I'M ASKING YOU TO BE STRONGER THAN I COULD BE.

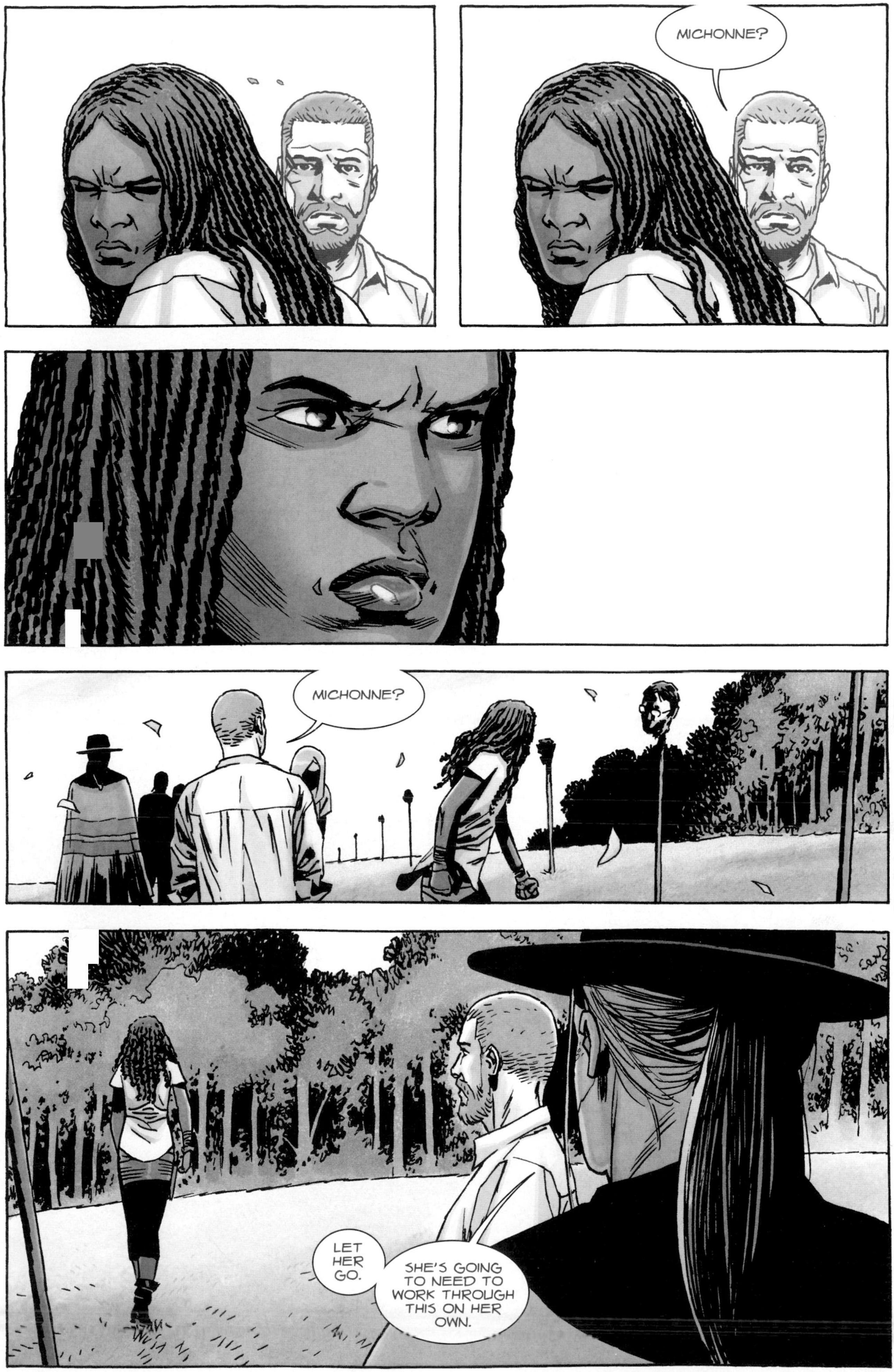
MICHONNE?
MICHONNE?
LET HER GO.
SHE'S GOING TO NEED TO WORK THROUGH THIS ON HER OWN.

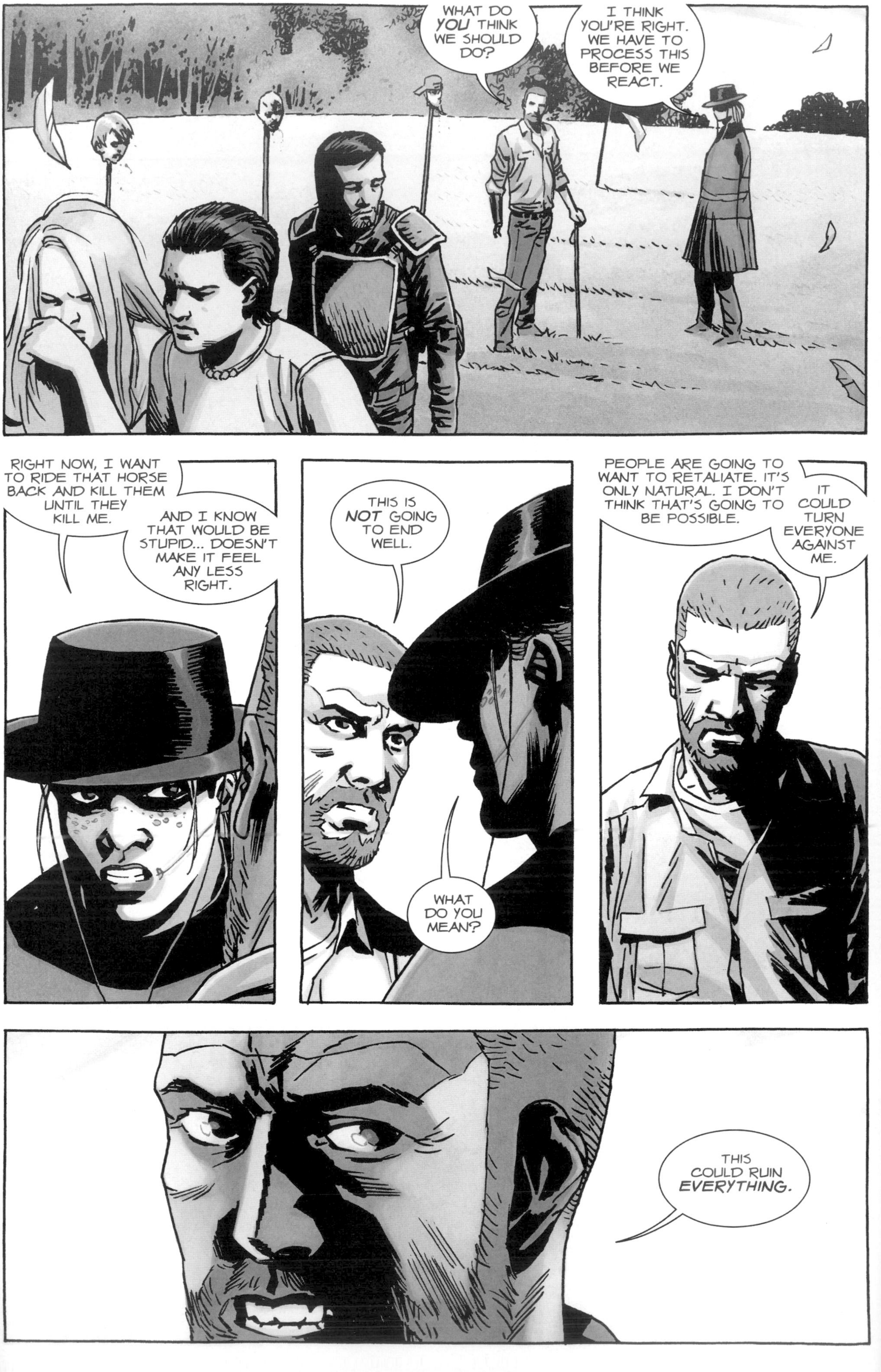
WHAT DO YOU THINK WE SHOULD DO?
I THINK YOU'RE RIGHT. WE HAVE TO PROCESS THIS BEFORE WE REACT.
RIGHT NOW, I WANT TO RIDE THAT HORSE BACK AND KILL THEM UNTIL THEY KILL ME.
AND I KNOW THAT WOULD BE STUPID... DOESN'T MAKE IT FEEL ANY LESS RIGHT.
THIS IS NOT GOING TO END WELL.
WHAT DO YOU MEAN?
PEOPLE ARE GOING TO WANT TO RETALIATE. IT'S ONLY NATURAL. I DON'T THINK THAT'S GOING TO BE POSSIBLE.
IT COULD TURN EVERYONE AGAINST ME.
THIS COULD RUIN EVERYTHING.

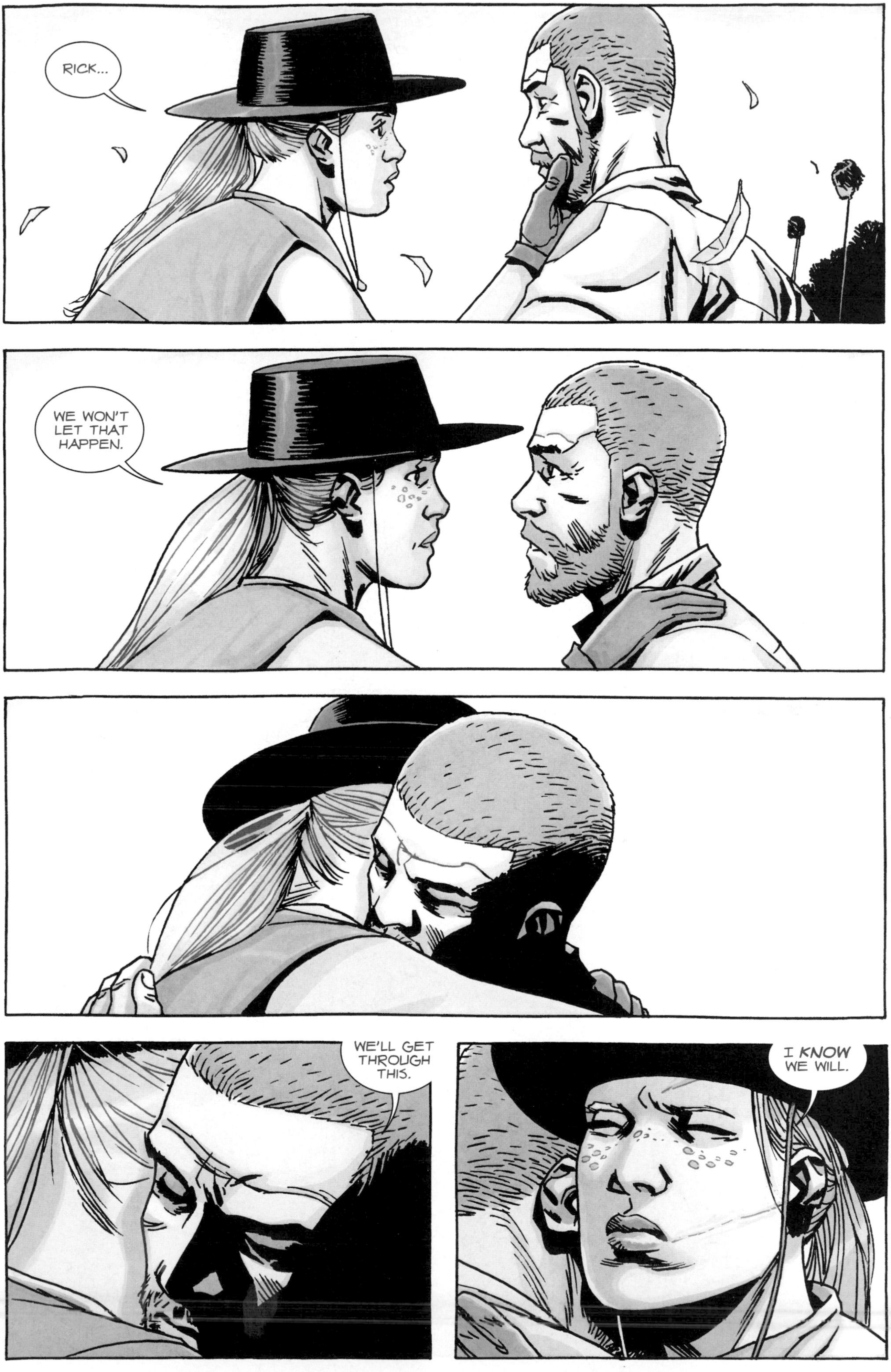
RICK...
WE WON'T LET THAT HAPPEN.
WE'LL GET THROUGH THIS.
I KNOW WE WILL.

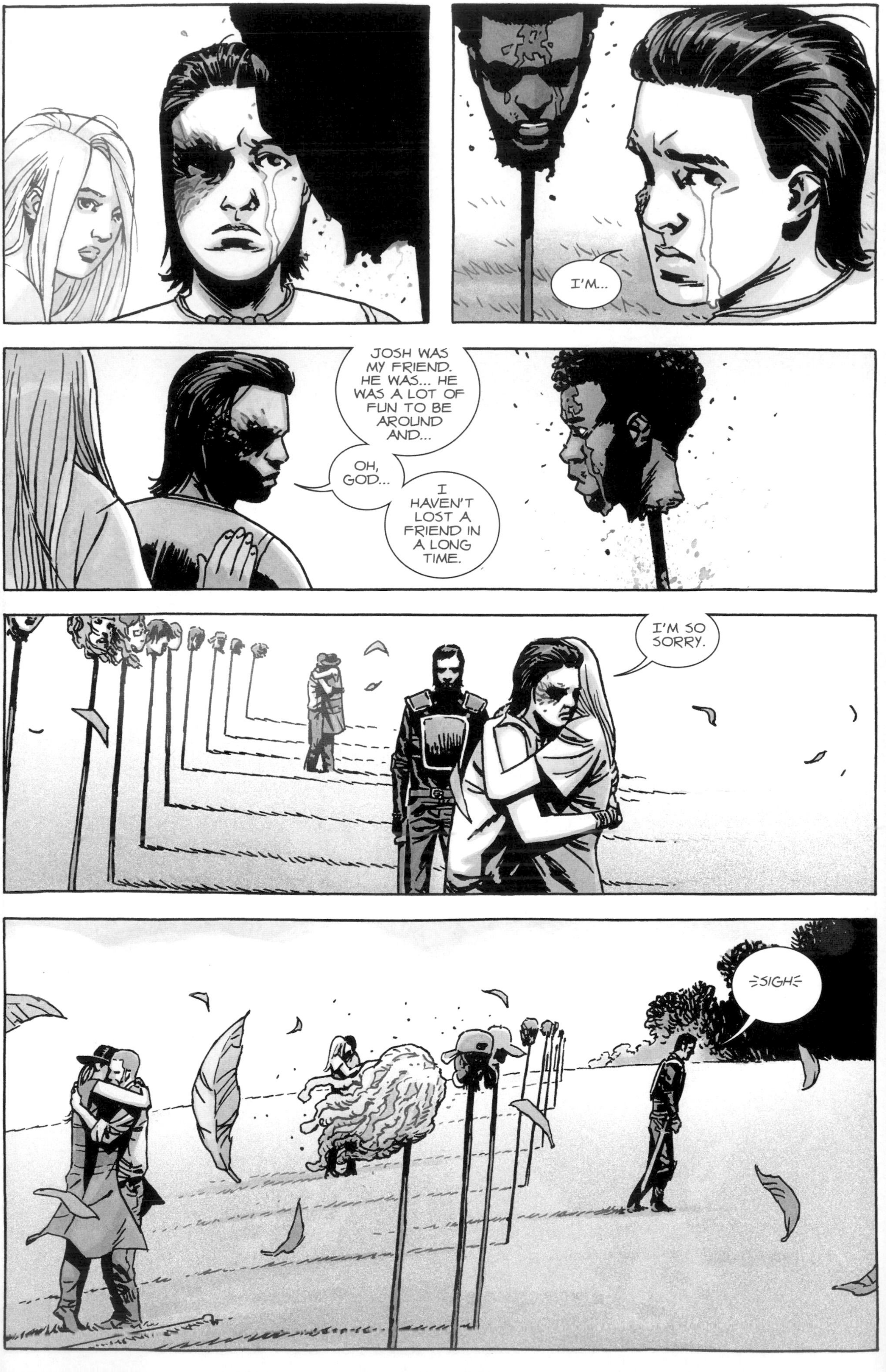
I'M...
JOSH WAS MY FRIEND. HE WAS... HE WAS A LOT OF FUN TO BE AROUND AND...
OH, GOD...
I HAVEN'T LOST A FRIEND IN A LONG TIME.
I'M SO SORRY.
SIGH

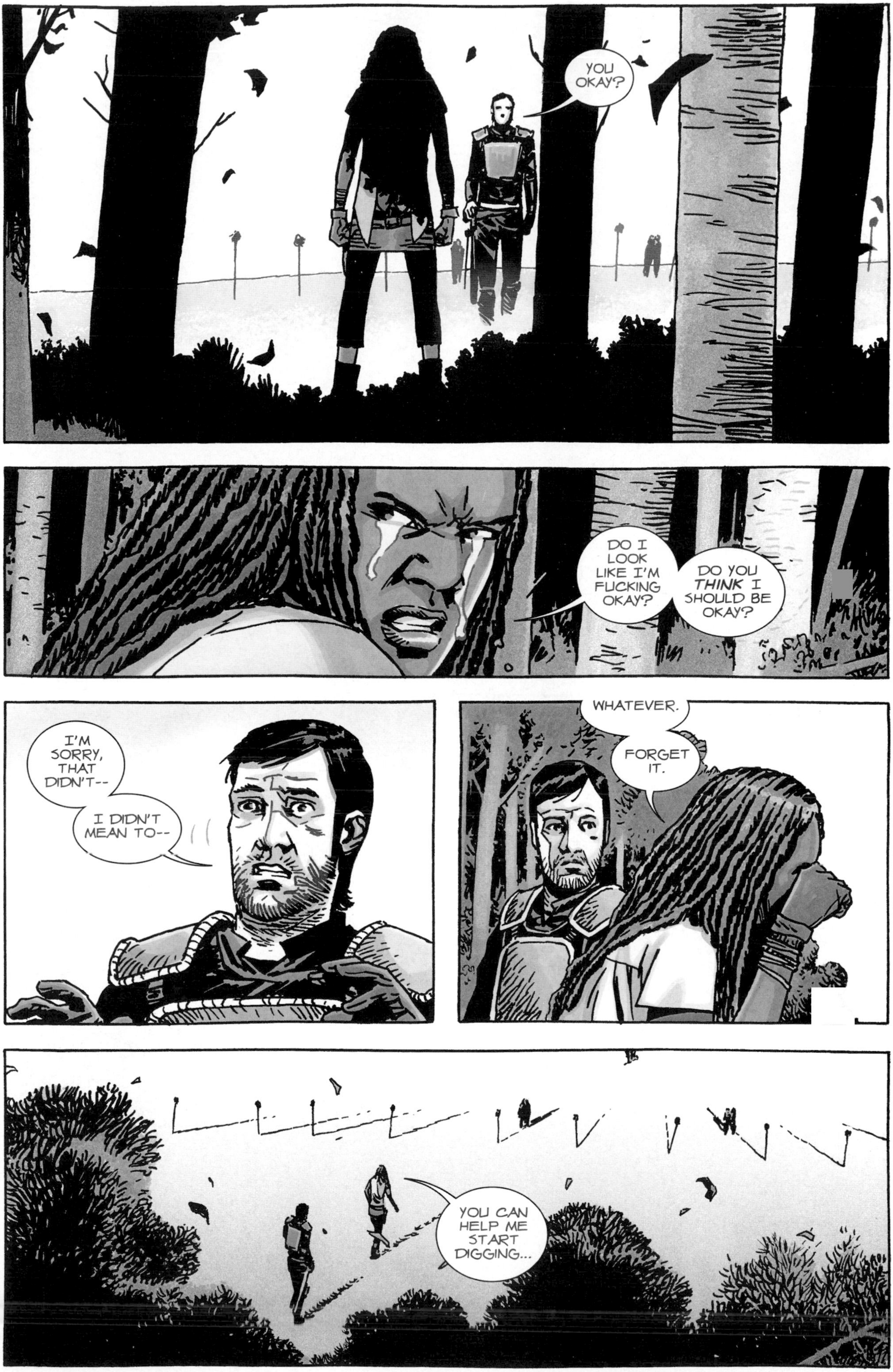
YOU OKAY?
DO I LOOK LIKE I'M FUCKING OKAY?
DO YOU THINK I SHOULD BE OKAY?
I'M SORRY, THAT DIDN'T--
I DIDN'T MEAN TO--
WHATEVER.
FORGET IT.
YOU CAN HELP ME START DIGGING...

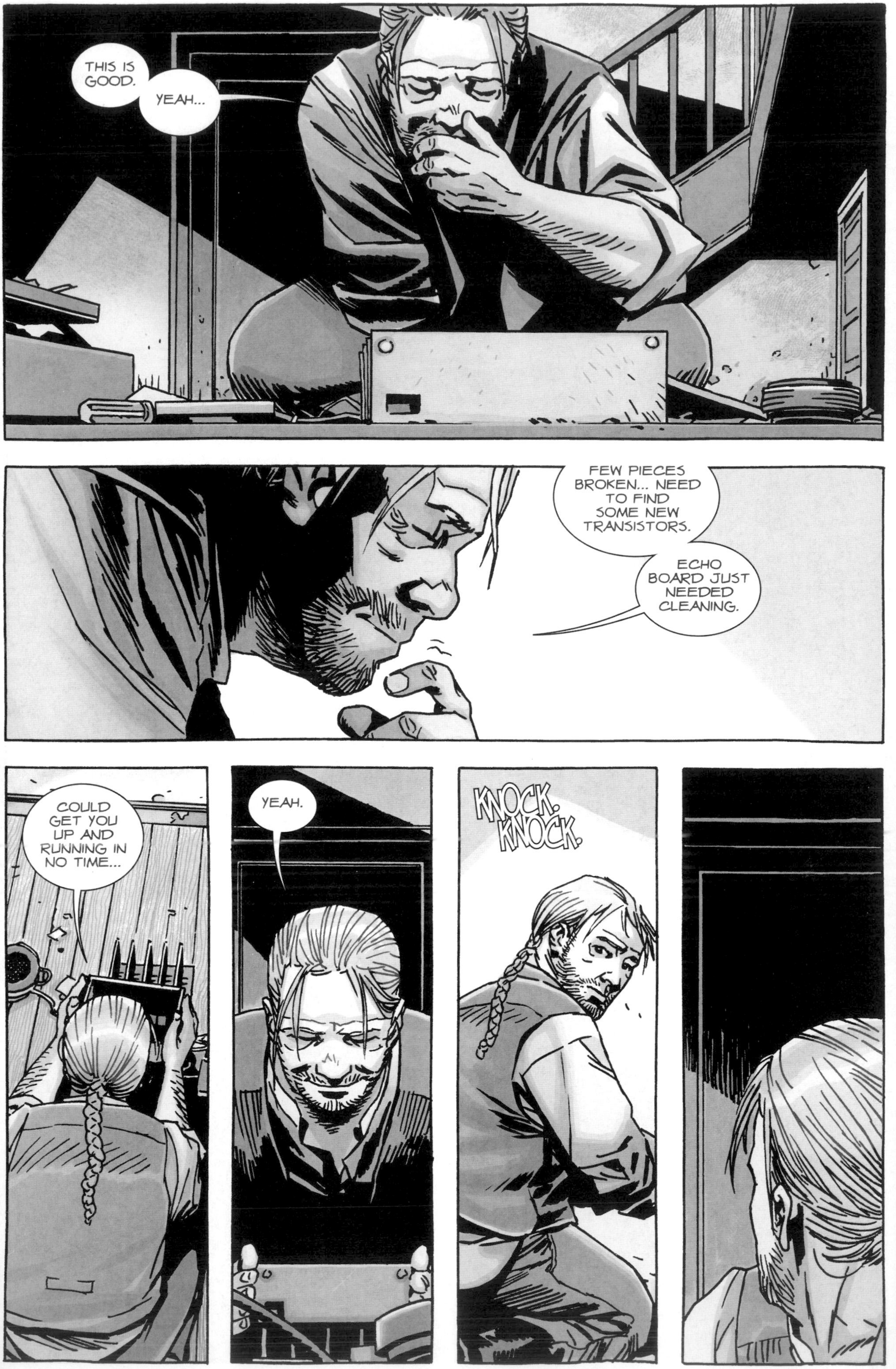
THIS IS GOOD.
YEAH...
FEW PIECES BROKEN... NEED TO FIND SOME NEW TRANSISTORS.
ECHO BOARD JUST NEEDED CLEANING.
COULD GET YOU UP AND RUNNING IN NO TIME...
YEAH.
KNOCK. KNOCK.

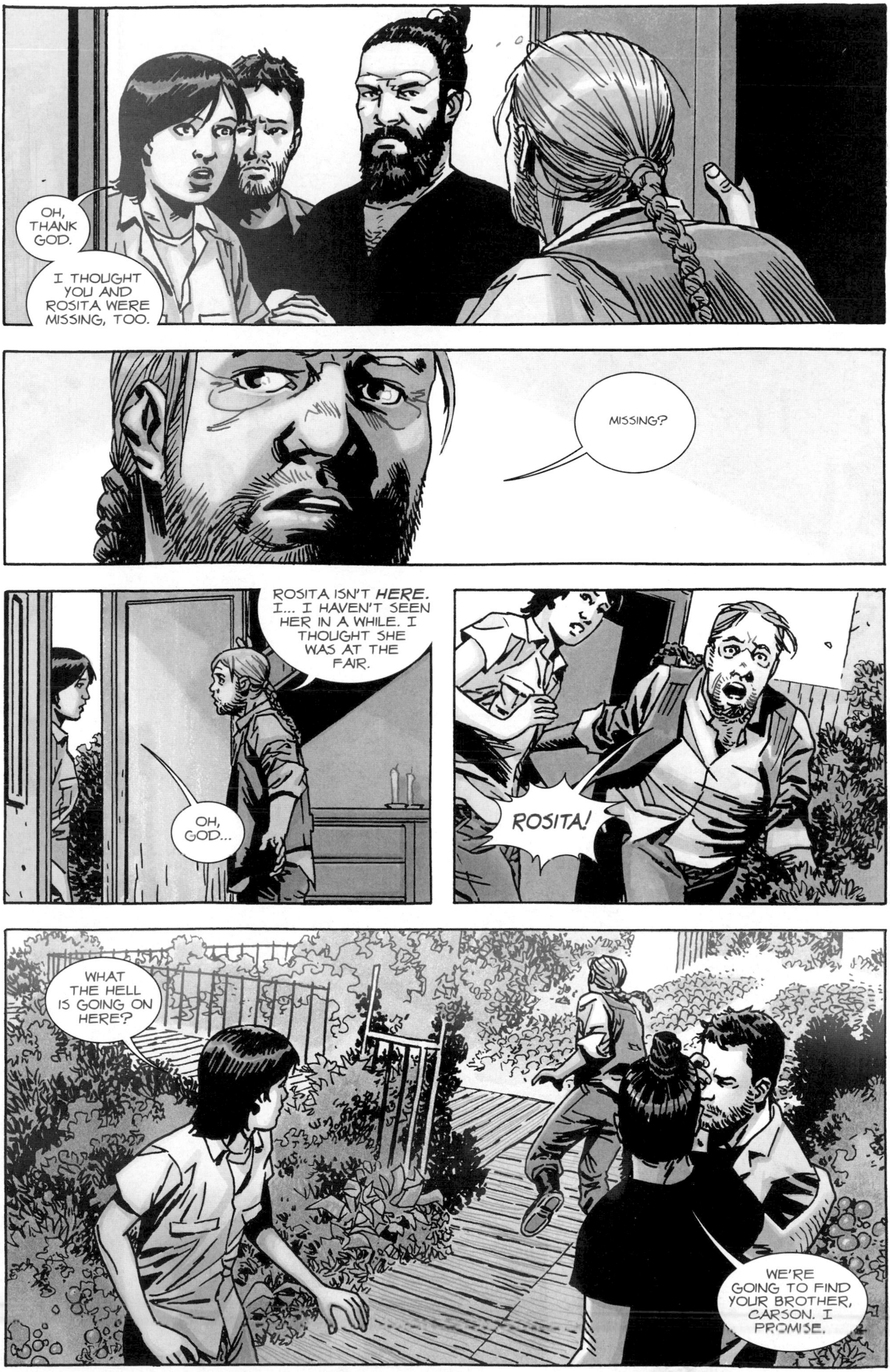
OH, THANK GOD.
I THOUGHT YOU AND ROSITA WERE MISSING, TOO.
MISSING?
ROSITA ISN'T *HERE.* I... I HAVEN'T SEEN HER IN A WHILE. I THOUGHT SHE WAS AT THE FAIR.
OH, GOD...
ROSITA!
WHAT THE HELL IS GOING ON HERE?
WE'RE GOING TO FIND YOUR BROTHER, CARSON. I PROMISE.

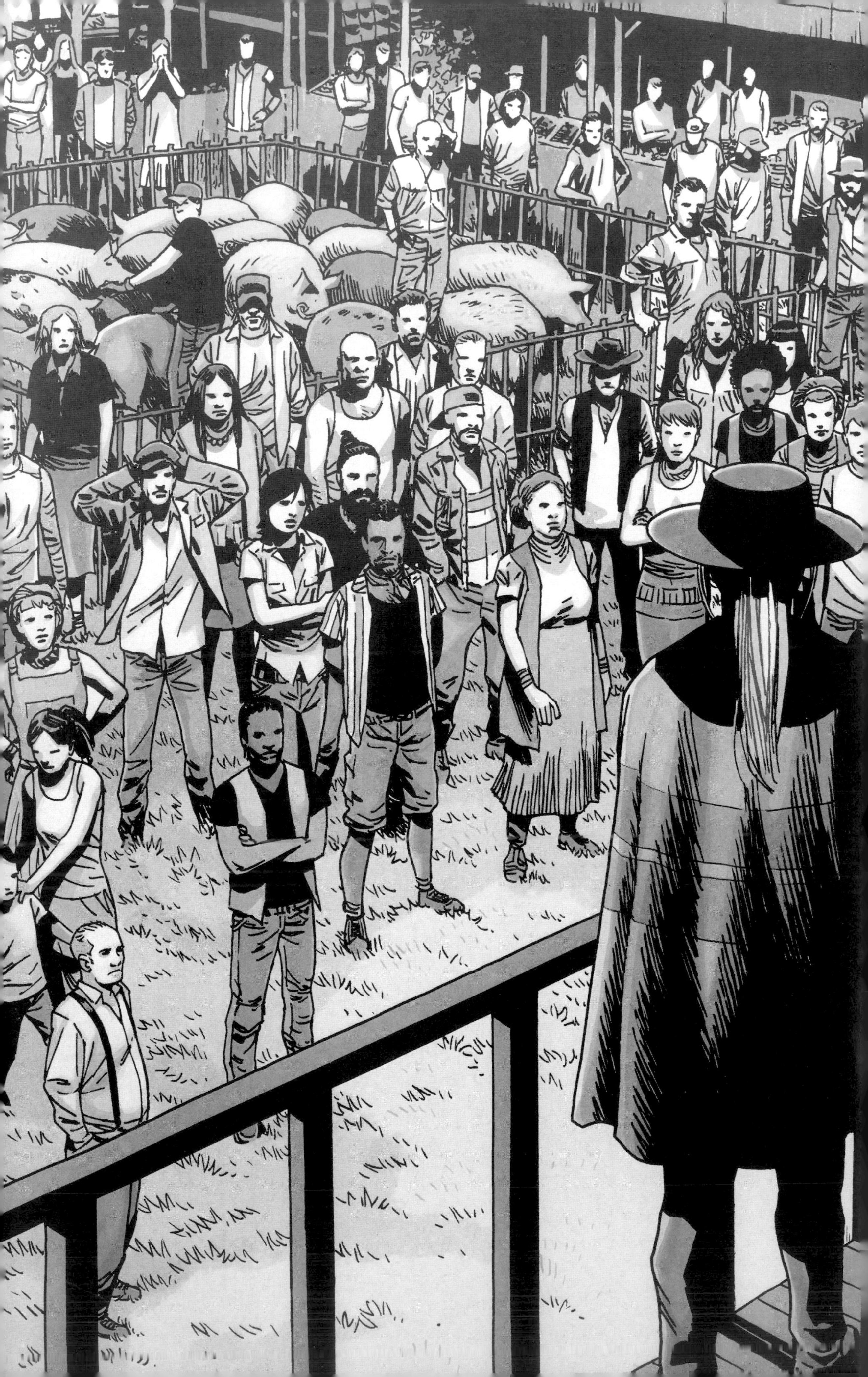

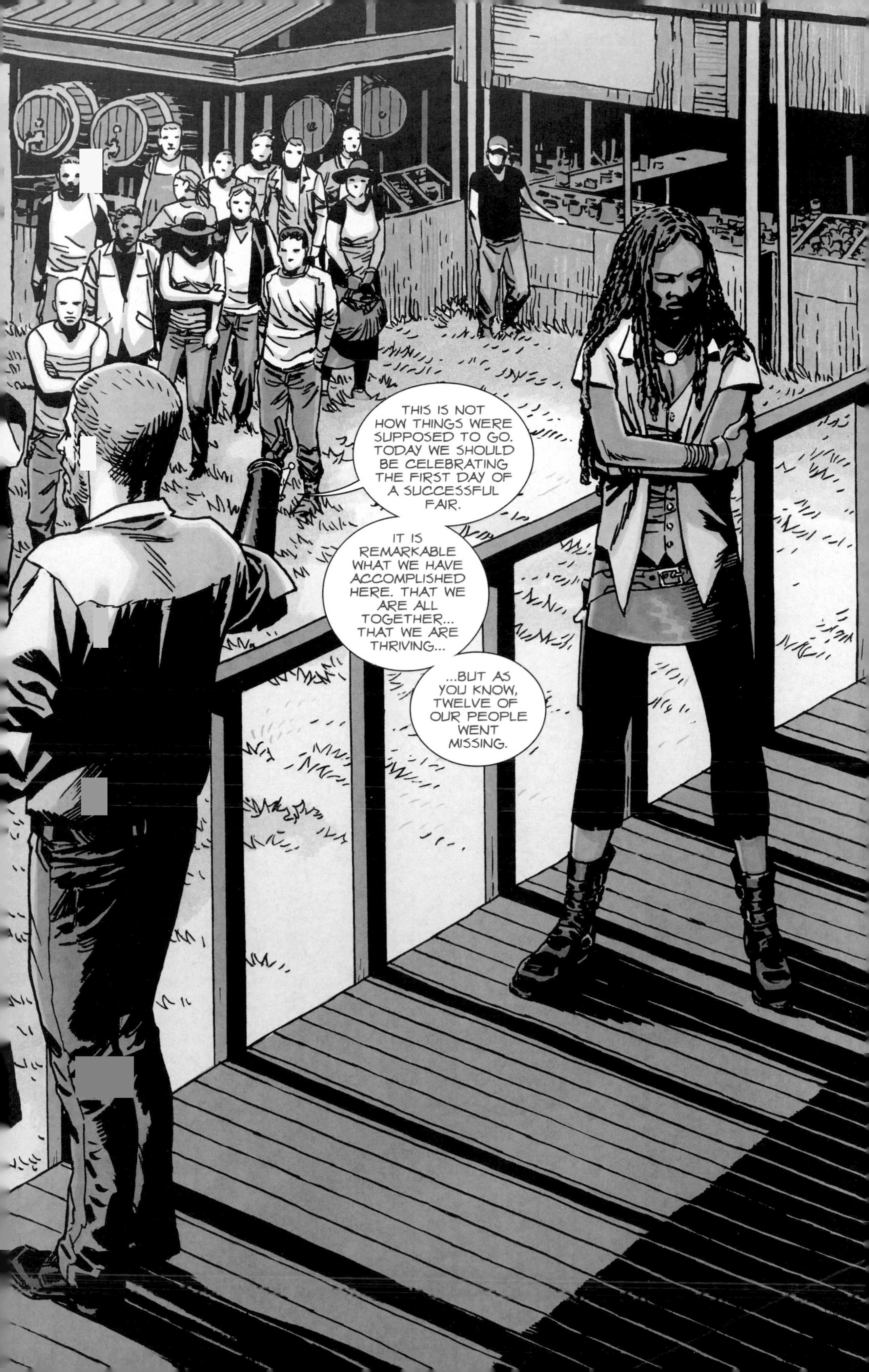
THIS IS NOT HOW THINGS WERE SUPPOSED TO GO. TODAY WE SHOULD BE CELEBRATING THE FIRST DAY OF A SUCCESSFUL FAIR.
IT IS REMARKABLE WHAT WE HAVE ACCOMPLISHED HERE. THAT WE ARE ALL TOGETHER... THAT WE ARE THRIVING...
...BUT AS YOU KNOW, TWELVE OF OUR PEOPLE WENT MISSING.

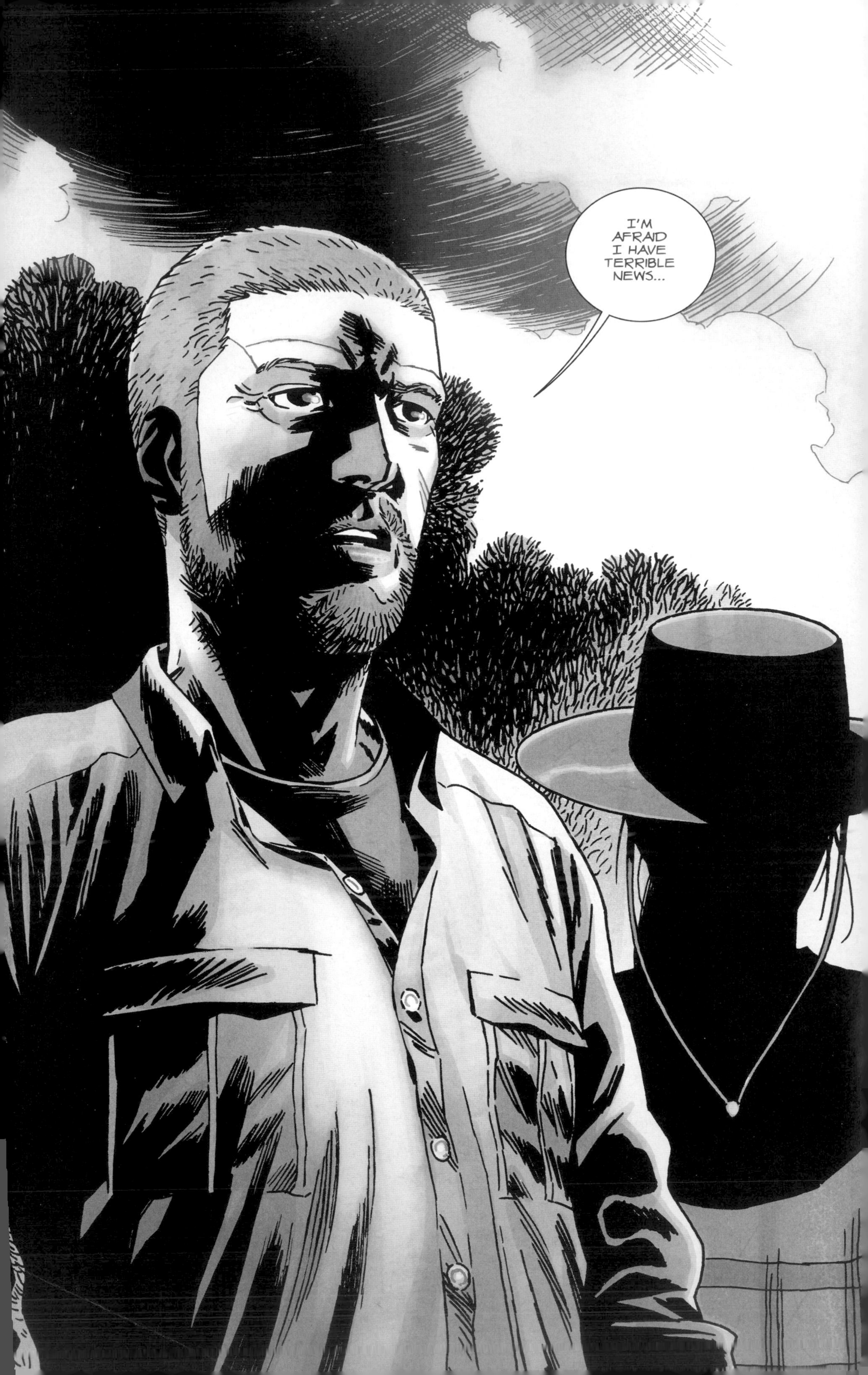
I'M AFRAID I HAVE TERRIBLE NEWS...

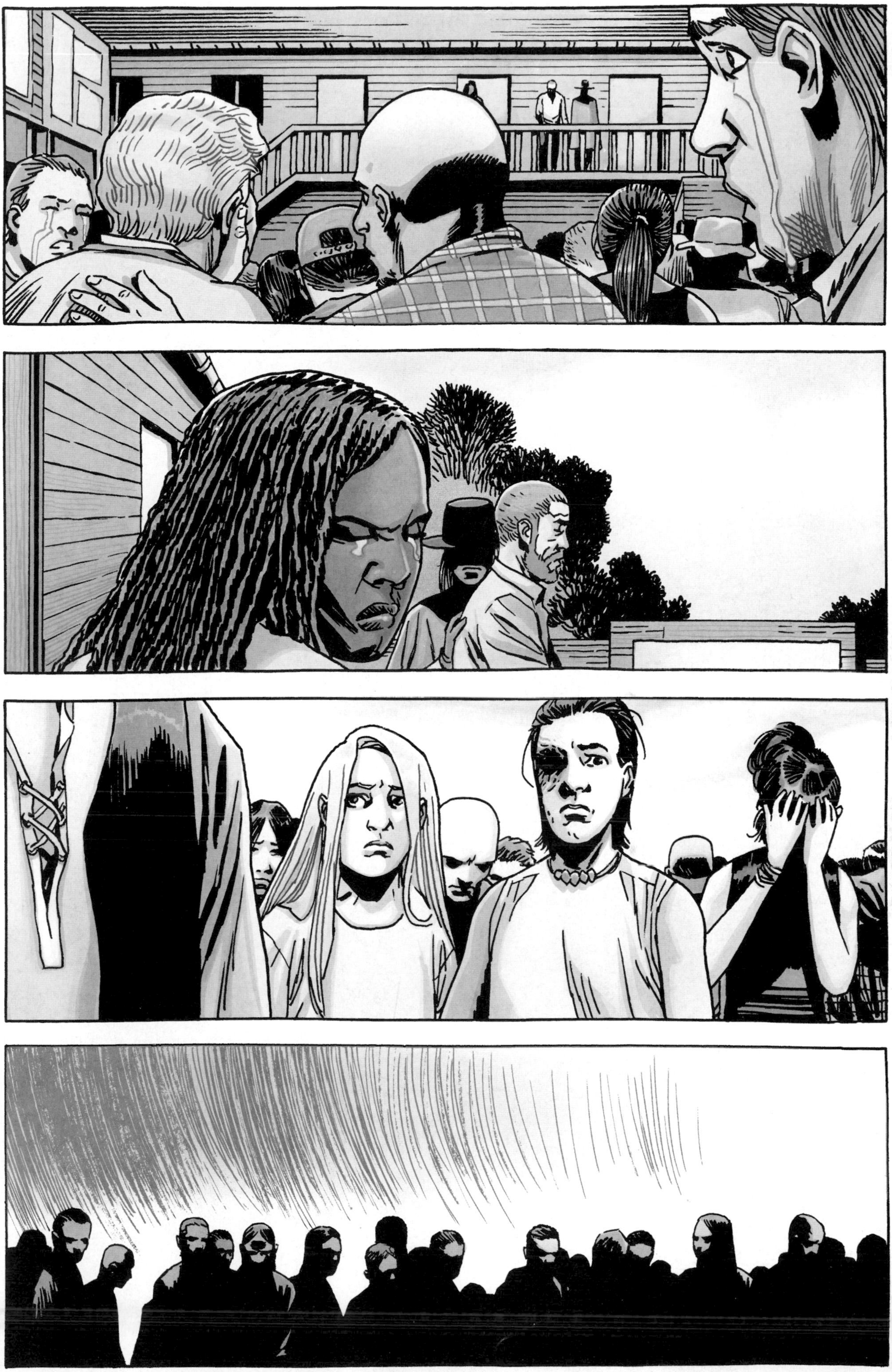

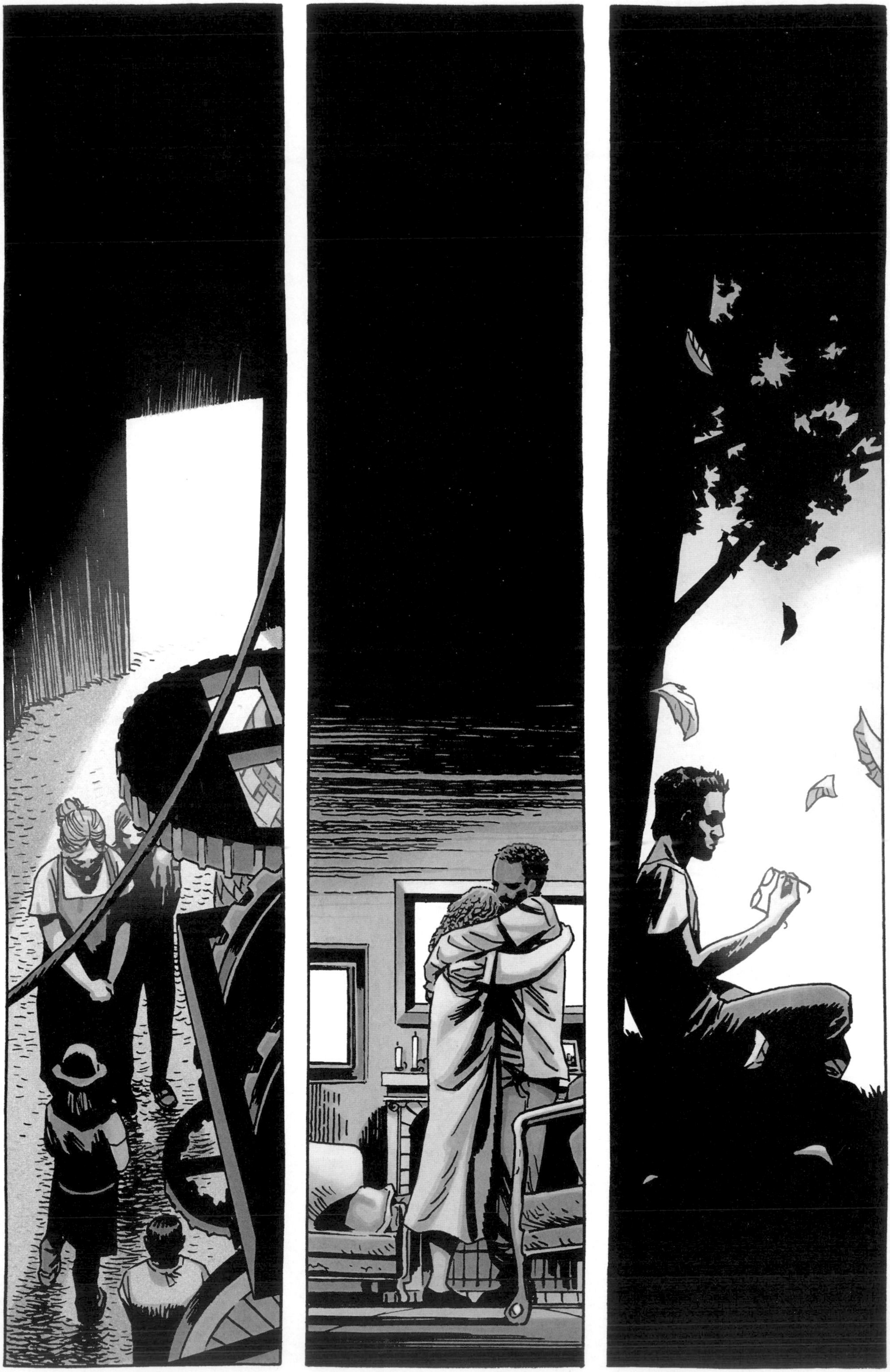

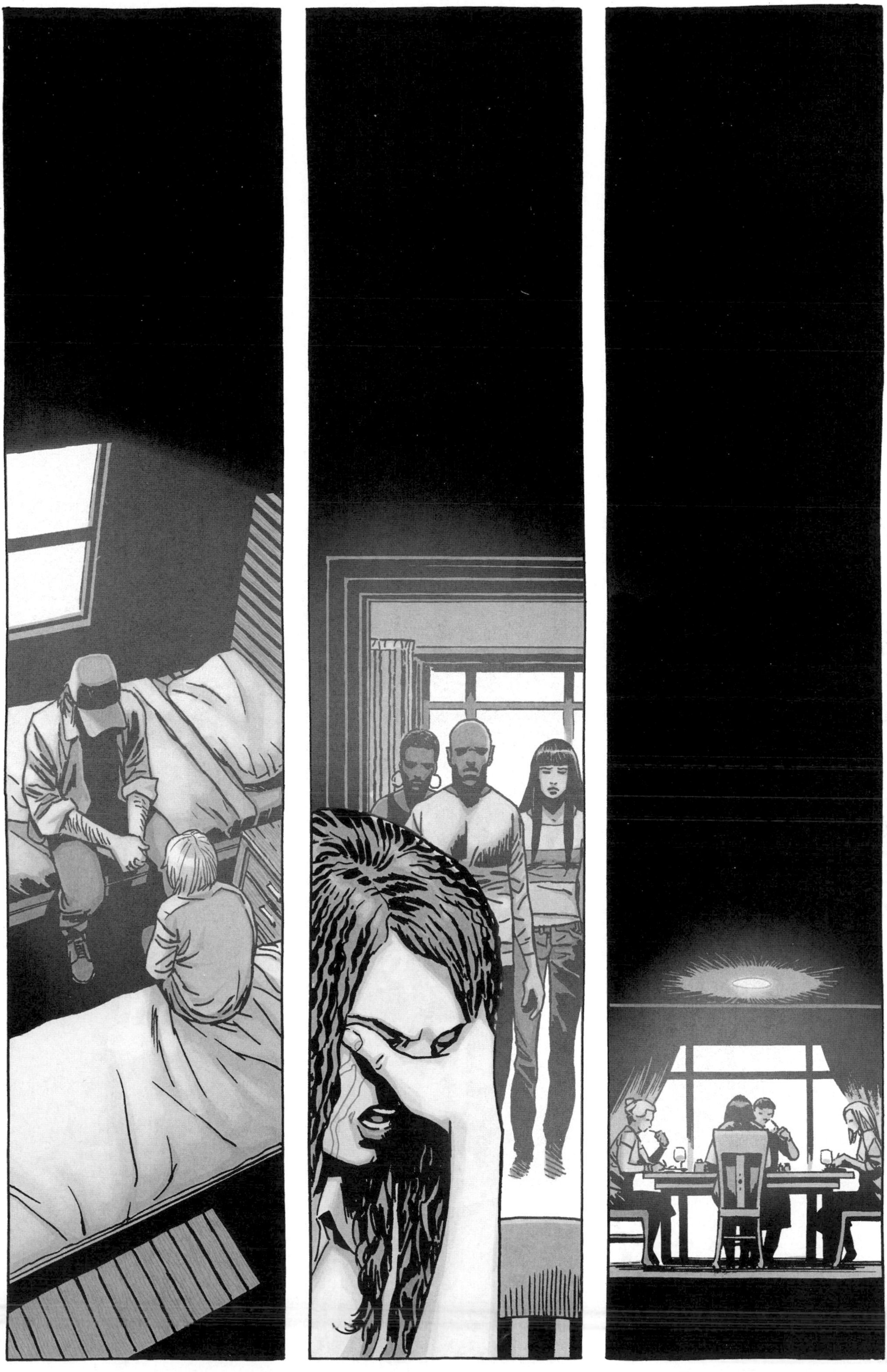

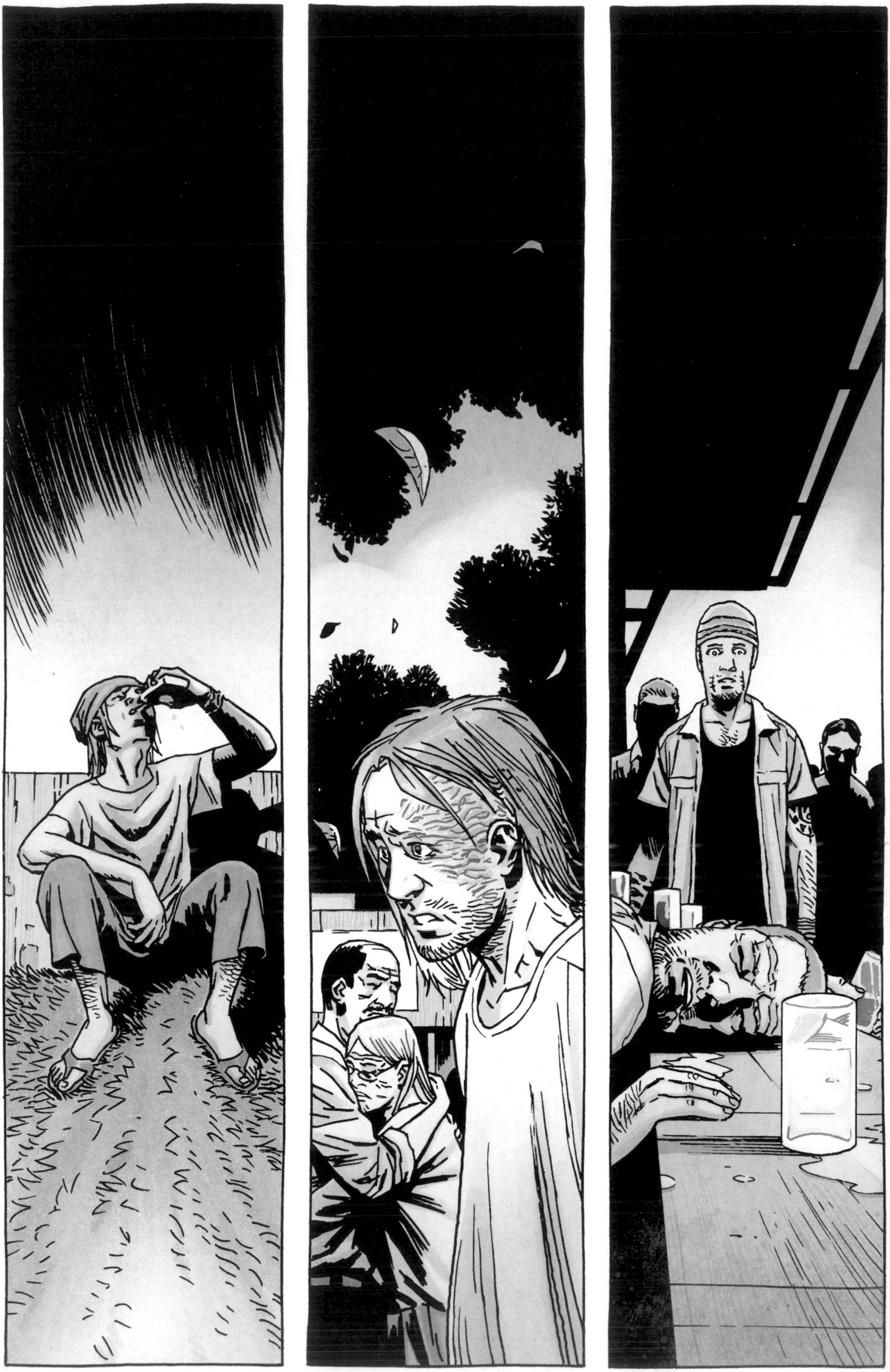

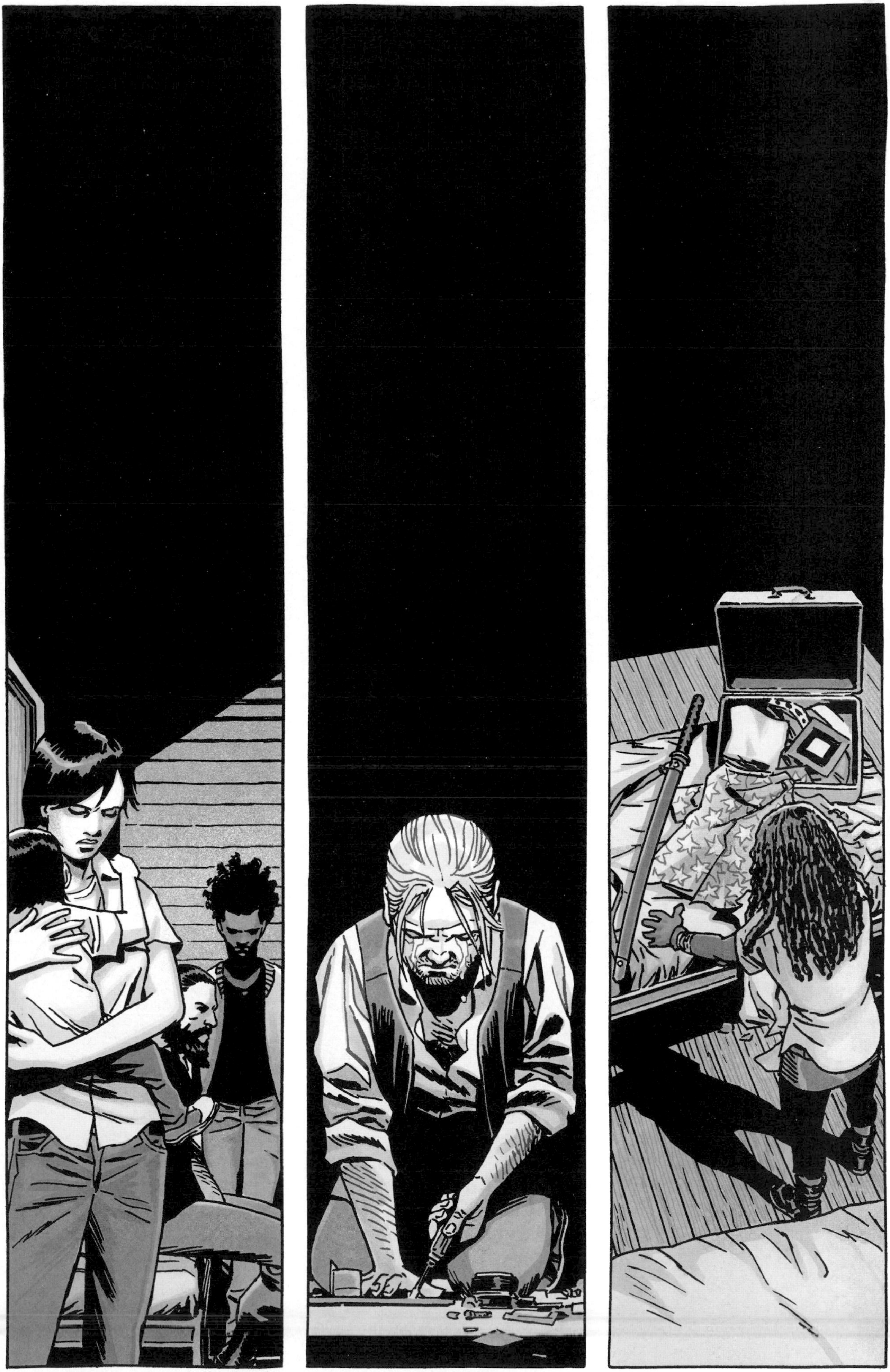

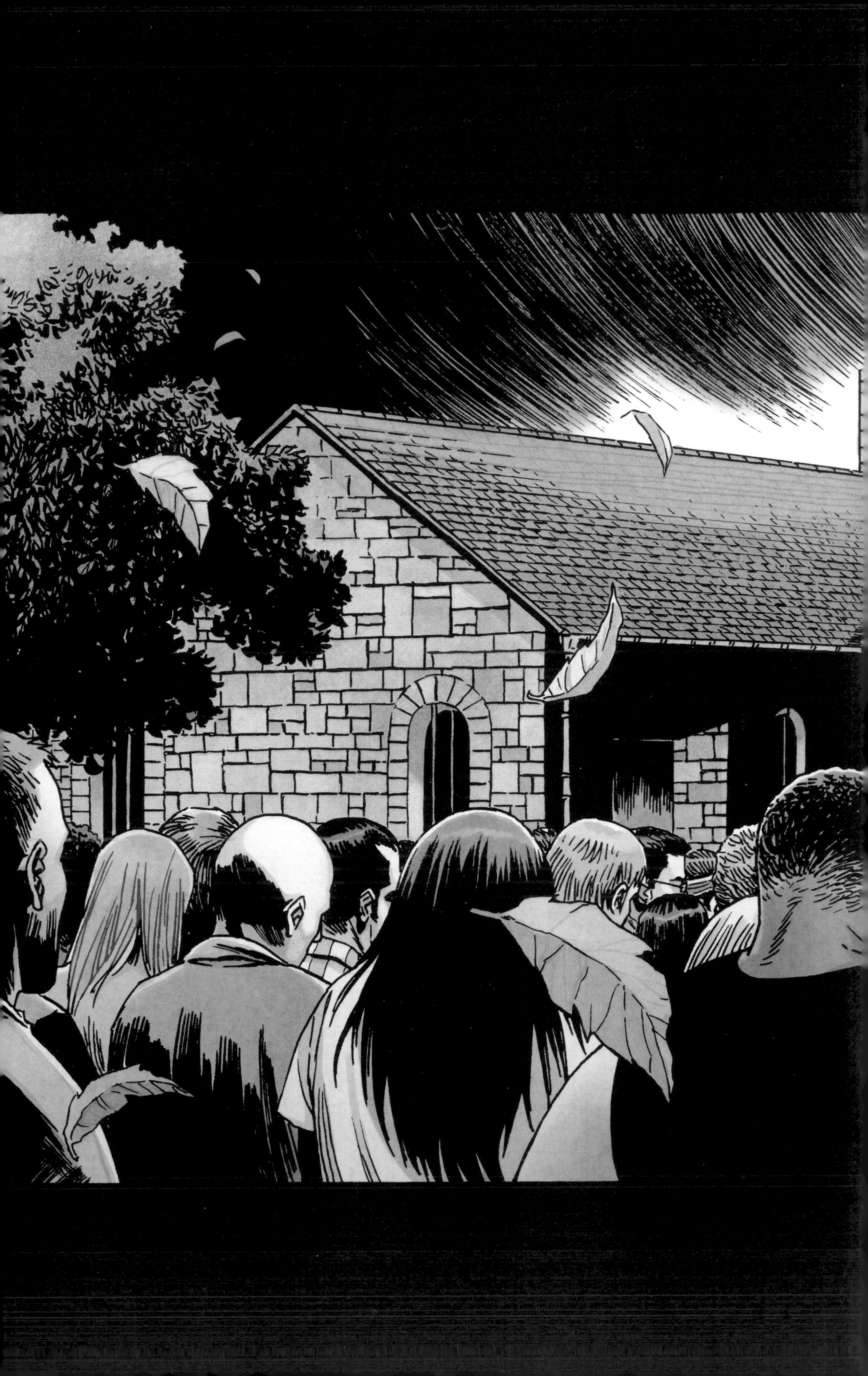

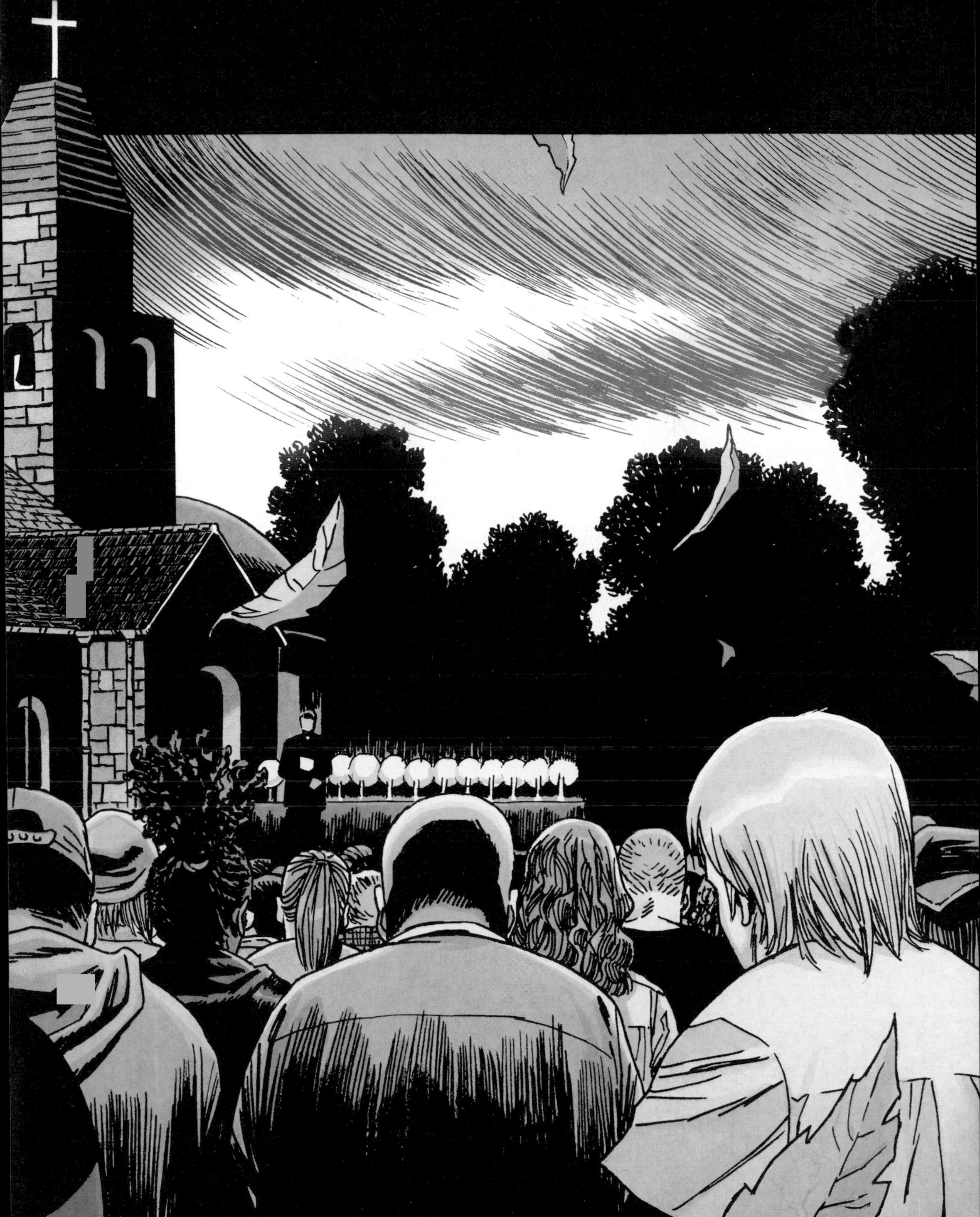

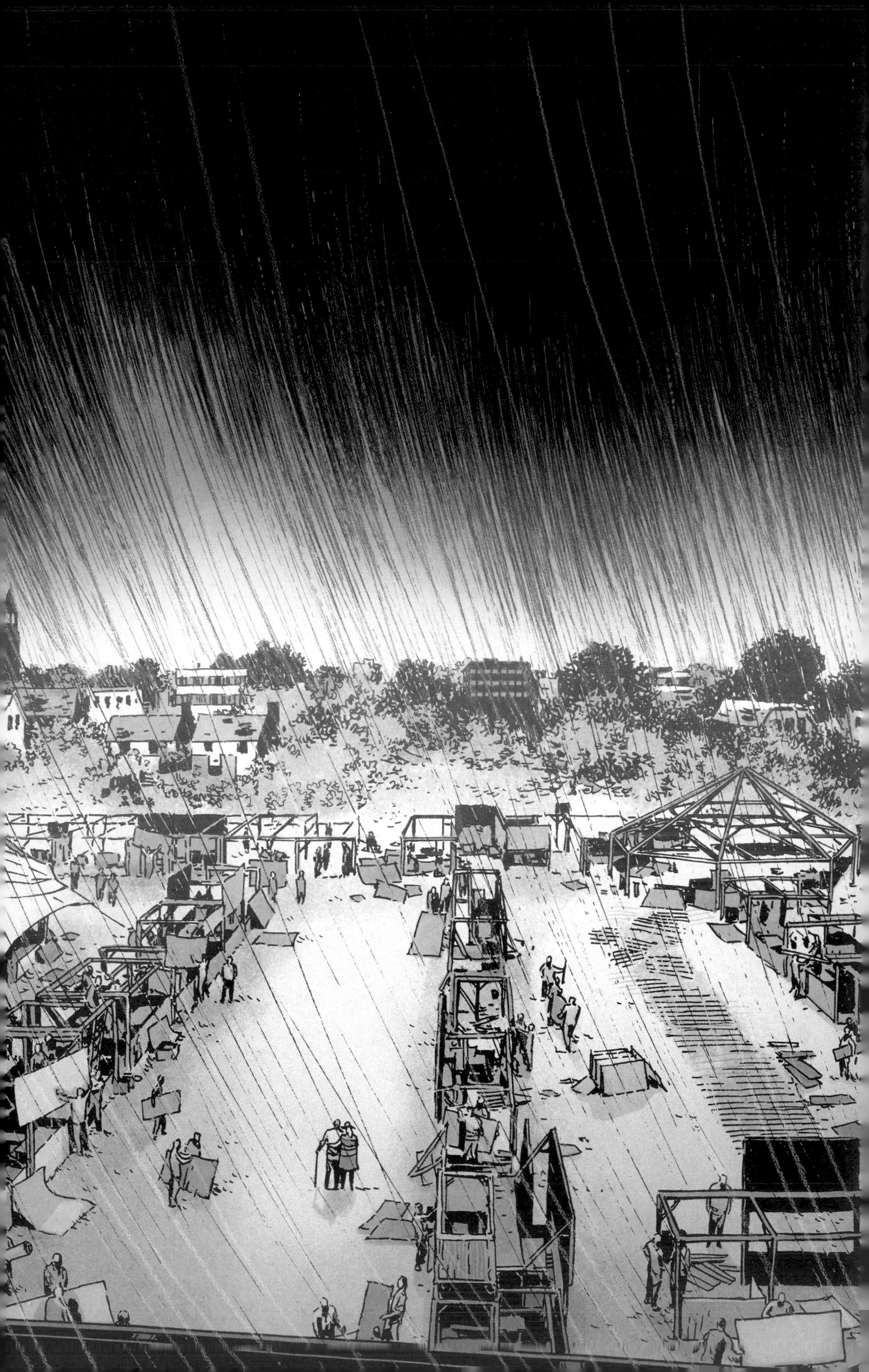

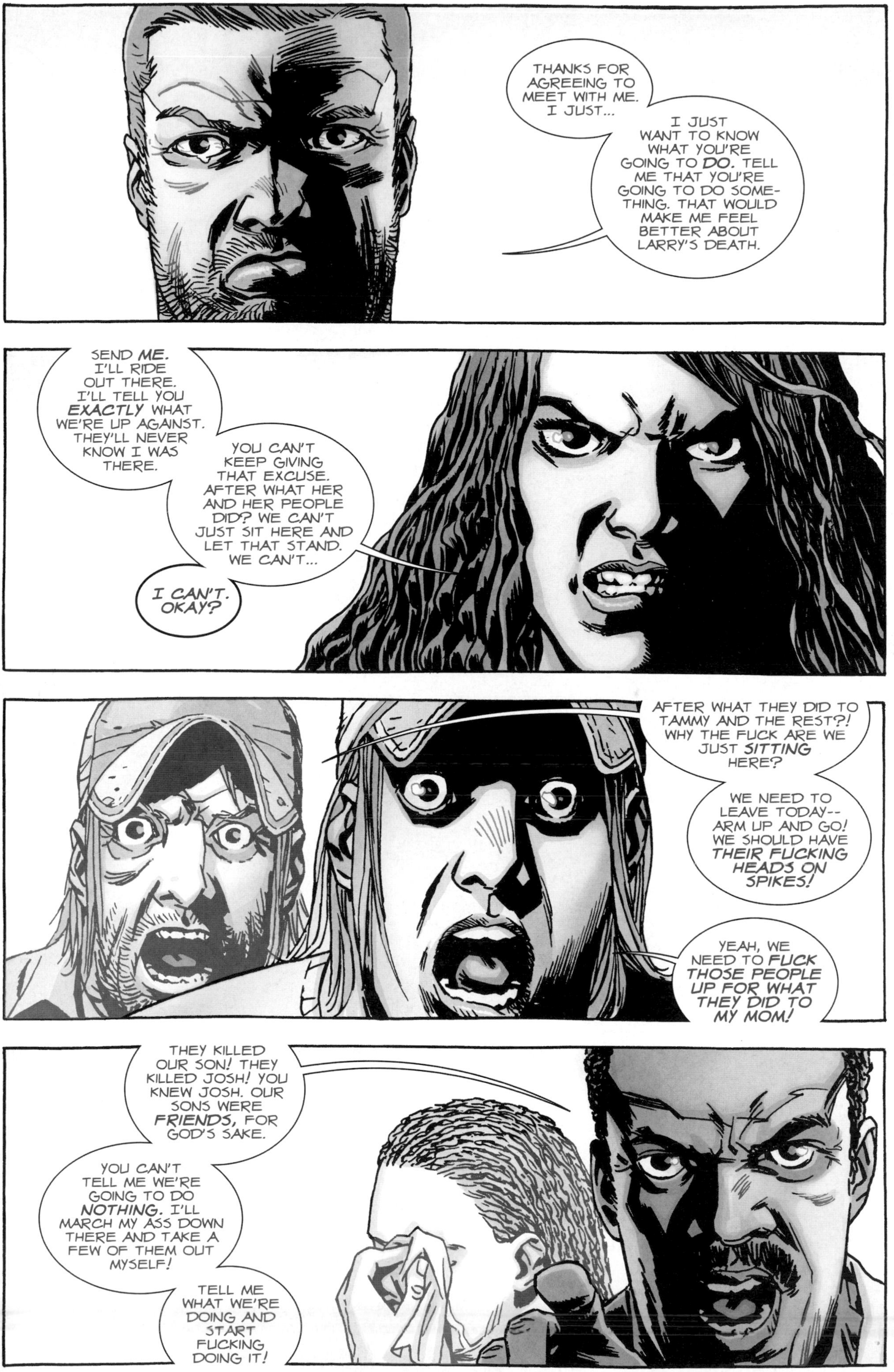

THANKS FOR AGREEING TO MEET WITH ME. I JUST...
I JUST WANT TO KNOW WHAT YOU'RE GOING TO DO. TELL ME THAT YOU'RE GOING TO DO SOME-THING. THAT WOULD MAKE ME FEEL BETTER ABOUT LARRY'S DEATH.
SEND ME. I'LL RIDE OUT THERE. I'LL TELL YOU EXACTLY WHAT WE'RE UP AGAINST. THEY'LL NEVER KNOW I WAS THERE.
YOU CAN'T KEEP GIVING THAT EXCUSE. AFTER WHAT HER AND HER PEOPLE DID? WE CAN'T JUST SIT HERE AND LET THAT STAND. WE CAN'T...
I CAN'T. OKAY?
AFTER WHAT THEY DID TO TAMMY AND THE REST?! WHY THE FUCK ARE WE JUST SITTING HERE?
WE NEED TO LEAVE TODAY-- ARM UP AND GO! WE SHOULD HAVE THEIR FUCKING HEADS ON SPIKES!
YEAH, WE NEED TO FUCK THOSE PEOPLE UP FOR WHAT THEY DID TO MY MOM!
THEY KILLED OUR SON! THEY KILLED JOSH! YOU KNEW JOSH. OUR SONS WERE FRIENDS, FOR GOD'S SAKE.
YOU CAN'T TELL ME WE'RE GOING TO DO NOTHING. I'LL MARCH MY ASS DOWN THERE AND TAKE A FEW OF THEM OUT MYSELF!
TELL ME WHAT WE'RE DOING AND START FUCKING DOING IT!

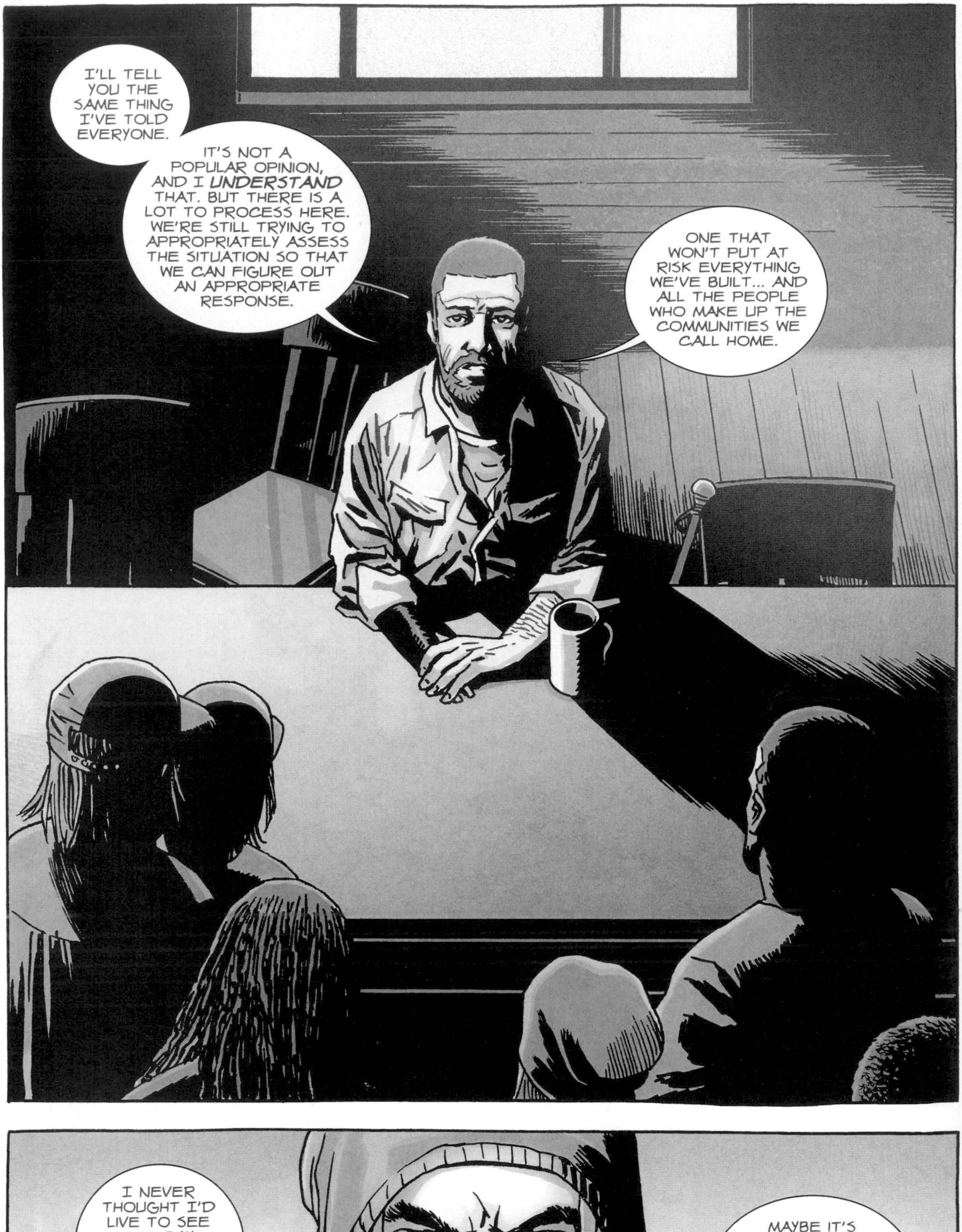
I'LL TELL YOU THE SAME THING I'VE TOLD EVERYONE.
IT'S NOT A POPULAR OPINION, AND I *UNDERSTAND* THAT. BUT THERE IS A LOT TO PROCESS HERE. WE'RE STILL TRYING TO APPROPRIATELY ASSESS THE SITUATION SO THAT WE CAN FIGURE OUT AN APPROPRIATE RESPONSE.
ONE THAT WON'T PUT AT RISK EVERYTHING WE'VE BUILT... AND ALL THE PEOPLE WHO MAKE UP THE COMMUNITIES WE CALL HOME.

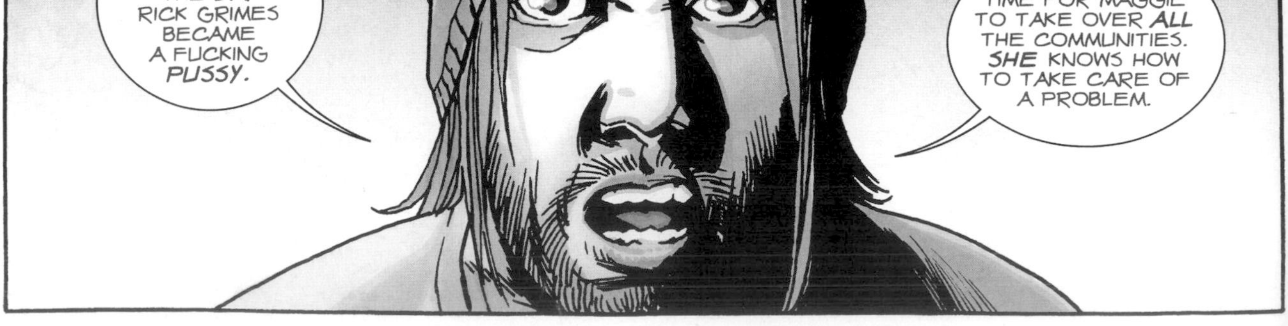
I NEVER THOUGHT I'D LIVE TO SEE THE DAY RICK GRIMES BECAME A FUCKING *PUSSY.*
MAYBE IT'S TIME FOR MAGGIE TO TAKE OVER *ALL* THE COMMUNITIES. *SHE* KNOWS HOW TO TAKE CARE OF A PROBLEM.

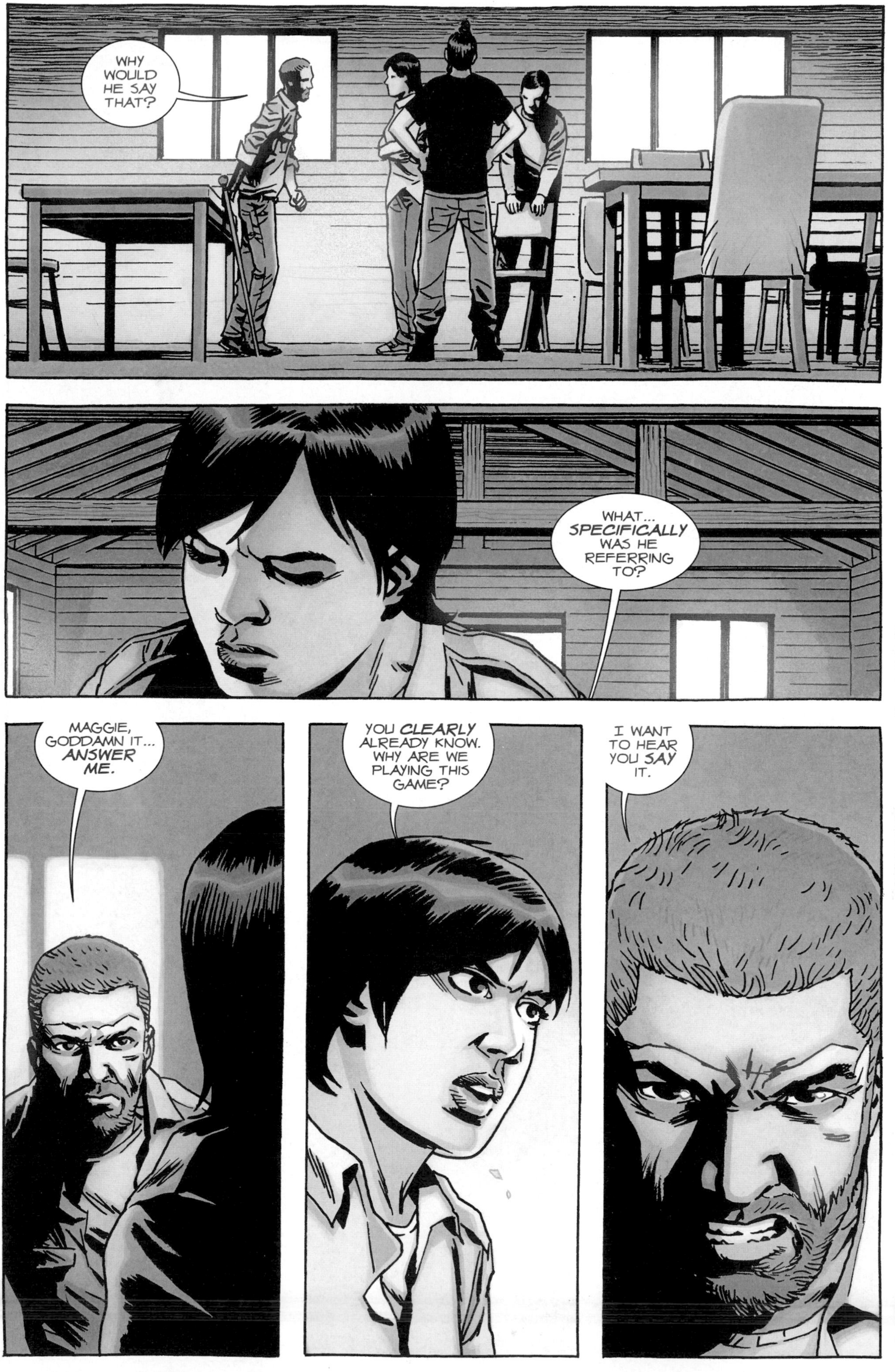
WHY WOULD HE SAY THAT?
WHAT... SPECIFICALLY WAS HE REFERRING TO?
MAGGIE, GODDAMN IT... ANSWER ME.
YOU CLEARLY ALREADY KNOW. WHY ARE WE PLAYING THIS GAME?
I WANT TO HEAR YOU SAY IT.

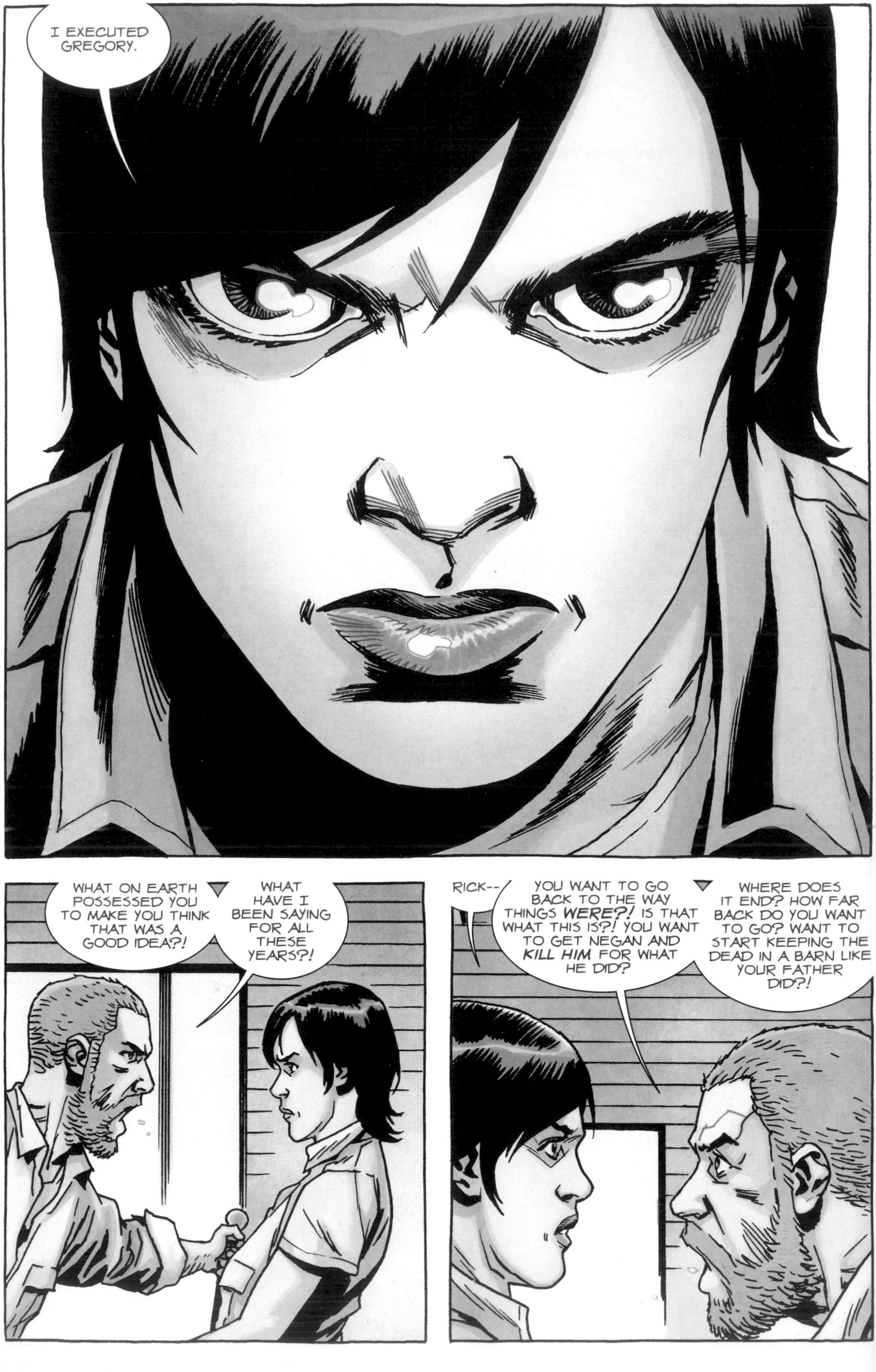
I EXECUTED GREGORY.
WHAT ON EARTH POSSESSED YOU TO MAKE YOU THINK THAT WAS A GOOD IDEA?!
WHAT HAVE I BEEN SAYING FOR ALL THESE YEARS?!
RICK--
YOU WANT TO GO BACK TO THE WAY THINGS WERE?! IS THAT WHAT THIS IS?! YOU WANT TO GET NEGAN AND KILL HIM FOR WHAT HE DID?
WHERE DOES IT END? HOW FAR BACK DO YOU WANT TO GO? WANT TO START KEEPING THE DEAD IN A BARN LIKE YOUR FATHER DID?!

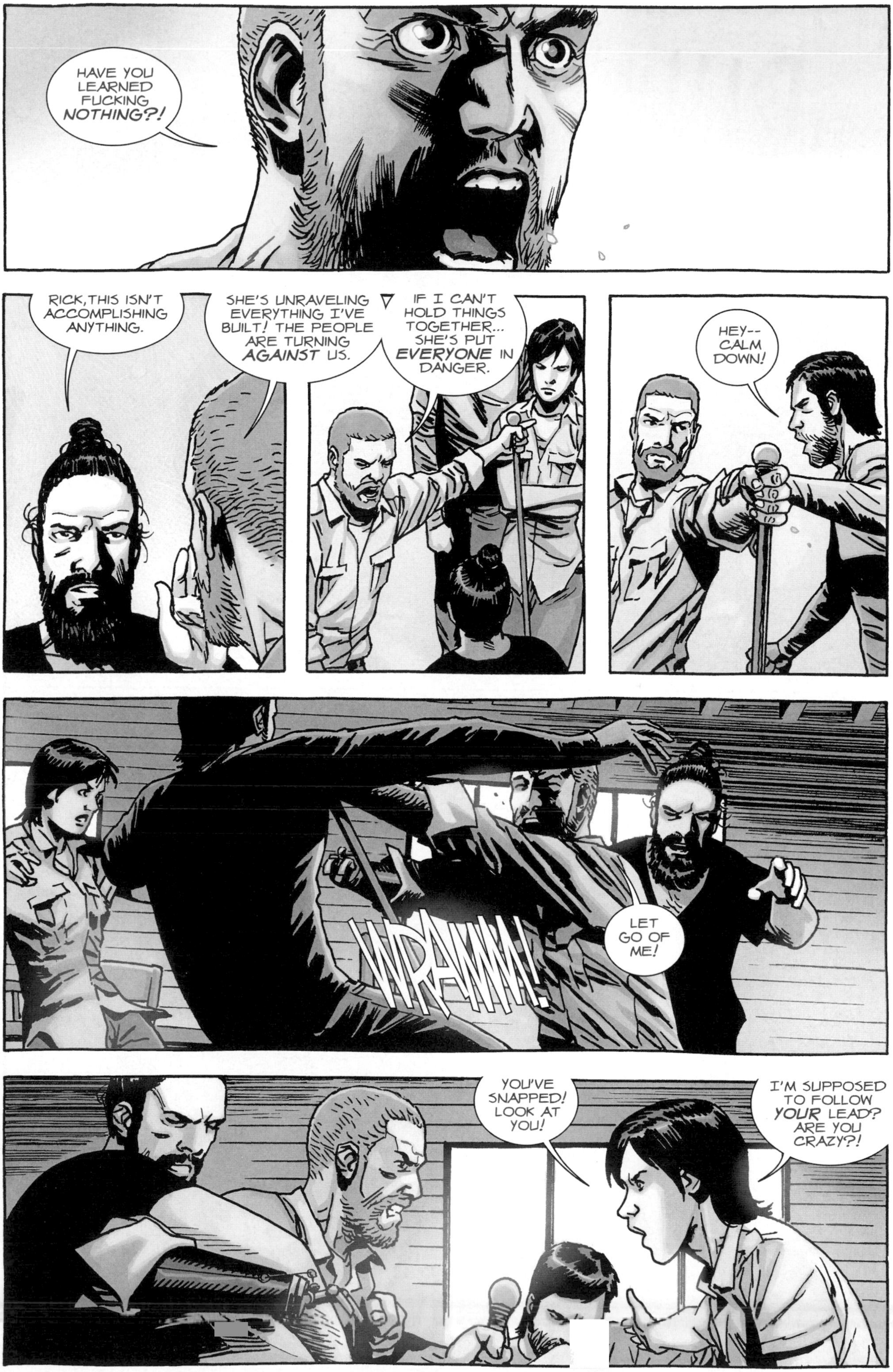
HAVE YOU LEARNED FUCKING NOTHING?!
RICK, THIS ISN'T ACCOMPLISHING ANYTHING.
SHE'S UNRAVELING EVERYTHING I'VE BUILT! THE PEOPLE ARE TURNING AGAINST US.
IF I CAN'T HOLD THINGS TOGETHER... SHE'S PUT EVERYONE IN DANGER.
HEY-- CALM DOWN!
WRANNN!
LET GO OF ME!
YOU'VE SNAPPED! LOOK AT YOU!
I'M SUPPOSED TO FOLLOW YOUR LEAD? ARE YOU CRAZY?!

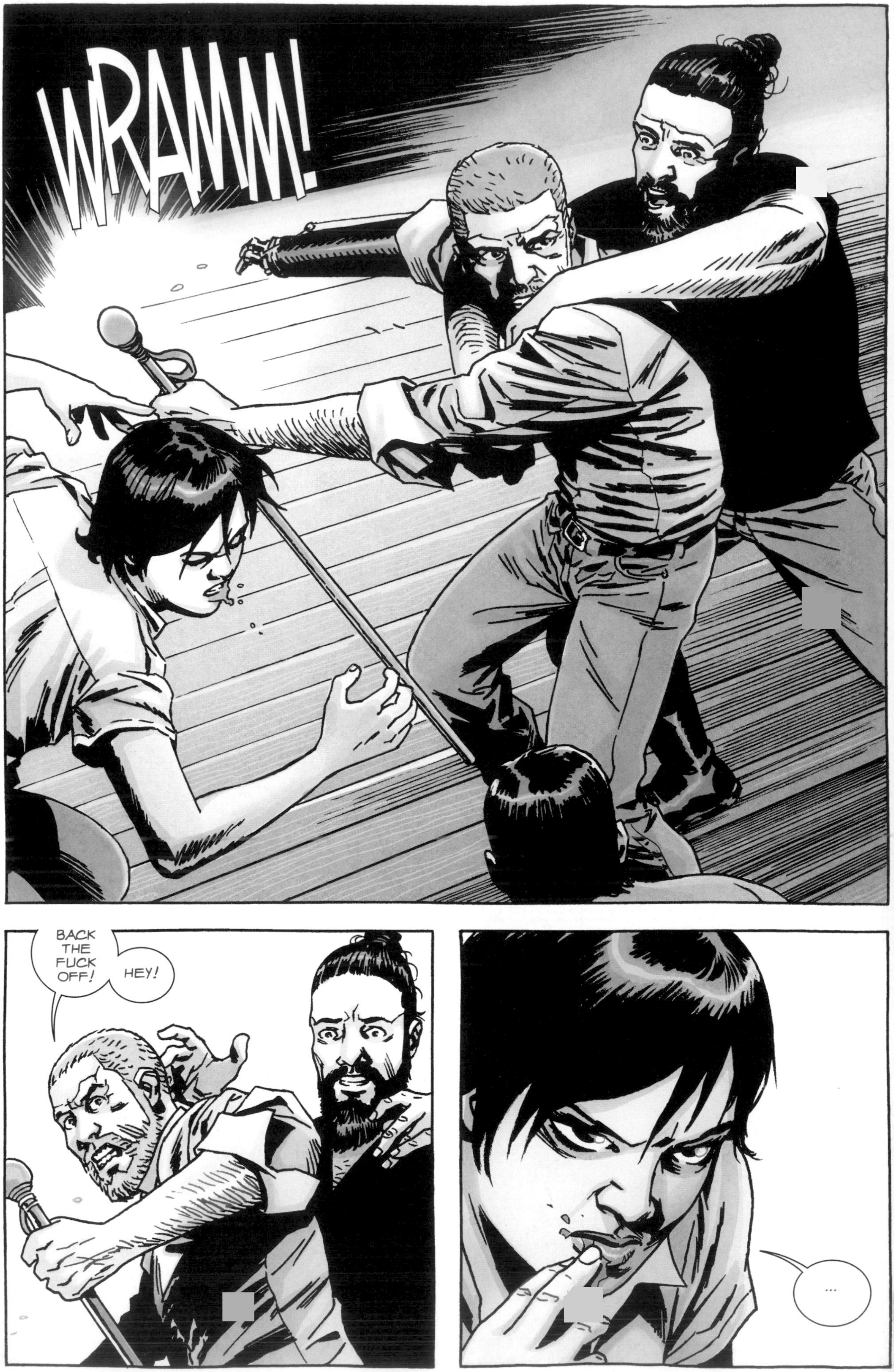
WRAMM!
BACK THE FUCK OFF!
HEY!
...

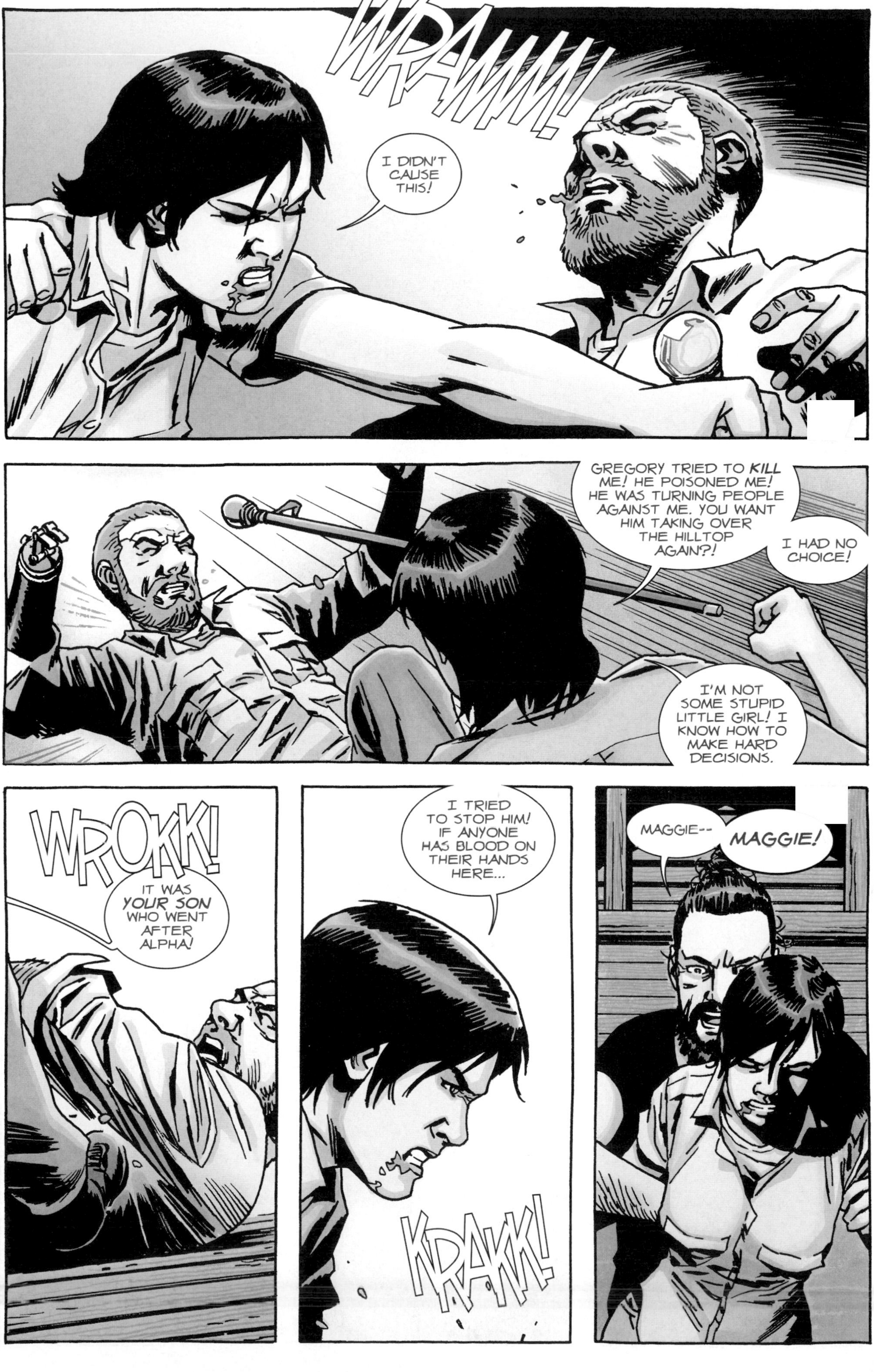
WRAMM!
I DIDN'T CAUSE THIS!
GREGORY TRIED TO *KILL* ME! HE POISONED ME! HE WAS TURNING PEOPLE AGAINST ME. YOU WANT HIM TAKING OVER THE HILLTOP AGAIN?!
I HAD NO CHOICE!
I'M NOT SOME STUPID LITTLE GIRL! I KNOW HOW TO MAKE HARD DECISIONS.
WROKK!
IT WAS *YOUR SON* WHO WENT AFTER ALPHA!
I TRIED TO STOP HIM! IF ANYONE HAS BLOOD ON THEIR HANDS HERE...
KRAKK!
MAGGIE--
MAGGIE!

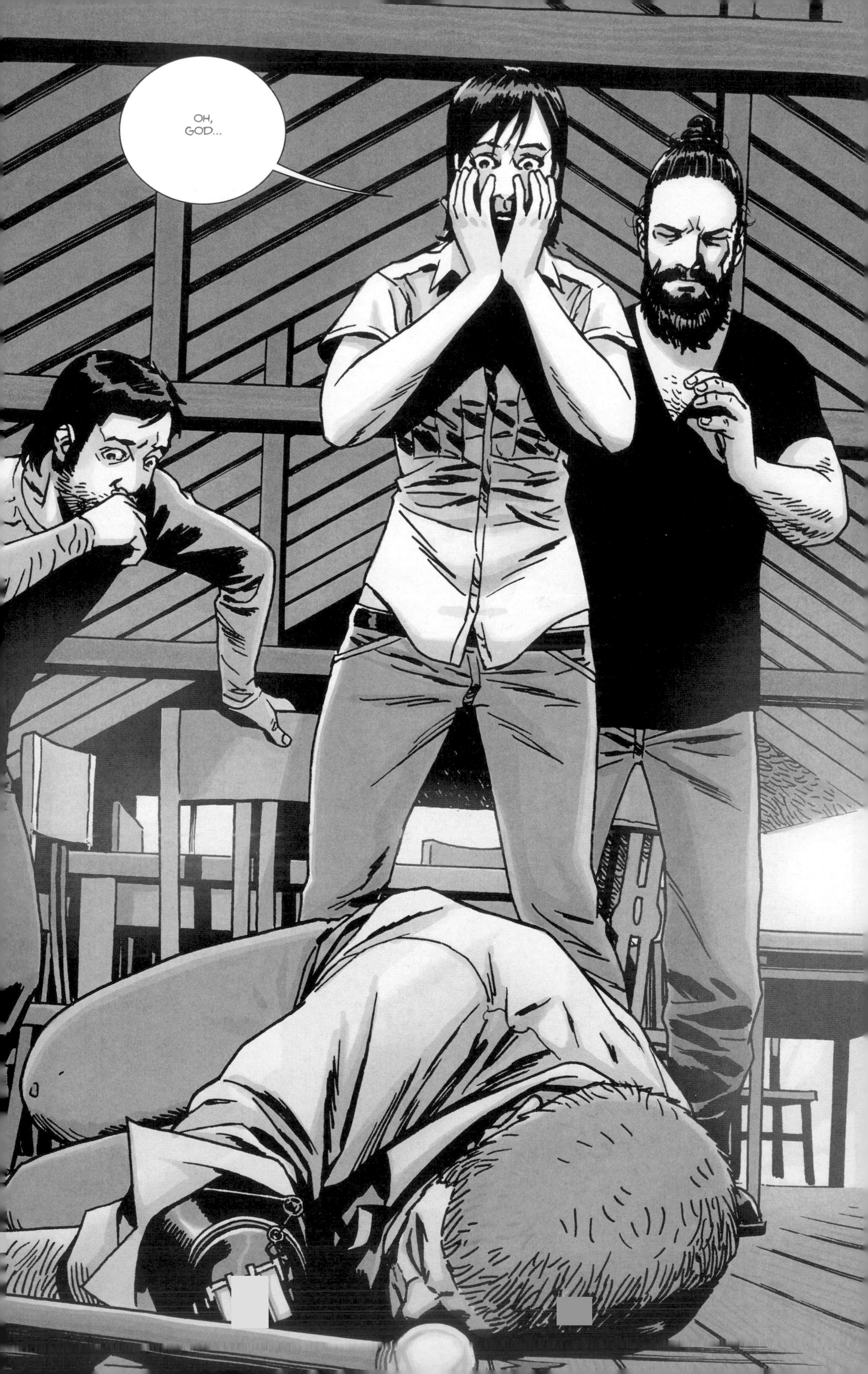
OH, GOD...

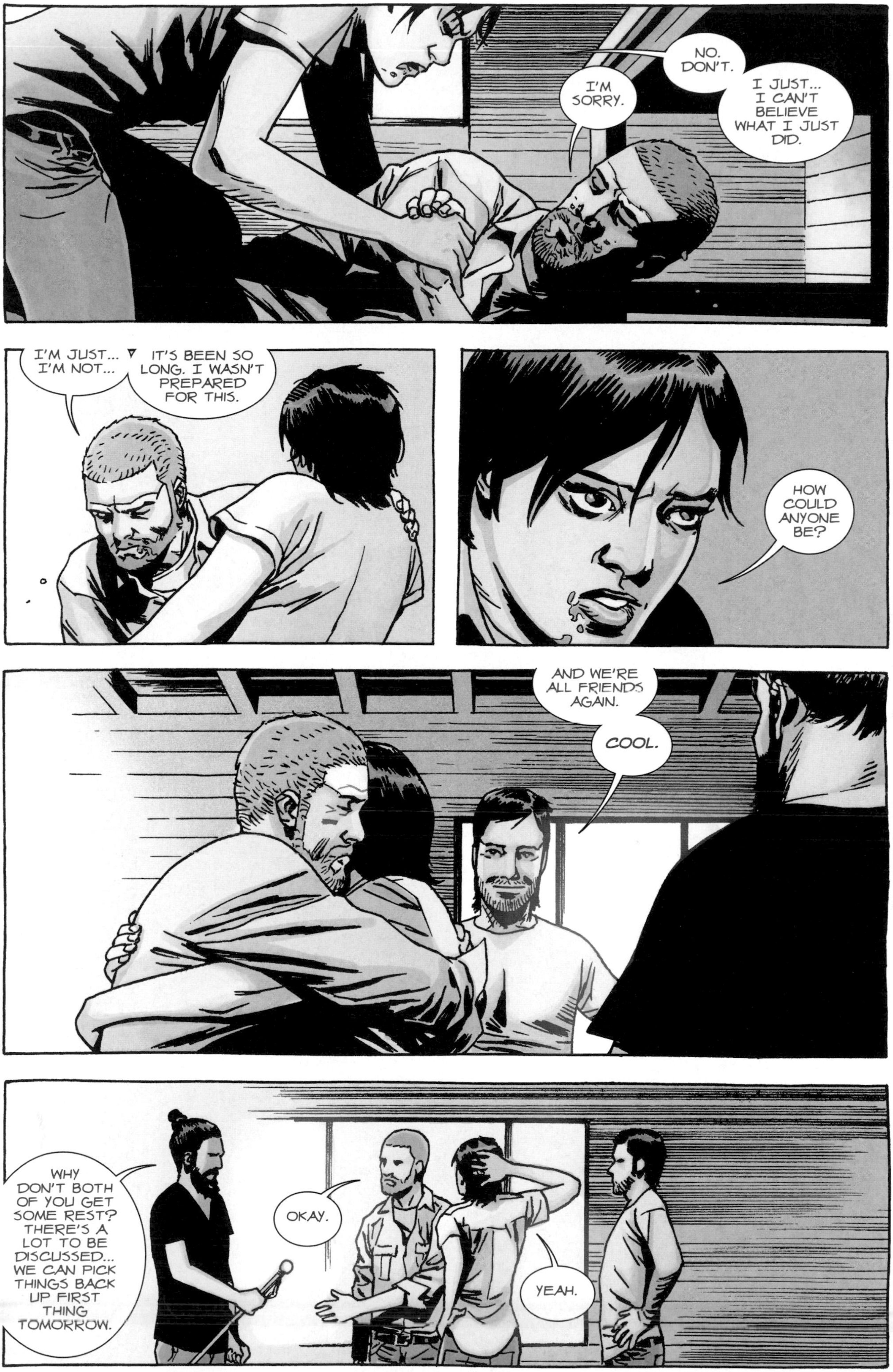
I'M SORRY.
NO. DON'T.
I JUST... I CAN'T BELIEVE WHAT I JUST DID.
I'M JUST... I'M NOT...
IT'S BEEN SO LONG. I WASN'T PREPARED FOR THIS.
HOW COULD ANYONE BE?
AND WE'RE ALL FRIENDS AGAIN.
COOL.
WHY DON'T BOTH OF YOU GET SOME REST? THERE'S A LOT TO BE DISCUSSED... WE CAN PICK THINGS BACK UP FIRST THING TOMORROW.
OKAY.
YEAH.

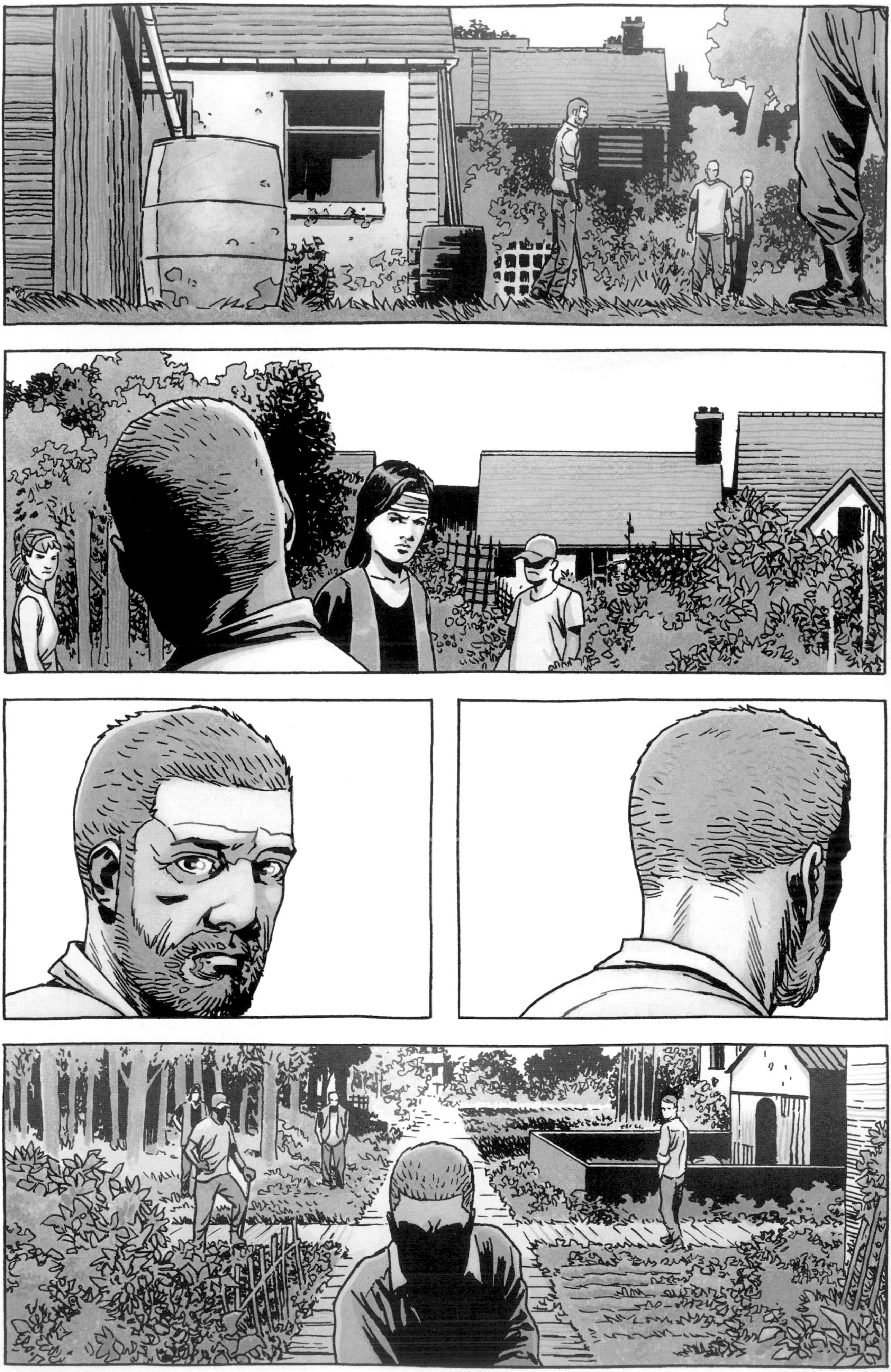

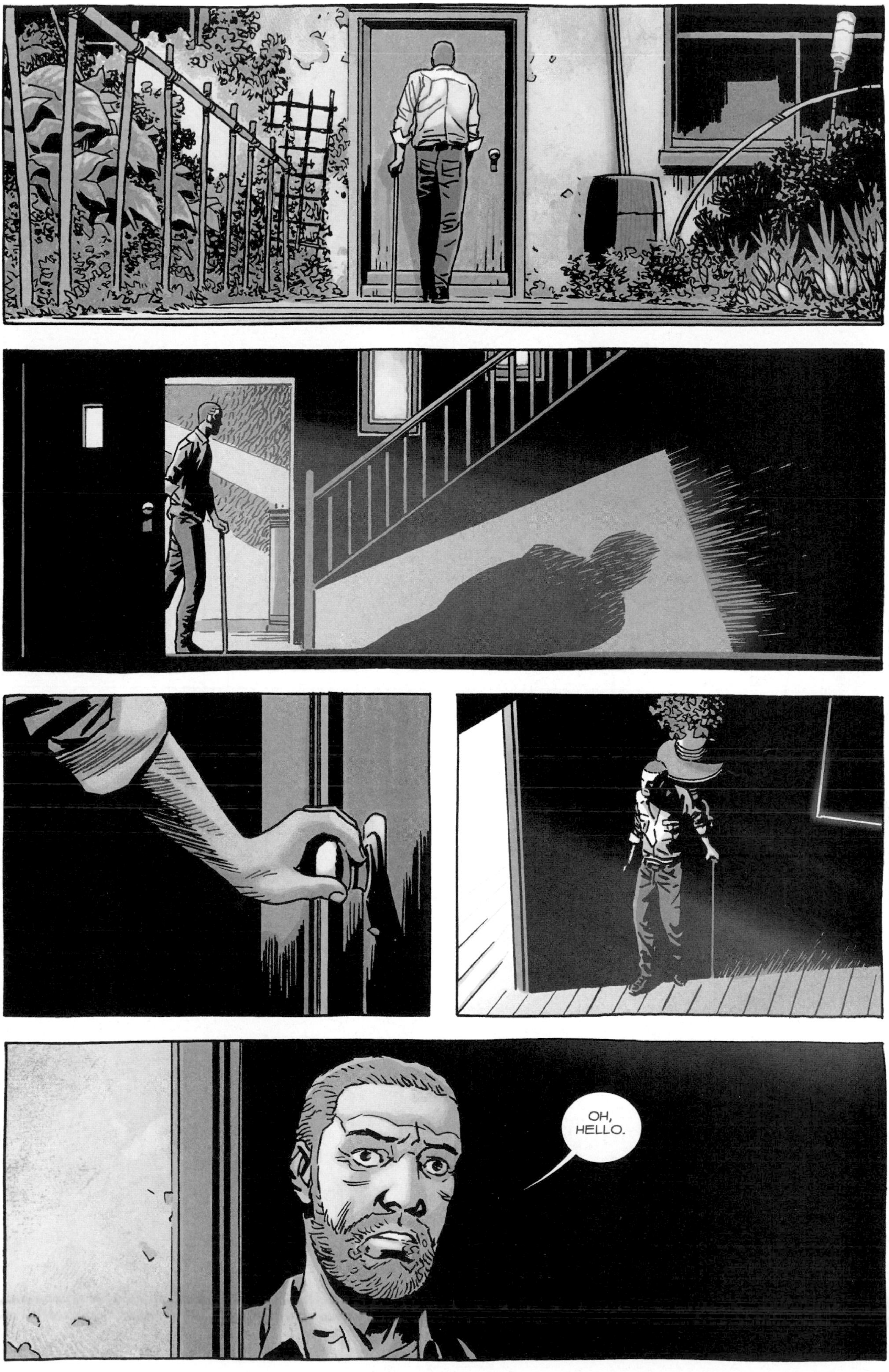
OH, HELLO.

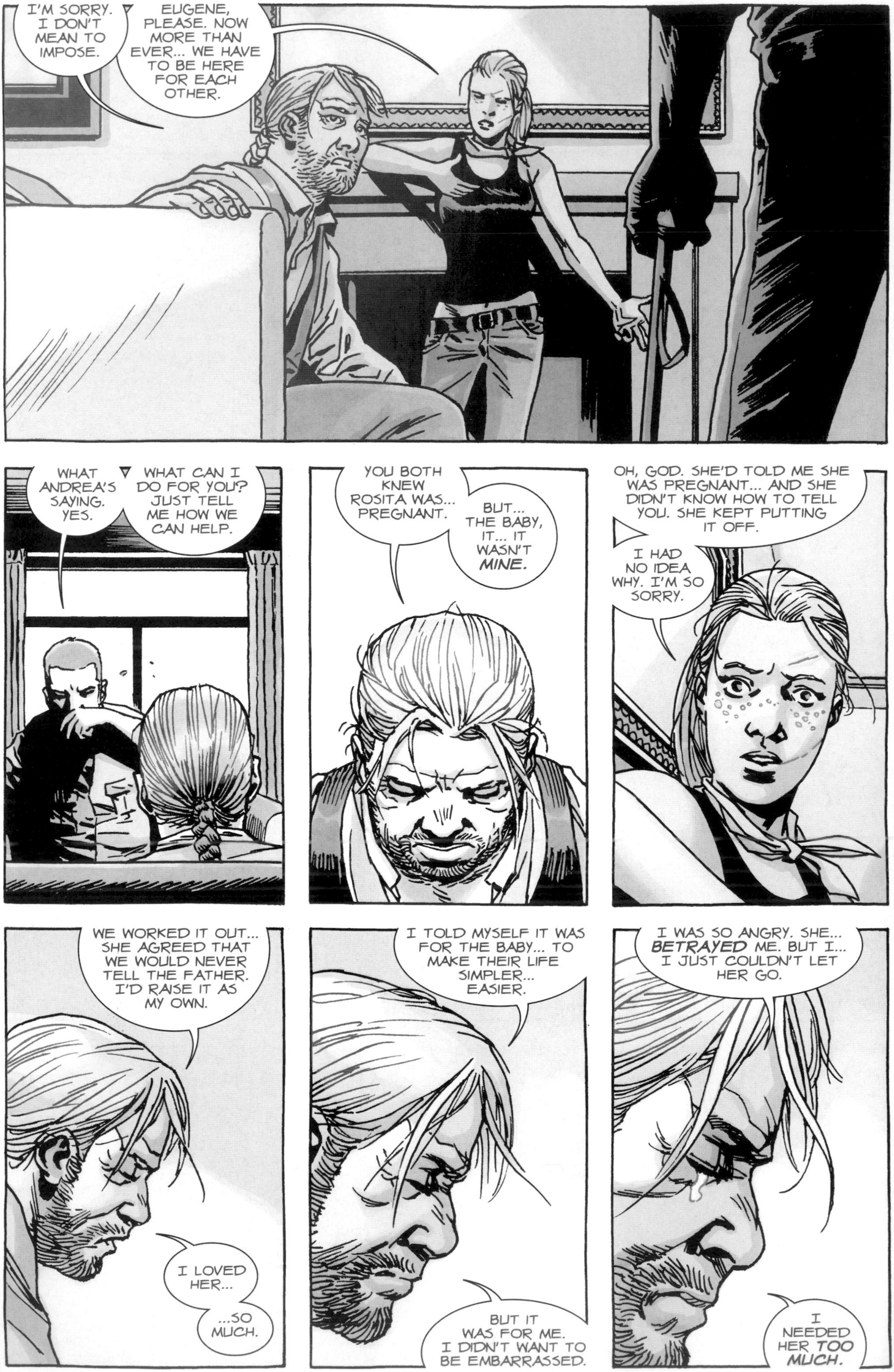
I'M SORRY. I DON'T MEAN TO IMPOSE.
EUGENE, PLEASE. NOW MORE THAN EVER... WE HAVE TO BE HERE FOR EACH OTHER.
WHAT ANDREA'S SAYING. YES.
WHAT CAN I DO FOR YOU? JUST TELL ME HOW WE CAN HELP.
YOU BOTH KNEW ROSITA WAS... PREGNANT.
BUT... THE BABY, IT... IT WASN'T MINE.
OH, GOD. SHE'D TOLD ME SHE WAS PREGNANT... AND SHE DIDN'T KNOW HOW TO TELL YOU. SHE KEPT PUTTING IT OFF.
I HAD NO IDEA WHY. I'M SO SORRY.
WE WORKED IT OUT... SHE AGREED THAT WE WOULD NEVER TELL THE FATHER. I'D RAISE IT AS MY OWN.
I LOVED HER...
...SO MUCH.
I TOLD MYSELF IT WAS FOR THE BABY... TO MAKE THEIR LIFE SIMPLER... EASIER.
BUT IT WAS FOR ME. I DIDN'T WANT TO BE EMBARRASSED.
I WAS SO ANGRY. SHE... BETRAYED ME. BUT I... I JUST COULDN'T LET HER GO.
I NEEDED HER TOO MUCH.

I KNOW THE PEOPLE... THEY'RE CALLING FOR WAR, THEY WANT TO ATTACK NOW... THEY WANT TO GET US ALL KILLED.

THEY'RE *NOT SMART* PEOPLE.

BUT I AM. I KNOW WE NEED TO PLAN. WE NEED TO WAIT... WE NEED TO GET THINGS RIGHT. BUT IN THE END... I JUST HAVE TO BE SURE...

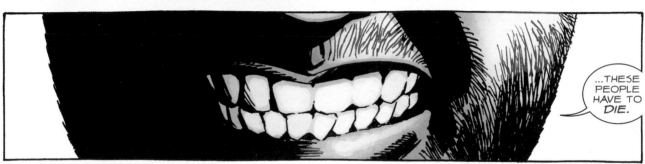

...THESE PEOPLE HAVE TO *DIE.*

I PROMISE YOU WE FEEL THE SAME WAY.

THIS... IT CANNOT GO *UNPUNISHED.*

I KNOW THAT DOESN'T BRING YOU MUCH COMFORT. BUT YOU'RE RIGHT. THIS HAS TO BE MANAGED VERY *CAREFULLY.*

YES, BUT... THAT'S WHY I'M HERE.

I KNOW HOW *DANGEROUS* THESE PEOPLE ARE... AND I'VE HEARD YOU TALK ABOUT THIS MASSIVE HERD THEY MANAGE... HOW THEY CONTROL IT.

BUT I THINK YOU'RE OVERLOOKING A MASSIVE ADVANTAGE WE HAVE OVER THEM RIGHT NOW. THEIR LEADER... THAT WOMAN... *ALPHA...*

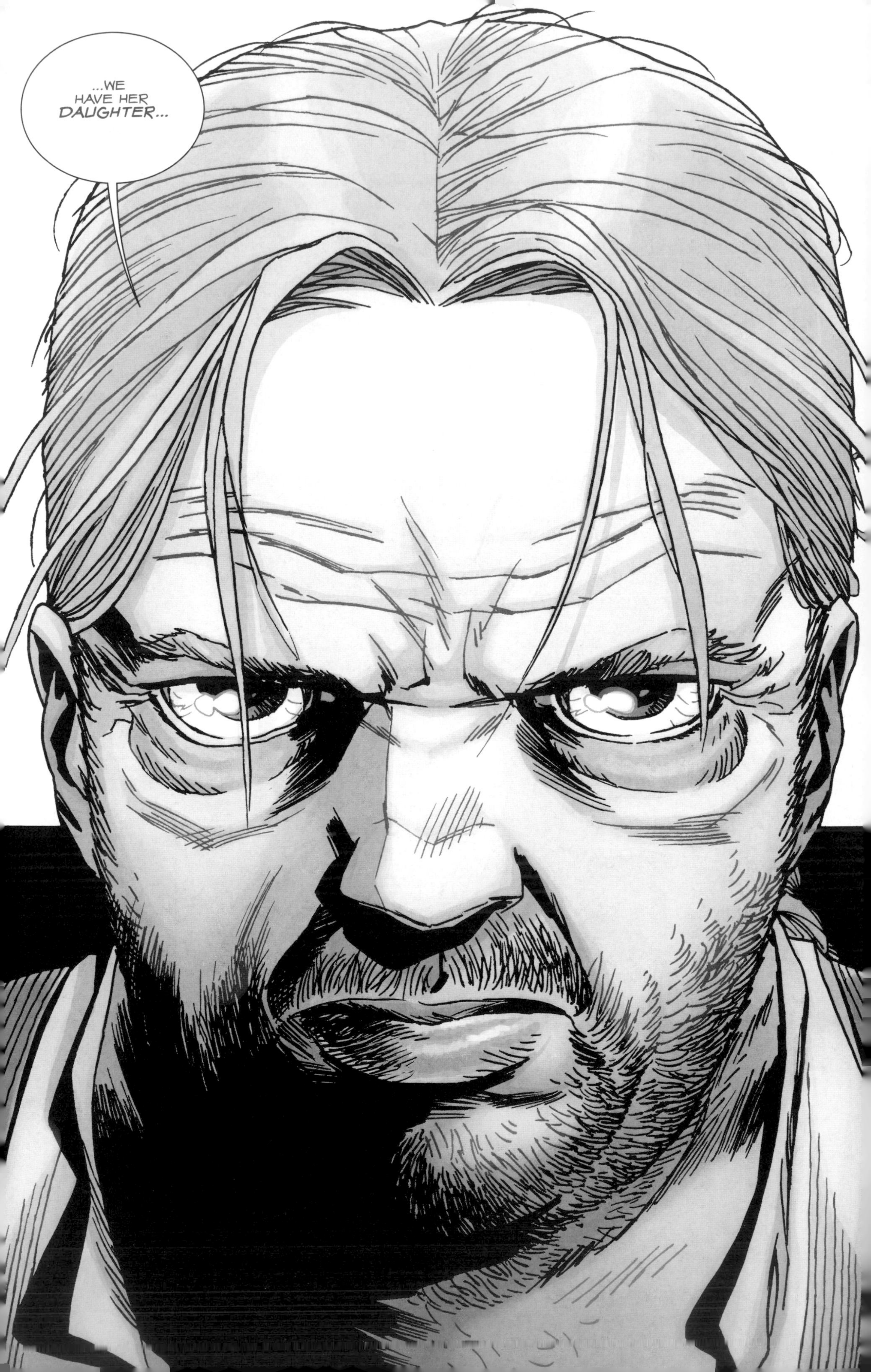
...WE HAVE HER DAUGHTER...

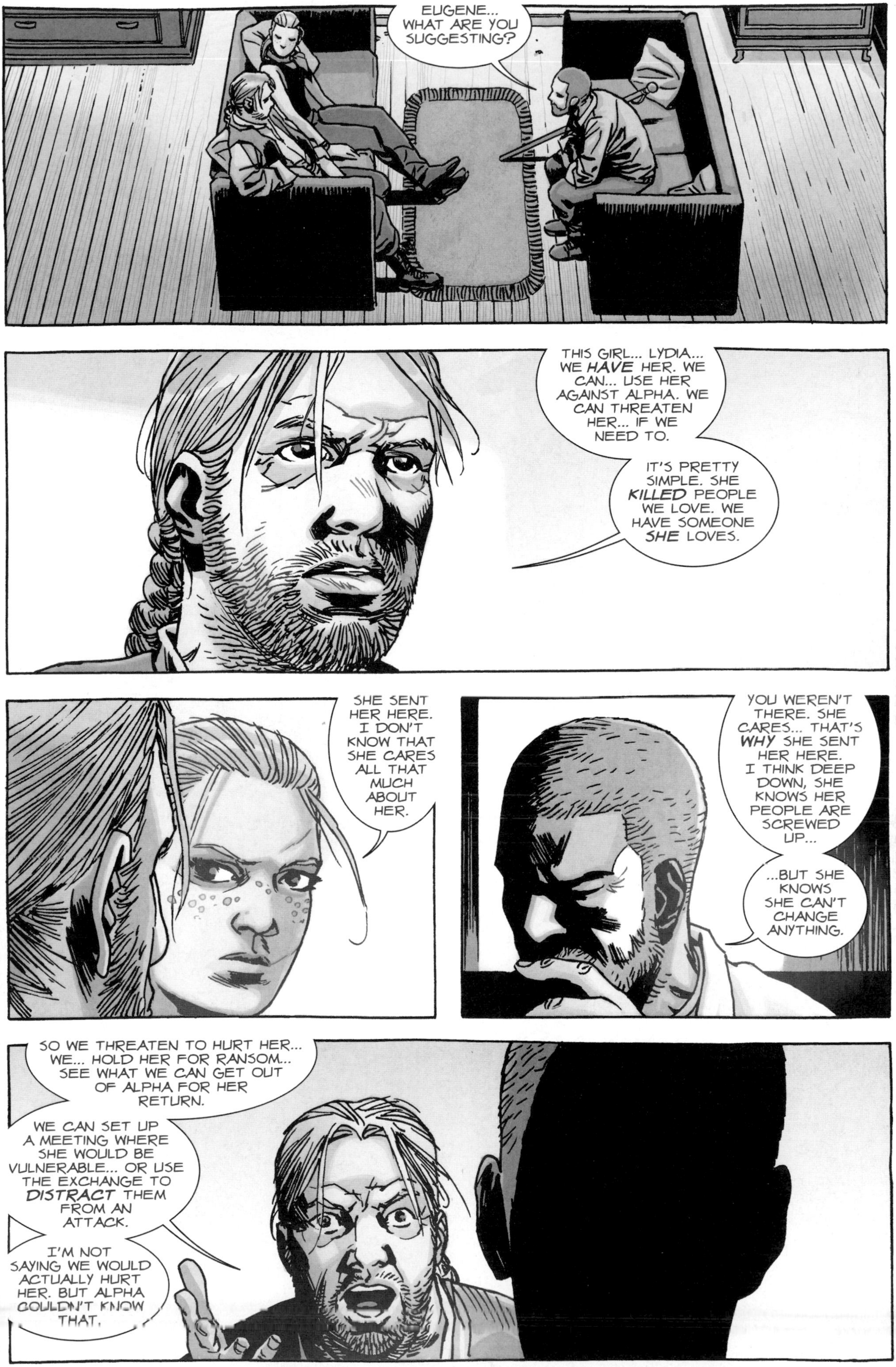
EUGENE... WHAT ARE YOU SUGGESTING?
THIS GIRL... LYDIA... WE HAVE HER. WE CAN... USE HER AGAINST ALPHA. WE CAN THREATEN HER... IF WE NEED TO.
IT'S PRETTY SIMPLE. SHE KILLED PEOPLE WE LOVE. WE HAVE SOMEONE SHE LOVES.
SHE SENT HER HERE. I DON'T KNOW THAT SHE CARES ALL THAT MUCH ABOUT HER.
YOU WEREN'T THERE. SHE CARES... THAT'S WHY SHE SENT HER HERE. I THINK DEEP DOWN, SHE KNOWS HER PEOPLE ARE SCREWED UP...
...BUT SHE KNOWS SHE CAN'T CHANGE ANYTHING.
SO WE THREATEN TO HURT HER... WE... HOLD HER FOR RANSOM... SEE WHAT WE CAN GET OUT OF ALPHA FOR HER RETURN.
WE CAN SET UP A MEETING WHERE SHE WOULD BE VULNERABLE... OR USE THE EXCHANGE TO DISTRACT THEM FROM AN ATTACK.
I'M NOT SAYING WE WOULD ACTUALLY HURT HER. BUT ALPHA COULDN'T KNOW THAT.

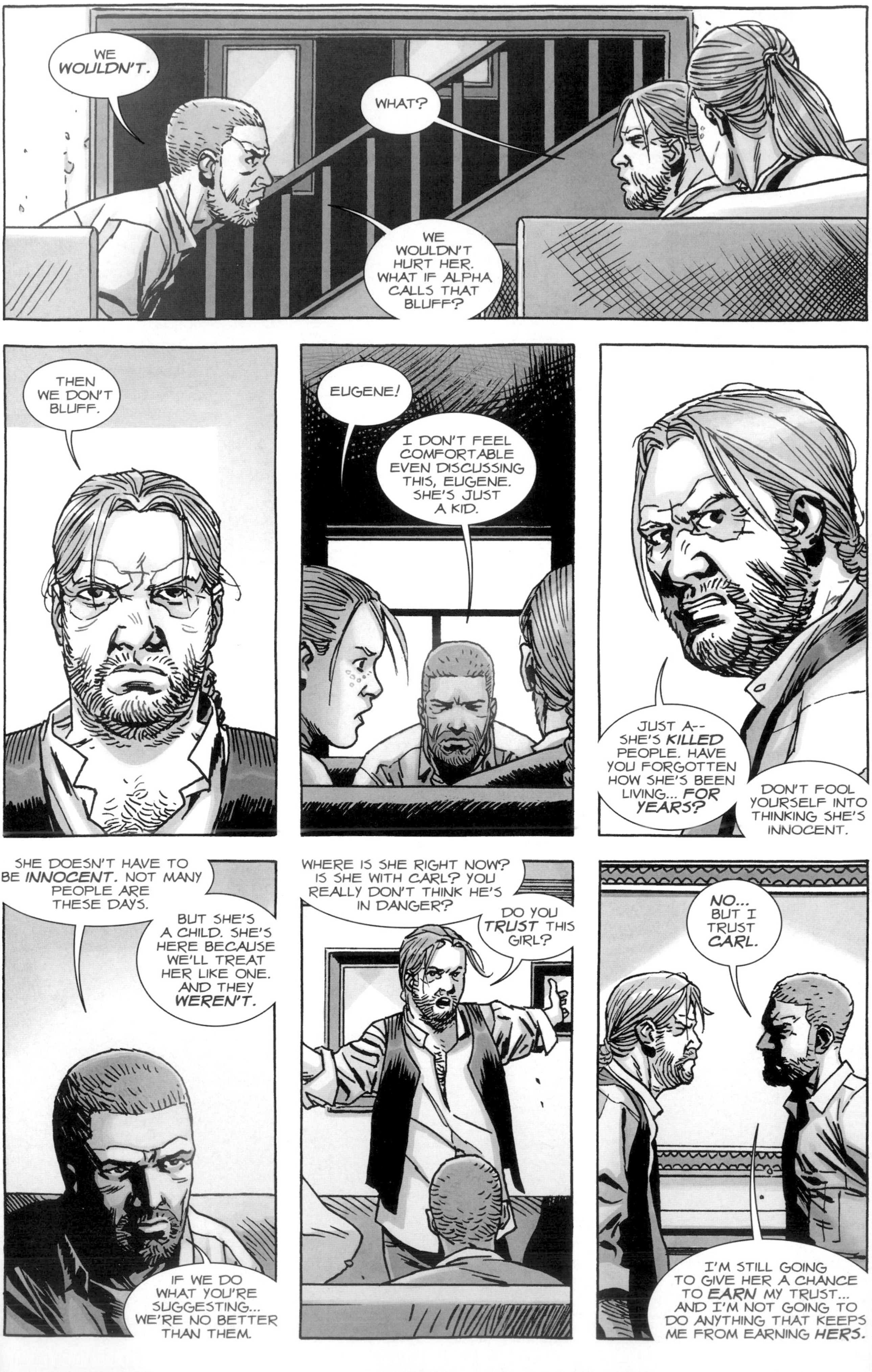
WE WOULDN'T.
WHAT?
WE WOULDN'T HURT HER. WHAT IF ALPHA CALLS THAT BLUFF?
THEN WE DON'T BLUFF.
EUGENE!
I DON'T FEEL COMFORTABLE EVEN DISCUSSING THIS, EUGENE. SHE'S JUST A KID.
JUST A-- SHE'S KILLED PEOPLE. HAVE YOU FORGOTTEN HOW SHE'S BEEN LIVING... FOR YEARS?
DON'T FOOL YOURSELF INTO THINKING SHE'S INNOCENT.
SHE DOESN'T HAVE TO BE INNOCENT. NOT MANY PEOPLE ARE THESE DAYS.
BUT SHE'S A CHILD. SHE'S HERE BECAUSE WE'LL TREAT HER LIKE ONE. AND THEY WEREN'T.
IF WE DO WHAT YOU'RE SUGGESTING... WE'RE NO BETTER THAN THEM.
WHERE IS SHE RIGHT NOW? IS SHE WITH CARL? YOU REALLY DON'T THINK HE'S IN DANGER?
DO YOU TRUST THIS GIRL?
NO... BUT I TRUST CARL.
I'M STILL GOING TO GIVE HER A CHANCE TO EARN MY TRUST... AND I'M NOT GOING TO DO ANYTHING THAT KEEPS ME FROM EARNING HERS.

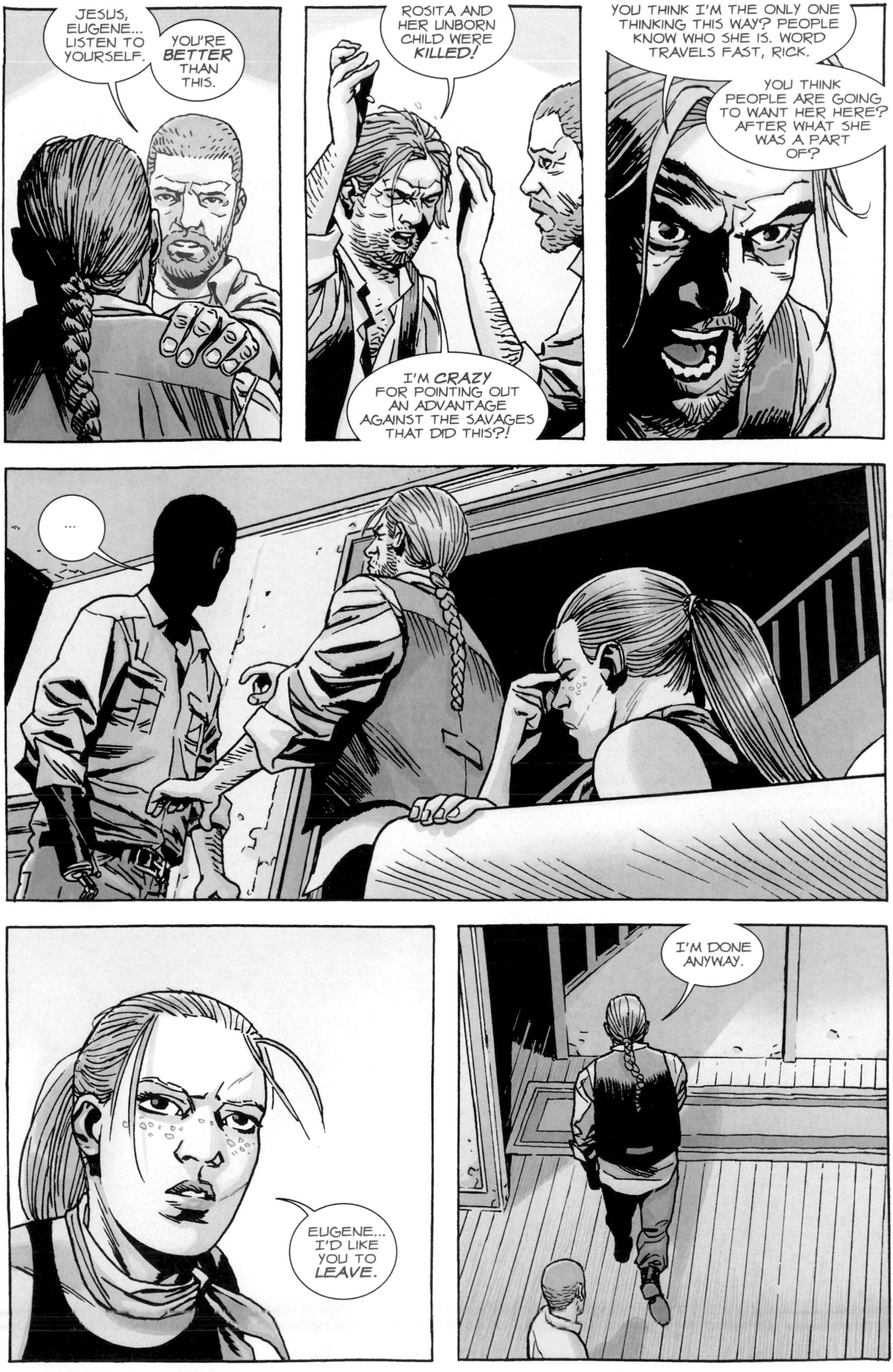
JESUS, EUGENE... LISTEN TO YOURSELF.
YOU'RE BETTER THAN THIS.
ROSITA AND HER UNBORN CHILD WERE KILLED!
I'M CRAZY FOR POINTING OUT AN ADVANTAGE AGAINST THE SAVAGES THAT DID THIS?!
YOU THINK I'M THE ONLY ONE THINKING THIS WAY? PEOPLE KNOW WHO SHE IS. WORD TRAVELS FAST, RICK.
YOU THINK PEOPLE ARE GOING TO WANT HER HERE? AFTER WHAT SHE WAS A PART OF?
...
EUGENE... I'D LIKE YOU TO LEAVE.
I'M DONE ANYWAY.

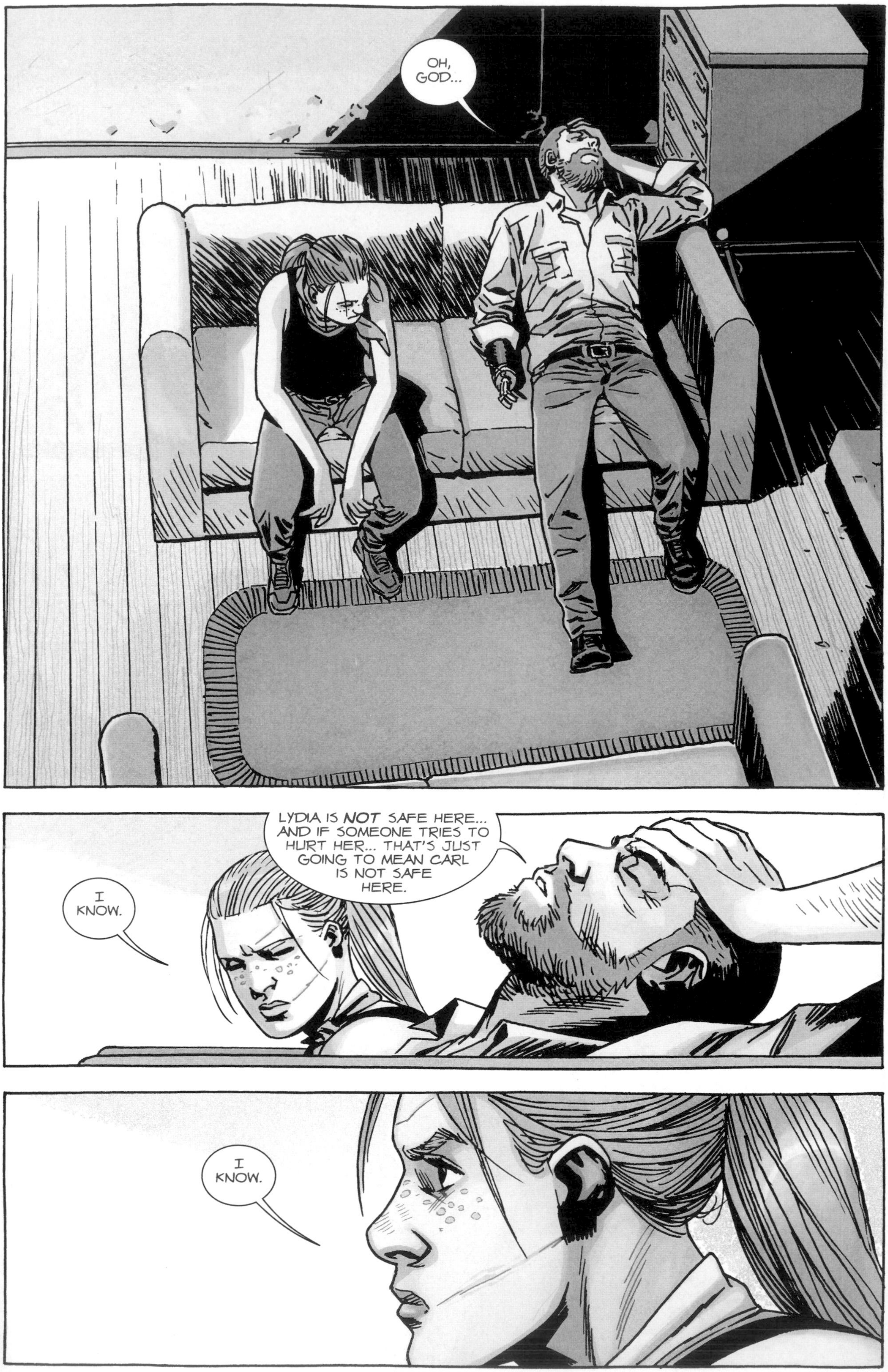

OH, GOD...
LYDIA IS NOT SAFE HERE... AND IF SOMEONE TRIES TO HURT HER... THAT'S JUST GOING TO MEAN CARL IS NOT SAFE HERE.
I KNOW.
I KNOW.

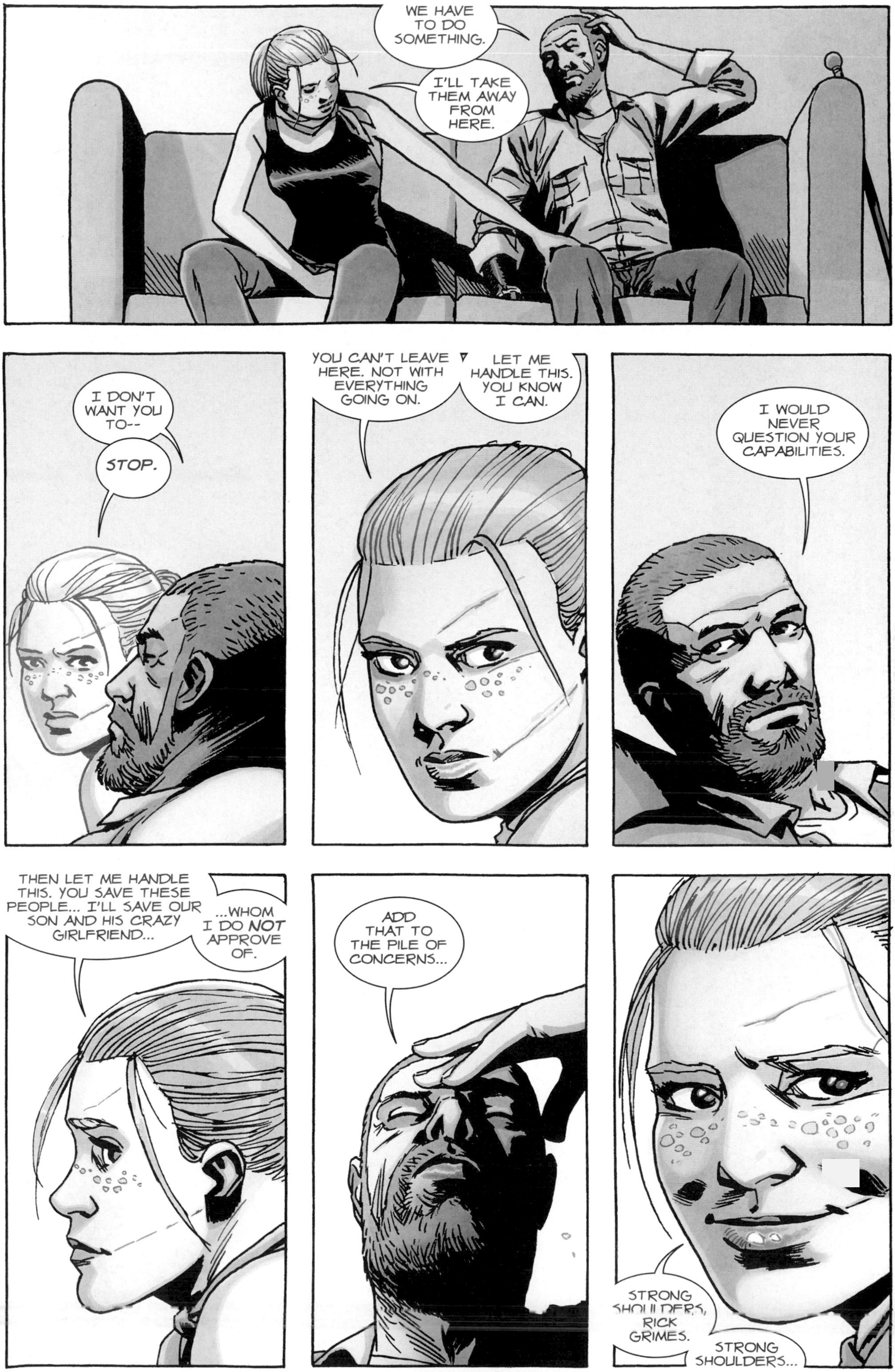
WE HAVE TO DO SOMETHING.
I'LL TAKE THEM AWAY FROM HERE.
I DON'T WANT YOU TO--
STOP.
YOU CAN'T LEAVE HERE. NOT WITH EVERYTHING GOING ON.
LET ME HANDLE THIS. YOU KNOW I CAN.
I WOULD NEVER QUESTION YOUR CAPABILITIES.
THEN LET ME HANDLE THIS. YOU SAVE THESE PEOPLE... I'LL SAVE OUR SON AND HIS CRAZY GIRLFRIEND...
...WHOM I DO NOT APPROVE OF.
ADD THAT TO THE PILE OF CONCERNS...
STRONG SHOULDERS, RICK GRIMES.
STRONG SHOULDERS...

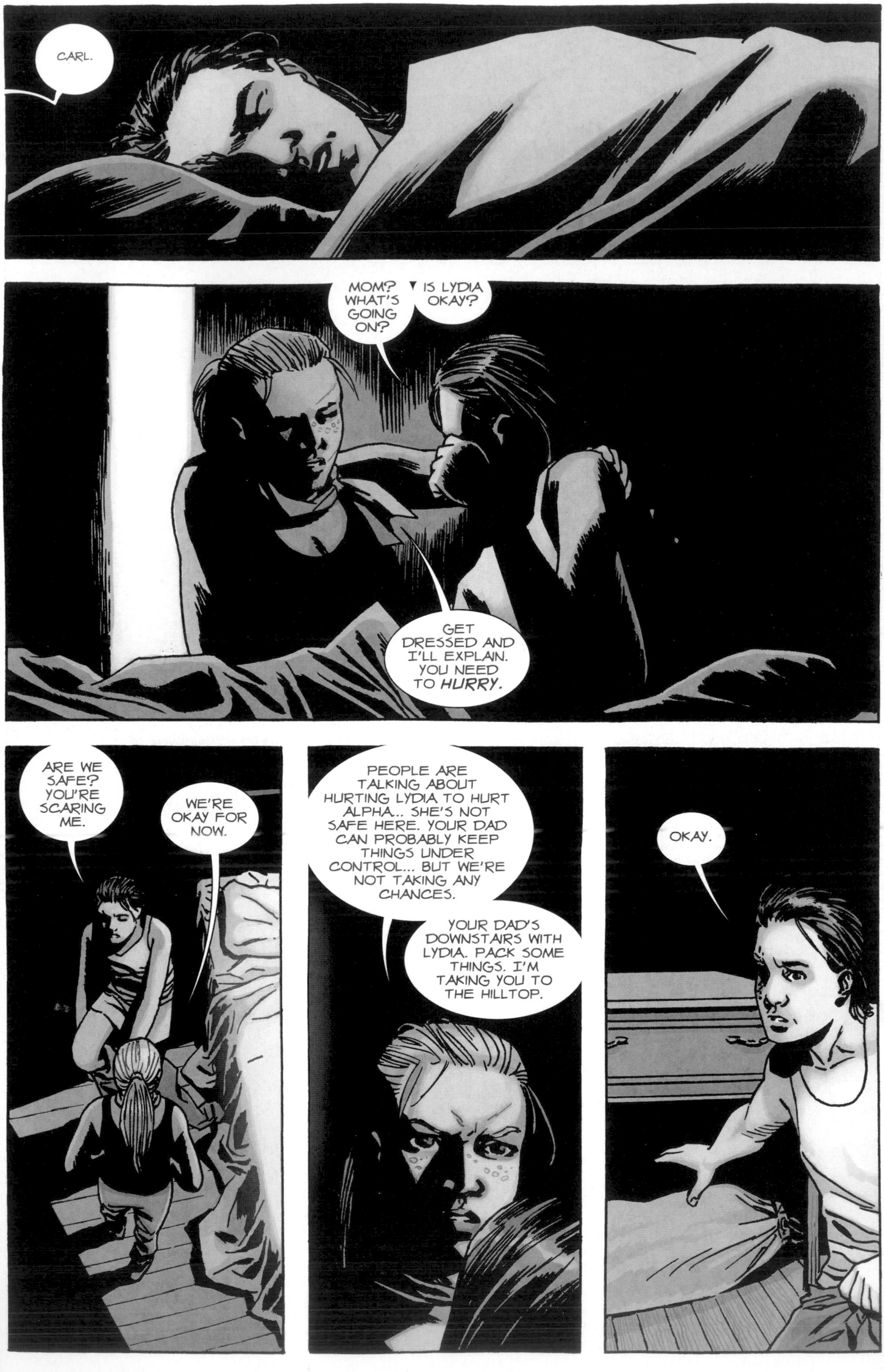
CARL.
MOM? WHAT'S GOING ON?
IS LYDIA OKAY?
GET DRESSED AND I'LL EXPLAIN. YOU NEED TO HURRY.
ARE WE SAFE? YOU'RE SCARING ME.
WE'RE OKAY FOR NOW.
PEOPLE ARE TALKING ABOUT HURTING LYDIA TO HURT ALPHA.. SHE'S NOT SAFE HERE. YOUR DAD CAN PROBABLY KEEP THINGS UNDER CONTROL... BUT WE'RE NOT TAKING ANY CHANCES.
YOUR DAD'S DOWNSTAIRS WITH LYDIA. PACK SOME THINGS. I'M TAKING YOU TO THE HILLTOP.
OKAY.

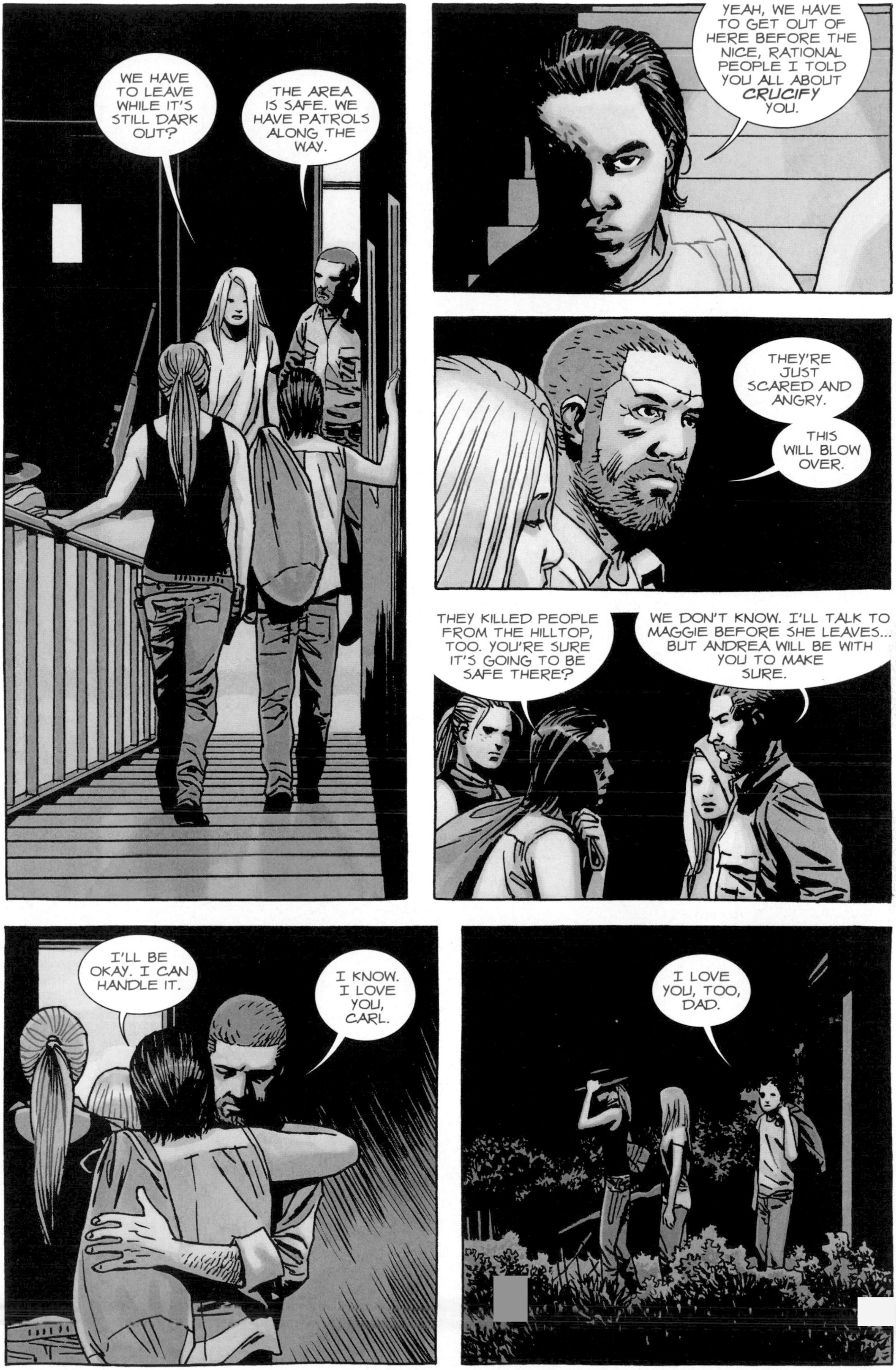

WE HAVE TO LEAVE WHILE IT'S STILL DARK OUT?
THE AREA IS SAFE. WE HAVE PATROLS ALONG THE WAY.
YEAH, WE HAVE TO GET OUT OF HERE BEFORE THE NICE, RATIONAL PEOPLE I TOLD YOU ALL ABOUT CRUCIFY YOU.
THEY'RE JUST SCARED AND ANGRY.
THIS WILL BLOW OVER.
THEY KILLED PEOPLE FROM THE HILLTOP, TOO. YOU'RE SURE IT'S GOING TO BE SAFE THERE?
WE DON'T KNOW. I'LL TALK TO MAGGIE BEFORE SHE LEAVES... BUT ANDREA WILL BE WITH YOU TO MAKE SURE.
I'LL BE OKAY. I CAN HANDLE IT.
I KNOW. I LOVE YOU, CARL.
I LOVE YOU, TOO, DAD.

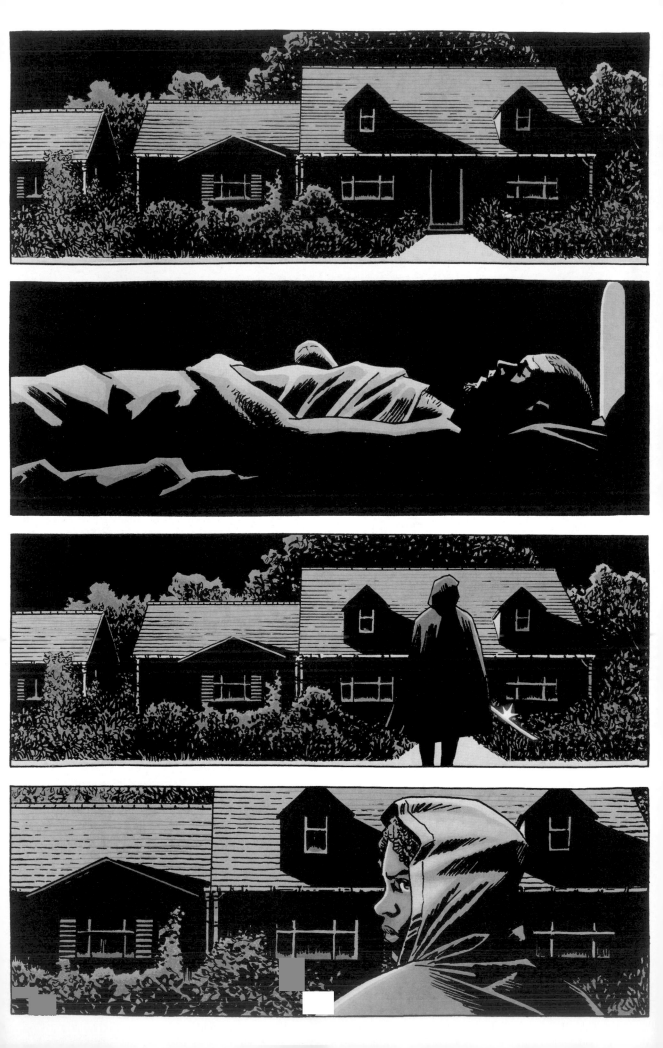

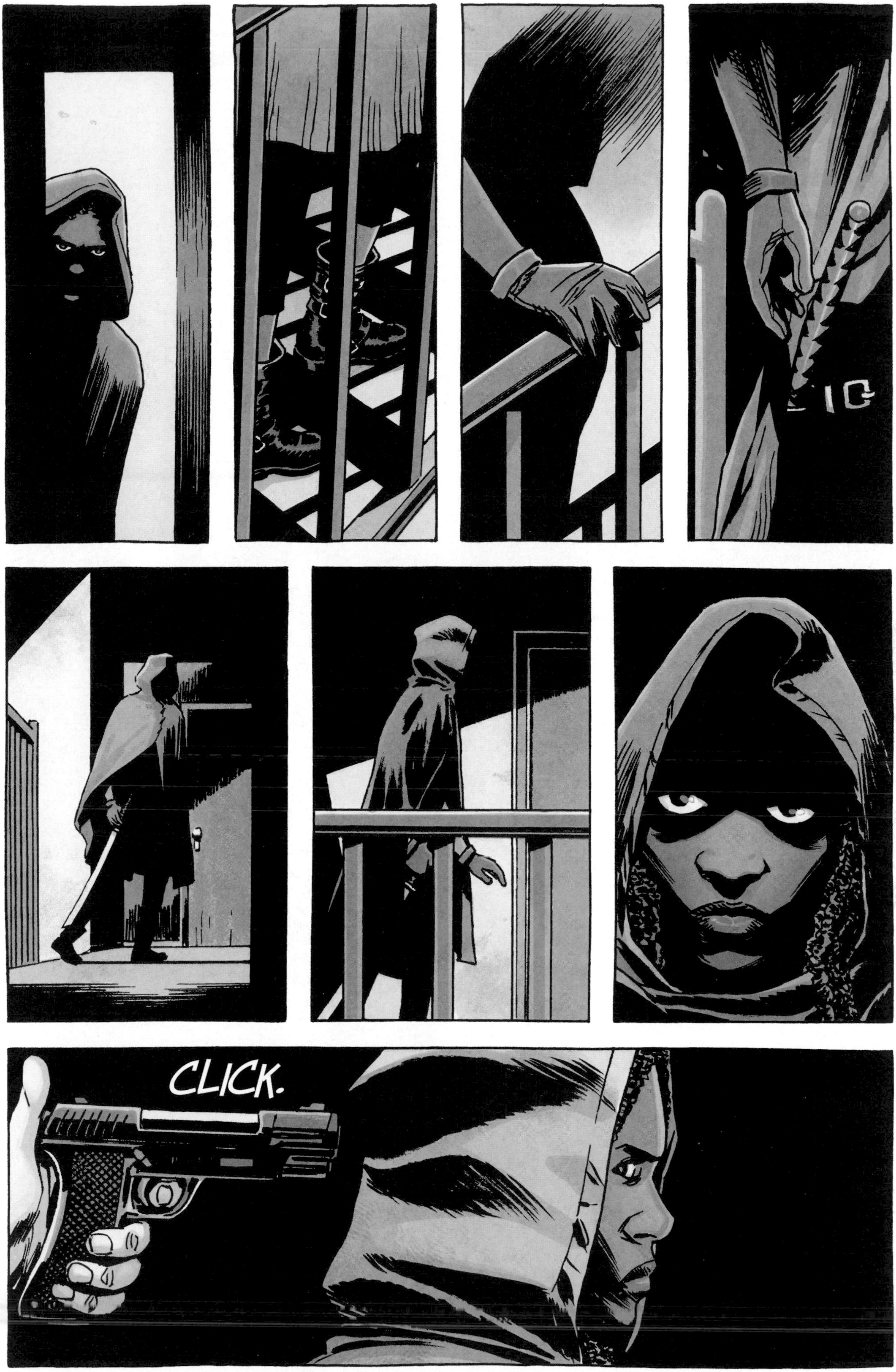
CLICK.

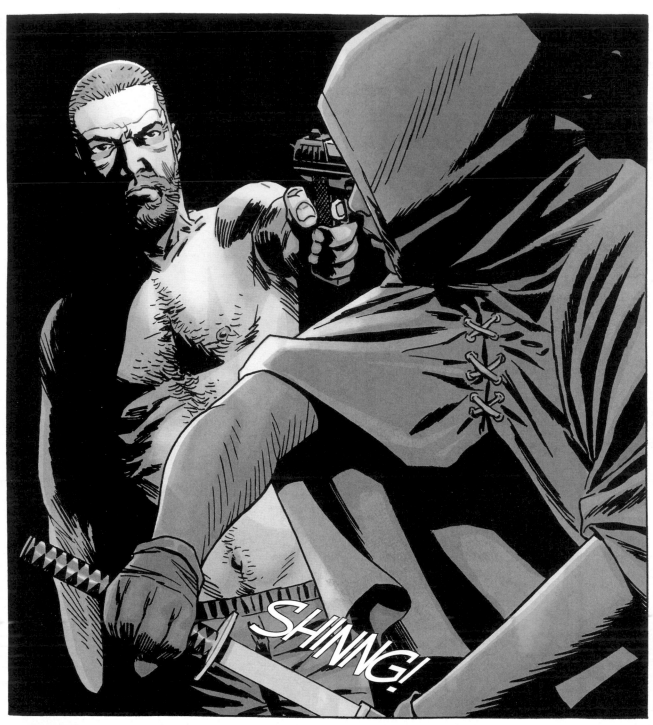

SHINNG!

YOU'RE NOT THE LEAST BIT RUSTY.

WHERE IS SHE?

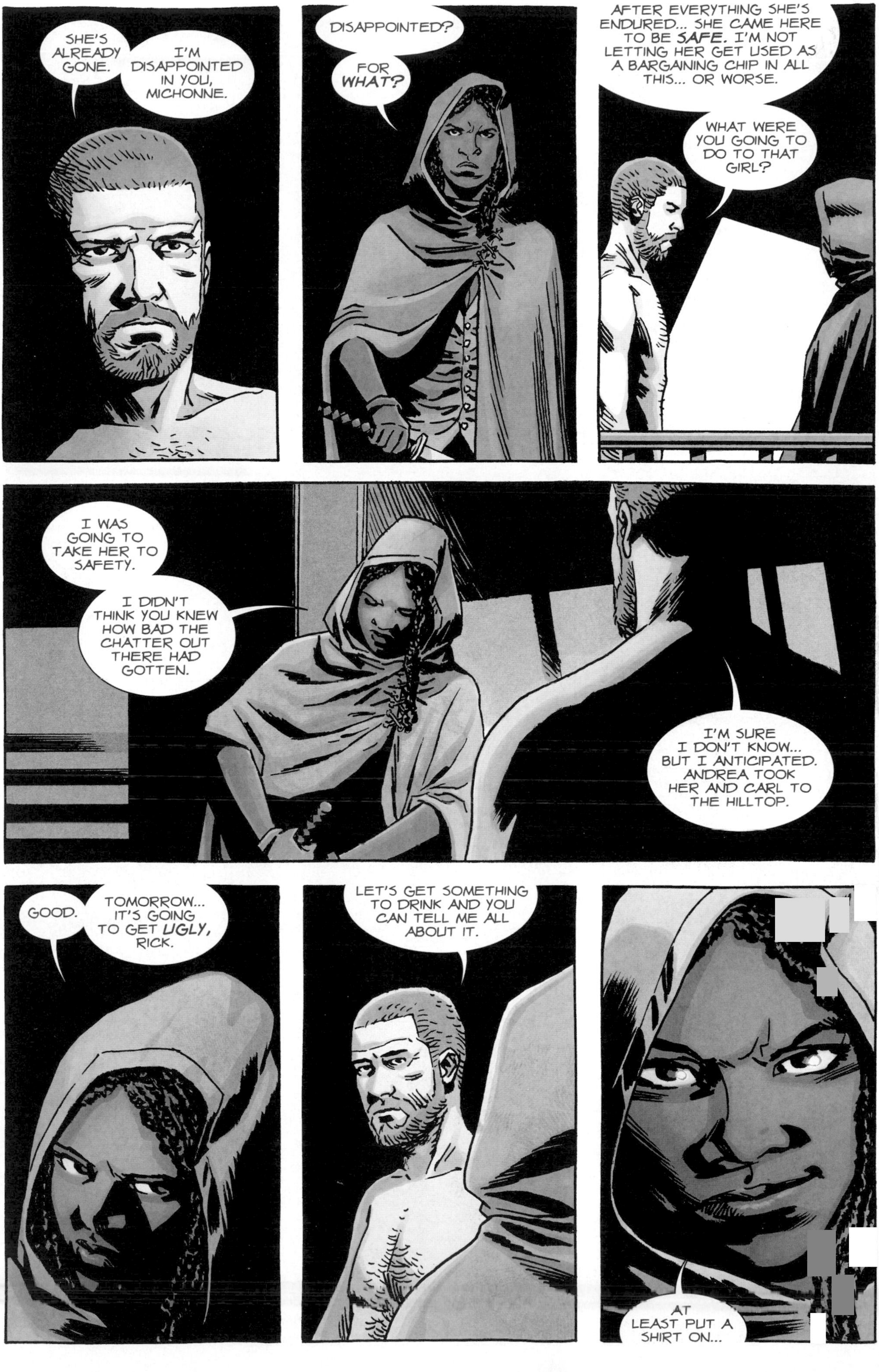
SHE'S ALREADY GONE.
I'M DISAPPOINTED IN YOU, MICHONNE.
DISAPPOINTED?
FOR WHAT?
AFTER EVERYTHING SHE'S ENDURED... SHE CAME HERE TO BE SAFE. I'M NOT LETTING HER GET USED AS A BARGAINING CHIP IN ALL THIS... OR WORSE.
WHAT WERE YOU GOING TO DO TO THAT GIRL?
I WAS GOING TO TAKE HER TO SAFETY.
I DIDN'T THINK YOU KNEW HOW BAD THE CHATTER OUT THERE HAD GOTTEN.
I'M SURE I DON'T KNOW... BUT I ANTICIPATED. ANDREA TOOK HER AND CARL TO THE HILLTOP.
GOOD.
TOMORROW... IT'S GOING TO GET UGLY, RICK.
LET'S GET SOMETHING TO DRINK AND YOU CAN TELL ME ALL ABOUT IT.
AT LEAST PUT A SHIRT ON...

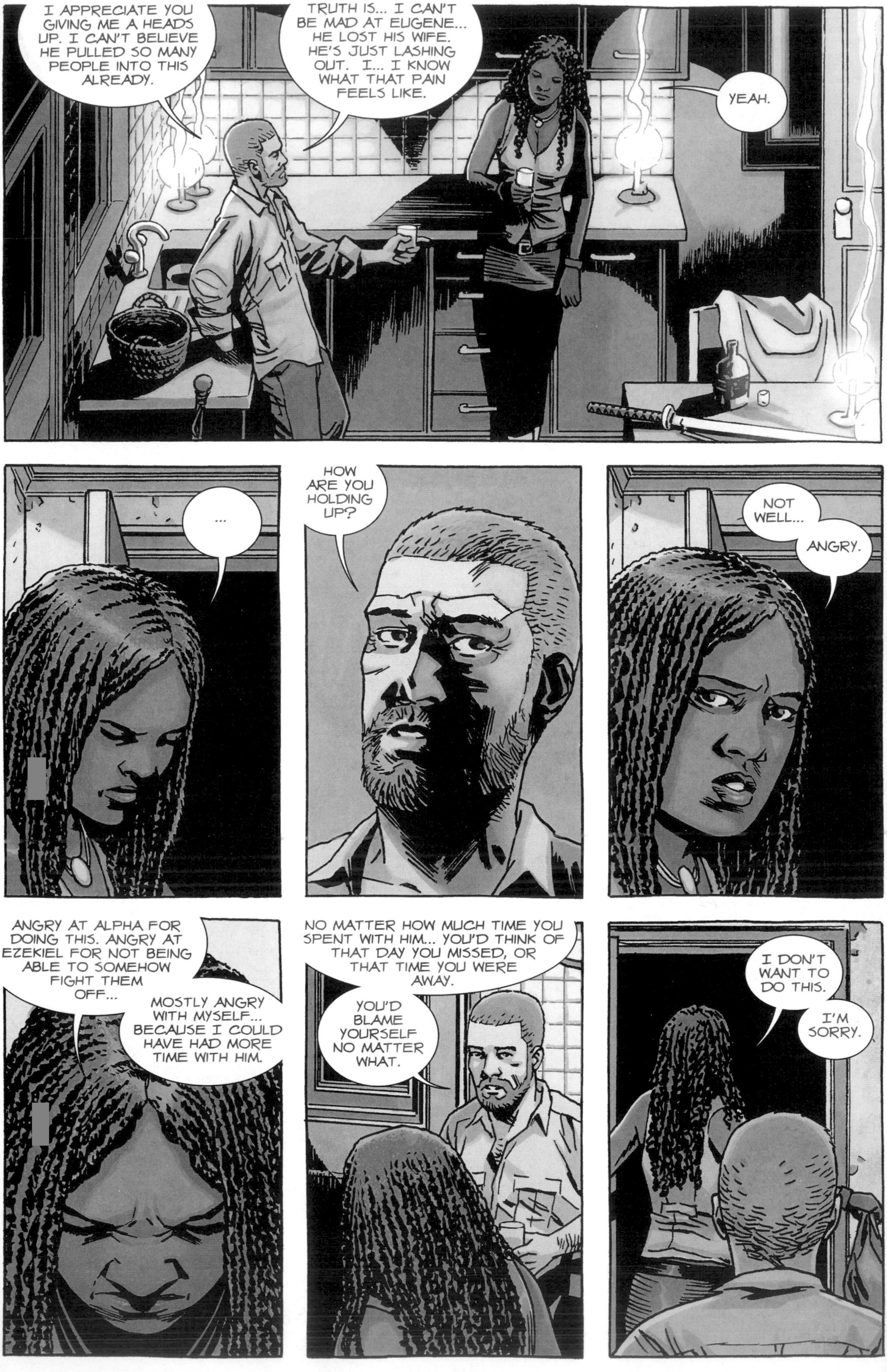
I APPRECIATE YOU GIVING ME A HEADS UP. I CAN'T BELIEVE HE PULLED SO MANY PEOPLE INTO THIS ALREADY.
TRUTH IS... I CAN'T BE MAD AT EUGENE... HE LOST HIS WIFE. HE'S JUST LASHING OUT. I... I KNOW WHAT THAT PAIN FEELS LIKE.
YEAH.
...
HOW ARE YOU HOLDING UP?
NOT WELL...
ANGRY.
ANGRY AT ALPHA FOR DOING THIS. ANGRY AT EZEKIEL FOR NOT BEING ABLE TO SOMEHOW FIGHT THEM OFF...
MOSTLY ANGRY WITH MYSELF... BECAUSE I COULD HAVE HAD MORE TIME WITH HIM.
NO MATTER HOW MUCH TIME YOU SPENT WITH HIM... YOU'D THINK OF THAT DAY YOU MISSED, OR THAT TIME YOU WERE AWAY.
YOU'D BLAME YOURSELF NO MATTER WHAT.
I DON'T WANT TO DO THIS.
I'M SORRY.

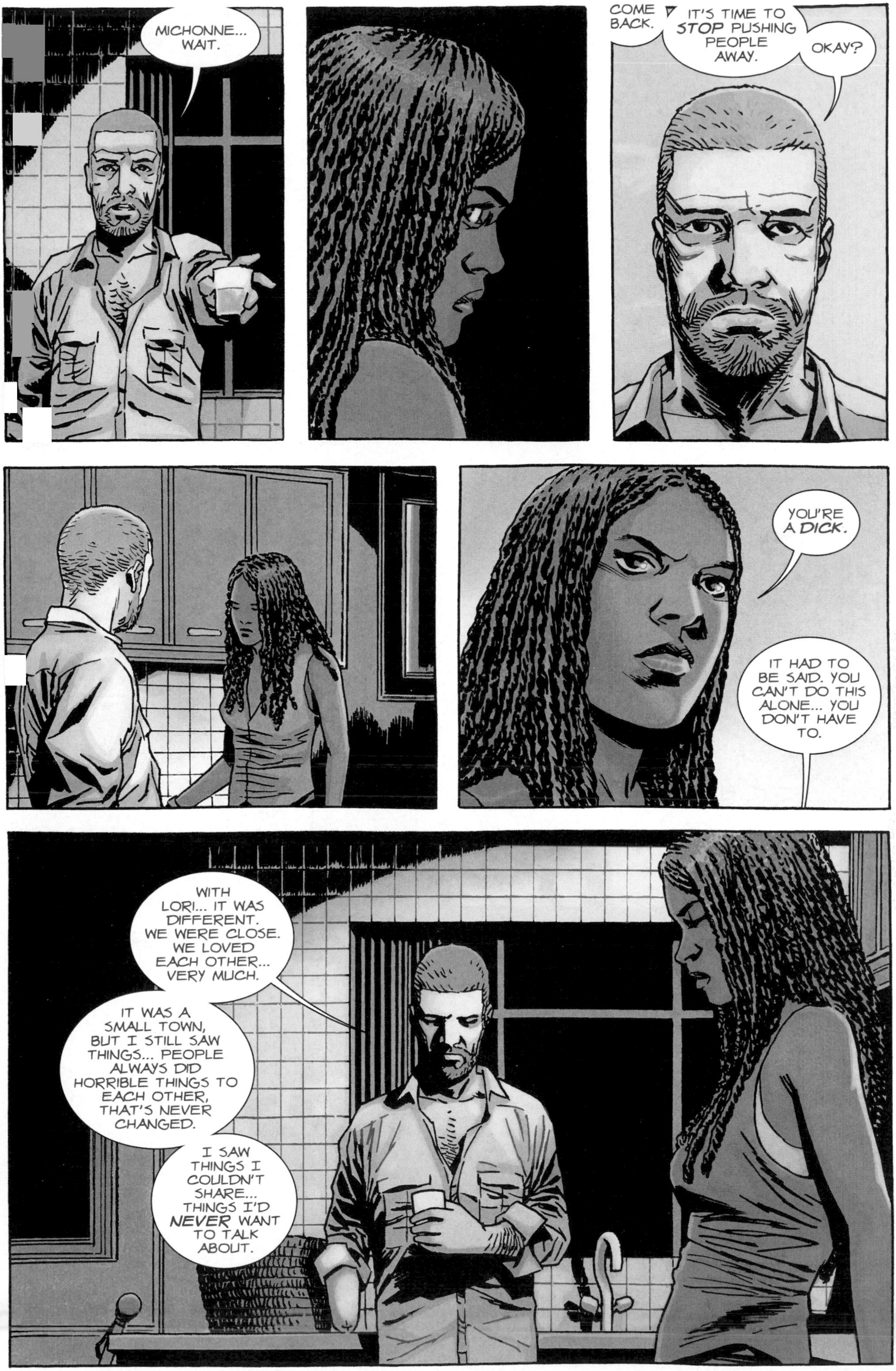
MICHONNE... WAIT.
COME BACK.
IT'S TIME TO STOP PUSHING PEOPLE AWAY.
OKAY?
YOU'RE A DICK.
IT HAD TO BE SAID. YOU CAN'T DO THIS ALONE... YOU DON'T HAVE TO.
WITH LORI... IT WAS DIFFERENT. WE WERE CLOSE. WE LOVED EACH OTHER... VERY MUCH.
IT WAS A SMALL TOWN, BUT I STILL SAW THINGS... PEOPLE ALWAYS DID HORRIBLE THINGS TO EACH OTHER, THAT'S NEVER CHANGED.
I SAW THINGS I COULDN'T SHARE... THINGS I'D NEVER WANT TO TALK ABOUT.

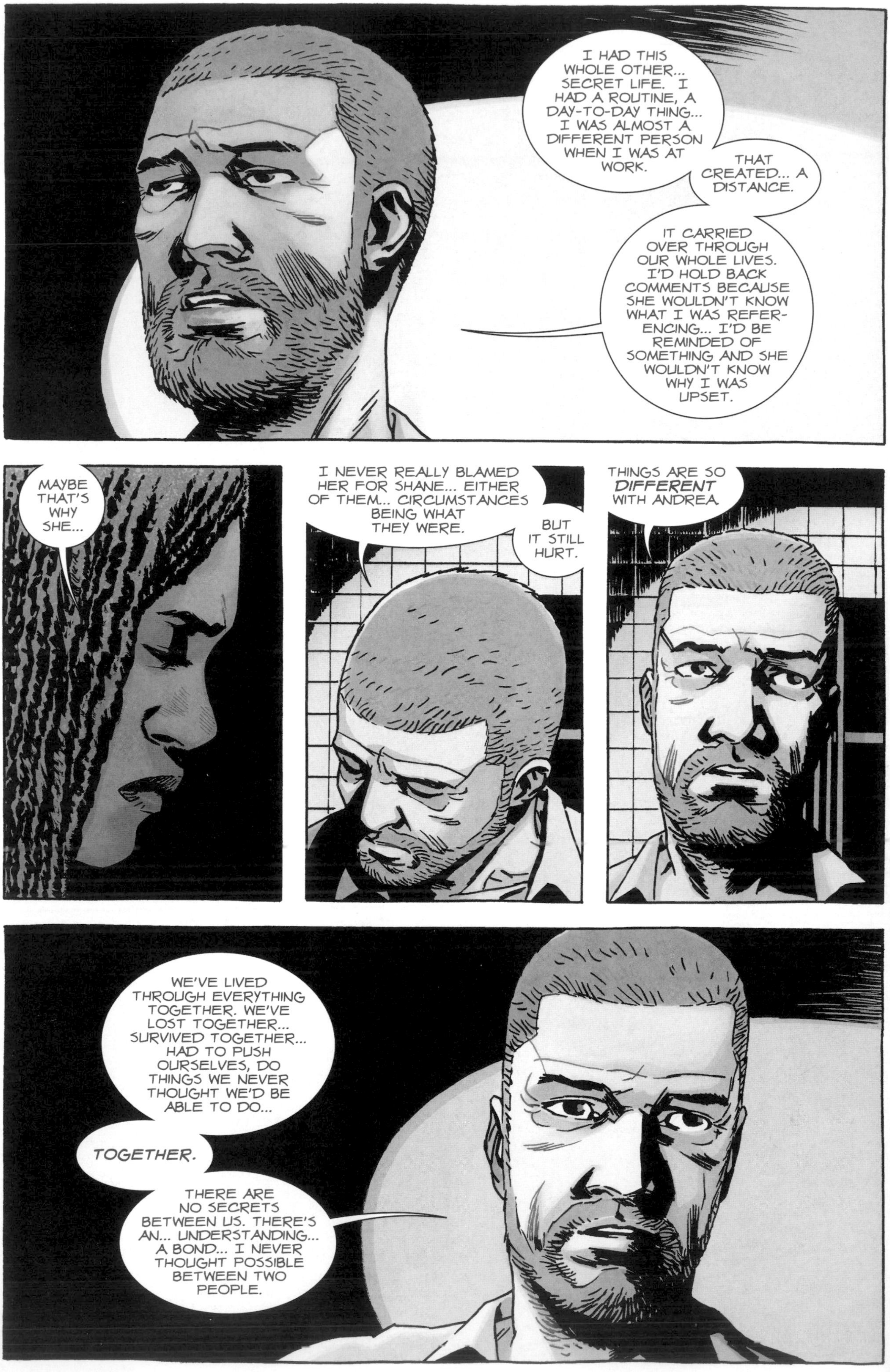

I HAD THIS WHOLE OTHER... SECRET LIFE. I HAD A ROUTINE, A DAY-TO-DAY THING... I WAS ALMOST A DIFFERENT PERSON WHEN I WAS AT WORK.
THAT CREATED... A DISTANCE.
IT CARRIED OVER THROUGH OUR WHOLE LIVES. I'D HOLD BACK COMMENTS BECAUSE SHE WOULDN'T KNOW WHAT I WAS REFER-ENCING... I'D BE REMINDED OF SOMETHING AND SHE WOULDN'T KNOW WHY I WAS UPSET.
MAYBE THAT'S WHY SHE...
I NEVER REALLY BLAMED HER FOR SHANE... EITHER OF THEM... CIRCUMSTANCES BEING WHAT THEY WERE.
BUT IT STILL HURT.
THINGS ARE SO *DIFFERENT* WITH ANDREA.
WE'VE LIVED THROUGH EVERYTHING TOGETHER. WE'VE LOST TOGETHER... SURVIVED TOGETHER... HAD TO PUSH OURSELVES, DO THINGS WE NEVER THOUGHT WE'D BE ABLE TO DO...
TOGETHER.
THERE ARE NO SECRETS BETWEEN US. THERE'S AN... UNDERSTANDING... A BOND... I NEVER THOUGHT POSSIBLE BETWEEN TWO PEOPLE.

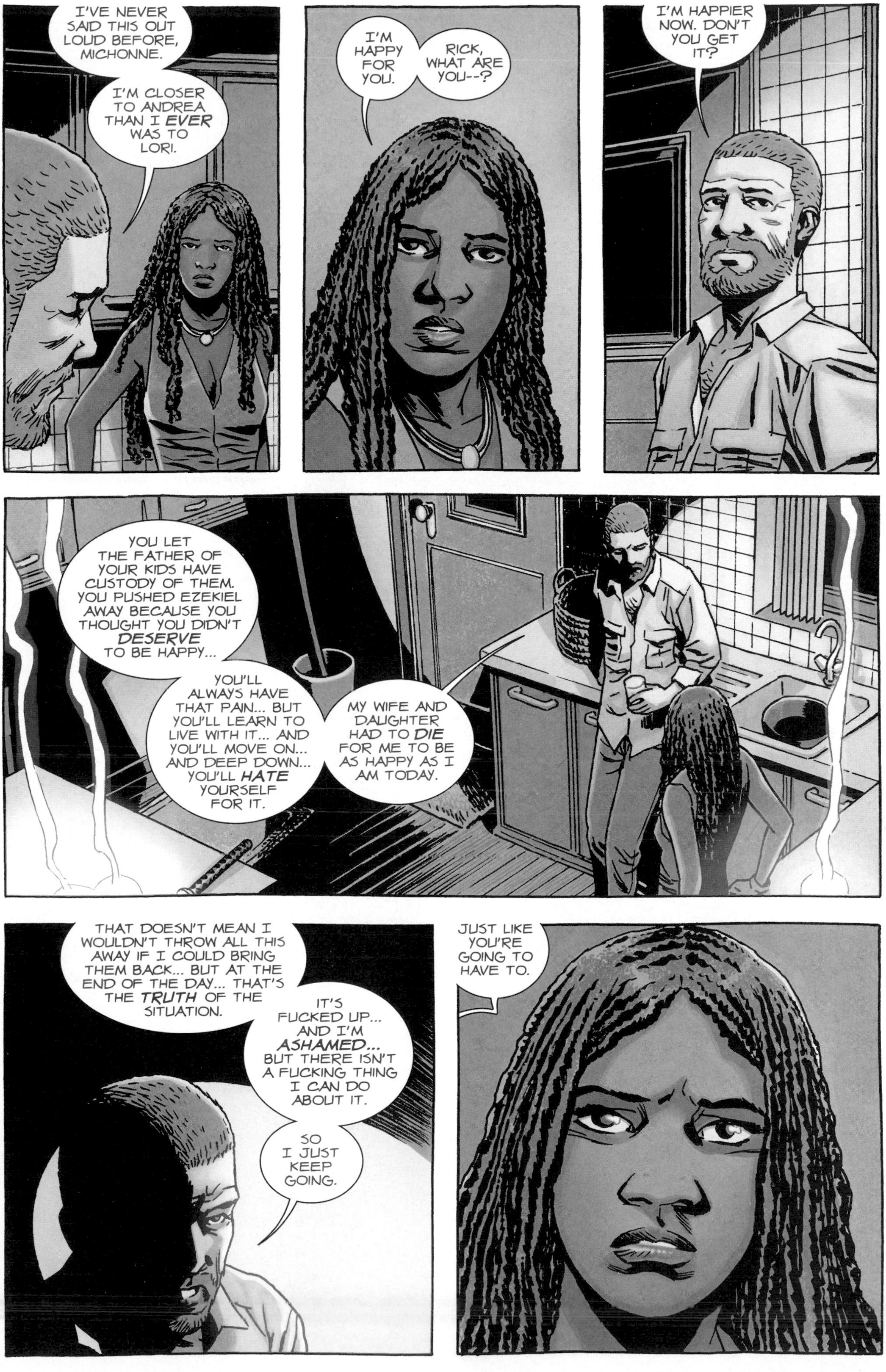
I'VE NEVER SAID THIS OUT LOUD BEFORE, MICHONNE.
I'M CLOSER TO ANDREA THAN I EVER WAS TO LORI.
I'M HAPPY FOR YOU.
RICK, WHAT ARE YOU--?
I'M HAPPIER NOW. DON'T YOU GET IT?
YOU LET THE FATHER OF YOUR KIDS HAVE CUSTODY OF THEM. YOU PUSHED EZEKIEL AWAY BECAUSE YOU THOUGHT YOU DIDN'T DESERVE TO BE HAPPY...
YOU'LL ALWAYS HAVE THAT PAIN... BUT YOU'LL LEARN TO LIVE WITH IT... AND YOU'LL MOVE ON... AND DEEP DOWN... YOU'LL HATE YOURSELF FOR IT.
MY WIFE AND DAUGHTER HAD TO DIE FOR ME TO BE AS HAPPY AS I AM TODAY.
THAT DOESN'T MEAN I WOULDN'T THROW ALL THIS AWAY IF I COULD BRING THEM BACK... BUT AT THE END OF THE DAY... THAT'S THE TRUTH OF THE SITUATION.
IT'S FUCKED UP... AND I'M ASHAMED... BUT THERE ISN'T A FUCKING THING I CAN DO ABOUT IT.
SO I JUST KEEP GOING.
JUST LIKE YOU'RE GOING TO HAVE TO.

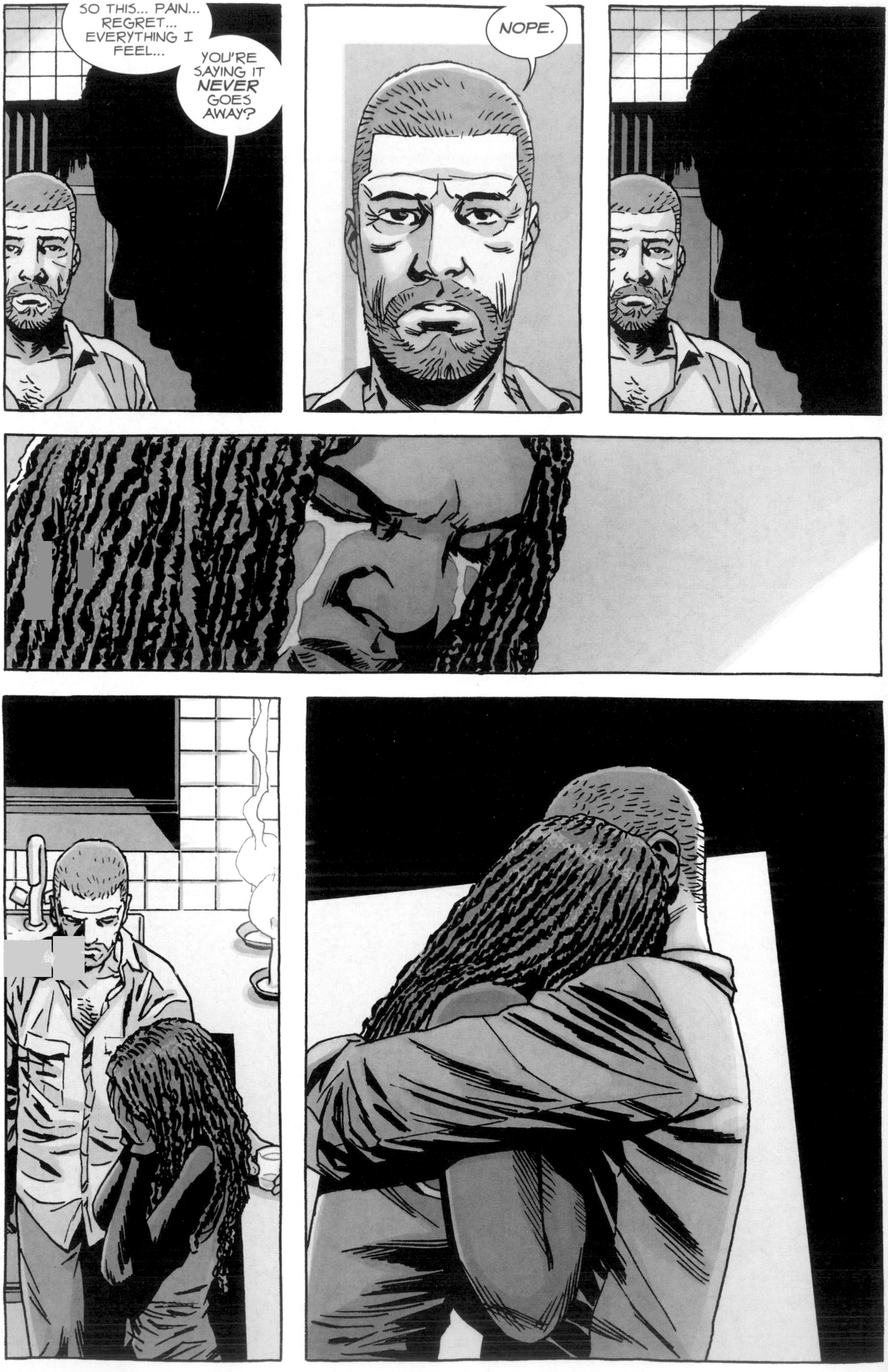
SO THIS... PAIN... REGRET... EVERYTHING I FEEL...
YOU'RE SAYING IT NEVER GOES AWAY?
NOPE.

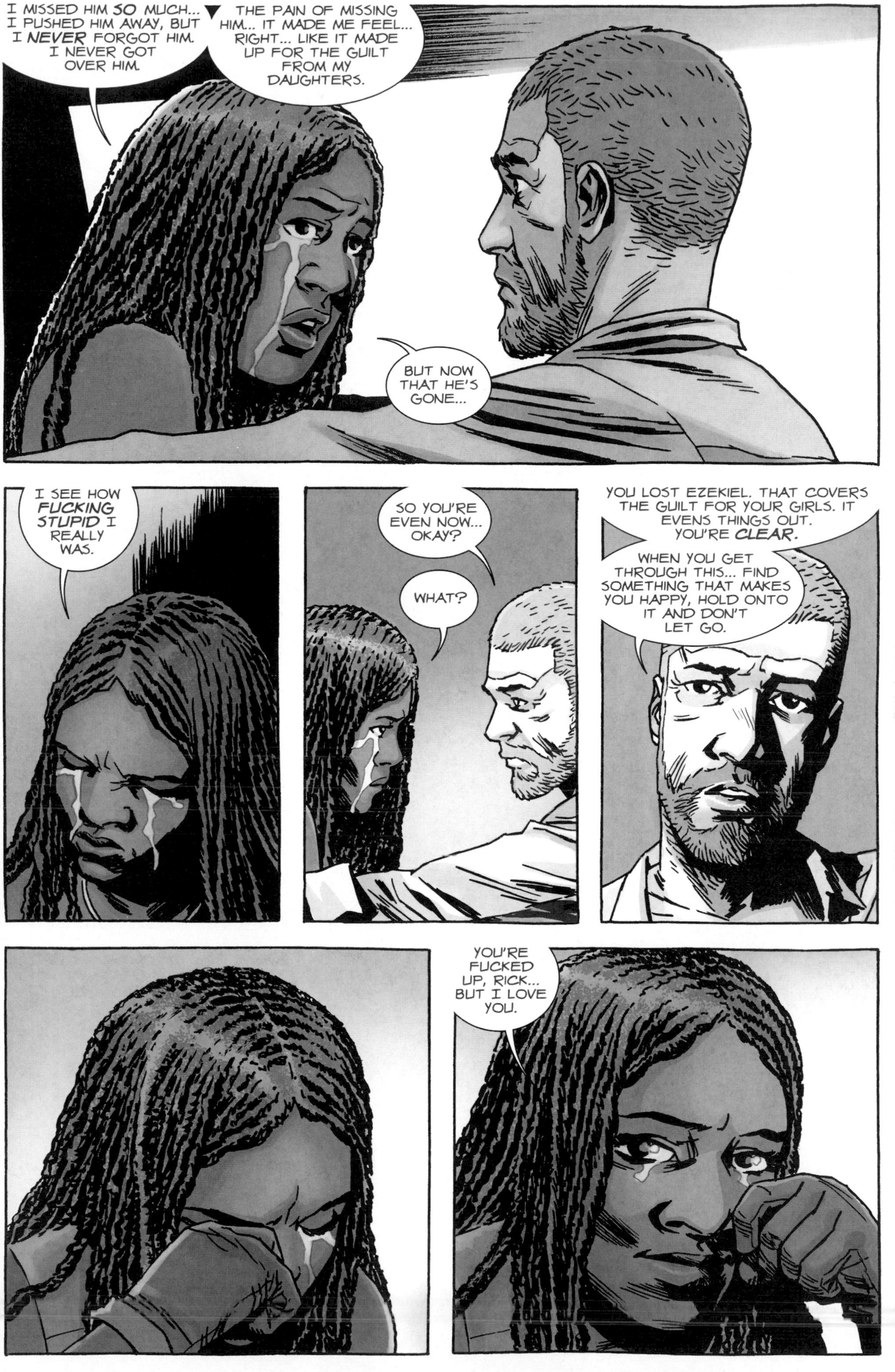
I MISSED HIM SO MUCH... I PUSHED HIM AWAY, BUT I NEVER FORGOT HIM. I NEVER GOT OVER HIM.
THE PAIN OF MISSING HIM... IT MADE ME FEEL... RIGHT... LIKE IT MADE UP FOR THE GUILT FROM MY DAUGHTERS.
BUT NOW THAT HE'S GONE...
I SEE HOW FUCKING STUPID I REALLY WAS.
SO YOU'RE EVEN NOW... OKAY?
WHAT?
YOU LOST EZEKIEL. THAT COVERS THE GUILT FOR YOUR GIRLS. IT EVENS THINGS OUT. YOU'RE CLEAR.
WHEN YOU GET THROUGH THIS... FIND SOMETHING THAT MAKES YOU HAPPY, HOLD ONTO IT AND DON'T LET GO.
YOU'RE FUCKED UP, RICK... BUT I LOVE YOU.

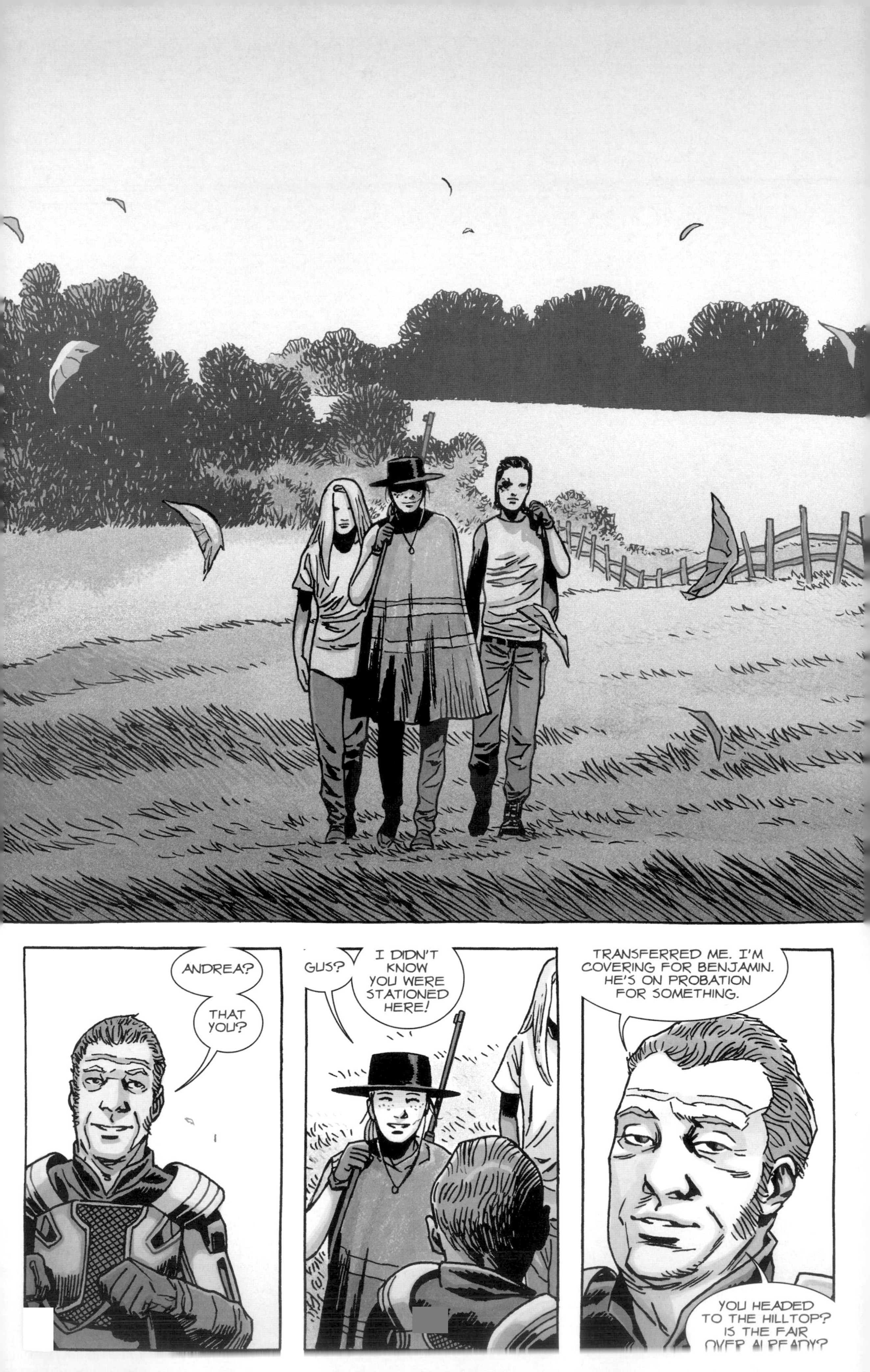
ANDREA?
THAT YOU?
GUS?
I DIDN'T KNOW YOU WERE STATIONED HERE!
TRANSFERRED ME. I'M COVERING FOR BENJAMIN. HE'S ON PROBATION FOR SOMETHING.
YOU HEADED TO THE HILLTOP? IS THE FAIR OVER ALREADY?

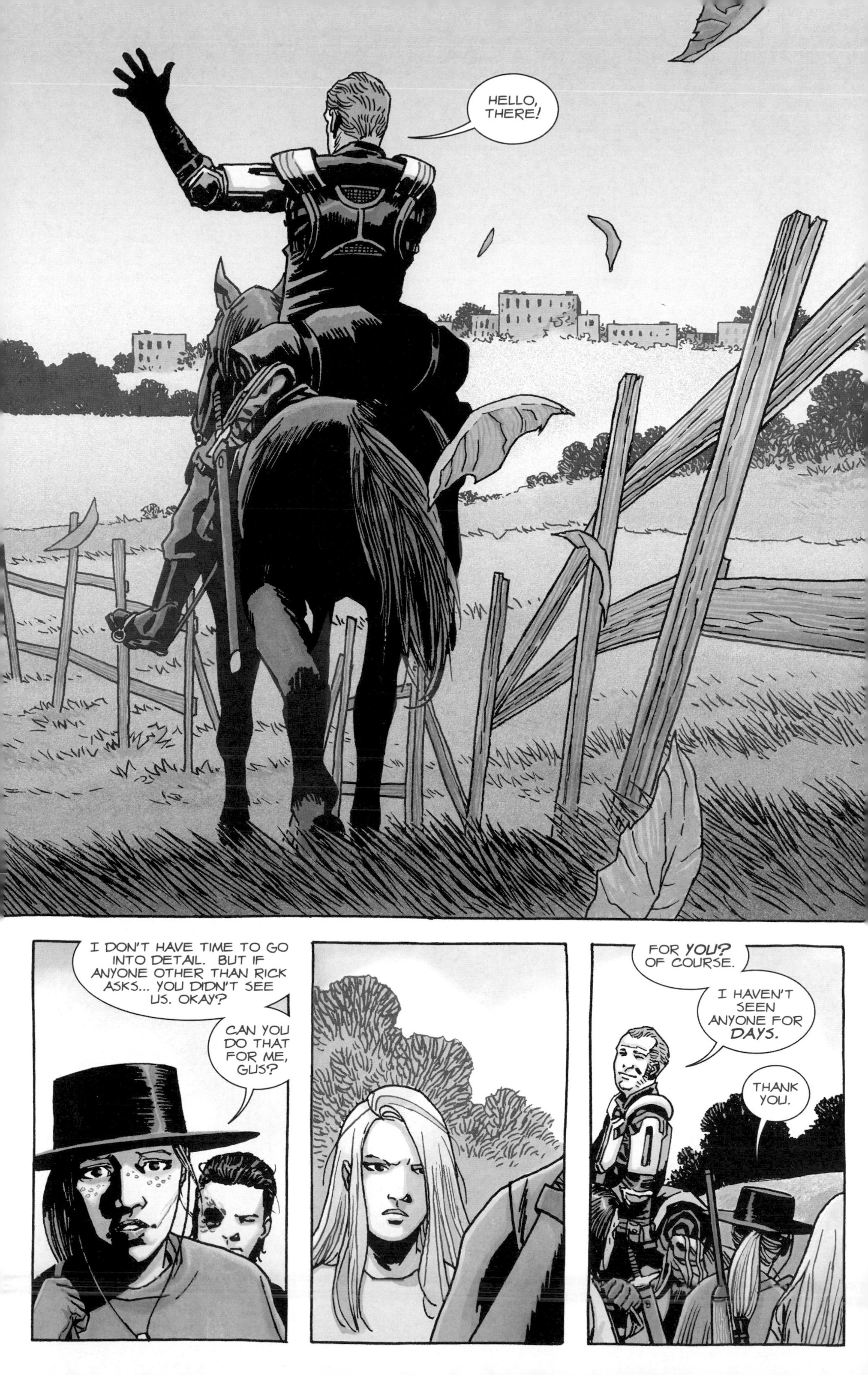
HELLO, THERE!
I DON'T HAVE TIME TO GO INTO DETAIL. BUT IF ANYONE OTHER THAN RICK ASKS... YOU DIDN'T SEE US. OKAY?
CAN YOU DO THAT FOR ME, GUS?
FOR YOU? OF COURSE.
I HAVEN'T SEEN ANYONE FOR DAYS.
THANK YOU.

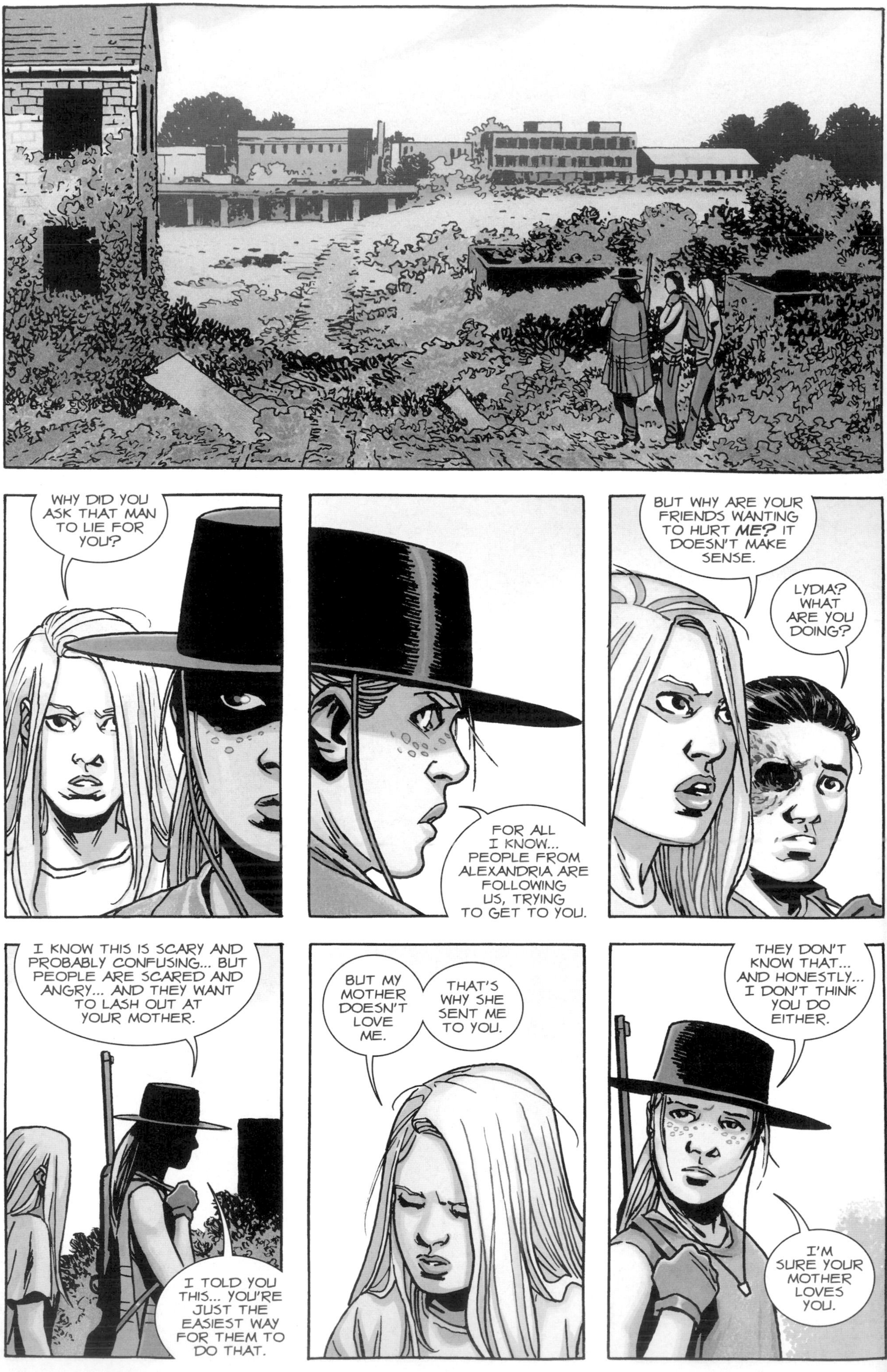
WHY DID YOU ASK THAT MAN TO LIE FOR YOU?
FOR ALL I KNOW... PEOPLE FROM ALEXANDRIA ARE FOLLOWING US, TRYING TO GET TO YOU.
BUT WHY ARE YOUR FRIENDS WANTING TO HURT ME? IT DOESN'T MAKE SENSE.
LYDIA? WHAT ARE YOU DOING?
I KNOW THIS IS SCARY AND PROBABLY CONFUSING... BUT PEOPLE ARE SCARED AND ANGRY... AND THEY WANT TO LASH OUT AT YOUR MOTHER.
I TOLD YOU THIS... YOU'RE JUST THE EASIEST WAY FOR THEM TO DO THAT.
BUT MY MOTHER DOESN'T LOVE ME.
THAT'S WHY SHE SENT ME TO YOU.
THEY DON'T KNOW THAT... AND HONESTLY... I DON'T THINK YOU DO EITHER.
I'M SURE YOUR MOTHER LOVES YOU.

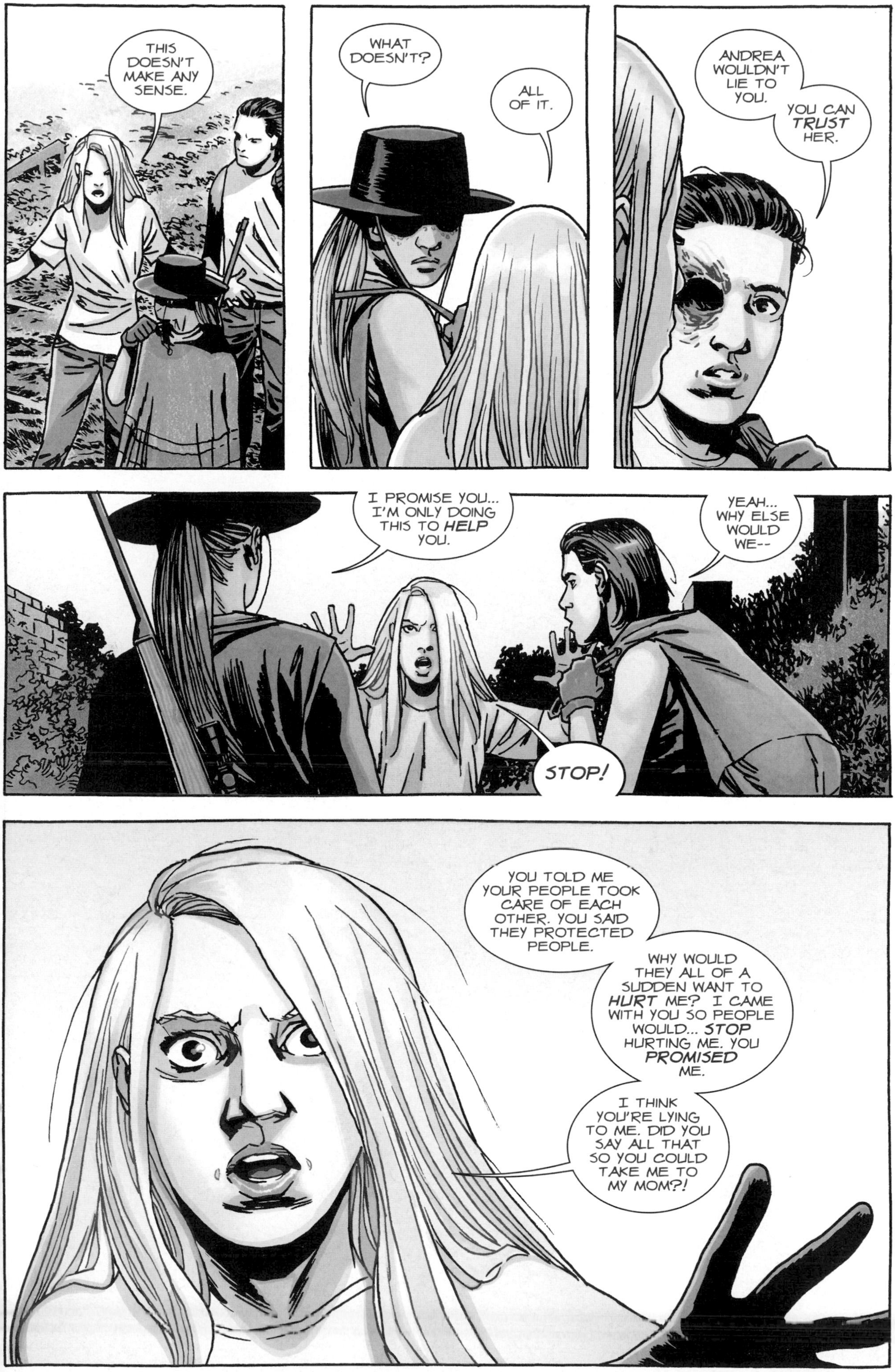
THIS DOESN'T MAKE ANY SENSE.
WHAT DOESN'T?
ALL OF IT.
ANDREA WOULDN'T LIE TO YOU.
YOU CAN TRUST HER.
I PROMISE YOU... I'M ONLY DOING THIS TO HELP YOU.
YEAH... WHY ELSE WOULD WE--
STOP!
YOU TOLD ME YOUR PEOPLE TOOK CARE OF EACH OTHER. YOU SAID THEY PROTECTED PEOPLE.
WHY WOULD THEY ALL OF A SUDDEN WANT TO HURT ME? I CAME WITH YOU SO PEOPLE WOULD... STOP HURTING ME. YOU PROMISED ME.
I THINK YOU'RE LYING TO ME. DID YOU SAY ALL THAT SO YOU COULD TAKE ME TO MY MOM?!

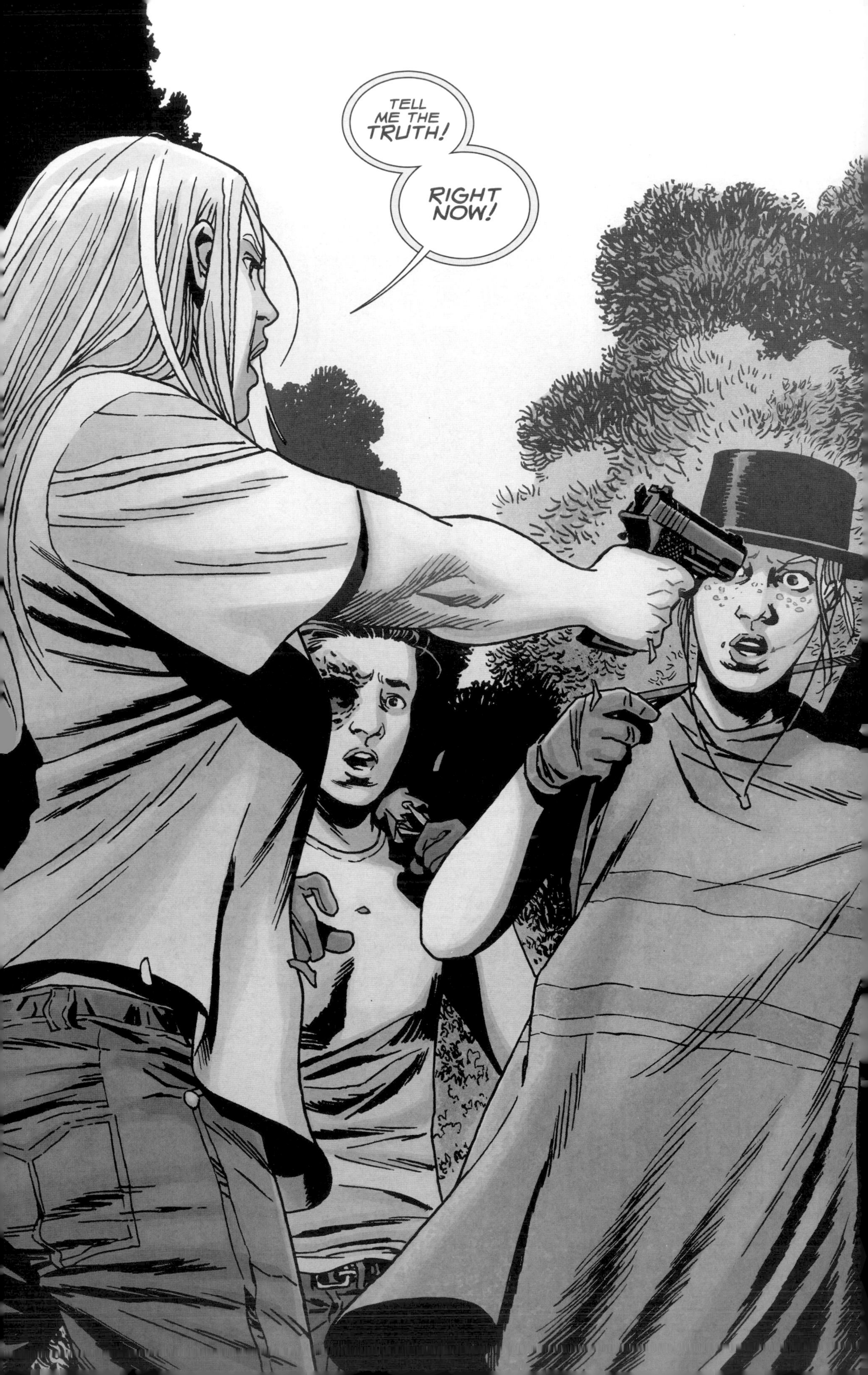
TELL ME THE TRUTH!
RIGHT NOW!

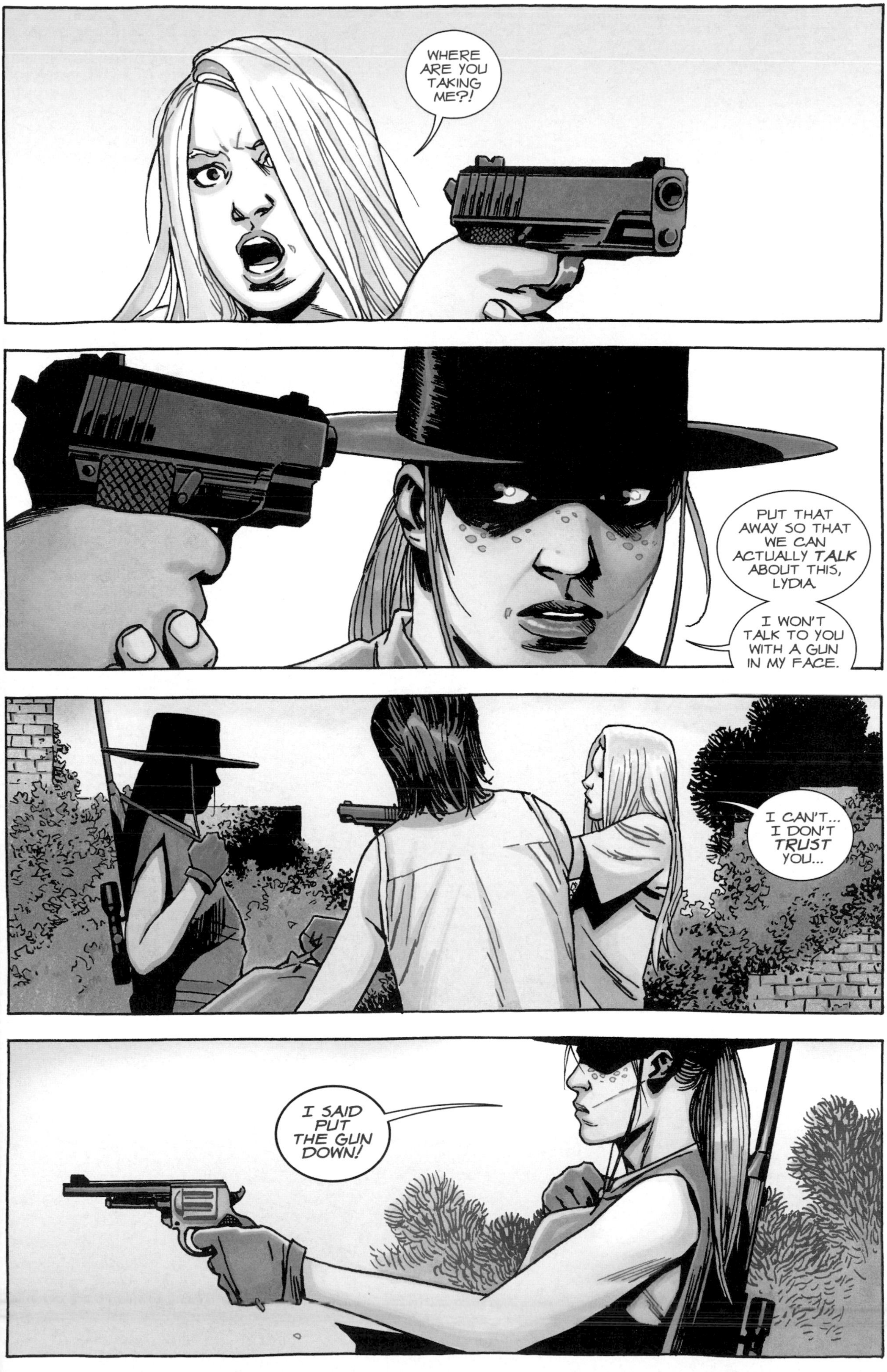
WHERE ARE YOU TAKING ME?!
PUT THAT AWAY SO THAT WE CAN ACTUALLY *TALK* ABOUT THIS, LYDIA.
I WON'T TALK TO YOU WITH A GUN IN MY FACE.
I CAN'T... I DON'T *TRUST* YOU...
I SAID PUT THE GUN DOWN!

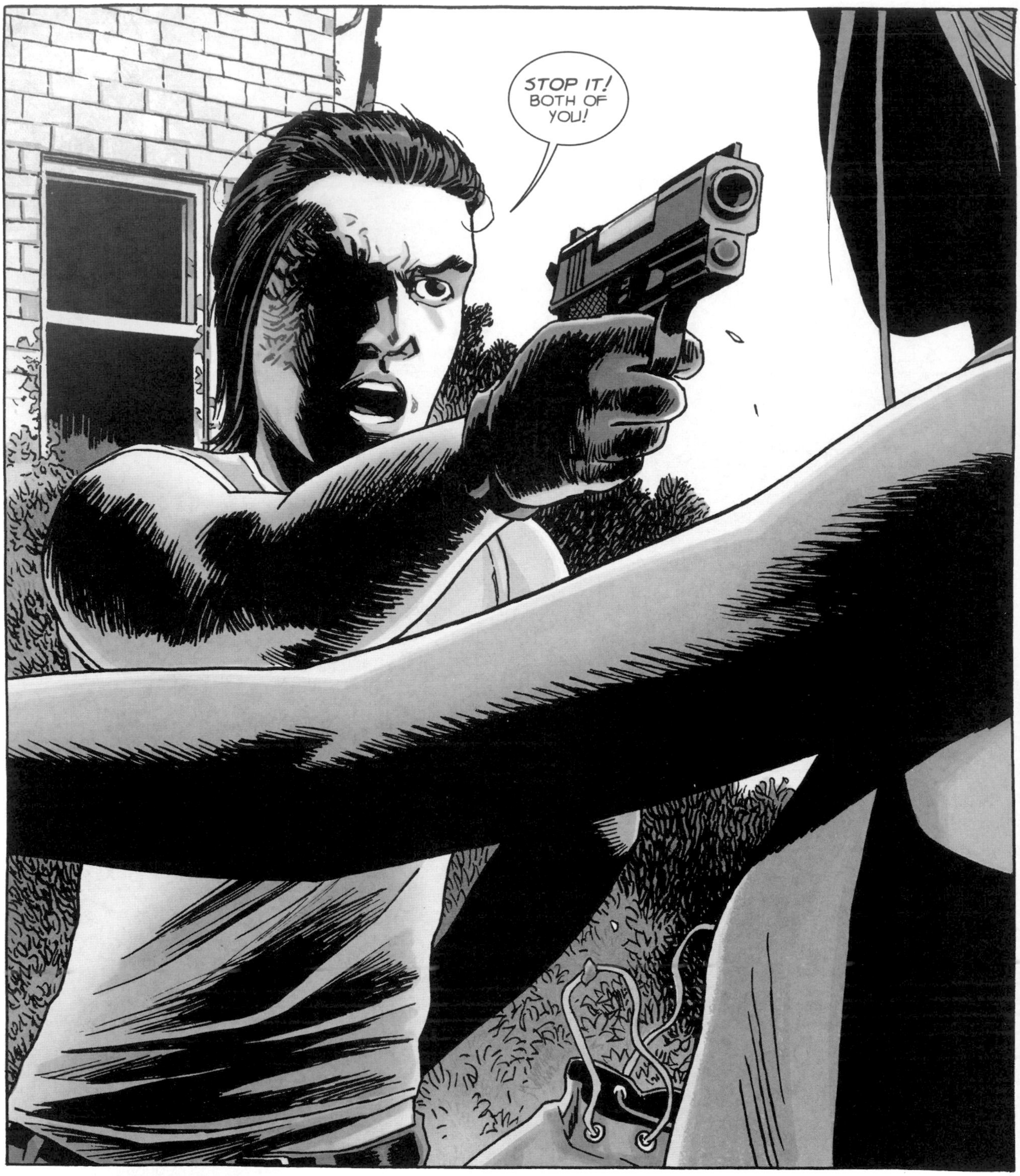
STOP IT! BOTH OF YOU!

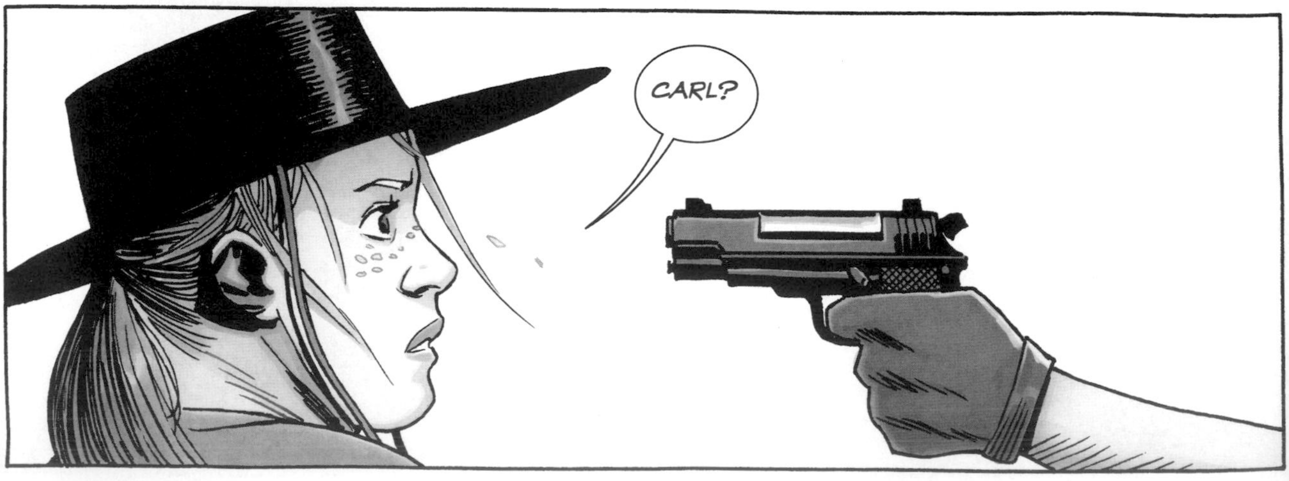
CARL?

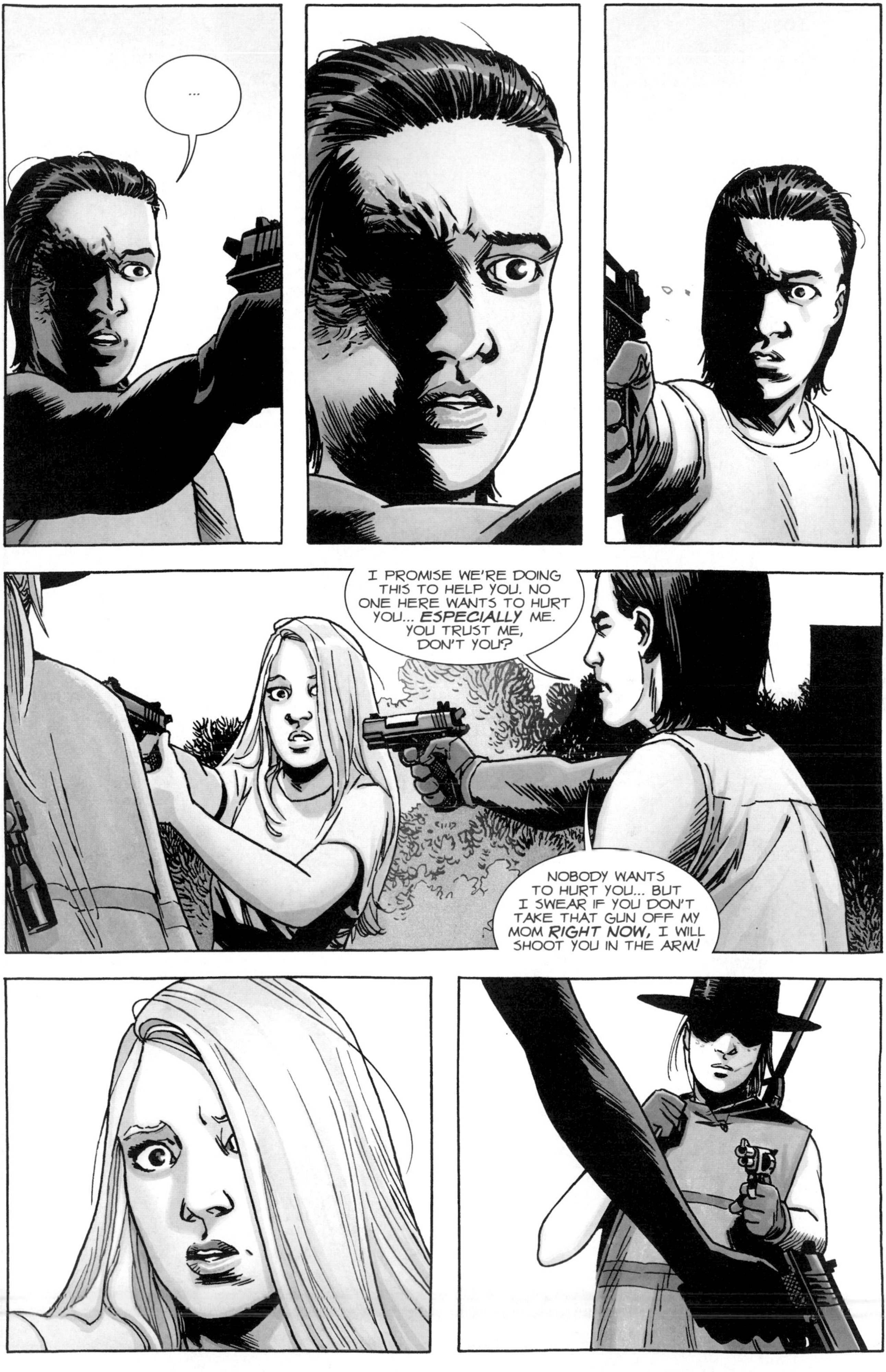
...
I PROMISE WE'RE DOING THIS TO HELP YOU. NO ONE HERE WANTS TO HURT YOU... *ESPECIALLY* ME. YOU TRUST ME, DON'T YOU?
NOBODY WANTS TO HURT YOU... BUT I SWEAR IF YOU DON'T TAKE THAT GUN OFF MY MOM *RIGHT NOW,* I WILL SHOOT YOU IN THE ARM!

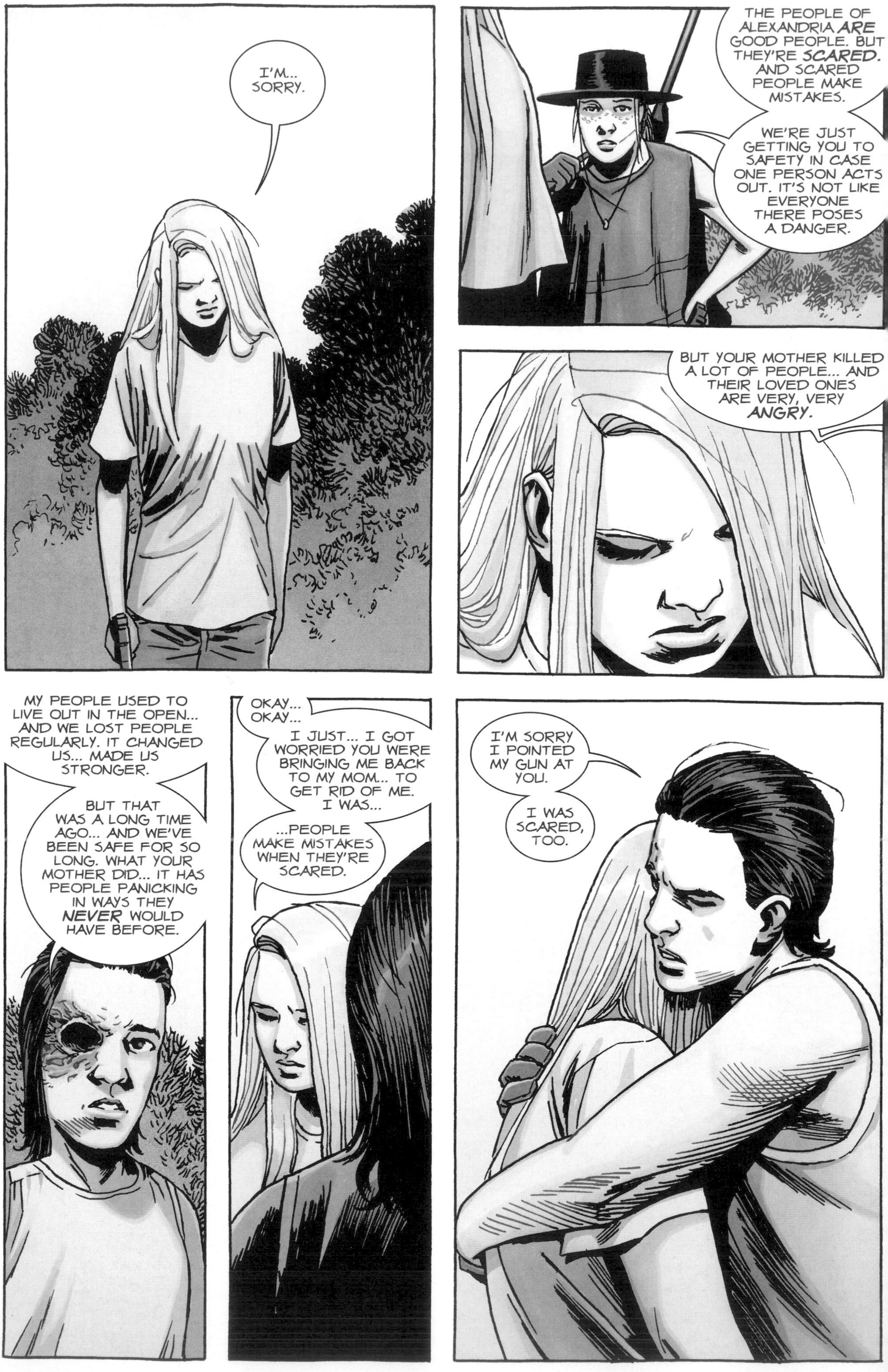
I'M... SORRY.
THE PEOPLE OF ALEXANDRIA ARE GOOD PEOPLE. BUT THEY'RE SCARED. AND SCARED PEOPLE MAKE MISTAKES.
WE'RE JUST GETTING YOU TO SAFETY IN CASE ONE PERSON ACTS OUT. IT'S NOT LIKE EVERYONE THERE POSES A DANGER.
BUT YOUR MOTHER KILLED A LOT OF PEOPLE... AND THEIR LOVED ONES ARE VERY, VERY ANGRY.
MY PEOPLE USED TO LIVE OUT IN THE OPEN... AND WE LOST PEOPLE REGULARLY. IT CHANGED US... MADE US STRONGER.
BUT THAT WAS A LONG TIME AGO... AND WE'VE BEEN SAFE FOR SO LONG. WHAT YOUR MOTHER DID... IT HAS PEOPLE PANICKING IN WAYS THEY NEVER WOULD HAVE BEFORE.
OKAY... OKAY...
I JUST... I GOT WORRIED YOU WERE BRINGING ME BACK TO MY MOM... TO GET RID OF ME. I WAS...
...PEOPLE MAKE MISTAKES WHEN THEY'RE SCARED.
I'M SORRY I POINTED MY GUN AT YOU.
I WAS SCARED, TOO.

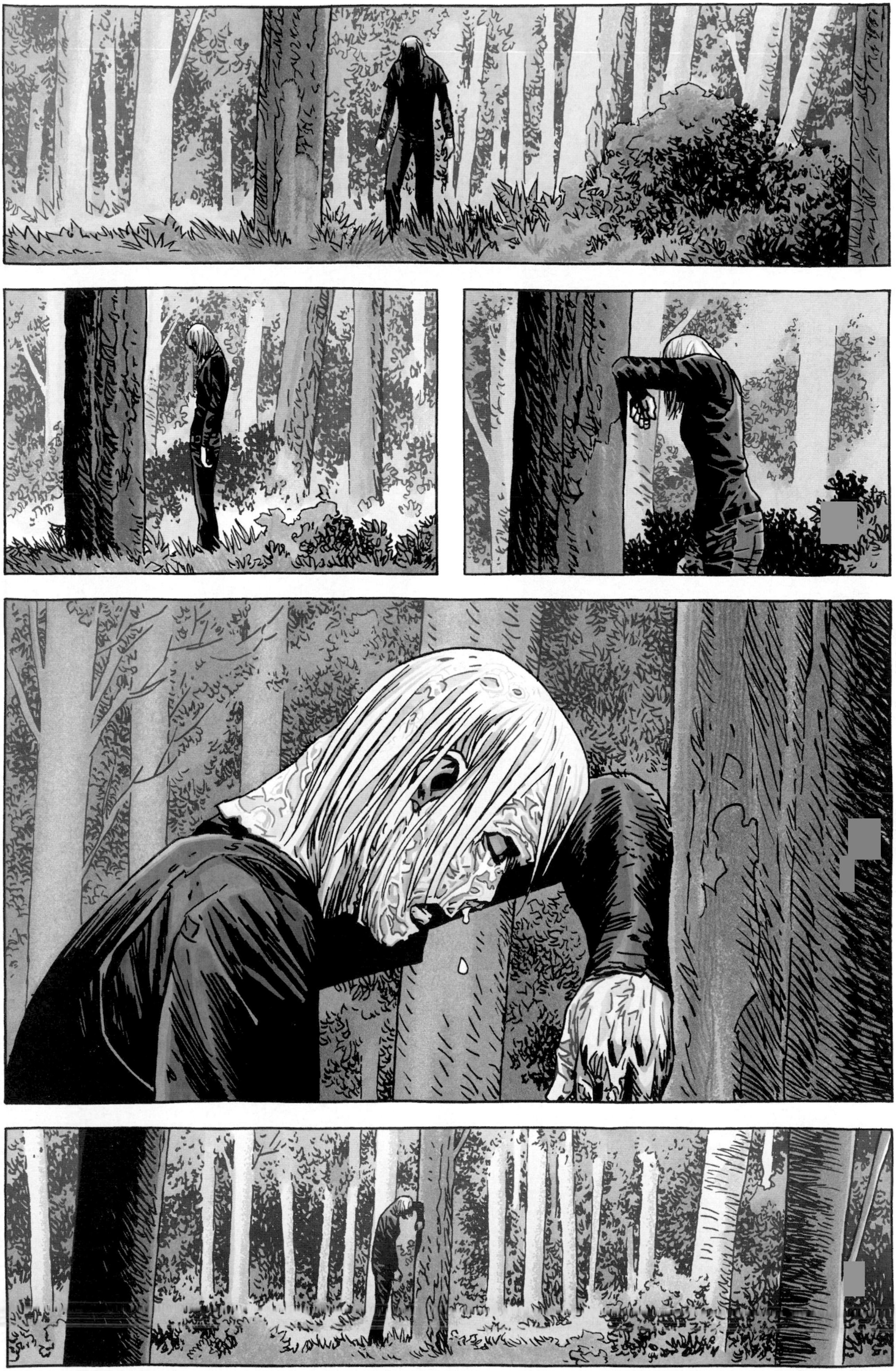

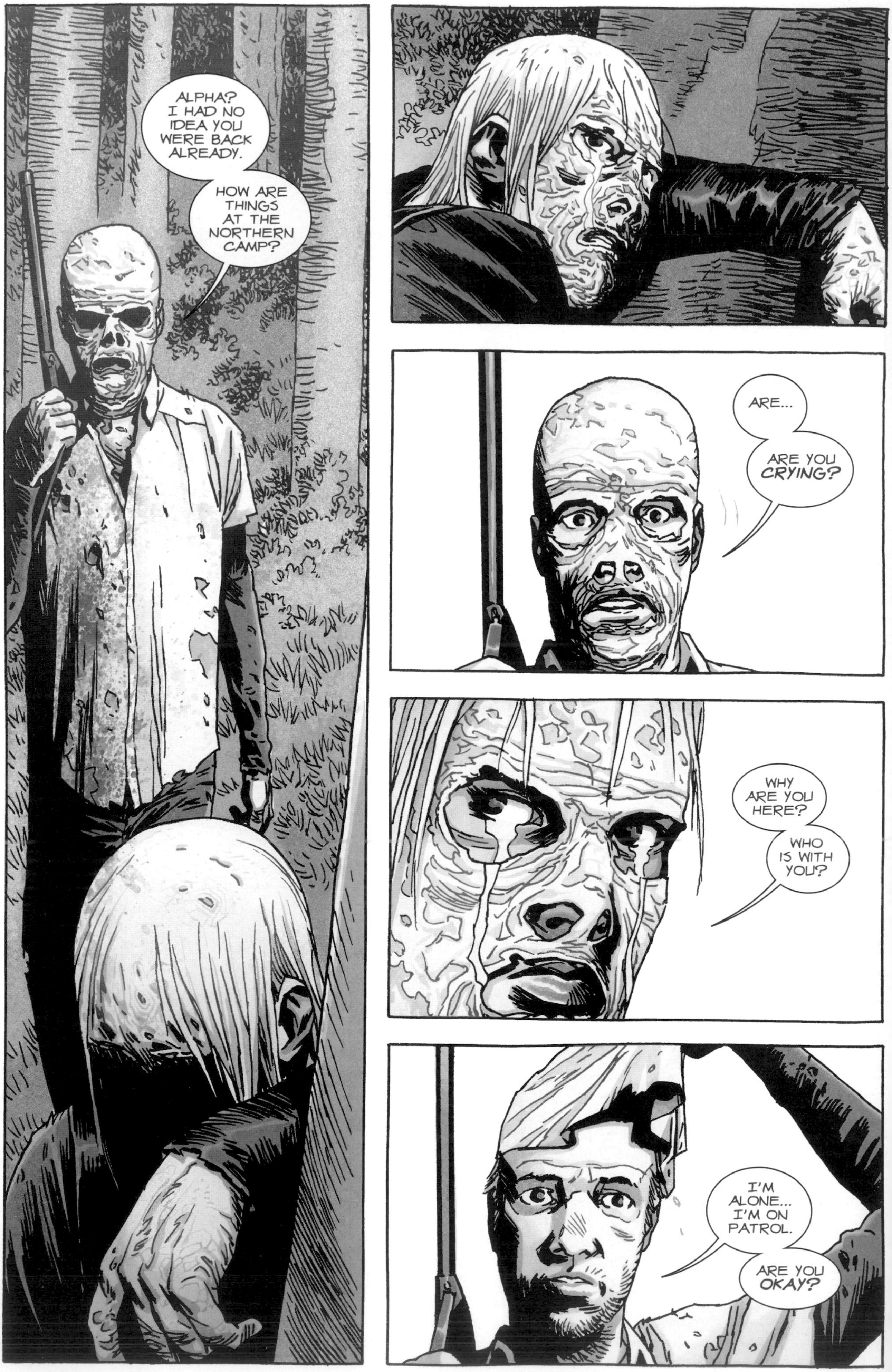
ALPHA? I HAD NO IDEA YOU WERE BACK ALREADY.
HOW ARE THINGS AT THE NORTHERN CAMP?
ARE...
ARE YOU CRYING?
WHY ARE YOU HERE?
WHO IS WITH YOU?
I'M ALONE... I'M ON PATROL.
ARE YOU OKAY?

I'M FINE.

YOUR DAUGHTER DIDN'T BELONG HERE. SHE WASN'T STRONG ENOUGH. YOU SENT HER AWAY.

I KNOW YOU KNOW IT WAS THE RIGHT THING TO DO... BUT I ALSO KNOW THAT'S GOTTA BE HARD.

YES...

I DIDN'T ANTICIPATE WORRYING ABOUT HER... THINKING ABOUT HER. I THOUGHT I WAS ABOVE IT.

I WAS STUPID... I'M BEING *STUPID* NOW.

YOU DON'T HAVE TO WORRY ABOUT ME. IT'S COOL.

BUT IF YOU DON'T WANT TO GET CHALLENGED... YOU BETTER MAKE SURE NOBODY ELSE FINDS OUT ABOUT THIS.

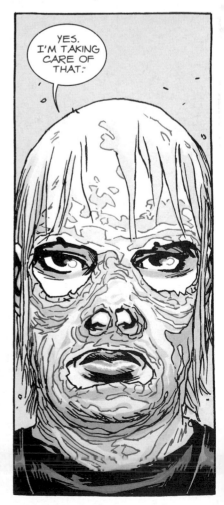

YES. I'M TAKING CARE OF THAT.

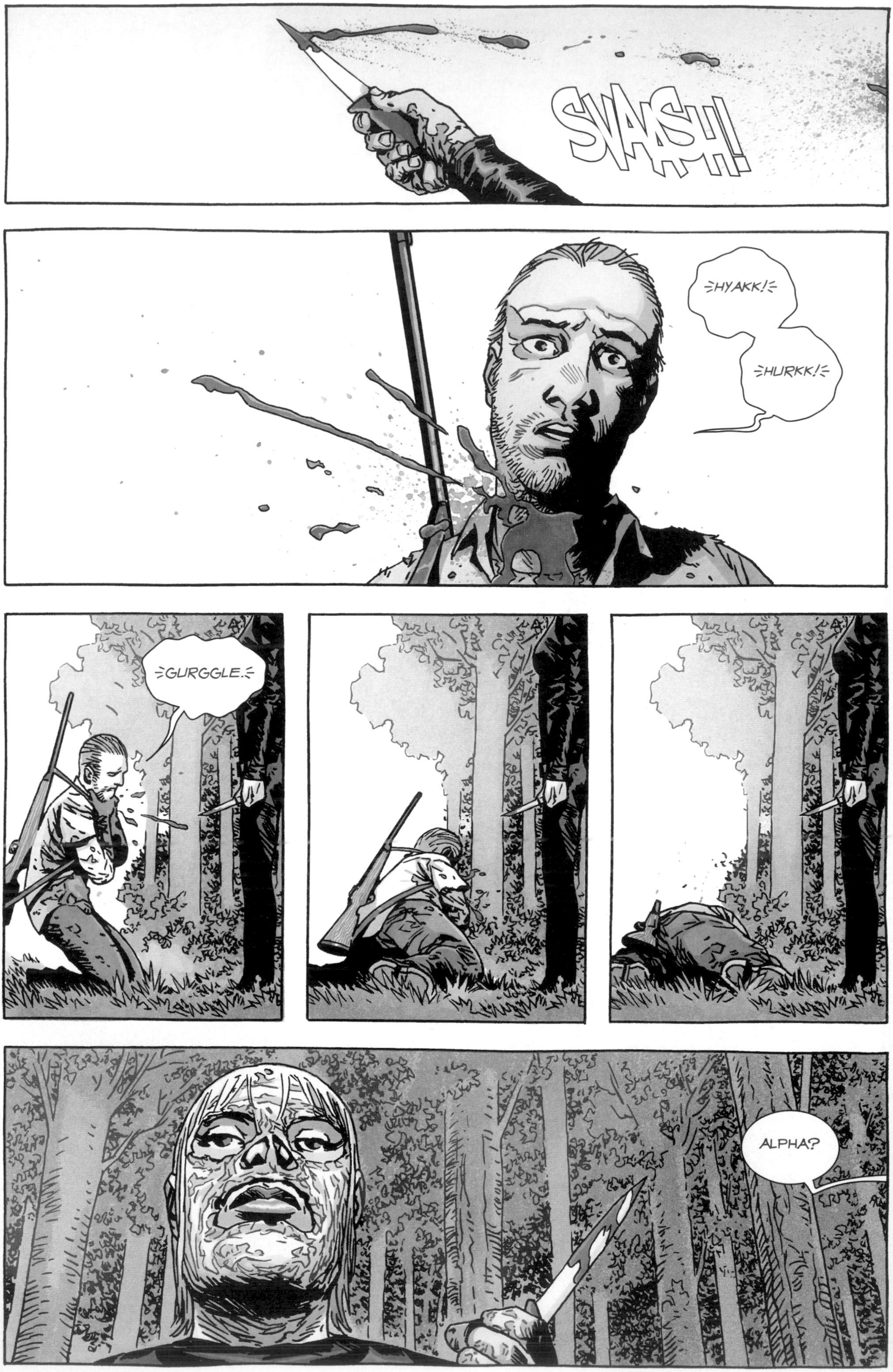
SVASH!
HYAKK!
HURKK!
GURGGLE.
ALPHA?

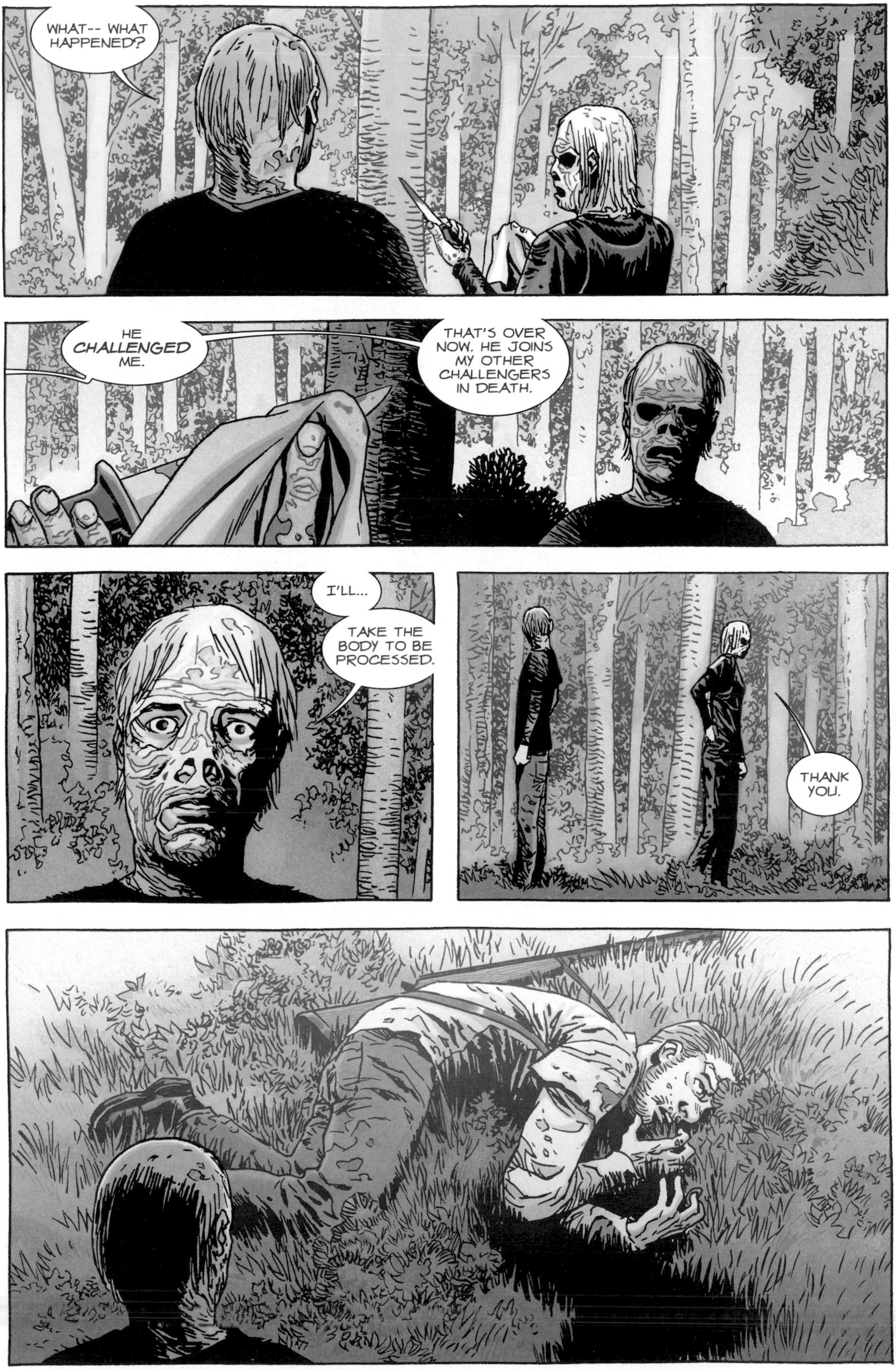
WHAT-- WHAT HAPPENED?
HE CHALLENGED ME.
THAT'S OVER NOW. HE JOINS MY OTHER CHALLENGERS IN DEATH.
I'LL...
TAKE THE BODY TO BE PROCESSED.
THANK YOU.

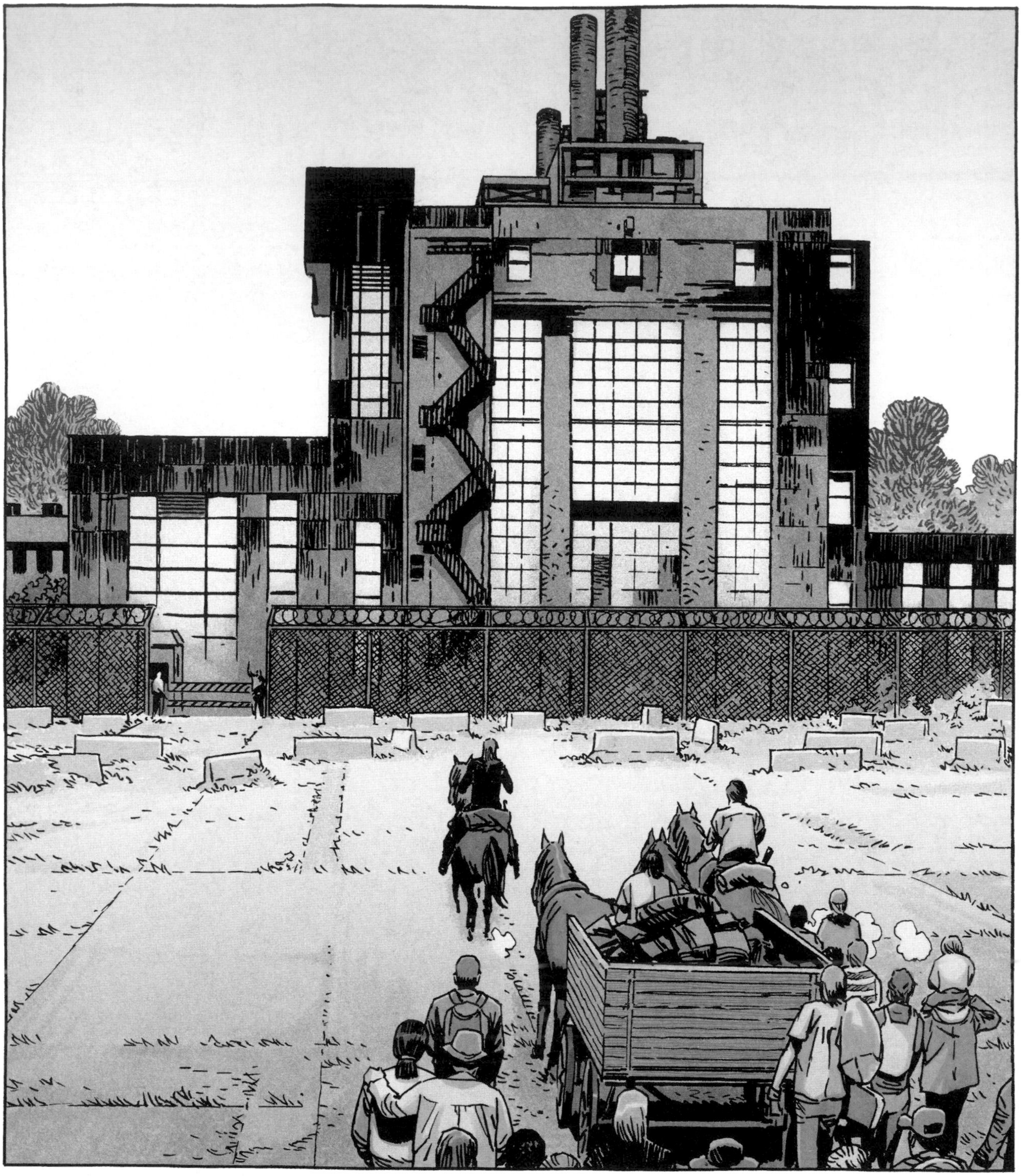

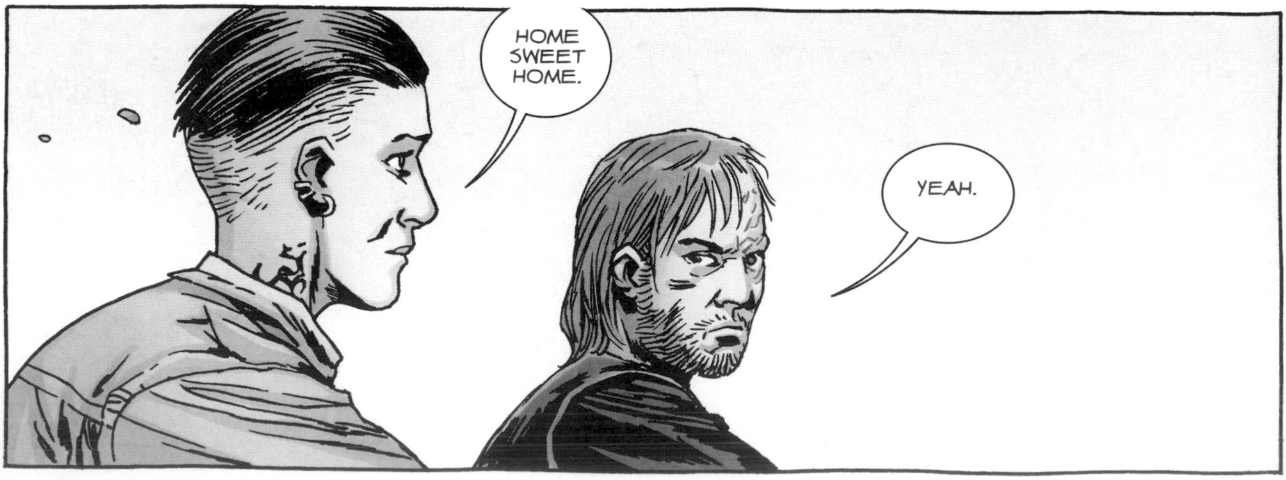
HOME SWEET HOME.
YEAH.

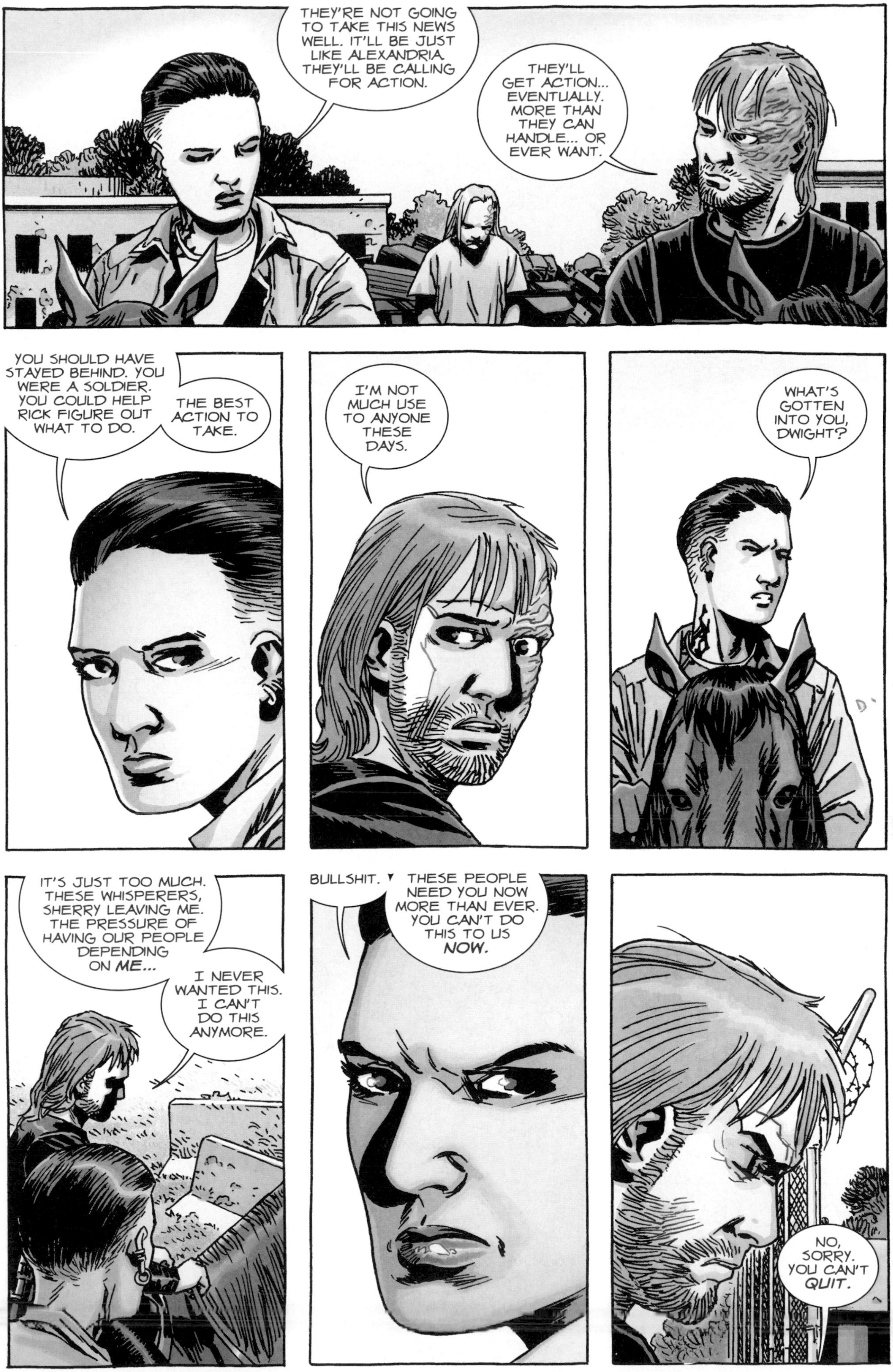
THEY'RE NOT GOING TO TAKE THIS NEWS WELL. IT'LL BE JUST LIKE ALEXANDRIA. THEY'LL BE CALLING FOR ACTION.
THEY'LL GET ACTION... EVENTUALLY. MORE THAN THEY CAN HANDLE... OR EVER WANT.
YOU SHOULD HAVE STAYED BEHIND. YOU WERE A SOLDIER. YOU COULD HELP RICK FIGURE OUT WHAT TO DO.
THE BEST ACTION TO TAKE.
I'M NOT MUCH USE TO ANYONE THESE DAYS.
WHAT'S GOTTEN INTO YOU, DWIGHT?
IT'S JUST TOO MUCH. THESE WHISPERERS, SHERRY LEAVING ME. THE PRESSURE OF HAVING OUR PEOPLE DEPENDING ON *ME*...
I NEVER WANTED THIS. I CAN'T DO THIS ANYMORE.
BULLSHIT.
THESE PEOPLE NEED YOU NOW MORE THAN EVER. YOU CAN'T DO THIS TO US *NOW.*
NO, SORRY. YOU CAN'T *QUIT.*

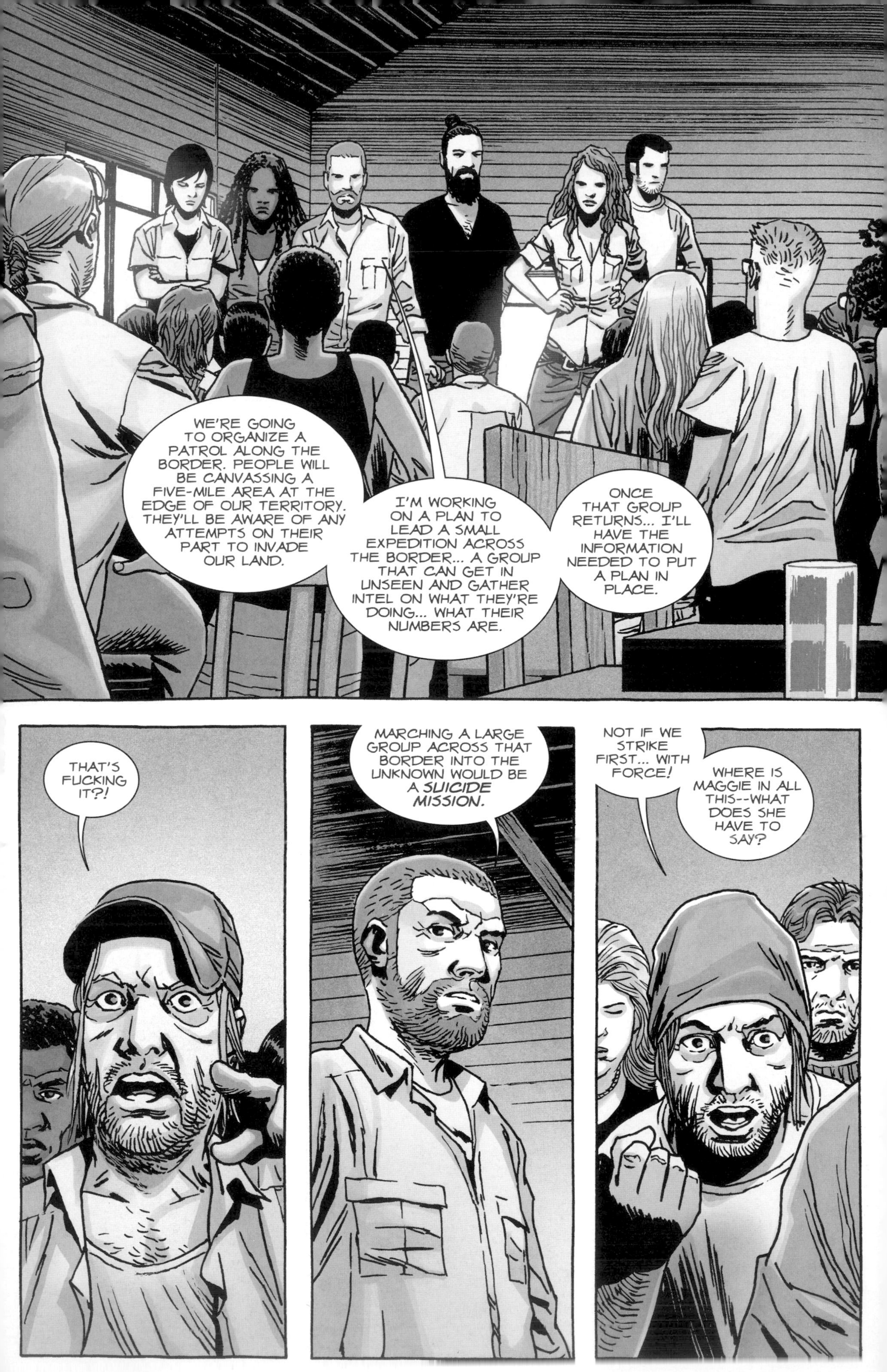
WE'RE GOING TO ORGANIZE A PATROL ALONG THE BORDER. PEOPLE WILL BE CANVASSING A FIVE-MILE AREA AT THE EDGE OF OUR TERRITORY. THEY'LL BE AWARE OF ANY ATTEMPTS ON THEIR PART TO INVADE OUR LAND.
I'M WORKING ON A PLAN TO LEAD A SMALL EXPEDITION ACROSS THE BORDER... A GROUP THAT CAN GET IN UNSEEN AND GATHER INTEL ON WHAT THEY'RE DOING... WHAT THEIR NUMBERS ARE.
ONCE THAT GROUP RETURNS... I'LL HAVE THE INFORMATION NEEDED TO PUT A PLAN IN PLACE.
THAT'S FUCKING IT?!
MARCHING A LARGE GROUP ACROSS THAT BORDER INTO THE UNKNOWN WOULD BE A *SUICIDE MISSION.*
NOT IF WE STRIKE FIRST... WITH FORCE!
WHERE IS MAGGIE IN ALL THIS--WHAT DOES SHE HAVE TO SAY?

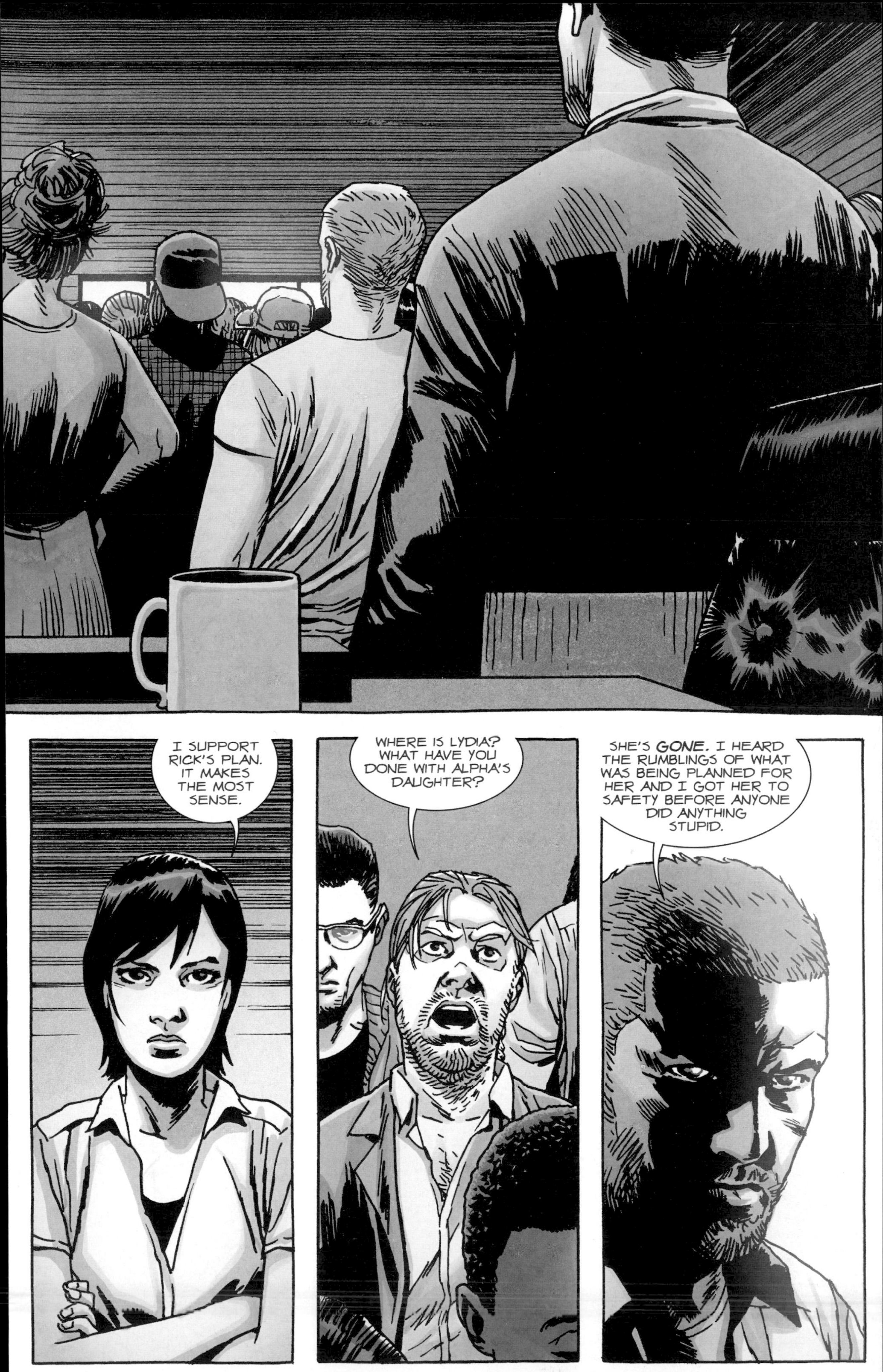
I SUPPORT RICK'S PLAN. IT MAKES THE MOST SENSE.
WHERE IS LYDIA? WHAT HAVE YOU DONE WITH ALPHA'S DAUGHTER?
SHE'S *GONE.* I HEARD THE RUMBLINGS OF WHAT WAS BEING PLANNED FOR HER AND I GOT HER TO SAFETY BEFORE ANYONE DID ANYTHING STUPID.

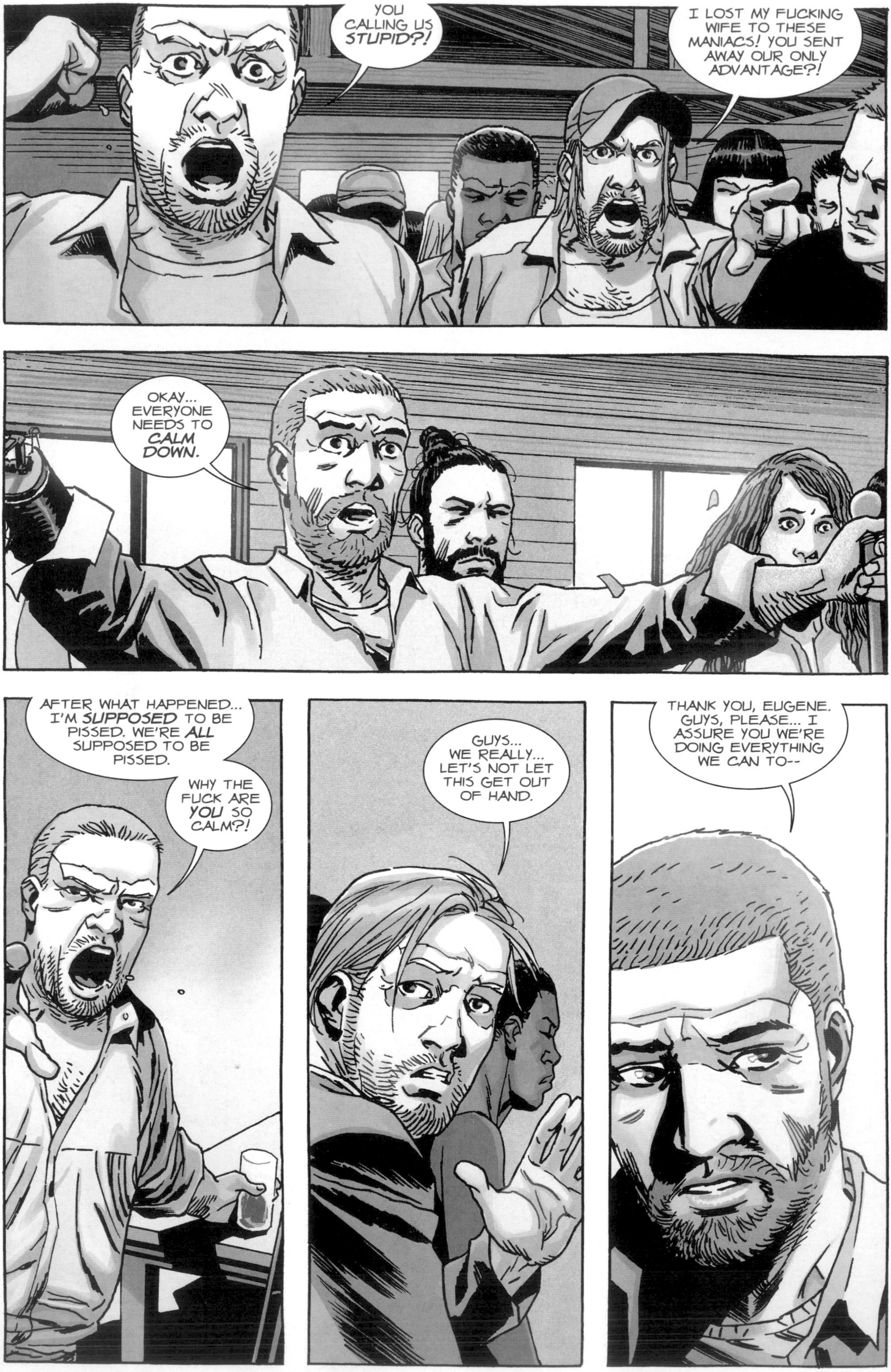
YOU CALLING US STUPID?!
I LOST MY FUCKING WIFE TO THESE MANIACS! YOU SENT AWAY OUR ONLY ADVANTAGE?!
OKAY... EVERYONE NEEDS TO CALM DOWN.
AFTER WHAT HAPPENED... I'M SUPPOSED TO BE PISSED. WE'RE ALL SUPPOSED TO BE PISSED.
WHY THE FUCK ARE YOU SO CALM?!
GUYS... WE REALLY... LET'S NOT LET THIS GET OUT OF HAND.
THANK YOU, EUGENE. GUYS, PLEASE... I ASSURE YOU WE'RE DOING EVERYTHING WE CAN TO--

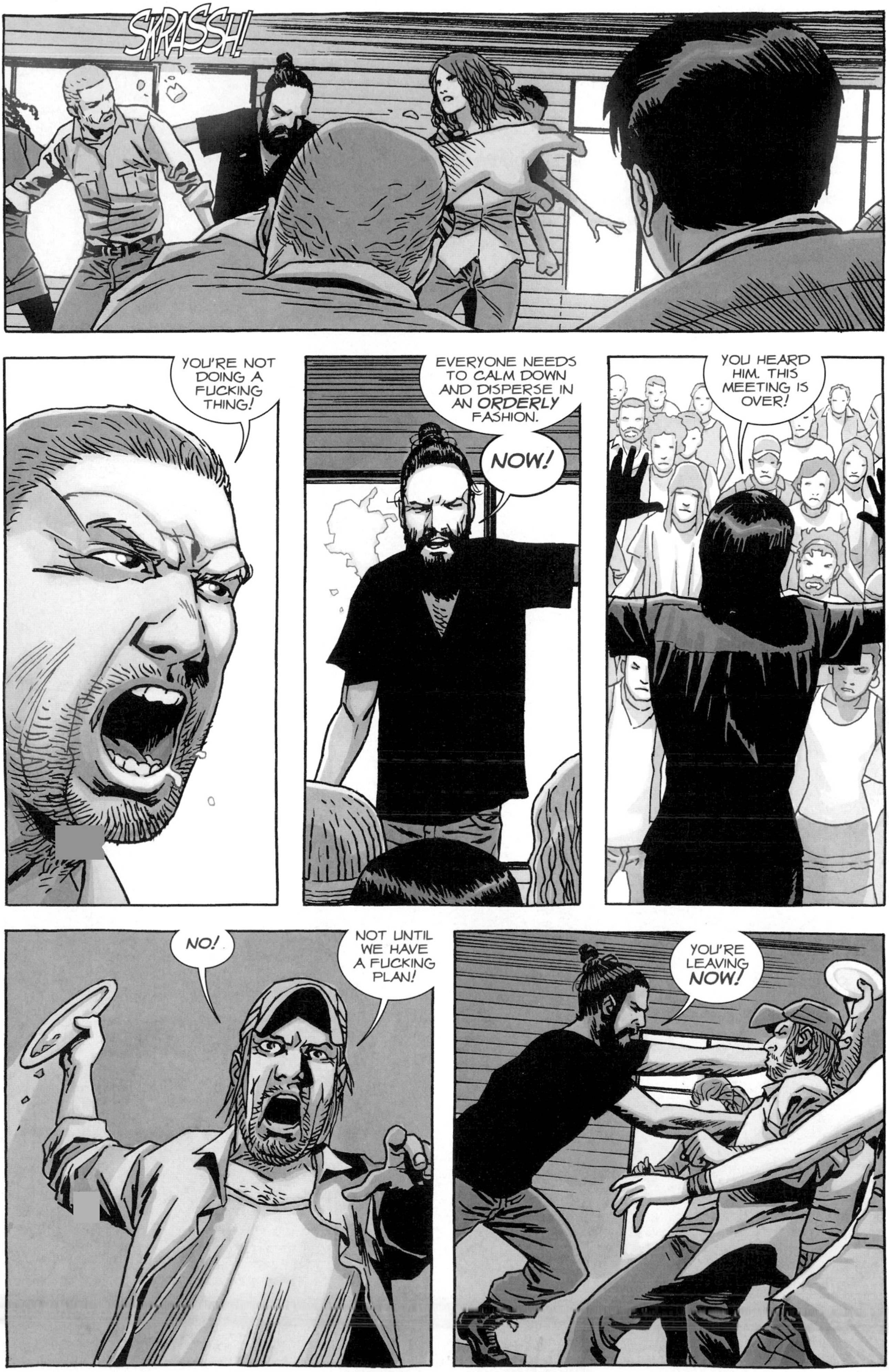
SKRASSH!
YOU'RE NOT DOING A FUCKING THING!
EVERYONE NEEDS TO CALM DOWN AND DISPERSE IN AN ORDERLY FASHION.
NOW!
YOU HEARD HIM. THIS MEETING IS OVER!
NO!
NOT UNTIL WE HAVE A FUCKING PLAN!
YOU'RE LEAVING NOW!

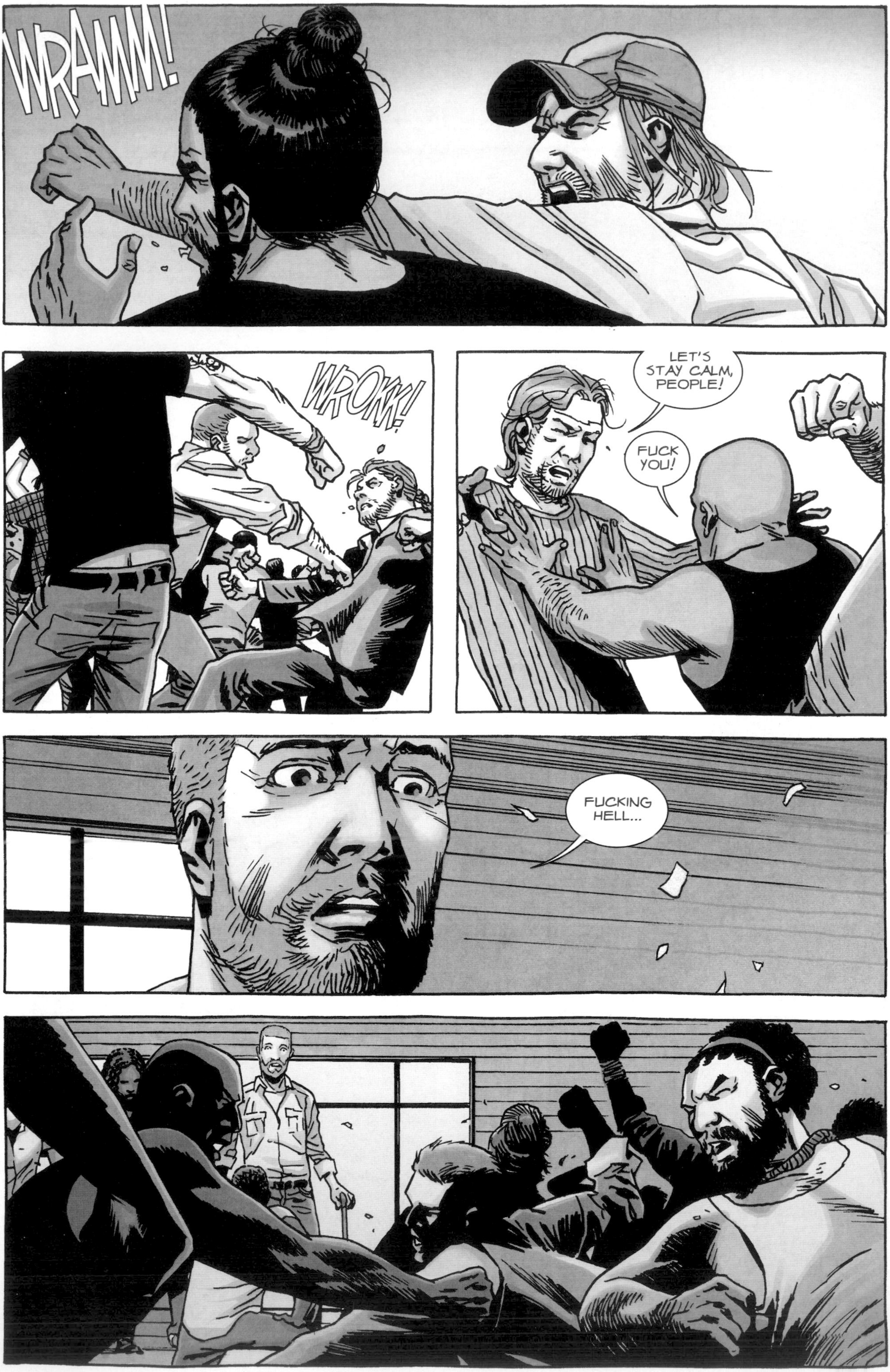
WRAMM!
WROKK!
LET'S STAY CALM, PEOPLE!
FUCK YOU!
FUCKING HELL...

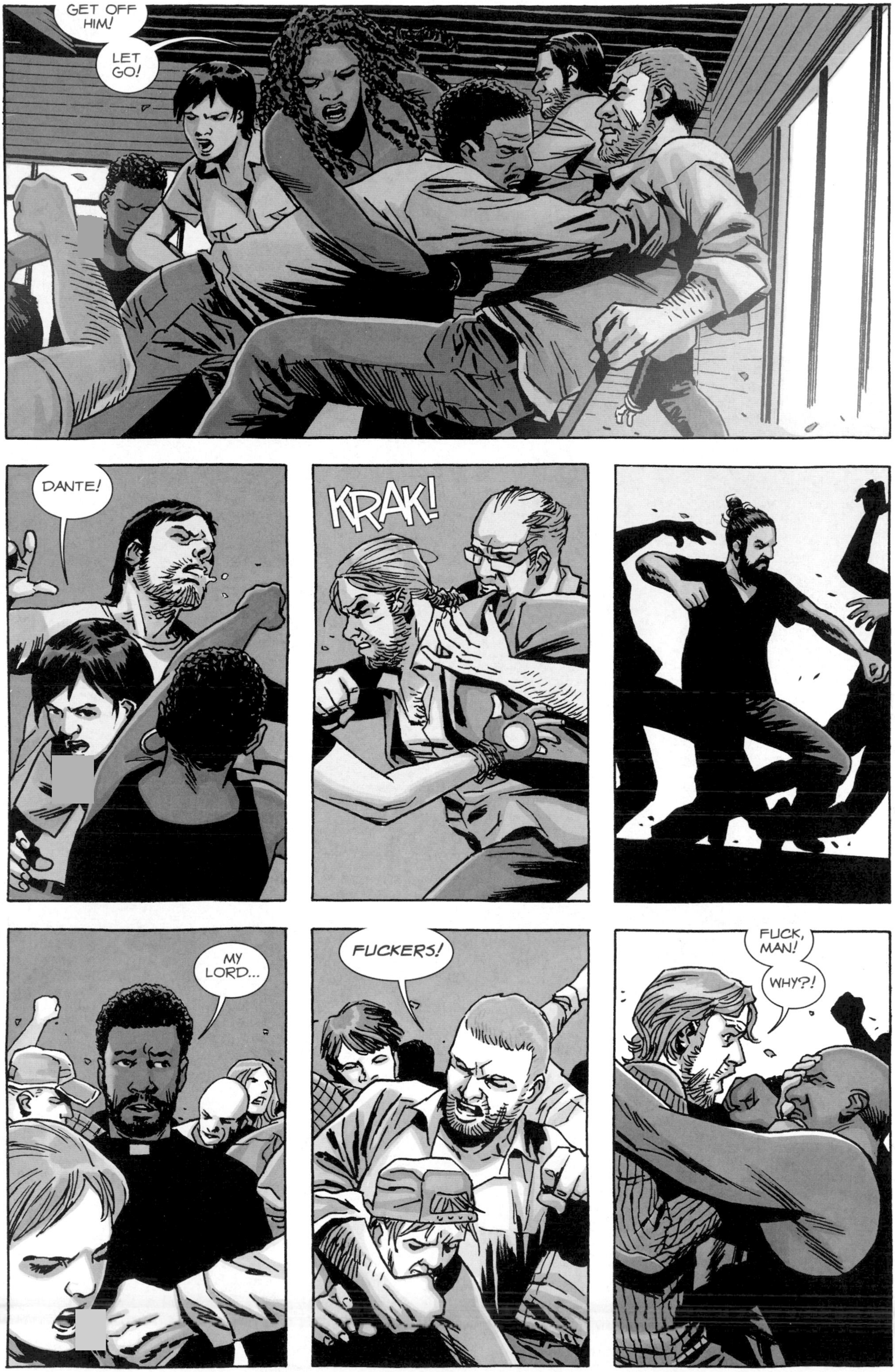
GET OFF HIM!
LET GO!
DANTE!
KRAK!
MY LORD...
FUCKERS!
FUCK, MAN!
WHY?!

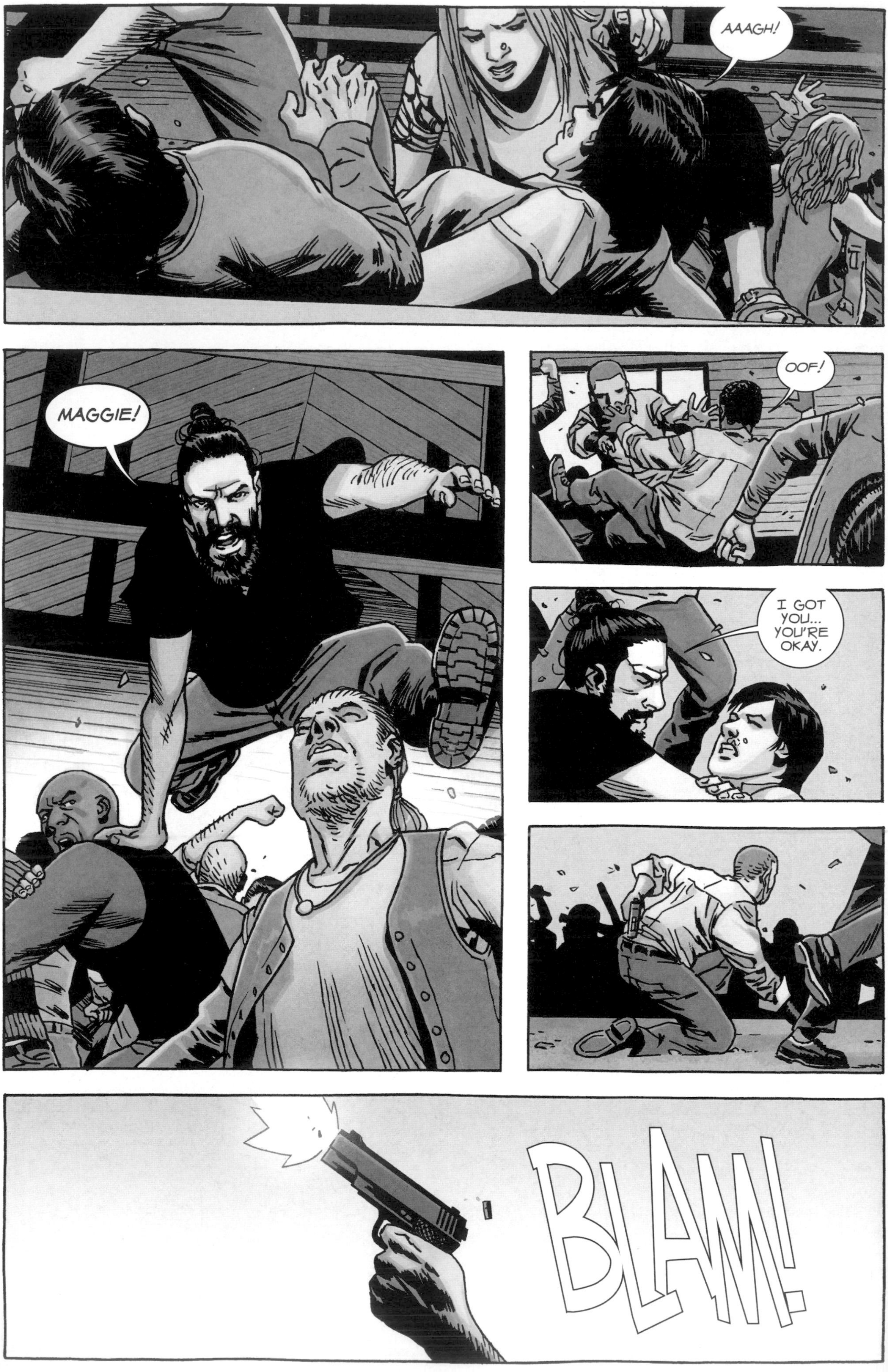
AAAGH!
MAGGIE!
OOF!
I GOT YOU... YOU'RE OKAY.
BLAM!

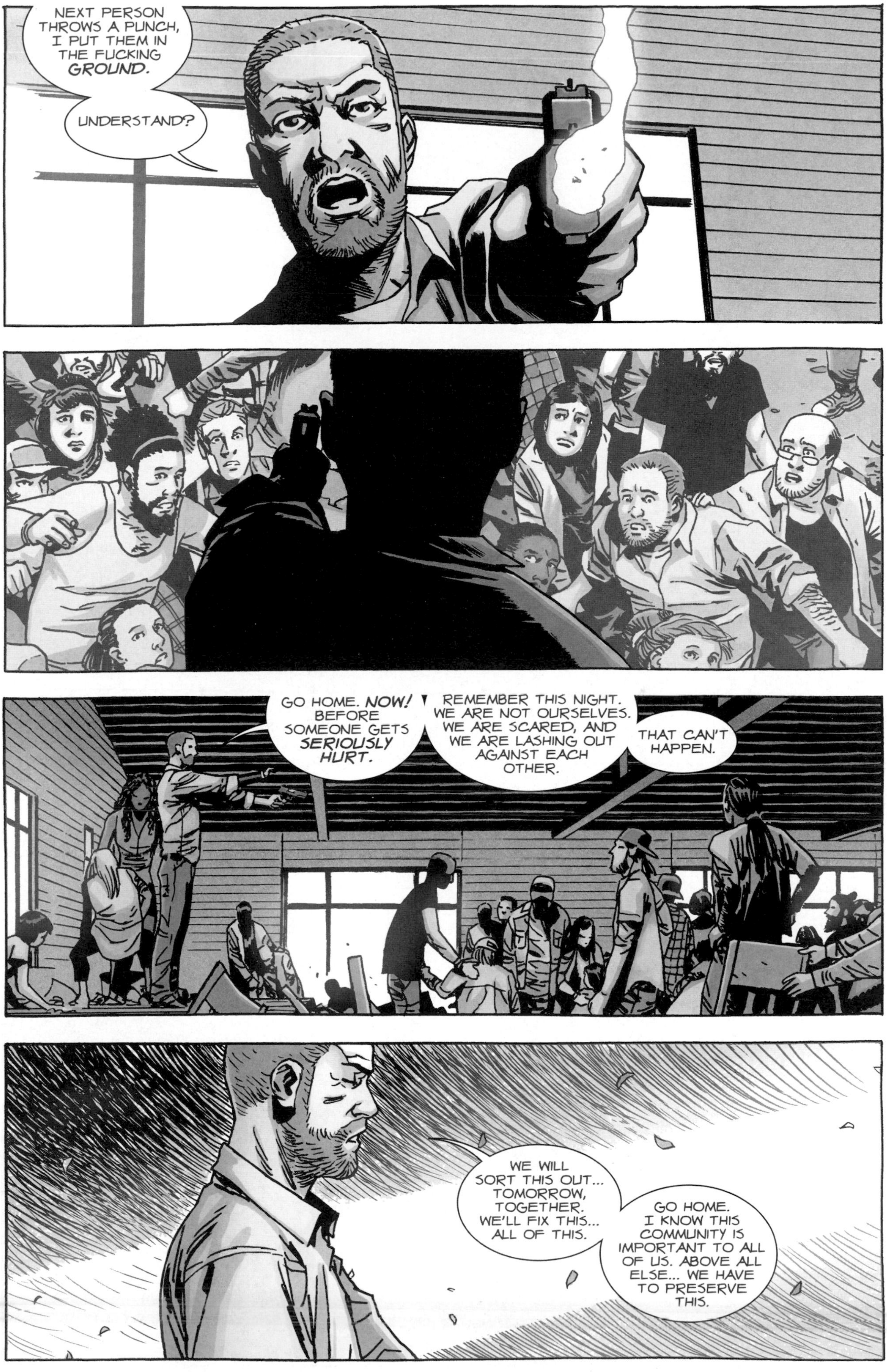
NEXT PERSON THROWS A PUNCH, I PUT THEM IN THE FUCKING **GROUND.**
UNDERSTAND?
GO HOME. **NOW!** BEFORE SOMEONE GETS ***SERIOUSLY HURT.***
REMEMBER THIS NIGHT. WE ARE NOT OURSELVES. WE ARE SCARED, AND WE ARE LASHING OUT AGAINST EACH OTHER.
THAT CAN'T HAPPEN.
WE WILL SORT THIS OUT... TOMORROW, TOGETHER. WE'LL FIX THIS... ALL OF THIS.
GO HOME. I KNOW THIS COMMUNITY IS IMPORTANT TO ALL OF US. ABOVE ALL ELSE... WE HAVE TO PRESERVE THIS.

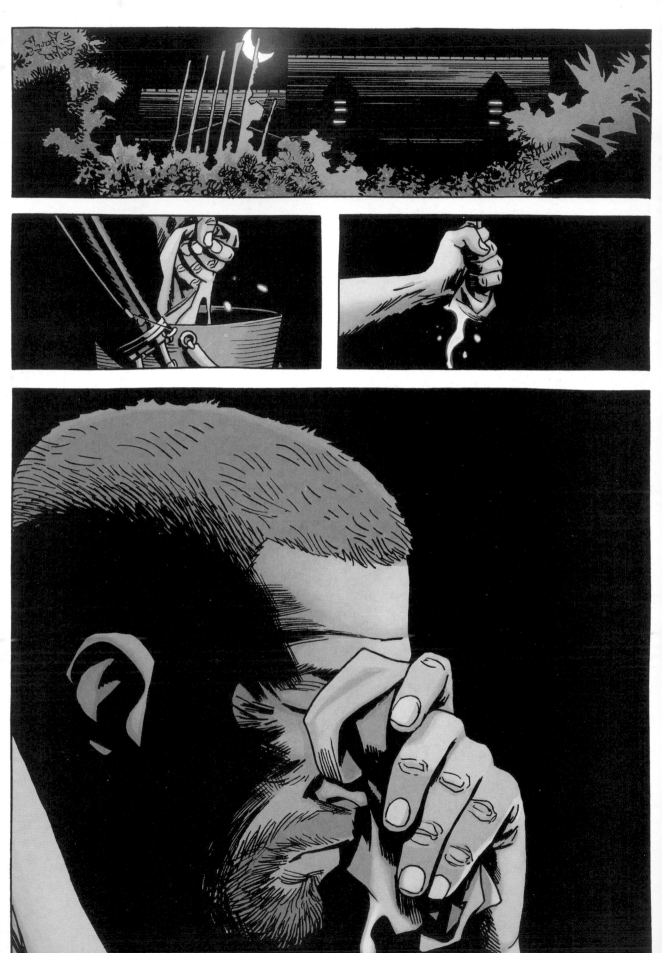

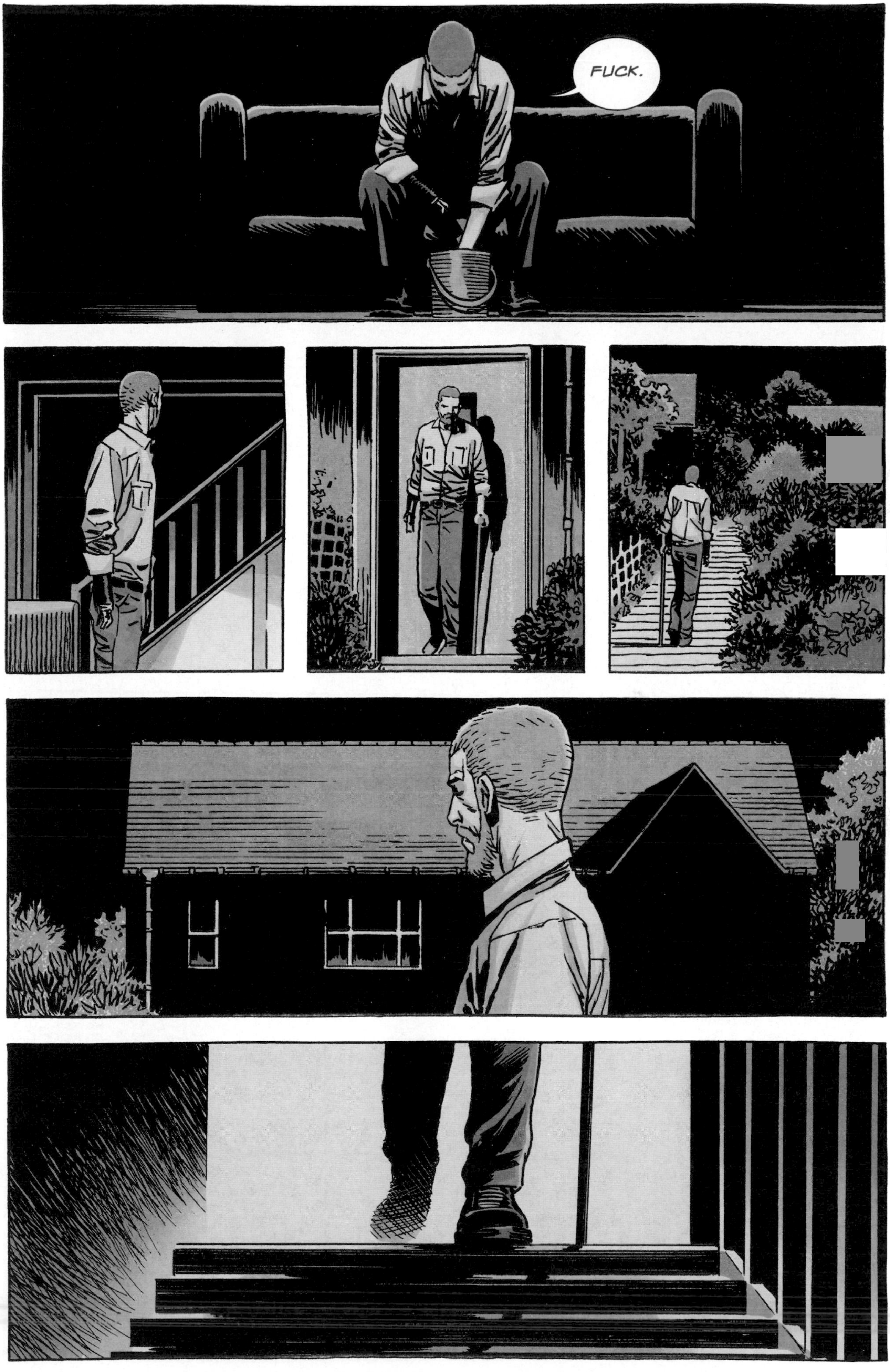
FUCK.

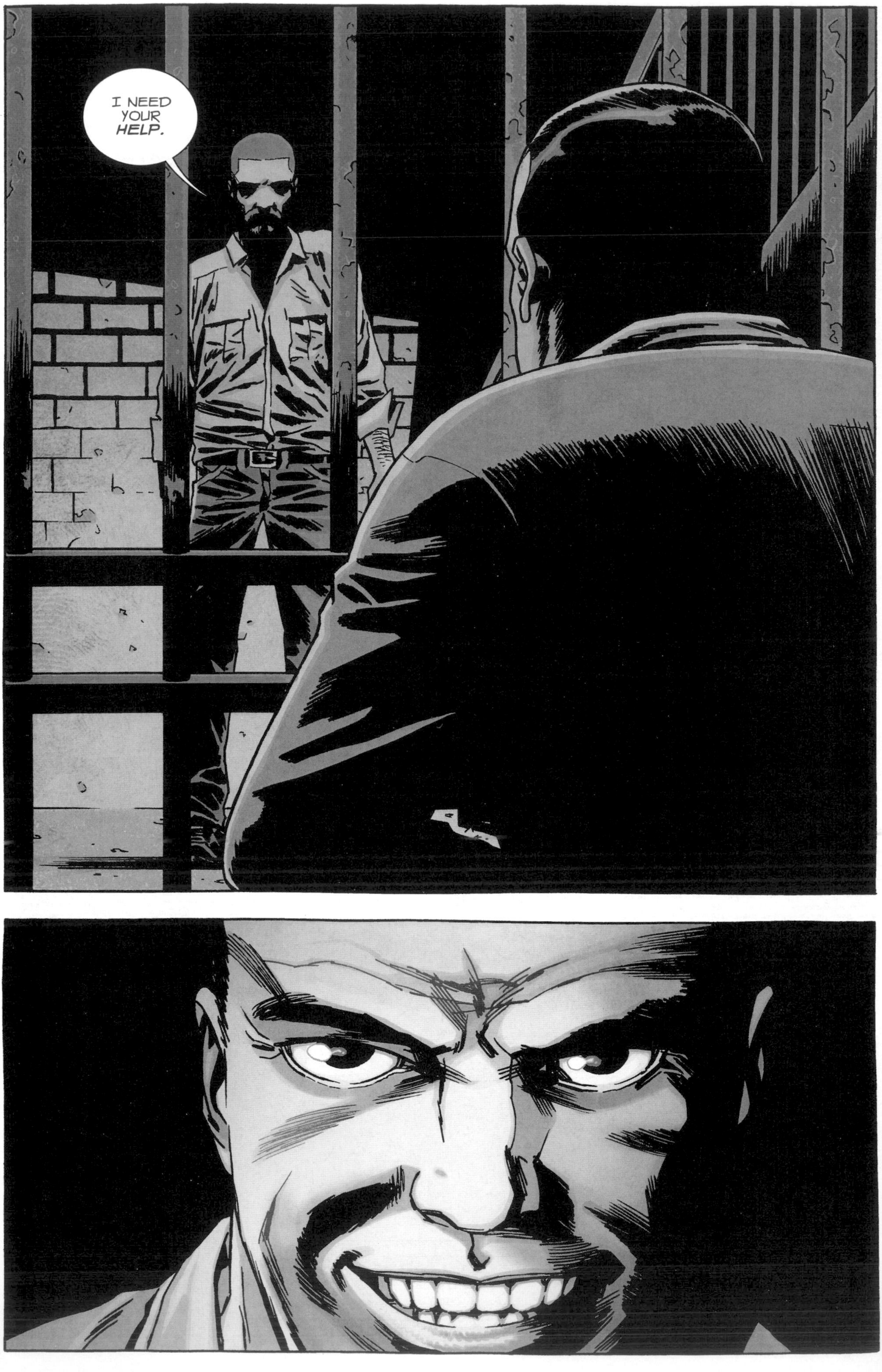
I NEED YOUR HELP.

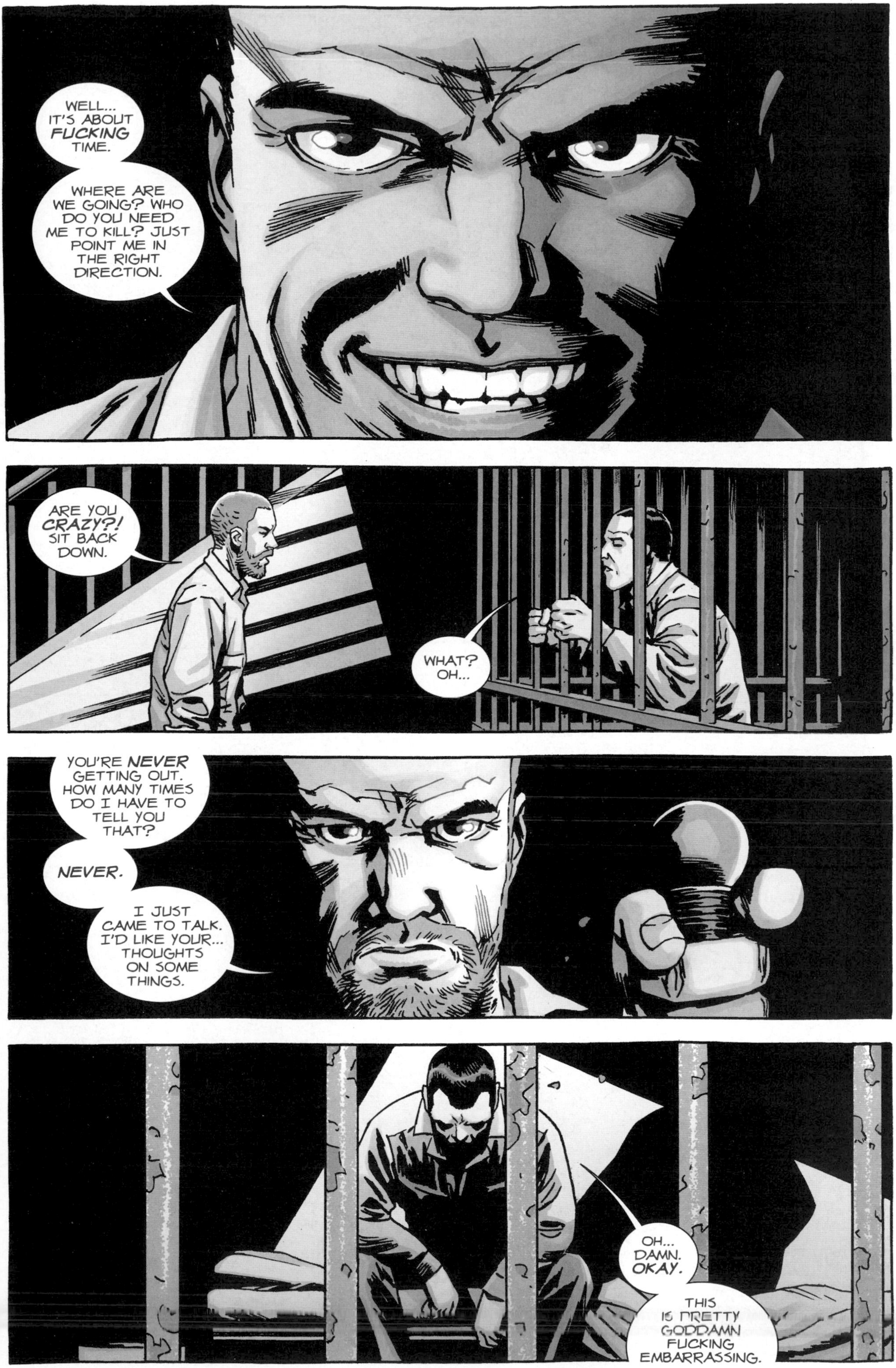
WELL... IT'S ABOUT FUCKING TIME.
WHERE ARE WE GOING? WHO DO YOU NEED ME TO KILL? JUST POINT ME IN THE RIGHT DIRECTION.
ARE YOU CRAZY?! SIT BACK DOWN.
WHAT? OH...
YOU'RE NEVER GETTING OUT. HOW MANY TIMES DO I HAVE TO TELL YOU THAT?
NEVER.
I JUST CAME TO TALK. I'D LIKE YOUR... THOUGHTS ON SOME THINGS.
OH... DAMN. OKAY.
THIS IS PRETTY GODDAMN FUCKING EMBARRASSING.

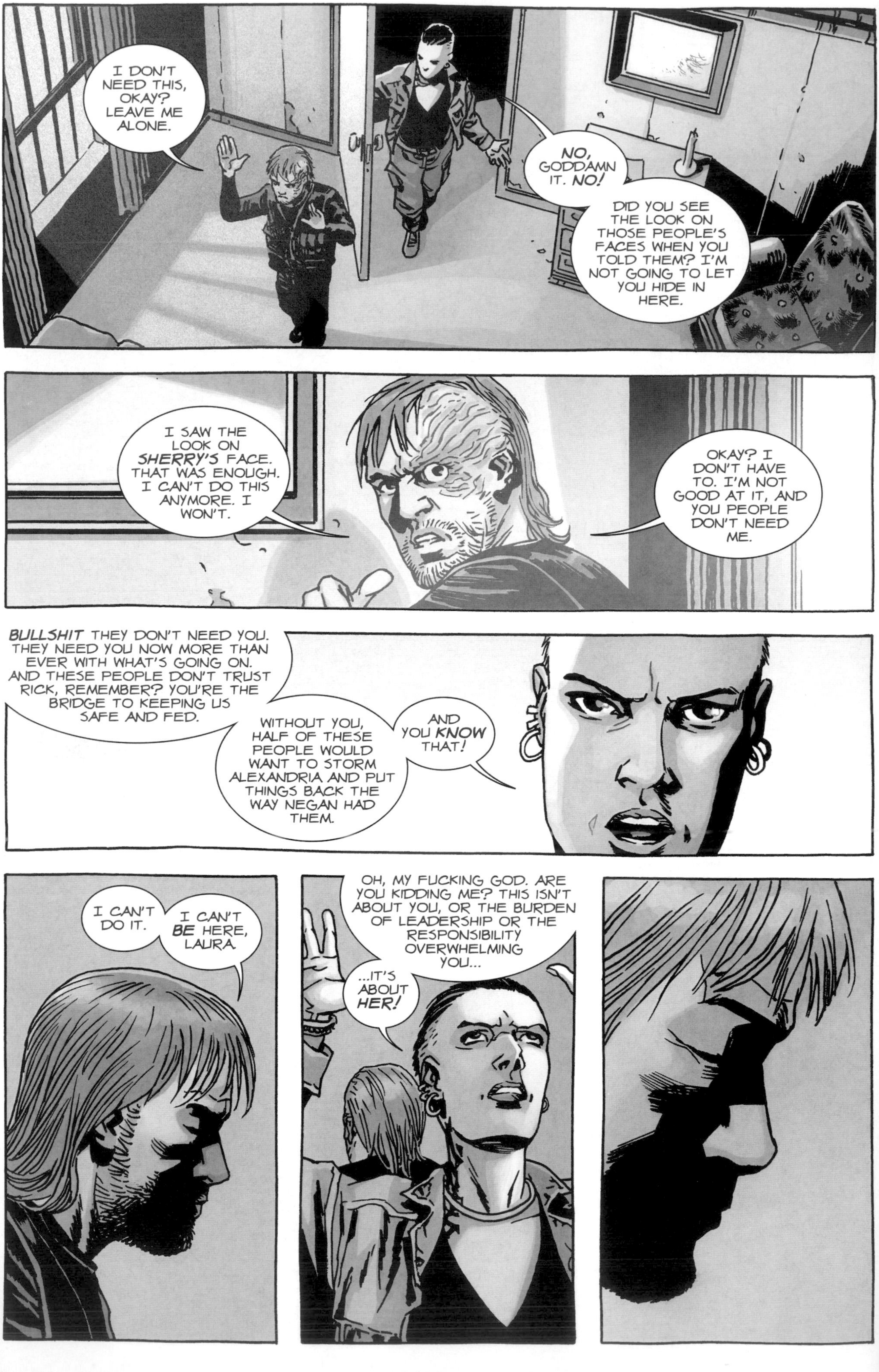
I DON'T NEED THIS, OKAY? LEAVE ME ALONE.
NO, GODDAMN IT. NO!
DID YOU SEE THE LOOK ON THOSE PEOPLE'S FACES WHEN YOU TOLD THEM? I'M NOT GOING TO LET YOU HIDE IN HERE.
I SAW THE LOOK ON SHERRY'S FACE. THAT WAS ENOUGH. I CAN'T DO THIS ANYMORE. I WON'T.
OKAY? I DON'T HAVE TO. I'M NOT GOOD AT IT, AND YOU PEOPLE DON'T NEED ME.
BULLSHIT THEY DON'T NEED YOU. THEY NEED YOU NOW MORE THAN EVER WITH WHAT'S GOING ON. AND THESE PEOPLE DON'T TRUST RICK, REMEMBER? YOU'RE THE BRIDGE TO KEEPING US SAFE AND FED.
WITHOUT YOU, HALF OF THESE PEOPLE WOULD WANT TO STORM ALEXANDRIA AND PUT THINGS BACK THE WAY NEGAN HAD THEM.
AND YOU KNOW THAT!
I CAN'T DO IT.
I CAN'T BE HERE, LAURA.
OH, MY FUCKING GOD. ARE YOU KIDDING ME? THIS ISN'T ABOUT YOU, OR THE BURDEN OF LEADERSHIP OR THE RESPONSIBILITY OVERWHELMING YOU...
...IT'S ABOUT HER!

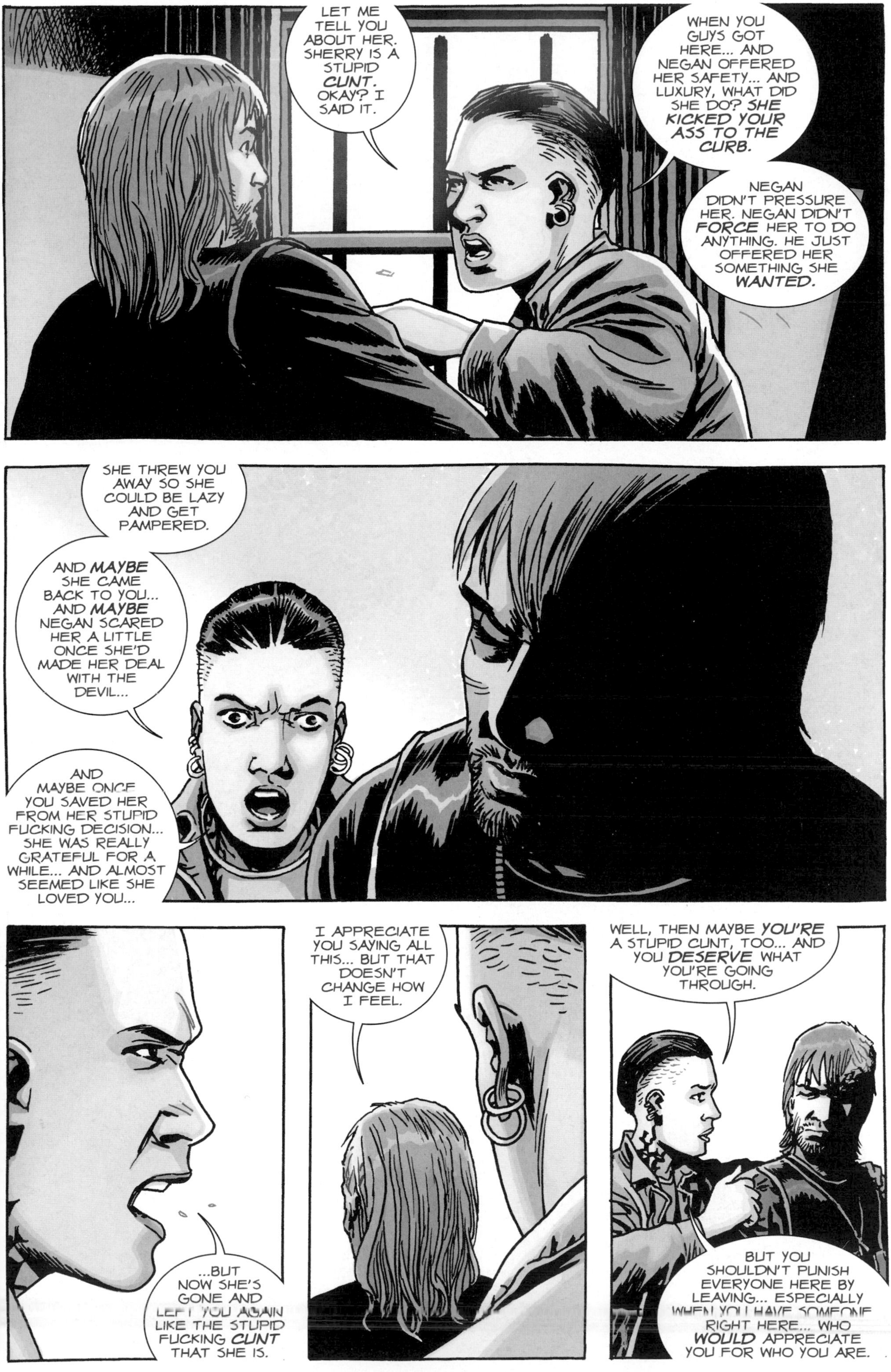
LET ME TELL YOU ABOUT HER. SHERRY IS A STUPID CUNT. OKAY? I SAID IT.
WHEN YOU GUYS GOT HERE... AND NEGAN OFFERED HER SAFETY... AND LUXURY, WHAT DID SHE DO? SHE KICKED YOUR ASS TO THE CURB.
NEGAN DIDN'T PRESSURE HER. NEGAN DIDN'T FORCE HER TO DO ANYTHING. HE JUST OFFERED HER SOMETHING SHE WANTED.
SHE THREW YOU AWAY SO SHE COULD BE LAZY AND GET PAMPERED.
AND MAYBE SHE CAME BACK TO YOU... AND MAYBE NEGAN SCARED HER A LITTLE ONCE SHE'D MADE HER DEAL WITH THE DEVIL...
AND MAYBE ONCE YOU SAVED HER FROM HER STUPID FUCKING DECISION... SHE WAS REALLY GRATEFUL FOR A WHILE... AND ALMOST SEEMED LIKE SHE LOVED YOU...
...BUT NOW SHE'S GONE AND LEFT YOU AGAIN LIKE THE STUPID FUCKING CUNT THAT SHE IS.
I APPRECIATE YOU SAYING ALL THIS... BUT THAT DOESN'T CHANGE HOW I FEEL.
WELL, THEN MAYBE YOU'RE A STUPID CUNT, TOO... AND YOU DESERVE WHAT YOU'RE GOING THROUGH.
BUT YOU SHOULDN'T PUNISH EVERYONE HERE BY LEAVING... ESPECIALLY WHEN YOU HAVE SOMEONE RIGHT HERE... WHO WOULD APPRECIATE YOU FOR WHO YOU ARE.

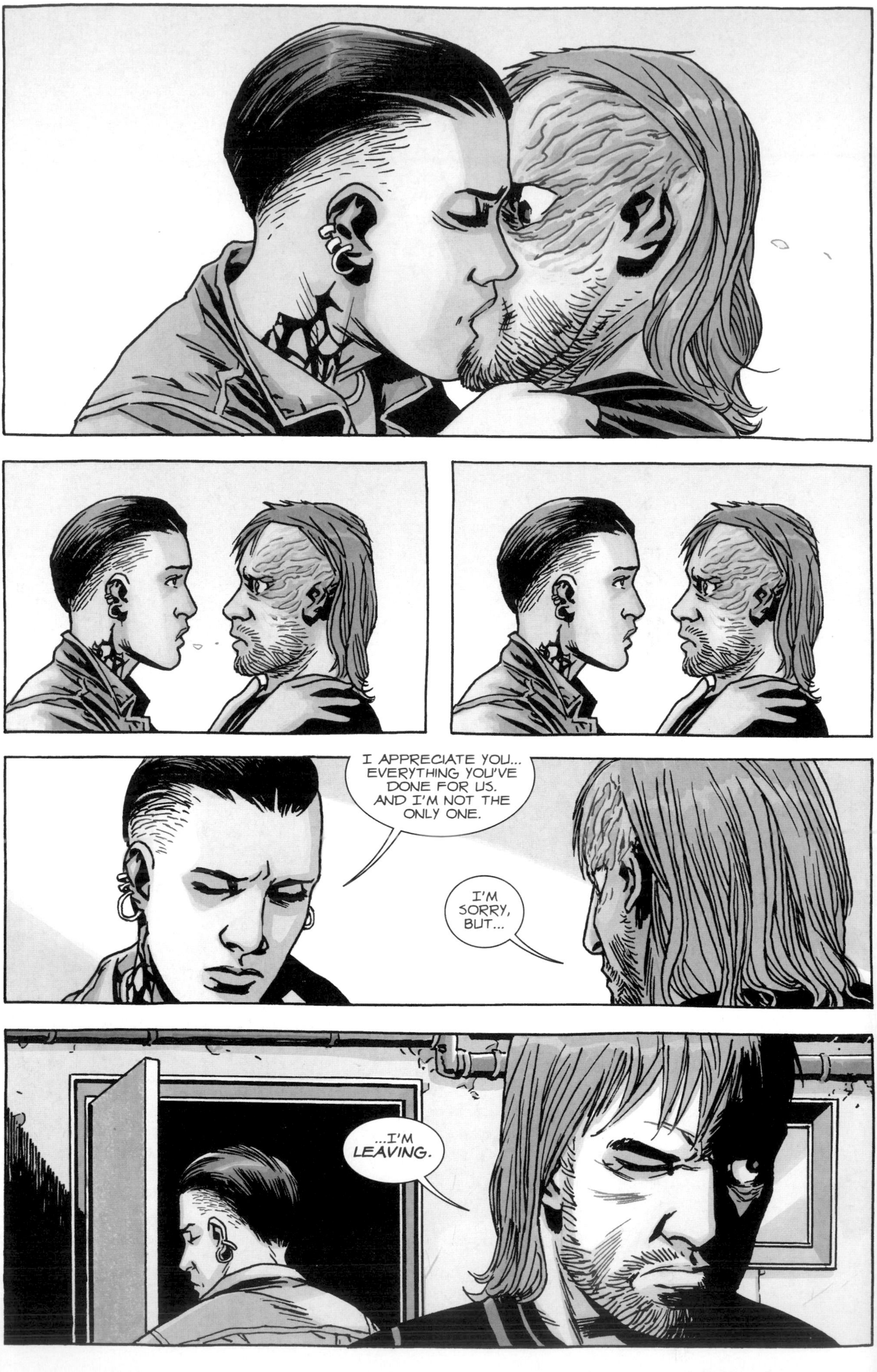
I APPRECIATE YOU... EVERYTHING YOU'VE DONE FOR US. AND I'M NOT THE ONLY ONE.
I'M SORRY, BUT...
...I'M LEAVING.

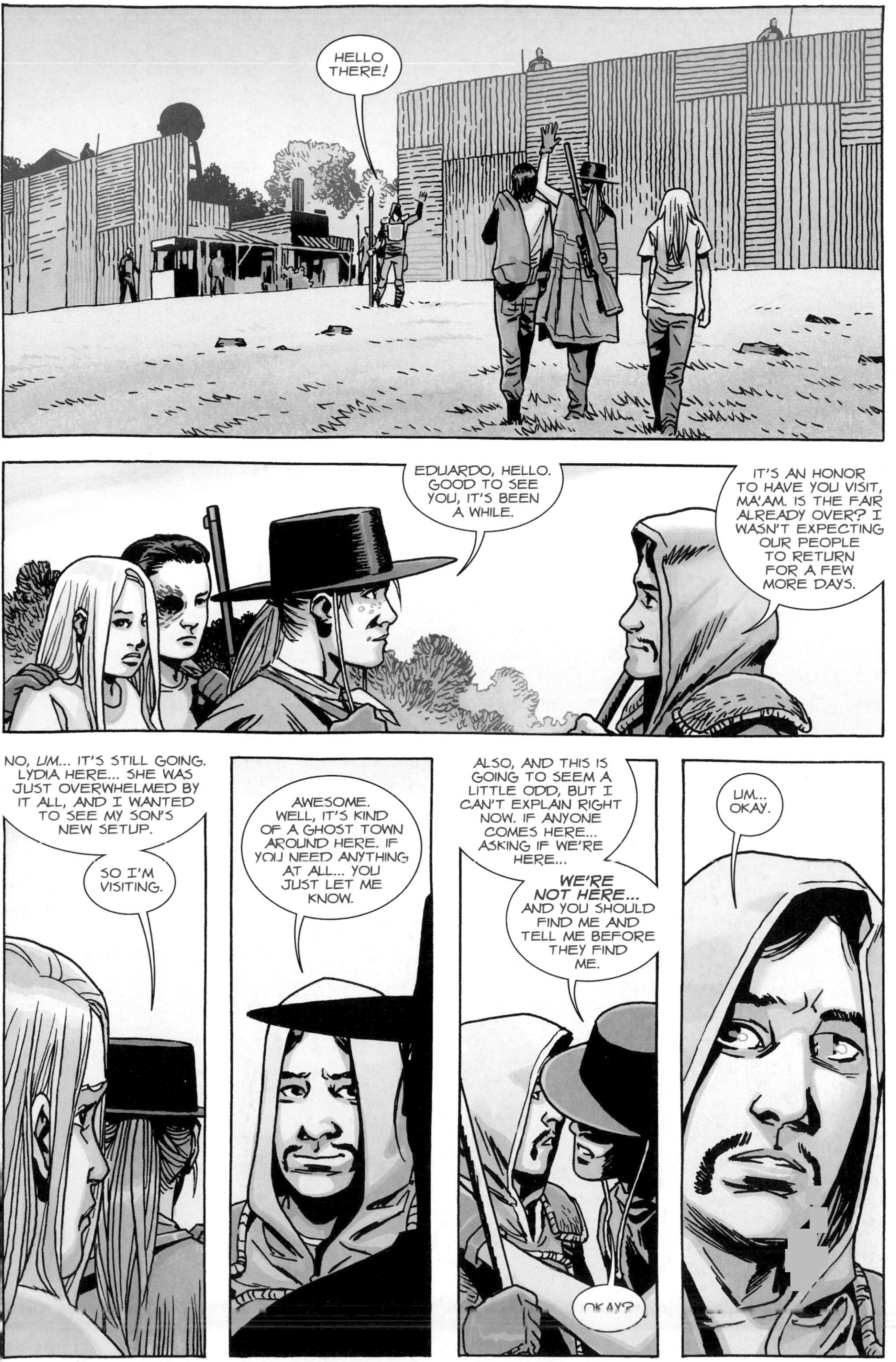
HELLO THERE!
EDUARDO, HELLO. GOOD TO SEE YOU, IT'S BEEN A WHILE.
IT'S AN HONOR TO HAVE YOU VISIT, MA'AM. IS THE FAIR ALREADY OVER? I WASN'T EXPECTING OUR PEOPLE TO RETURN FOR A FEW MORE DAYS.
NO, *UM*... IT'S STILL GOING. LYDIA HERE... SHE WAS JUST OVERWHELMED BY IT ALL, AND I WANTED TO SEE MY SON'S NEW SETUP.
SO I'M VISITING.
AWESOME. WELL, IT'S KIND OF A GHOST TOWN AROUND HERE. IF YOU NEED ANYTHING AT ALL... YOU JUST LET ME KNOW.
ALSO, AND THIS IS GOING TO SEEM A LITTLE ODD, BUT I CAN'T EXPLAIN RIGHT NOW. IF ANYONE COMES HERE... ASKING IF WE'RE HERE...
WE'RE NOT HERE... AND YOU SHOULD FIND ME AND TELL ME BEFORE THEY FIND ME.
OKAY?
UM... OKAY.

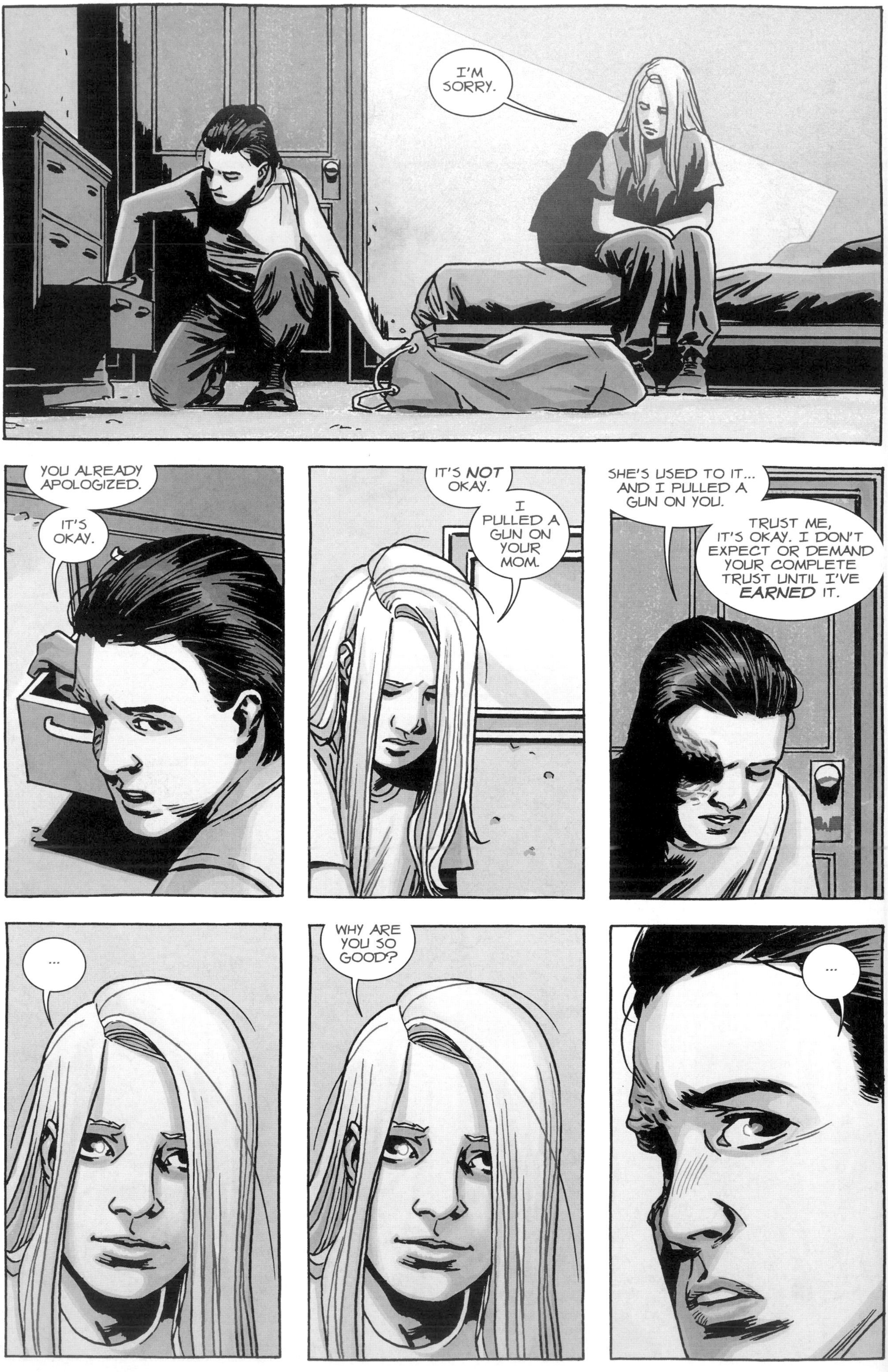
I'M SORRY.
YOU ALREADY APOLOGIZED.
IT'S OKAY.
IT'S NOT OKAY.
I PULLED A GUN ON YOUR MOM.
SHE'S USED TO IT... AND I PULLED A GUN ON YOU.
TRUST ME, IT'S OKAY. I DON'T EXPECT OR DEMAND YOUR COMPLETE TRUST UNTIL I'VE EARNED IT.
...
WHY ARE YOU SO GOOD?
...

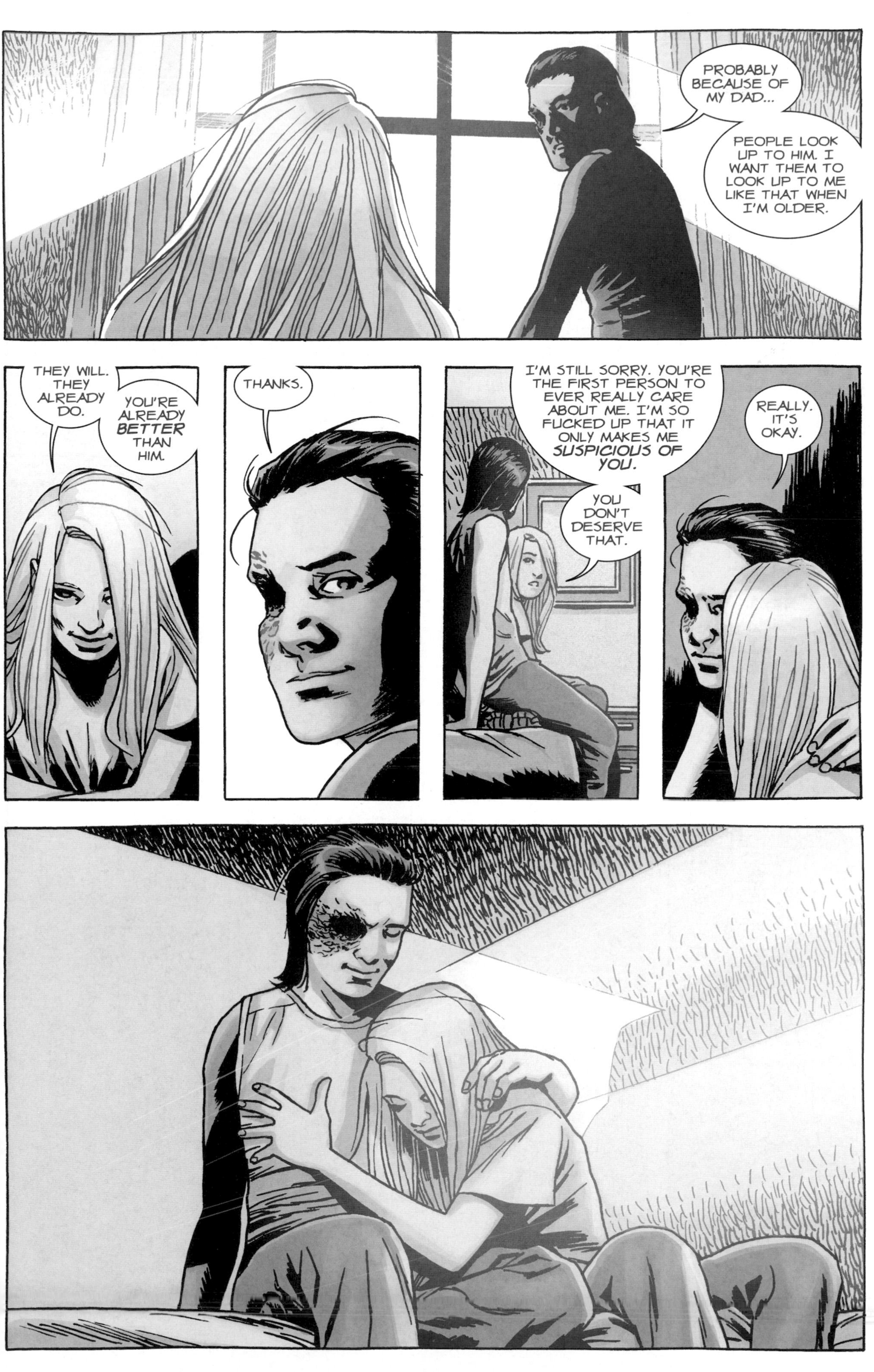
PROBABLY BECAUSE OF MY DAD...
PEOPLE LOOK UP TO HIM. I WANT THEM TO LOOK UP TO ME LIKE THAT WHEN I'M OLDER.
THEY WILL. THEY ALREADY DO.
YOU'RE ALREADY *BETTER* THAN HIM.
THANKS.
I'M STILL SORRY. YOU'RE THE FIRST PERSON TO EVER REALLY CARE ABOUT ME. I'M SO FUCKED UP THAT IT ONLY MAKES ME *SUSPICIOUS OF YOU.*
YOU DON'T DESERVE THAT.
REALLY. IT'S OKAY.

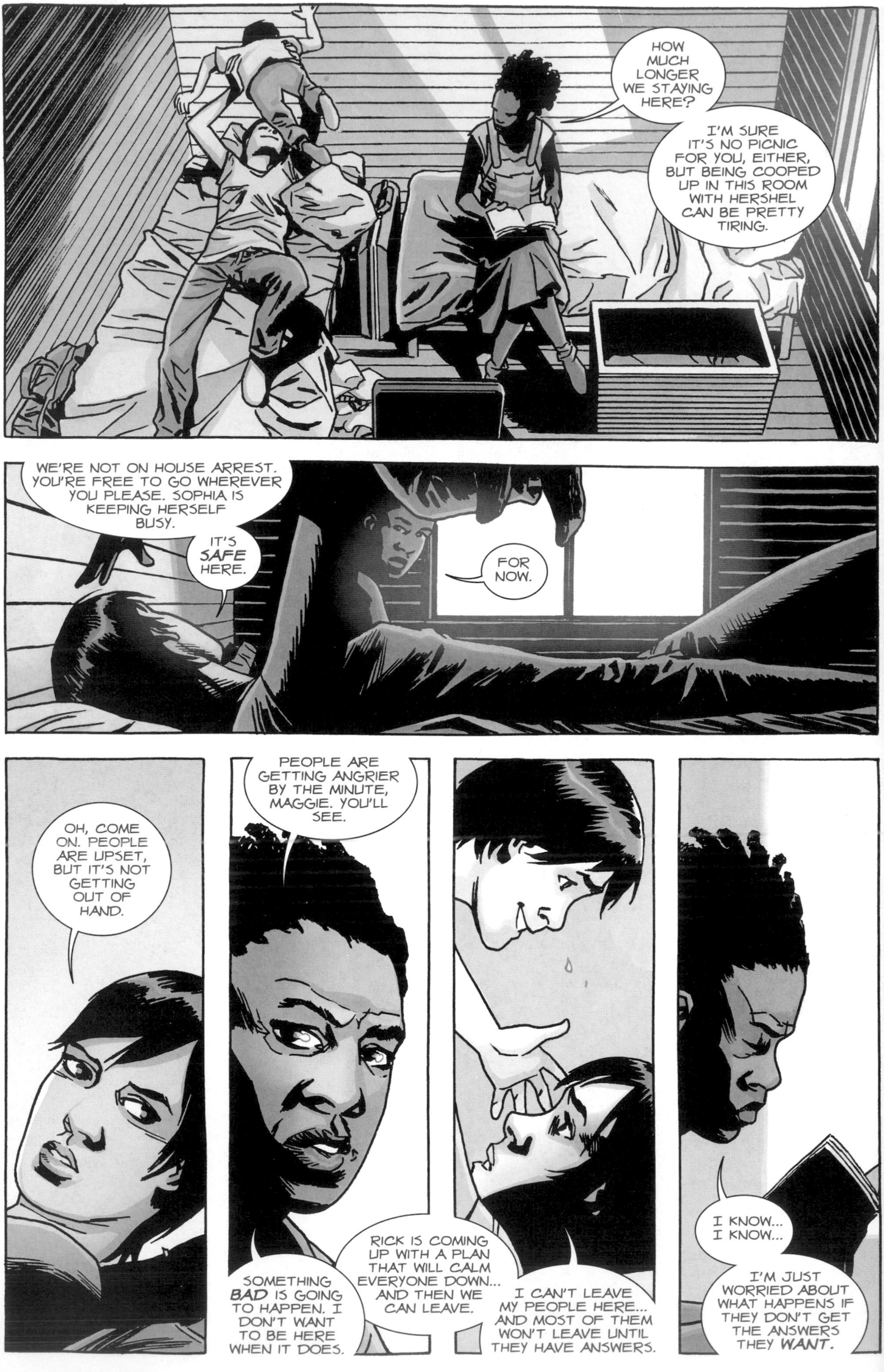
HOW MUCH LONGER WE STAYING HERE?
I'M SURE IT'S NO PICNIC FOR YOU, EITHER, BUT BEING COOPED UP IN THIS ROOM WITH HERSHEL CAN BE PRETTY TIRING.
WE'RE NOT ON HOUSE ARREST. YOU'RE FREE TO GO WHEREVER YOU PLEASE. SOPHIA IS KEEPING HERSELF BUSY.
IT'S *SAFE* HERE.
FOR NOW.
OH, COME ON. PEOPLE ARE UPSET, BUT IT'S NOT GETTING OUT OF HAND.
PEOPLE ARE GETTING ANGRIER BY THE MINUTE, MAGGIE. YOU'LL SEE.
SOMETHING ***BAD*** IS GOING TO HAPPEN. I DON'T WANT TO BE HERE WHEN IT DOES.
RICK IS COMING UP WITH A PLAN THAT WILL CALM EVERYONE DOWN... AND THEN WE CAN LEAVE.
I CAN'T LEAVE MY PEOPLE HERE... AND MOST OF THEM WON'T LEAVE UNTIL THEY HAVE ANSWERS.
I KNOW... I KNOW...
I'M JUST WORRIED ABOUT WHAT HAPPENS IF THEY DON'T GET THE ANSWERS THEY ***WANT***.

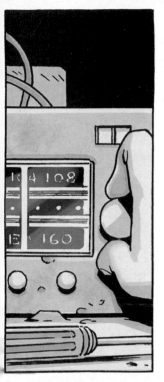

SKEEEEE.

SKK-SHHHHH.

SHHH–

KLICK.

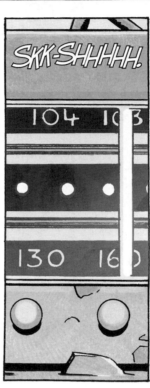

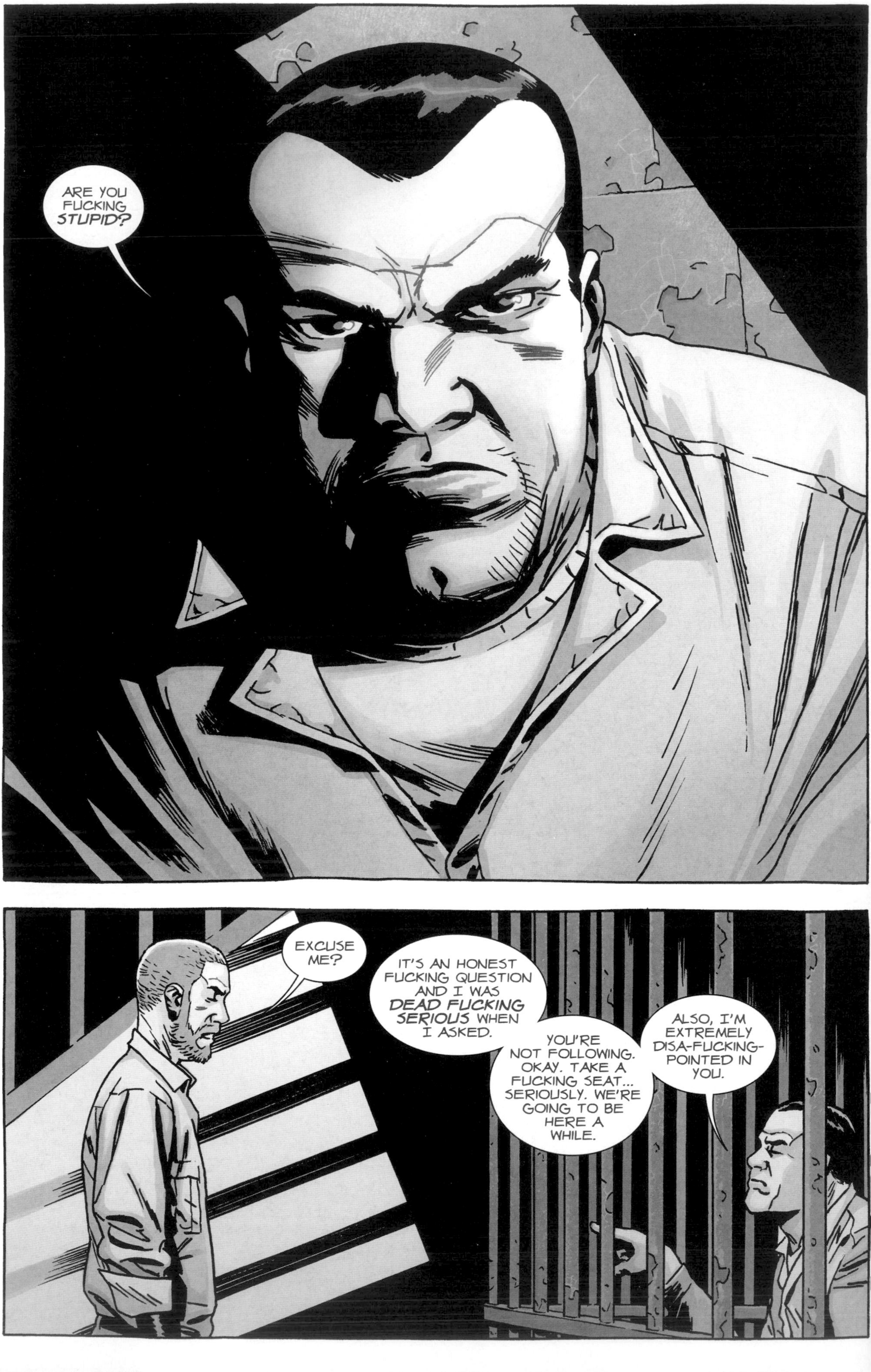
ARE YOU FUCKING STUPID?
EXCUSE ME?
IT'S AN HONEST FUCKING QUESTION AND I WAS DEAD FUCKING SERIOUS WHEN I ASKED.
YOU'RE NOT FOLLOWING. OKAY. TAKE A FUCKING SEAT... SERIOUSLY. WE'RE GOING TO BE HERE A WHILE.
ALSO, I'M EXTREMELY DISA-FUCKING-POINTED IN YOU.

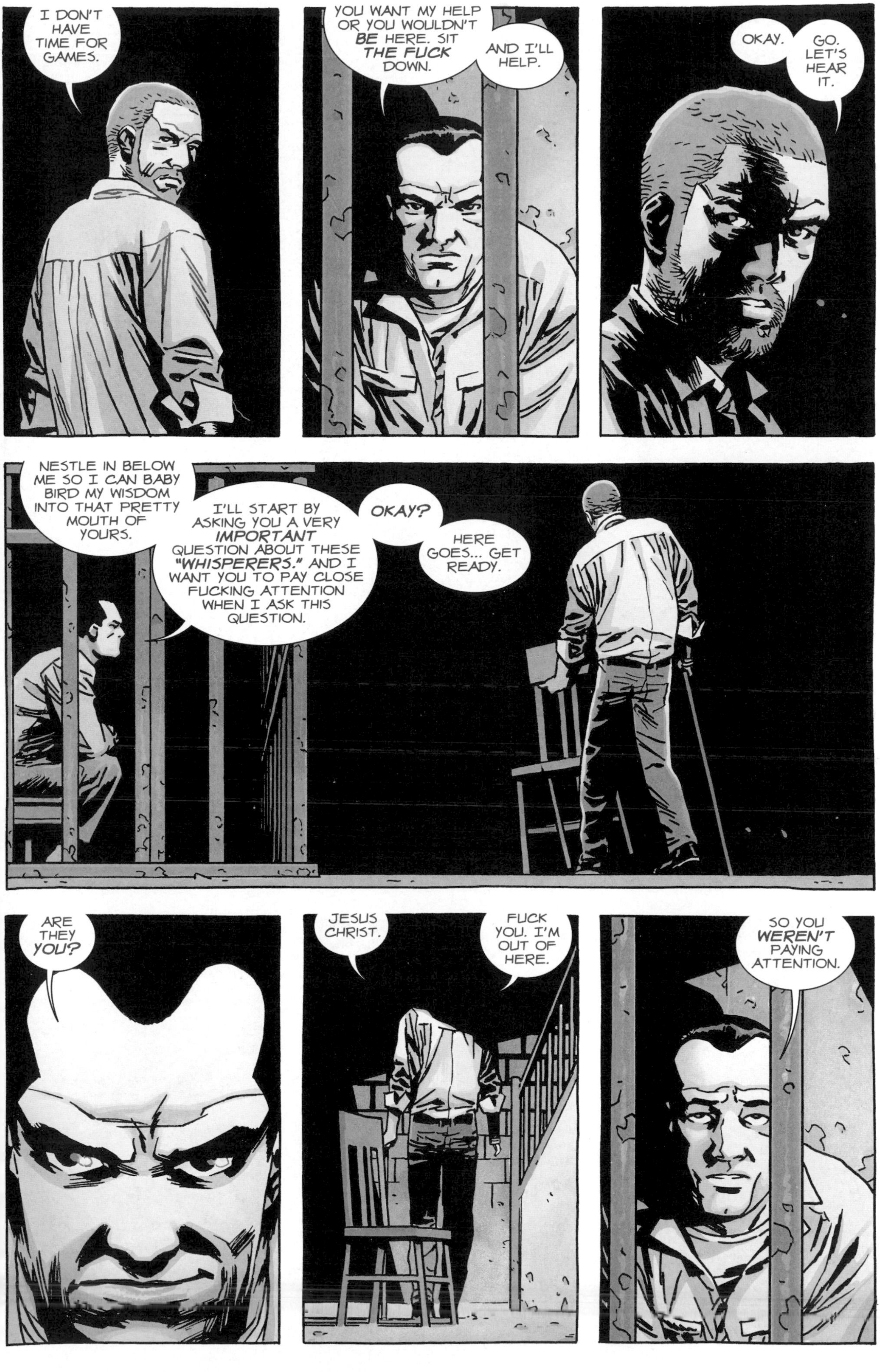
I DON'T HAVE TIME FOR GAMES.
YOU WANT MY HELP OR YOU WOULDN'T BE HERE. SIT THE FUCK DOWN.
AND I'LL HELP.
OKAY.
GO. LET'S HEAR IT.
NESTLE IN BELOW ME SO I CAN BABY BIRD MY WISDOM INTO THAT PRETTY MOUTH OF YOURS.
I'LL START BY ASKING YOU A VERY IMPORTANT QUESTION ABOUT THESE "WHISPERERS." AND I WANT YOU TO PAY CLOSE FUCKING ATTENTION WHEN I ASK THIS QUESTION.
OKAY?
HERE GOES... GET READY.
ARE THEY YOU?
JESUS CHRIST.
FUCK YOU. I'M OUT OF HERE.
SO YOU WEREN'T PAYING ATTENTION.

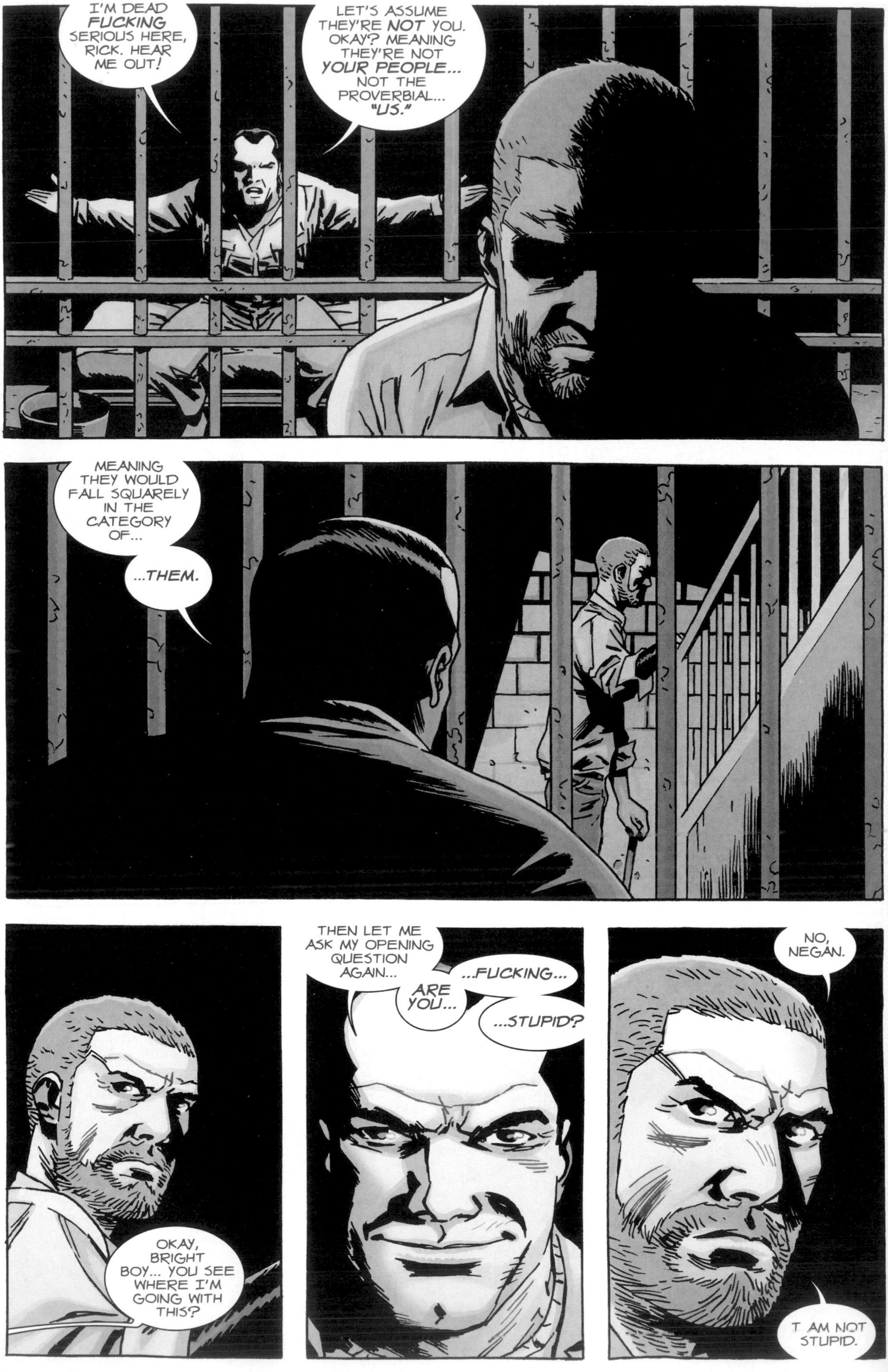
I'M DEAD FUCKING SERIOUS HERE, RICK. HEAR ME OUT!
LET'S ASSUME THEY'RE NOT YOU. OKAY? MEANING THEY'RE NOT YOUR PEOPLE... NOT THE PROVERBIAL... "US."
MEANING THEY WOULD FALL SQUARELY IN THE CATEGORY OF...
...THEM.
OKAY, BRIGHT BOY... YOU SEE WHERE I'M GOING WITH THIS?
THEN LET ME ASK MY OPENING QUESTION AGAIN...
ARE YOU...
...FUCKING...
...STUPID?
NO, NEGAN.
I AM NOT STUPID.

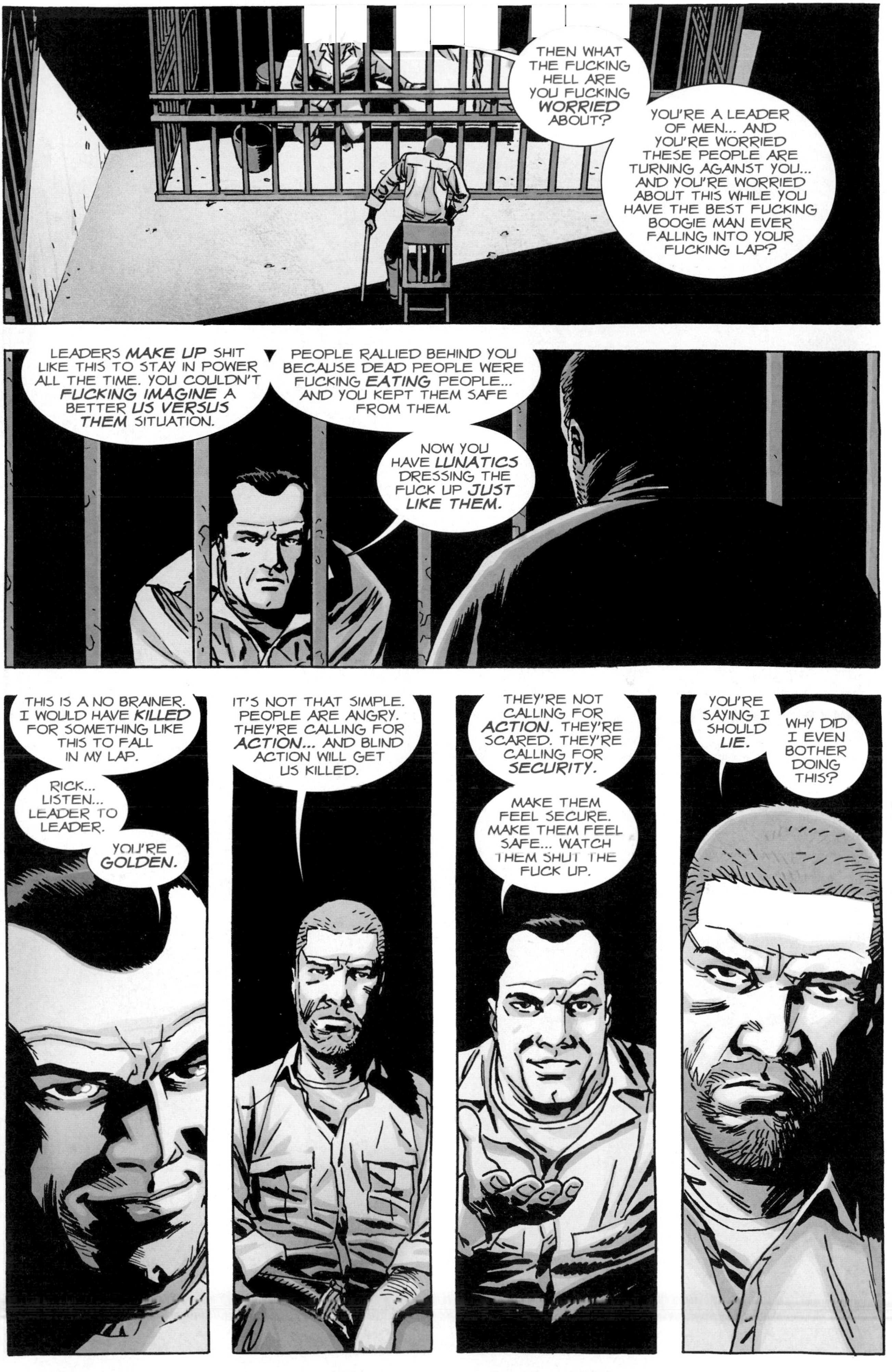
THEN WHAT THE FUCKING HELL ARE YOU FUCKING WORRIED ABOUT?
YOU'RE A LEADER OF MEN... AND YOU'RE WORRIED THESE PEOPLE ARE TURNING AGAINST YOU... AND YOU'RE WORRIED ABOUT THIS WHILE YOU HAVE THE BEST FUCKING BOOGIE MAN EVER FALLING INTO YOUR FUCKING LAP?
LEADERS MAKE UP SHIT LIKE THIS TO STAY IN POWER ALL THE TIME. YOU COULDN'T FUCKING IMAGINE A BETTER US VERSUS THEM SITUATION.
PEOPLE RALLIED BEHIND YOU BECAUSE DEAD PEOPLE WERE FUCKING EATING PEOPLE... AND YOU KEPT THEM SAFE FROM THEM.
NOW YOU HAVE LUNATICS DRESSING THE FUCK UP JUST LIKE THEM.
THIS IS A NO BRAINER. I WOULD HAVE KILLED FOR SOMETHING LIKE THIS TO FALL IN MY LAP.
RICK... LISTEN... LEADER TO LEADER.
YOU'RE GOLDEN.
IT'S NOT THAT SIMPLE. PEOPLE ARE ANGRY. THEY'RE CALLING FOR ACTION... AND BLIND ACTION WILL GET US KILLED.
THEY'RE NOT CALLING FOR ACTION. THEY'RE SCARED. THEY'RE CALLING FOR SECURITY.
MAKE THEM FEEL SECURE. MAKE THEM FEEL SAFE... WATCH THEM SHUT THE FUCK UP.
YOU'RE SAYING I SHOULD LIE.
WHY DID I EVEN BOTHER DOING THIS?

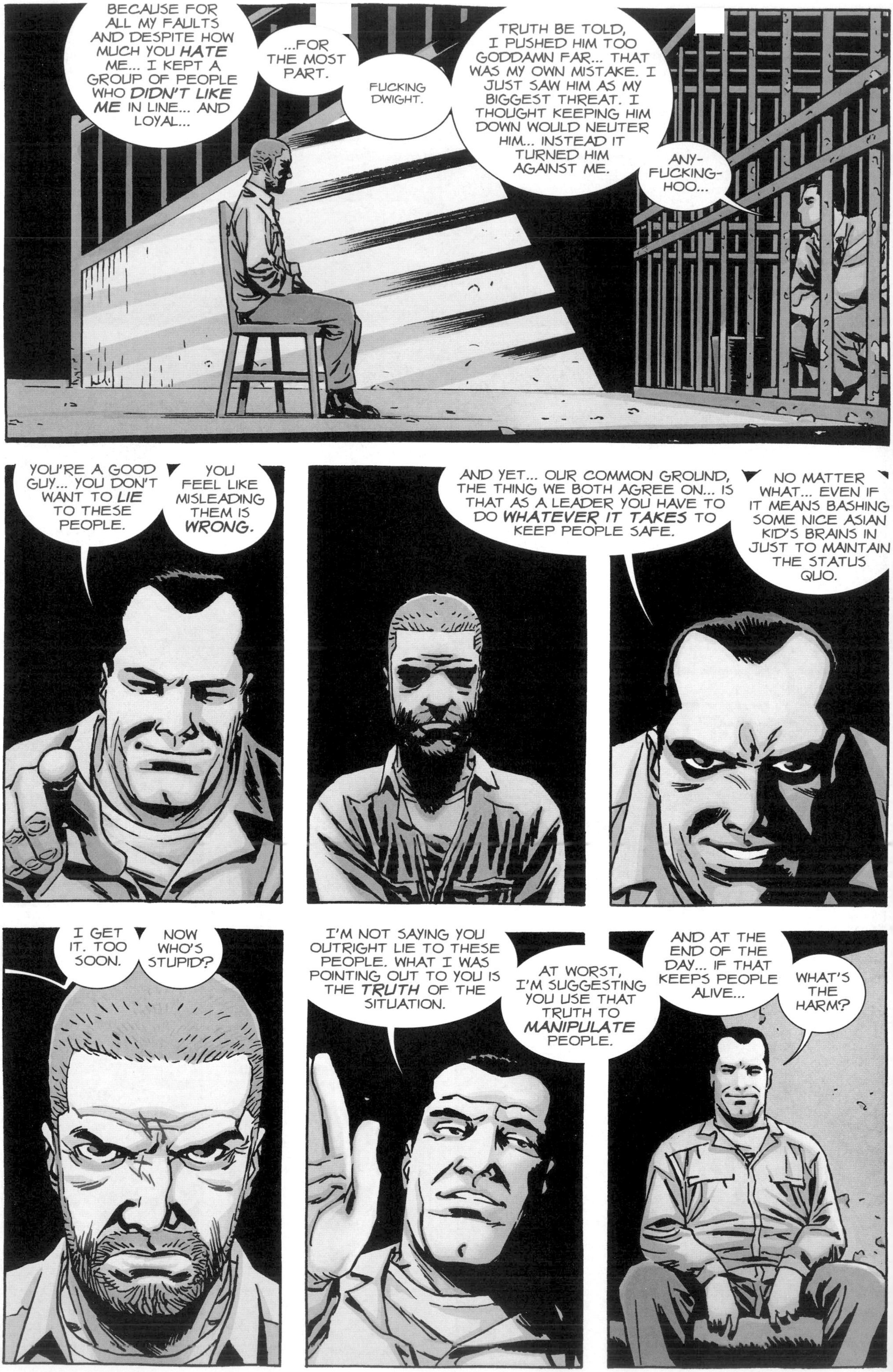
BECAUSE FOR ALL MY FAULTS AND DESPITE HOW MUCH YOU *HATE* ME... I KEPT A GROUP OF PEOPLE WHO *DIDN'T LIKE ME* IN LINE... AND LOYAL...
...FOR THE MOST PART.
FUCKING DWIGHT.
TRUTH BE TOLD, I PUSHED HIM TOO GODDAMN FAR... THAT WAS MY OWN MISTAKE. I JUST SAW HIM AS MY BIGGEST THREAT. I THOUGHT KEEPING HIM DOWN WOULD NEUTER HIM... INSTEAD IT TURNED HIM AGAINST ME.
ANY-FUCKING-HOO...
YOU'RE A GOOD GUY... YOU DON'T WANT TO *LIE* TO THESE PEOPLE.
YOU FEEL LIKE MISLEADING THEM IS *WRONG.*
AND YET... OUR COMMON GROUND, THE THING WE BOTH AGREE ON... IS THAT AS A LEADER YOU HAVE TO DO *WHATEVER IT TAKES* TO KEEP PEOPLE SAFE.
NO MATTER WHAT... EVEN IF IT MEANS BASHING SOME NICE ASIAN KID'S BRAINS IN JUST TO MAINTAIN THE STATUS QUO.
I GET IT. TOO SOON.
NOW WHO'S STUPID?
I'M NOT SAYING YOU OUTRIGHT LIE TO THESE PEOPLE. WHAT I WAS POINTING OUT TO YOU IS THE *TRUTH* OF THE SITUATION.
AT WORST, I'M SUGGESTING YOU USE THAT TRUTH TO *MANIPULATE* PEOPLE.
AND AT THE END OF THE DAY... IF THAT KEEPS PEOPLE ALIVE...
WHAT'S THE HARM?

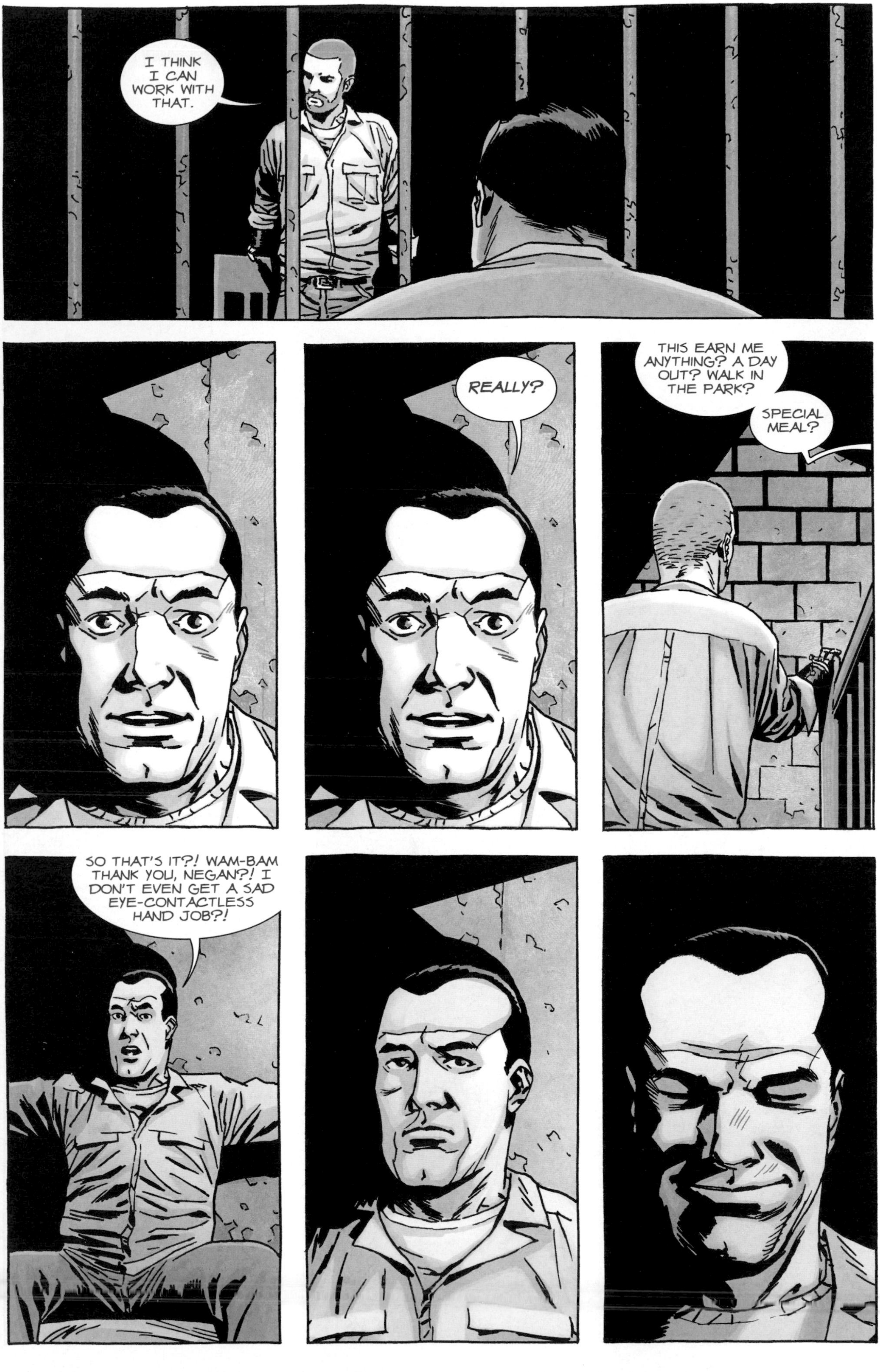
I THINK I CAN WORK WITH THAT.
REALLY?
THIS EARN ME ANYTHING? A DAY OUT? WALK IN THE PARK?
SPECIAL MEAL?
SO THAT'S IT?! WAM-BAM THANK YOU, NEGAN?! I DON'T EVEN GET A SAD EYE-CONTACTLESS HAND JOB?!

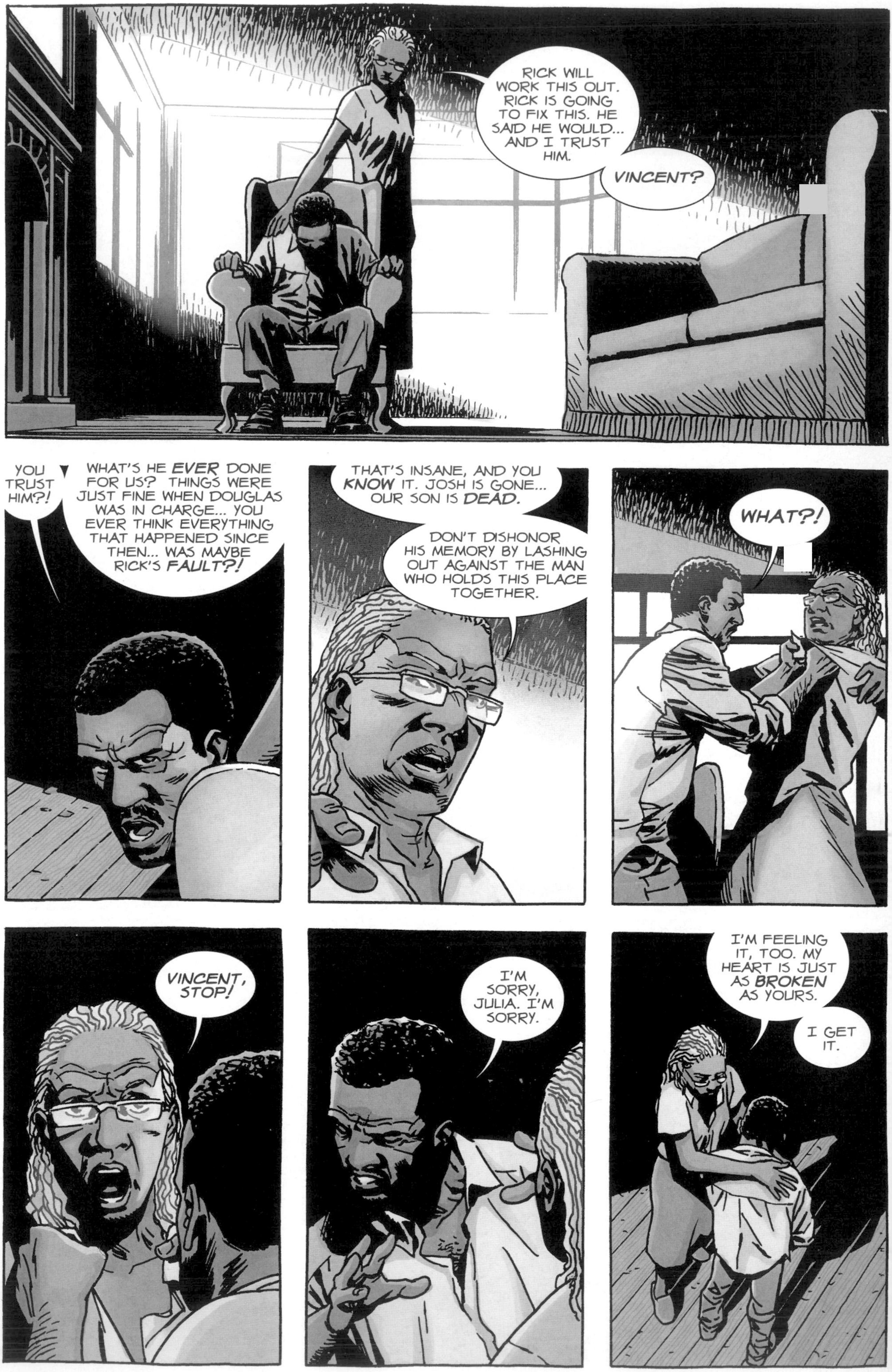
RICK WILL WORK THIS OUT. RICK IS GOING TO FIX THIS. HE SAID HE WOULD... AND I TRUST HIM.
VINCENT?
YOU TRUST HIM?!
WHAT'S HE EVER DONE FOR US? THINGS WERE JUST FINE WHEN DOUGLAS WAS IN CHARGE... YOU EVER THINK EVERYTHING THAT HAPPENED SINCE THEN... WAS MAYBE RICK'S FAULT?!
THAT'S INSANE, AND YOU KNOW IT. JOSH IS GONE... OUR SON IS DEAD.
DON'T DISHONOR HIS MEMORY BY LASHING OUT AGAINST THE MAN WHO HOLDS THIS PLACE TOGETHER.
WHAT?!
VINCENT, STOP!
I'M SORRY, JULIA. I'M SORRY.
I'M FEELING IT, TOO. MY HEART IS JUST AS BROKEN AS YOURS.
I GET IT.

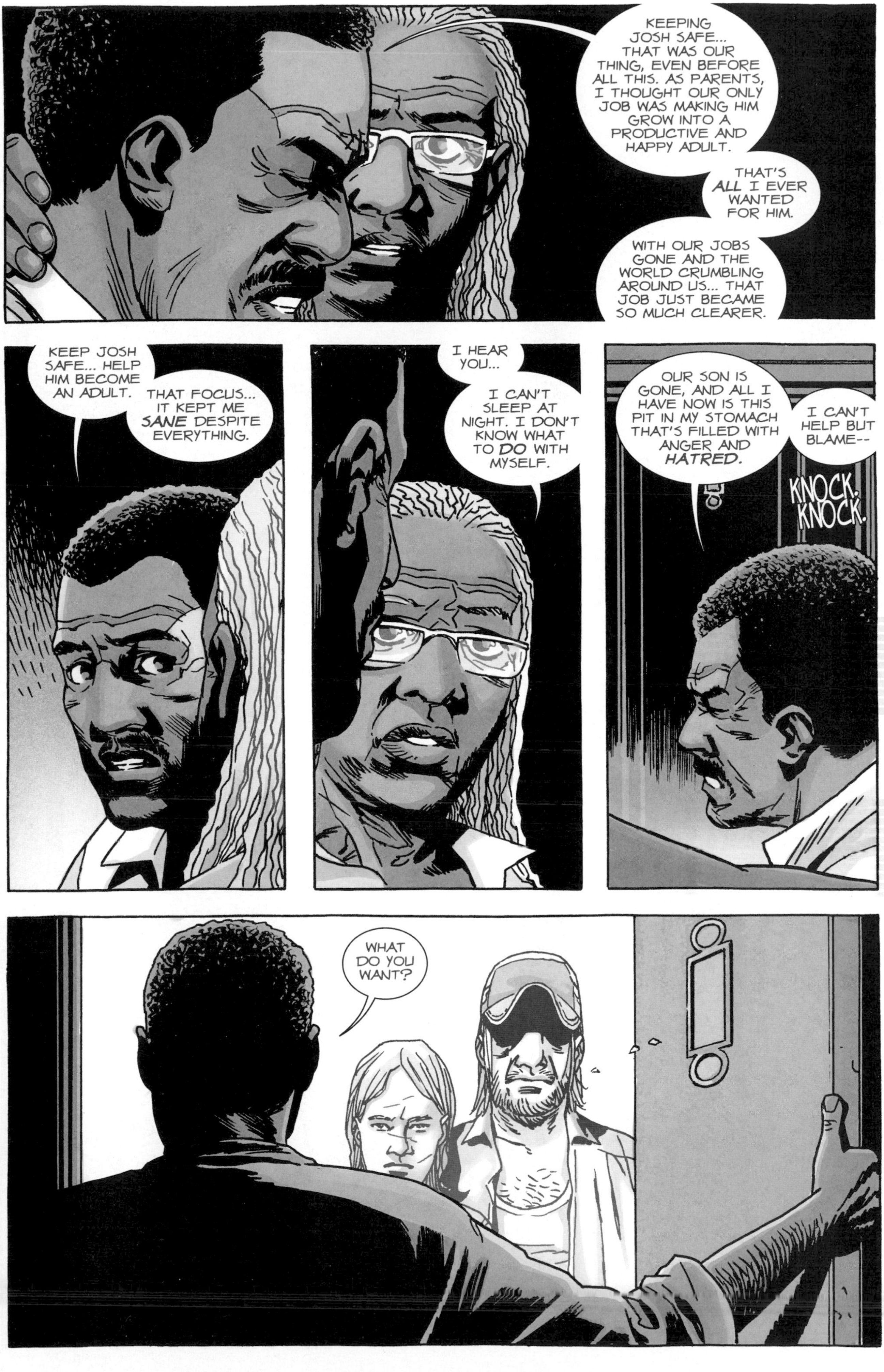
KEEPING JOSH SAFE... THAT WAS OUR THING, EVEN BEFORE ALL THIS. AS PARENTS, I THOUGHT OUR ONLY JOB WAS MAKING HIM GROW INTO A PRODUCTIVE AND HAPPY ADULT.
THAT'S ALL I EVER WANTED FOR HIM.
WITH OUR JOBS GONE AND THE WORLD CRUMBLING AROUND US... THAT JOB JUST BECAME SO MUCH CLEARER.
KEEP JOSH SAFE... HELP HIM BECOME AN ADULT.
THAT FOCUS... IT KEPT ME SANE DESPITE EVERYTHING.
I HEAR YOU...
I CAN'T SLEEP AT NIGHT. I DON'T KNOW WHAT TO DO WITH MYSELF.
OUR SON IS GONE, AND ALL I HAVE NOW IS THIS PIT IN MY STOMACH THAT'S FILLED WITH ANGER AND HATRED.
I CAN'T HELP BUT BLAME--
KNOCK. KNOCK.
WHAT DO YOU WANT?

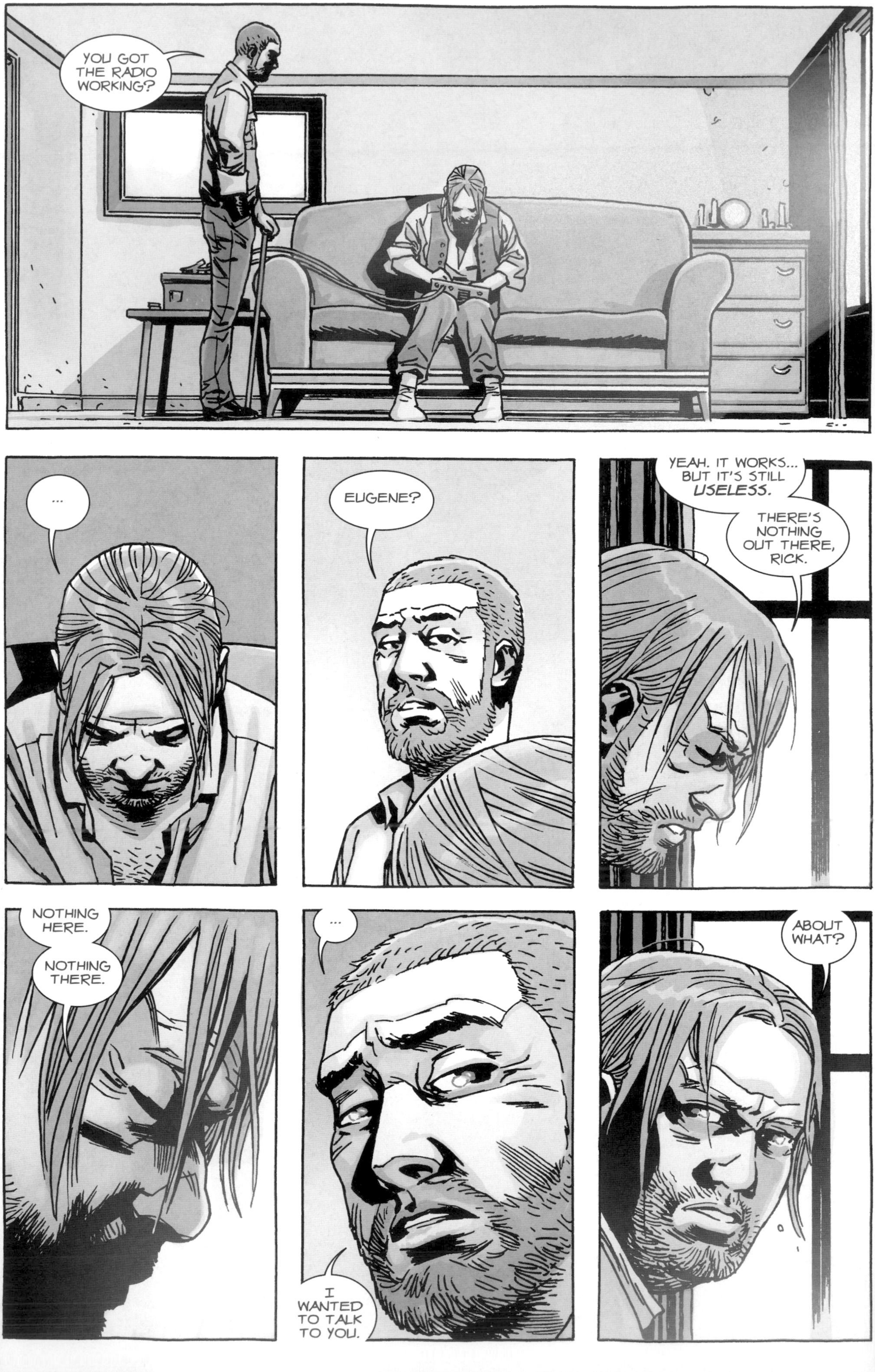
YOU GOT THE RADIO WORKING?
...
EUGENE?
YEAH. IT WORKS... BUT IT'S STILL USELESS.
THERE'S NOTHING OUT THERE, RICK.
NOTHING HERE.
NOTHING THERE.
...
I WANTED TO TALK TO YOU.
ABOUT WHAT?

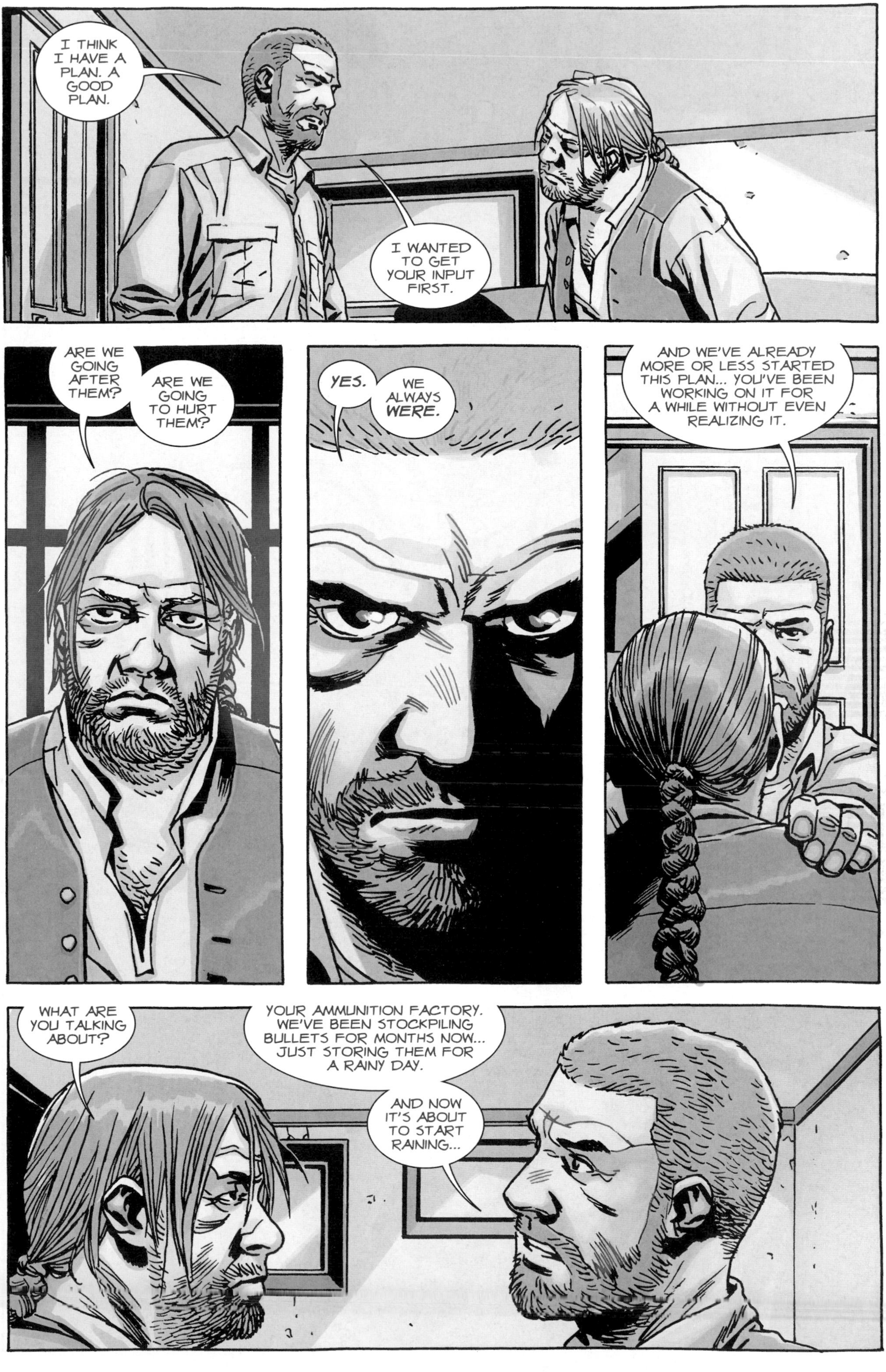
I THINK I HAVE A PLAN. A GOOD PLAN.
I WANTED TO GET YOUR INPUT FIRST.
ARE WE GOING AFTER THEM?
ARE WE GOING TO HURT THEM?
YES.
WE ALWAYS WERE.
AND WE'VE ALREADY MORE OR LESS STARTED THIS PLAN... YOU'VE BEEN WORKING ON IT FOR A WHILE WITHOUT EVEN REALIZING IT.
WHAT ARE YOU TALKING ABOUT?
YOUR AMMUNITION FACTORY. WE'VE BEEN STOCKPILING BULLETS FOR MONTHS NOW... JUST STORING THEM FOR A RAINY DAY.
AND NOW IT'S ABOUT TO START RAINING...

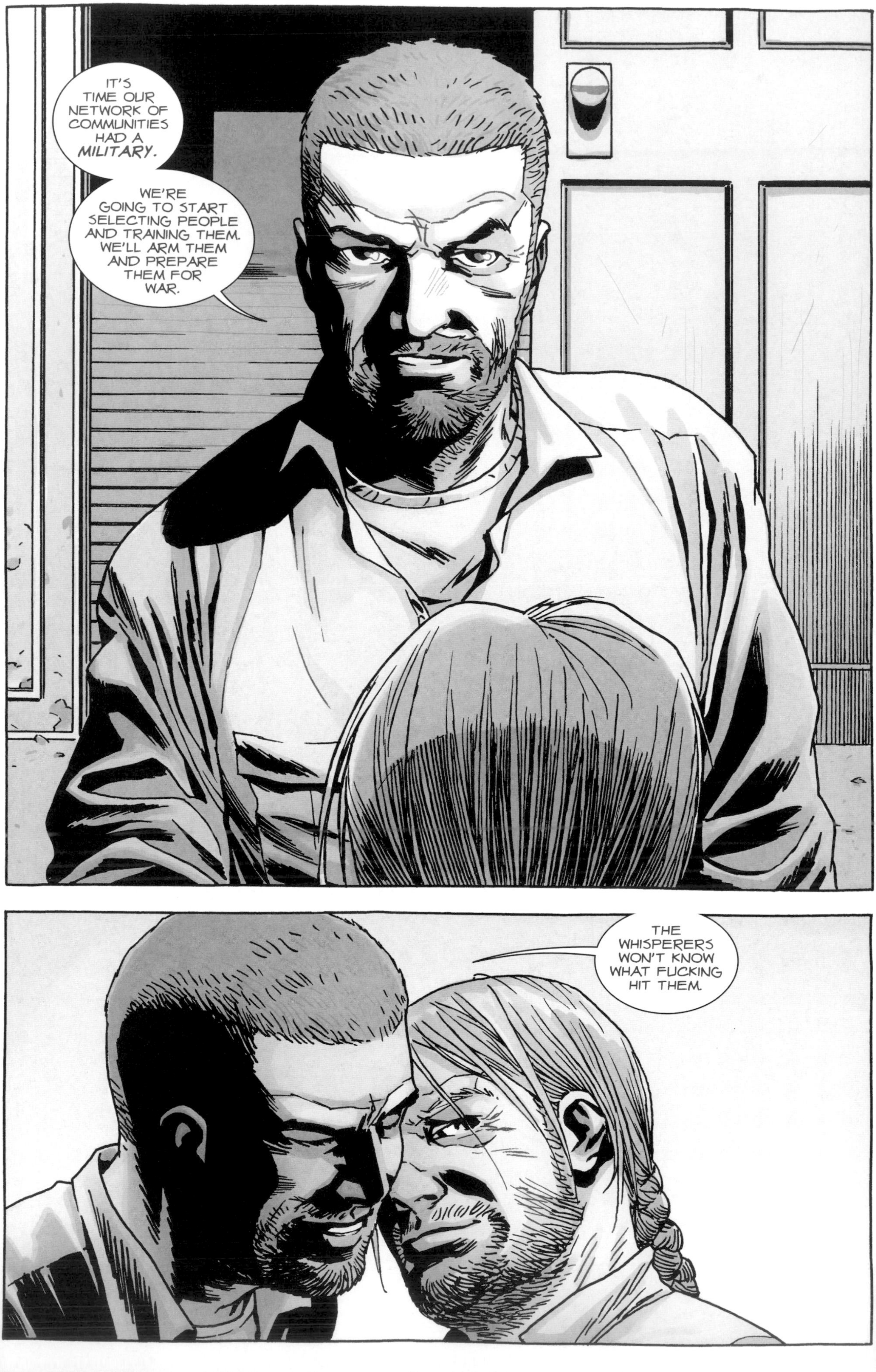
IT'S TIME OUR NETWORK OF COMMUNITIES HAD A *MILITARY*.
WE'RE GOING TO START SELECTING PEOPLE AND TRAINING THEM. WE'LL ARM THEM AND PREPARE THEM FOR WAR.
THE WHISPERERS WON'T KNOW WHAT FUCKING HIT THEM.

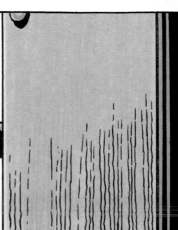

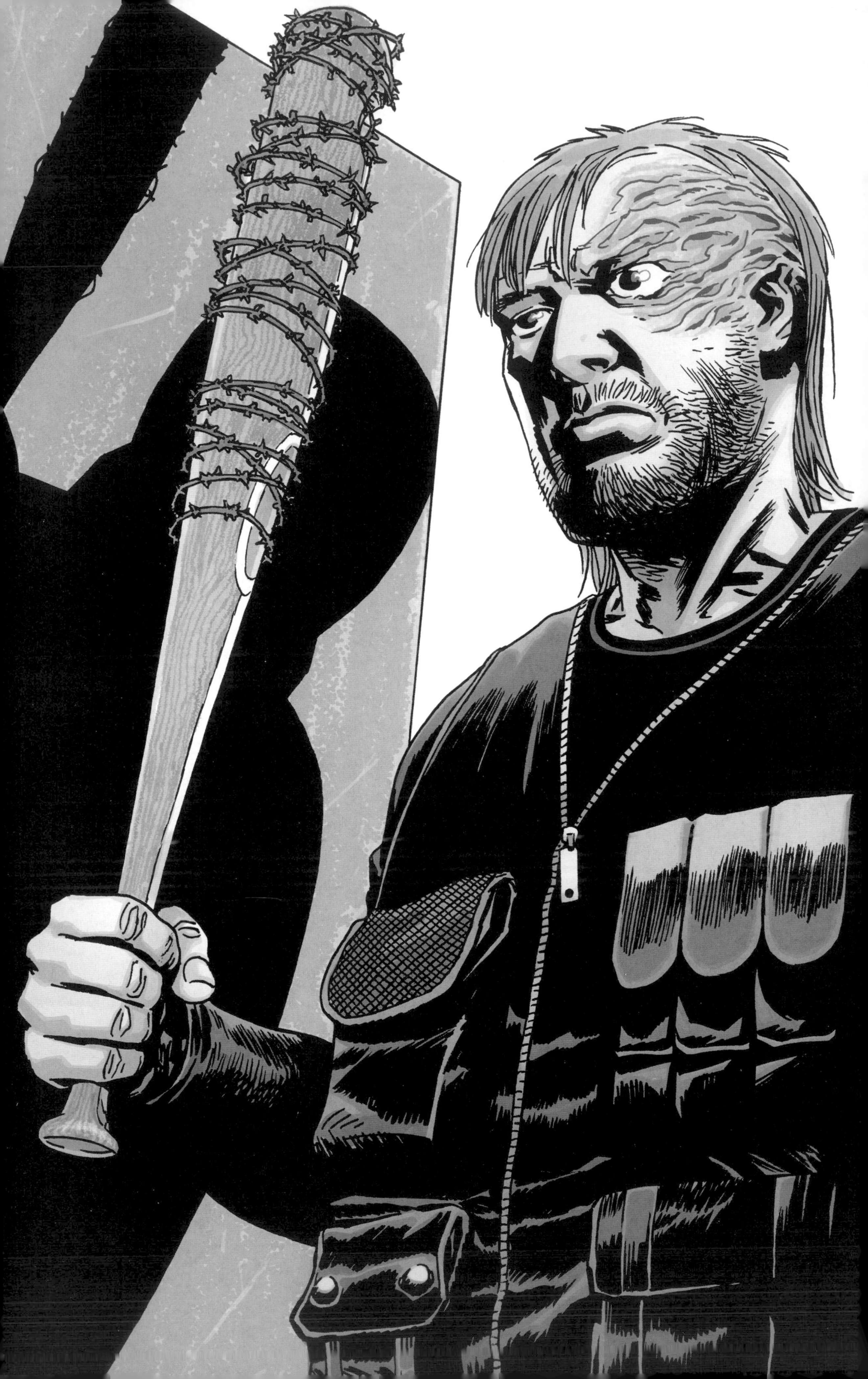

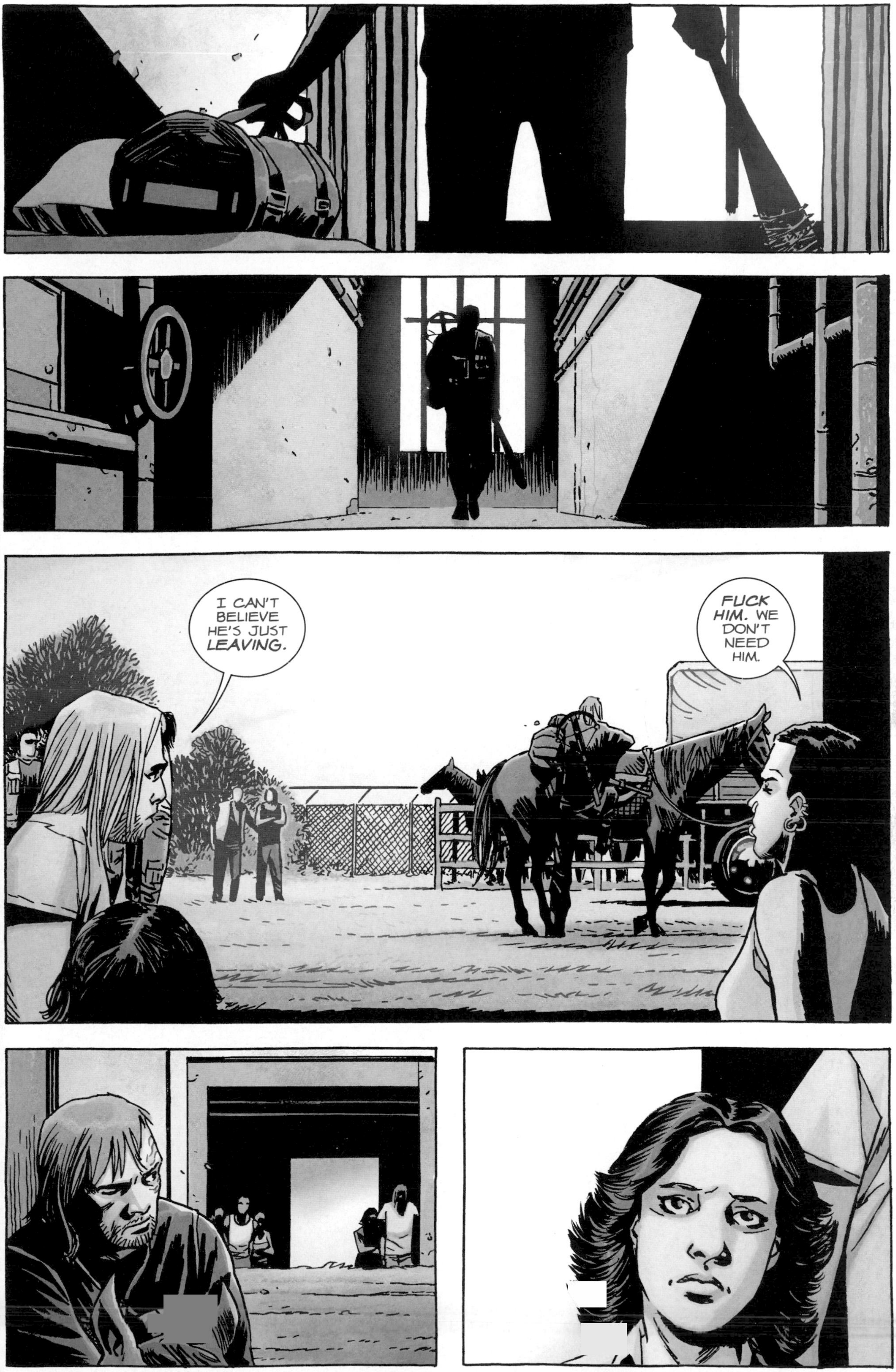
I CAN'T BELIEVE HE'S JUST LEAVING.
FUCK HIM. WE DON'T NEED HIM.

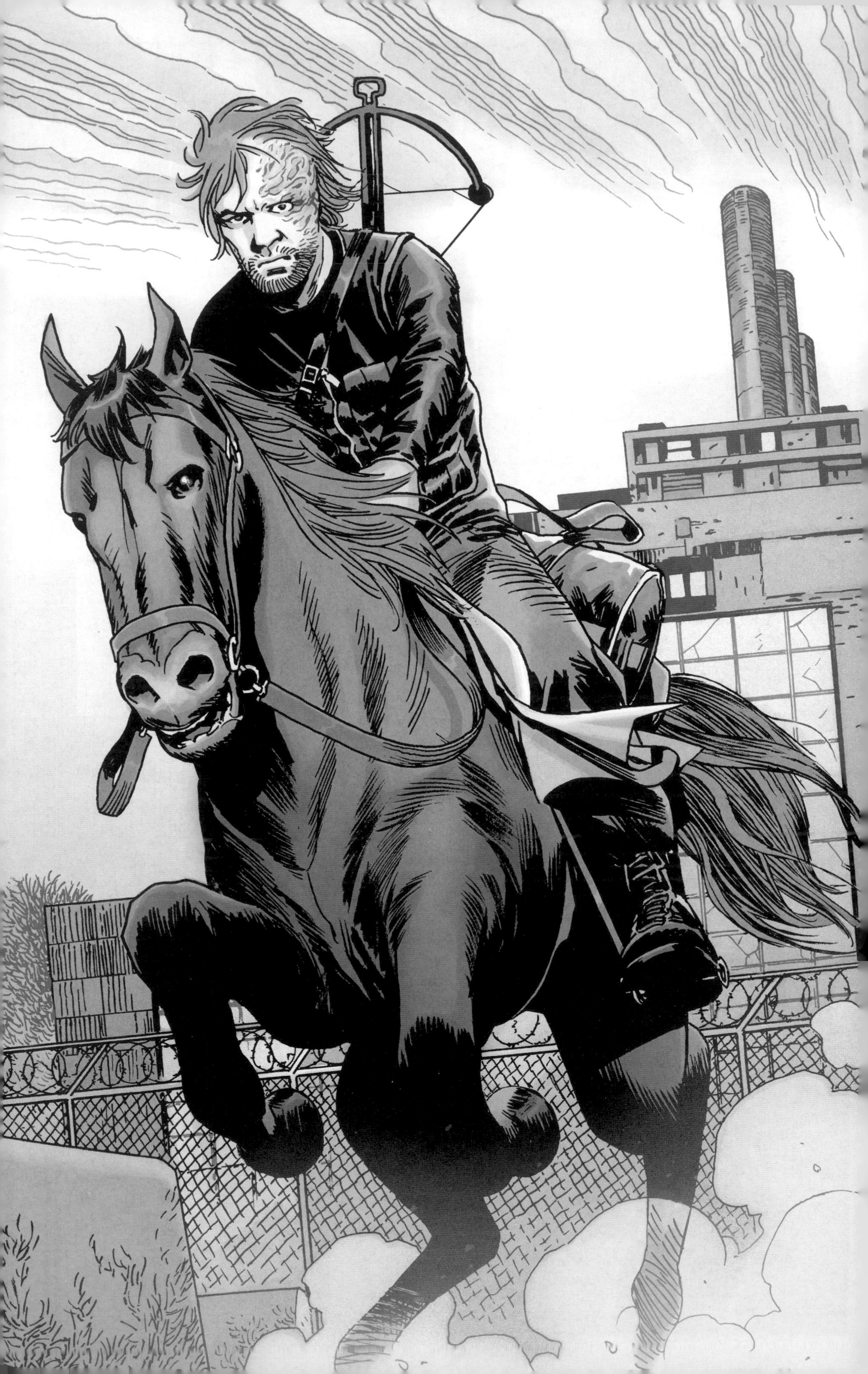

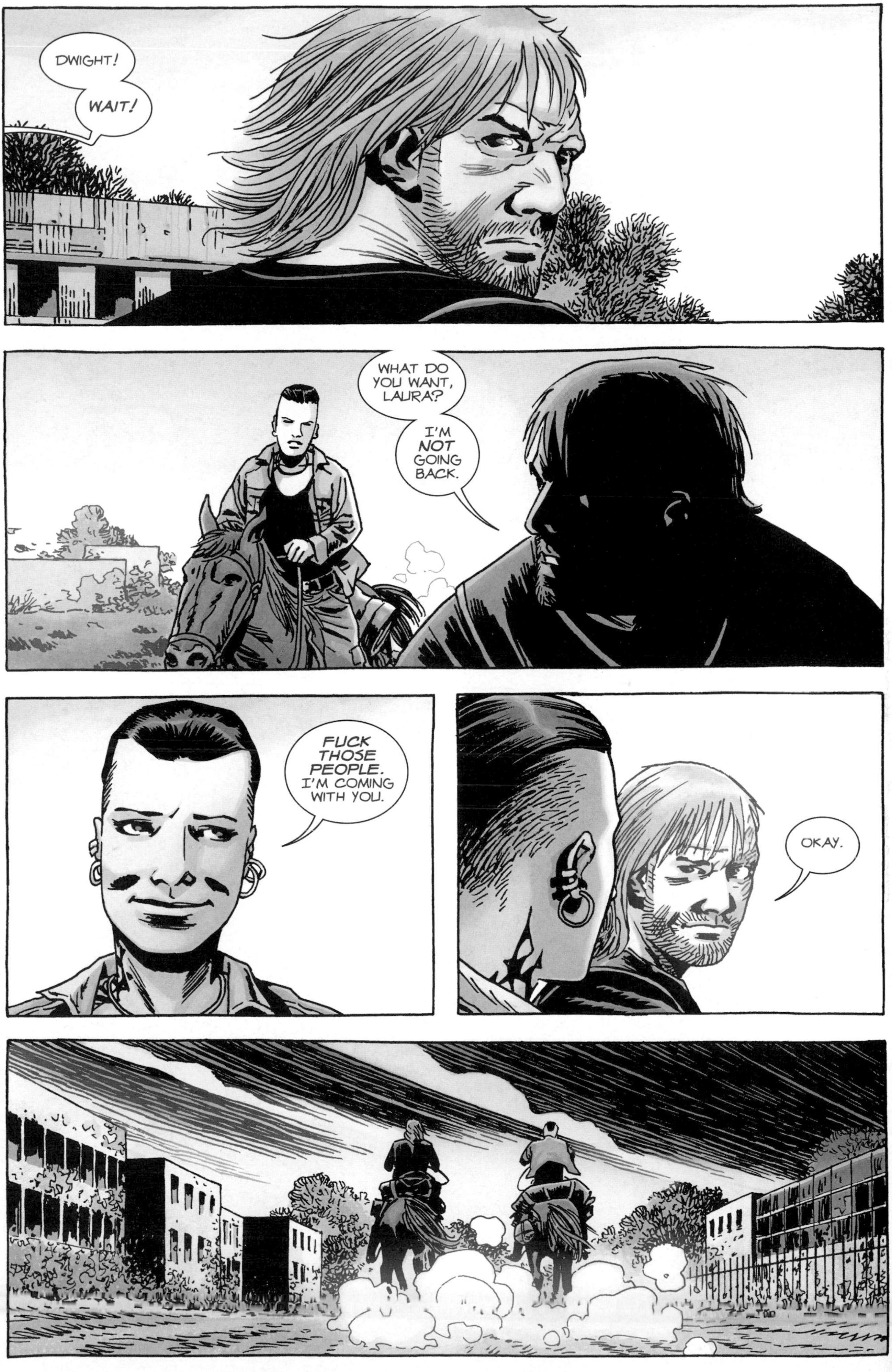
DWIGHT!
WAIT!
WHAT DO YOU WANT, LAURA?
I'M NOT GOING BACK.
FUCK THOSE PEOPLE. I'M COMING WITH YOU.
OKAY.

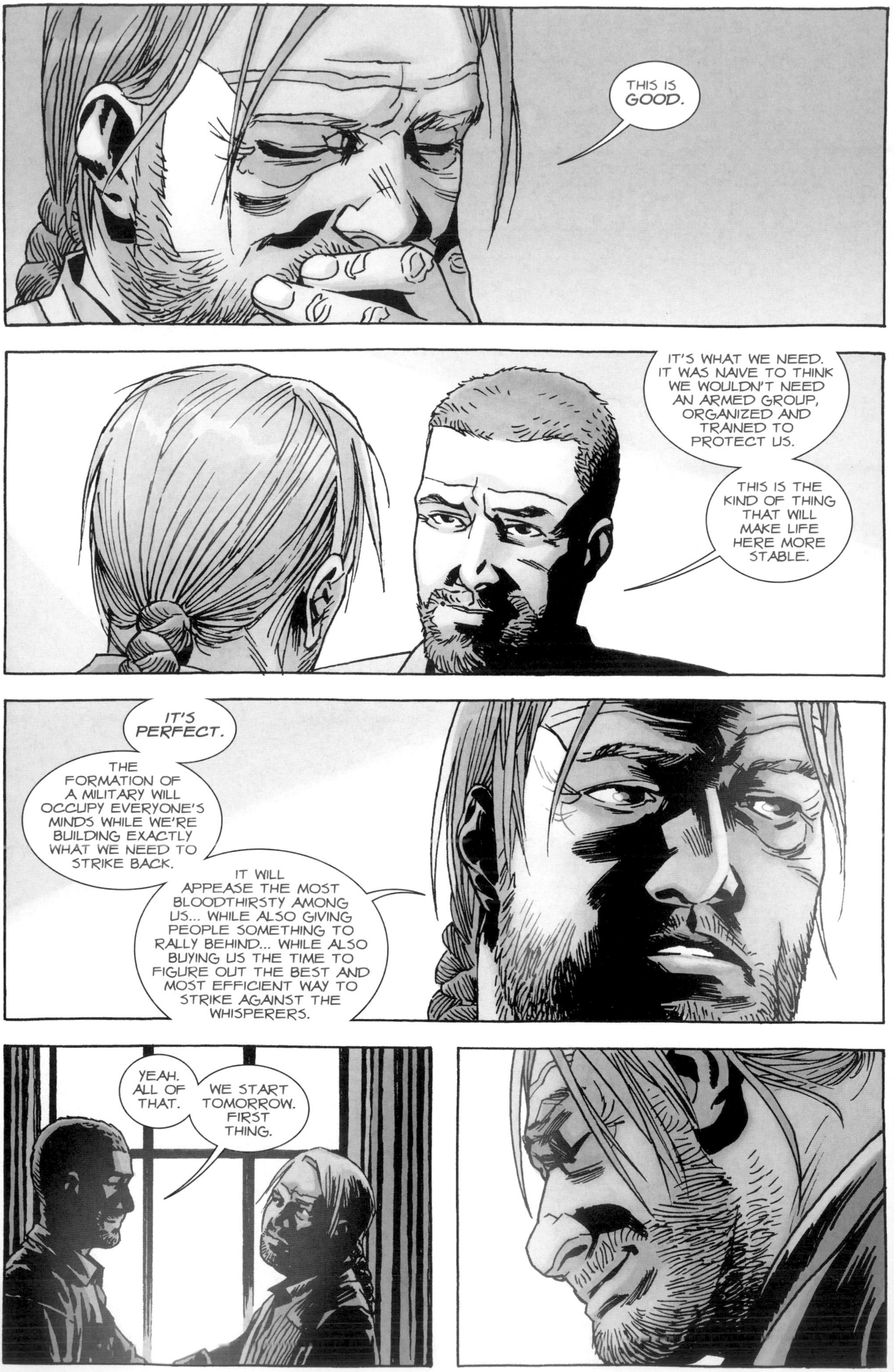
THIS IS GOOD.
IT'S WHAT WE NEED. IT WAS NAIVE TO THINK WE WOULDN'T NEED AN ARMED GROUP, ORGANIZED AND TRAINED TO PROTECT US.
THIS IS THE KIND OF THING THAT WILL MAKE LIFE HERE MORE STABLE.
IT'S PERFECT.
THE FORMATION OF A MILITARY WILL OCCUPY EVERYONE'S MINDS WHILE WE'RE BUILDING EXACTLY WHAT WE NEED TO STRIKE BACK.
IT WILL APPEASE THE MOST BLOODTHIRSTY AMONG US... WHILE ALSO GIVING PEOPLE SOMETHING TO RALLY BEHIND... WHILE ALSO BUYING US THE TIME TO FIGURE OUT THE BEST AND MOST EFFICIENT WAY TO STRIKE AGAINST THE WHISPERERS.
YEAH. ALL OF THAT.
WE START TOMORROW. FIRST THING.

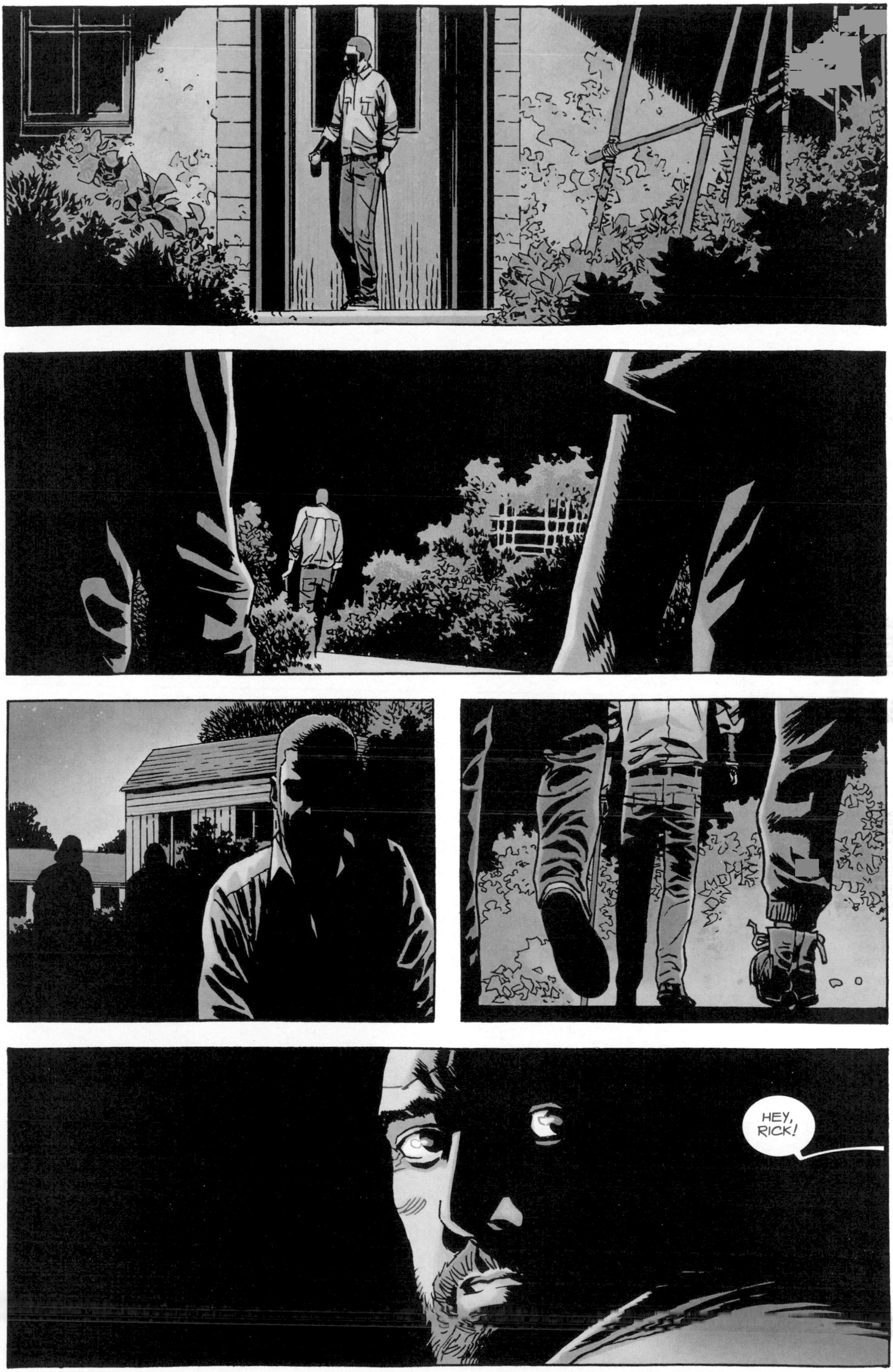
HEY, RICK!

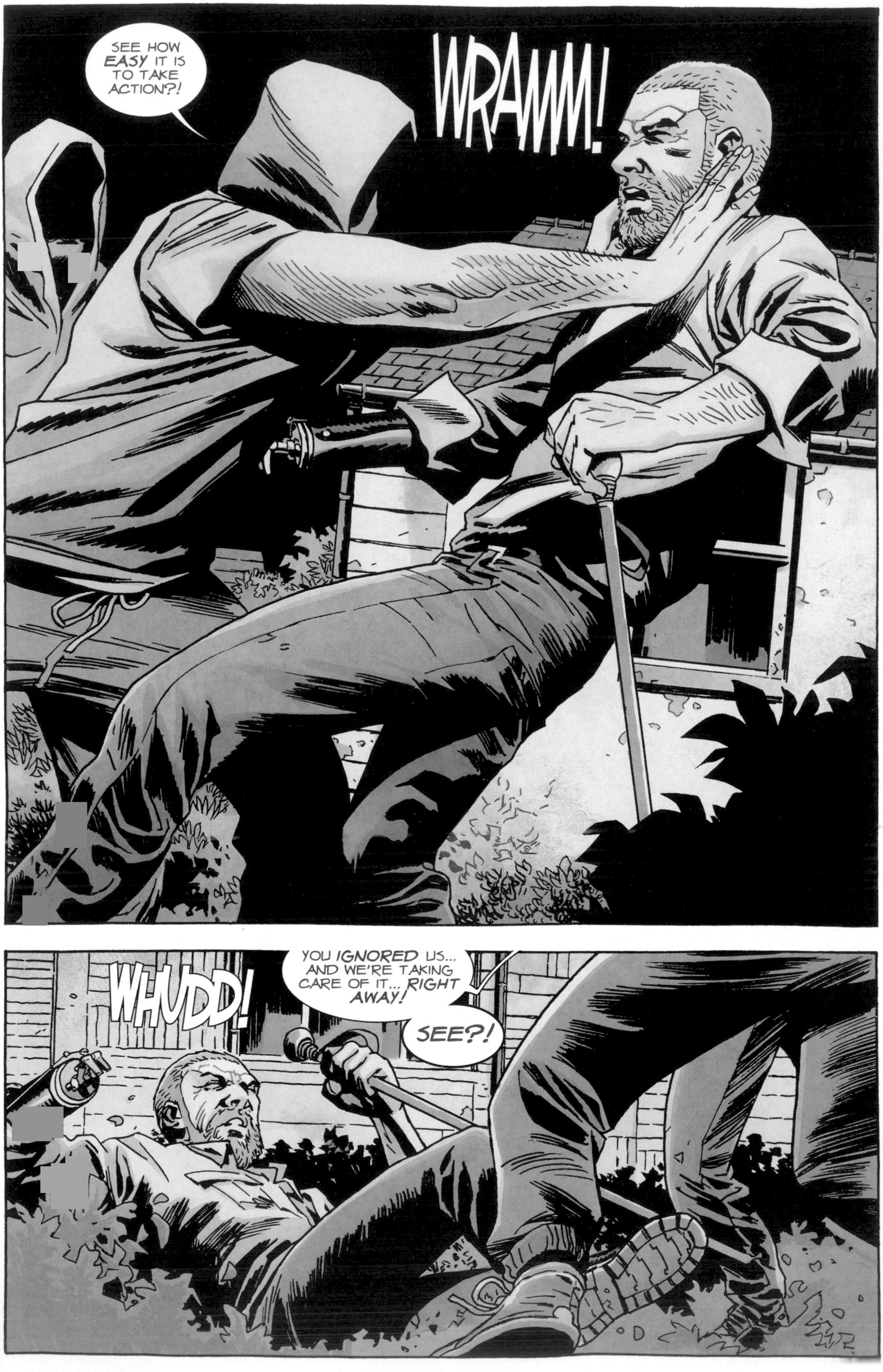
SEE HOW EASY IT IS TO TAKE ACTION?!
WRAMM!
WHUDD!
YOU IGNORED US... AND WE'RE TAKING CARE OF IT... RIGHT AWAY!
SEE?!

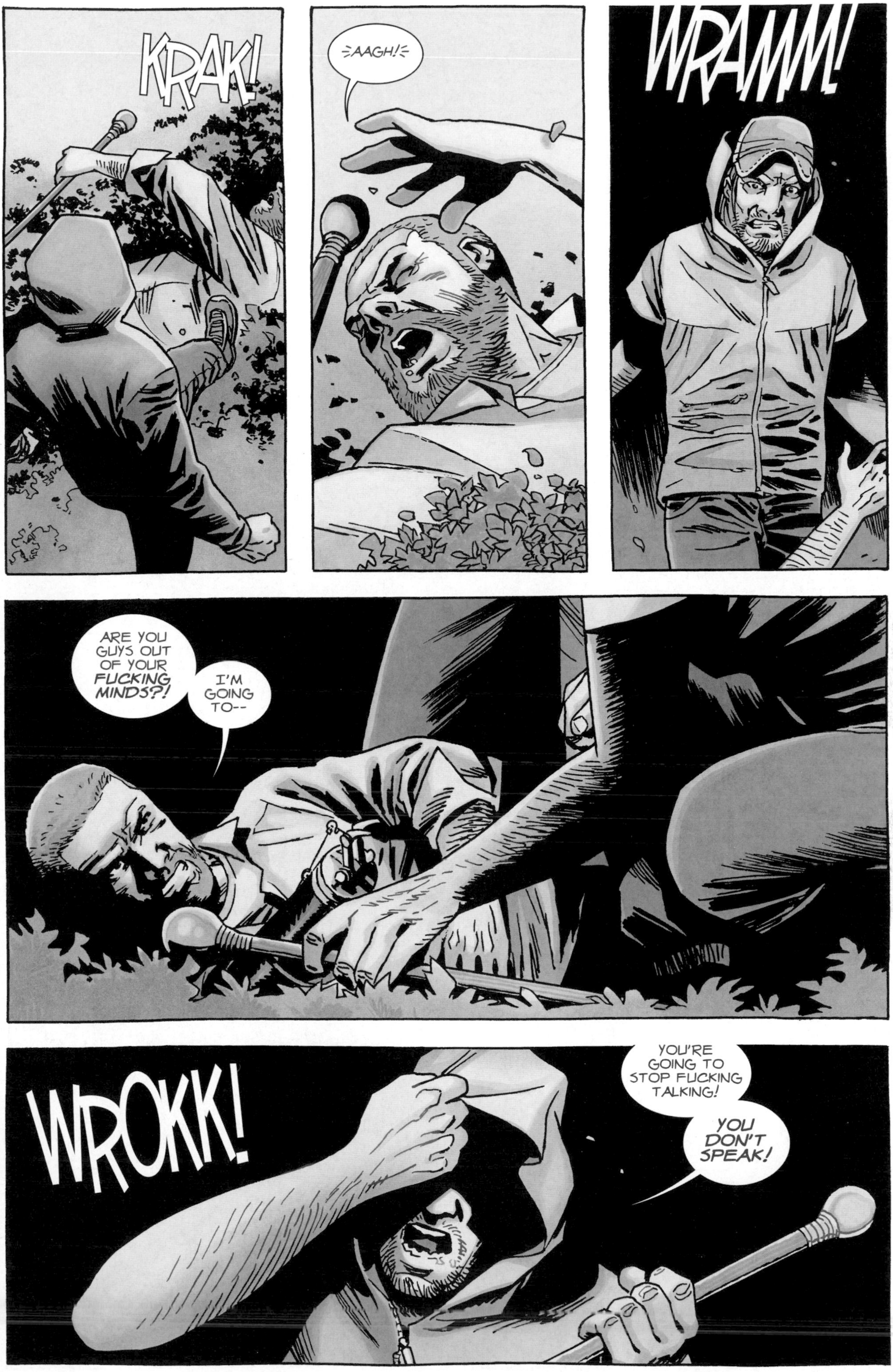
KRAK!
AAGH!
WRAMM!
ARE YOU GUYS OUT OF YOUR FUCKING MINDS?!
I'M GOING TO--
WROKK!
YOU'RE GOING TO STOP FUCKING TALKING!
YOU DON'T SPEAK!

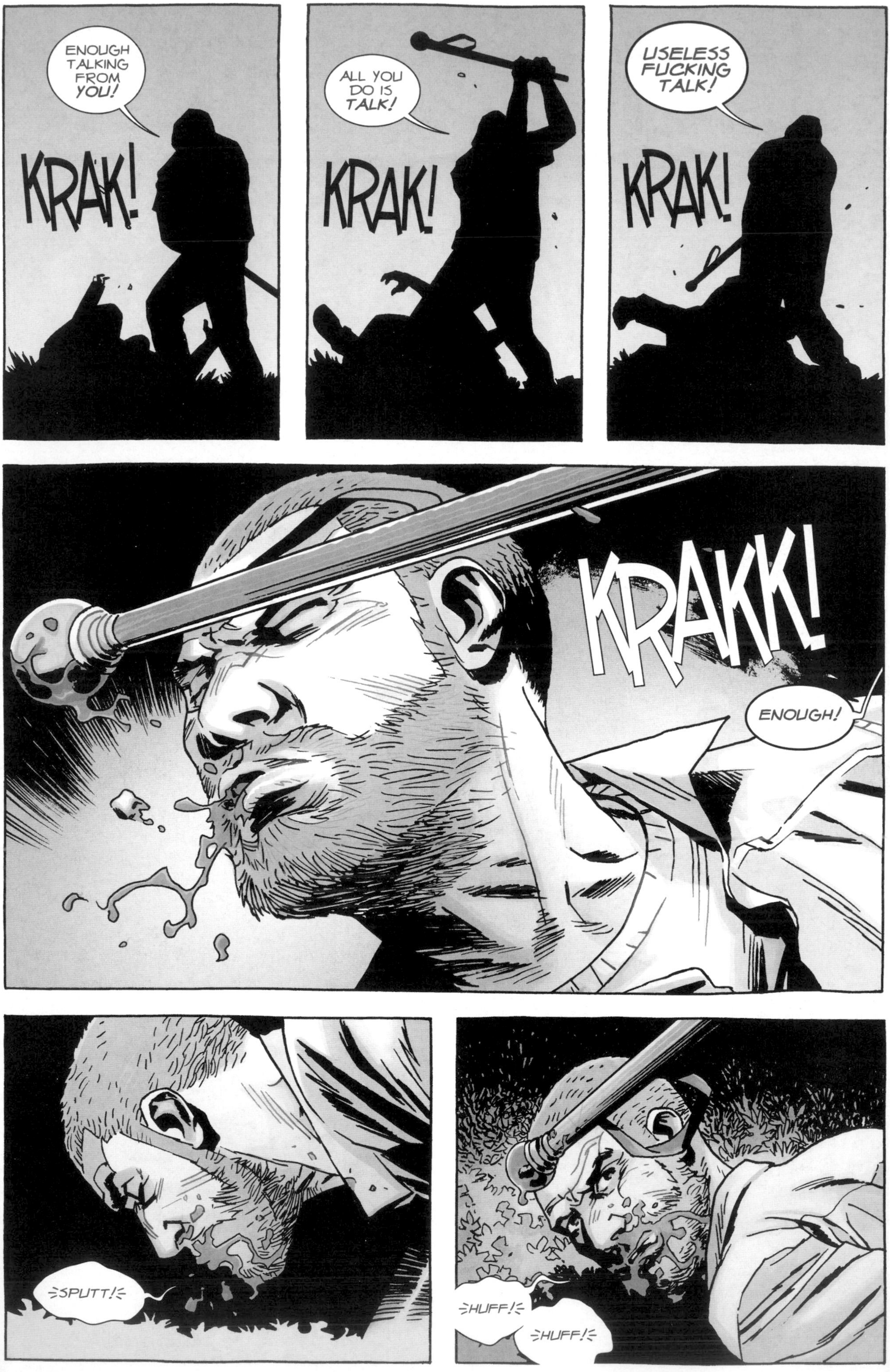
ENOUGH TALKING FROM YOU!
KRAK!
ALL YOU DO IS TALK!
KRAK!
USELESS FUCKING TALK!
KRAK!
KRAKK!
ENOUGH!
SPUTT!
HUFF!
HUFF!

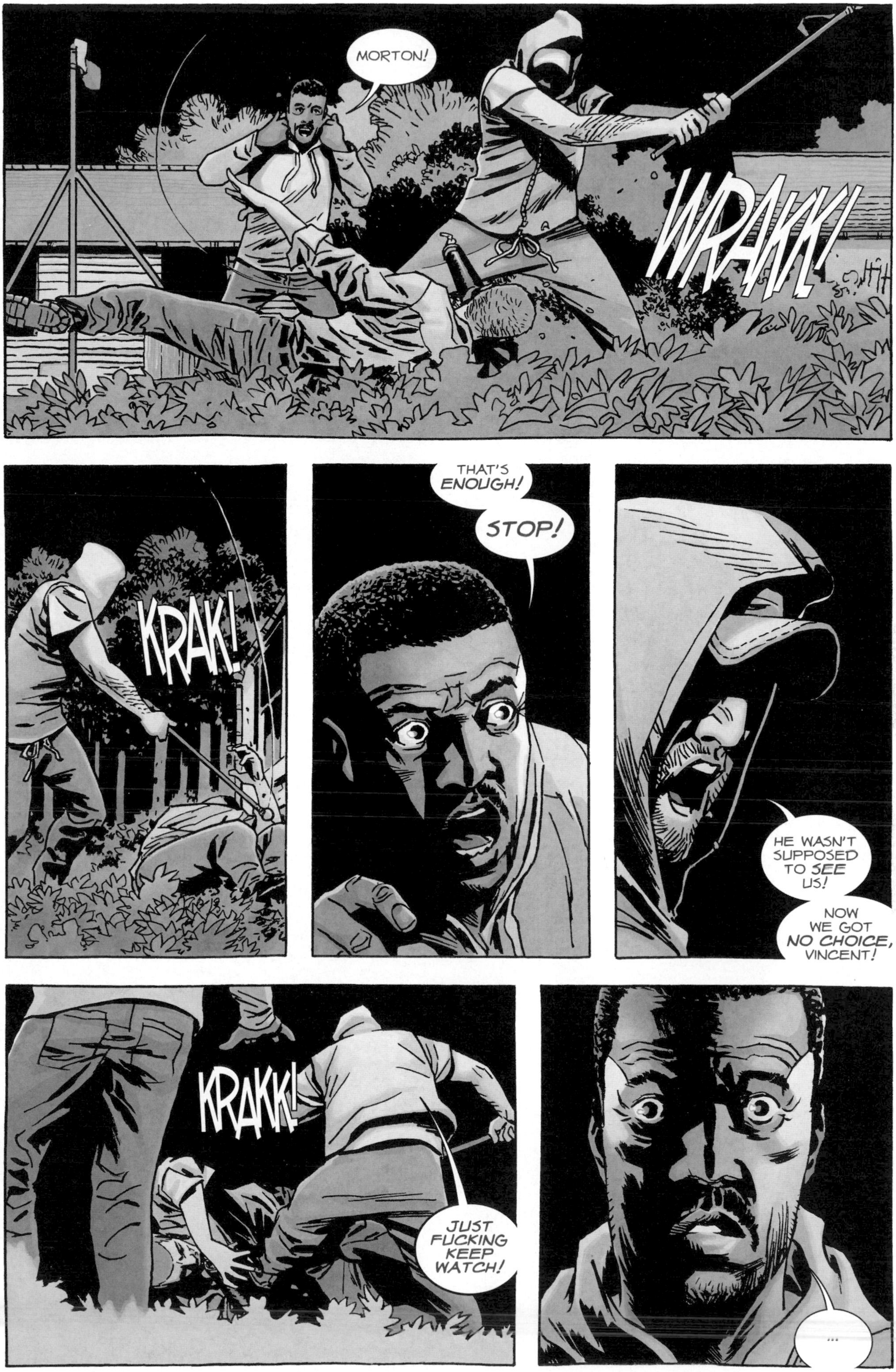
MORTON!
WRAKK!
KRAK!
THAT'S ENOUGH!
STOP!
HE WASN'T SUPPOSED TO SEE US!
NOW WE GOT NO CHOICE, VINCENT!
KRAKK!
JUST FUCKING KEEP WATCH!
...

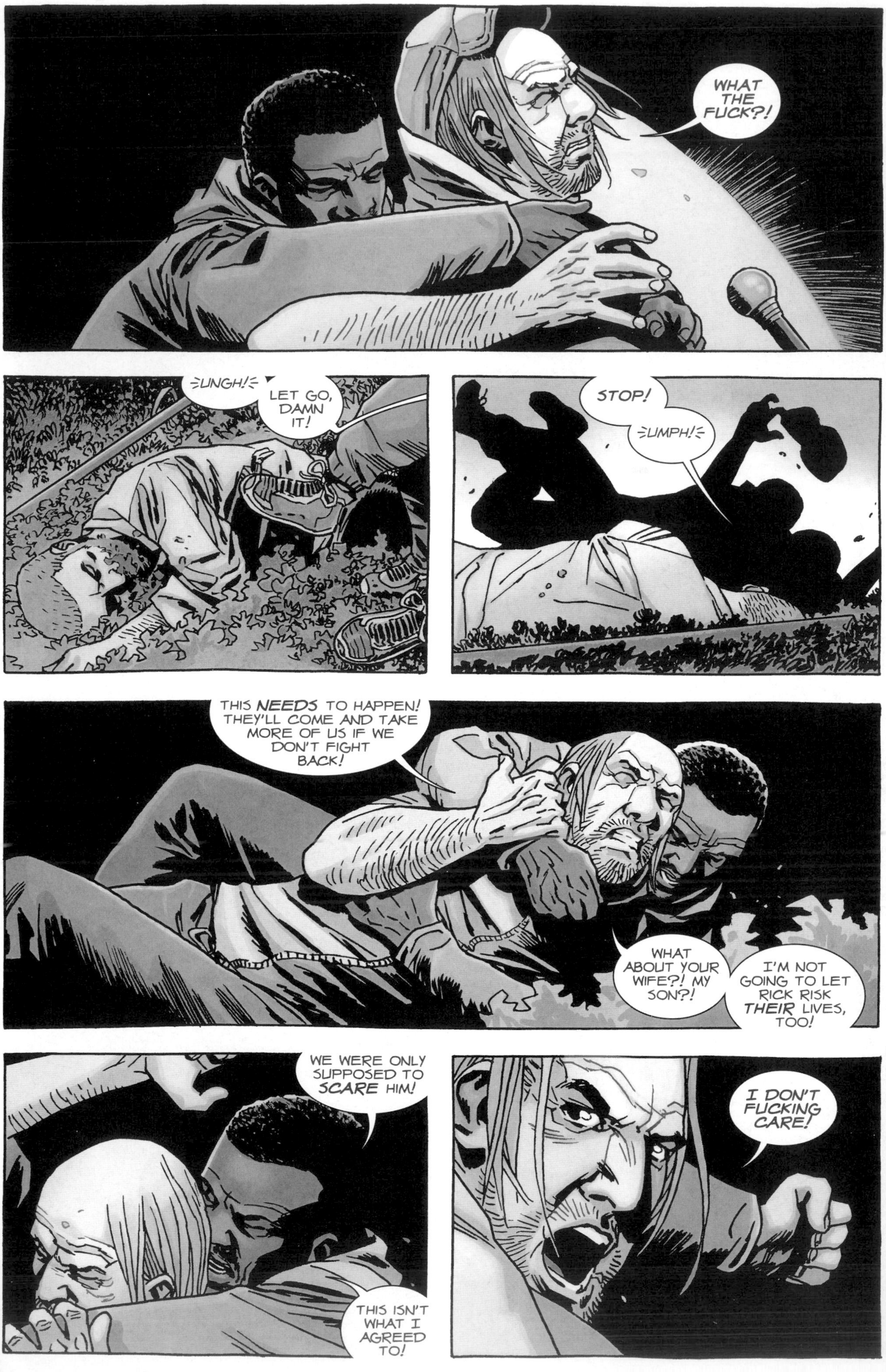
WHAT THE FUCK?!
UNGH!
LET GO, DAMN IT!
STOP!
UMPH!
THIS NEEDS TO HAPPEN! THEY'LL COME AND TAKE MORE OF US IF WE DON'T FIGHT BACK!
WHAT ABOUT YOUR WIFE?! MY SON?!
I'M NOT GOING TO LET RICK RISK THEIR LIVES, TOO!
WE WERE ONLY SUPPOSED TO SCARE HIM!
THIS ISN'T WHAT I AGREED TO!
I DON'T FUCKING CARE!

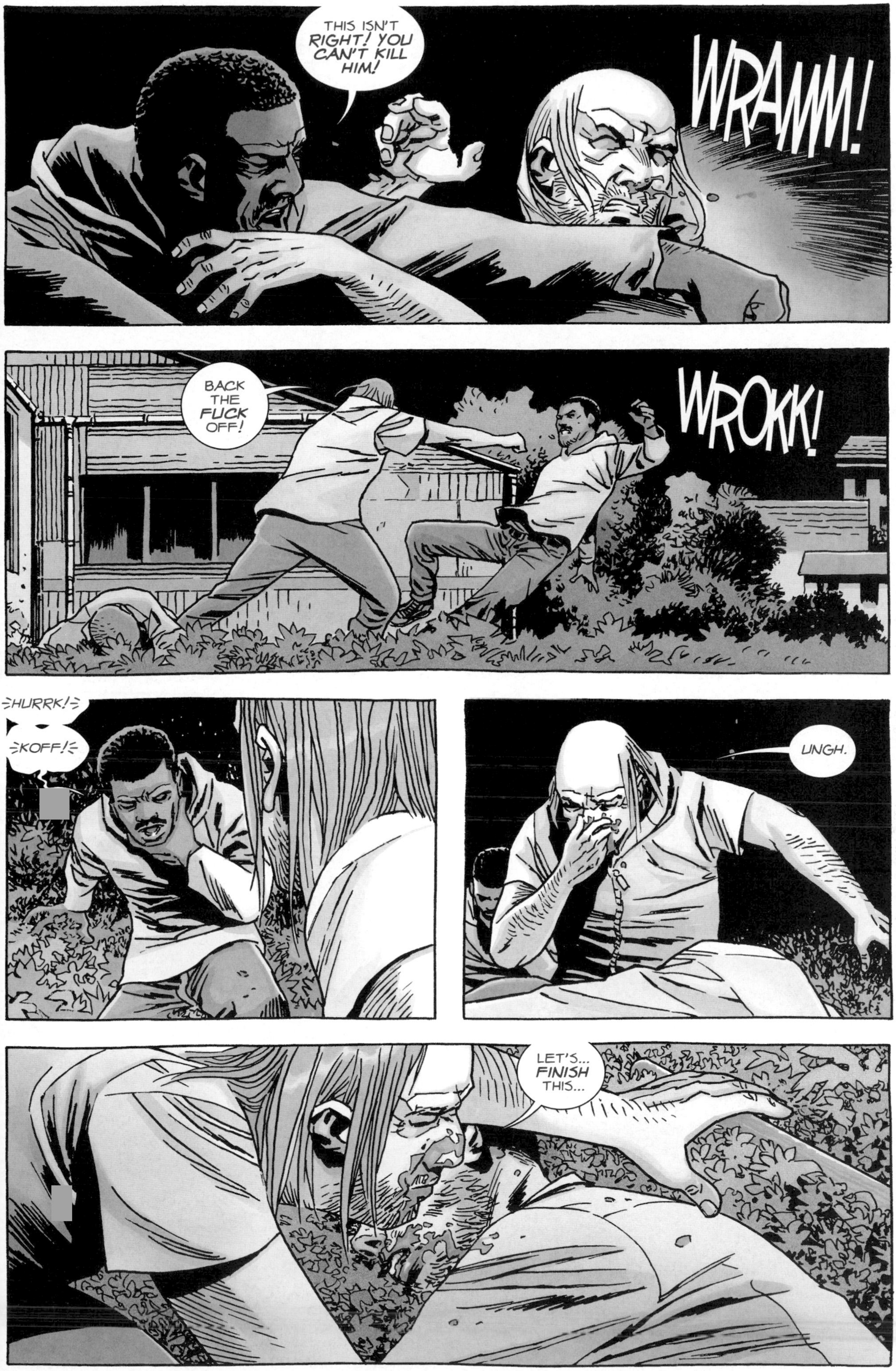
THIS ISN'T RIGHT! YOU CAN'T KILL HIM!
WRAMM!
BACK THE FUCK OFF!
WROKK!
HURRK!
KOFF!
UNGH.
LET'S... FINISH THIS...

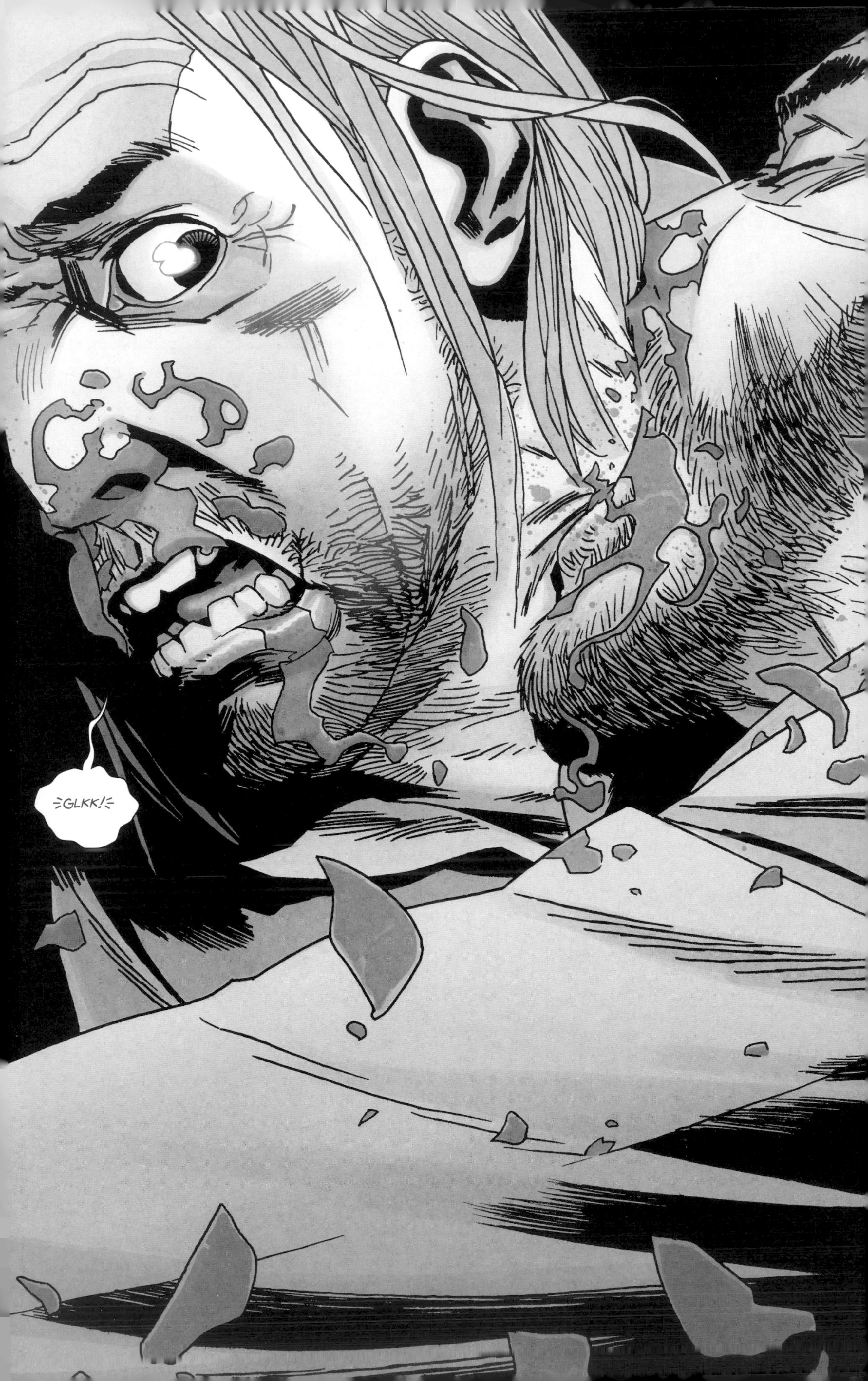
GLKK!

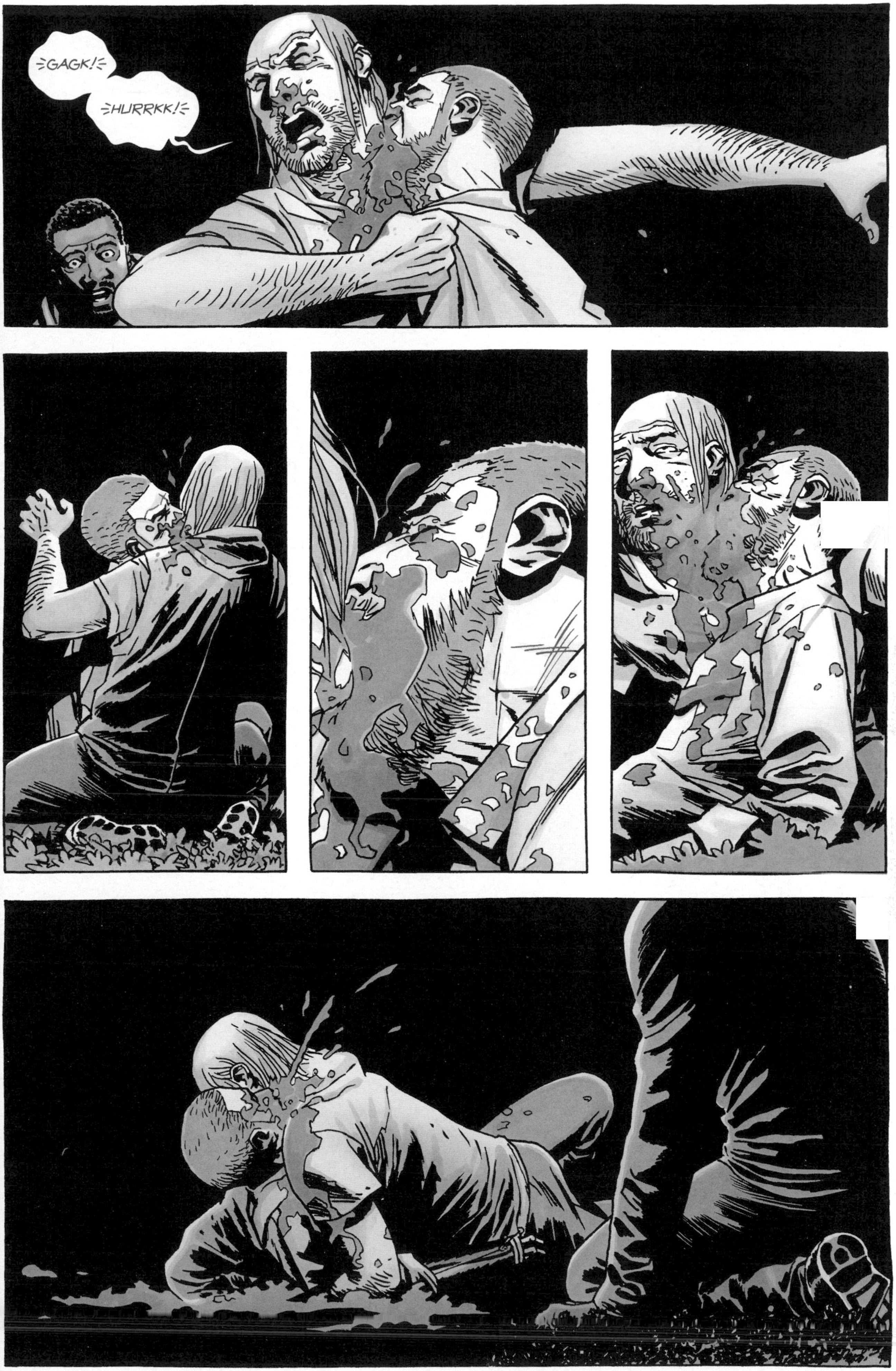
GAGK!
HURRKK!

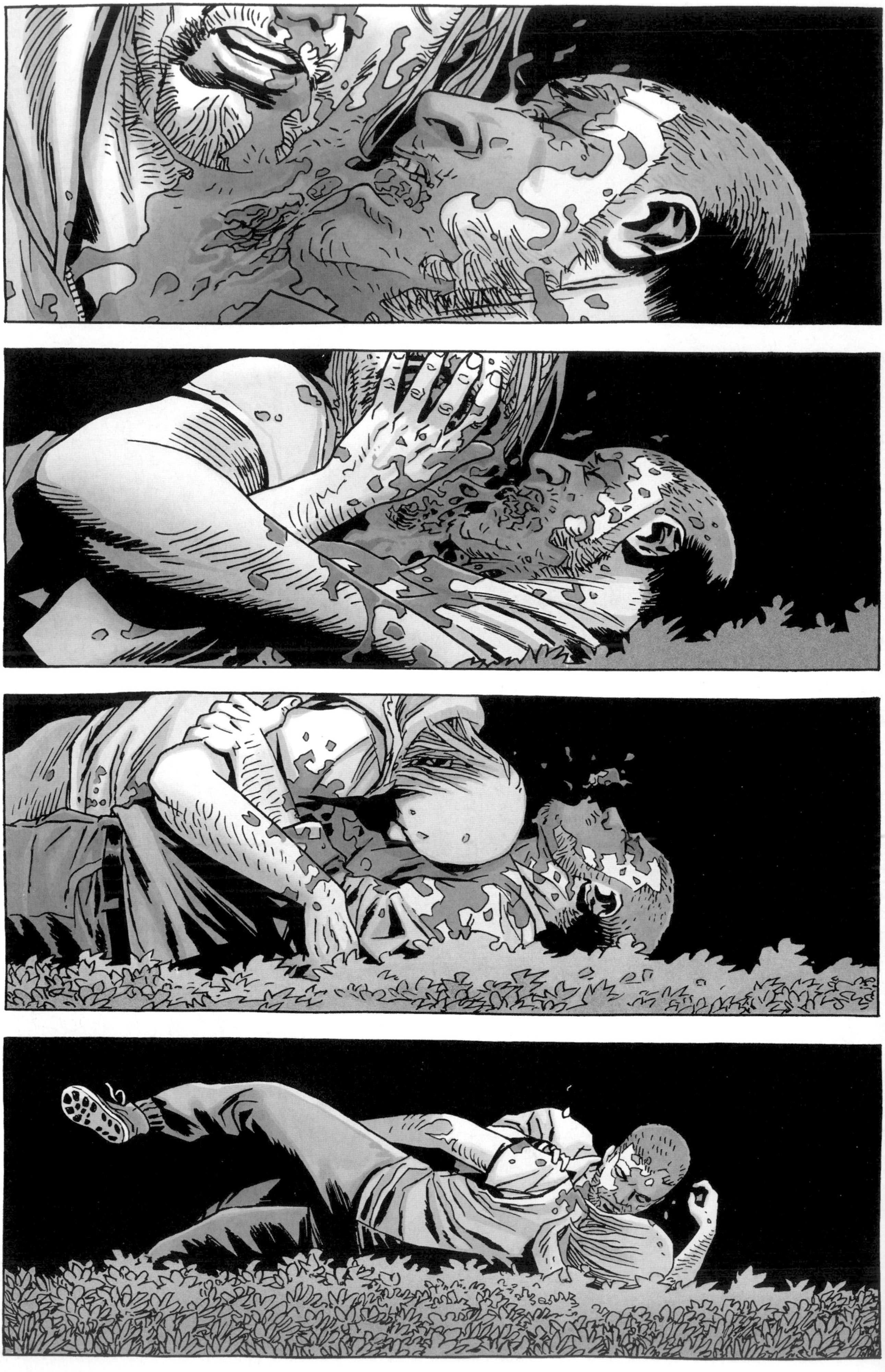

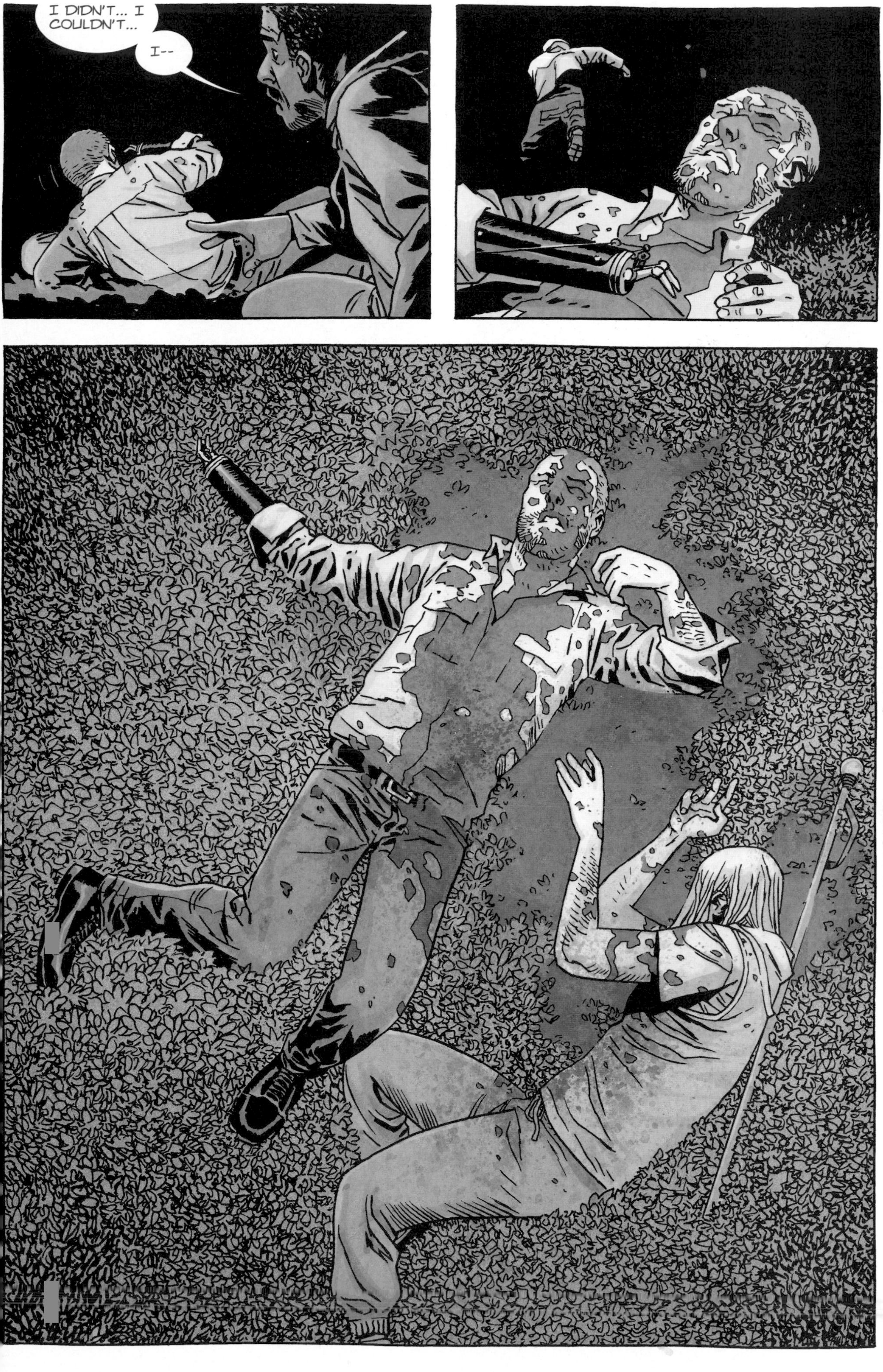
I DIDN'T... I COULDN'T...
I--

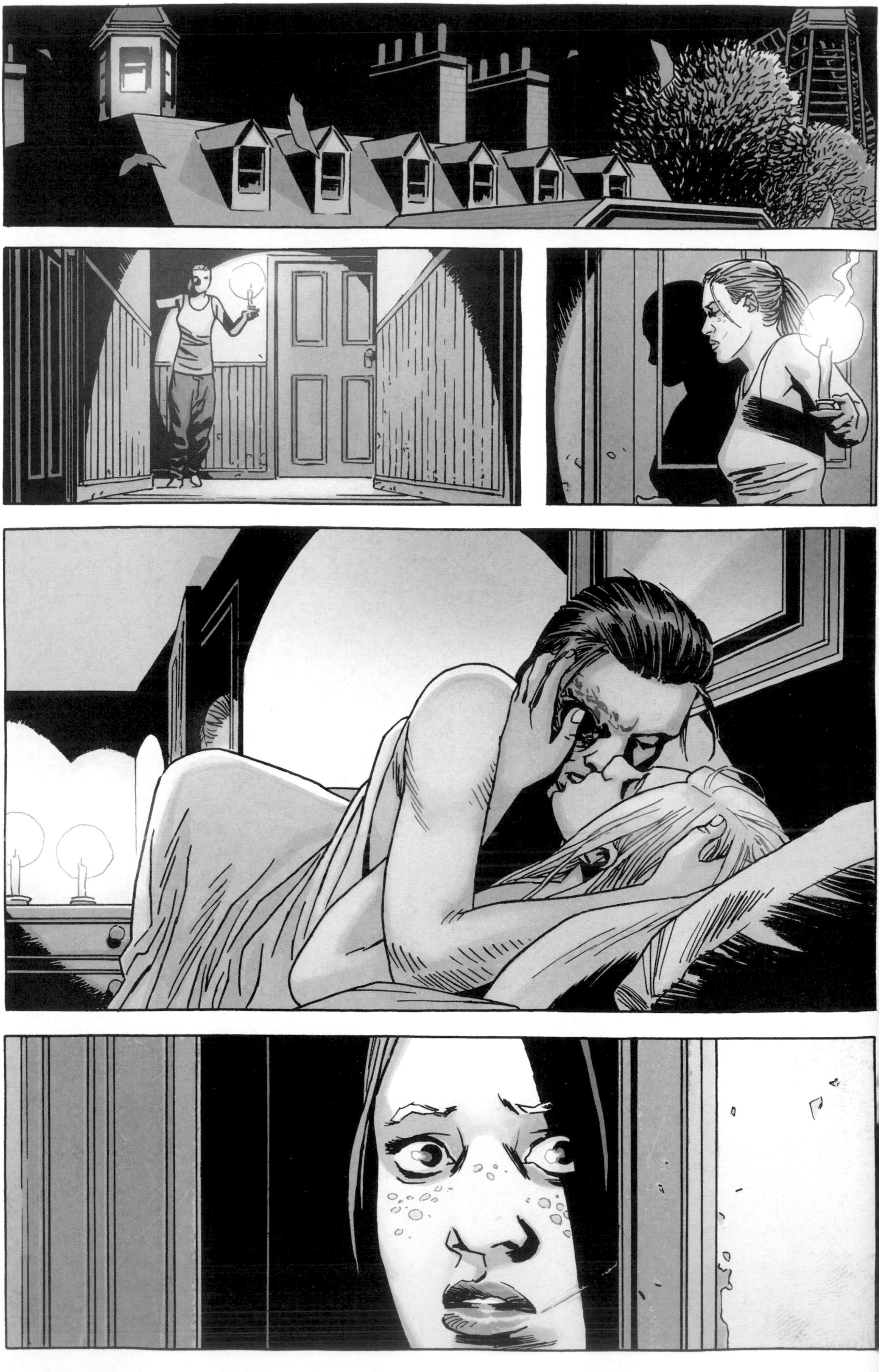

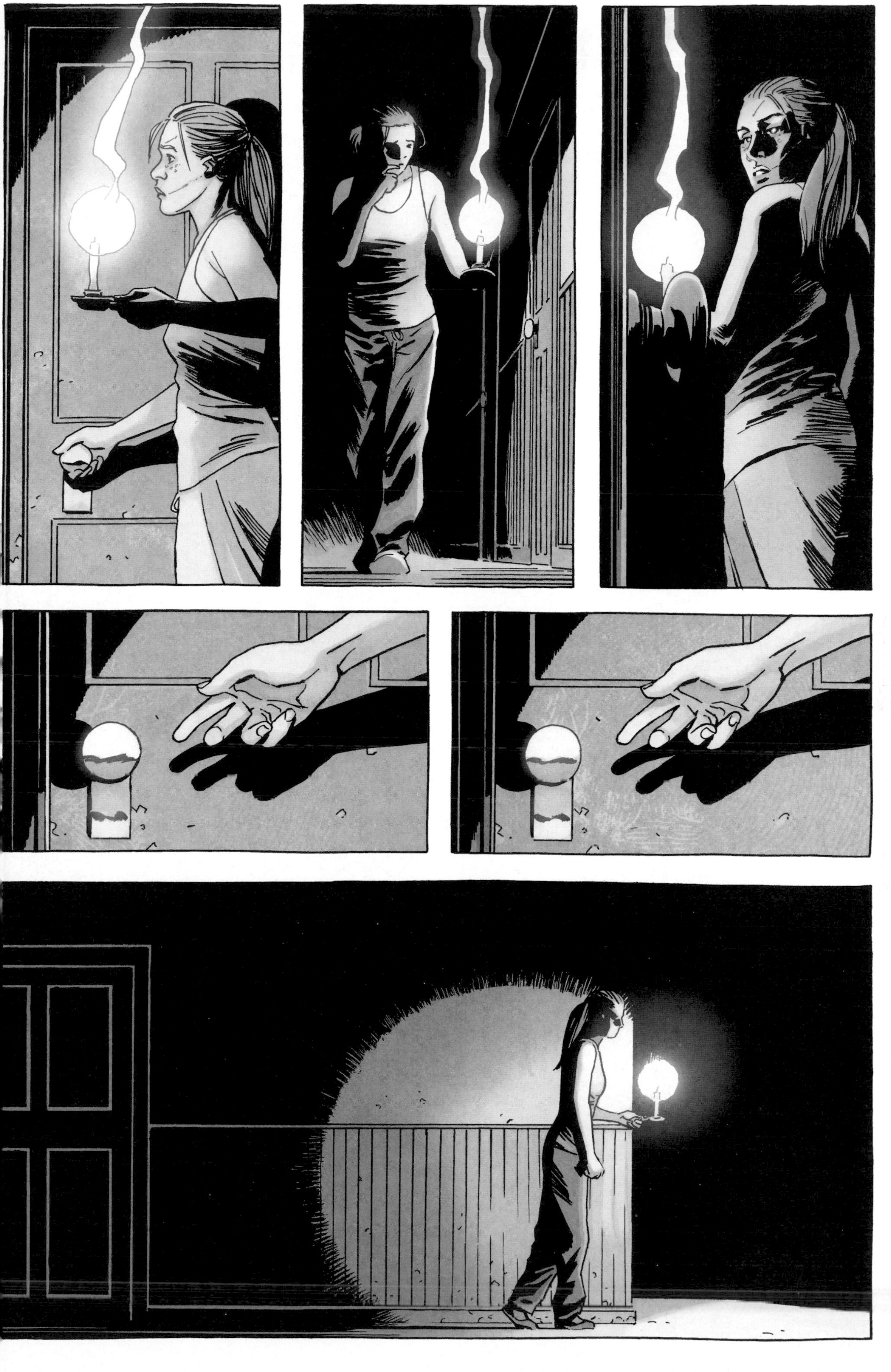

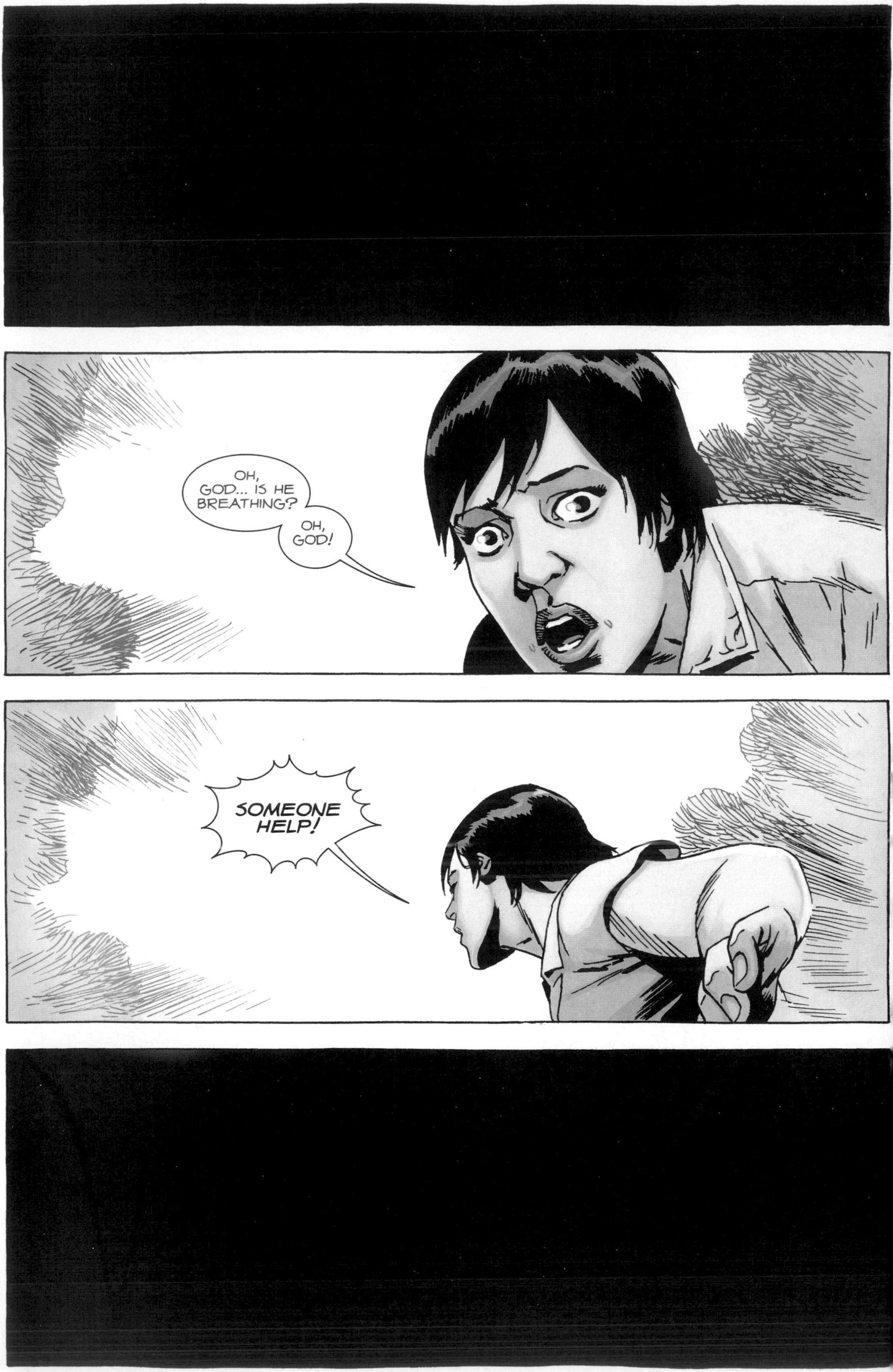
OH, GOD... IS HE BREATHING?
OH, GOD!
SOMEONE HELP!

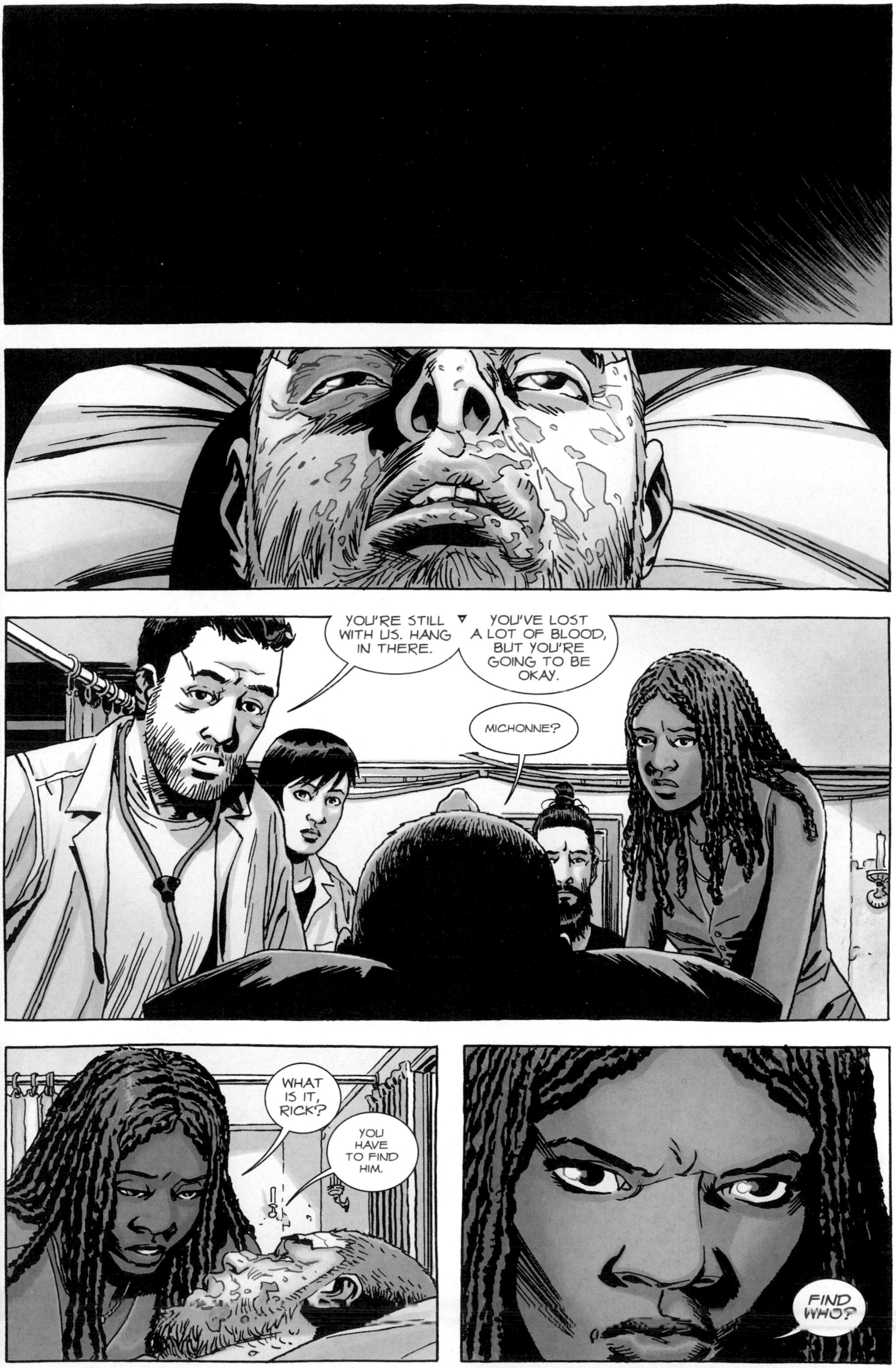
YOU'RE STILL WITH US. HANG IN THERE.
YOU'VE LOST A LOT OF BLOOD, BUT YOU'RE GOING TO BE OKAY.
MICHONNE?
WHAT IS IT, RICK?
YOU HAVE TO FIND HIM.
FIND WHO?

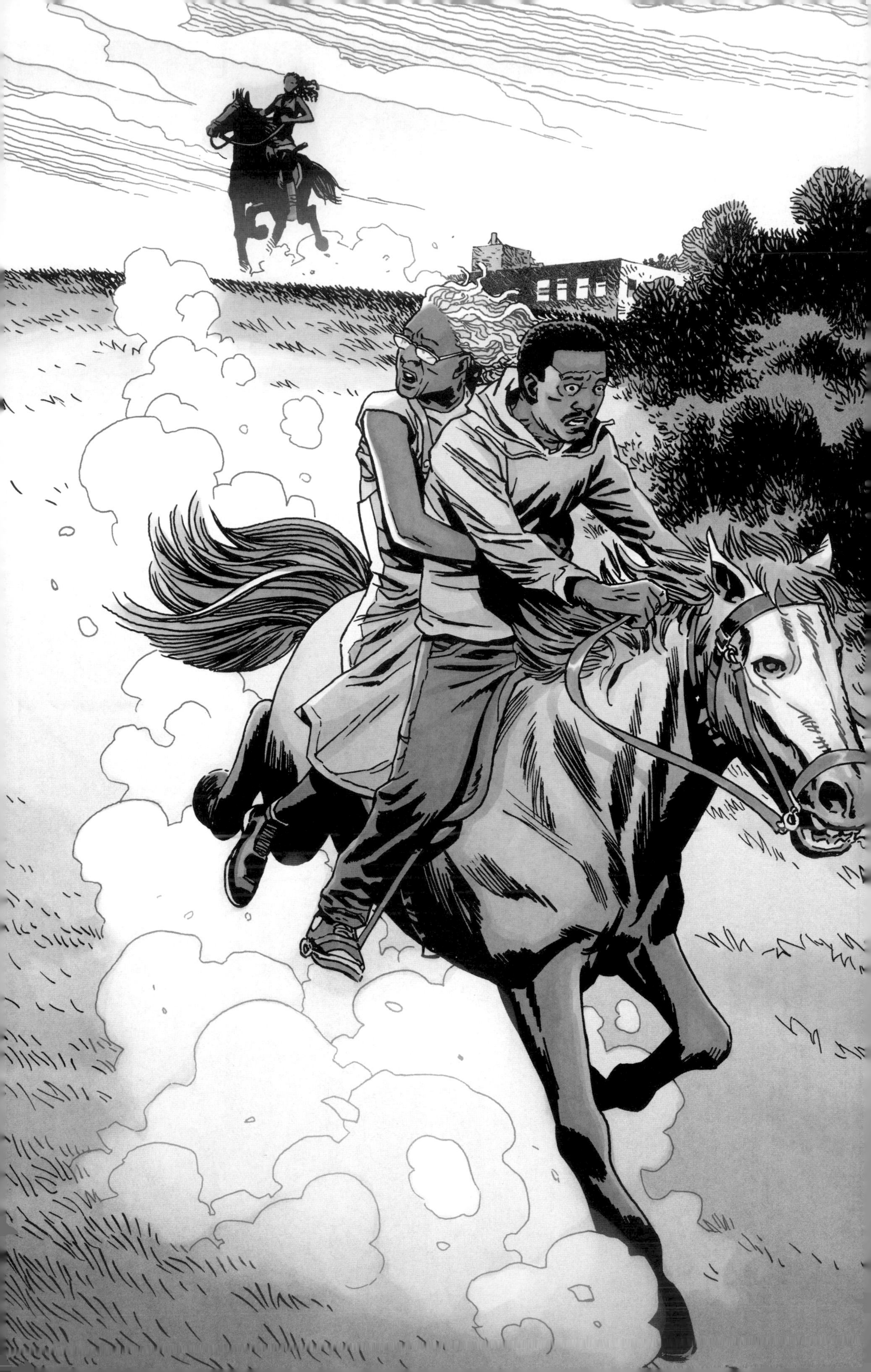

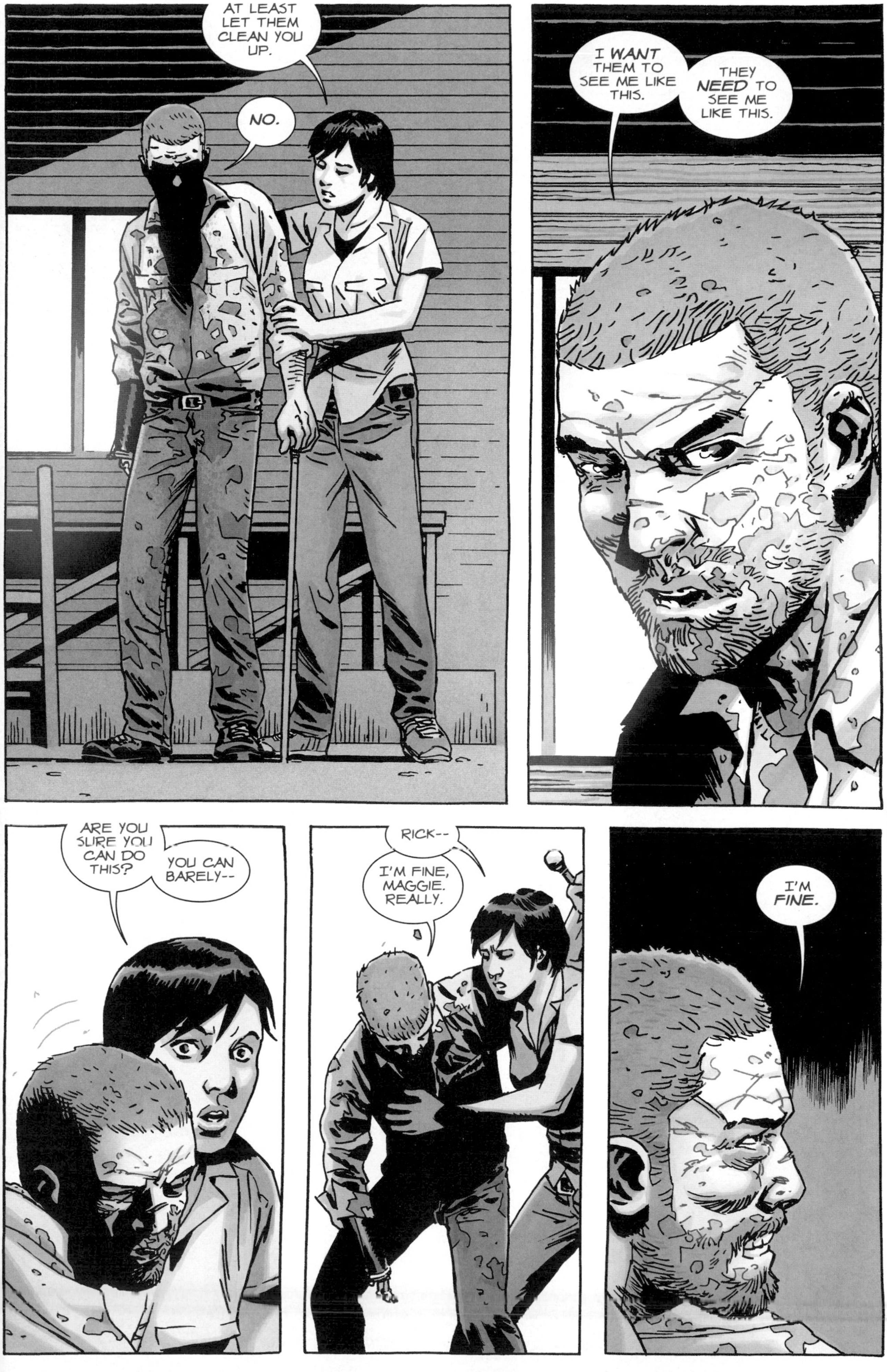
AT LEAST LET THEM CLEAN YOU UP.
NO.
I *WANT* THEM TO SEE ME LIKE THIS.
THEY *NEED* TO SEE ME LIKE THIS.
ARE YOU SURE YOU CAN DO THIS?
YOU CAN BARELY--
RICK--
I'M FINE, MAGGIE. REALLY.
I'M *FINE*.

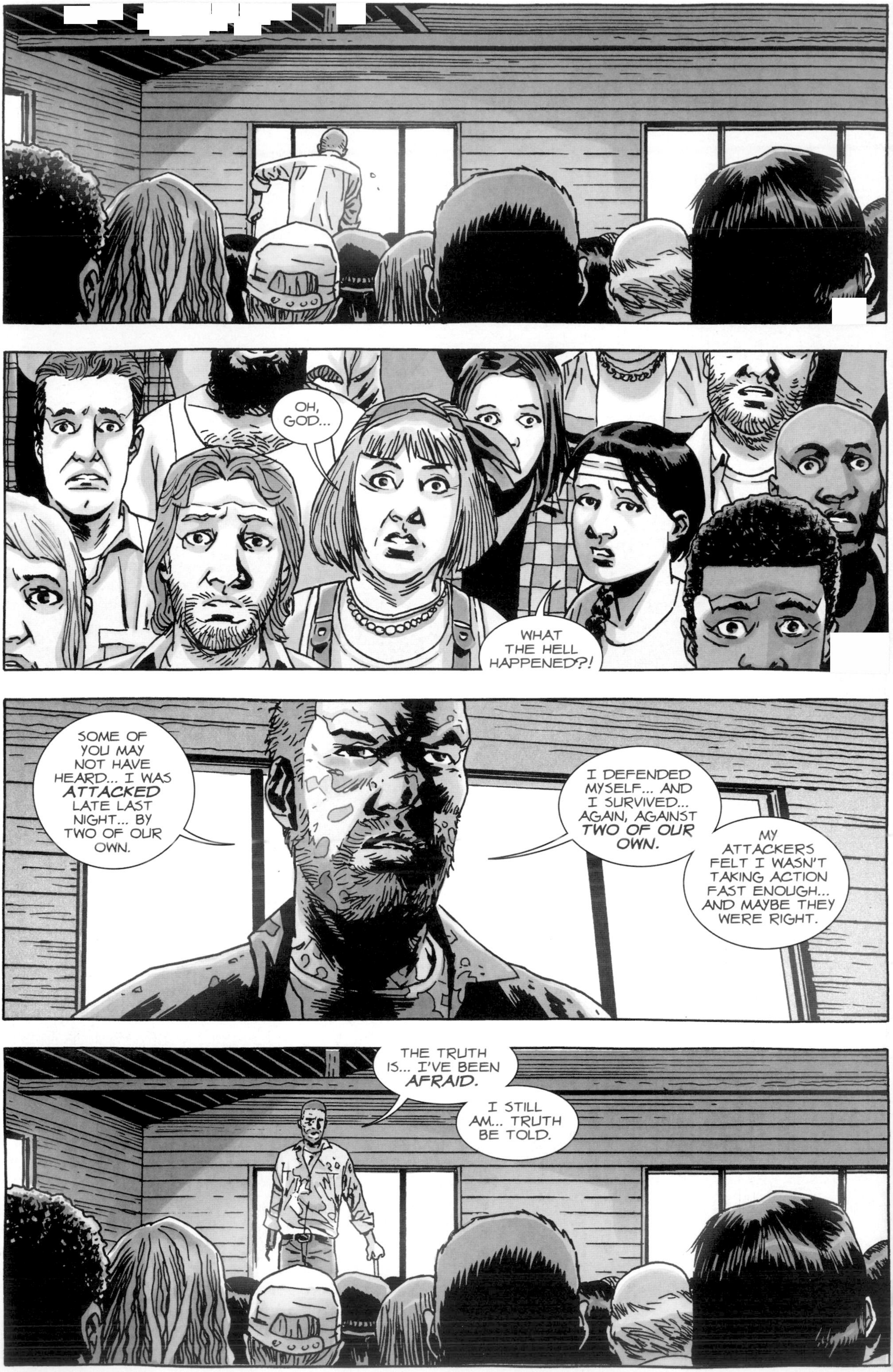
OH, GOD...
WHAT THE HELL HAPPENED?!
SOME OF YOU MAY NOT HAVE HEARD... I WAS ATTACKED LATE LAST NIGHT... BY TWO OF OUR OWN.
I DEFENDED MYSELF... AND I SURVIVED... AGAIN, AGAINST TWO OF OUR OWN.
MY ATTACKERS FELT I WASN'T TAKING ACTION FAST ENOUGH... AND MAYBE THEY WERE RIGHT.
THE TRUTH IS... I'VE BEEN AFRAID.
I STILL AM... TRUTH BE TOLD.

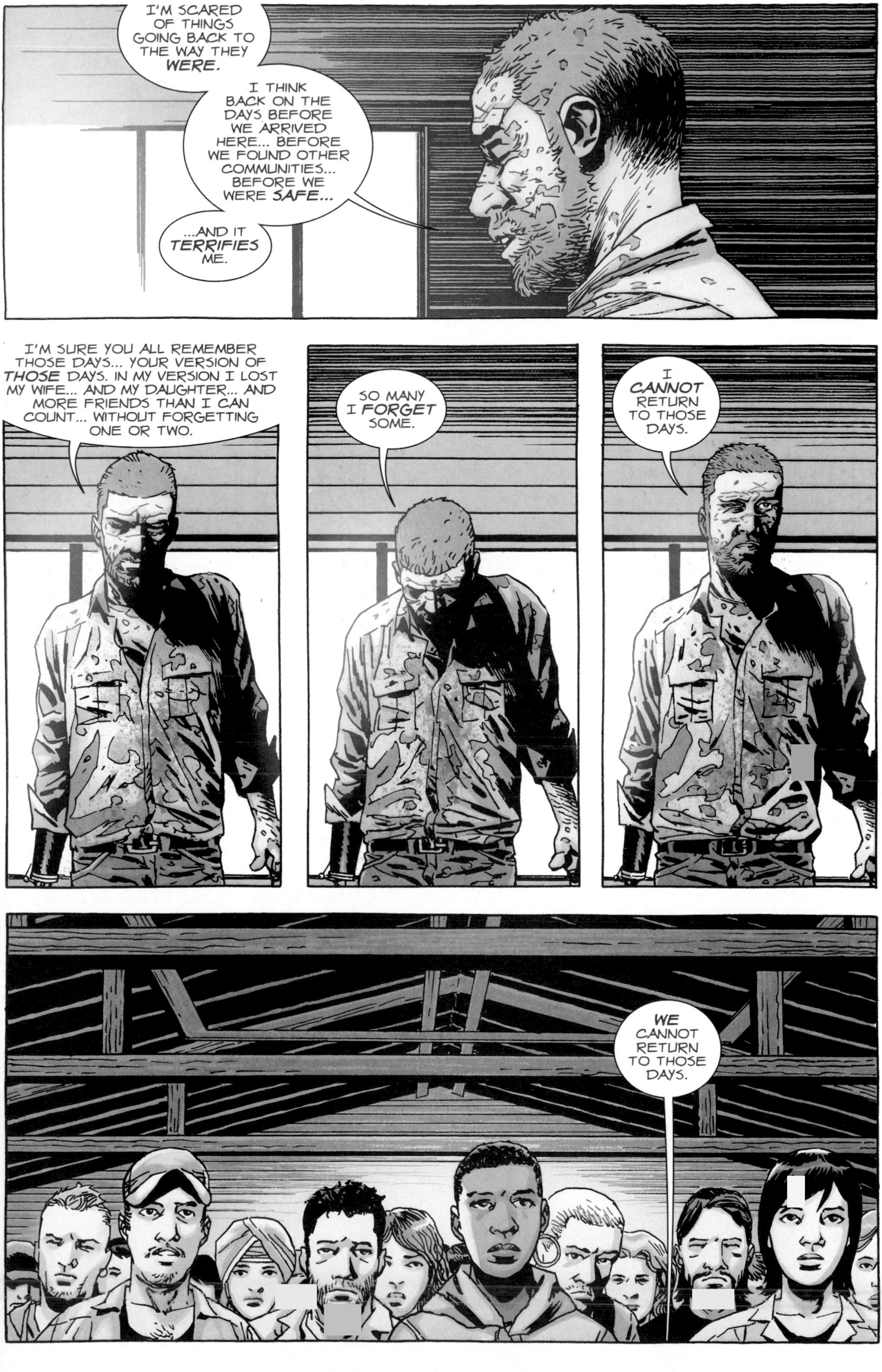
I'M SCARED OF THINGS GOING BACK TO THE WAY THEY WERE.
I THINK BACK ON THE DAYS BEFORE WE ARRIVED HERE... BEFORE WE FOUND OTHER COMMUNITIES... BEFORE WE WERE SAFE...
...AND IT TERRIFIES ME.
I'M SURE YOU ALL REMEMBER THOSE DAYS... YOUR VERSION OF THOSE DAYS. IN MY VERSION I LOST MY WIFE... AND MY DAUGHTER... AND MORE FRIENDS THAN I CAN COUNT... WITHOUT FORGETTING ONE OR TWO.
SO MANY I FORGET SOME.
I CANNOT RETURN TO THOSE DAYS.
WE CANNOT RETURN TO THOSE DAYS.

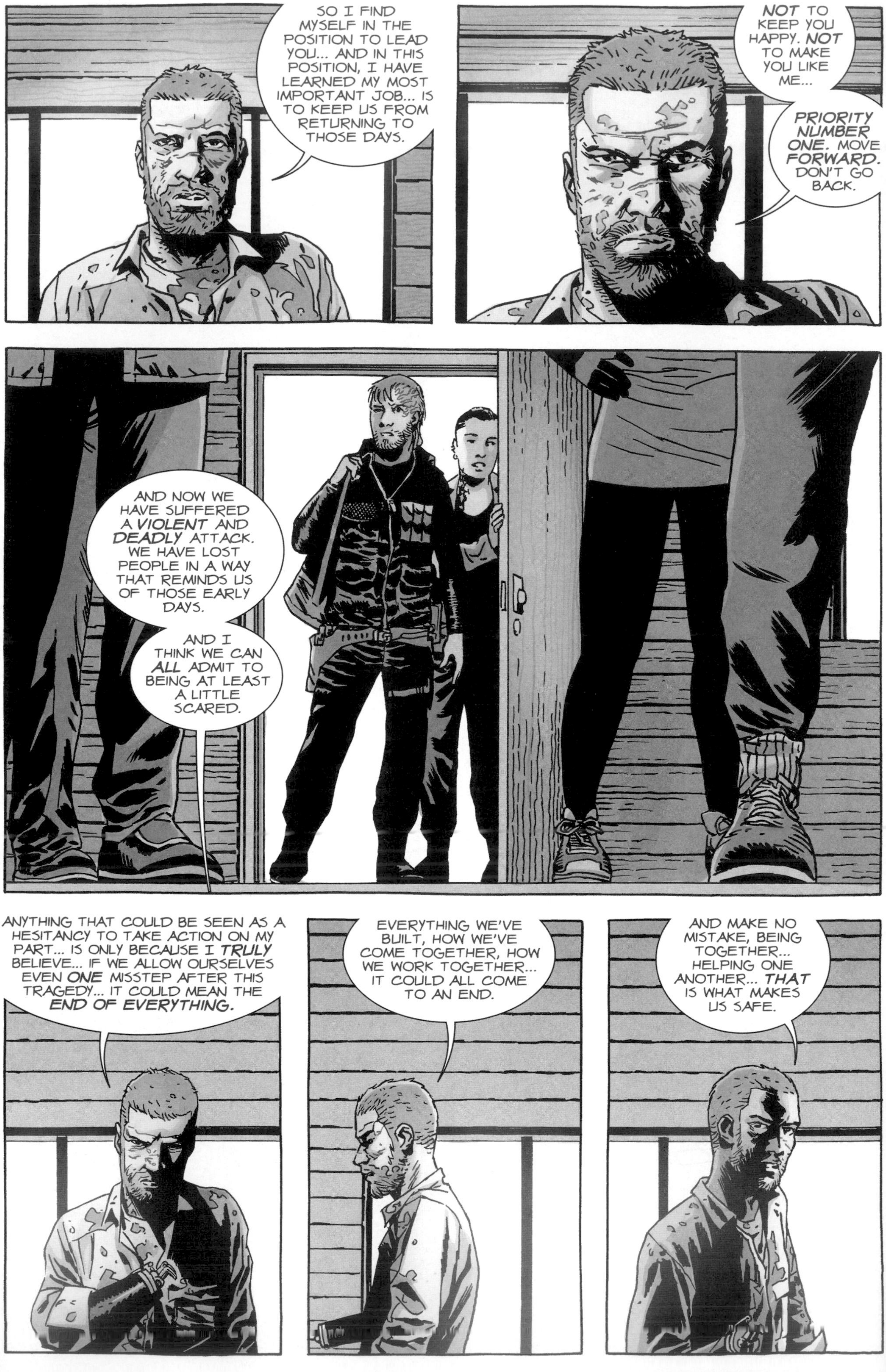
SO I FIND MYSELF IN THE POSITION TO LEAD YOU... AND IN THIS POSITION, I HAVE LEARNED MY MOST IMPORTANT JOB... IS TO KEEP US FROM RETURNING TO THOSE DAYS.
NOT TO KEEP YOU HAPPY. NOT TO MAKE YOU LIKE ME...
PRIORITY NUMBER ONE. MOVE FORWARD. DON'T GO BACK.
AND NOW WE HAVE SUFFERED A VIOLENT AND DEADLY ATTACK. WE HAVE LOST PEOPLE IN A WAY THAT REMINDS US OF THOSE EARLY DAYS.
AND I THINK WE CAN ALL ADMIT TO BEING AT LEAST A LITTLE SCARED.
ANYTHING THAT COULD BE SEEN AS A HESITANCY TO TAKE ACTION ON MY PART... IS ONLY BECAUSE I TRULY BELIEVE... IF WE ALLOW OURSELVES EVEN ONE MISSTEP AFTER THIS TRAGEDY... IT COULD MEAN THE END OF EVERYTHING.
EVERYTHING WE'VE BUILT, HOW WE'VE COME TOGETHER, HOW WE WORK TOGETHER... IT COULD ALL COME TO AN END.
AND MAKE NO MISTAKE, BEING TOGETHER... HELPING ONE ANOTHER... THAT IS WHAT MAKES US SAFE.

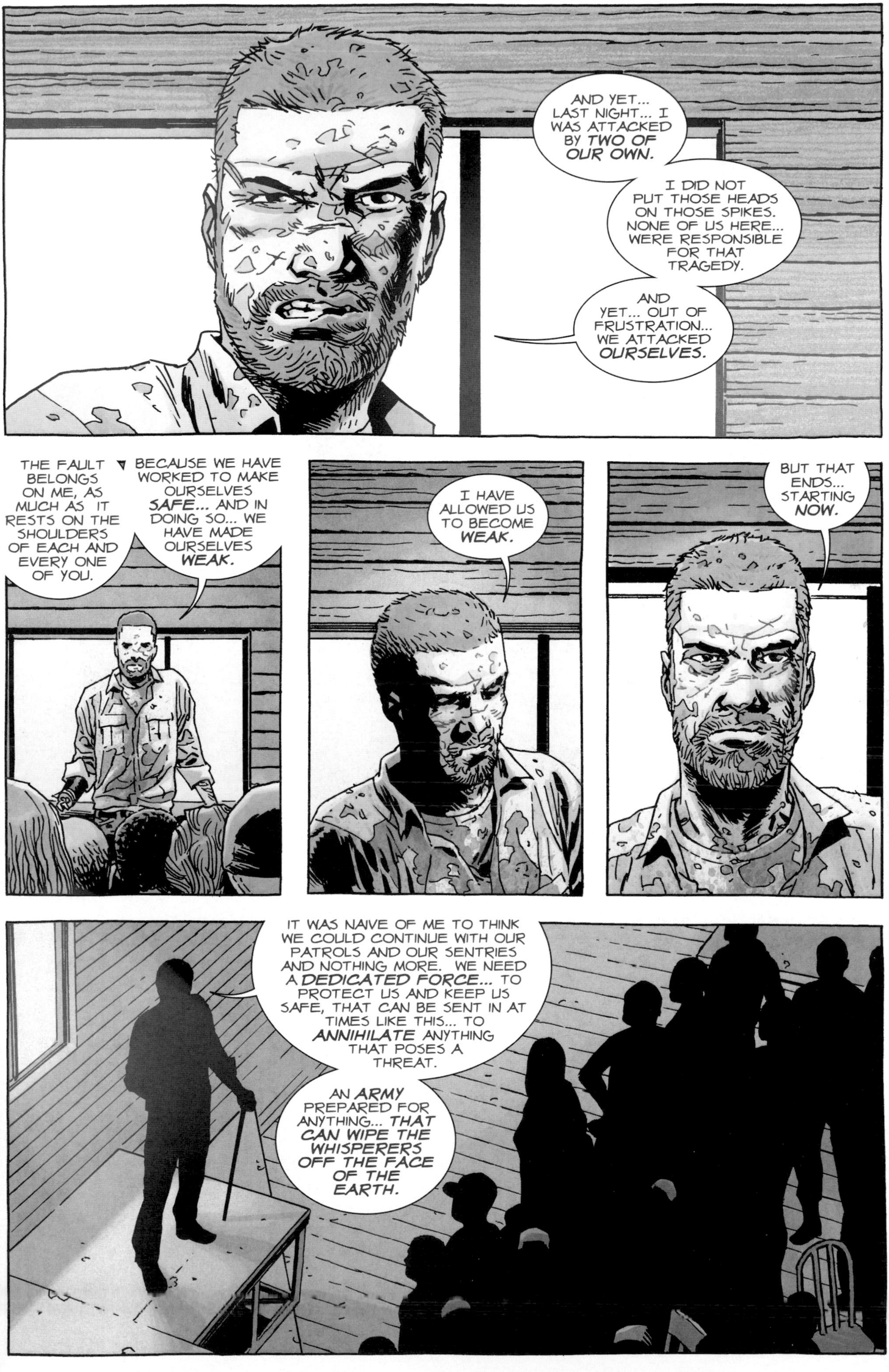

AND YET... LAST NIGHT... I WAS ATTACKED BY TWO OF OUR OWN.
I DID NOT PUT THOSE HEADS ON THOSE SPIKES. NONE OF US HERE... WERE RESPONSIBLE FOR THAT TRAGEDY.
AND YET... OUT OF FRUSTRATION... WE ATTACKED OURSELVES.
THE FAULT BELONGS ON ME, AS MUCH AS IT RESTS ON THE SHOULDERS OF EACH AND EVERY ONE OF YOU.
BECAUSE WE HAVE WORKED TO MAKE OURSELVES SAFE... AND IN DOING SO... WE HAVE MADE OURSELVES WEAK.
I HAVE ALLOWED US TO BECOME WEAK.
BUT THAT ENDS... STARTING NOW.
IT WAS NAIVE OF ME TO THINK WE COULD CONTINUE WITH OUR PATROLS AND OUR SENTRIES AND NOTHING MORE. WE NEED A DEDICATED FORCE... TO PROTECT US AND KEEP US SAFE, THAT CAN BE SENT IN AT TIMES LIKE THIS... TO ANNIHILATE ANYTHING THAT POSES A THREAT.
AN ARMY PREPARED FOR ANYTHING... THAT CAN WIPE THE WHISPERERS OFF THE FACE OF THE EARTH.

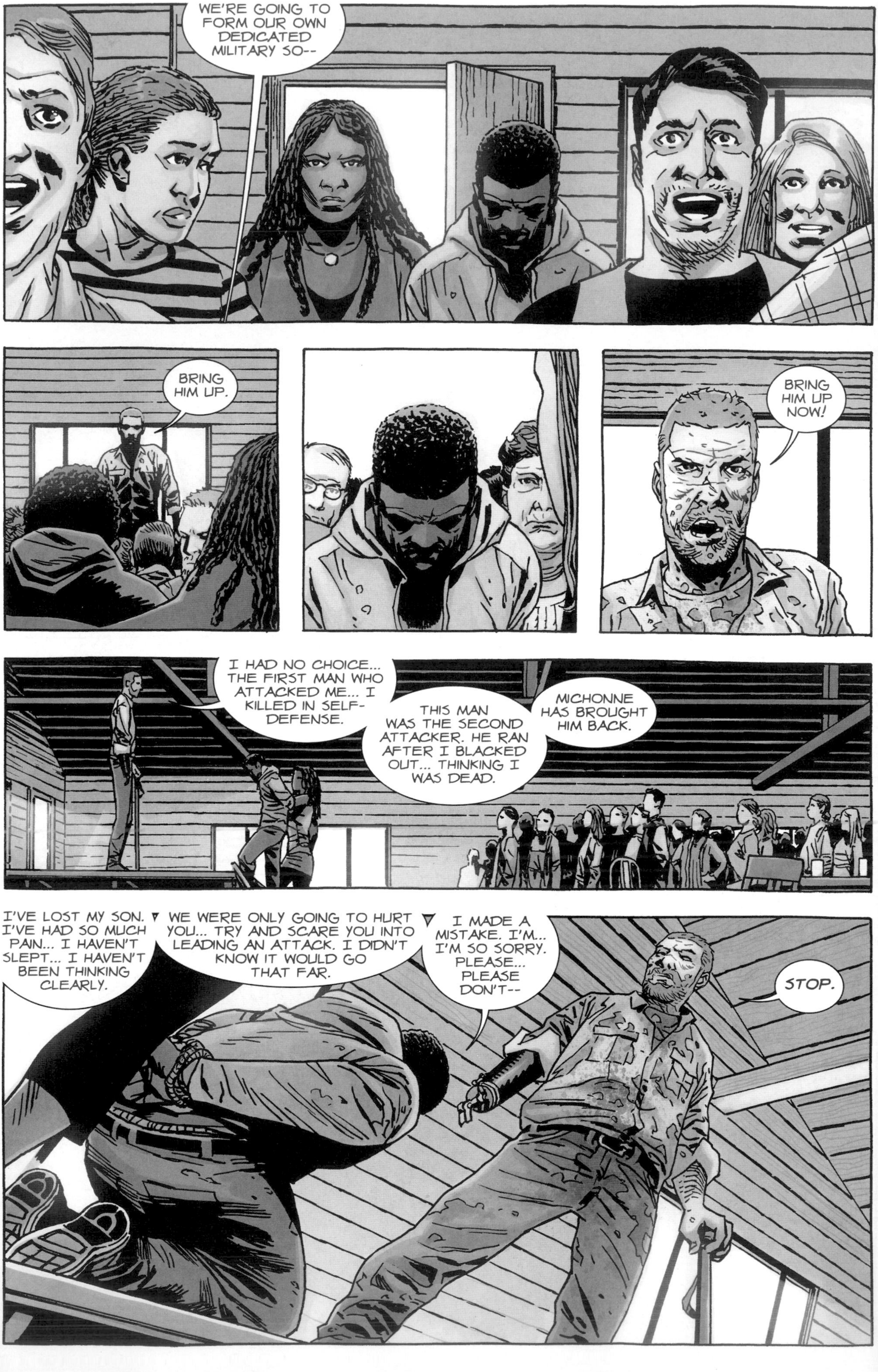
WE'RE GOING TO FORM OUR OWN DEDICATED MILITARY SO--
BRING HIM UP.
BRING HIM UP NOW!
I HAD NO CHOICE... THE FIRST MAN WHO ATTACKED ME... I KILLED IN SELF-DEFENSE.
THIS MAN WAS THE SECOND ATTACKER. HE RAN AFTER I BLACKED OUT... THINKING I WAS DEAD.
MICHONNE HAS BROUGHT HIM BACK.
I'VE LOST MY SON. I'VE HAD SO MUCH PAIN... I HAVEN'T SLEPT... I HAVEN'T BEEN THINKING CLEARLY.
WE WERE ONLY GOING TO HURT YOU... TRY AND SCARE YOU INTO LEADING AN ATTACK. I DIDN'T KNOW IT WOULD GO THAT FAR.
I MADE A MISTAKE. I'M... I'M SO SORRY. PLEASE... PLEASE DON'T--
STOP.

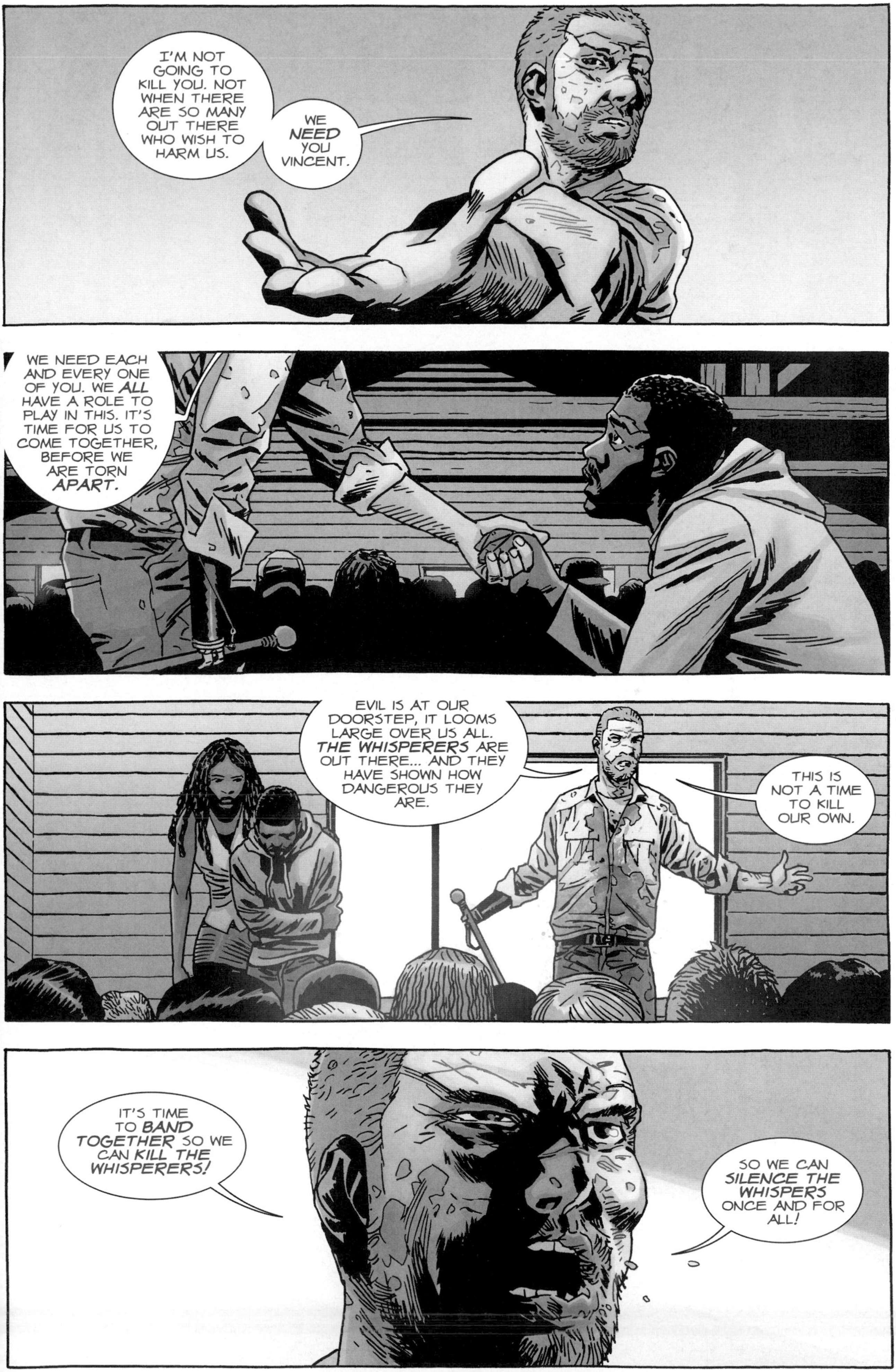
I'M NOT GOING TO KILL YOU. NOT WHEN THERE ARE SO MANY OUT THERE WHO WISH TO HARM US.
WE NEED YOU VINCENT.
WE NEED EACH AND EVERY ONE OF YOU. WE ALL HAVE A ROLE TO PLAY IN THIS. IT'S TIME FOR US TO COME TOGETHER, BEFORE WE ARE TORN APART.
EVIL IS AT OUR DOORSTEP, IT LOOMS LARGE OVER US ALL. THE WHISPERERS ARE OUT THERE... AND THEY HAVE SHOWN HOW DANGEROUS THEY ARE.
THIS IS NOT A TIME TO KILL OUR OWN.
IT'S TIME TO BAND TOGETHER SO WE CAN KILL THE WHISPERERS!
SO WE CAN SILENCE THE WHISPERS ONCE AND FOR ALL!

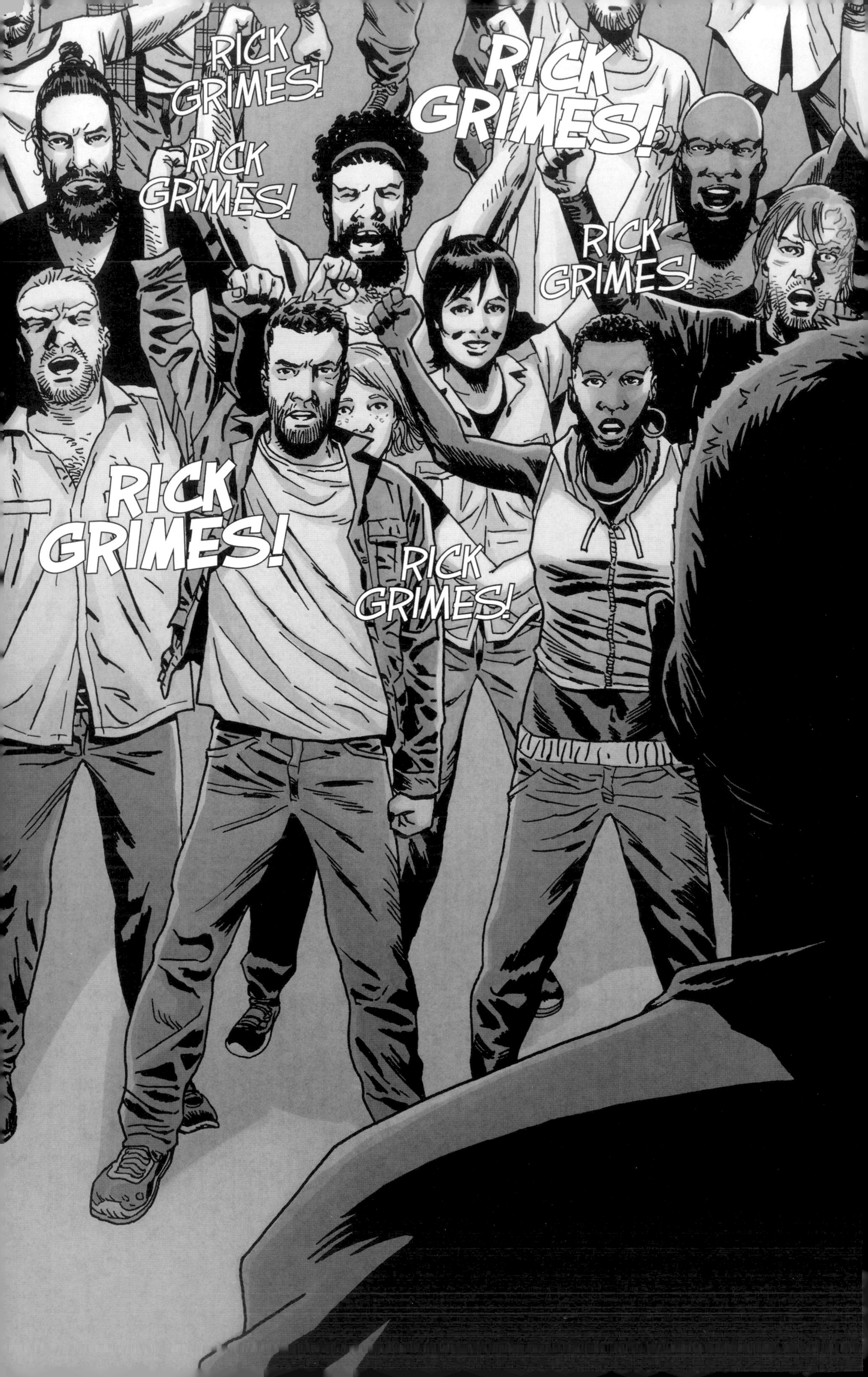
RICK GRIMES!
RICK GRIMES!
RICK GRIMES!
RICK GRIMES!
RICK GRIMES!
RICK GRIMES!

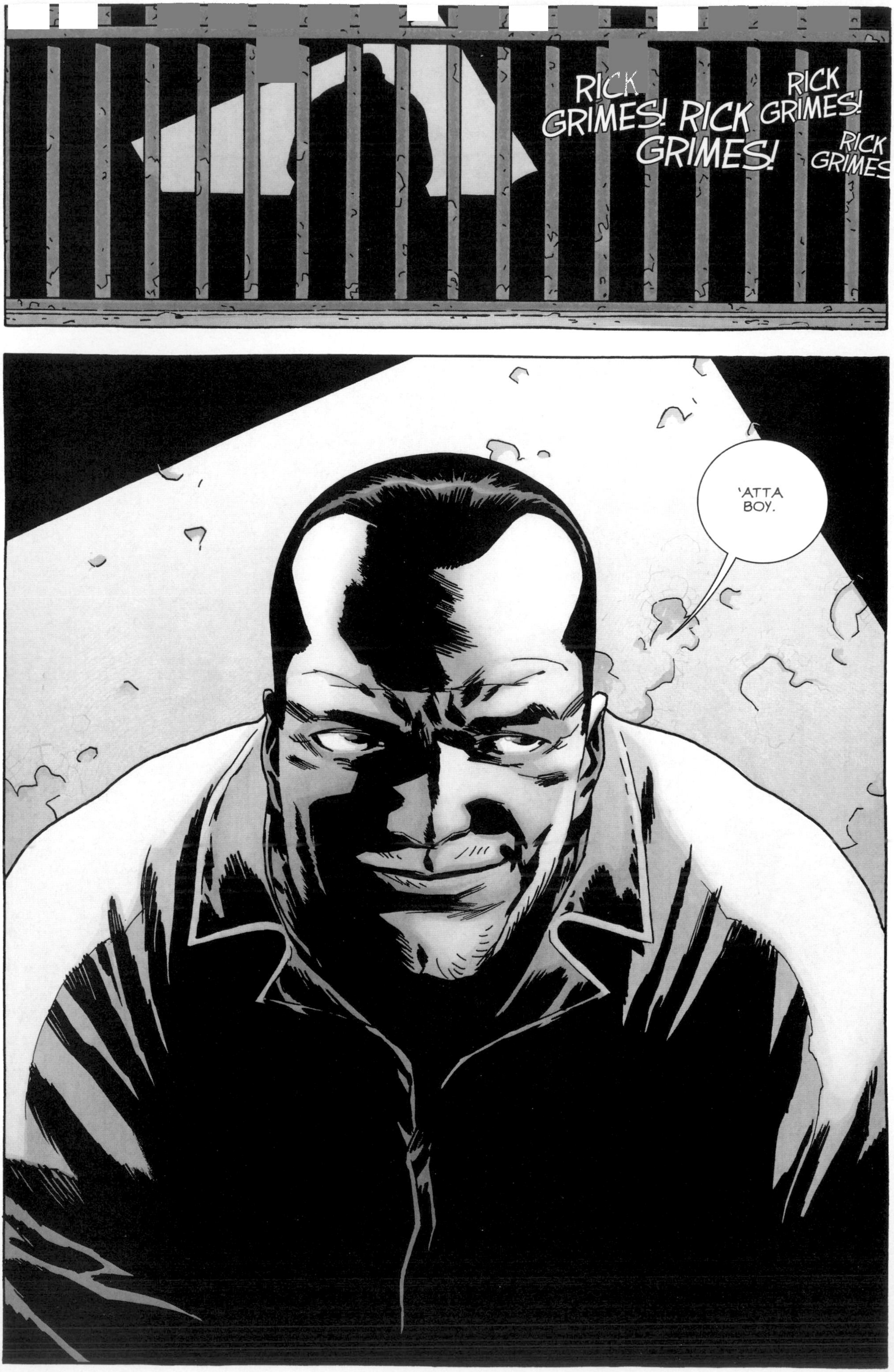
RICK GRIMES!
RICK GRIMES!
RICK GRIMES!
RICK GRIMES
'ATTA BOY.

Chapter Twenty-Six:
Call To Arms

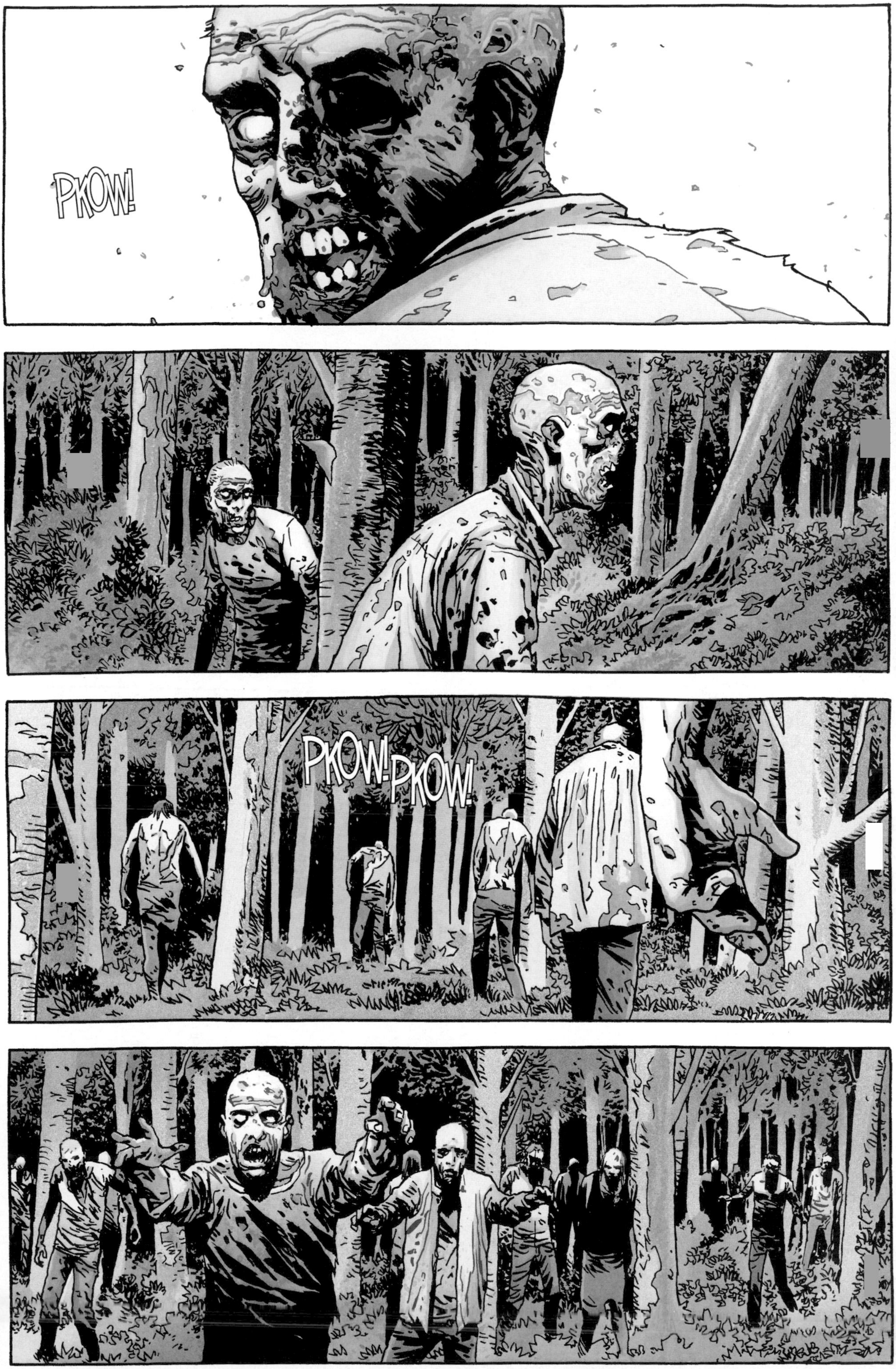
PKOW!
PKOW! PKOW!

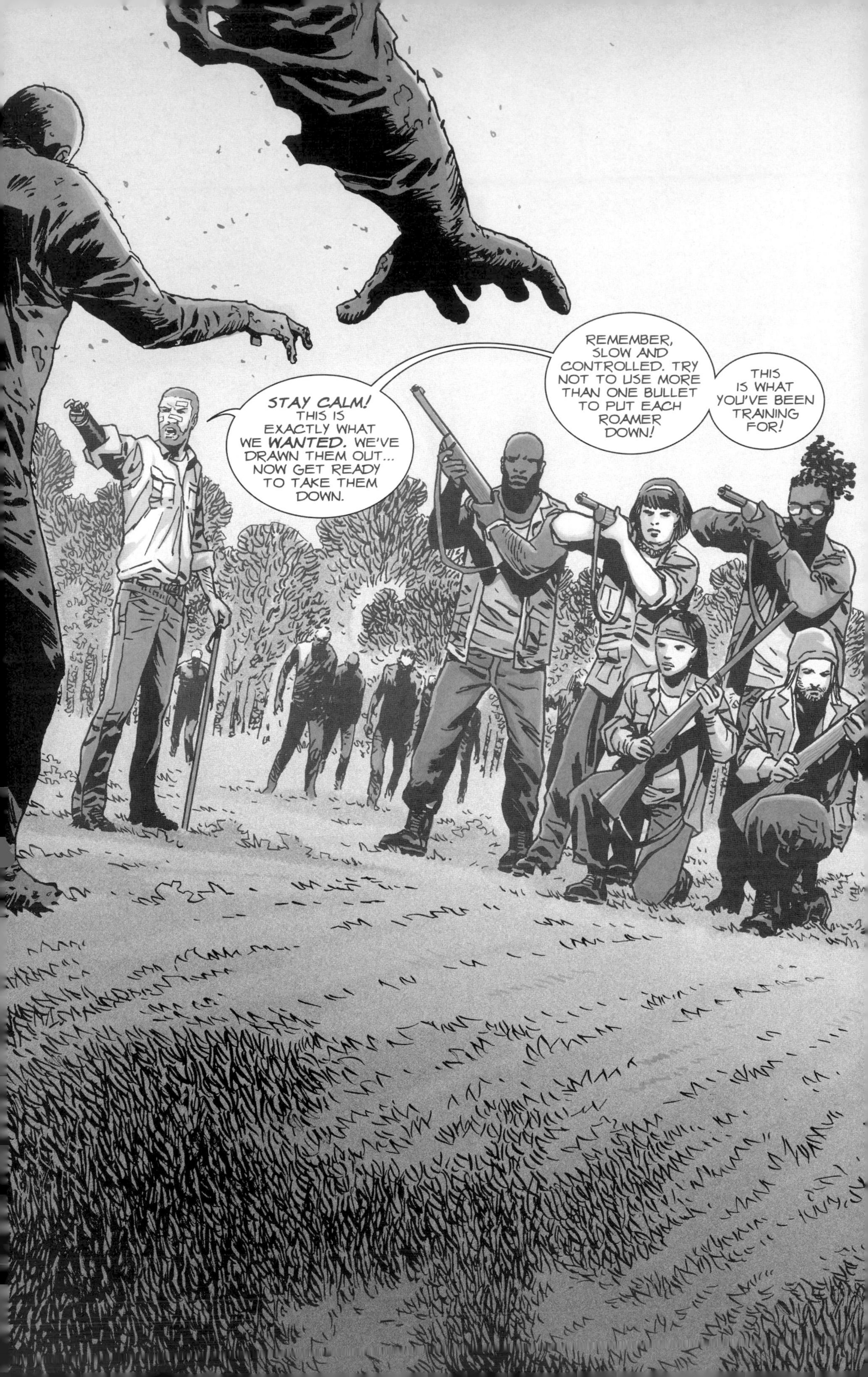
STAY CALM! THIS IS EXACTLY WHAT WE WANTED. WE'VE DRAWN THEM OUT... NOW GET READY TO TAKE THEM DOWN.
REMEMBER, SLOW AND CONTROLLED. TRY NOT TO USE MORE THAN ONE BULLET TO PUT EACH ROAMER DOWN!
THIS IS WHAT YOU'VE BEEN TRAINING FOR!

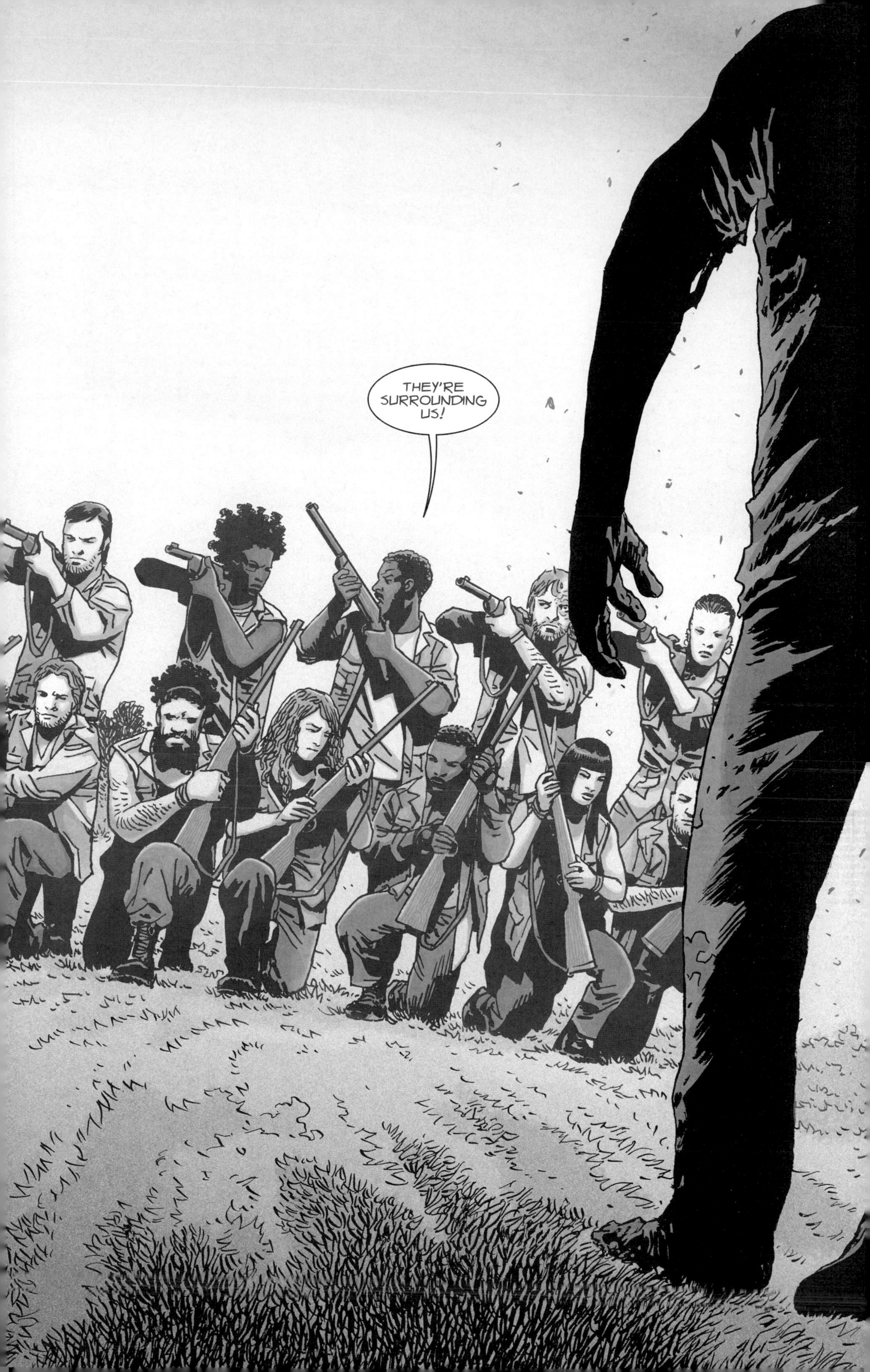
THEY'RE SURROUNDING US!

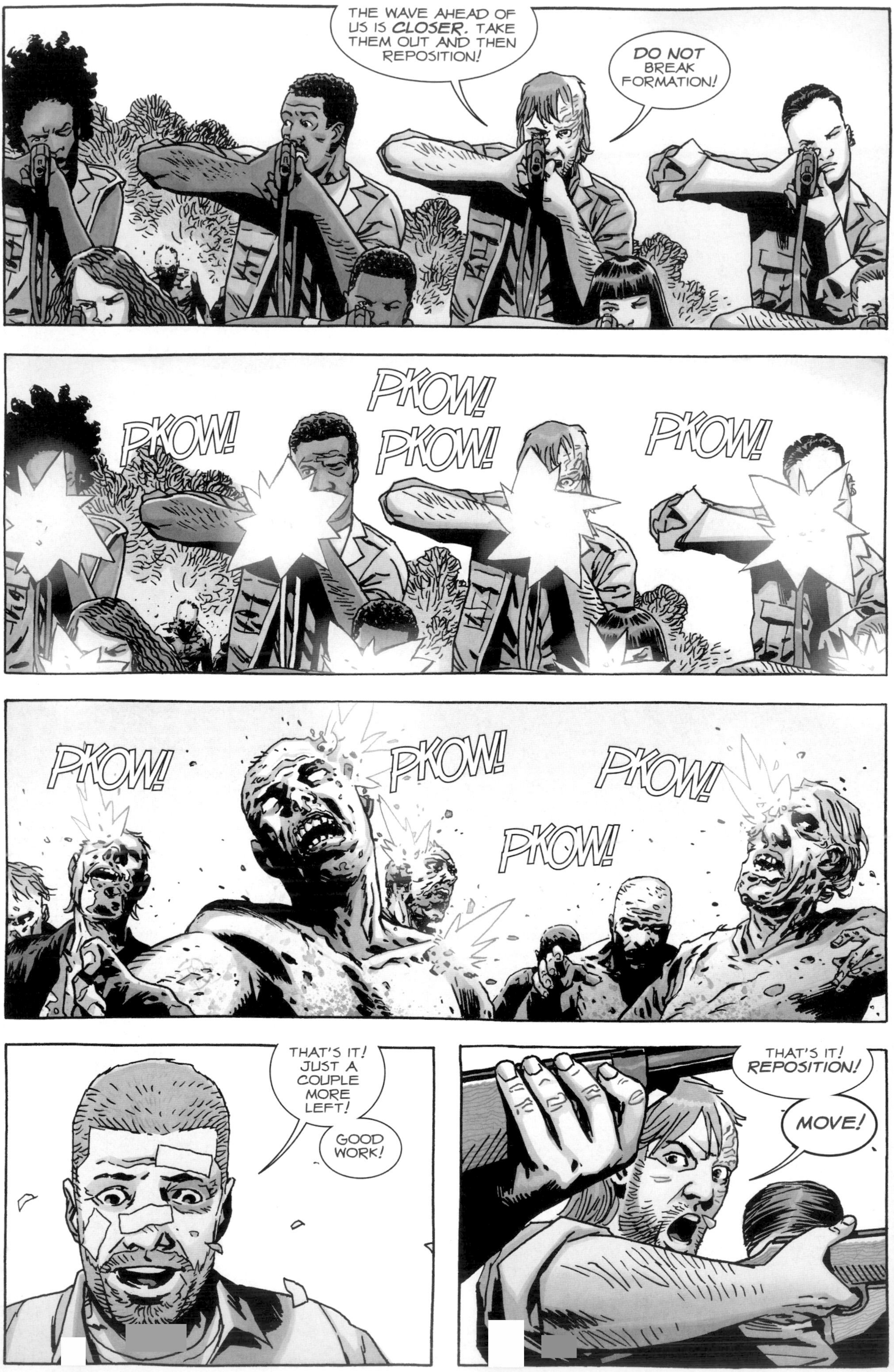
THE WAVE AHEAD OF US IS CLOSER. TAKE THEM OUT AND THEN REPOSITION!
DO NOT BREAK FORMATION!
PKOW!
PKOW!
PKOW!
PKOW!
PKOW!
PKOW!
PKOW!
PKOW!
THAT'S IT! JUST A COUPLE MORE LEFT!
GOOD WORK!
THAT'S IT! REPOSITION!
MOVE!

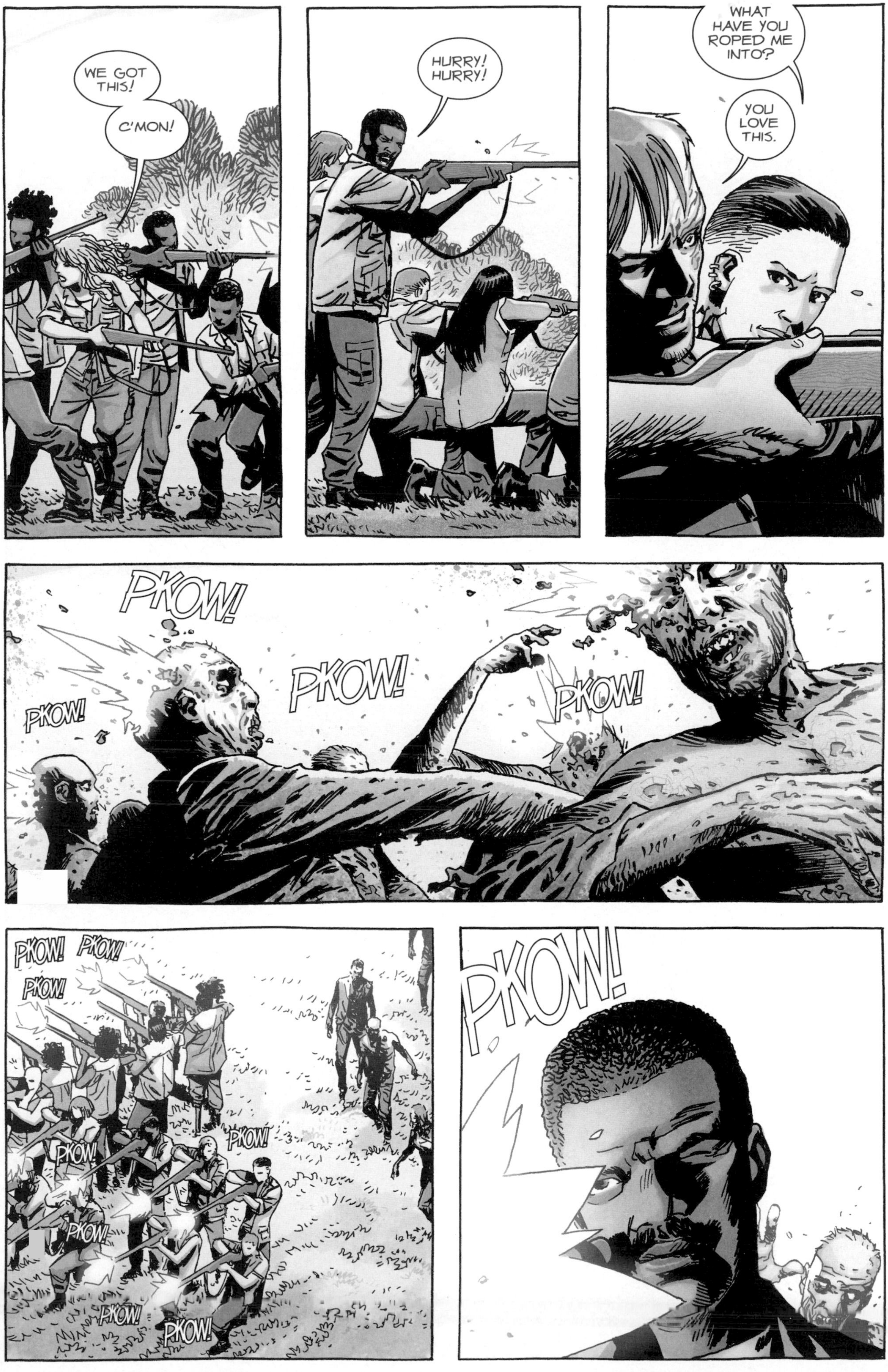
WE GOT THIS!
C'MON!
HURRY! HURRY!
WHAT HAVE YOU ROPED ME INTO?
YOU LOVE THIS.
PKOW!
PKOW!
PKOW!
PKOW!
PKOW! PKOW!
PKOW!
PKOW!
PKOW!
PKOW!
PKOW!
PKOW!
PKOW!

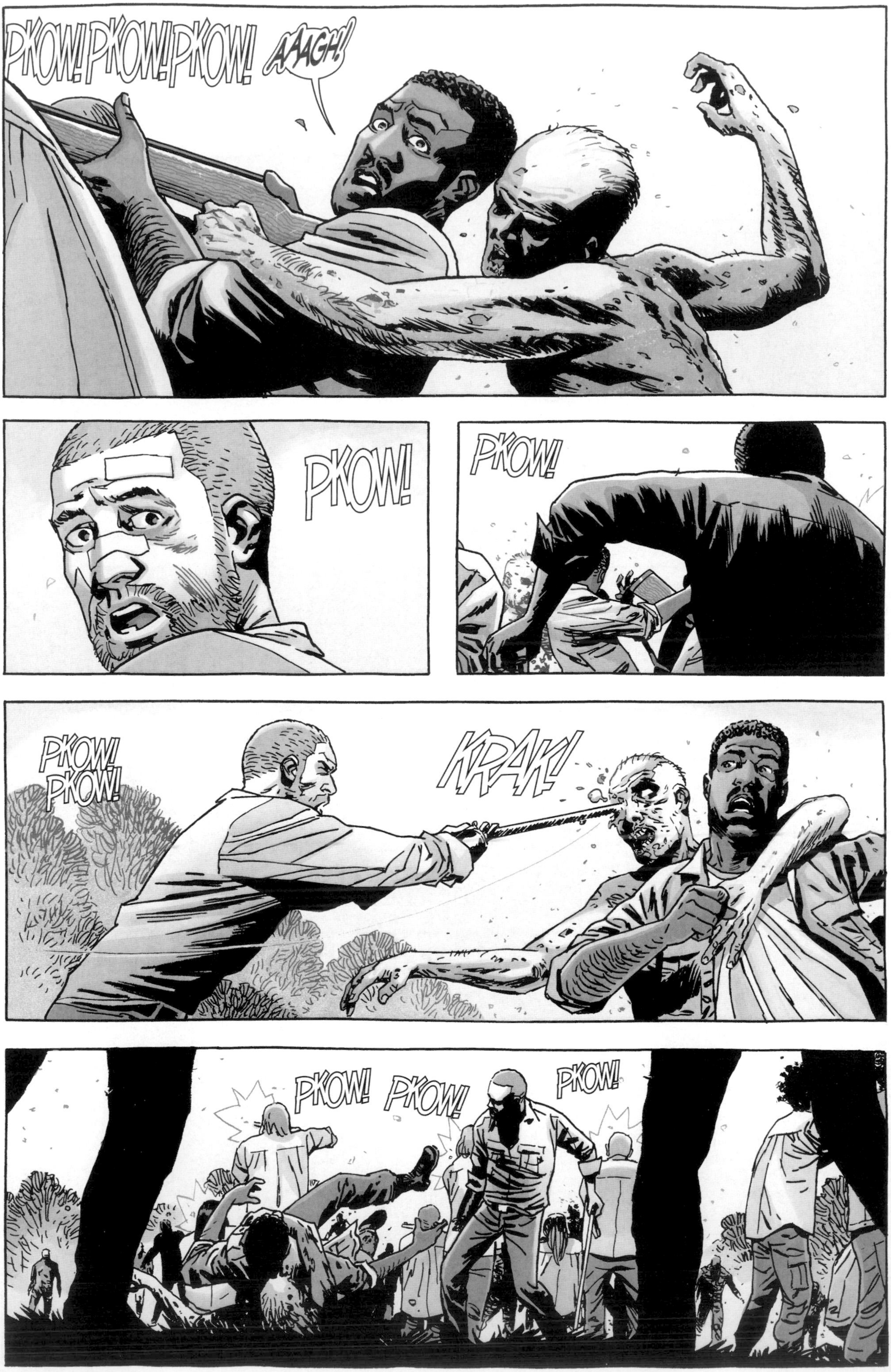
PKOW! PKOW! PKOW!
AAAGH!
PKOW!
PKOW!
PKOW! PKOW!
KRAK!
PKOW!
PKOW!
PKOW!

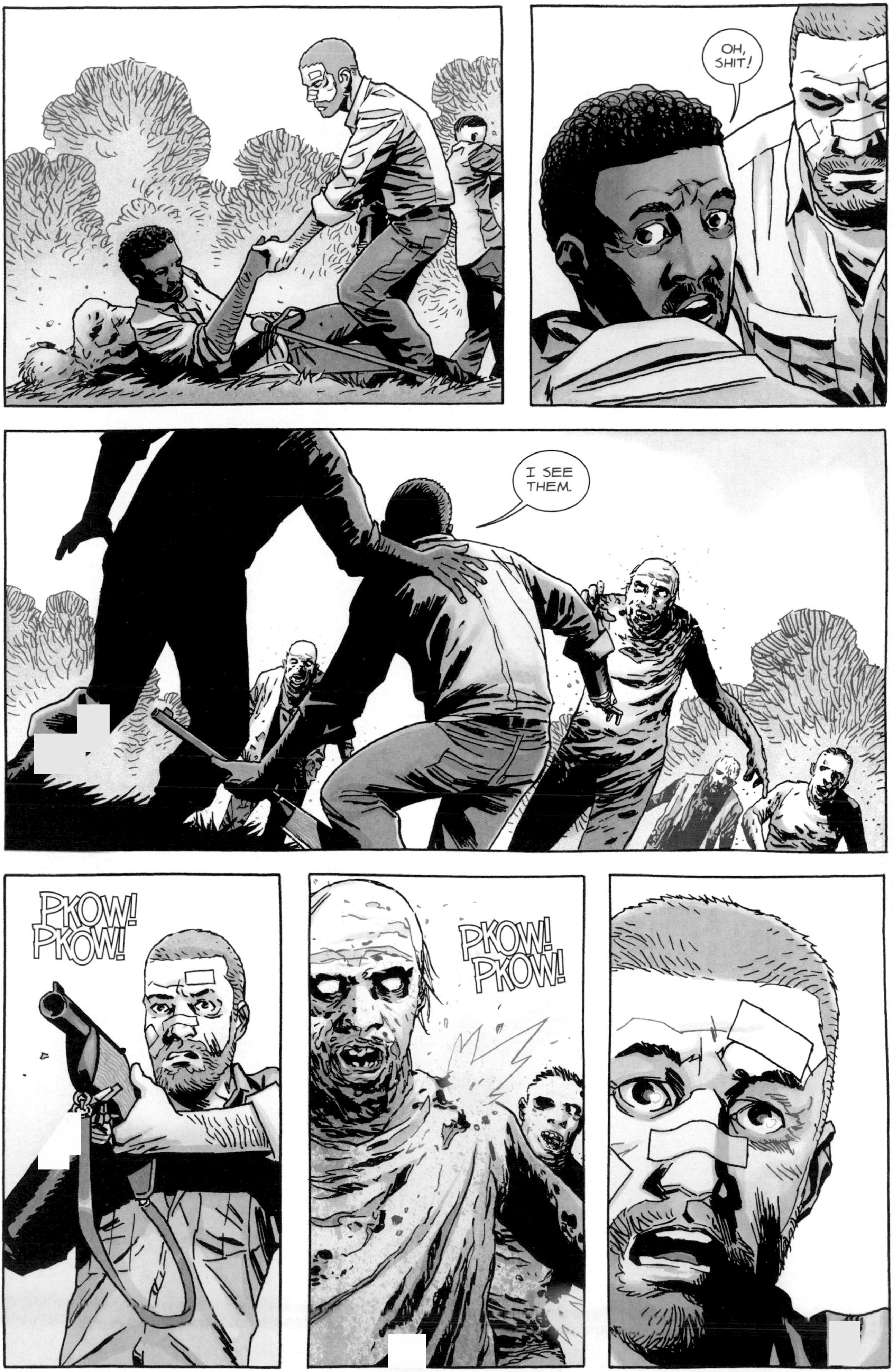
OH, SHIT!
I SEE THEM.
PKOW! PKOW!
PKOW! PKOW!

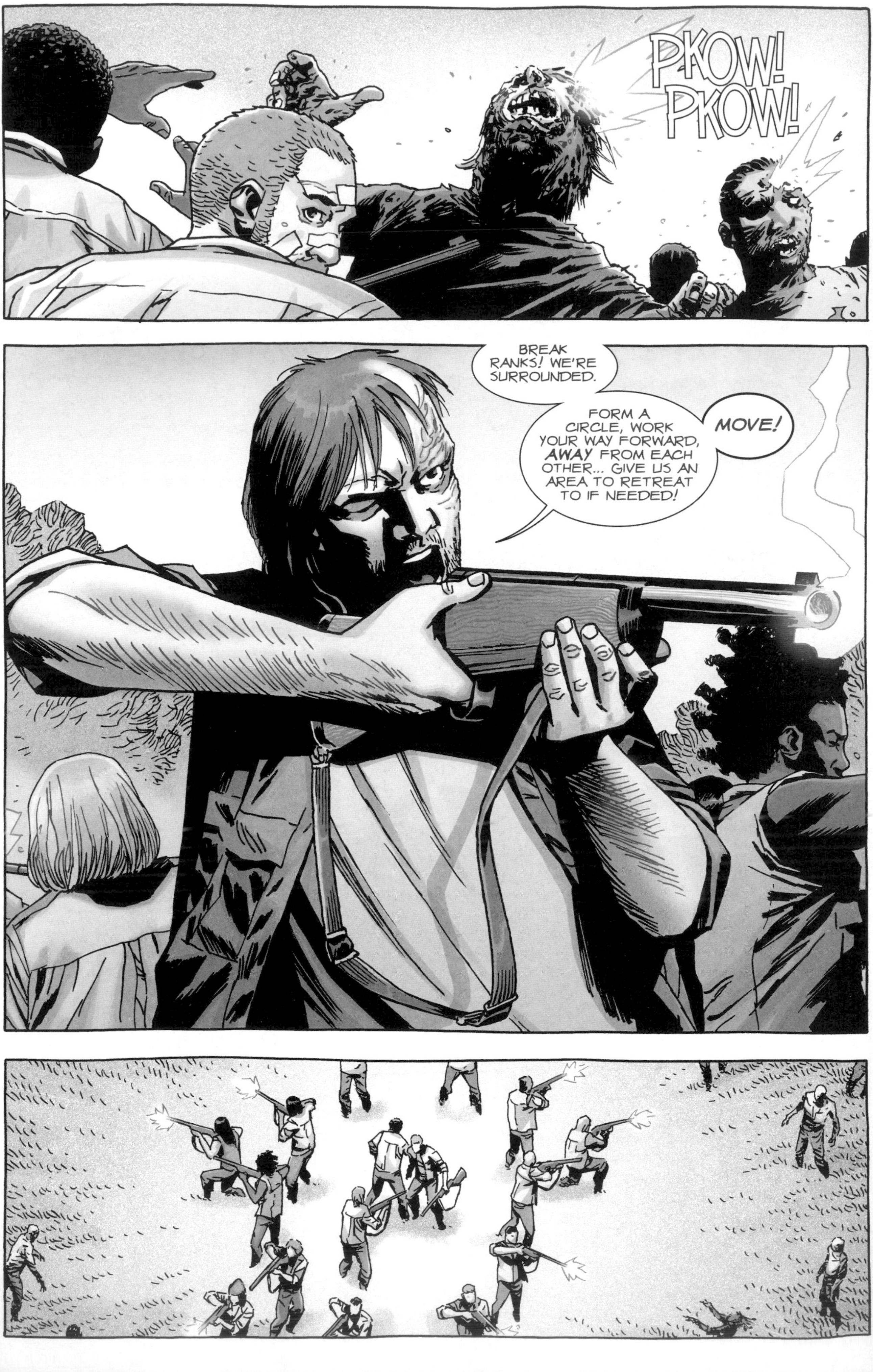
PKOW! PKOW!
BREAK RANKS! WE'RE SURROUNDED.
FORM A CIRCLE, WORK YOUR WAY FORWARD, AWAY FROM EACH OTHER... GIVE US AN AREA TO RETREAT TO IF NEEDED!
MOVE!

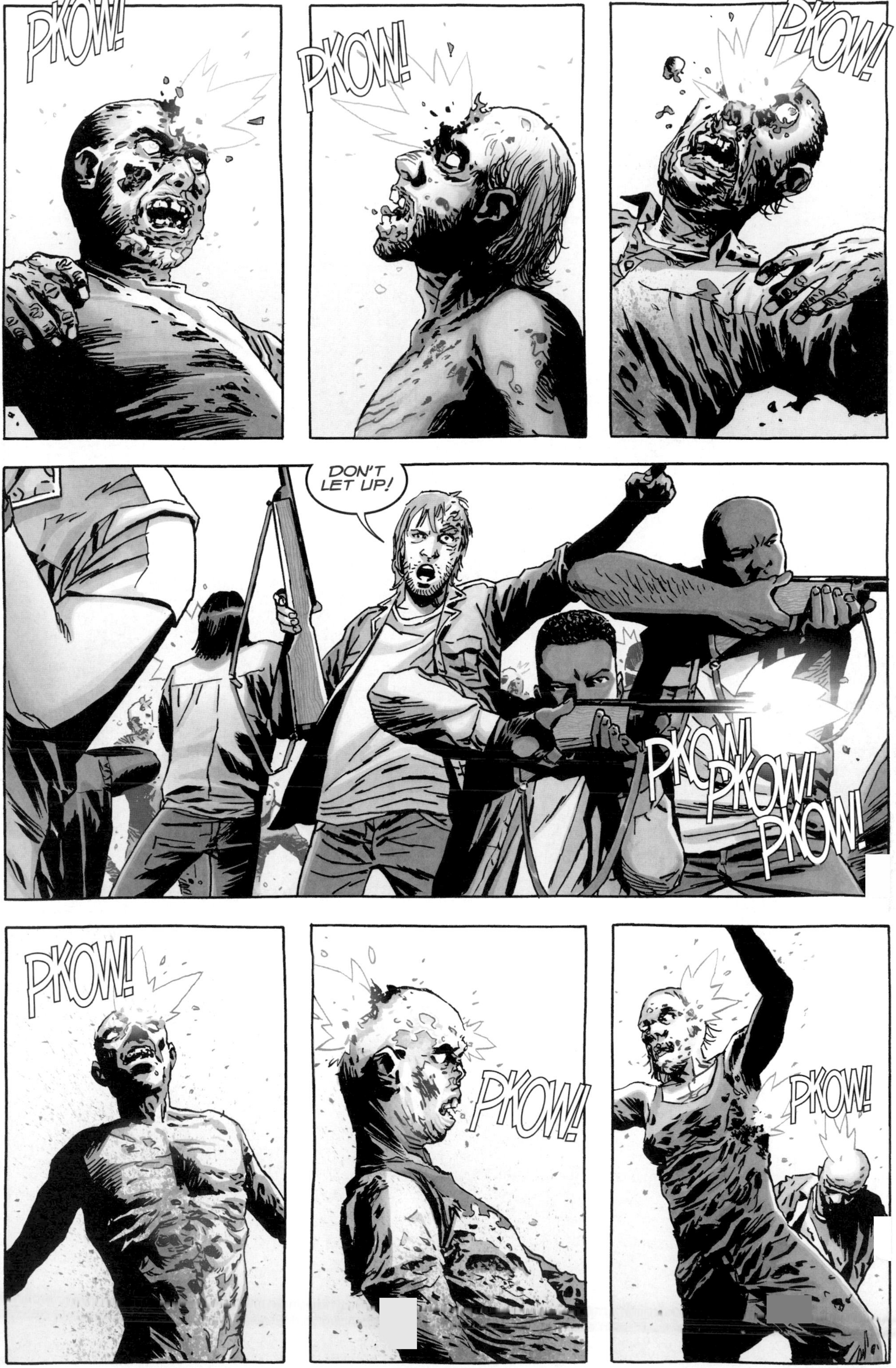
PKOW!
PKOW!
PKOW!
DON'T LET UP!
PKOW!
PKOW!
PKOW!
PKOW!
PKOW!
PKOW!

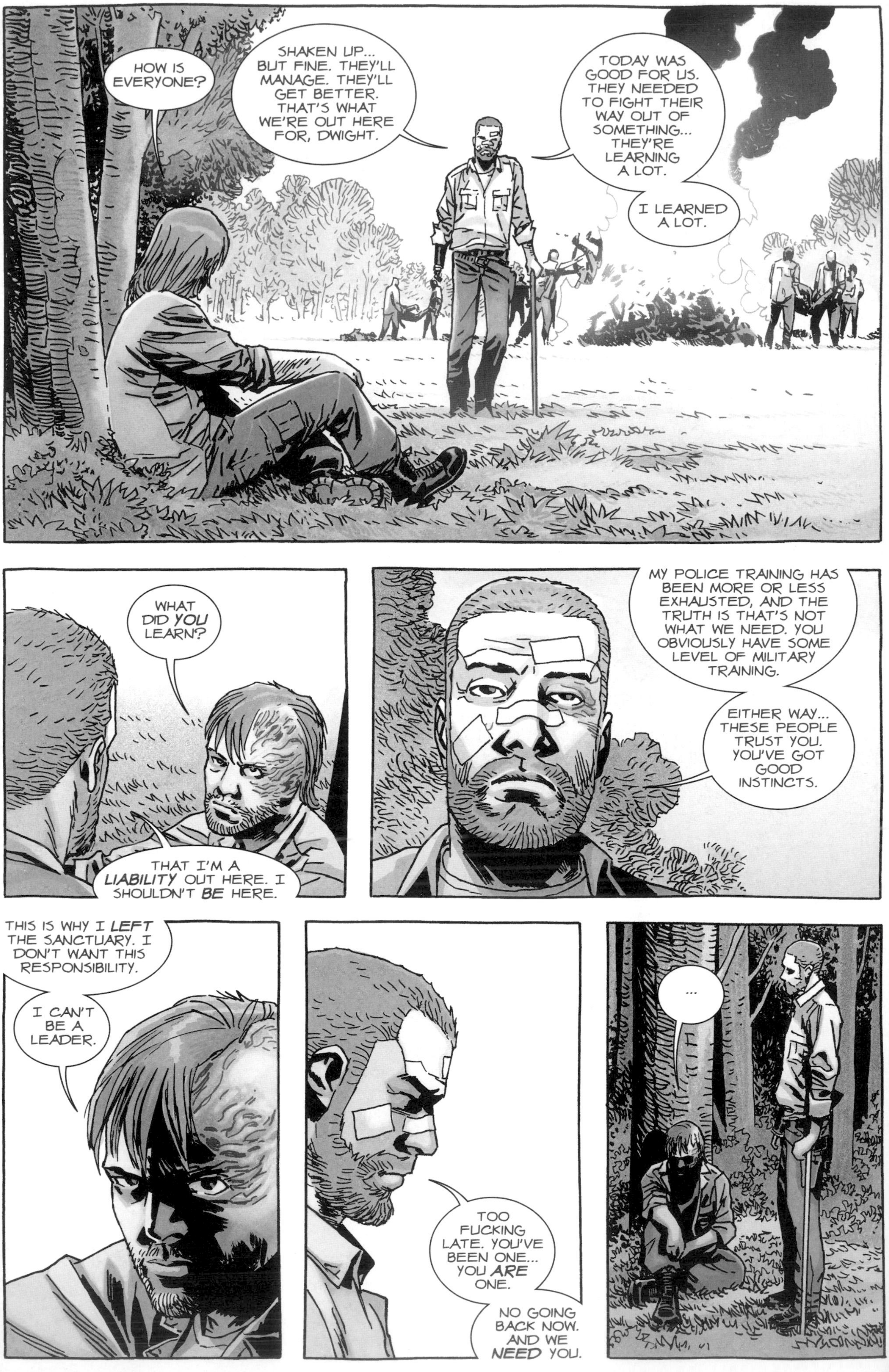
HOW IS EVERYONE?
SHAKEN UP... BUT FINE. THEY'LL MANAGE. THEY'LL GET BETTER. THAT'S WHAT WE'RE OUT HERE FOR, DWIGHT.
TODAY WAS GOOD FOR US. THEY NEEDED TO FIGHT THEIR WAY OUT OF SOMETHING... THEY'RE LEARNING A LOT.
I LEARNED A LOT.
WHAT DID YOU LEARN?
THAT I'M A LIABILITY OUT HERE. I SHOULDN'T BE HERE.
MY POLICE TRAINING HAS BEEN MORE OR LESS EXHAUSTED, AND THE TRUTH IS THAT'S NOT WHAT WE NEED. YOU OBVIOUSLY HAVE SOME LEVEL OF MILITARY TRAINING.
EITHER WAY... THESE PEOPLE TRUST YOU. YOU'VE GOT GOOD INSTINCTS.
THIS IS WHY I LEFT THE SANCTUARY. I DON'T WANT THIS RESPONSIBILITY.
I CAN'T BE A LEADER.
TOO FUCKING LATE. YOU'VE BEEN ONE... YOU ARE ONE.
NO GOING BACK NOW. AND WE NEED YOU.
...

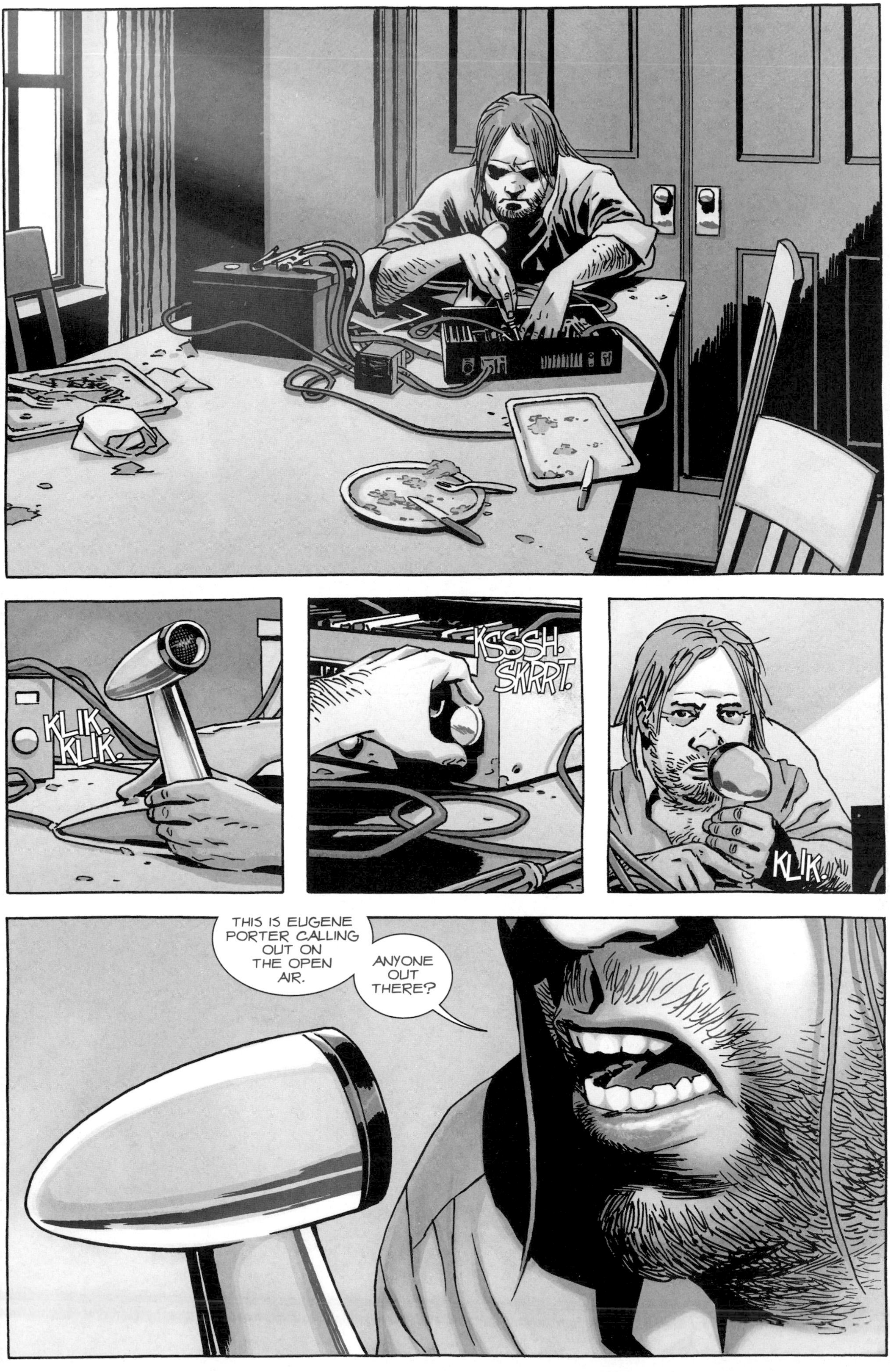
KLIK. KLIK.
KSSSH. SKRRT.
KLIK.
THIS IS EUGENE PORTER CALLING OUT ON THE OPEN AIR.
ANYONE OUT THERE?

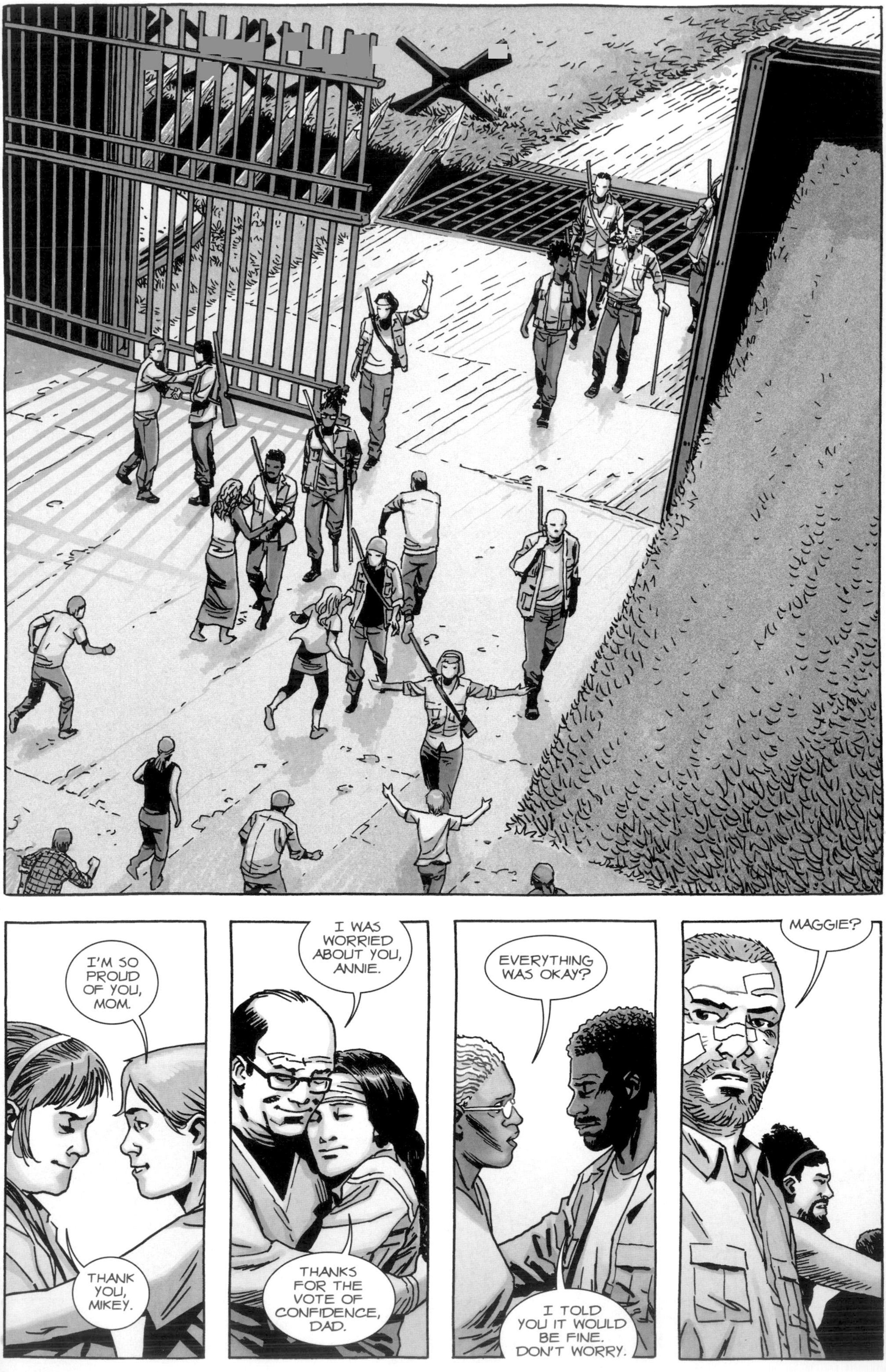
I'M SO PROUD OF YOU, MOM.
THANK YOU, MIKEY.
I WAS WORRIED ABOUT YOU, ANNIE.
THANKS FOR THE VOTE OF CONFIDENCE, DAD.
EVERYTHING WAS OKAY?
I TOLD YOU IT WOULD BE FINE. DON'T WORRY.
MAGGIE?

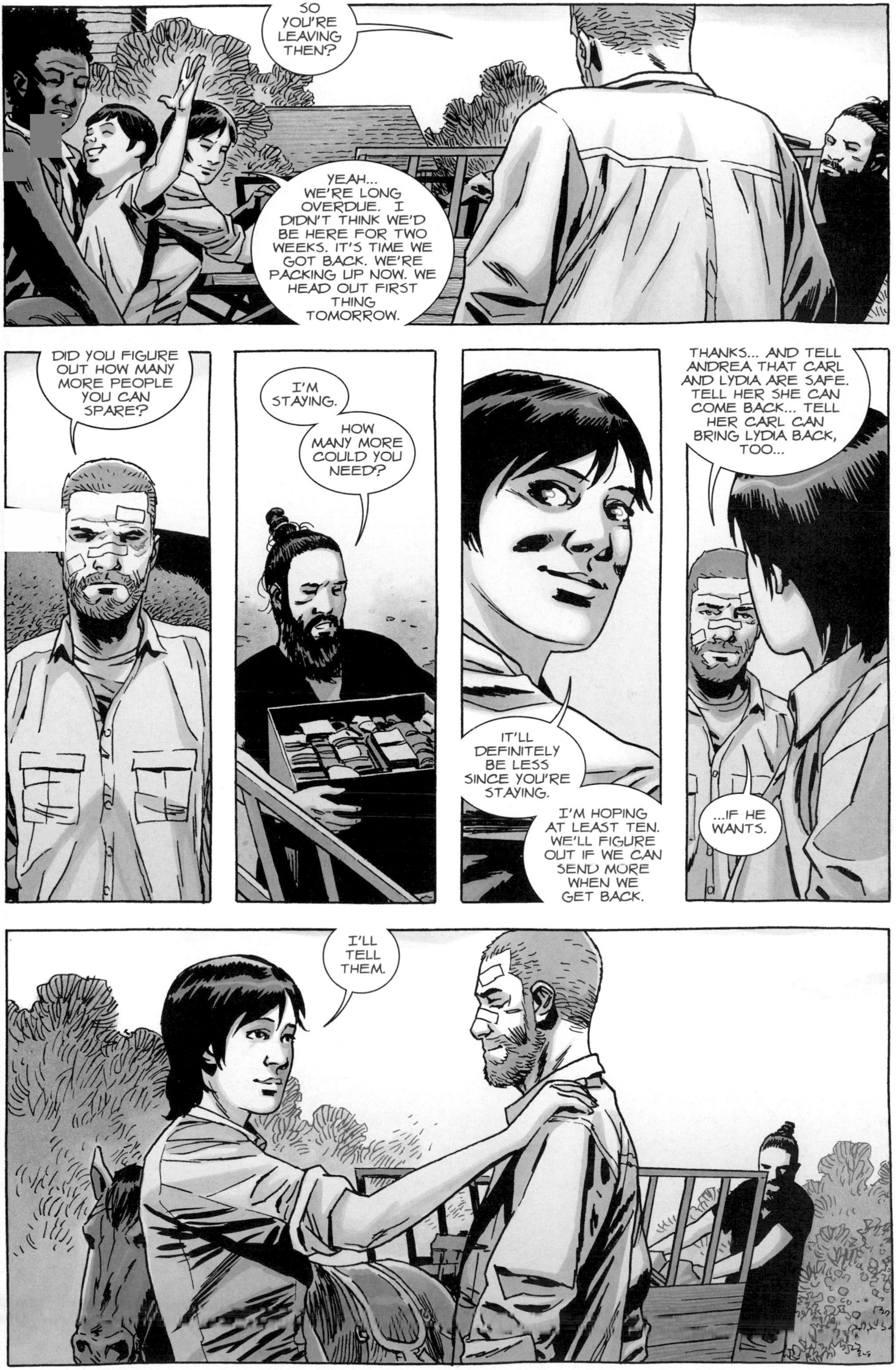
SO YOU'RE LEAVING THEN?
YEAH... WE'RE LONG OVERDUE. I DIDN'T THINK WE'D BE HERE FOR TWO WEEKS. IT'S TIME WE GOT BACK. WE'RE PACKING UP NOW. WE HEAD OUT FIRST THING TOMORROW.
DID YOU FIGURE OUT HOW MANY MORE PEOPLE YOU CAN SPARE?
I'M STAYING.
HOW MANY MORE COULD YOU NEED?
IT'LL DEFINITELY BE LESS SINCE YOU'RE STAYING.
I'M HOPING AT LEAST TEN. WE'LL FIGURE OUT IF WE CAN SEND MORE WHEN WE GET BACK.
THANKS... AND TELL ANDREA THAT CARL AND LYDIA ARE SAFE. TELL HER SHE CAN COME BACK... TELL HER CARL CAN BRING LYDIA BACK, TOO...
...IF HE WANTS.
I'LL TELL THEM.

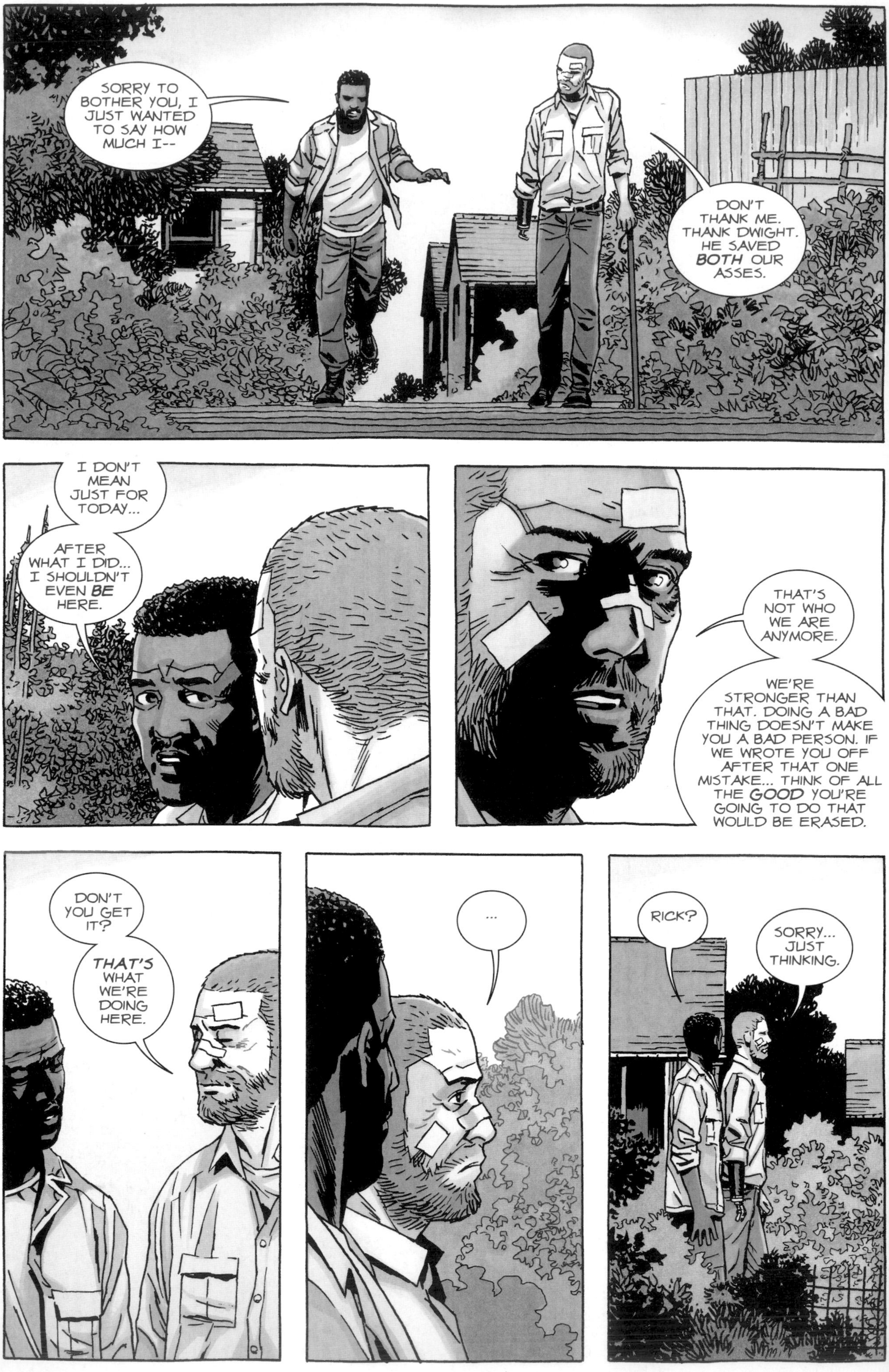
SORRY TO BOTHER YOU, I JUST WANTED TO SAY HOW MUCH I--
DON'T THANK ME. THANK DWIGHT. HE SAVED BOTH OUR ASSES.
I DON'T MEAN JUST FOR TODAY...
AFTER WHAT I DID... I SHOULDN'T EVEN BE HERE.
THAT'S NOT WHO WE ARE ANYMORE.
WE'RE STRONGER THAN THAT. DOING A BAD THING DOESN'T MAKE YOU A BAD PERSON. IF WE WROTE YOU OFF AFTER THAT ONE MISTAKE... THINK OF ALL THE GOOD YOU'RE GOING TO DO THAT WOULD BE ERASED.
DON'T YOU GET IT?
THAT'S WHAT WE'RE DOING HERE.
...
RICK?
SORRY... JUST THINKING.

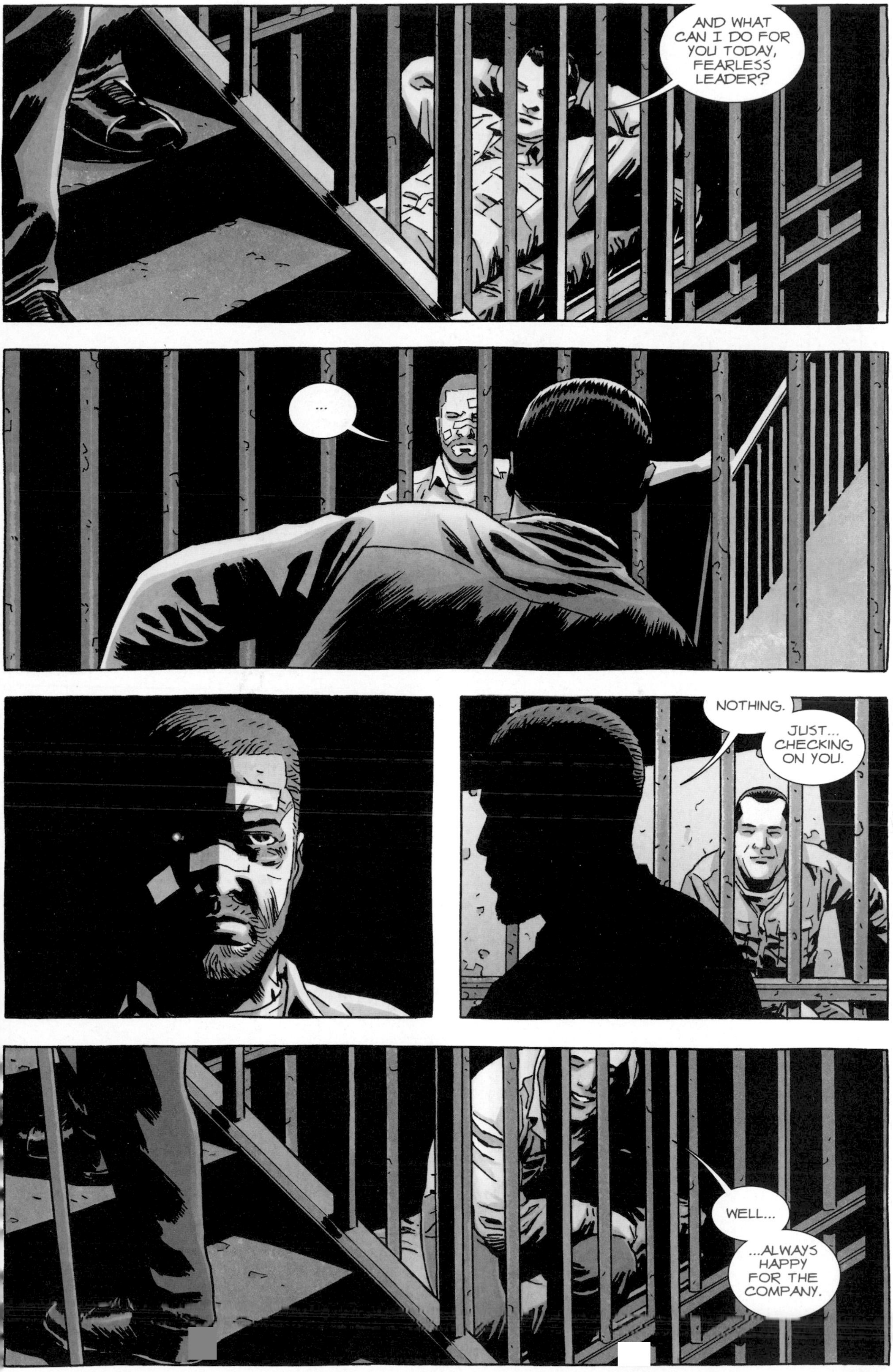
AND WHAT CAN I DO FOR YOU TODAY, FEARLESS LEADER?
...
NOTHING.
JUST... CHECKING ON YOU.
WELL...
...ALWAYS HAPPY FOR THE COMPANY.

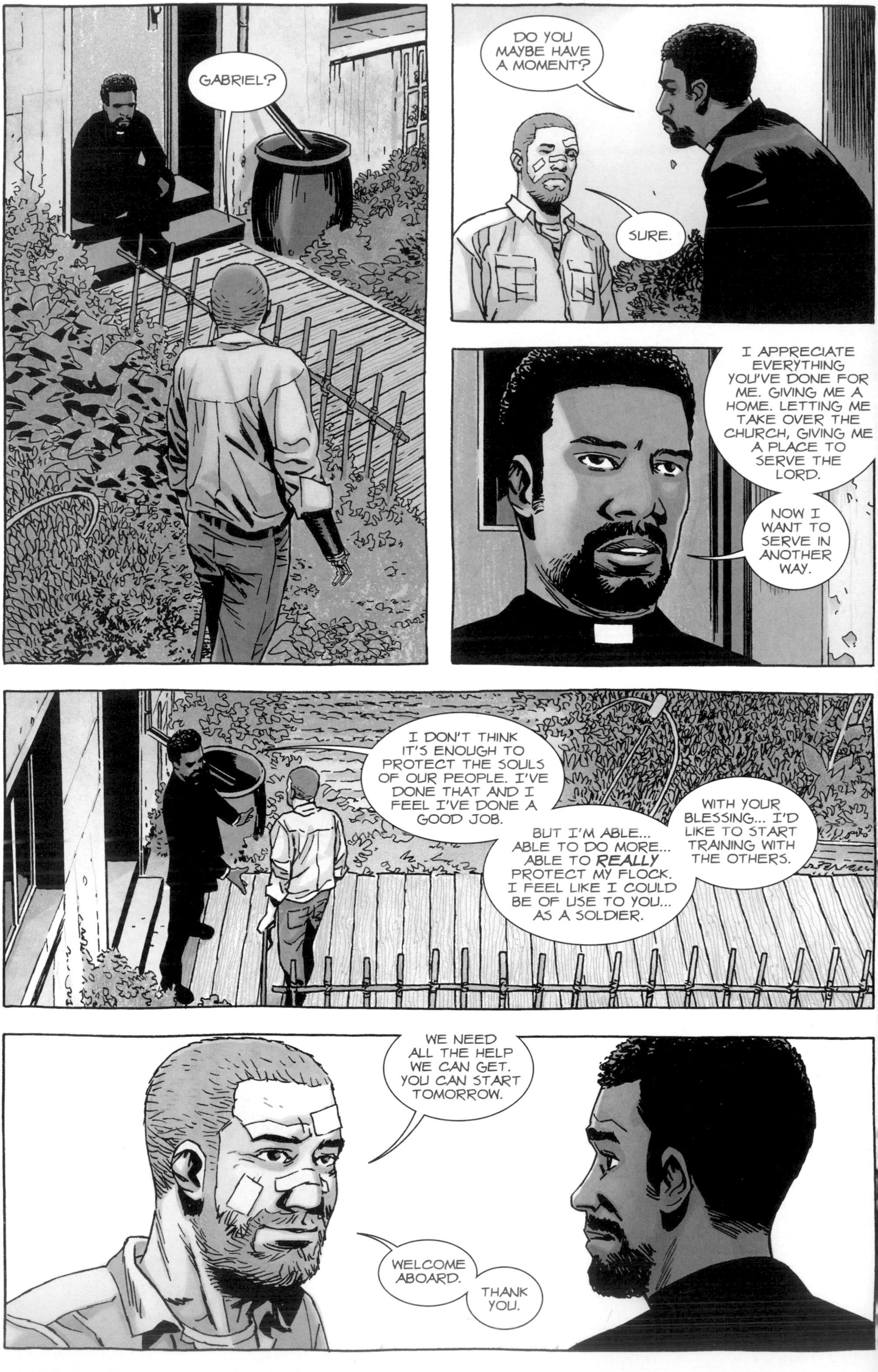
GABRIEL?
DO YOU MAYBE HAVE A MOMENT?
SURE.
I APPRECIATE EVERYTHING YOU'VE DONE FOR ME. GIVING ME A HOME. LETTING ME TAKE OVER THE CHURCH, GIVING ME A PLACE TO SERVE THE LORD.
NOW I WANT TO SERVE IN ANOTHER WAY.
I DON'T THINK IT'S ENOUGH TO PROTECT THE SOULS OF OUR PEOPLE. I'VE DONE THAT AND I FEEL I'VE DONE A GOOD JOB.
BUT I'M ABLE... ABLE TO DO MORE... ABLE TO *REALLY* PROTECT MY FLOCK. I FEEL LIKE I COULD BE OF USE TO YOU... AS A SOLDIER.
WITH YOUR BLESSING... I'D LIKE TO START TRAINING WITH THE OTHERS.
WE NEED ALL THE HELP WE CAN GET. YOU CAN START TOMORROW.
WELCOME ABOARD.
THANK YOU.

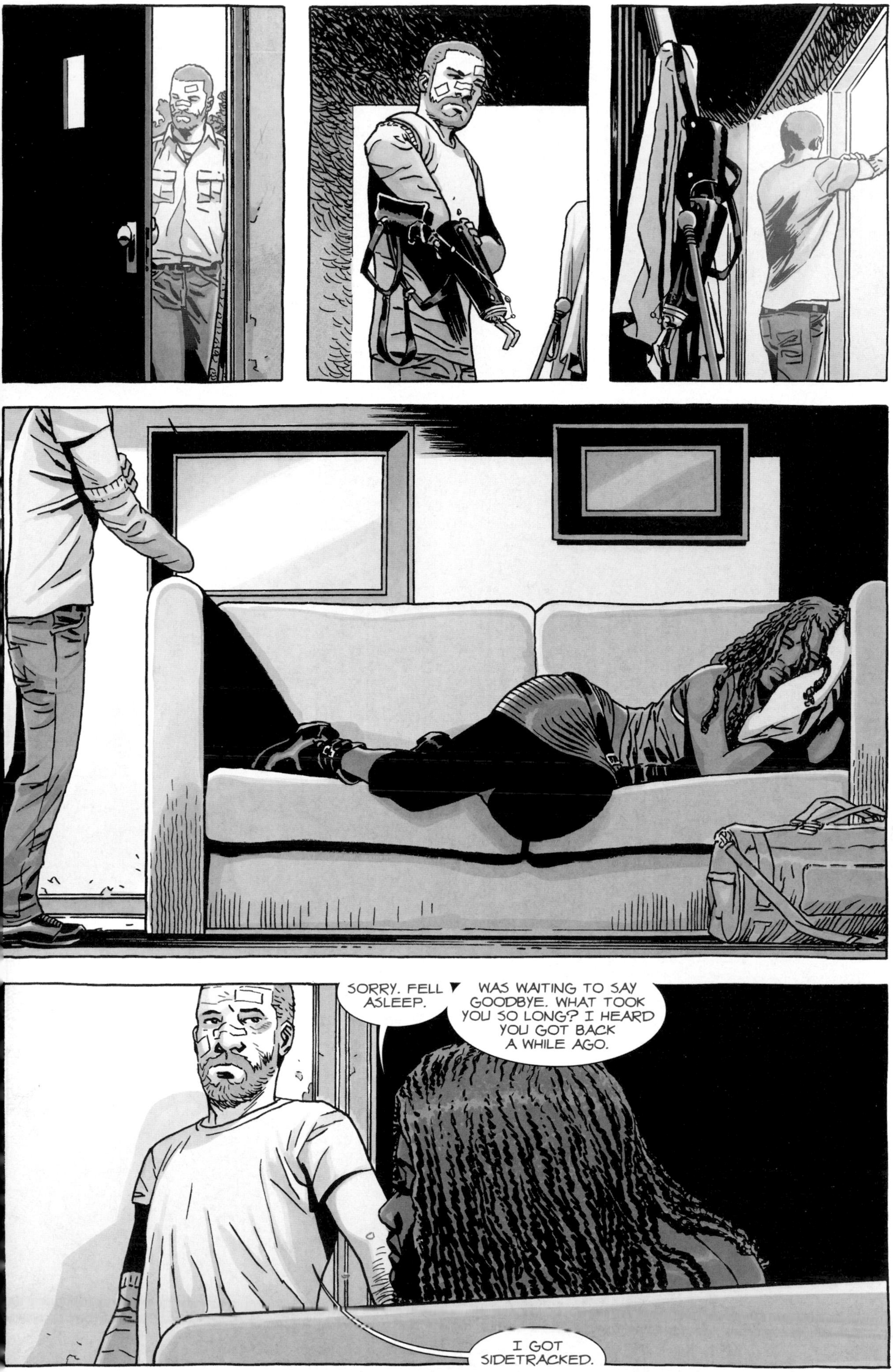
SORRY. FELL ASLEEP.
WAS WAITING TO SAY GOODBYE. WHAT TOOK YOU SO LONG? I HEARD YOU GOT BACK A WHILE AGO.
I GOT SIDETRACKED.

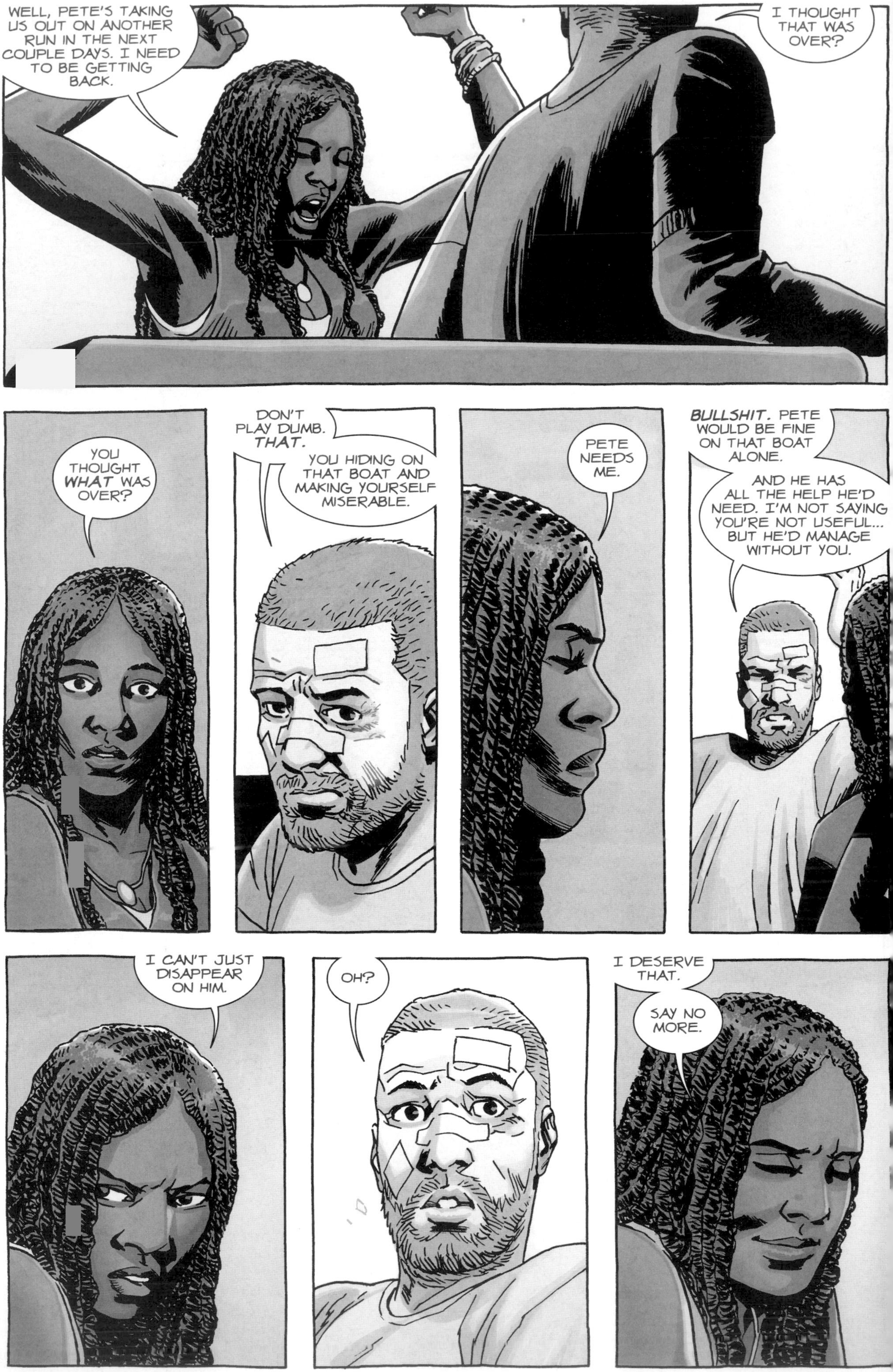
WELL, PETE'S TAKING US OUT ON ANOTHER RUN IN THE NEXT COUPLE DAYS. I NEED TO BE GETTING BACK.
I THOUGHT THAT WAS OVER?
YOU THOUGHT WHAT WAS OVER?
DON'T PLAY DUMB. THAT.
YOU HIDING ON THAT BOAT AND MAKING YOURSELF MISERABLE.
PETE NEEDS ME.
BULLSHIT. PETE WOULD BE FINE ON THAT BOAT ALONE.
AND HE HAS ALL THE HELP HE'D NEED. I'M NOT SAYING YOU'RE NOT USEFUL... BUT HE'D MANAGE WITHOUT YOU.
I CAN'T JUST DISAPPEAR ON HIM.
OH?
I DESERVE THAT.
SAY NO MORE.

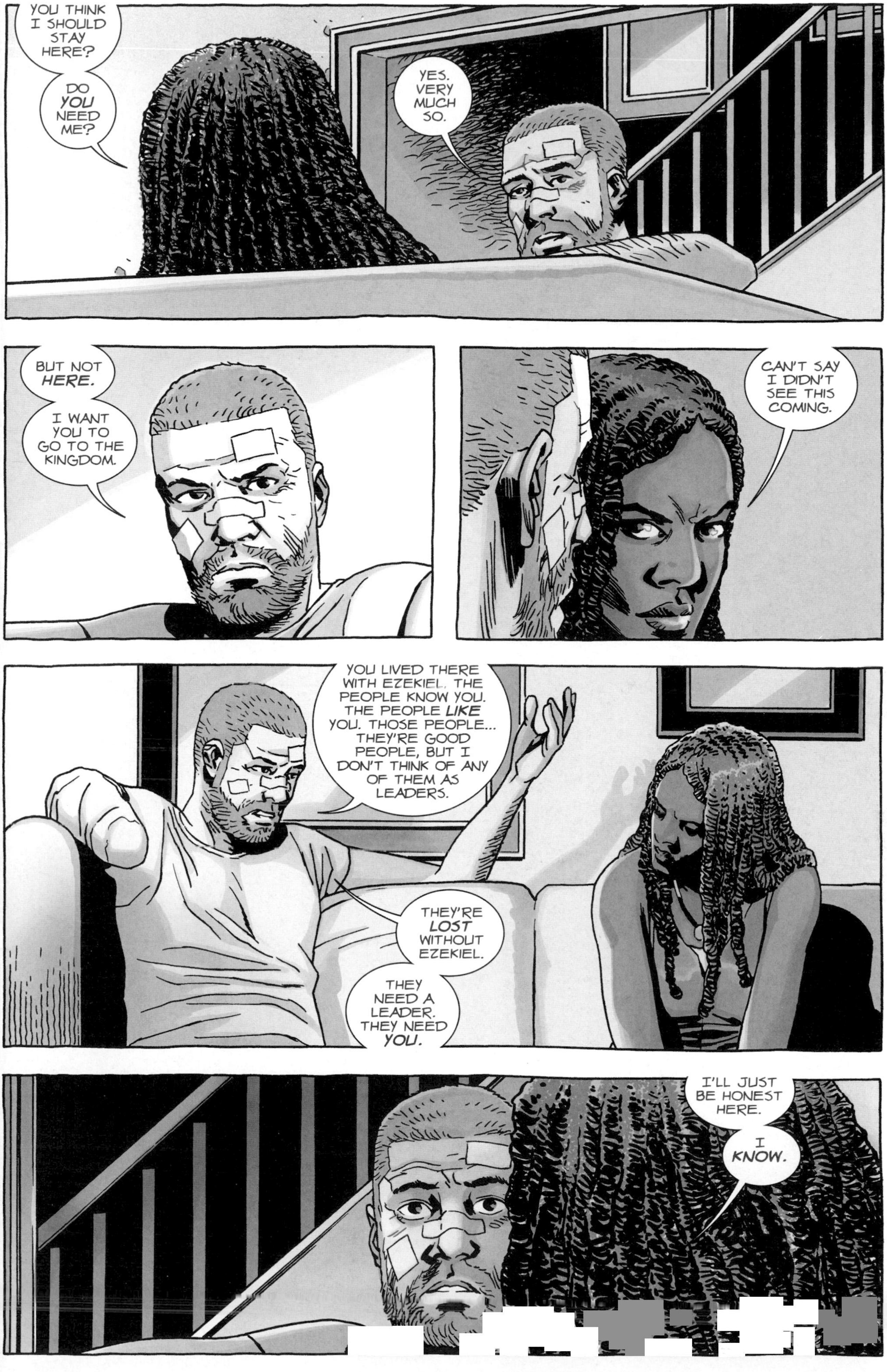
YOU THINK I SHOULD STAY HERE?
DO YOU NEED ME?
YES. VERY MUCH SO.
BUT NOT HERE.
I WANT YOU TO GO TO THE KINGDOM.
CAN'T SAY I DIDN'T SEE THIS COMING.
YOU LIVED THERE WITH EZEKIEL. THE PEOPLE KNOW YOU. THE PEOPLE LIKE YOU. THOSE PEOPLE... THEY'RE GOOD PEOPLE, BUT I DON'T THINK OF ANY OF THEM AS LEADERS.
THEY'RE LOST WITHOUT EZEKIEL.
THEY NEED A LEADER. THEY NEED YOU.
I'LL JUST BE HONEST HERE.
I KNOW.

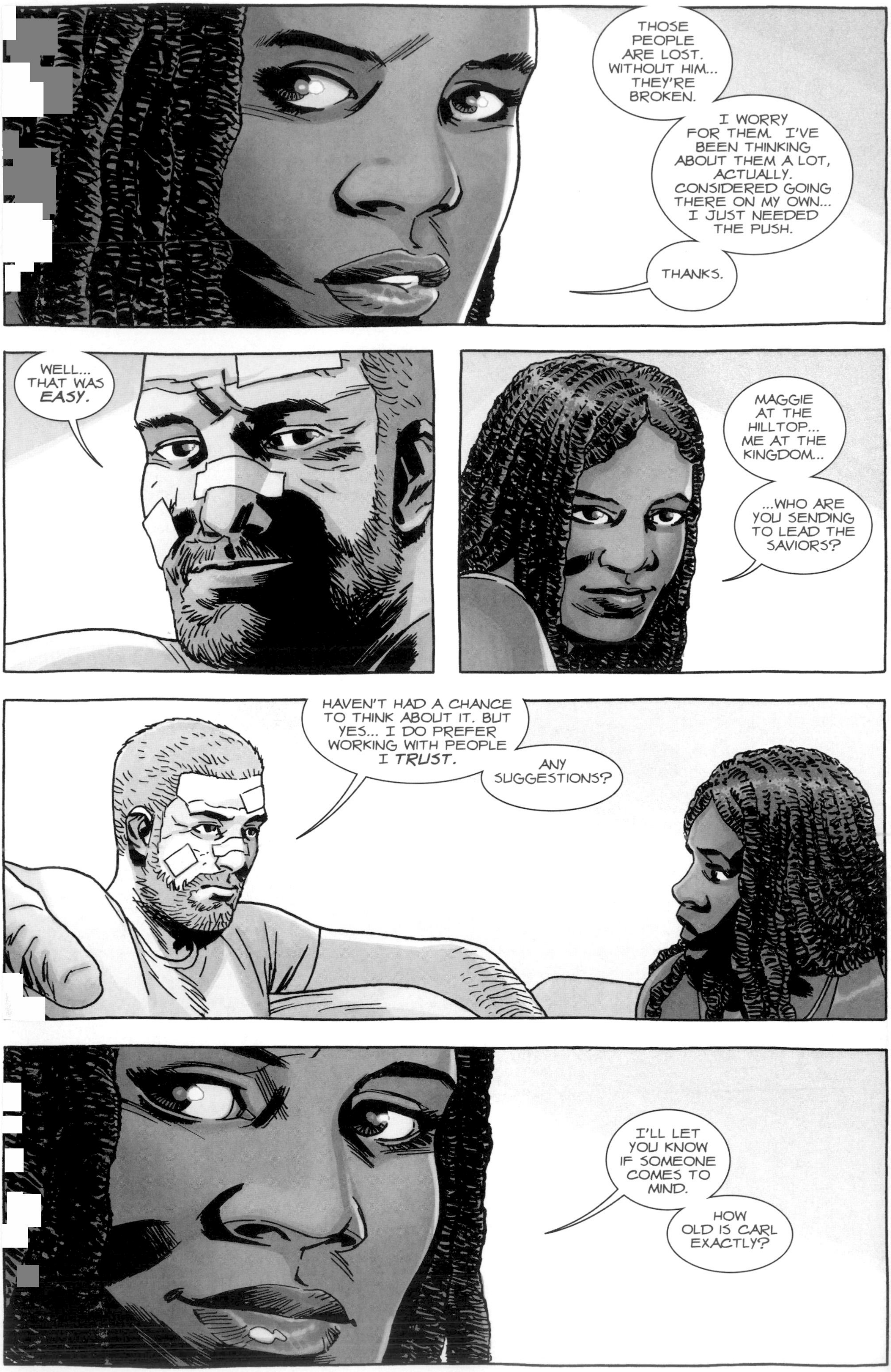
THOSE PEOPLE ARE LOST. WITHOUT HIM... THEY'RE BROKEN.
I WORRY FOR THEM. I'VE BEEN THINKING ABOUT THEM A LOT, ACTUALLY. CONSIDERED GOING THERE ON MY OWN... I JUST NEEDED THE PUSH.
THANKS.
WELL... THAT WAS *EASY.*
MAGGIE AT THE HILLTOP... ME AT THE KINGDOM...
...WHO ARE YOU SENDING TO LEAD THE SAVIORS?
HAVEN'T HAD A CHANCE TO THINK ABOUT IT. BUT YES... I DO PREFER WORKING WITH PEOPLE I *TRUST.*
ANY SUGGESTIONS?
I'LL LET YOU KNOW IF SOMEONE COMES TO MIND.
HOW OLD IS CARL EXACTLY?

THIS IS EUGENE PORTER CALLING OUT LIVE ON THE OPEN AIR.

IS ANYONE OUT THERE?

KLIK.

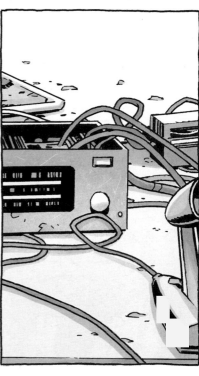

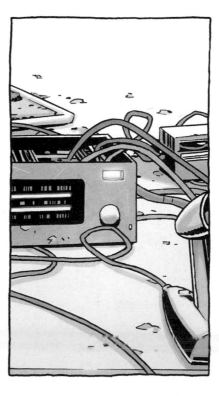

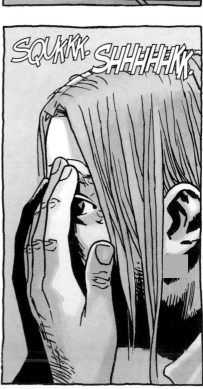

SQUKK. SHHHHHK.

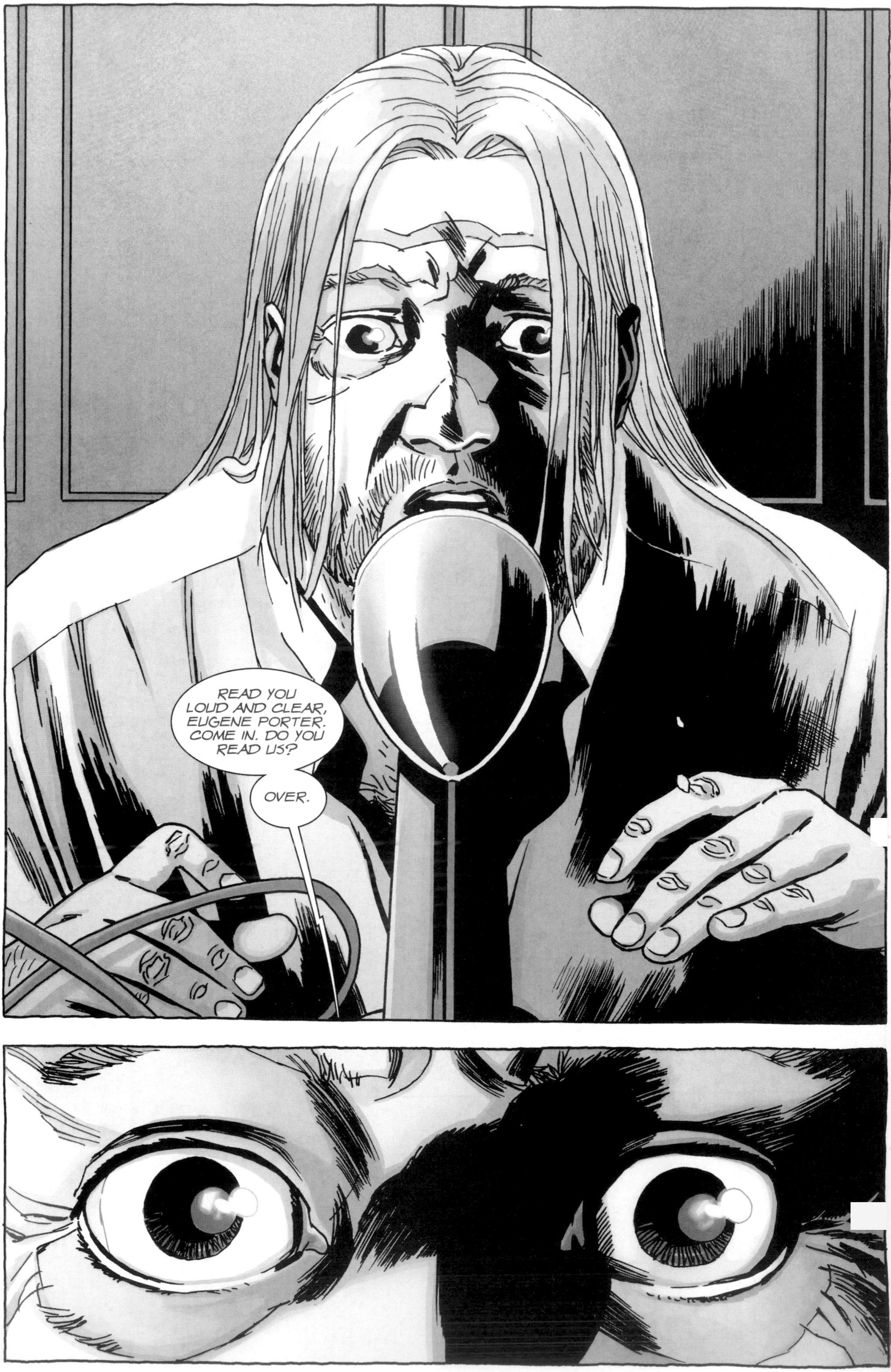
READ YOU LOUD AND CLEAR, EUGENE PORTER. COME IN. DO YOU READ US?
OVER.

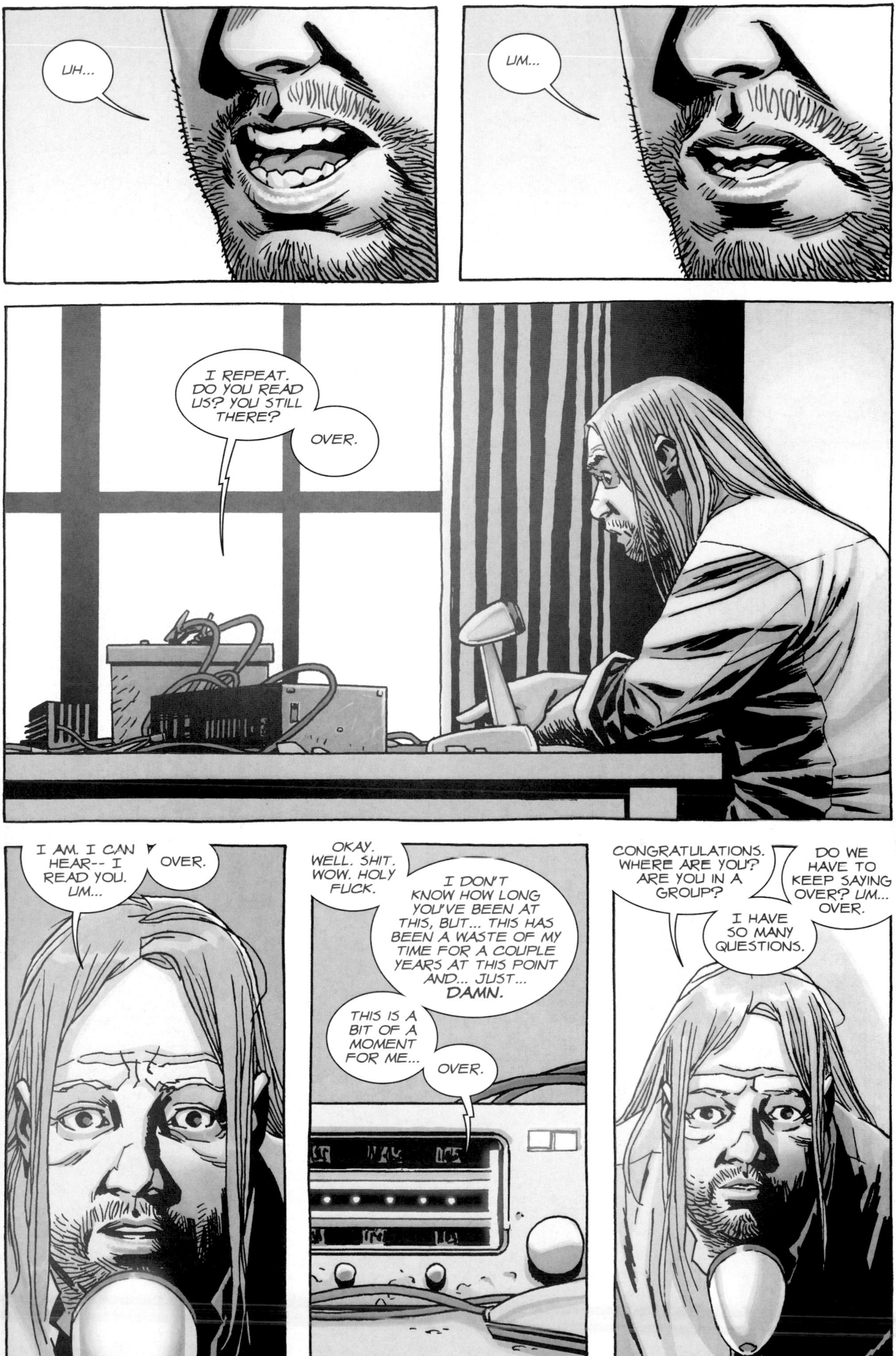
UH...
UM...
I REPEAT. DO YOU READ US? YOU STILL THERE?
OVER.
I AM. I CAN HEAR-- I READ YOU. UM...
OVER.
OKAY. WELL. SHIT. WOW. HOLY FUCK.
I DON'T KNOW HOW LONG YOU'VE BEEN AT THIS, BUT... THIS HAS BEEN A WASTE OF MY TIME FOR A COUPLE YEARS AT THIS POINT AND... JUST... DAMN.
THIS IS A BIT OF A MOMENT FOR ME...
OVER.
CONGRATULATIONS. WHERE ARE YOU? ARE YOU IN A GROUP?
I HAVE SO MANY QUESTIONS.
DO WE HAVE TO KEEP SAYING OVER? UM... OVER.

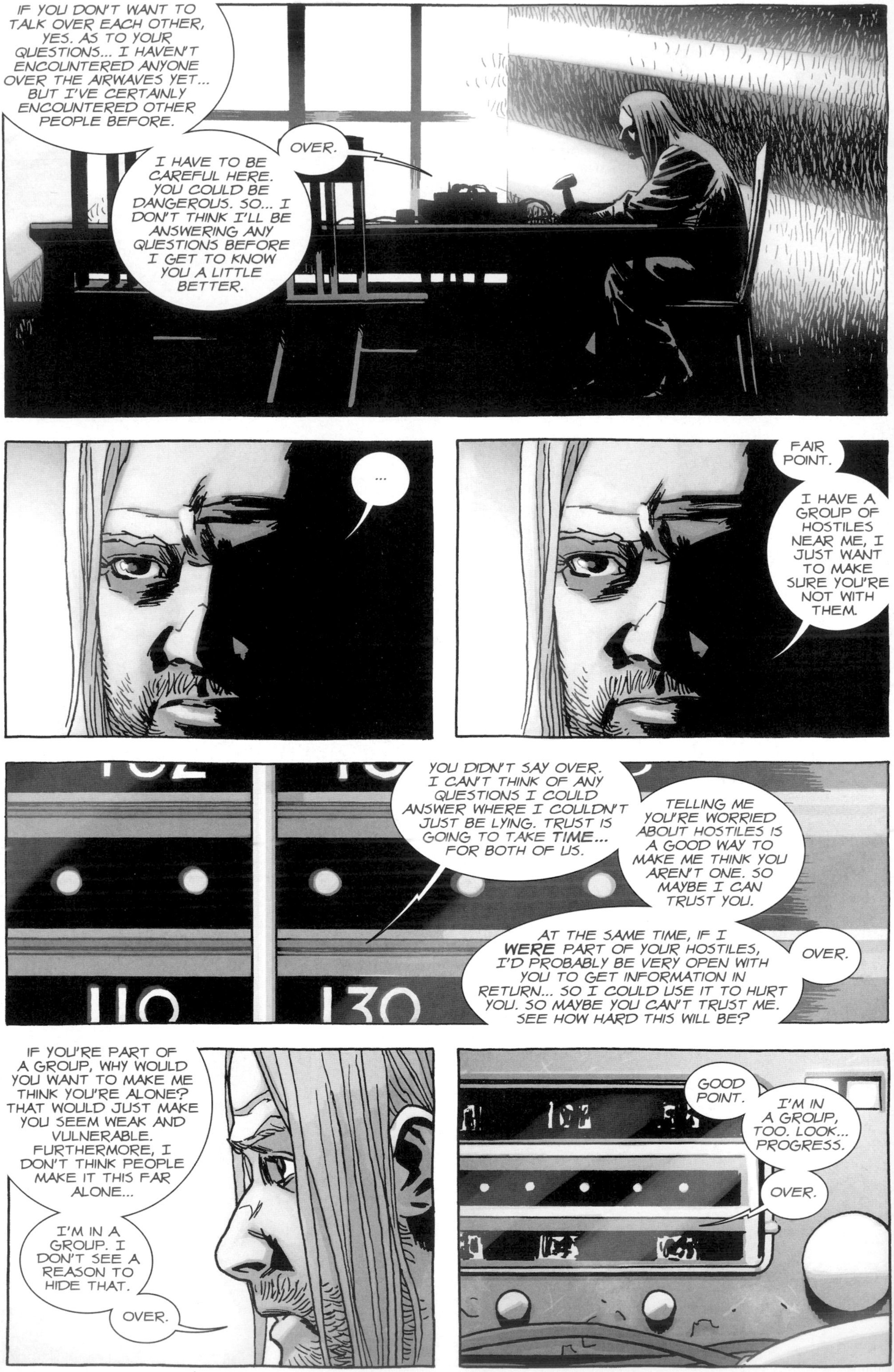
IF YOU DON'T WANT TO TALK OVER EACH OTHER, YES. AS TO YOUR QUESTIONS... I HAVEN'T ENCOUNTERED ANYONE OVER THE AIRWAVES YET... BUT I'VE CERTAINLY ENCOUNTERED OTHER PEOPLE BEFORE.
OVER.
I HAVE TO BE CAREFUL HERE. YOU COULD BE DANGEROUS. SO... I DON'T THINK I'LL BE ANSWERING ANY QUESTIONS BEFORE I GET TO KNOW YOU A LITTLE BETTER.
...
FAIR POINT.
I HAVE A GROUP OF HOSTILES NEAR ME, I JUST WANT TO MAKE SURE YOU'RE NOT WITH THEM.
110
130
YOU DIDN'T SAY OVER. I CAN'T THINK OF ANY QUESTIONS I COULD ANSWER WHERE I COULDN'T JUST BE LYING. TRUST IS GOING TO TAKE TIME... FOR BOTH OF US.
TELLING ME YOU'RE WORRIED ABOUT HOSTILES IS A GOOD WAY TO MAKE ME THINK YOU AREN'T ONE. SO MAYBE I CAN TRUST YOU.
AT THE SAME TIME, IF I WERE PART OF YOUR HOSTILES, I'D PROBABLY BE VERY OPEN WITH YOU TO GET INFORMATION IN RETURN... SO I COULD USE IT TO HURT YOU. SO MAYBE YOU CAN'T TRUST ME. SEE HOW HARD THIS WILL BE?
OVER.
IF YOU'RE PART OF A GROUP, WHY WOULD YOU WANT TO MAKE ME THINK YOU'RE ALONE? THAT WOULD JUST MAKE YOU SEEM WEAK AND VULNERABLE. FURTHERMORE, I DON'T THINK PEOPLE MAKE IT THIS FAR ALONE...
I'M IN A GROUP. I DON'T SEE A REASON TO HIDE THAT.
OVER.
GOOD POINT.
I'M IN A GROUP, TOO. LOOK... PROGRESS.
OVER.

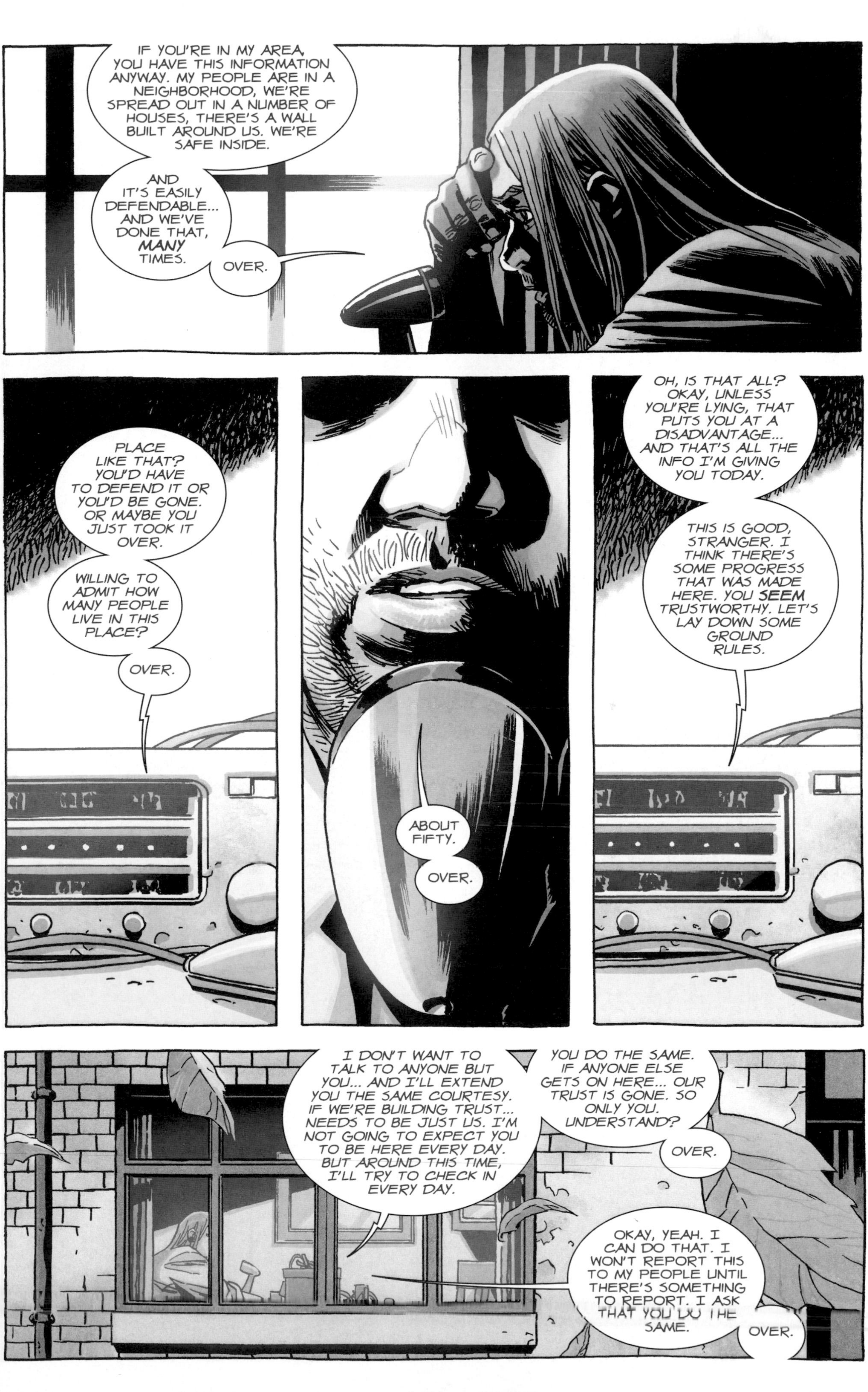
IF YOU'RE IN MY AREA, YOU HAVE THIS INFORMATION ANYWAY. MY PEOPLE ARE IN A NEIGHBORHOOD, WE'RE SPREAD OUT IN A NUMBER OF HOUSES, THERE'S A WALL BUILT AROUND US. WE'RE SAFE INSIDE.
AND IT'S EASILY DEFENDABLE... AND WE'VE DONE THAT, MANY TIMES.
OVER.
PLACE LIKE THAT? YOU'D HAVE TO DEFEND IT OR YOU'D BE GONE. OR MAYBE YOU JUST TOOK IT OVER.
WILLING TO ADMIT HOW MANY PEOPLE LIVE IN THIS PLACE?
OVER.
ABOUT FIFTY.
OVER.
OH, IS THAT ALL? OKAY, UNLESS YOU'RE LYING, THAT PUTS YOU AT A DISADVANTAGE... AND THAT'S ALL THE INFO I'M GIVING YOU TODAY.
THIS IS GOOD, STRANGER. I THINK THERE'S SOME PROGRESS THAT WAS MADE HERE. YOU SEEM TRUSTWORTHY. LET'S LAY DOWN SOME GROUND RULES.
I DON'T WANT TO TALK TO ANYONE BUT YOU... AND I'LL EXTEND YOU THE SAME COURTESY. IF WE'RE BUILDING TRUST... NEEDS TO BE JUST US. I'M NOT GOING TO EXPECT YOU TO BE HERE EVERY DAY. BUT AROUND THIS TIME, I'LL TRY TO CHECK IN EVERY DAY.
YOU DO THE SAME. IF ANYONE ELSE GETS ON HERE... OUR TRUST IS GONE. SO ONLY YOU. UNDERSTAND?
OVER.
OKAY, YEAH. I CAN DO THAT. I WON'T REPORT THIS TO MY PEOPLE UNTIL THERE'S SOMETHING TO REPORT. I ASK THAT YOU DO THE SAME.
OVER.

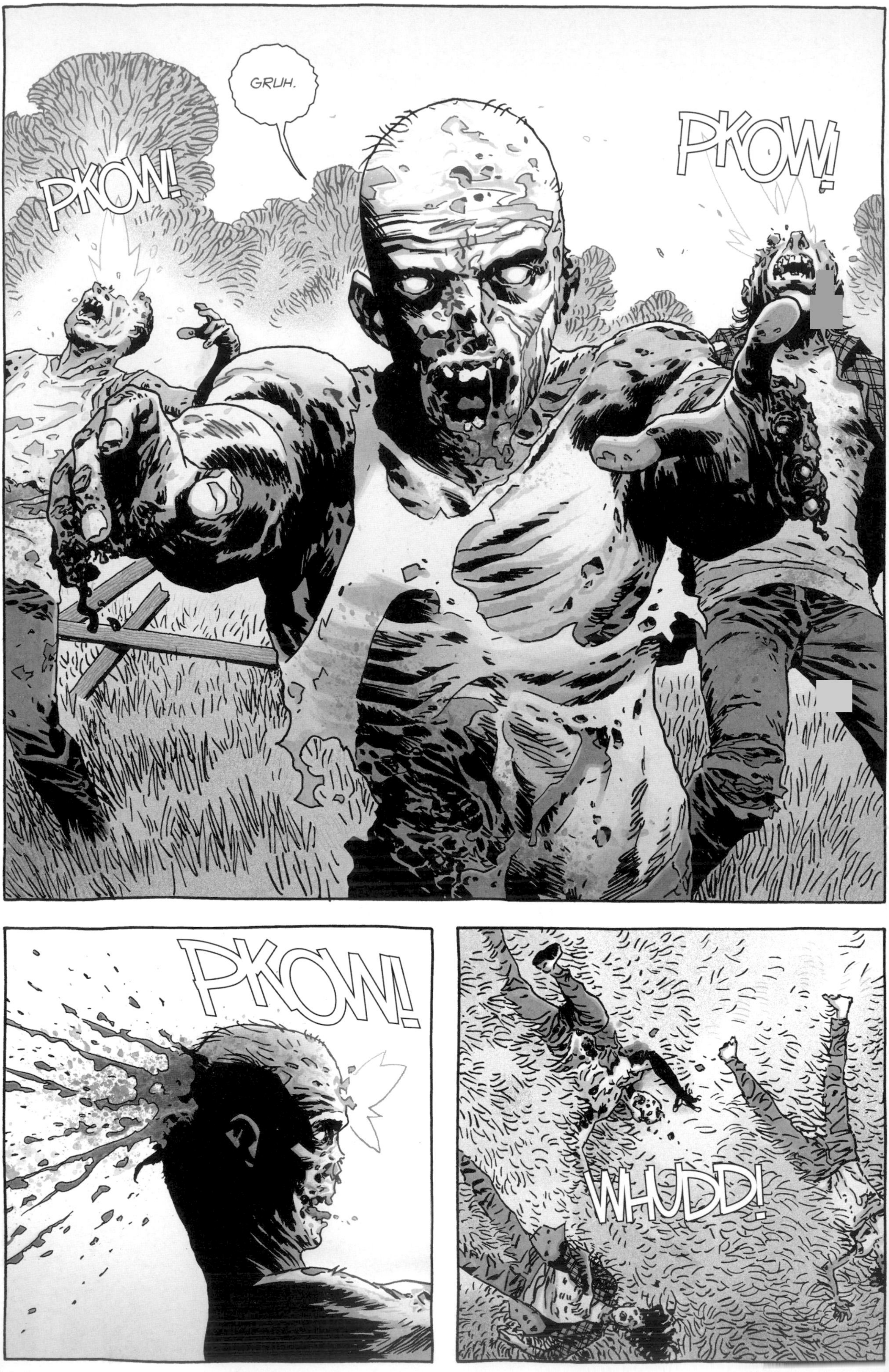
PKOW!
GRUH.
PKOW!
PKOW!
WHUDD!

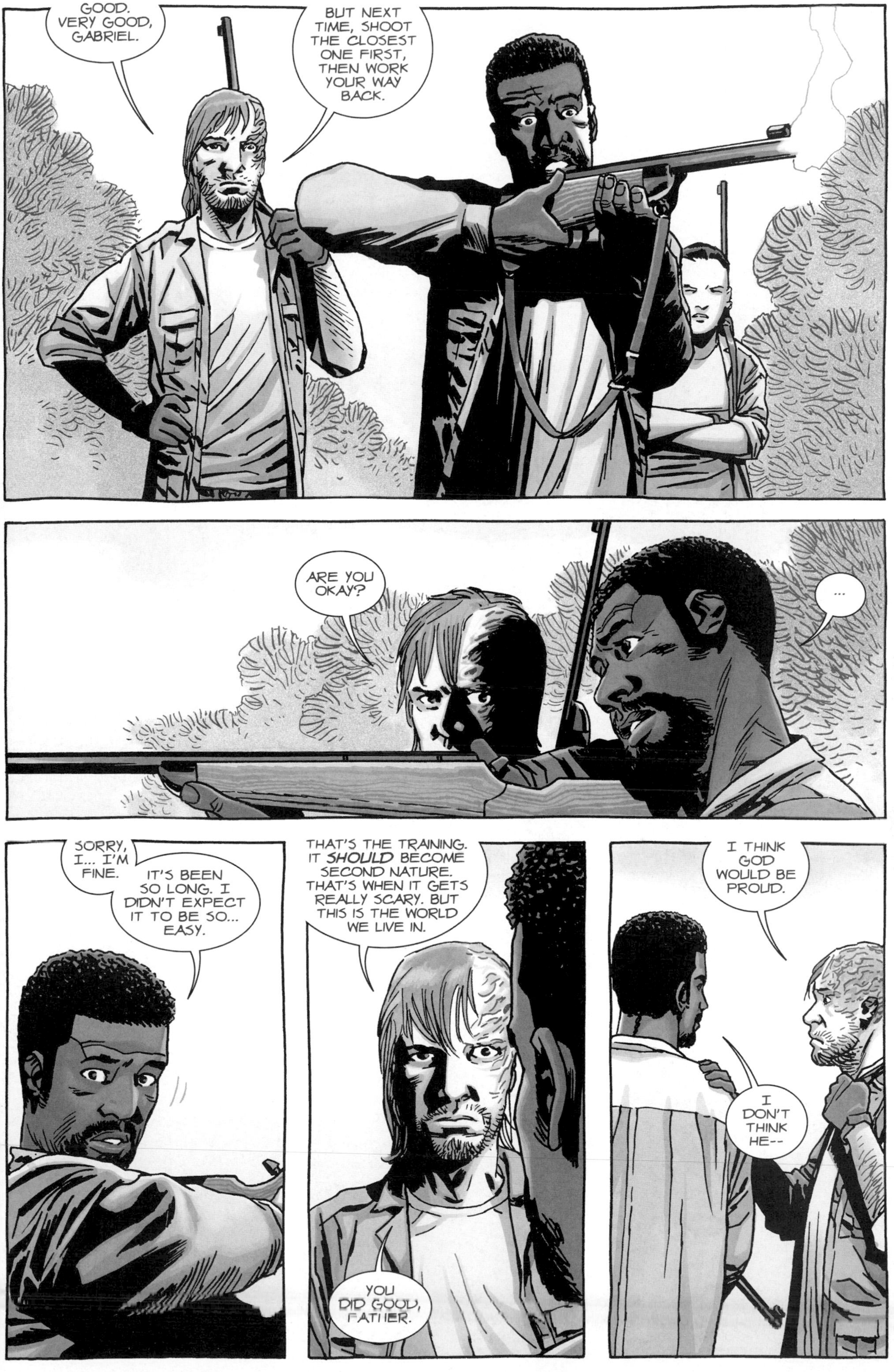
GOOD. VERY GOOD, GABRIEL.
BUT NEXT TIME, SHOOT THE CLOSEST ONE FIRST, THEN WORK YOUR WAY BACK.
ARE YOU OKAY?
...
SORRY, I... I'M FINE.
IT'S BEEN SO LONG. I DIDN'T EXPECT IT TO BE SO... EASY.
THAT'S THE TRAINING. IT *SHOULD* BECOME SECOND NATURE. THAT'S WHEN IT GETS REALLY SCARY. BUT THIS IS THE WORLD WE LIVE IN.
YOU DID GOOD, FATHER.
I THINK GOD WOULD BE PROUD.
I DON'T THINK HE--

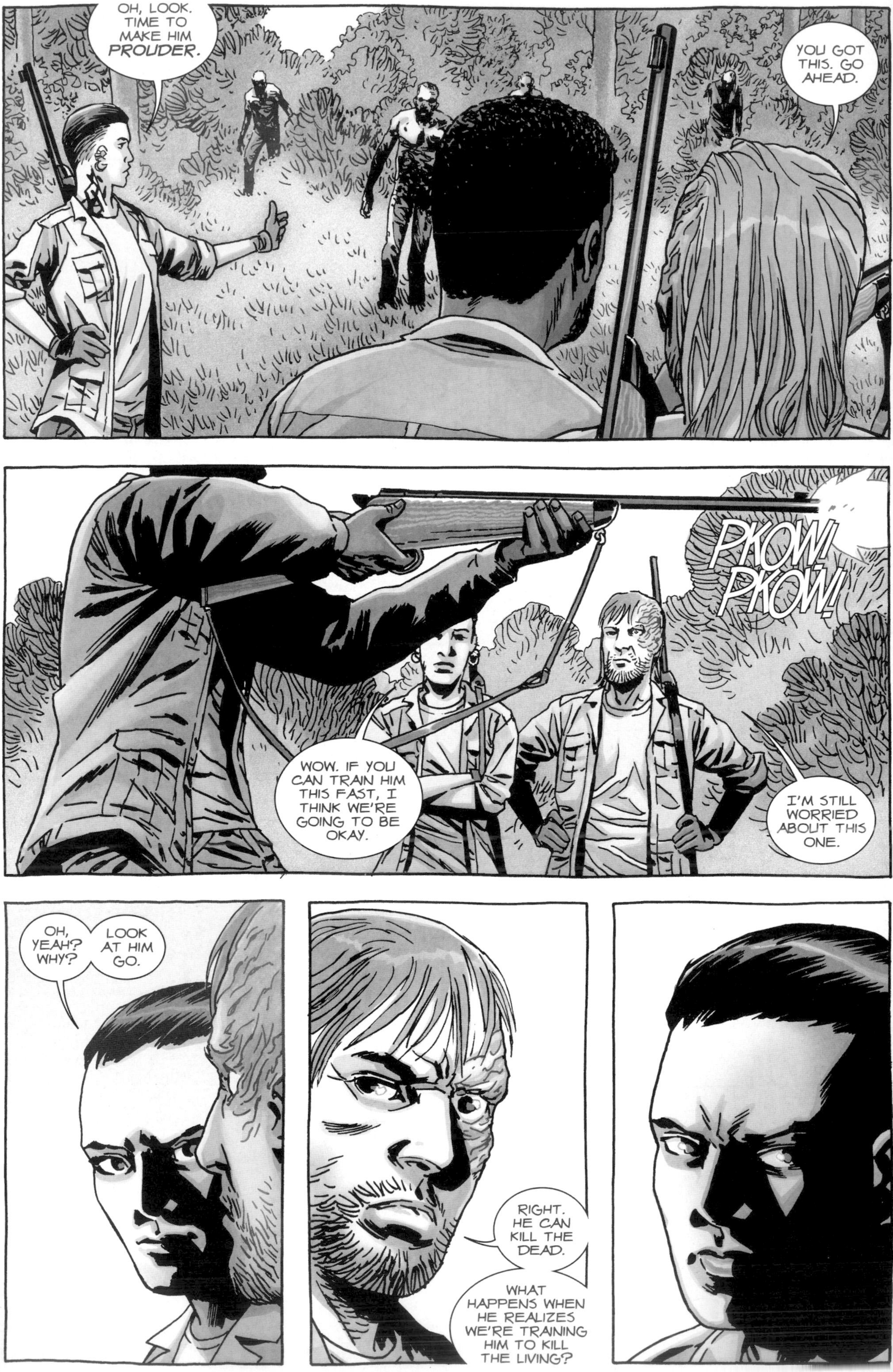

OH, LOOK. TIME TO MAKE HIM PROUDER.
YOU GOT THIS. GO AHEAD.
PKOW! PKOW!
WOW. IF YOU CAN TRAIN HIM THIS FAST, I THINK WE'RE GOING TO BE OKAY.
I'M STILL WORRIED ABOUT THIS ONE.
OH, YEAH? WHY?
LOOK AT HIM GO.
RIGHT. HE CAN KILL THE DEAD.
WHAT HAPPENS WHEN HE REALIZES WE'RE TRAINING HIM TO KILL THE LIVING?

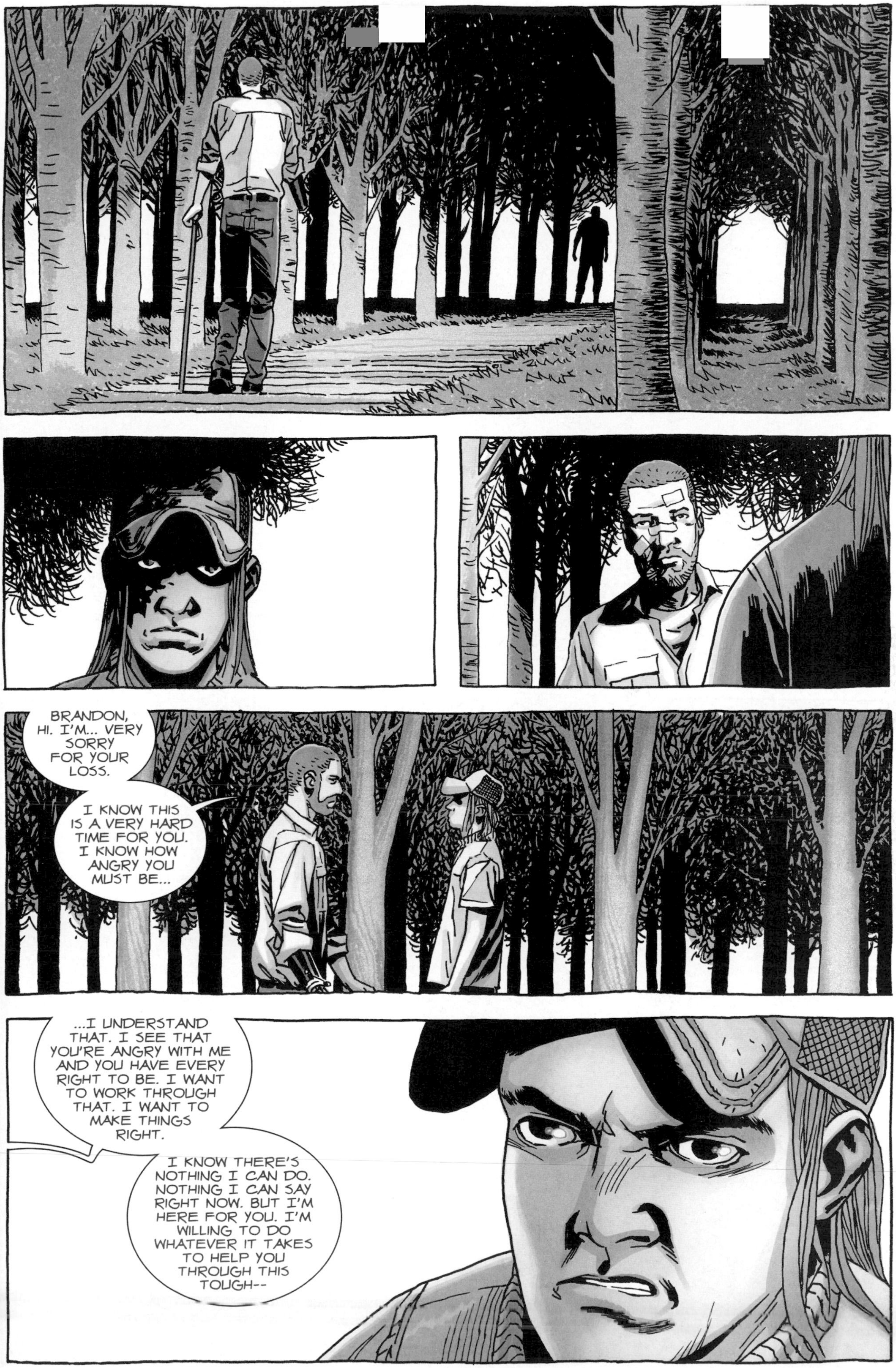

BRANDON, HI. I'M... VERY SORRY FOR YOUR LOSS.
I KNOW THIS IS A VERY HARD TIME FOR YOU. I KNOW HOW ANGRY YOU MUST BE...
...I UNDERSTAND THAT. I SEE THAT YOU'RE ANGRY WITH ME AND YOU HAVE EVERY RIGHT TO BE. I WANT TO WORK THROUGH THAT. I WANT TO MAKE THINGS RIGHT.
I KNOW THERE'S NOTHING I CAN DO. NOTHING I CAN SAY RIGHT NOW. BUT I'M HERE FOR YOU. I'M WILLING TO DO WHATEVER IT TAKES TO HELP YOU THROUGH THIS TOUGH--

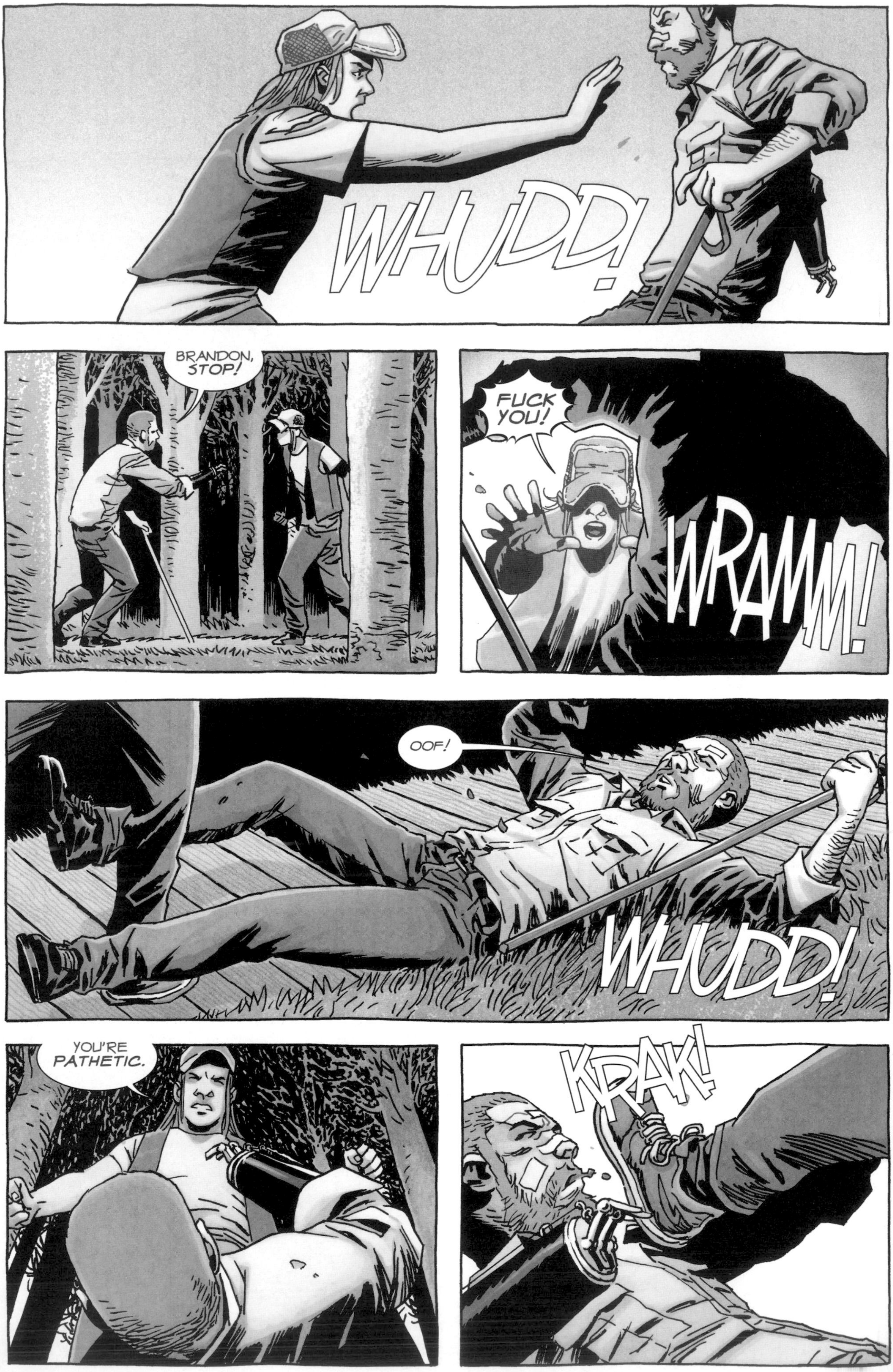
WHUDD!
BRANDON, STOP!
FUCK YOU!
WRAMM!
OOF!
WHUDD!
YOU'RE PATHETIC.
KRAK!

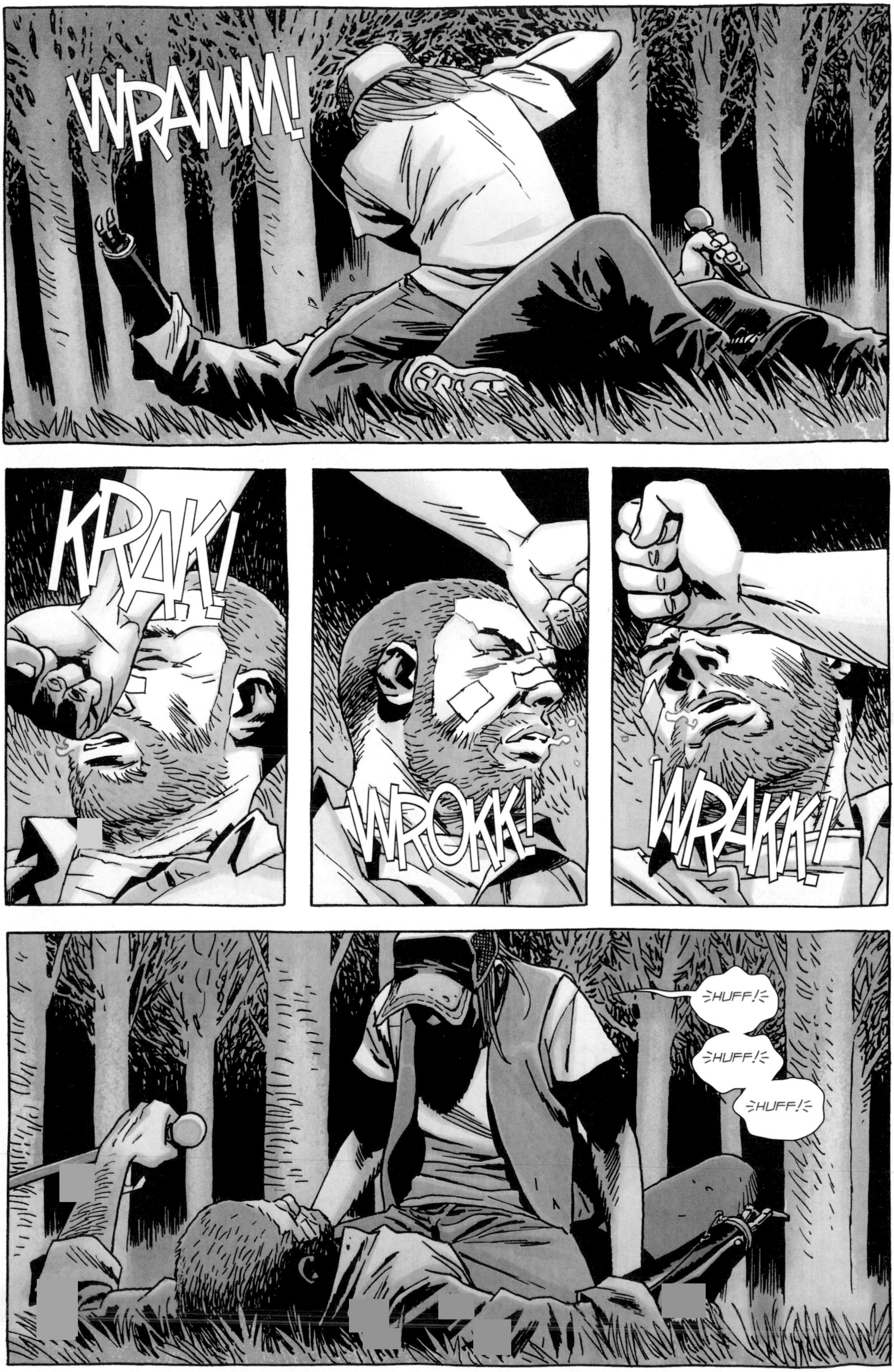
WRAMM!
KRAK!
WROKK!
WRAKK!
HUFF!
HUFF!
HUFF!

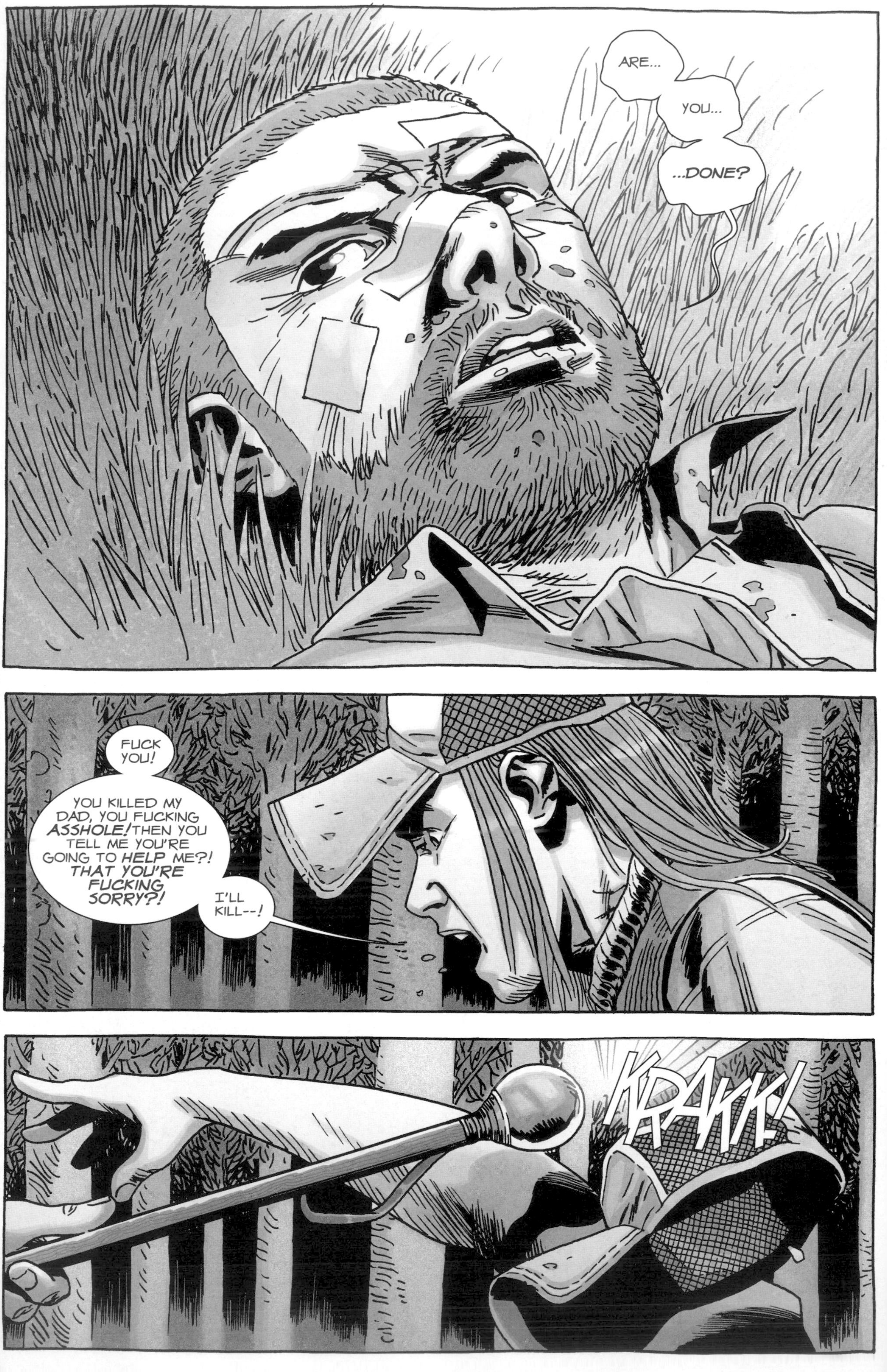
ARE...
YOU...
...DONE?
FUCK YOU!
YOU KILLED MY DAD, YOU FUCKING ASSHOLE! THEN YOU TELL ME YOU'RE GOING TO HELP ME?! THAT YOU'RE FUCKING SORRY?!
I'LL KILL--!
KRAKK!

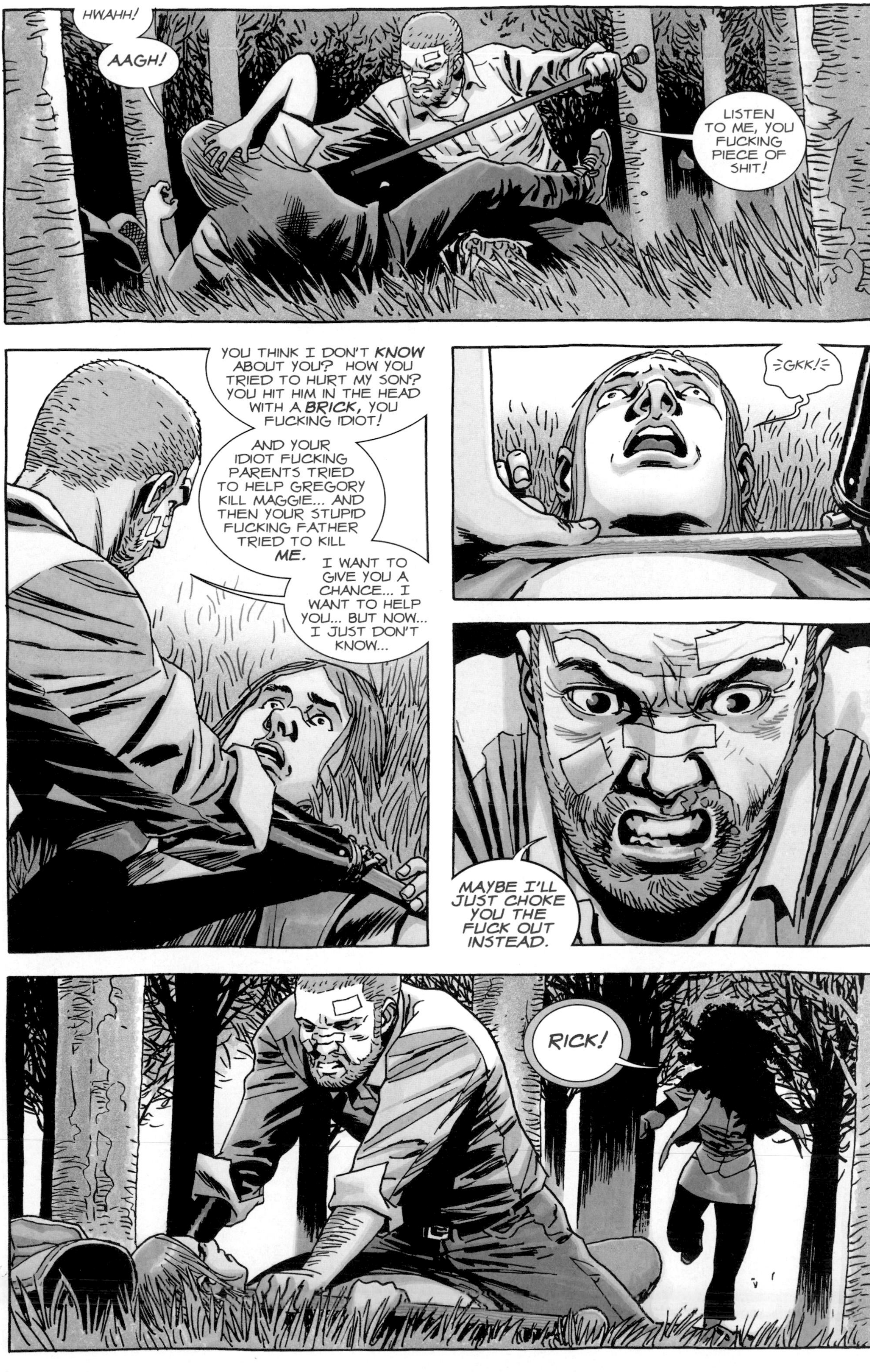
HWAHH!
AAGH!
LISTEN TO ME, YOU FUCKING PIECE OF SHIT!
YOU THINK I DON'T KNOW ABOUT YOU? HOW YOU TRIED TO HURT MY SON? YOU HIT HIM IN THE HEAD WITH A BRICK, YOU FUCKING IDIOT!
AND YOUR IDIOT FUCKING PARENTS TRIED TO HELP GREGORY KILL MAGGIE... AND THEN YOUR STUPID FUCKING FATHER TRIED TO KILL ME.
I WANT TO GIVE YOU A CHANCE... I WANT TO HELP YOU... BUT NOW... I JUST DON'T KNOW...
GKK!
MAYBE I'LL JUST CHOKE YOU THE FUCK OUT INSTEAD.
RICK!

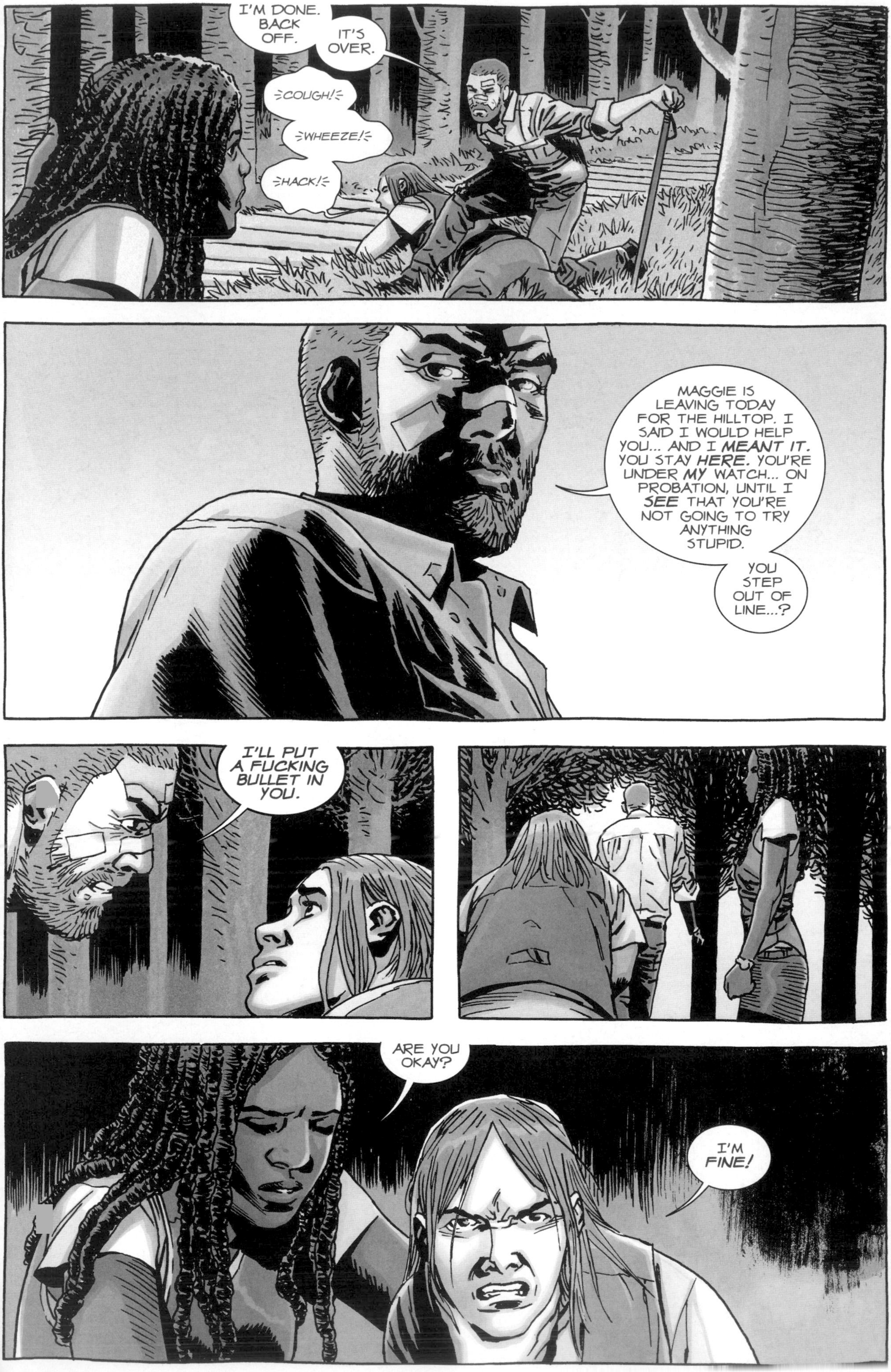

I'M DONE. BACK OFF.
IT'S OVER.
COUGH!
WHEEZE!
HACK!
MAGGIE IS LEAVING TODAY FOR THE HILLTOP. I SAID I WOULD HELP YOU... AND I MEANT IT. YOU STAY HERE. YOU'RE UNDER MY WATCH... ON PROBATION, UNTIL I SEE THAT YOU'RE NOT GOING TO TRY ANYTHING STUPID.
YOU STEP OUT OF LINE...?
I'LL PUT A FUCKING BULLET IN YOU.
ARE YOU OKAY?
I'M FINE!

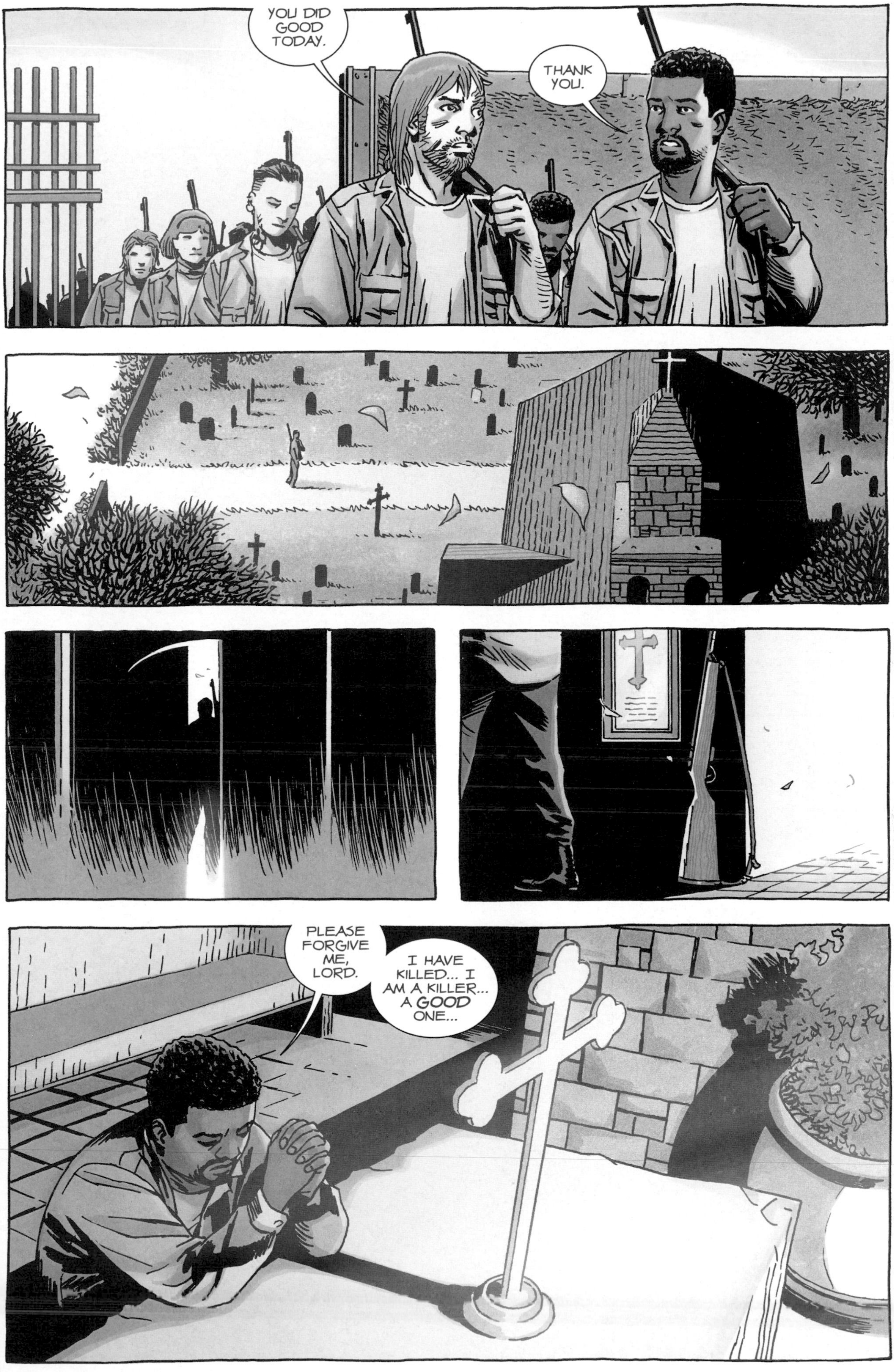
YOU DID GOOD TODAY.
THANK YOU.
PLEASE FORGIVE ME, LORD.
I HAVE KILLED... I AM A KILLER... A GOOD ONE...

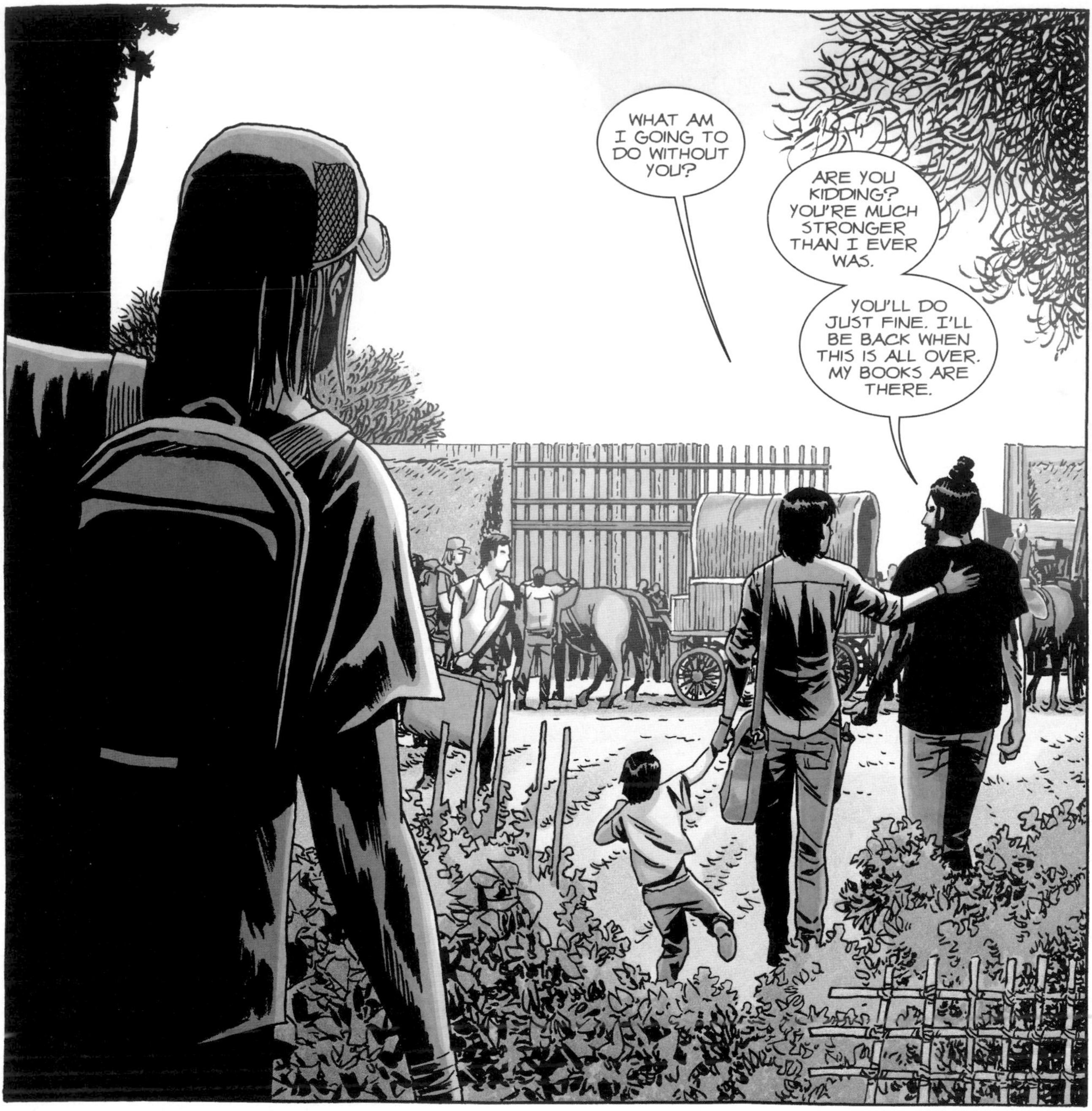
WHAT AM I GOING TO DO WITHOUT YOU?
ARE YOU KIDDING? YOU'RE MUCH STRONGER THAN I EVER WAS.
YOU'LL DO JUST FINE. I'LL BE BACK WHEN THIS IS ALL OVER. MY BOOKS ARE THERE.

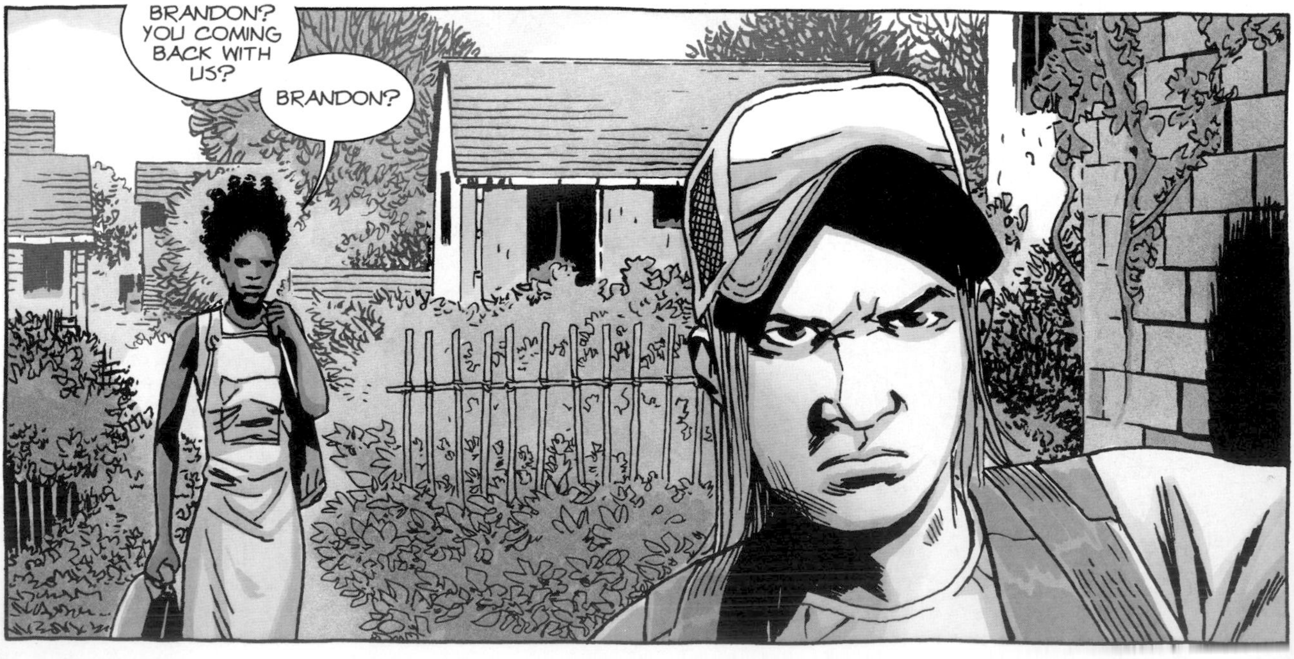
BRANDON? YOU COMING BACK WITH US?
BRANDON?

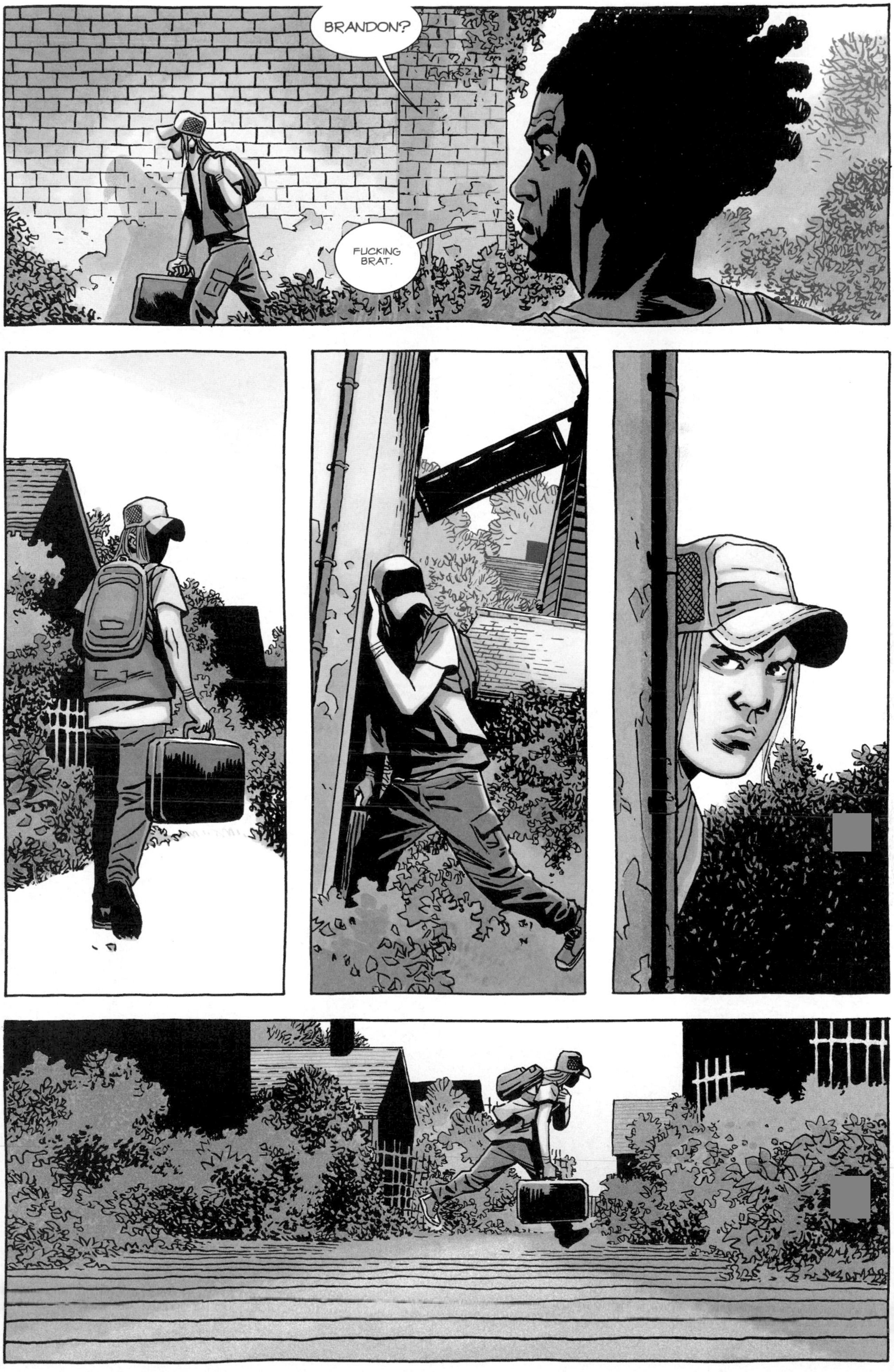
BRANDON?
FUCKING BRAT.

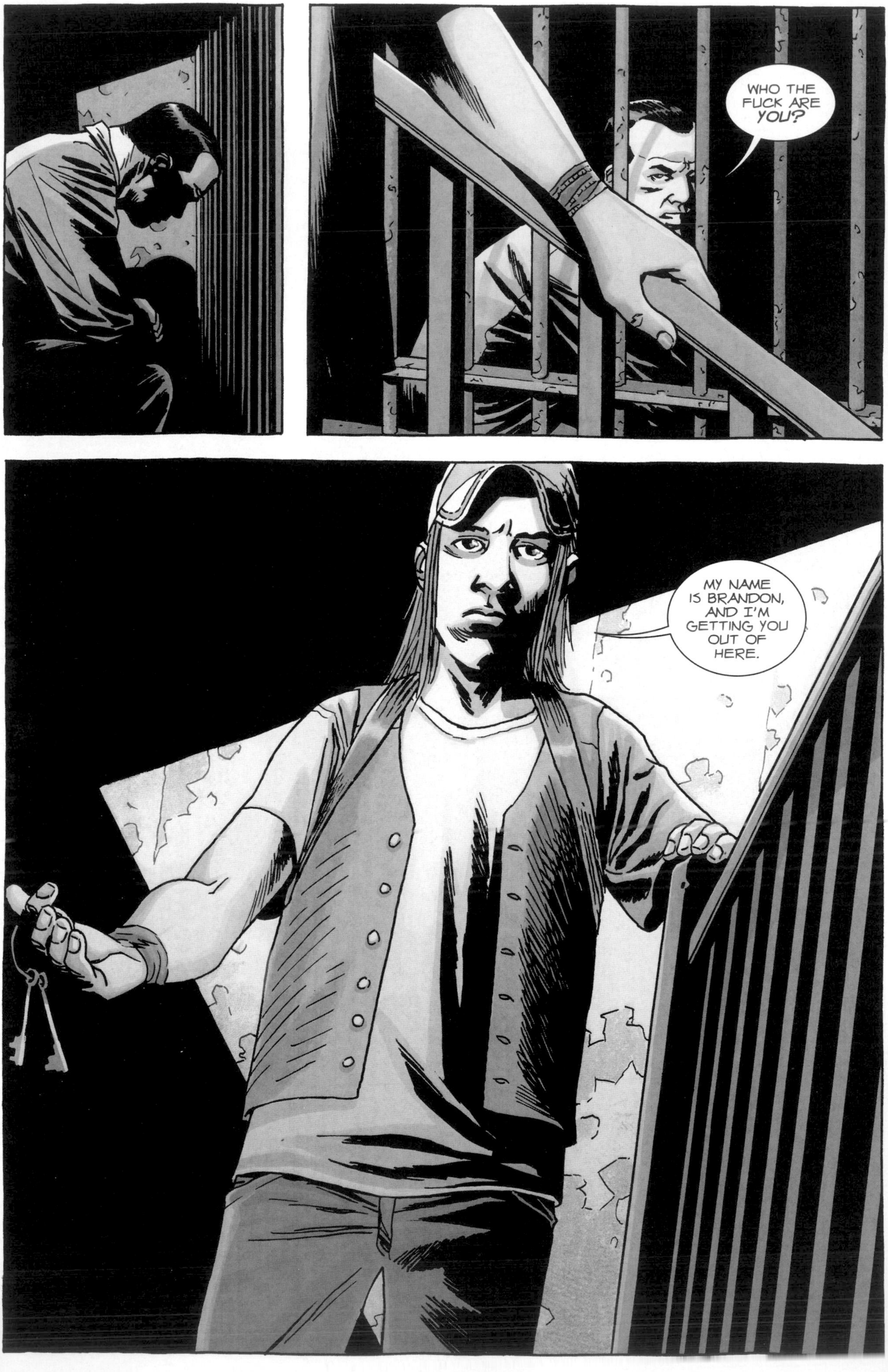
WHO THE FUCK ARE YOU?
MY NAME IS BRANDON, AND I'M GETTING YOU OUT OF HERE.

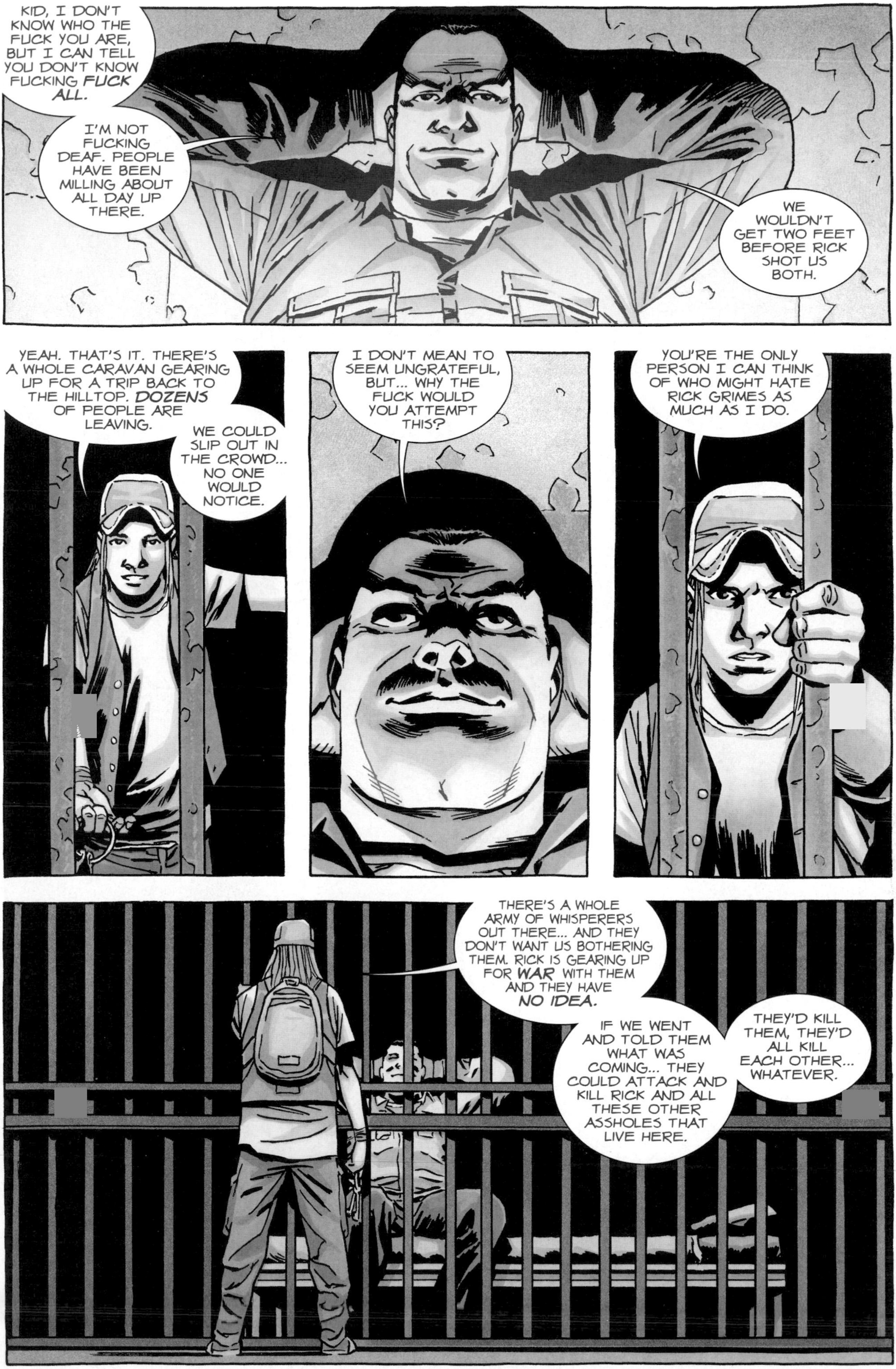
KID, I DON'T KNOW WHO THE FUCK YOU ARE, BUT I CAN TELL YOU DON'T KNOW FUCKING FUCK ALL.
I'M NOT FUCKING DEAF. PEOPLE HAVE BEEN MILLING ABOUT ALL DAY UP THERE.
WE WOULDN'T GET TWO FEET BEFORE RICK SHOT US BOTH.
YEAH. THAT'S IT. THERE'S A WHOLE CARAVAN GEARING UP FOR A TRIP BACK TO THE HILLTOP. DOZENS OF PEOPLE ARE LEAVING.
WE COULD SLIP OUT IN THE CROWD... NO ONE WOULD NOTICE.
I DON'T MEAN TO SEEM UNGRATEFUL, BUT... WHY THE FUCK WOULD YOU ATTEMPT THIS?
YOU'RE THE ONLY PERSON I CAN THINK OF WHO MIGHT HATE RICK GRIMES AS MUCH AS I DO.
THERE'S A WHOLE ARMY OF WHISPERERS OUT THERE... AND THEY DON'T WANT US BOTHERING THEM. RICK IS GEARING UP FOR WAR WITH THEM AND THEY HAVE NO IDEA.
IF WE WENT AND TOLD THEM WHAT WAS COMING... THEY COULD ATTACK AND KILL RICK AND ALL THESE OTHER ASSHOLES THAT LIVE HERE.
THEY'D KILL THEM, THEY'D ALL KILL EACH OTHER... WHATEVER.

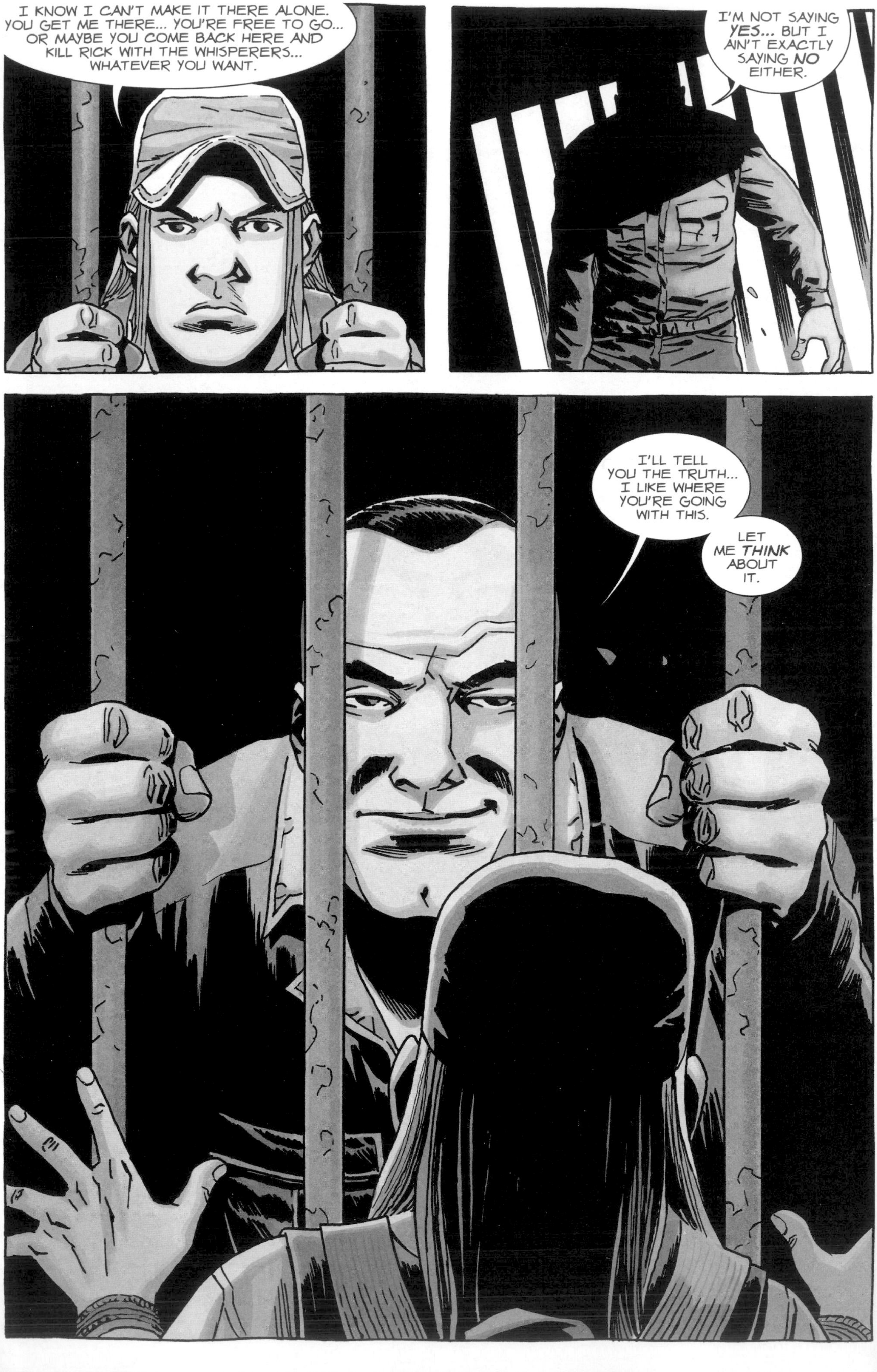
I KNOW I CAN'T MAKE IT THERE ALONE. YOU GET ME THERE... YOU'RE FREE TO GO... OR MAYBE YOU COME BACK HERE AND KILL RICK WITH THE WHISPERERS... WHATEVER YOU WANT.
I'M NOT SAYING YES... BUT I AIN'T EXACTLY SAYING NO EITHER.
I'LL TELL YOU THE TRUTH... I LIKE WHERE YOU'RE GOING WITH THIS.
LET ME THINK ABOUT IT.

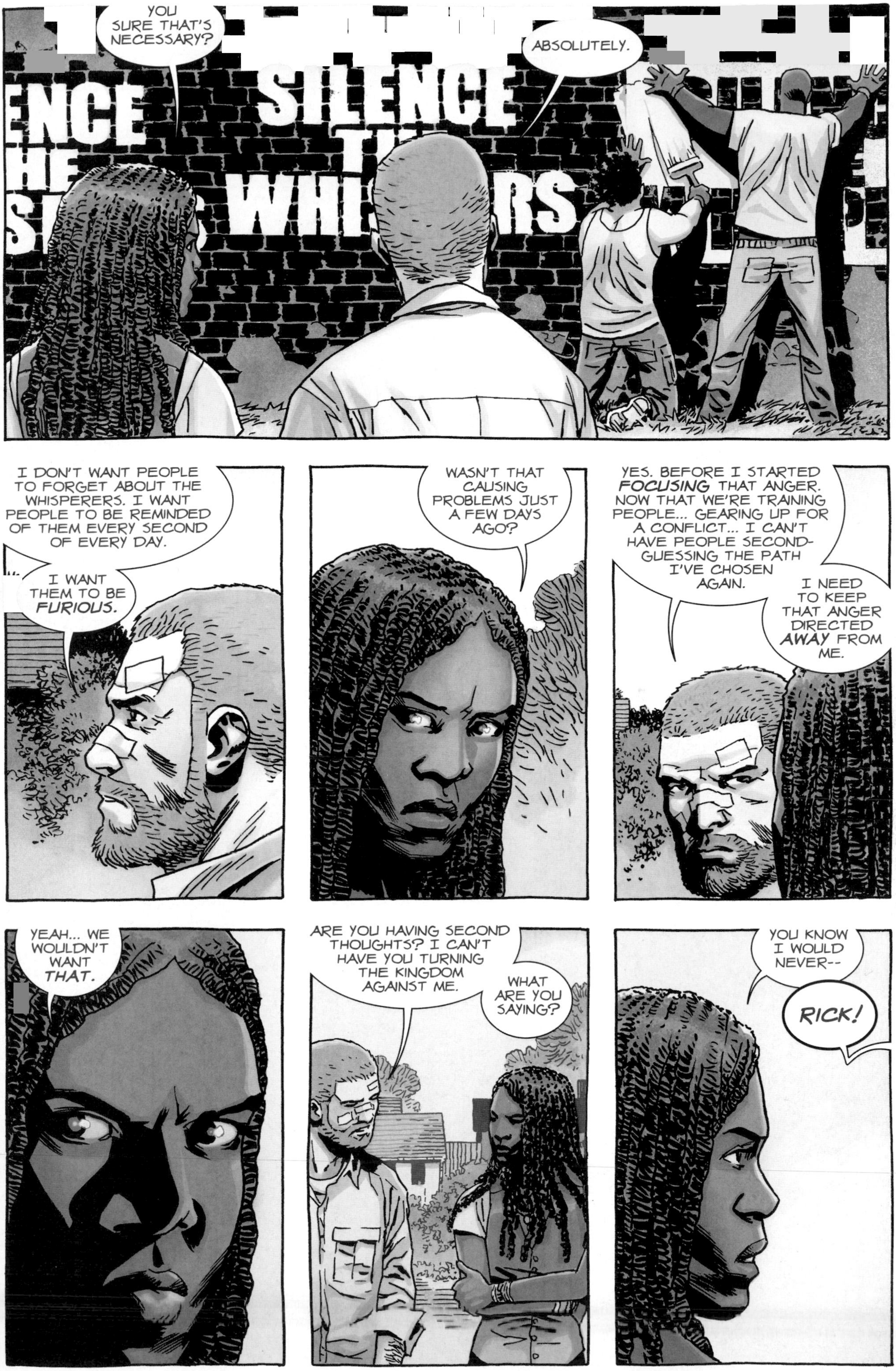
YOU SURE THAT'S NECESSARY?
ABSOLUTELY.
SILENCE
I DON'T WANT PEOPLE TO FORGET ABOUT THE WHISPERERS. I WANT PEOPLE TO BE REMINDED OF THEM EVERY SECOND OF EVERY DAY.
I WANT THEM TO BE FURIOUS.
WASN'T THAT CAUSING PROBLEMS JUST A FEW DAYS AGO?
YES. BEFORE I STARTED FOCUSING THAT ANGER. NOW THAT WE'RE TRAINING PEOPLE... GEARING UP FOR A CONFLICT... I CAN'T HAVE PEOPLE SECOND-GUESSING THE PATH I'VE CHOSEN AGAIN.
I NEED TO KEEP THAT ANGER DIRECTED AWAY FROM ME.
YEAH... WE WOULDN'T WANT THAT.
ARE YOU HAVING SECOND THOUGHTS? I CAN'T HAVE YOU TURNING THE KINGDOM AGAINST ME.
WHAT ARE YOU SAYING?
YOU KNOW I WOULD NEVER--
RICK!

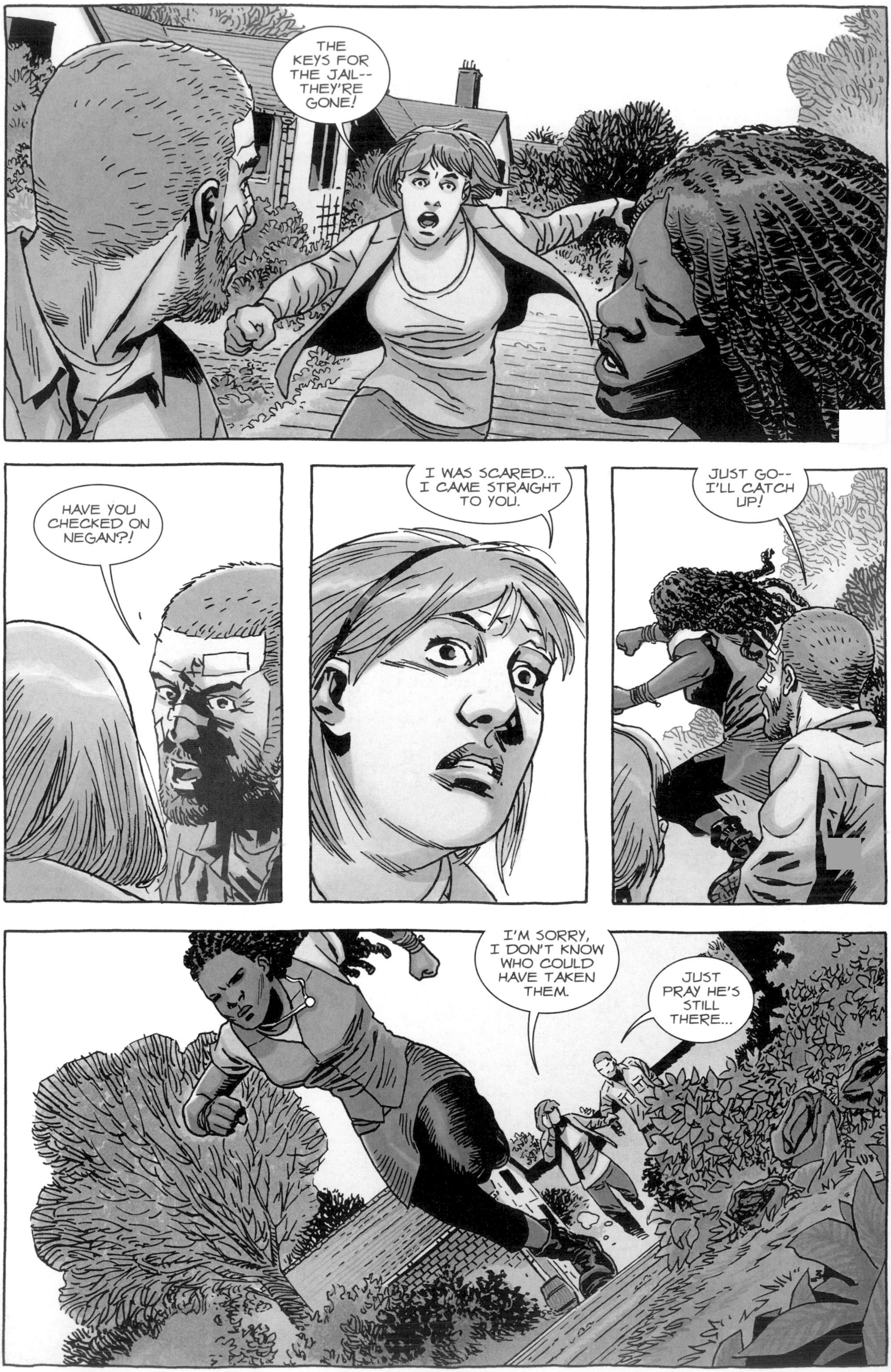
THE KEYS FOR THE JAIL-- THEY'RE GONE!
HAVE YOU CHECKED ON NEGAN?!
I WAS SCARED... I CAME STRAIGHT TO YOU.
JUST GO-- I'LL CATCH UP!
I'M SORRY, I DON'T KNOW WHO COULD HAVE TAKEN THEM.
JUST PRAY HE'S STILL THERE...

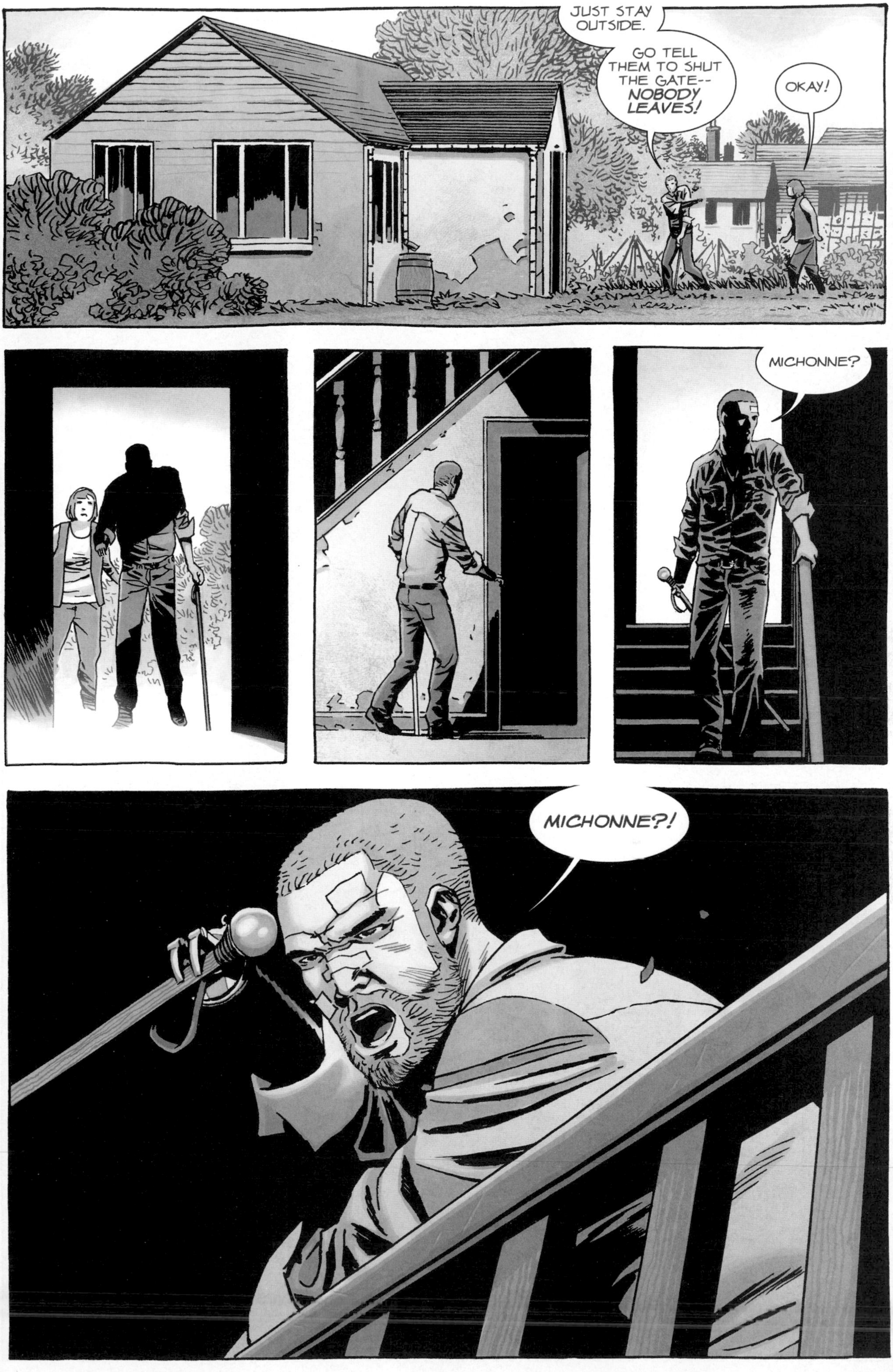
JUST STAY OUTSIDE.
GO TELL THEM TO SHUT THE GATE-- NOBODY LEAVES!
OKAY!
MICHONNE?
MICHONNE?!

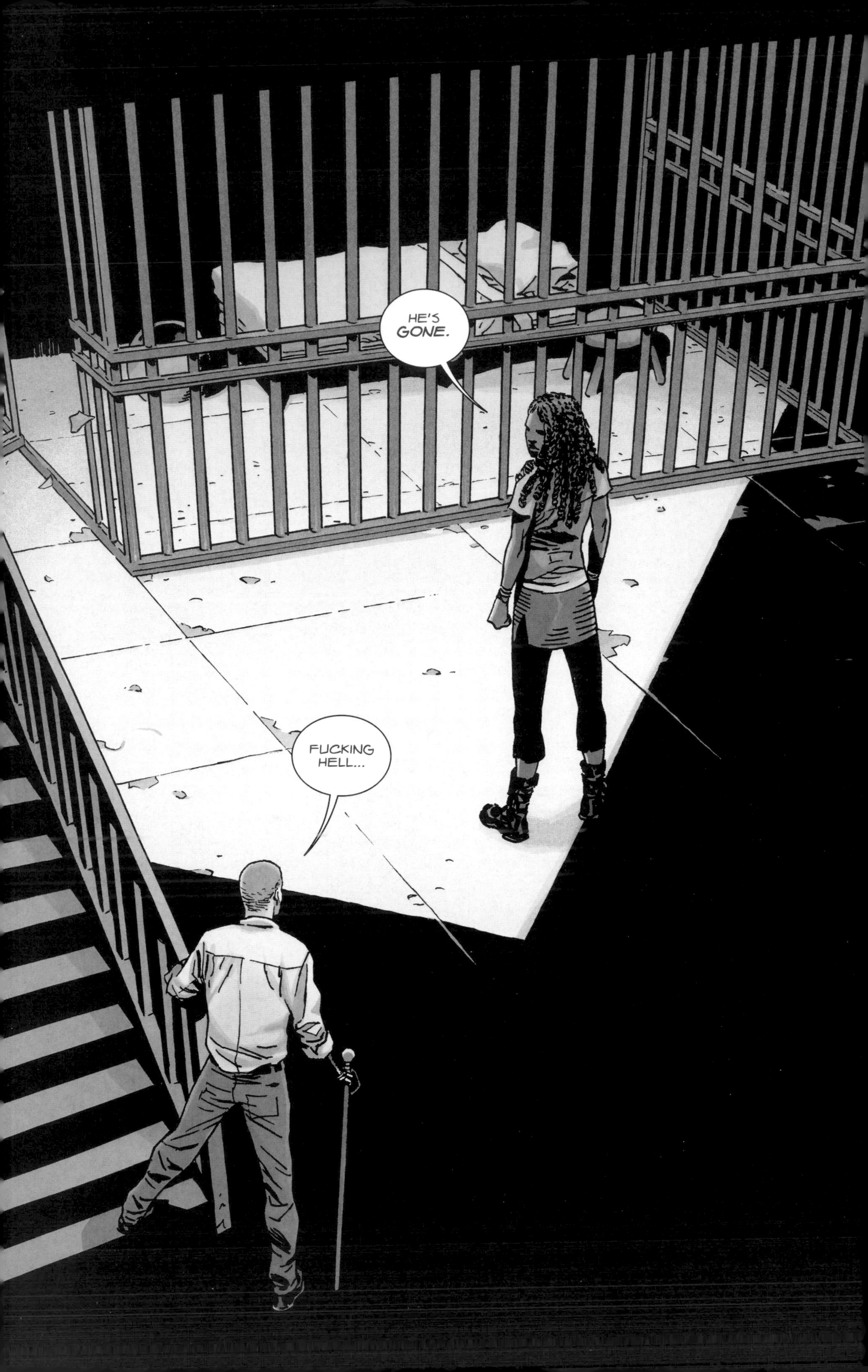
HE'S GONE.
FUCKING HELL...

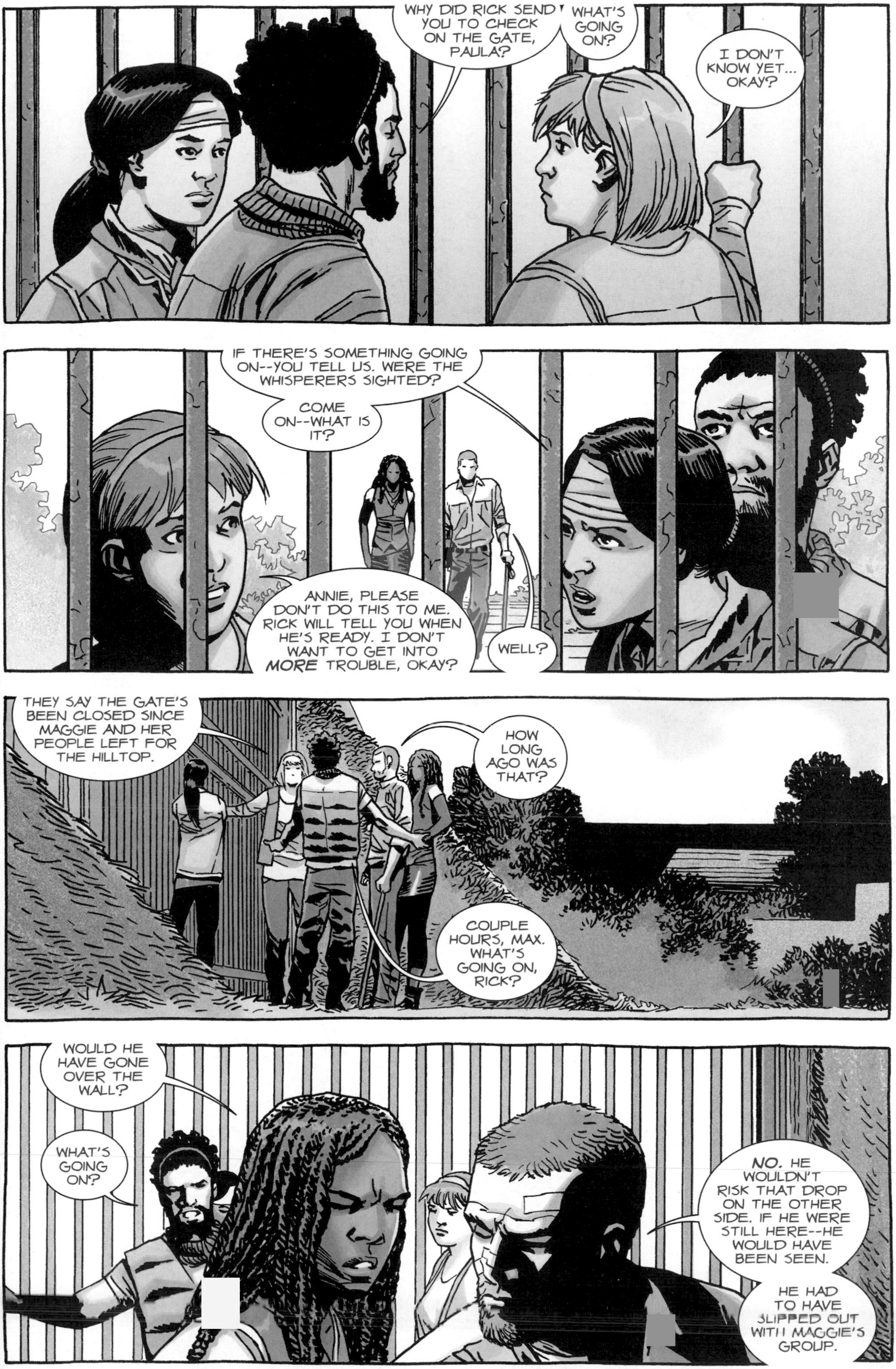
WHY DID RICK SEND YOU TO CHECK ON THE GATE, PAULA?
WHAT'S GOING ON?
I DON'T KNOW YET... OKAY?
IF THERE'S SOMETHING GOING ON--YOU TELL US. WERE THE WHISPERERS SIGHTED?
COME ON--WHAT IS IT?
ANNIE, PLEASE DON'T DO THIS TO ME. RICK WILL TELL YOU WHEN HE'S READY. I DON'T WANT TO GET INTO MORE TROUBLE, OKAY?
WELL?
THEY SAY THE GATE'S BEEN CLOSED SINCE MAGGIE AND HER PEOPLE LEFT FOR THE HILLTOP.
HOW LONG AGO WAS THAT?
COUPLE HOURS, MAX. WHAT'S GOING ON, RICK?
WOULD HE HAVE GONE OVER THE WALL?
WHAT'S GOING ON?
NO. HE WOULDN'T RISK THAT DROP ON THE OTHER SIDE. IF HE WERE STILL HERE--HE WOULD HAVE BEEN SEEN.
HE HAD TO HAVE SLIPPED OUT WITH MAGGIE'S GROUP.

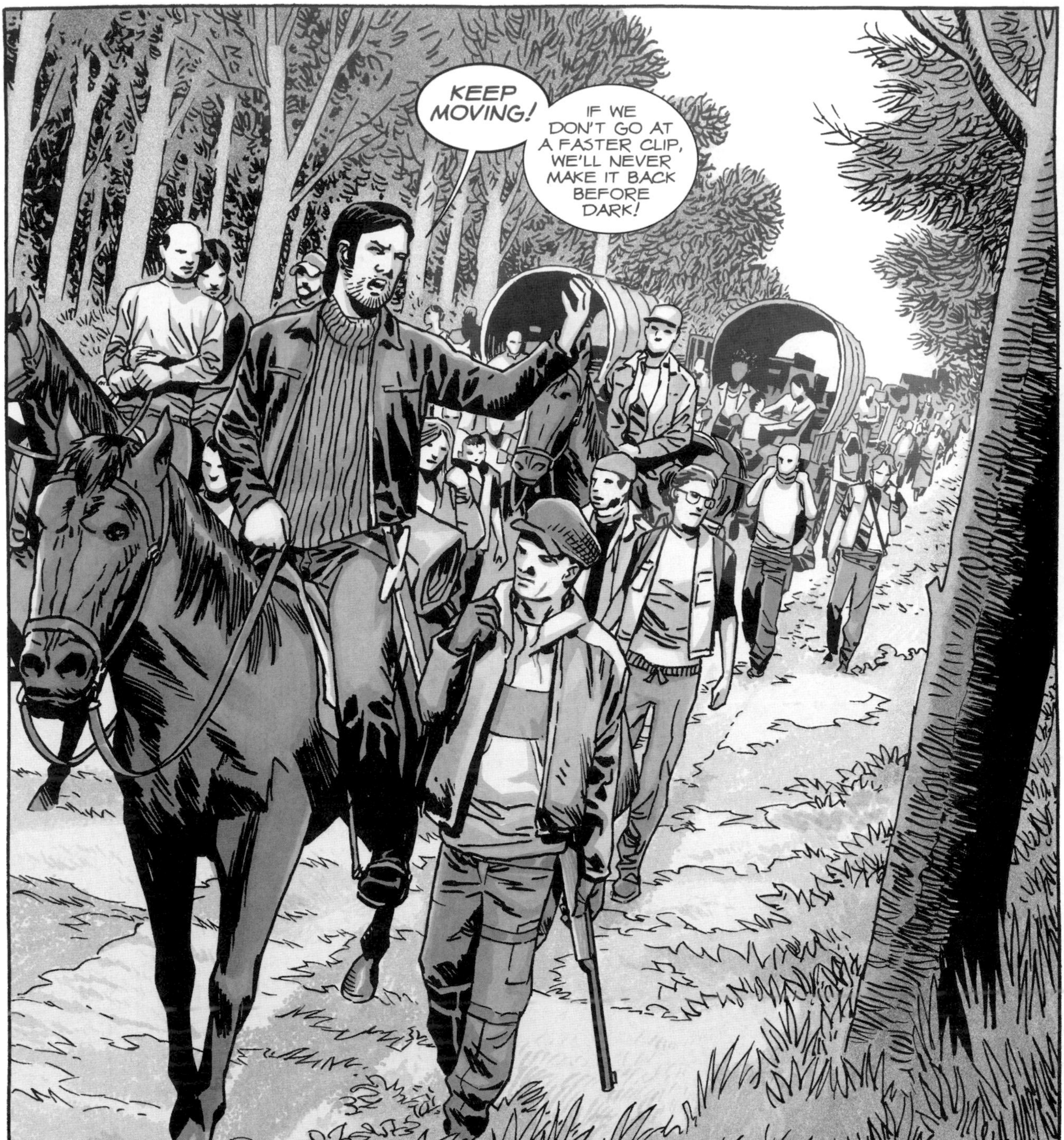
KEEP MOVING!
IF WE DON'T GO AT A FASTER CLIP, WE'LL NEVER MAKE IT BACK BEFORE DARK!

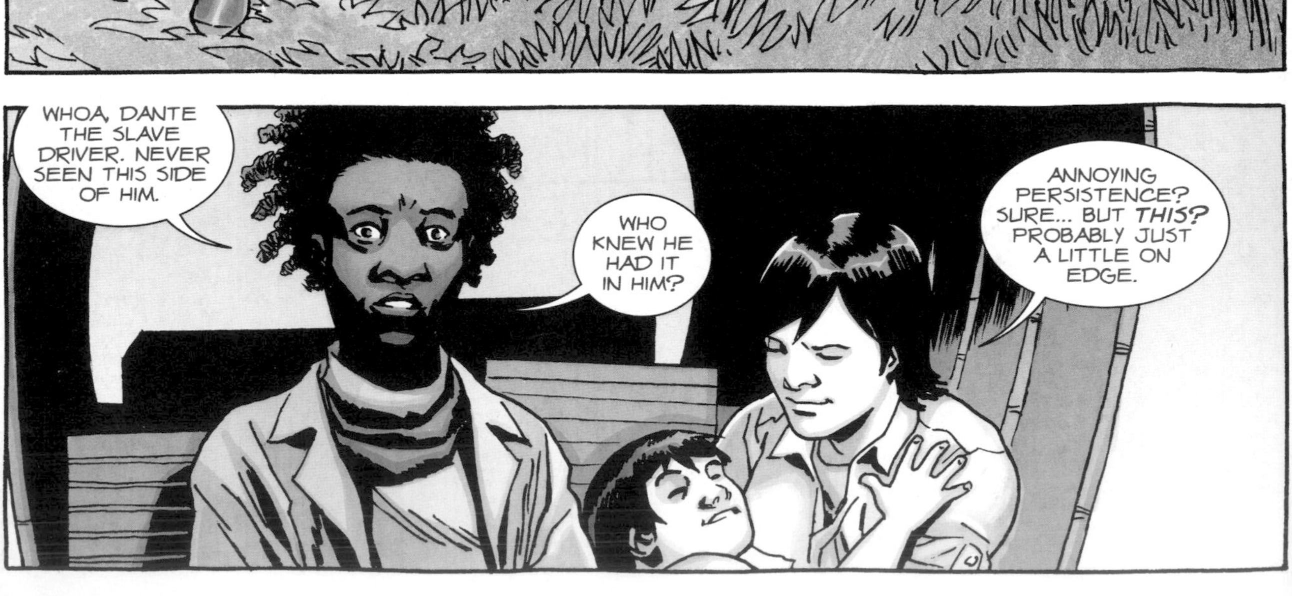
WHOA, DANTE THE SLAVE DRIVER. NEVER SEEN THIS SIDE OF HIM.
WHO KNEW HE HAD IT IN HIM?
ANNOYING PERSISTENCE? SURE... BUT THIS? PROBABLY JUST A LITTLE ON EDGE.

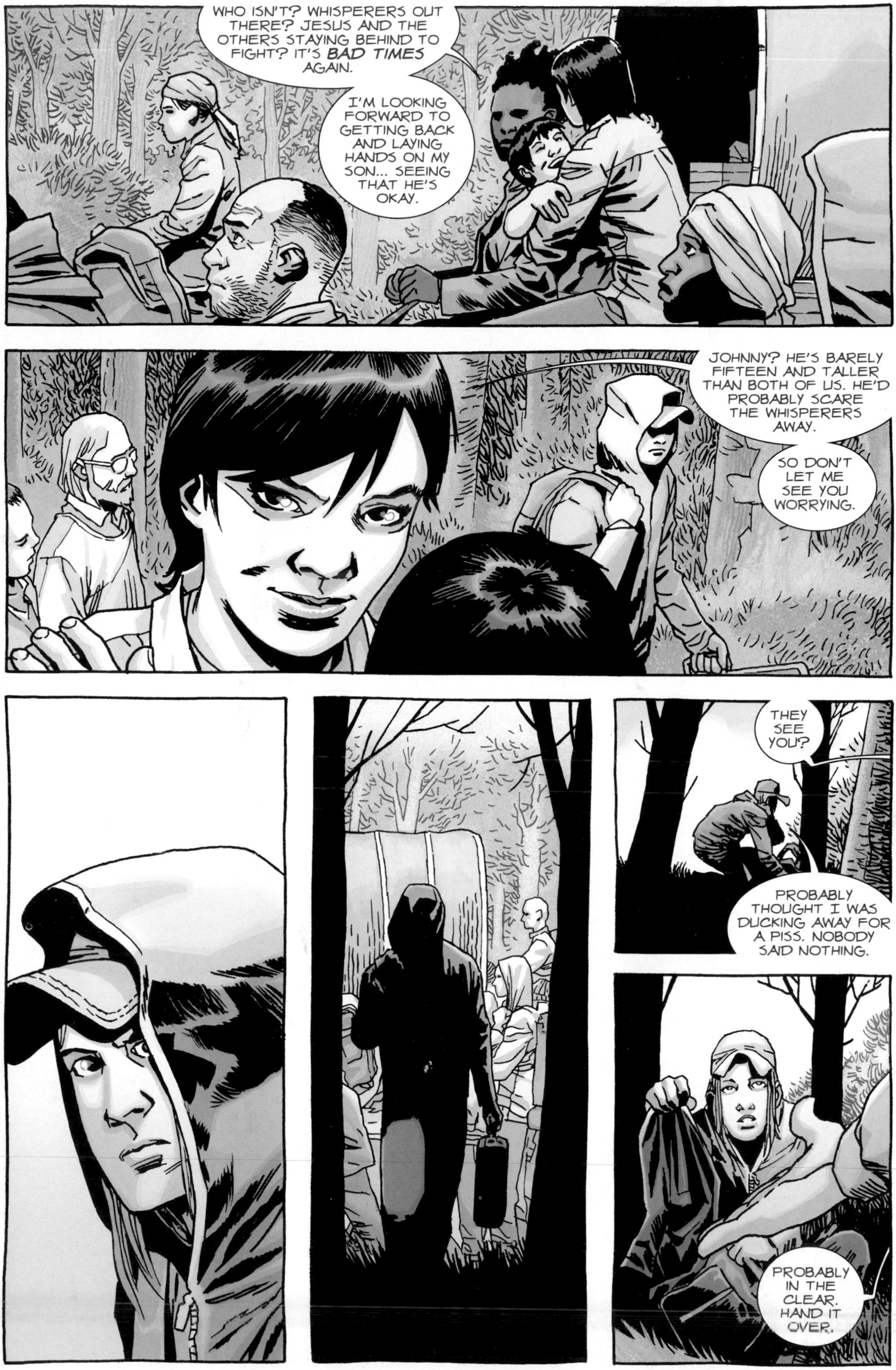
WHO ISN'T? WHISPERERS OUT THERE? JESUS AND THE OTHERS STAYING BEHIND TO FIGHT? IT'S BAD TIMES AGAIN.
I'M LOOKING FORWARD TO GETTING BACK AND LAYING HANDS ON MY SON... SEEING THAT HE'S OKAY.
JOHNNY? HE'S BARELY FIFTEEN AND TALLER THAN BOTH OF US. HE'D PROBABLY SCARE THE WHISPERERS AWAY.
SO DON'T LET ME SEE YOU WORRYING.
THEY SEE YOU?
PROBABLY THOUGHT I WAS DUCKING AWAY FOR A PISS. NOBODY SAID NOTHING.
PROBABLY IN THE CLEAR. HAND IT OVER.

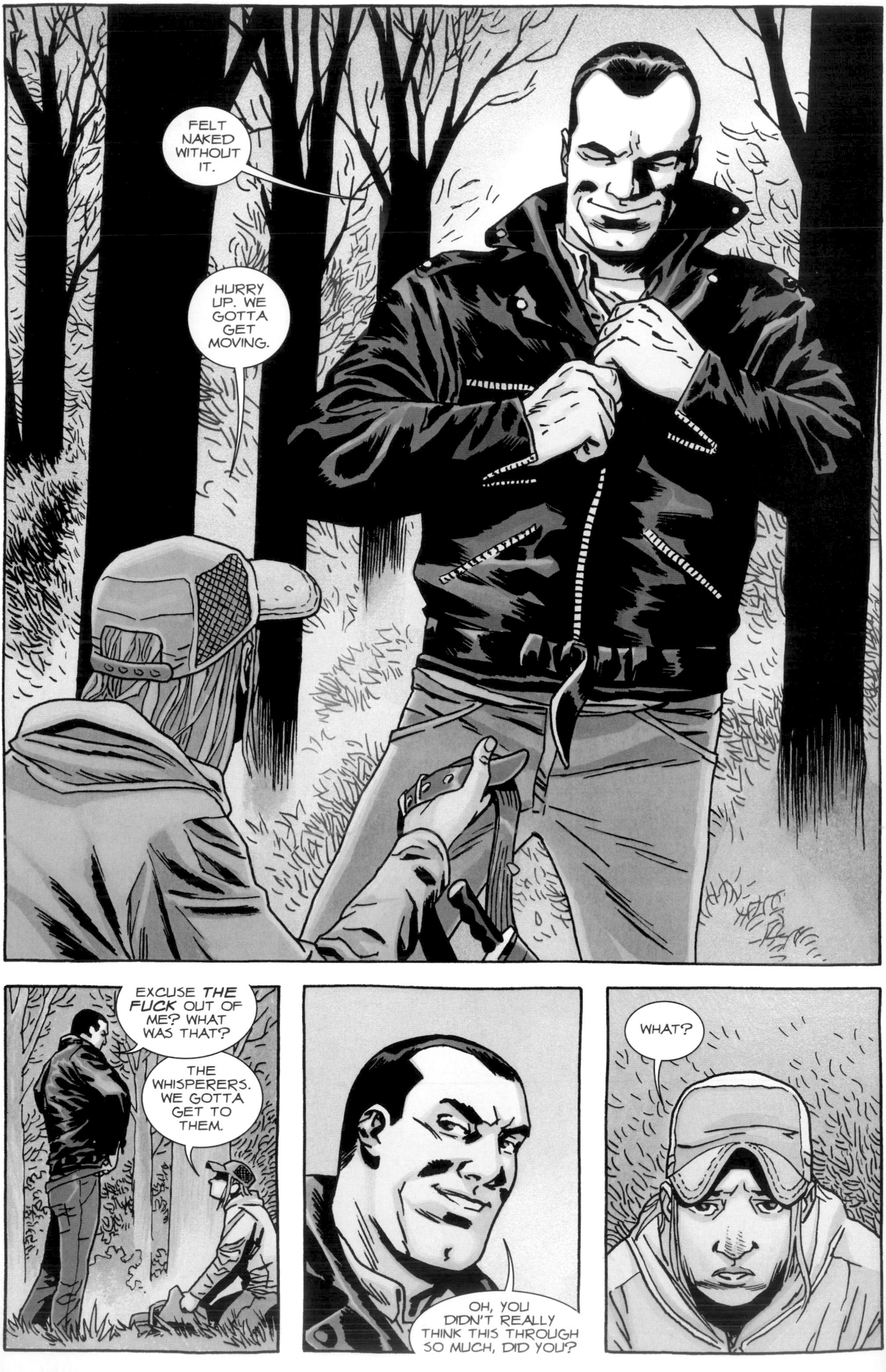
FELT NAKED WITHOUT IT.
HURRY UP. WE GOTTA GET MOVING.
EXCUSE *THE FUCK* OUT OF ME? WHAT WAS THAT?
THE WHISPERERS. WE GOTTA GET TO THEM.
OH, YOU DIDN'T REALLY THINK THIS THROUGH SO MUCH, DID YOU?
WHAT?

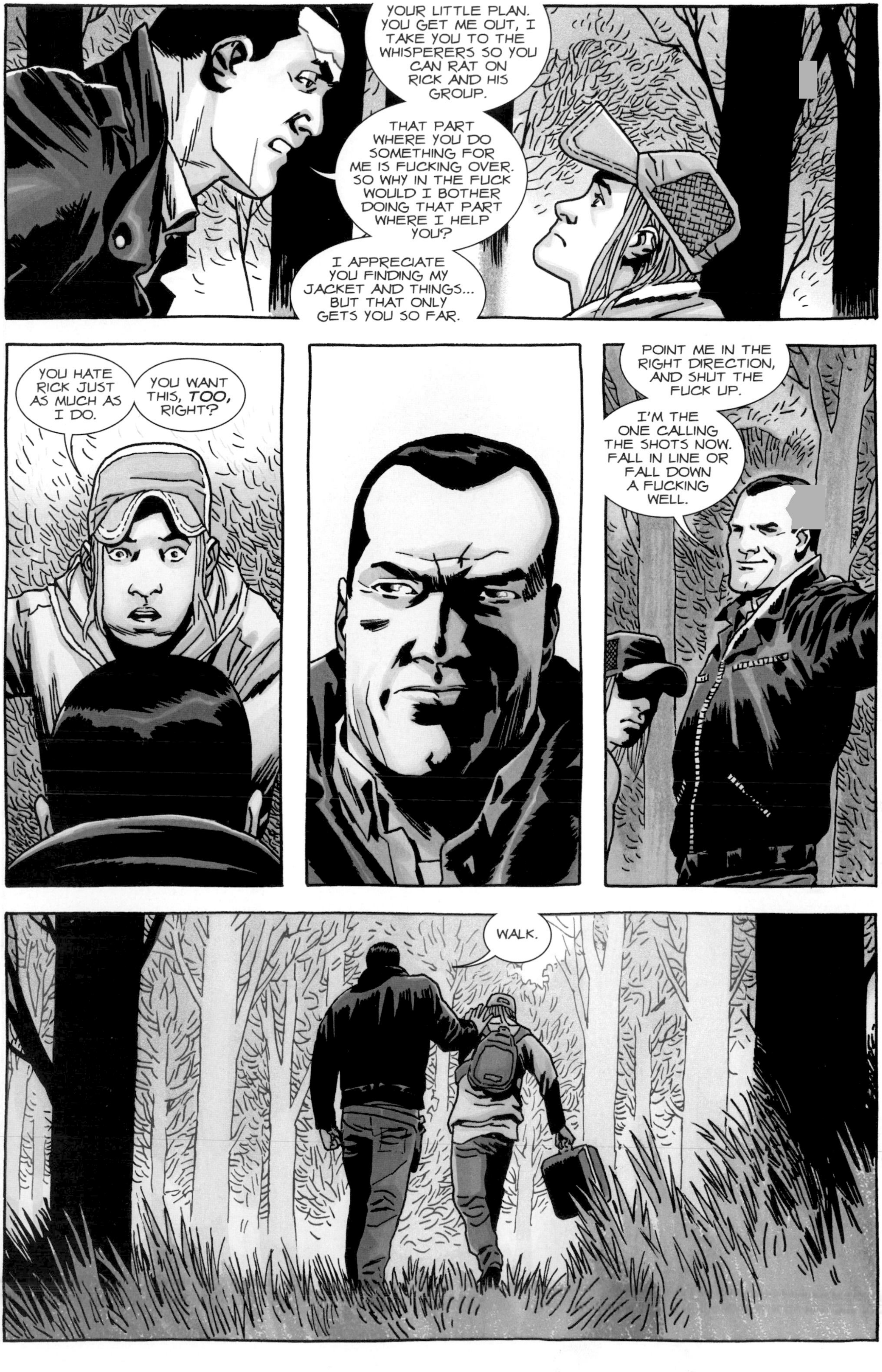
YOUR LITTLE PLAN. YOU GET ME OUT, I TAKE YOU TO THE WHISPERERS SO YOU CAN RAT ON RICK AND HIS GROUP.
THAT PART WHERE YOU DO SOMETHING FOR ME IS FUCKING OVER. SO WHY IN THE FUCK WOULD I BOTHER DOING THAT PART WHERE I HELP YOU?
I APPRECIATE YOU FINDING MY JACKET AND THINGS... BUT THAT ONLY GETS YOU SO FAR.
YOU HATE RICK JUST AS MUCH AS I DO.
YOU WANT THIS, TOO, RIGHT?
POINT ME IN THE RIGHT DIRECTION, AND SHUT THE FUCK UP.
I'M THE ONE CALLING THE SHOTS NOW. FALL IN LINE OR FALL DOWN A FUCKING WELL.
WALK.

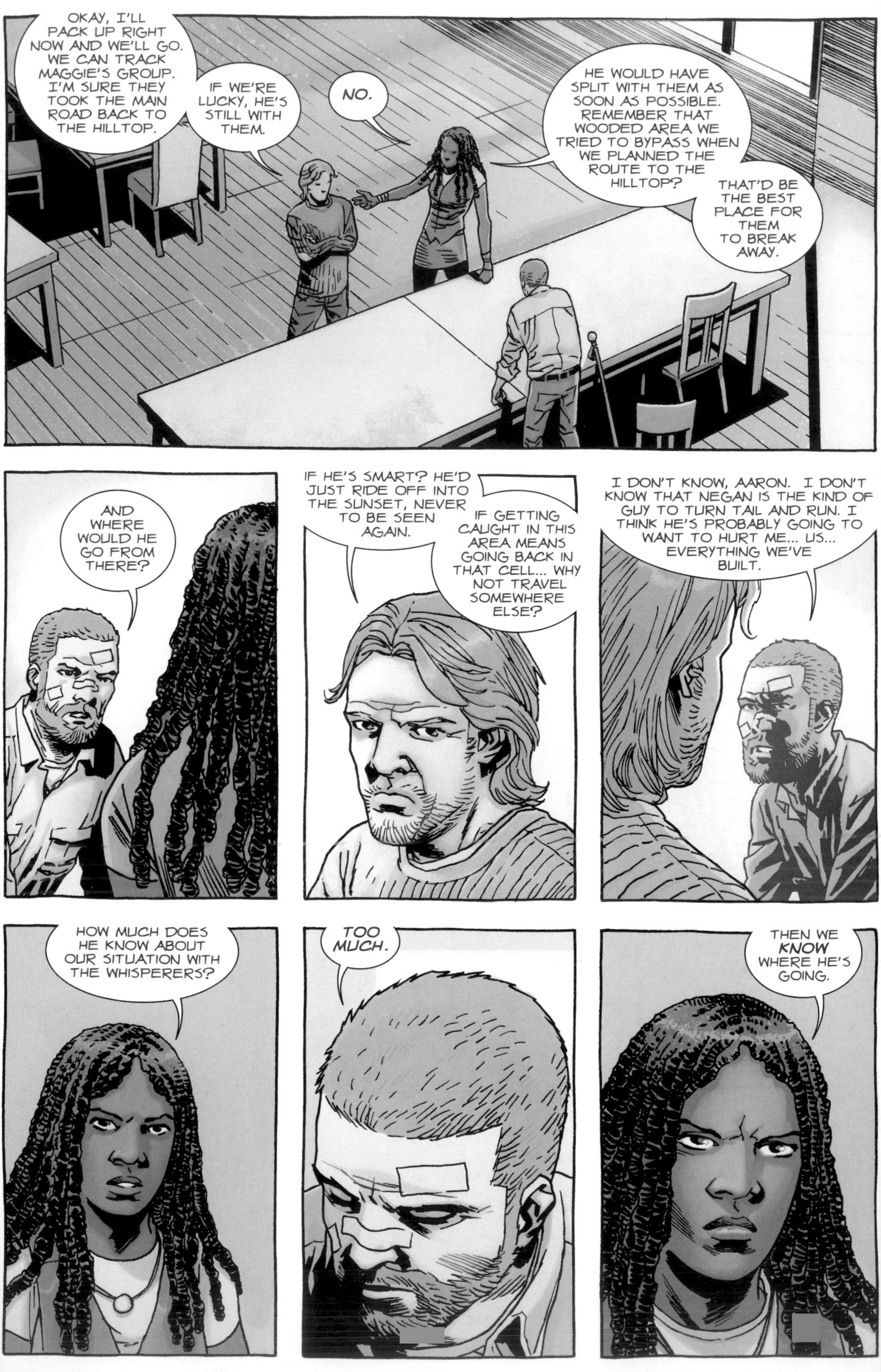
OKAY, I'LL PACK UP RIGHT NOW AND WE'LL GO. WE CAN TRACK MAGGIE'S GROUP. I'M SURE THEY TOOK THE MAIN ROAD BACK TO THE HILLTOP.
IF WE'RE LUCKY, HE'S STILL WITH THEM.
NO.
HE WOULD HAVE SPLIT WITH THEM AS SOON AS POSSIBLE. REMEMBER THAT WOODED AREA WE TRIED TO BYPASS WHEN WE PLANNED THE ROUTE TO THE HILLTOP?
THAT'D BE THE BEST PLACE FOR THEM TO BREAK AWAY.
AND WHERE WOULD HE GO FROM THERE?
IF HE'S SMART? HE'D JUST RIDE OFF INTO THE SUNSET, NEVER TO BE SEEN AGAIN.
IF GETTING CAUGHT IN THIS AREA MEANS GOING BACK IN THAT CELL... WHY NOT TRAVEL SOMEWHERE ELSE?
I DON'T KNOW, AARON. I DON'T KNOW THAT NEGAN IS THE KIND OF GUY TO TURN TAIL AND RUN. I THINK HE'S PROBABLY GOING TO WANT TO HURT ME... US... EVERYTHING WE'VE BUILT.
HOW MUCH DOES HE KNOW ABOUT OUR SITUATION WITH THE WHISPERERS?
TOO MUCH.
THEN WE KNOW WHERE HE'S GOING.

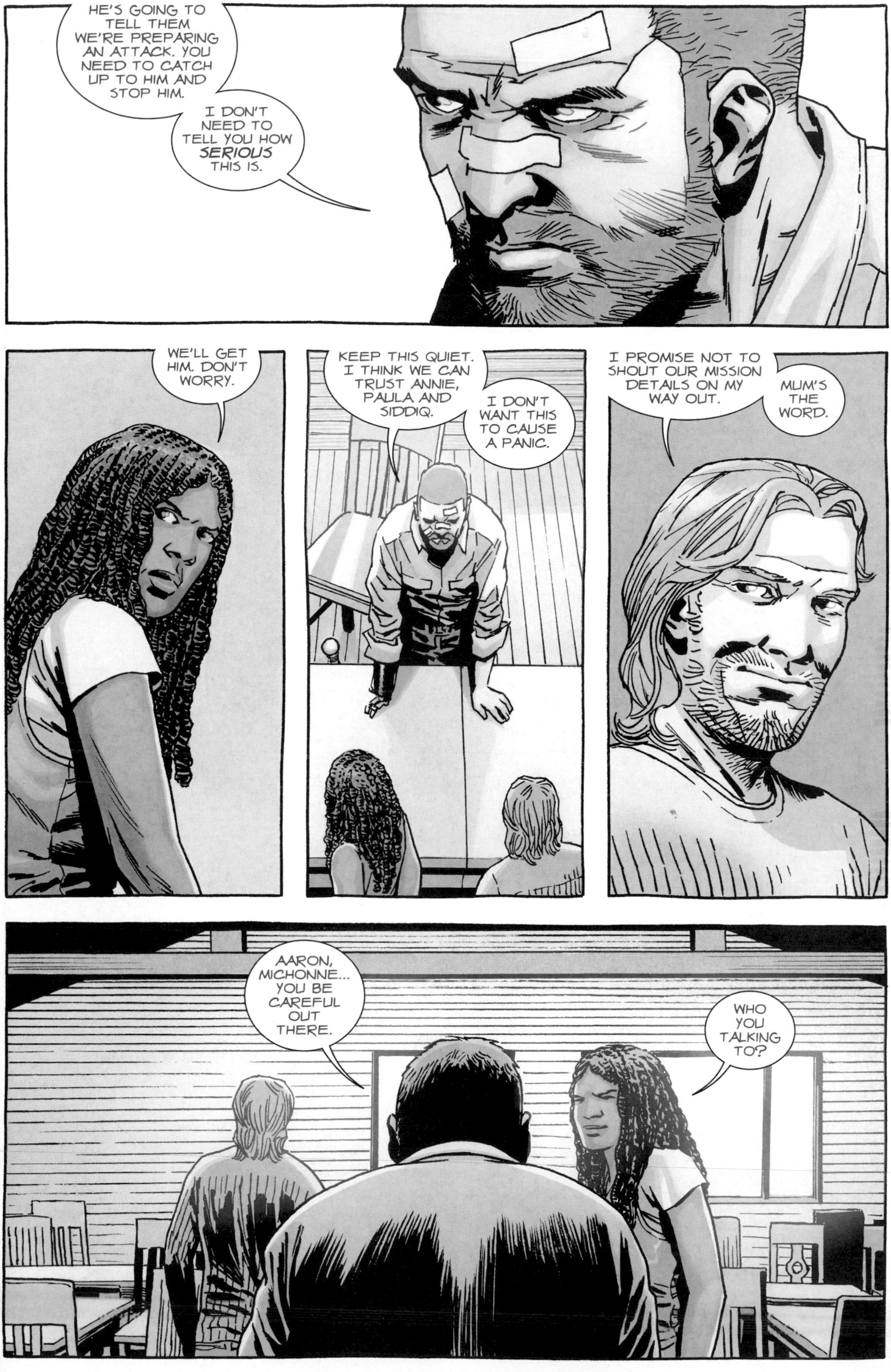

HE'S GOING TO TELL THEM WE'RE PREPARING AN ATTACK. YOU NEED TO CATCH UP TO HIM AND STOP HIM.
I DON'T NEED TO TELL YOU HOW SERIOUS THIS IS.
WE'LL GET HIM. DON'T WORRY.
KEEP THIS QUIET. I THINK WE CAN TRUST ANNIE, PAULA AND SIDDIQ.
I DON'T WANT THIS TO CAUSE A PANIC.
I PROMISE NOT TO SHOUT OUR MISSION DETAILS ON MY WAY OUT.
MUM'S THE WORD.
AARON, MICHONNE... YOU BE CAREFUL OUT THERE.
WHO YOU TALKING TO?

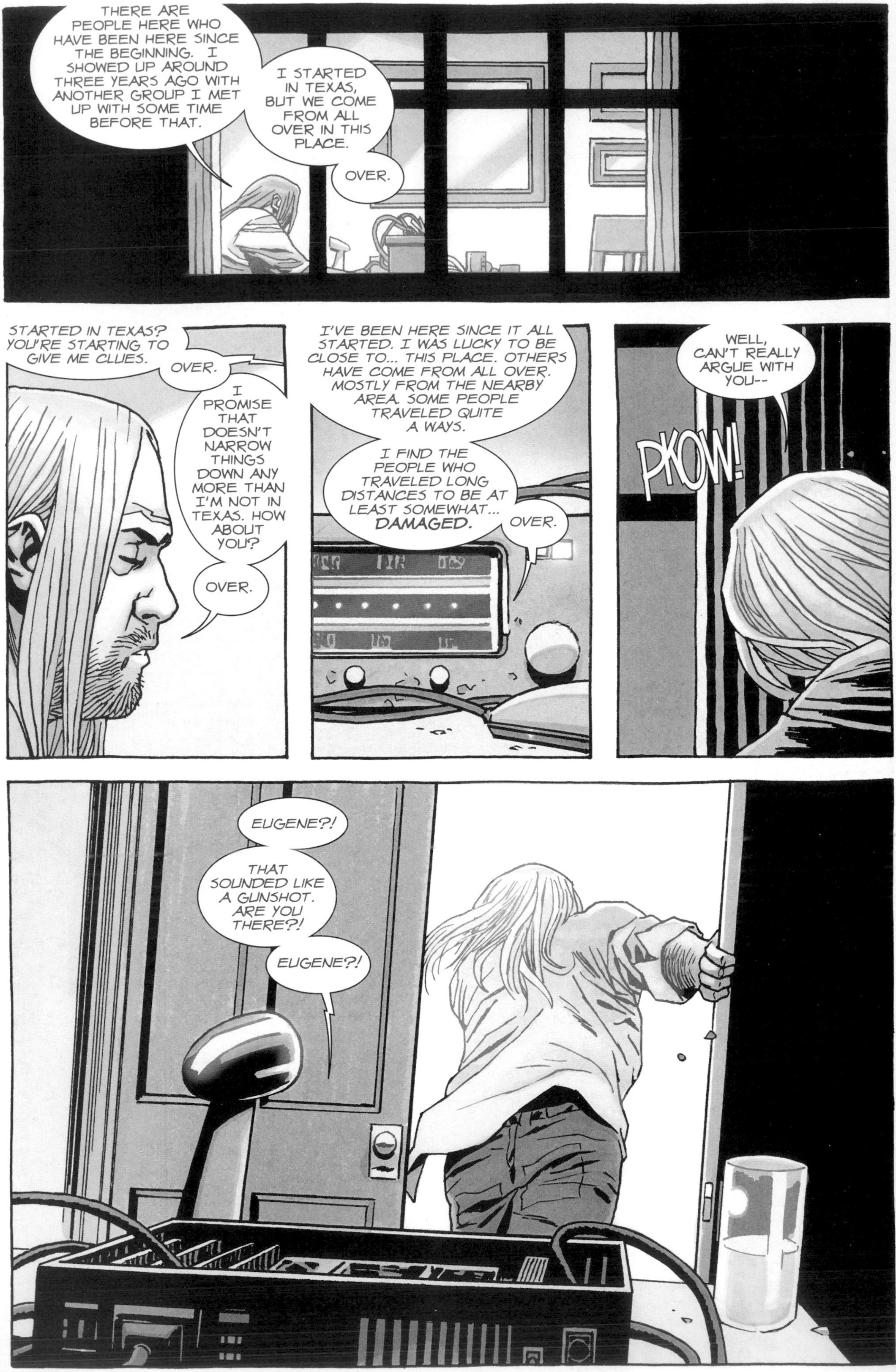
THERE ARE PEOPLE HERE WHO HAVE BEEN HERE SINCE THE BEGINNING. I SHOWED UP AROUND THREE YEARS AGO WITH ANOTHER GROUP I MET UP WITH SOME TIME BEFORE THAT.
I STARTED IN TEXAS, BUT WE COME FROM ALL OVER IN THIS PLACE.
OVER.
STARTED IN TEXAS? YOU'RE STARTING TO GIVE ME CLUES.
OVER.
I PROMISE THAT DOESN'T NARROW THINGS DOWN ANY MORE THAN I'M NOT IN TEXAS. HOW ABOUT YOU?
OVER.
I'VE BEEN HERE SINCE IT ALL STARTED. I WAS LUCKY TO BE CLOSE TO... THIS PLACE. OTHERS HAVE COME FROM ALL OVER. MOSTLY FROM THE NEARBY AREA. SOME PEOPLE TRAVELED QUITE A WAYS.
I FIND THE PEOPLE WHO TRAVELED LONG DISTANCES TO BE AT LEAST SOMEWHAT... **DAMAGED.**
OVER.
WELL, CAN'T REALLY ARGUE WITH YOU--
PKOW!
EUGENE?!
THAT SOUNDED LIKE A GUNSHOT. ARE YOU THERE?!
EUGENE?!

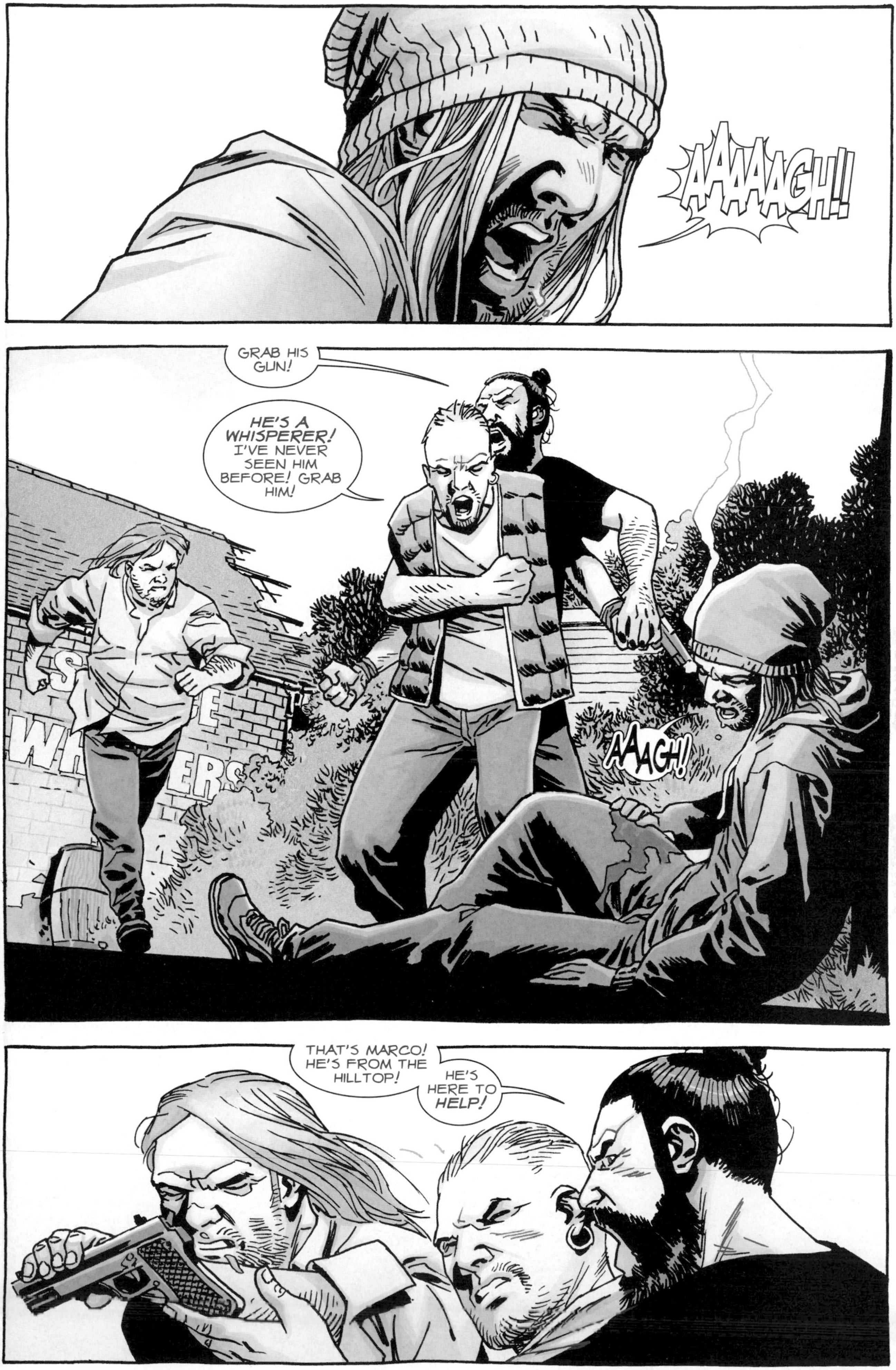
AAAAAGH!!
GRAB HIS GUN!
HE'S A WHISPERER! I'VE NEVER SEEN HIM BEFORE! GRAB HIM!
AAAGH!
THAT'S MARCO! HE'S FROM THE HILLTOP!
HE'S HERE TO HELP!

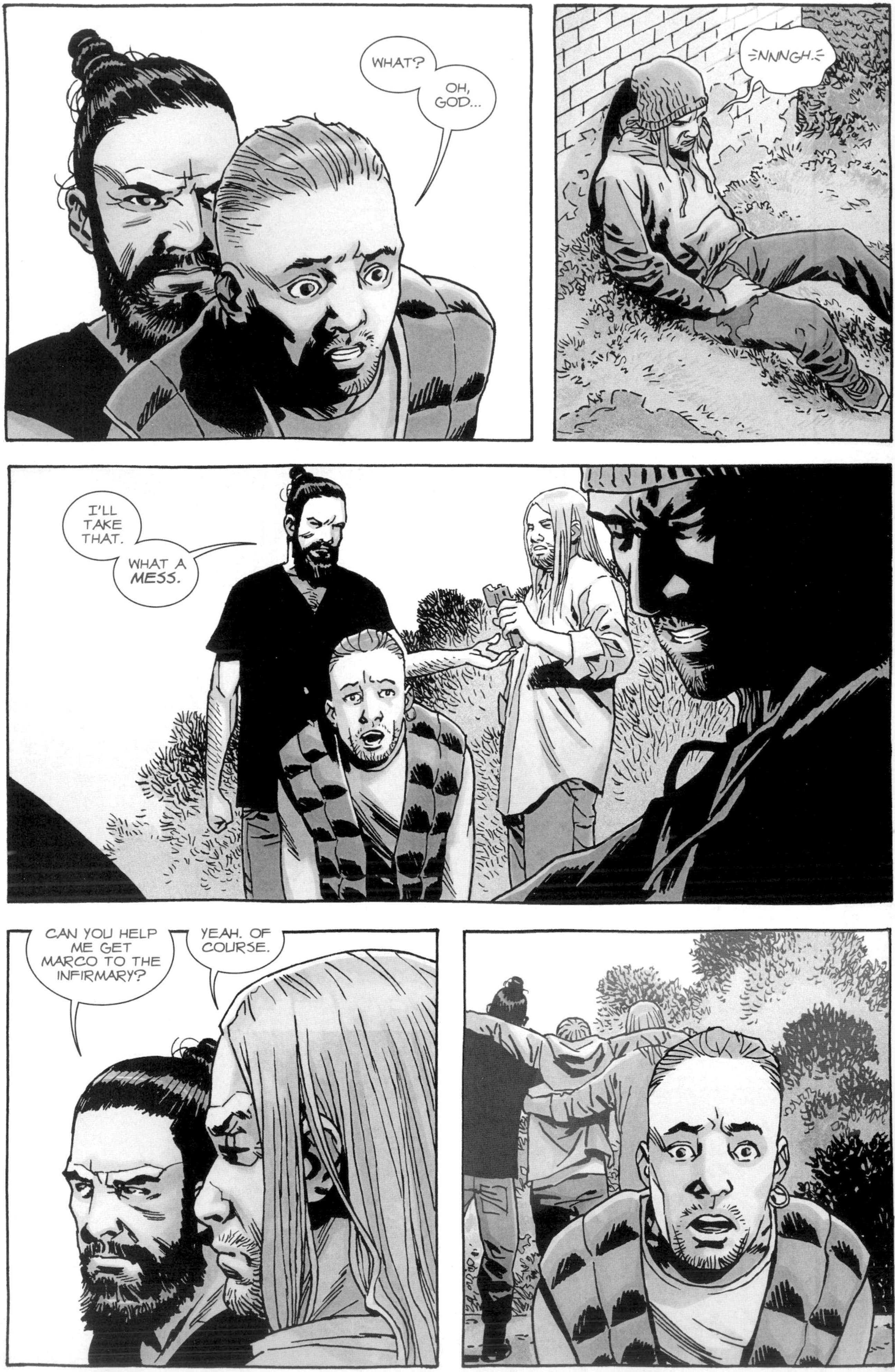
WHAT?
OH, GOD...
NNNGH.
I'LL TAKE THAT.
WHAT A MESS.
CAN YOU HELP ME GET MARCO TO THE INFIRMARY?
YEAH. OF COURSE.

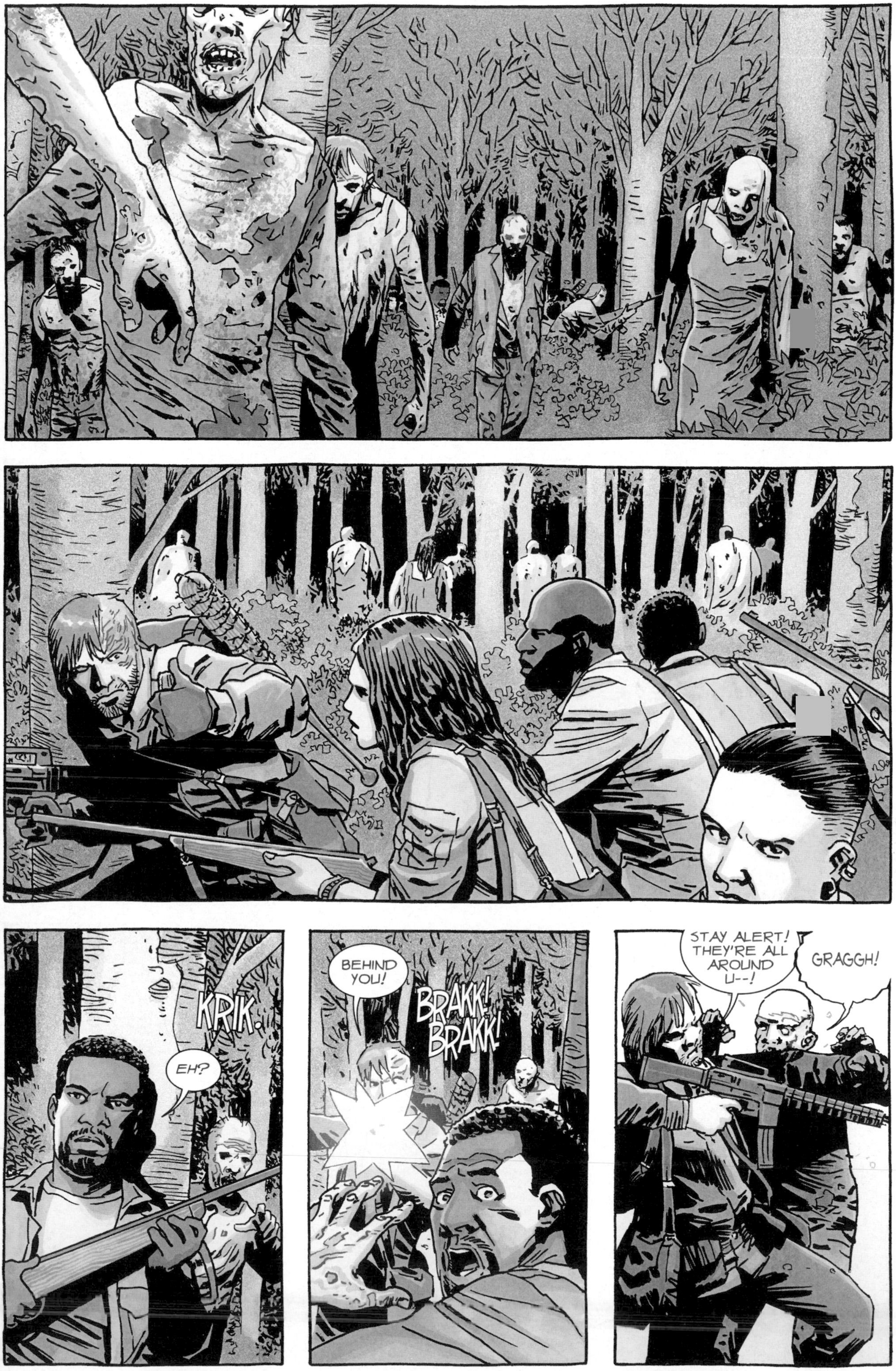
KRIK.
EH?
BEHIND YOU!
BRAKK! BRAKK!
STAY ALERT! THEY'RE ALL AROUND U--!
GRAGGH!

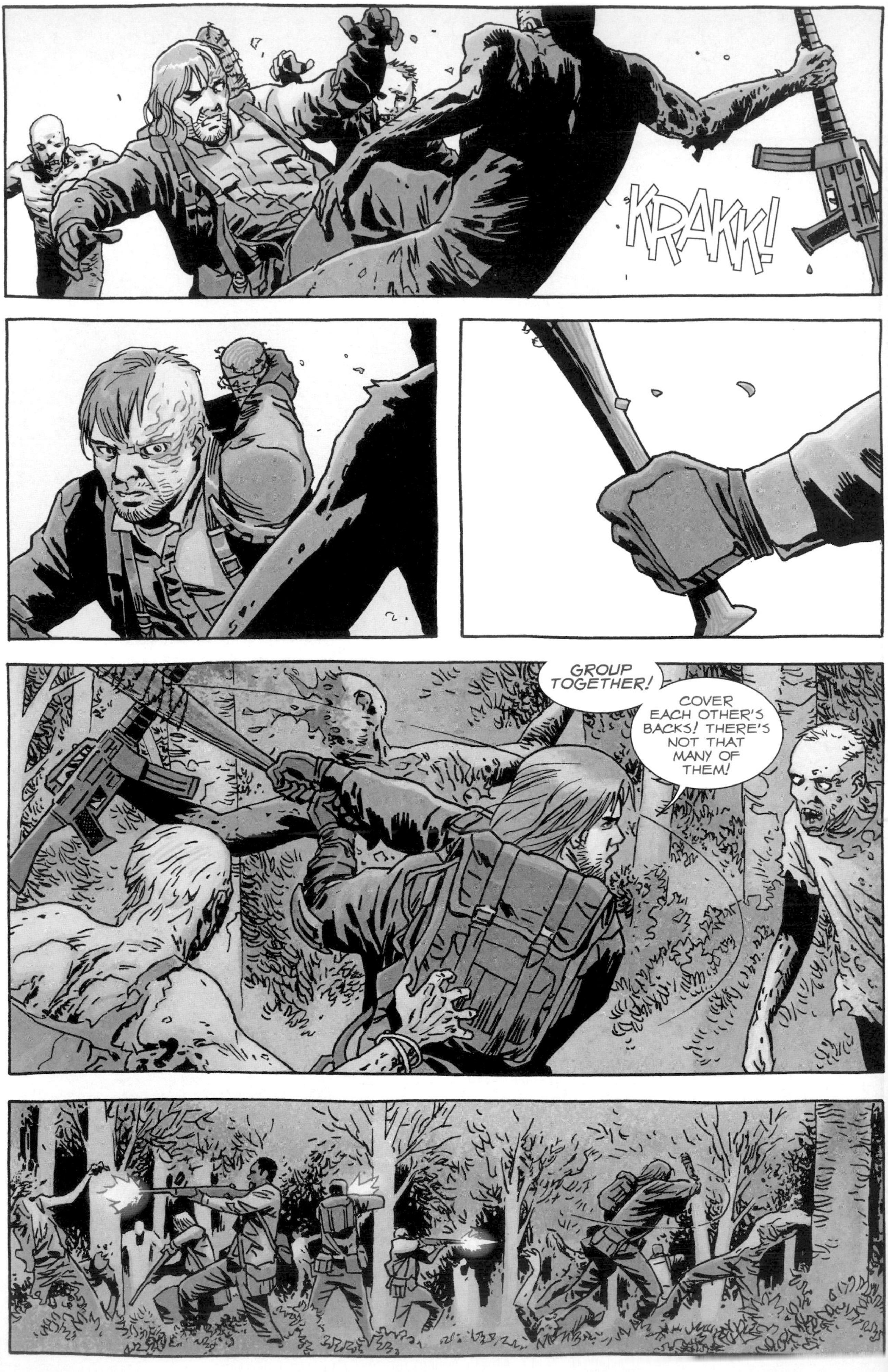
KRAKK!
GROUP TOGETHER!
COVER EACH OTHER'S BACKS! THERE'S NOT THAT MANY OF THEM!

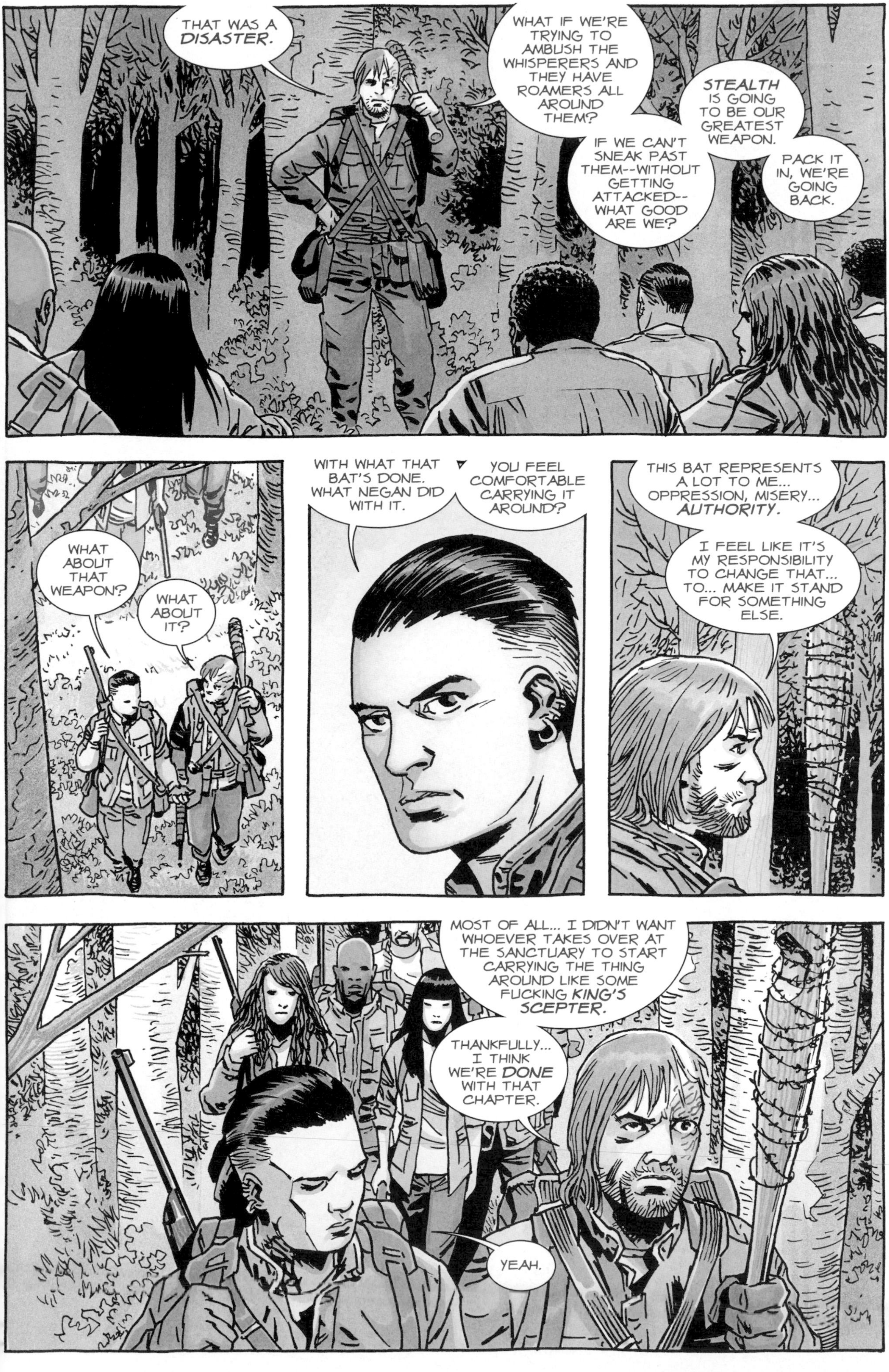
THAT WAS A DISASTER.
WHAT IF WE'RE TRYING TO AMBUSH THE WHISPERERS AND THEY HAVE ROAMERS ALL AROUND THEM?
IF WE CAN'T SNEAK PAST THEM--WITHOUT GETTING ATTACKED-- WHAT GOOD ARE WE?
STEALTH IS GOING TO BE OUR GREATEST WEAPON.
PACK IT IN, WE'RE GOING BACK.
WHAT ABOUT THAT WEAPON?
WHAT ABOUT IT?
WITH WHAT THAT BAT'S DONE. WHAT NEGAN DID WITH IT.
YOU FEEL COMFORTABLE CARRYING IT AROUND?
THIS BAT REPRESENTS A LOT TO ME... OPPRESSION, MISERY... AUTHORITY.
I FEEL LIKE IT'S MY RESPONSIBILITY TO CHANGE THAT... TO... MAKE IT STAND FOR SOMETHING ELSE.
MOST OF ALL... I DIDN'T WANT WHOEVER TAKES OVER AT THE SANCTUARY TO START CARRYING THE THING AROUND LIKE SOME FUCKING KING'S SCEPTER.
THANKFULLY... I THINK WE'RE DONE WITH THAT CHAPTER.
YEAH.

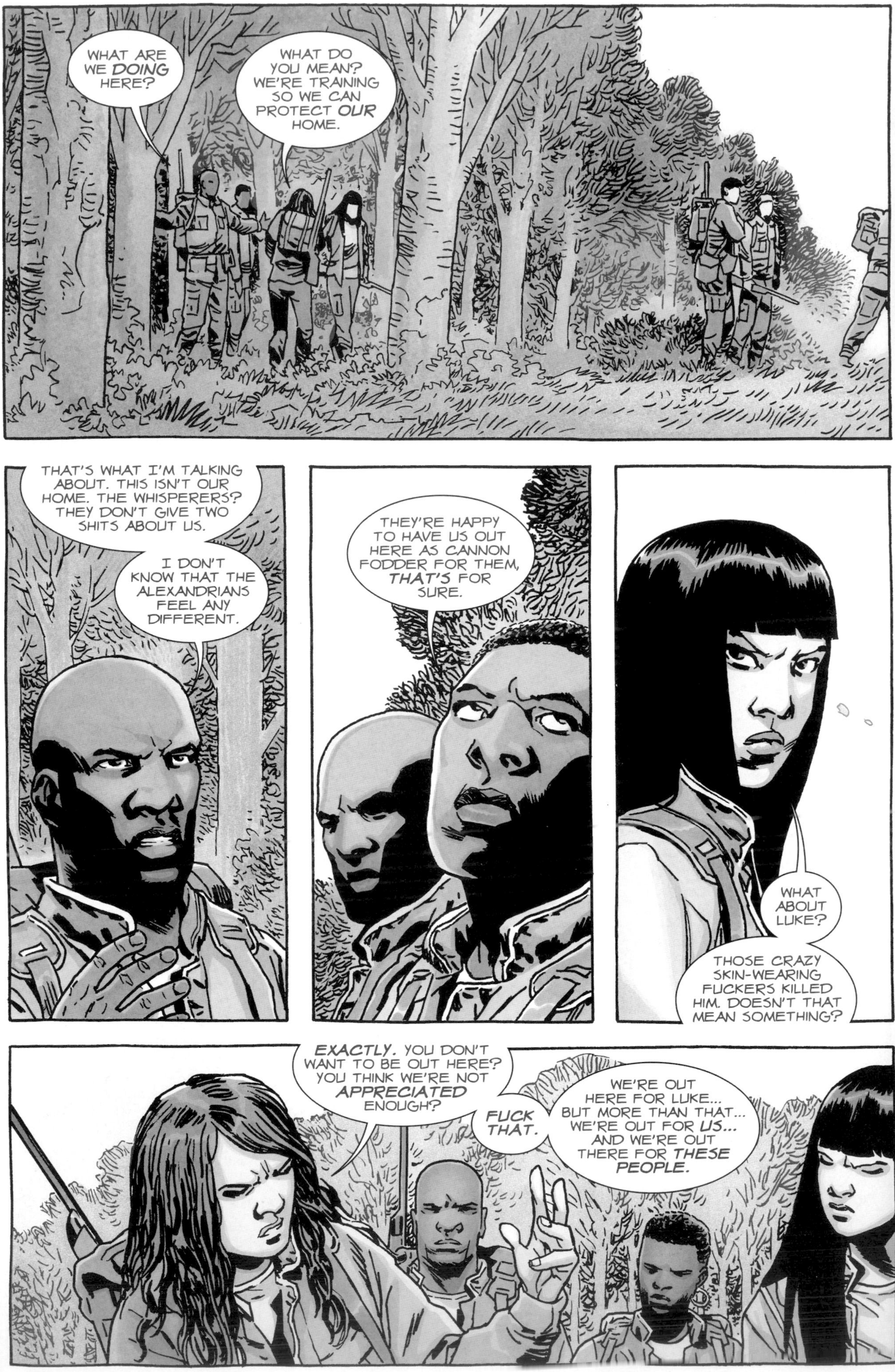
WHAT ARE WE DOING HERE?
WHAT DO YOU MEAN? WE'RE TRAINING SO WE CAN PROTECT OUR HOME.
THAT'S WHAT I'M TALKING ABOUT. THIS ISN'T OUR HOME. THE WHISPERERS? THEY DON'T GIVE TWO SHITS ABOUT US.
I DON'T KNOW THAT THE ALEXANDRIANS FEEL ANY DIFFERENT.
THEY'RE HAPPY TO HAVE US OUT HERE AS CANNON FODDER FOR THEM, THAT'S FOR SURE.
WHAT ABOUT LUKE?
THOSE CRAZY SKIN-WEARING FUCKERS KILLED HIM. DOESN'T THAT MEAN SOMETHING?
EXACTLY. YOU DON'T WANT TO BE OUT HERE? YOU THINK WE'RE NOT APPRECIATED ENOUGH?
FUCK THAT.
WE'RE OUT HERE FOR LUKE... BUT MORE THAN THAT... WE'RE OUT FOR US... AND WE'RE OUT THERE FOR THESE PEOPLE.

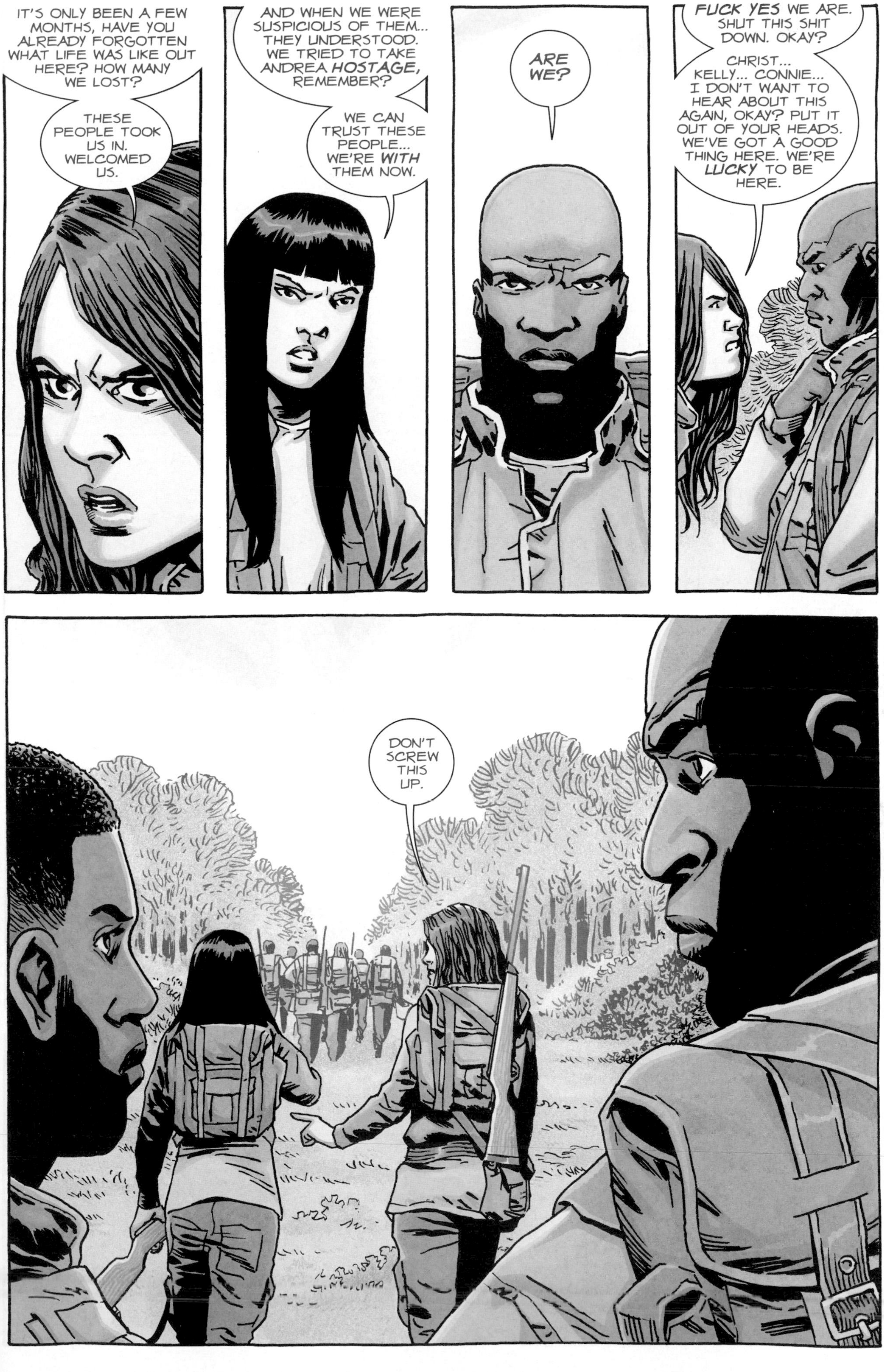
IT'S ONLY BEEN A FEW MONTHS, HAVE YOU ALREADY FORGOTTEN WHAT LIFE WAS LIKE OUT HERE? HOW MANY WE LOST?
THESE PEOPLE TOOK US IN. WELCOMED US.
AND WHEN WE WERE SUSPICIOUS OF THEM... THEY UNDERSTOOD. WE TRIED TO TAKE ANDREA HOSTAGE, REMEMBER?
WE CAN TRUST THESE PEOPLE... WE'RE WITH THEM NOW.
ARE WE?
FUCK YES WE ARE. SHUT THIS SHIT DOWN. OKAY?
CHRIST... KELLY... CONNIE... I DON'T WANT TO HEAR ABOUT THIS AGAIN, OKAY? PUT IT OUT OF YOUR HEADS. WE'VE GOT A GOOD THING HERE. WE'RE LUCKY TO BE HERE.
DON'T SCREW THIS UP.

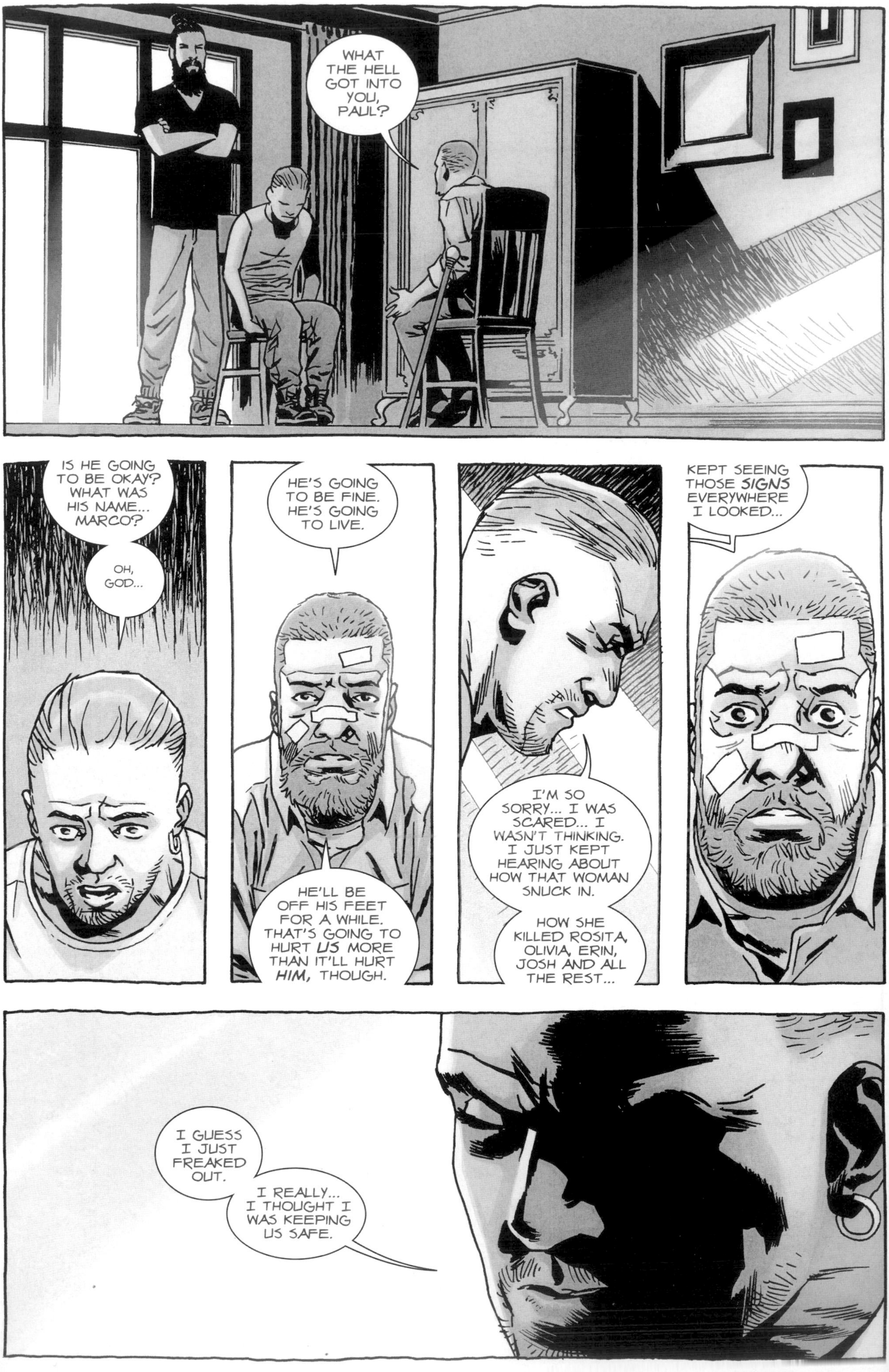
WHAT THE HELL GOT INTO YOU, PAUL?
IS HE GOING TO BE OKAY? WHAT WAS HIS NAME... MARCO?
OH, GOD...
HE'S GOING TO BE FINE. HE'S GOING TO LIVE.
HE'LL BE OFF HIS FEET FOR A WHILE. THAT'S GOING TO HURT US MORE THAN IT'LL HURT HIM, THOUGH.
I'M SO SORRY... I WAS SCARED... I WASN'T THINKING. I JUST KEPT HEARING ABOUT HOW THAT WOMAN SNUCK IN.
HOW SHE KILLED ROSITA, OLIVIA, ERIN, JOSH AND ALL THE REST...
KEPT SEEING THOSE SIGNS EVERYWHERE I LOOKED...
I GUESS I JUST FREAKED OUT.
I REALLY... I THOUGHT I WAS KEEPING US SAFE.

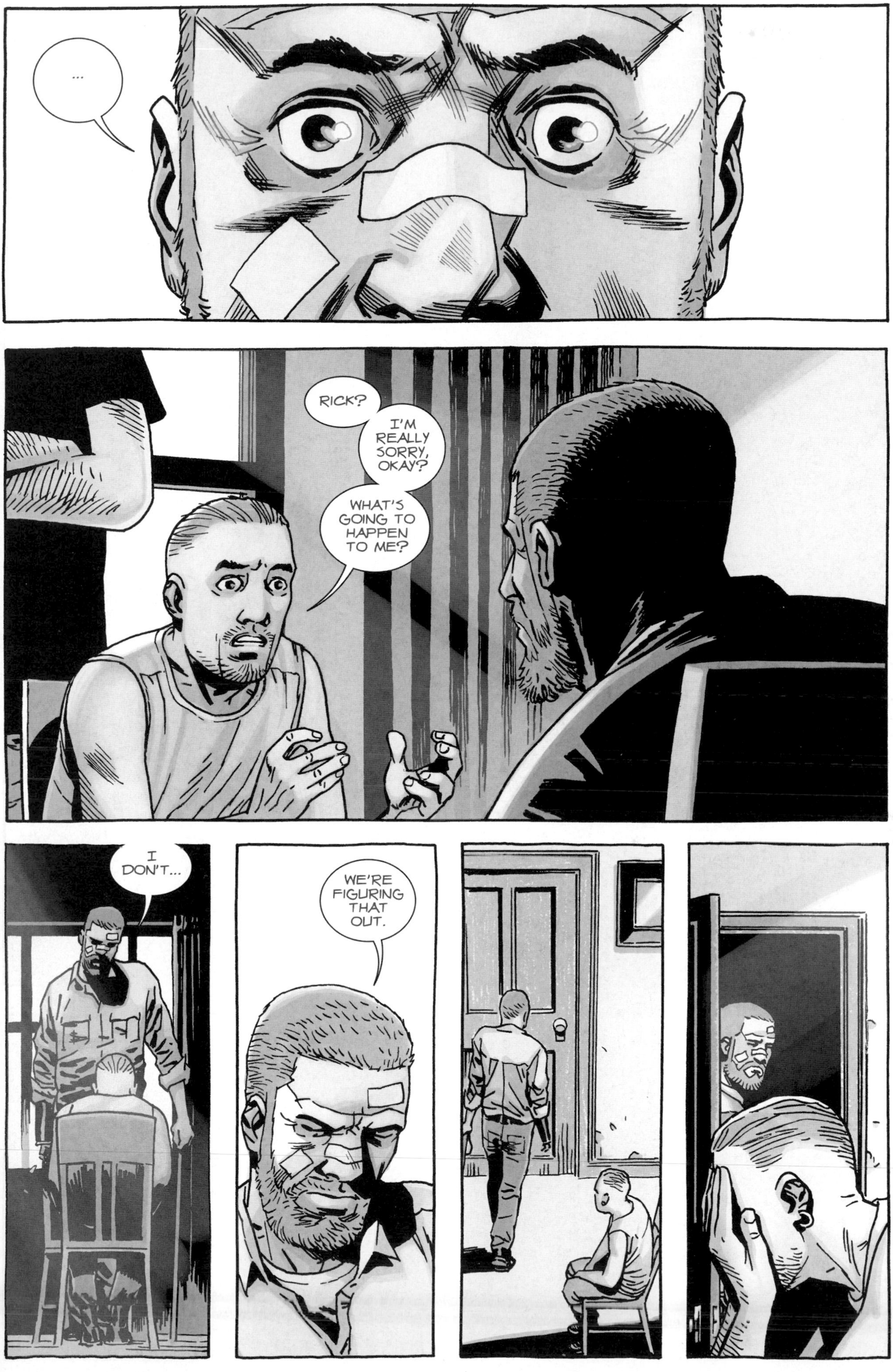
...
RICK?
I'M REALLY SORRY, OKAY?
WHAT'S GOING TO HAPPEN TO ME?
I DON'T...
WE'RE FIGURING THAT OUT.

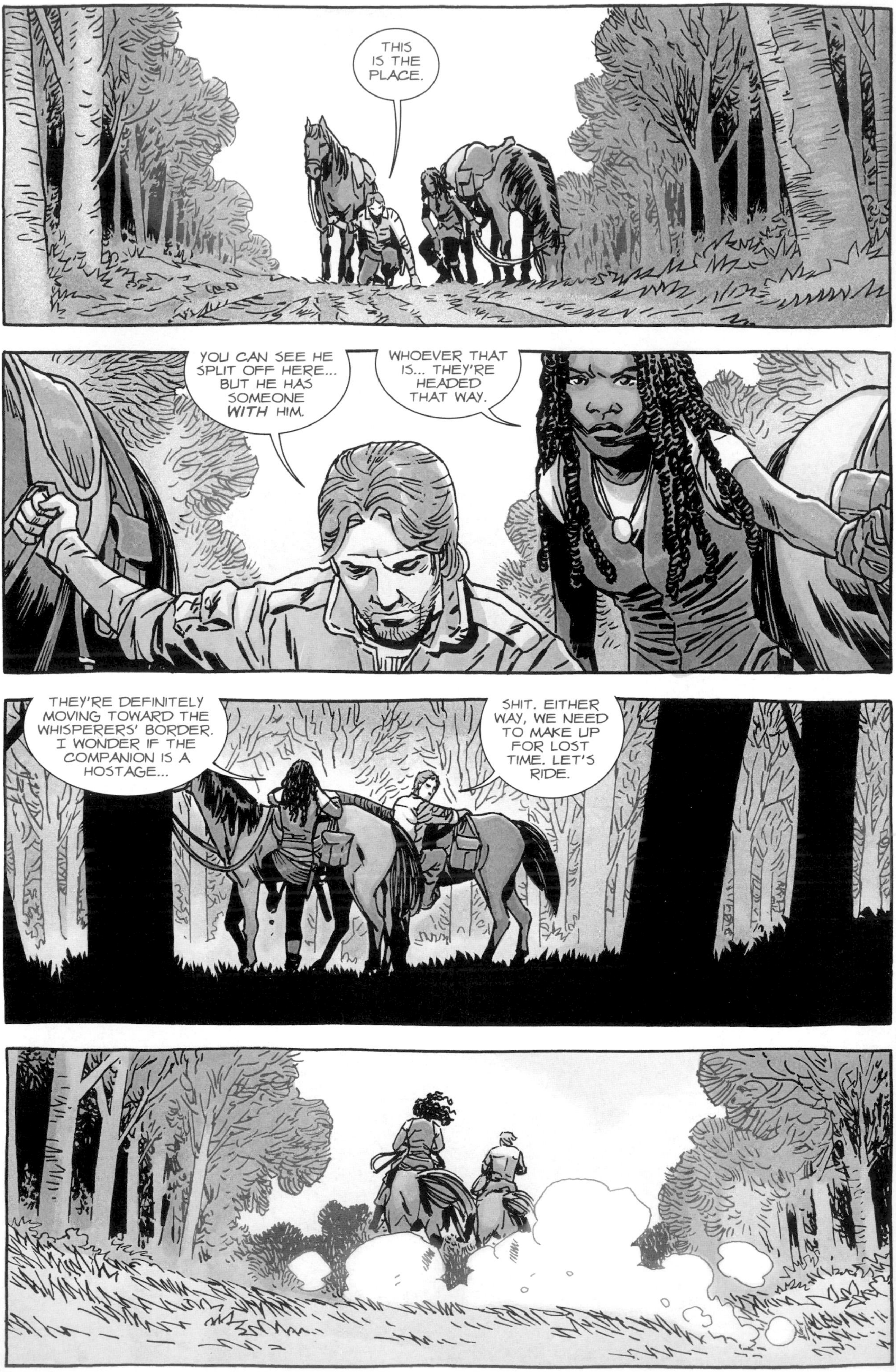
THIS IS THE PLACE.
YOU CAN SEE HE SPLIT OFF HERE... BUT HE HAS SOMEONE WITH HIM.
WHOEVER THAT IS... THEY'RE HEADED THAT WAY.
THEY'RE DEFINITELY MOVING TOWARD THE WHISPERERS' BORDER. I WONDER IF THE COMPANION IS A HOSTAGE...
SHIT. EITHER WAY, WE NEED TO MAKE UP FOR LOST TIME. LET'S RIDE.

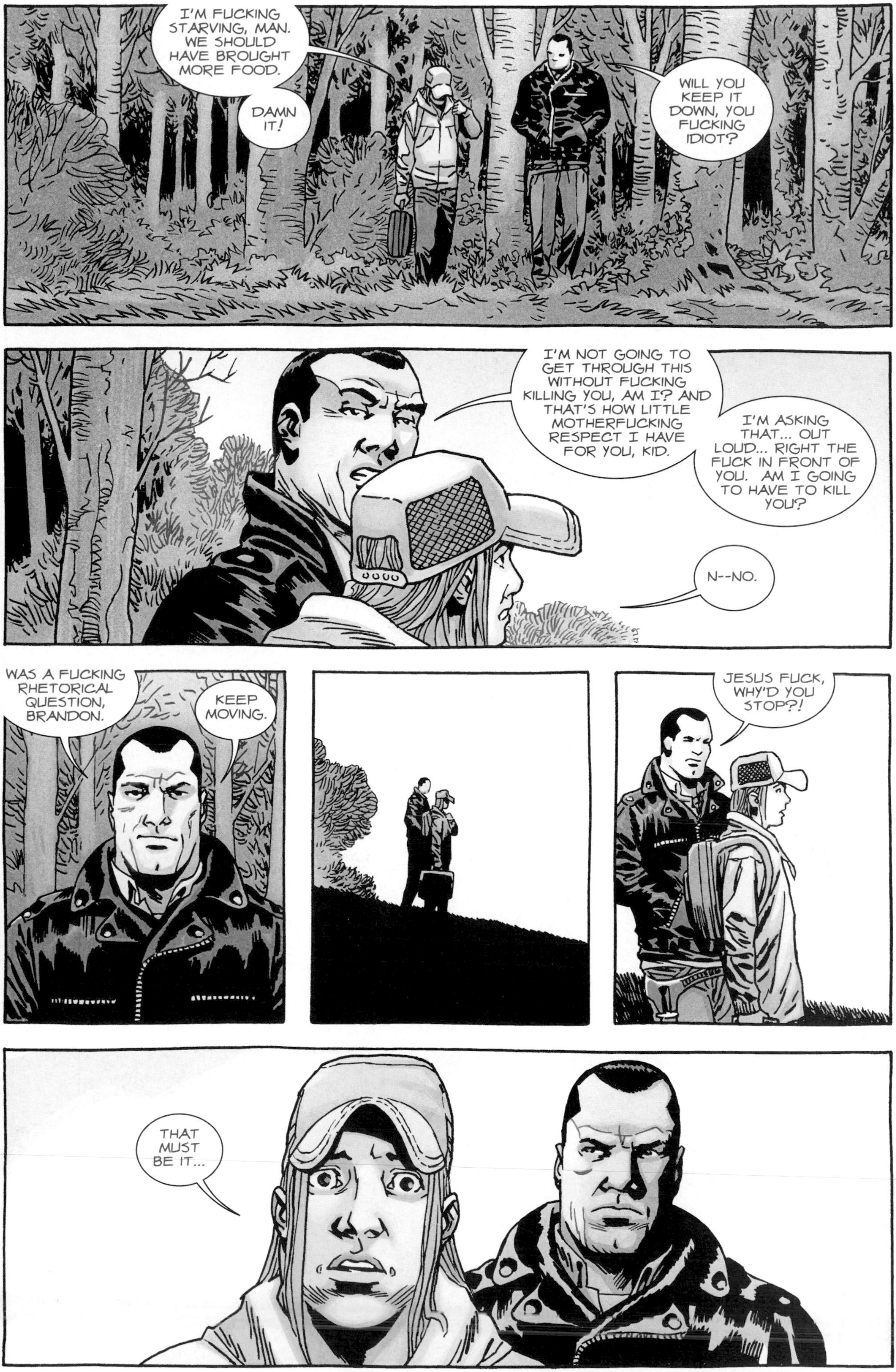
I'M FUCKING STARVING, MAN. WE SHOULD HAVE BROUGHT MORE FOOD.
DAMN IT!
WILL YOU KEEP IT DOWN, YOU FUCKING IDIOT?
I'M NOT GOING TO GET THROUGH THIS WITHOUT FUCKING KILLING YOU, AM I? AND THAT'S HOW LITTLE MOTHERFUCKING RESPECT I HAVE FOR YOU, KID.
I'M ASKING THAT... OUT LOUD... RIGHT THE FUCK IN FRONT OF YOU. AM I GOING TO HAVE TO KILL YOU?
N--NO.
WAS A FUCKING RHETORICAL QUESTION, BRANDON.
KEEP MOVING.
JESUS FUCK, WHY'D YOU STOP?!
THAT MUST BE IT...

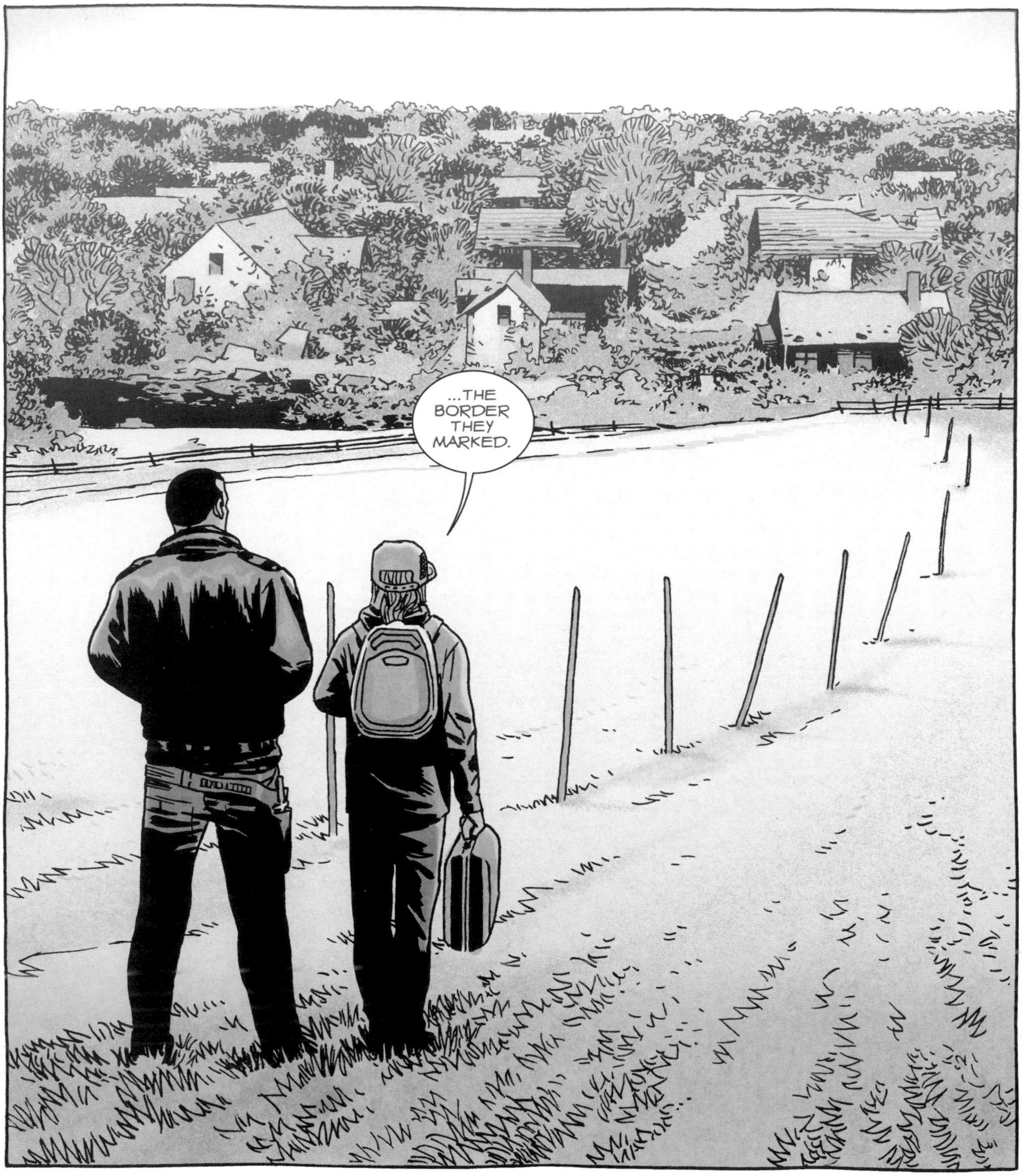
...THE BORDER THEY MARKED.

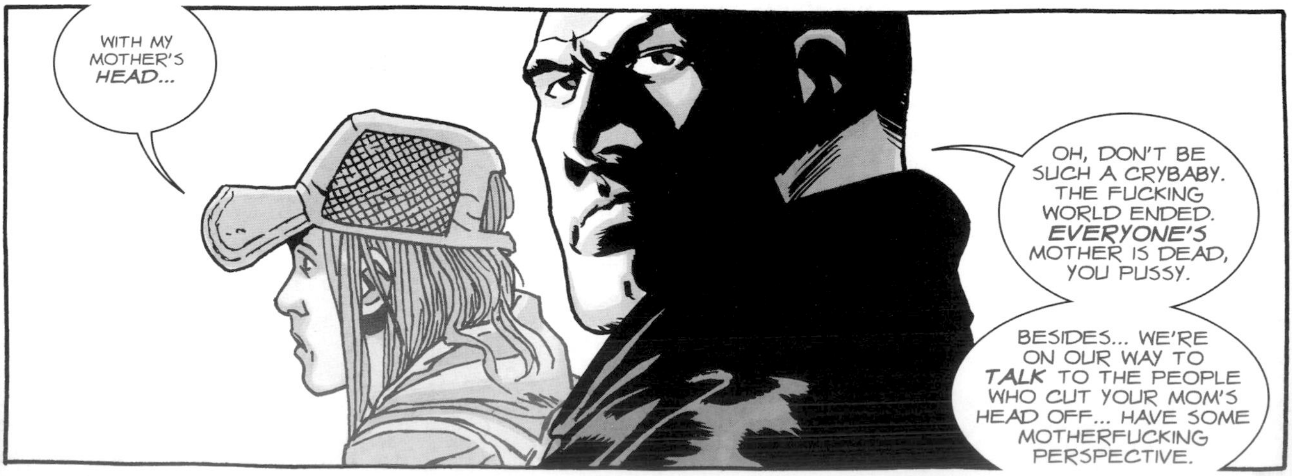
WITH MY MOTHER'S HEAD...
OH, DON'T BE SUCH A CRYBABY. THE FUCKING WORLD ENDED. EVERYONE'S MOTHER IS DEAD, YOU PUSSY.
BESIDES... WE'RE ON OUR WAY TO TALK TO THE PEOPLE WHO CUT YOUR MOM'S HEAD OFF... HAVE SOME MOTHERFUCKING PERSPECTIVE.

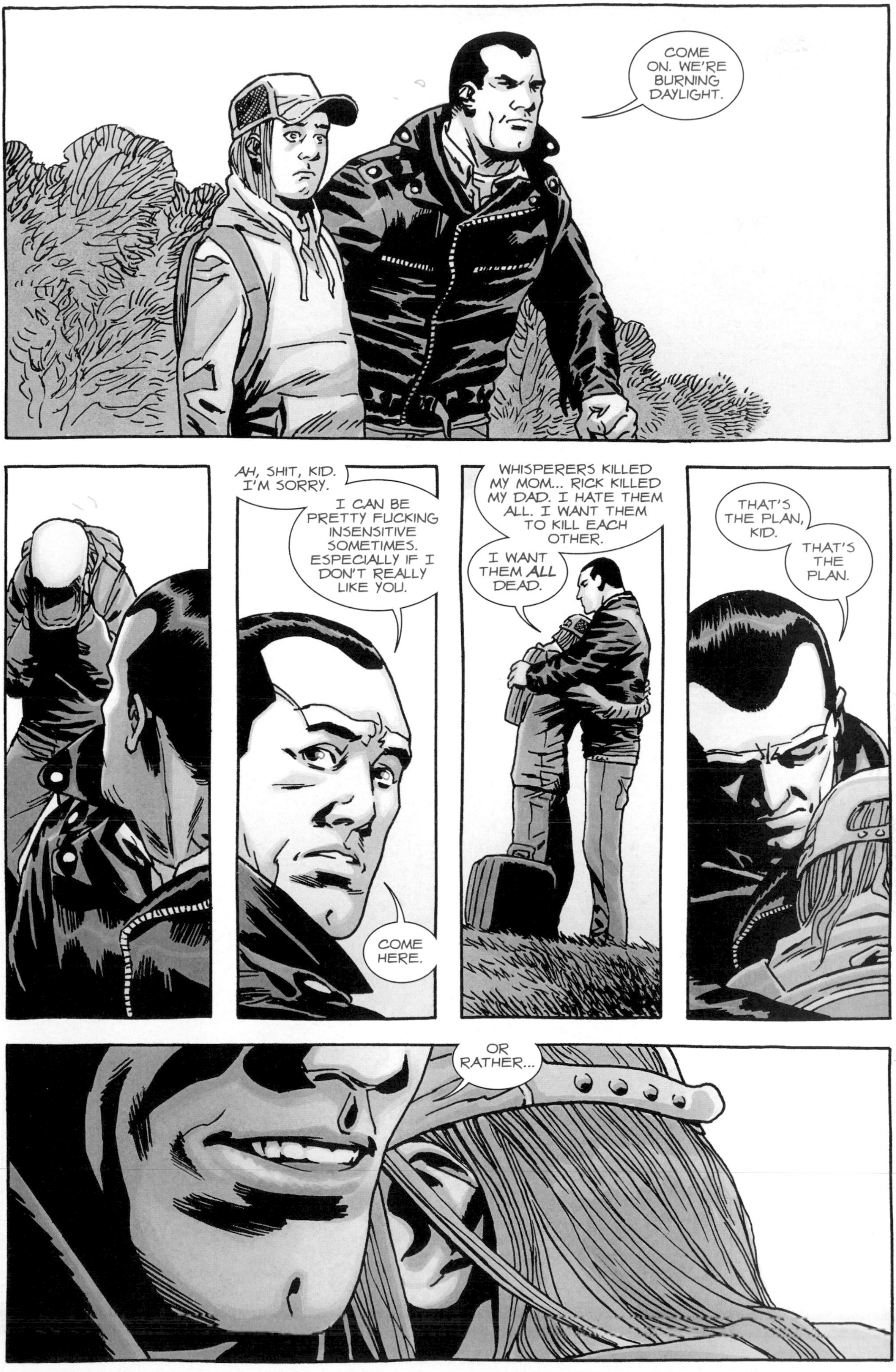
COME ON. WE'RE BURNING DAYLIGHT.
AH, SHIT, KID. I'M SORRY.
I CAN BE PRETTY FUCKING INSENSITIVE SOMETIMES. ESPECIALLY IF I DON'T REALLY LIKE YOU.
COME HERE.
WHISPERERS KILLED MY MOM... RICK KILLED MY DAD. I HATE THEM ALL. I WANT THEM TO KILL EACH OTHER.
I WANT THEM *ALL* DEAD.
THAT'S THE PLAN, KID.
THAT'S THE PLAN.
OR RATHER...

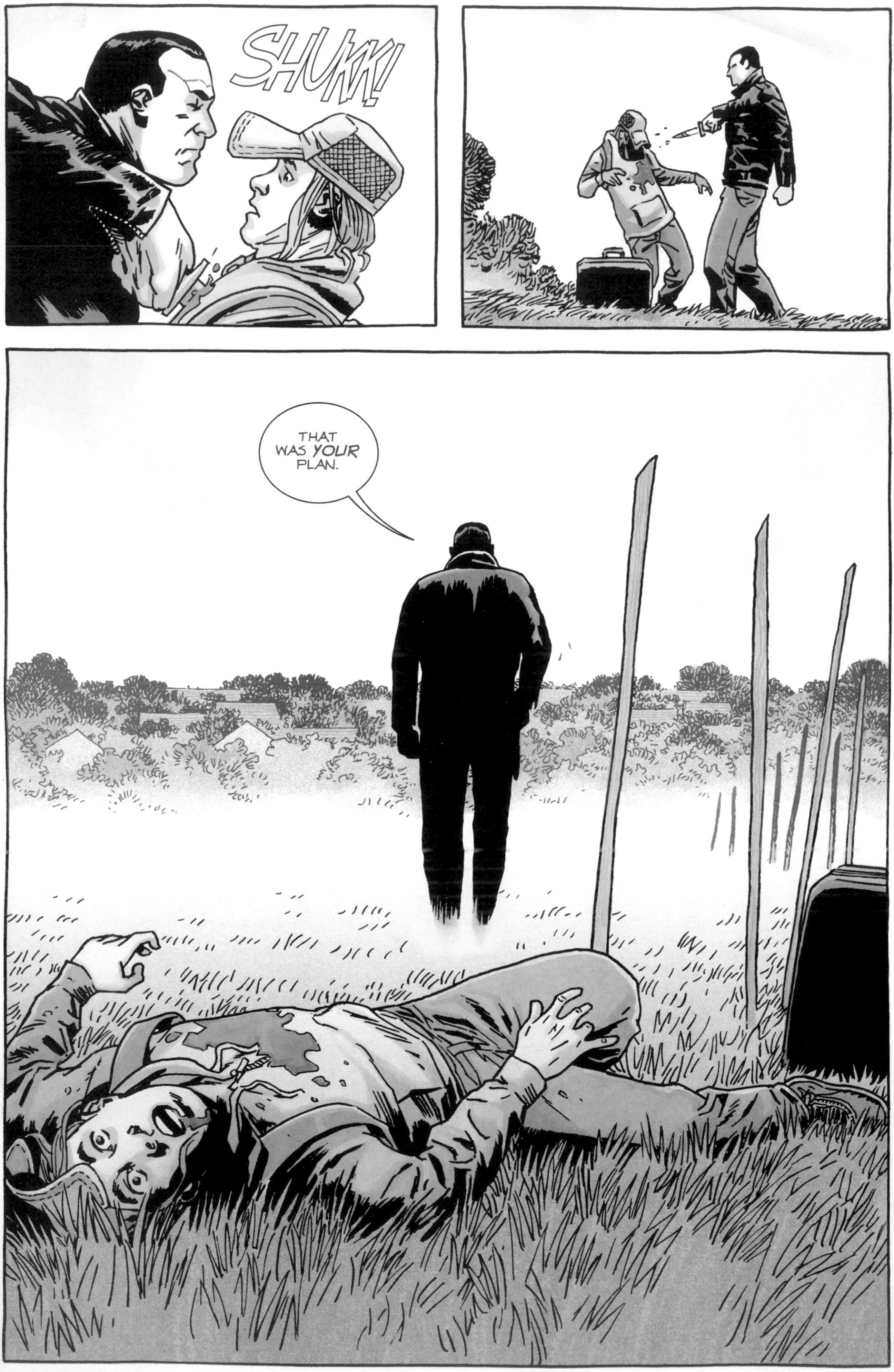
SHUKK!
THAT WAS YOUR PLAN.

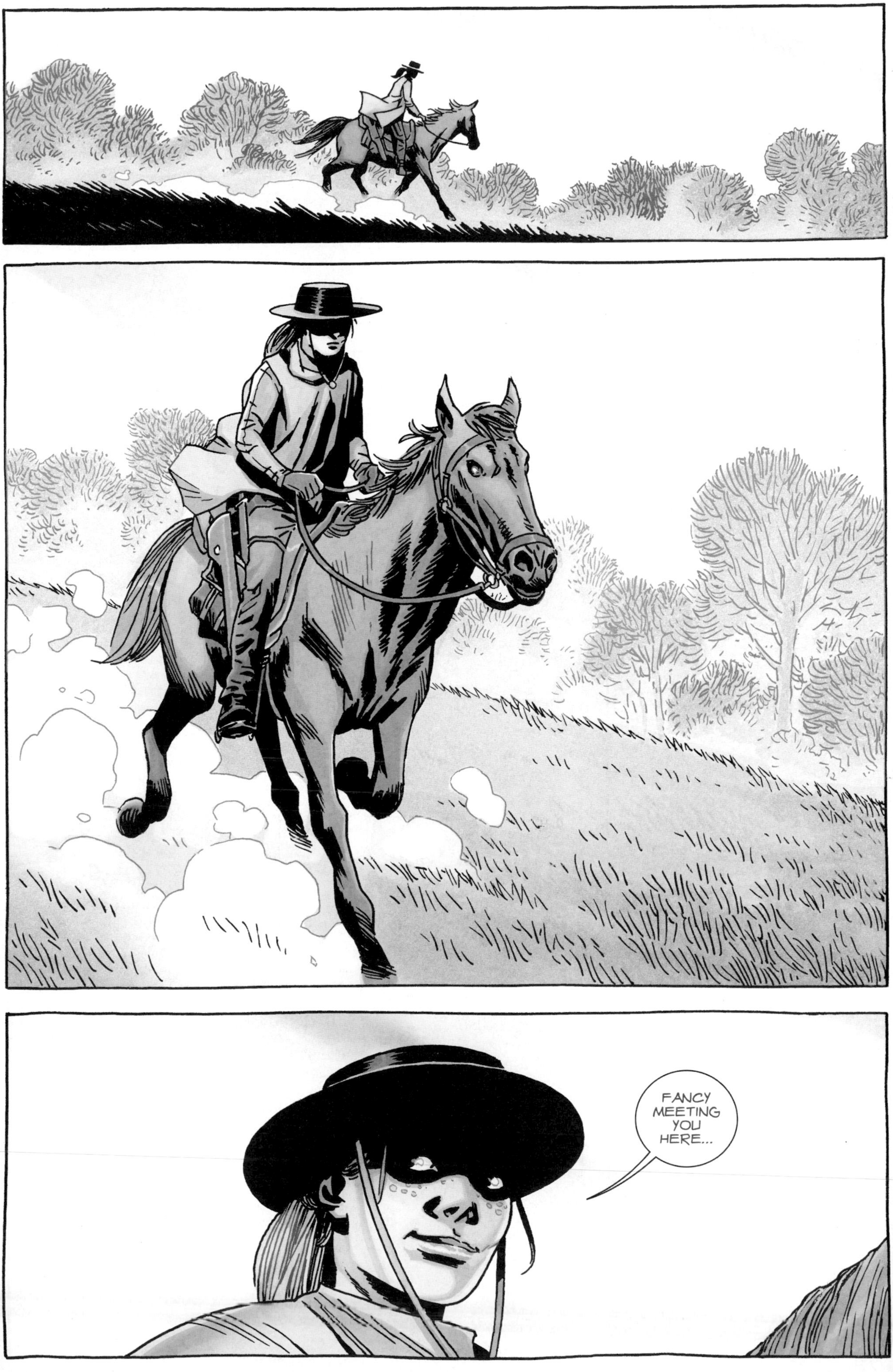
FANCY MEETING YOU HERE...

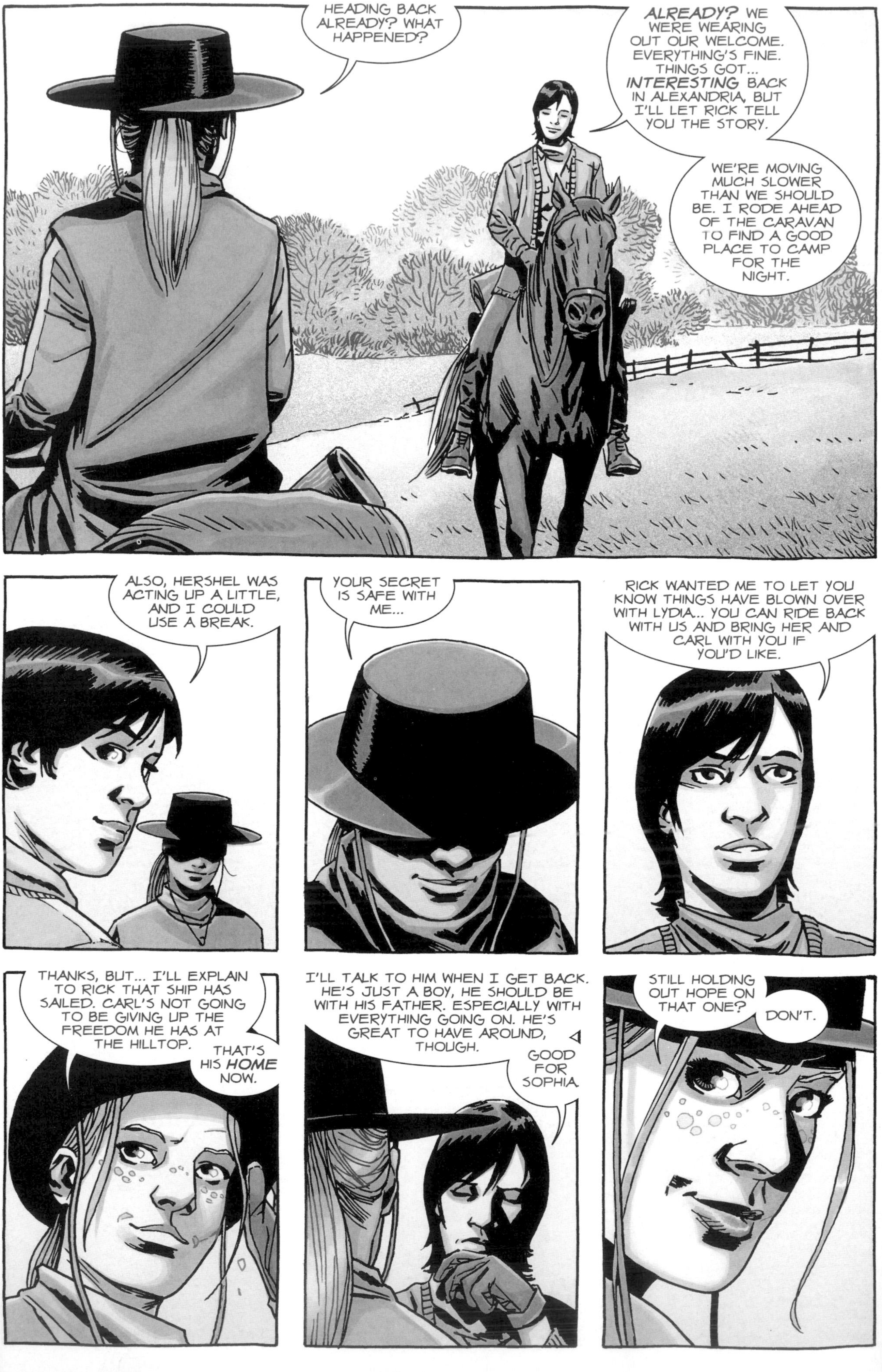
HEADING BACK ALREADY? WHAT HAPPENED?
ALREADY? WE WERE WEARING OUT OUR WELCOME. EVERYTHING'S FINE. THINGS GOT... INTERESTING BACK IN ALEXANDRIA, BUT I'LL LET RICK TELL YOU THE STORY.
WE'RE MOVING MUCH SLOWER THAN WE SHOULD BE. I RODE AHEAD OF THE CARAVAN TO FIND A GOOD PLACE TO CAMP FOR THE NIGHT.
ALSO, HERSHEL WAS ACTING UP A LITTLE, AND I COULD USE A BREAK.
YOUR SECRET IS SAFE WITH ME...
RICK WANTED ME TO LET YOU KNOW THINGS HAVE BLOWN OVER WITH LYDIA.. YOU CAN RIDE BACK WITH US AND BRING HER AND CARL WITH YOU IF YOU'D LIKE.
THANKS, BUT... I'LL EXPLAIN TO RICK THAT SHIP HAS SAILED. CARL'S NOT GOING TO BE GIVING UP THE FREEDOM HE HAS AT THE HILLTOP.
THAT'S HIS HOME NOW.
I'LL TALK TO HIM WHEN I GET BACK. HE'S JUST A BOY, HE SHOULD BE WITH HIS FATHER. ESPECIALLY WITH EVERYTHING GOING ON. HE'S GREAT TO HAVE AROUND, THOUGH.
GOOD FOR SOPHIA.
STILL HOLDING OUT HOPE ON THAT ONE?
DON'T.

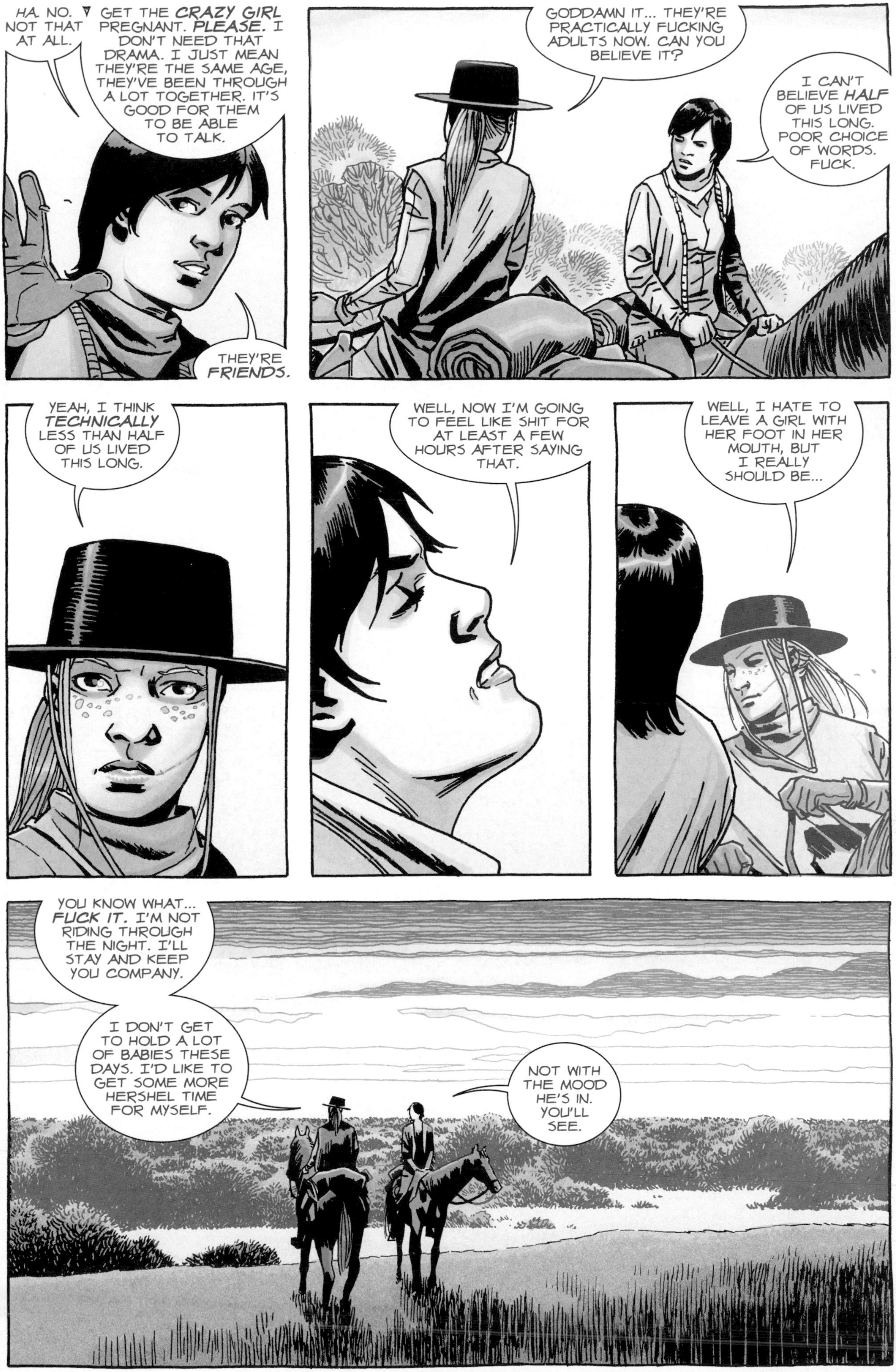
HA. NO. NOT THAT AT ALL.
GET THE CRAZY GIRL PREGNANT. PLEASE. I DON'T NEED THAT DRAMA. I JUST MEAN THEY'RE THE SAME AGE, THEY'VE BEEN THROUGH A LOT TOGETHER. IT'S GOOD FOR THEM TO BE ABLE TO TALK.
THEY'RE FRIENDS.
GODDAMN IT... THEY'RE PRACTICALLY FUCKING ADULTS NOW. CAN YOU BELIEVE IT?
I CAN'T BELIEVE HALF OF US LIVED THIS LONG. POOR CHOICE OF WORDS. FUCK.
YEAH, I THINK TECHNICALLY LESS THAN HALF OF US LIVED THIS LONG.
WELL, NOW I'M GOING TO FEEL LIKE SHIT FOR AT LEAST A FEW HOURS AFTER SAYING THAT.
WELL, I HATE TO LEAVE A GIRL WITH HER FOOT IN HER MOUTH, BUT I REALLY SHOULD BE...
YOU KNOW WHAT... FUCK IT. I'M NOT RIDING THROUGH THE NIGHT. I'LL STAY AND KEEP YOU COMPANY.
I DON'T GET TO HOLD A LOT OF BABIES THESE DAYS. I'D LIKE TO GET SOME MORE HERSHEL TIME FOR MYSELF.
NOT WITH THE MOOD HE'S IN. YOU'LL SEE.

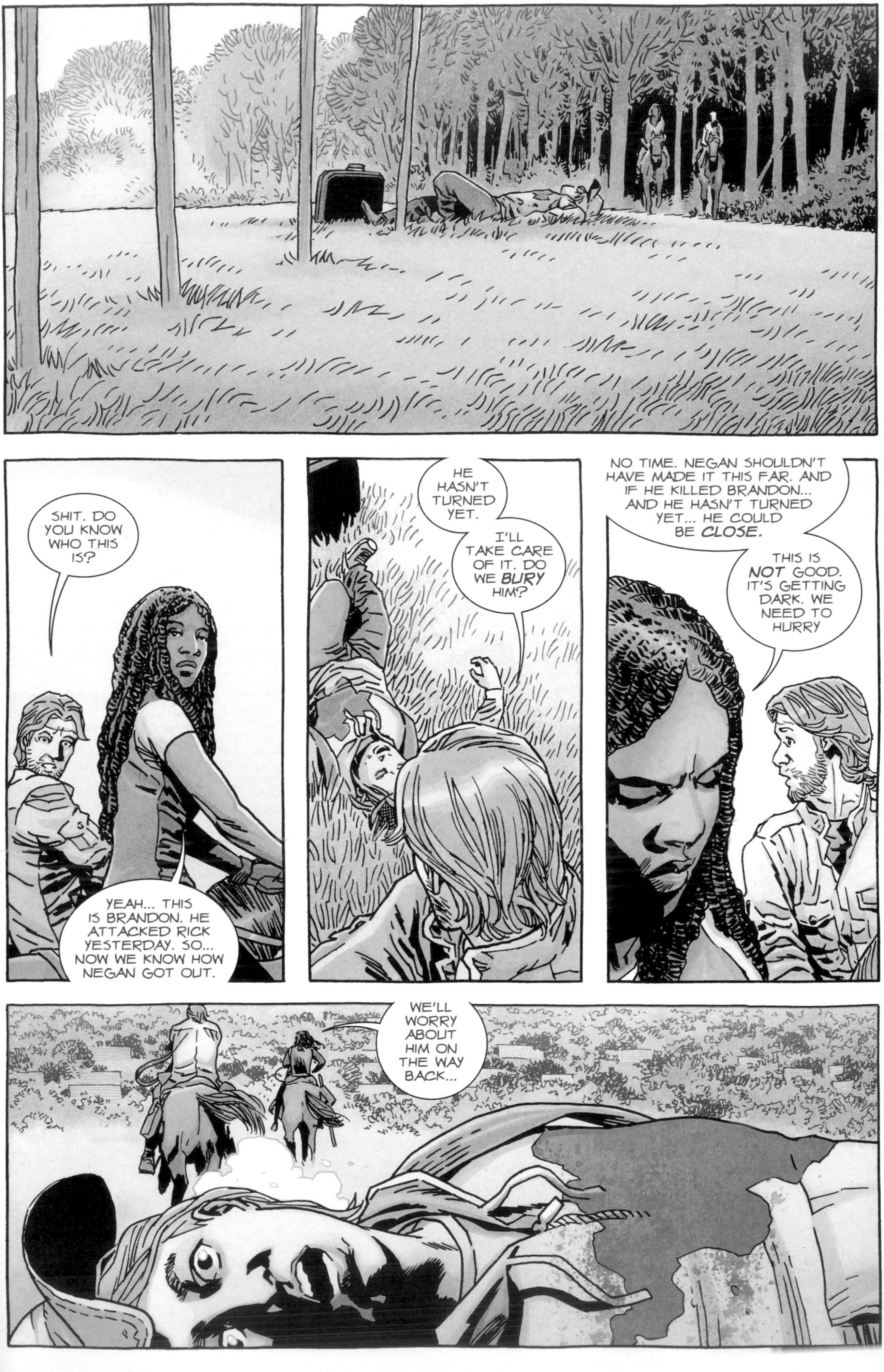
SHIT. DO YOU KNOW WHO THIS IS?
YEAH... THIS IS BRANDON. HE ATTACKED RICK YESTERDAY. SO... NOW WE KNOW HOW NEGAN GOT OUT.
HE HASN'T TURNED YET.
I'LL TAKE CARE OF IT. DO WE BURY HIM?
NO TIME. NEGAN SHOULDN'T HAVE MADE IT THIS FAR. AND IF HE KILLED BRANDON... AND HE HASN'T TURNED YET... HE COULD BE CLOSE.
THIS IS NOT GOOD. IT'S GETTING DARK. WE NEED TO HURRY
WE'LL WORRY ABOUT HIM ON THE WAY BACK...

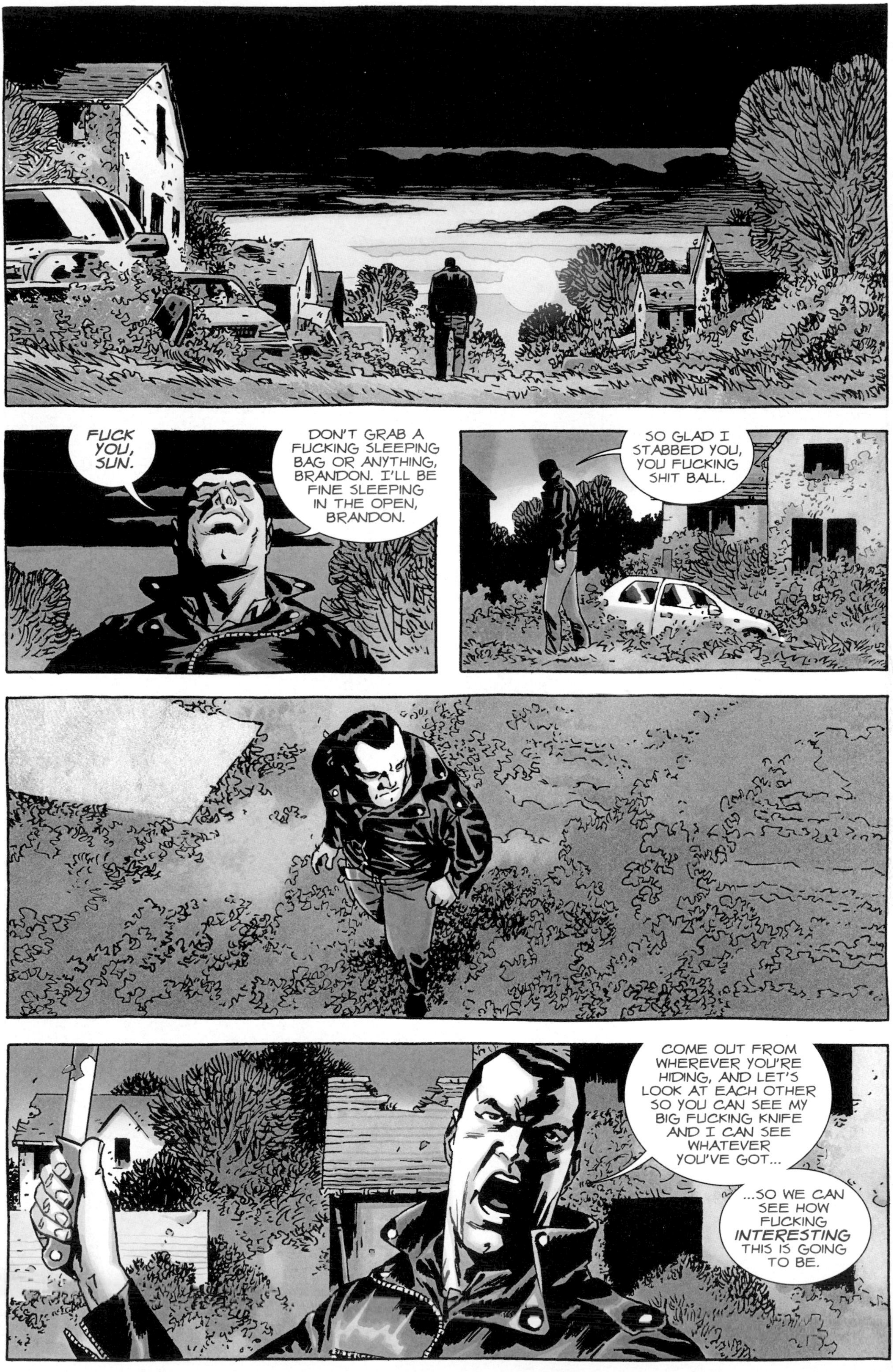
FUCK YOU, SUN.
DON'T GRAB A FUCKING SLEEPING BAG OR ANYTHING, BRANDON. I'LL BE FINE SLEEPING IN THE OPEN, BRANDON.
SO GLAD I STABBED YOU, YOU FUCKING SHIT BALL.
COME OUT FROM WHEREVER YOU'RE HIDING, AND LET'S LOOK AT EACH OTHER SO YOU CAN SEE MY BIG FUCKING KNIFE AND I CAN SEE WHATEVER YOU'VE GOT...
...SO WE CAN SEE HOW FUCKING INTERESTING THIS IS GOING TO BE.

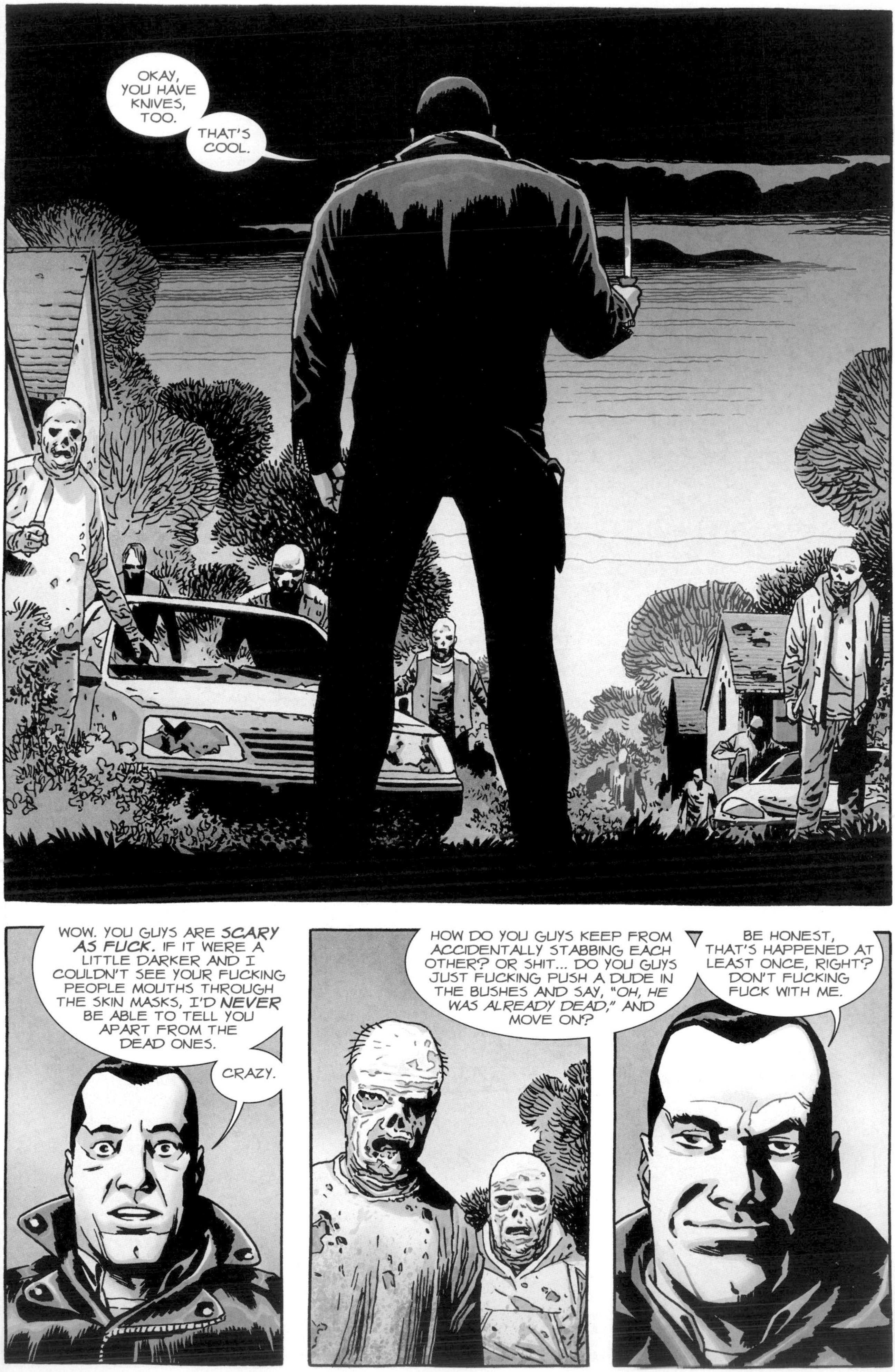
OKAY, YOU HAVE KNIVES, TOO.
THAT'S COOL.
WOW. YOU GUYS ARE SCARY AS FUCK. IF IT WERE A LITTLE DARKER AND I COULDN'T SEE YOUR FUCKING PEOPLE MOUTHS THROUGH THE SKIN MASKS, I'D NEVER BE ABLE TO TELL YOU APART FROM THE DEAD ONES.
CRAZY.
HOW DO YOU GUYS KEEP FROM ACCIDENTALLY STABBING EACH OTHER? OR SHIT... DO YOU GUYS JUST FUCKING PUSH A DUDE IN THE BUSHES AND SAY, "OH, HE WAS ALREADY DEAD," AND MOVE ON?
BE HONEST, THAT'S HAPPENED AT LEAST ONCE, RIGHT? DON'T FUCKING FUCK WITH ME.

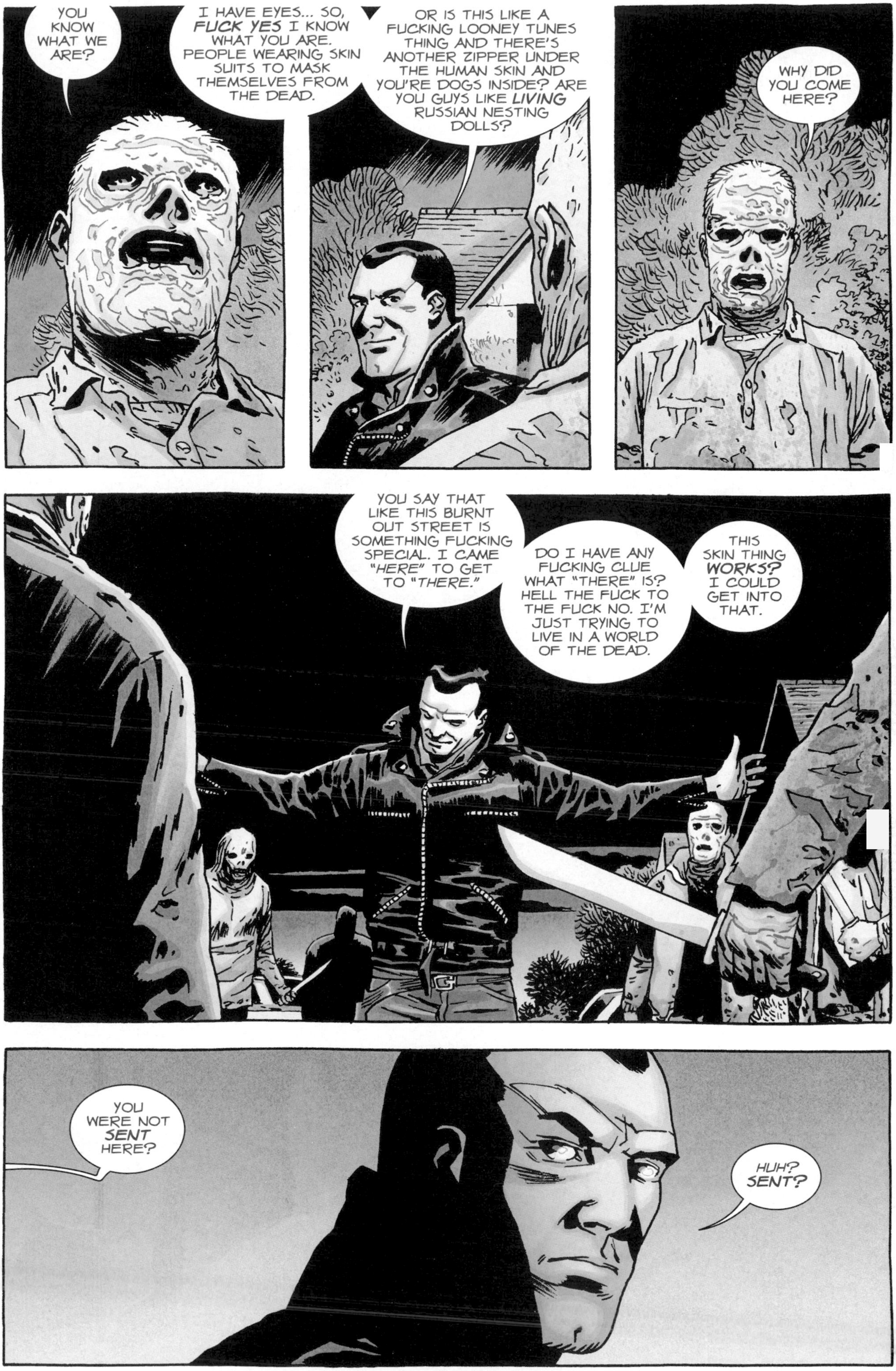
YOU KNOW WHAT WE ARE?
I HAVE EYES... SO, FUCK YES I KNOW WHAT YOU ARE. PEOPLE WEARING SKIN SUITS TO MASK THEMSELVES FROM THE DEAD.
OR IS THIS LIKE A FUCKING LOONEY TUNES THING AND THERE'S ANOTHER ZIPPER UNDER THE HUMAN SKIN AND YOU'RE DOGS INSIDE? ARE YOU GUYS LIKE LIVING RUSSIAN NESTING DOLLS?
WHY DID YOU COME HERE?
YOU SAY THAT LIKE THIS BURNT OUT STREET IS SOMETHING FUCKING SPECIAL. I CAME "HERE" TO GET TO "THERE."
DO I HAVE ANY FUCKING CLUE WHAT "THERE" IS? HELL THE FUCK TO THE FUCK NO. I'M JUST TRYING TO LIVE IN A WORLD OF THE DEAD.
THIS SKIN THING WORKS? I COULD GET INTO THAT.
YOU WERE NOT SENT HERE?
HUH? SENT?

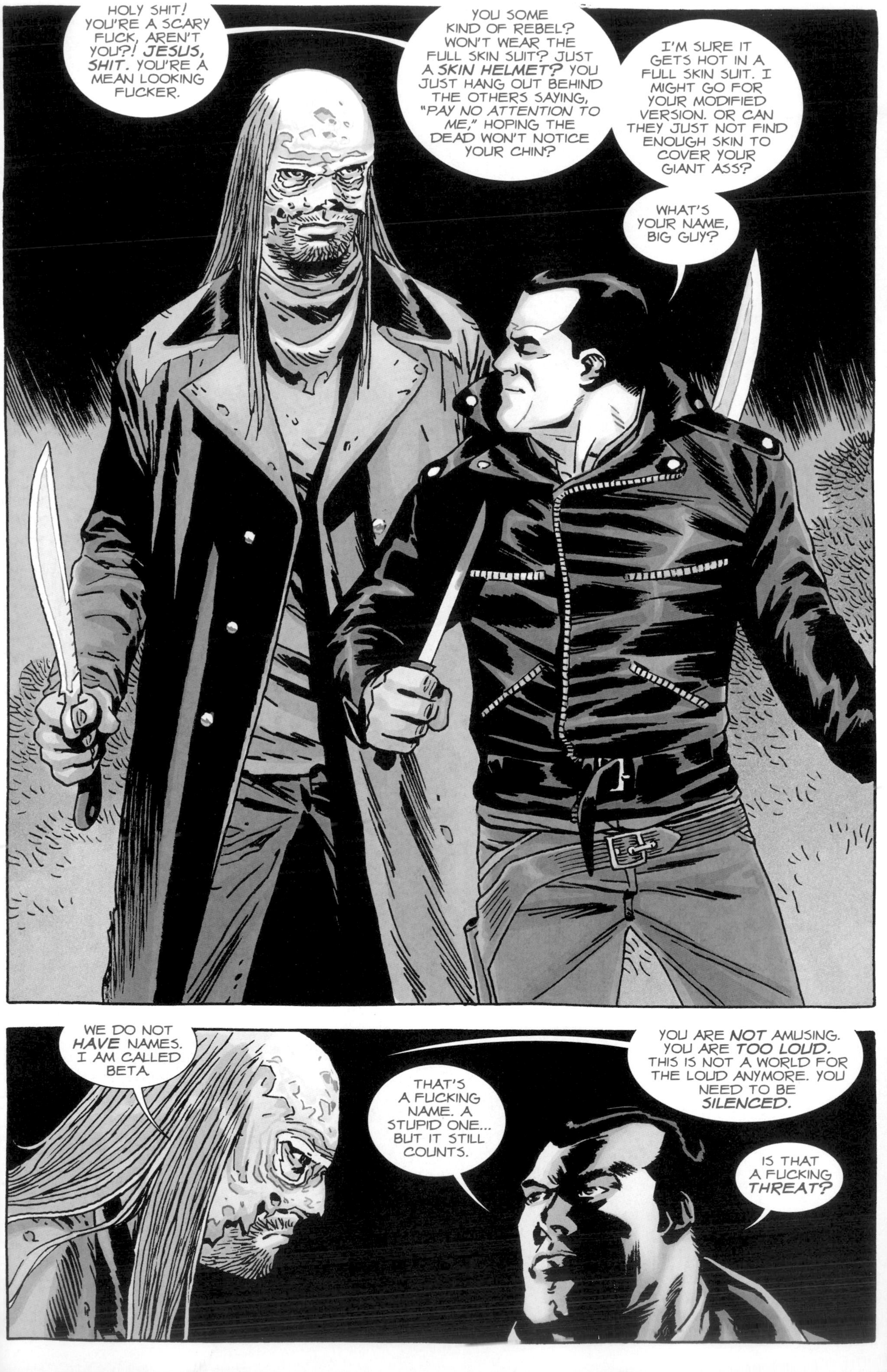
HOLY SHIT! YOU'RE A SCARY FUCK, AREN'T YOU?! JESUS, SHIT. YOU'RE A MEAN LOOKING FUCKER.
YOU SOME KIND OF REBEL? WON'T WEAR THE FULL SKIN SUIT? JUST A SKIN HELMET? YOU JUST HANG OUT BEHIND THE OTHERS SAYING, "PAY NO ATTENTION TO ME," HOPING THE DEAD WON'T NOTICE YOUR CHIN?
I'M SURE IT GETS HOT IN A FULL SKIN SUIT. I MIGHT GO FOR YOUR MODIFIED VERSION. OR CAN THEY JUST NOT FIND ENOUGH SKIN TO COVER YOUR GIANT ASS?
WHAT'S YOUR NAME, BIG GUY?
WE DO NOT HAVE NAMES. I AM CALLED BETA.
THAT'S A FUCKING NAME. A STUPID ONE... BUT IT STILL COUNTS.
YOU ARE NOT AMUSING. YOU ARE TOO LOUD. THIS IS NOT A WORLD FOR THE LOUD ANYMORE. YOU NEED TO BE SILENCED.
IS THAT A FUCKING THREAT?

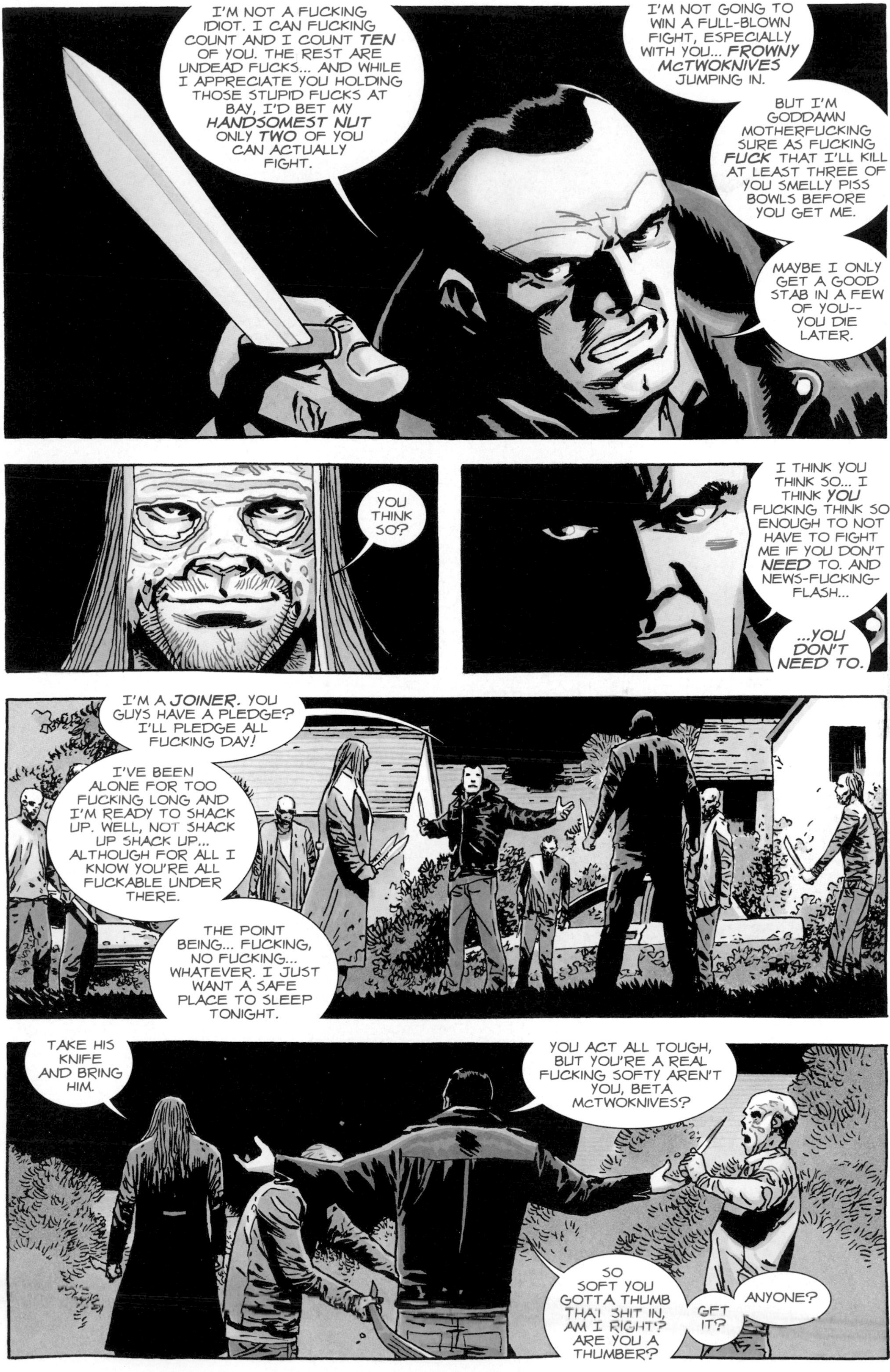
I'M NOT A FUCKING IDIOT. I CAN FUCKING COUNT AND I COUNT TEN OF YOU. THE REST ARE UNDEAD FUCKS... AND WHILE I APPRECIATE YOU HOLDING THOSE STUPID FUCKS AT BAY, I'D BET MY HANDSOMEST NUT ONLY TWO OF YOU CAN ACTUALLY FIGHT.
I'M NOT GOING TO WIN A FULL-BLOWN FIGHT, ESPECIALLY WITH YOU... FROWNY McTWOKNIVES JUMPING IN.
BUT I'M GODDAMN MOTHERFUCKING SURE AS FUCKING FUCK THAT I'LL KILL AT LEAST THREE OF YOU SMELLY PISS BOWLS BEFORE YOU GET ME.
MAYBE I ONLY GET A GOOD STAB IN A FEW OF YOU-- YOU DIE LATER.
YOU THINK SO?
I THINK YOU THINK SO... I THINK YOU FUCKING THINK SO ENOUGH TO NOT HAVE TO FIGHT ME IF YOU DON'T NEED TO. AND NEWS-FUCKING-FLASH...
...YOU DON'T NEED TO.
I'M A JOINER. YOU GUYS HAVE A PLEDGE? I'LL PLEDGE ALL FUCKING DAY!
I'VE BEEN ALONE FOR TOO FUCKING LONG AND I'M READY TO SHACK UP. WELL, NOT SHACK UP SHACK UP... ALTHOUGH FOR ALL I KNOW YOU'RE ALL FUCKABLE UNDER THERE.
THE POINT BEING... FUCKING, NO FUCKING... WHATEVER. I JUST WANT A SAFE PLACE TO SLEEP TONIGHT.
TAKE HIS KNIFE AND BRING HIM.
YOU ACT ALL TOUGH, BUT YOU'RE A REAL FUCKING SOFTY AREN'T YOU, BETA McTWOKNIVES?
SO SOFT YOU GOTTA THUMB THAT SHIT IN, AM I RIGHT? ARE YOU A THUMBER?
GET IT?
ANYONE?

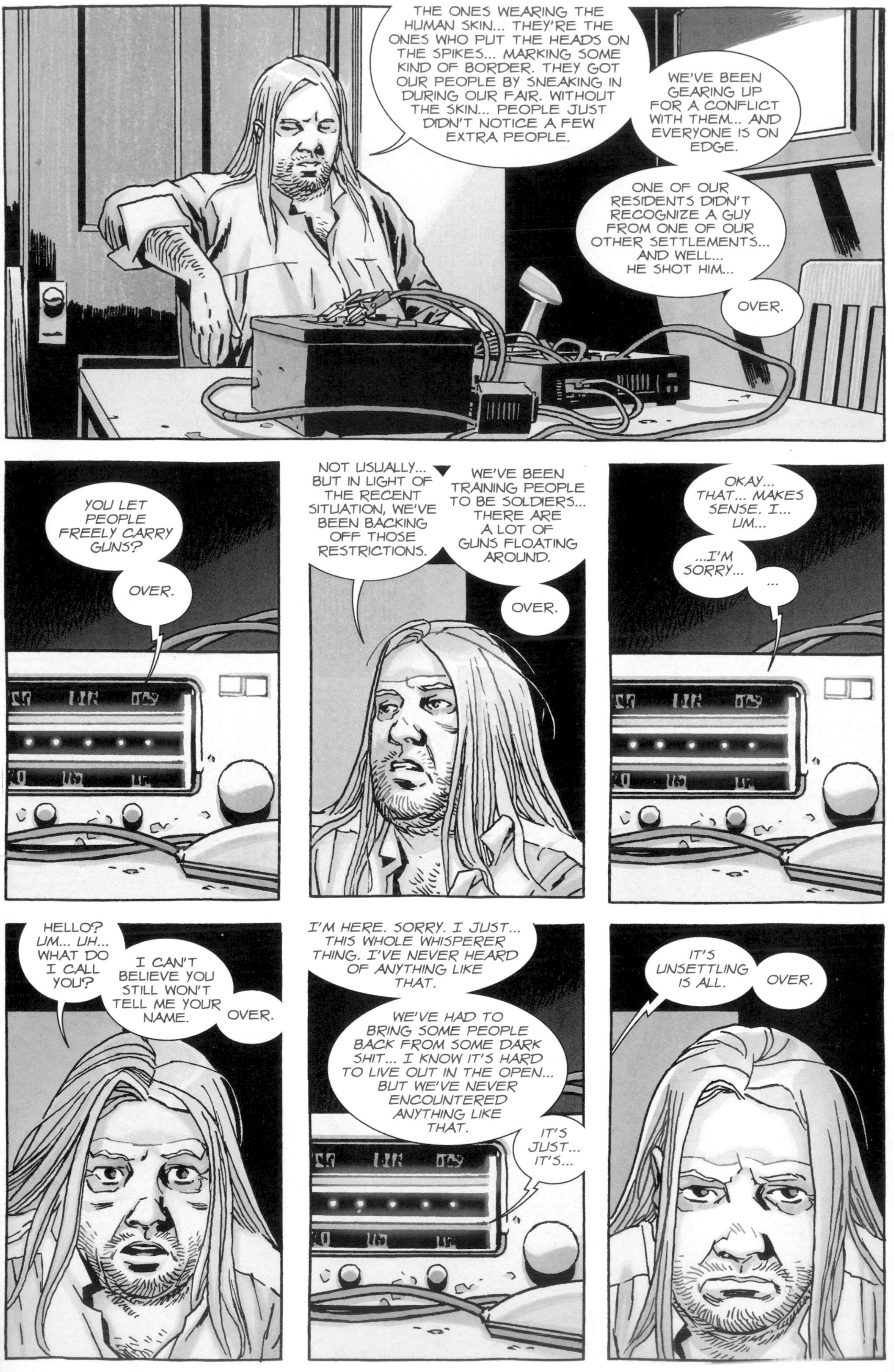
THE ONES WEARING THE HUMAN SKIN... THEY'RE THE ONES WHO PUT THE HEADS ON THE SPIKES... MARKING SOME KIND OF BORDER. THEY GOT OUR PEOPLE BY SNEAKING IN DURING OUR FAIR. WITHOUT THE SKIN... PEOPLE JUST DIDN'T NOTICE A FEW EXTRA PEOPLE.
WE'VE BEEN GEARING UP FOR A CONFLICT WITH THEM... AND EVERYONE IS ON EDGE.
ONE OF OUR RESIDENTS DIDN'T RECOGNIZE A GUY FROM ONE OF OUR OTHER SETTLEMENTS... AND WELL... HE SHOT HIM...
OVER.
YOU LET PEOPLE FREELY CARRY GUNS?
OVER.
NOT USUALLY... BUT IN LIGHT OF THE RECENT SITUATION, WE'VE BEEN BACKING OFF THOSE RESTRICTIONS.
WE'VE BEEN TRAINING PEOPLE TO BE SOLDIERS... THERE ARE A LOT OF GUNS FLOATING AROUND.
OVER.
OKAY... THAT... MAKES SENSE. I... UM...
...I'M SORRY...
...
HELLO? UM... UH... WHAT DO I CALL YOU?
I CAN'T BELIEVE YOU STILL WON'T TELL ME YOUR NAME.
OVER.
I'M HERE. SORRY. I JUST... THIS WHOLE WHISPERER THING. I'VE NEVER HEARD OF ANYTHING LIKE THAT.
WE'VE HAD TO BRING SOME PEOPLE BACK FROM SOME DARK SHIT... I KNOW IT'S HARD TO LIVE OUT IN THE OPEN... BUT WE'VE NEVER ENCOUNTERED ANYTHING LIKE THAT.
IT'S JUST... IT'S...
IT'S UNSETTLING IS ALL.
OVER.

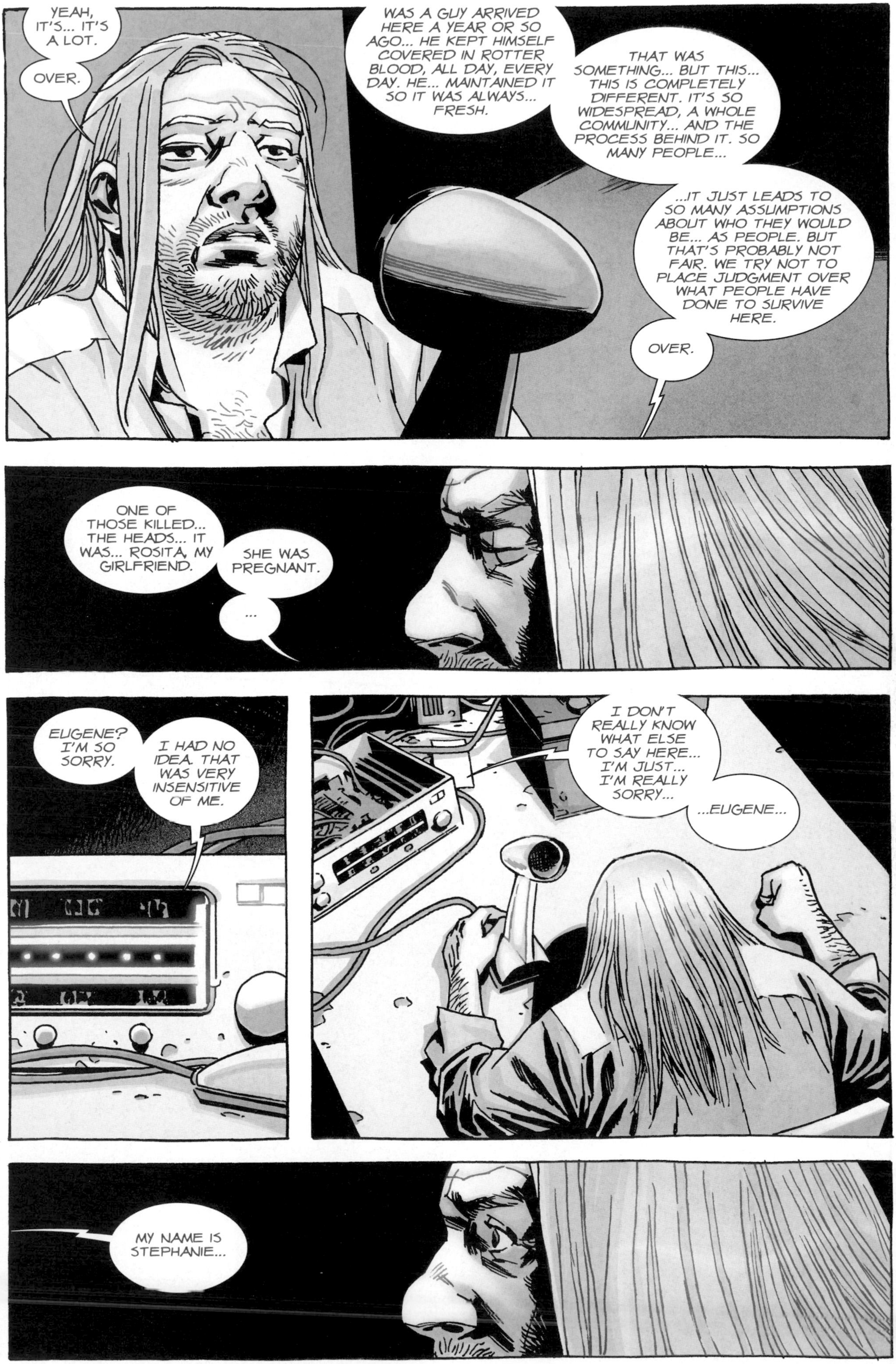
YEAH, IT'S... IT'S A LOT.
OVER.
WAS A GUY ARRIVED HERE A YEAR OR SO AGO... HE KEPT HIMSELF COVERED IN ROTTER BLOOD, ALL DAY, EVERY DAY. HE... MAINTAINED IT SO IT WAS ALWAYS... FRESH.
THAT WAS SOMETHING... BUT THIS... THIS IS COMPLETELY DIFFERENT. IT'S SO WIDESPREAD, A WHOLE COMMUNITY... AND THE PROCESS BEHIND IT. SO MANY PEOPLE...
...IT JUST LEADS TO SO MANY ASSUMPTIONS ABOUT WHO THEY WOULD BE... AS PEOPLE. BUT THAT'S PROBABLY NOT FAIR. WE TRY NOT TO PLACE JUDGMENT OVER WHAT PEOPLE HAVE DONE TO SURVIVE HERE.
OVER.
ONE OF THOSE KILLED... THE HEADS... IT WAS... ROSITA, MY GIRLFRIEND.
SHE WAS PREGNANT.
...
EUGENE? I'M SO SORRY.
I HAD NO IDEA. THAT WAS VERY INSENSITIVE OF ME.
I DON'T REALLY KNOW WHAT ELSE TO SAY HERE... I'M JUST... I'M REALLY SORRY...
...EUGENE...
MY NAME IS STEPHANIE...

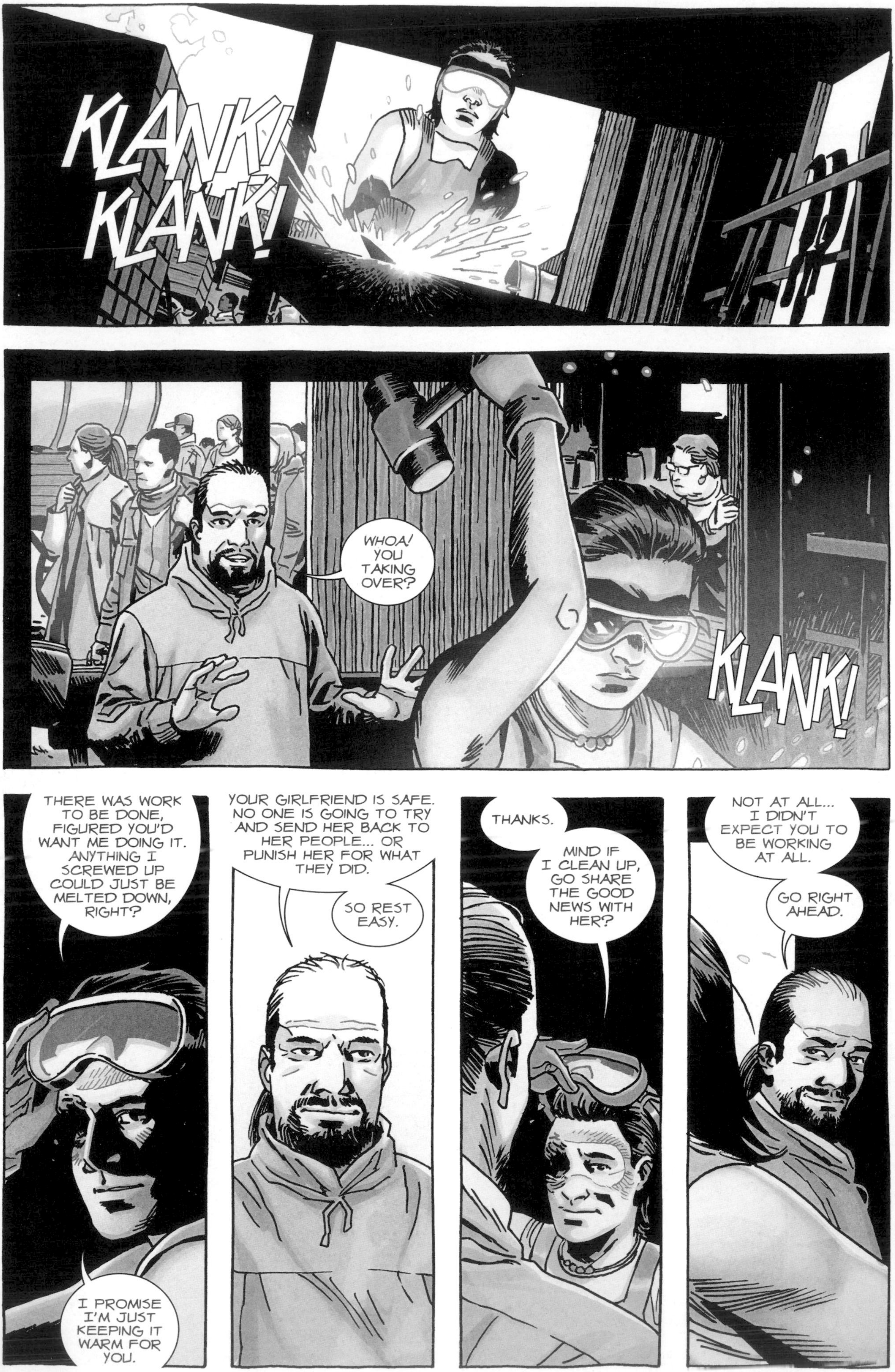
KLANK! KLANK!
WHOA! YOU TAKING OVER?
KLANK!
THERE WAS WORK TO BE DONE, FIGURED YOU'D WANT ME DOING IT. ANYTHING I SCREWED UP COULD JUST BE MELTED DOWN, RIGHT?
I PROMISE I'M JUST KEEPING IT WARM FOR YOU.
YOUR GIRLFRIEND IS SAFE. NO ONE IS GOING TO TRY AND SEND HER BACK TO HER PEOPLE... OR PUNISH HER FOR WHAT THEY DID.
SO REST EASY.
THANKS.
MIND IF I CLEAN UP, GO SHARE THE GOOD NEWS WITH HER?
NOT AT ALL... I DIDN'T EXPECT YOU TO BE WORKING AT ALL.
GO RIGHT AHEAD.

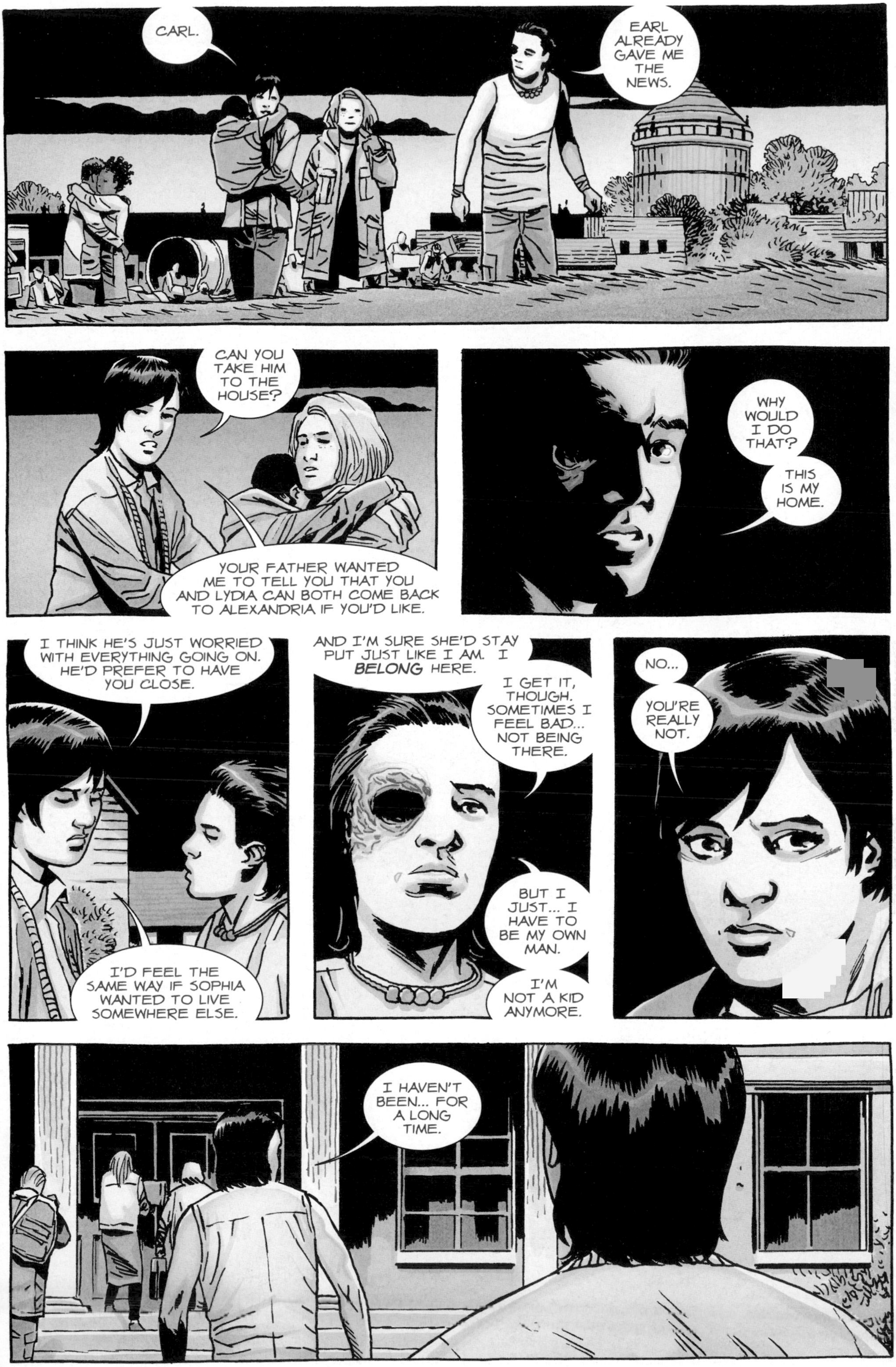
CARL.
EARL ALREADY GAVE ME THE NEWS.
CAN YOU TAKE HIM TO THE HOUSE?
YOUR FATHER WANTED ME TO TELL YOU THAT YOU AND LYDIA CAN BOTH COME BACK TO ALEXANDRIA IF YOU'D LIKE.
WHY WOULD I DO THAT?
THIS IS MY HOME.
I THINK HE'S JUST WORRIED WITH EVERYTHING GOING ON. HE'D PREFER TO HAVE YOU CLOSE.
I'D FEEL THE SAME WAY IF SOPHIA WANTED TO LIVE SOMEWHERE ELSE.
AND I'M SURE SHE'D STAY PUT JUST LIKE I AM. I *BELONG* HERE.
I GET IT, THOUGH. SOMETIMES I FEEL BAD... NOT BEING THERE.
BUT I JUST... I HAVE TO BE MY OWN MAN.
I'M NOT A KID ANYMORE.
NO...
YOU'RE REALLY NOT.
I HAVEN'T BEEN... FOR A LONG TIME.

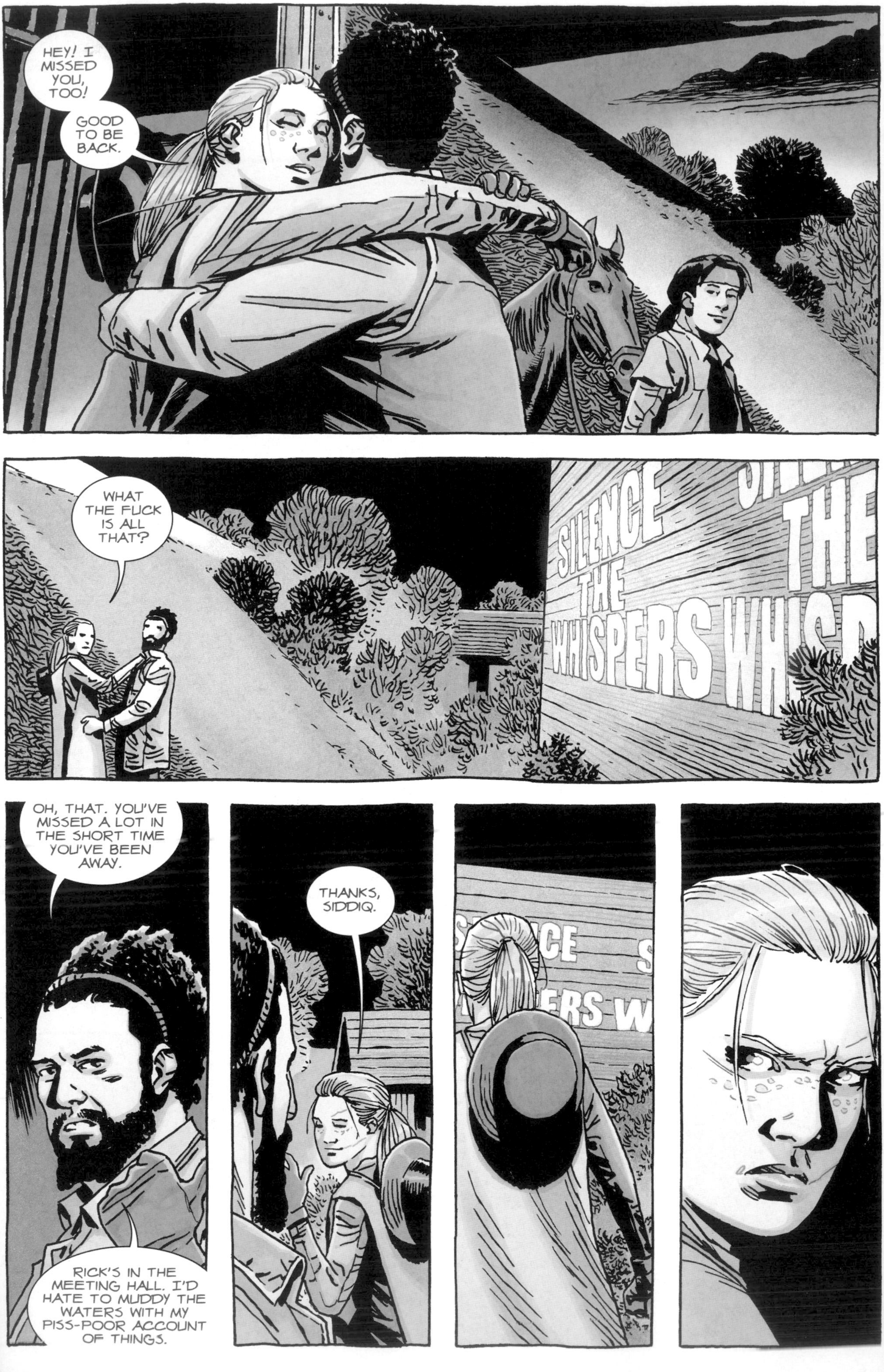
HEY! I MISSED YOU, TOO!
GOOD TO BE BACK.
WHAT THE FUCK IS ALL THAT?
SILENCE THE WHISPERS
OH, THAT. YOU'VE MISSED A LOT IN THE SHORT TIME YOU'VE BEEN AWAY.
RICK'S IN THE MEETING HALL. I'D HATE TO MUDDY THE WATERS WITH MY PISS-POOR ACCOUNT OF THINGS.
THANKS, SIDDIQ.

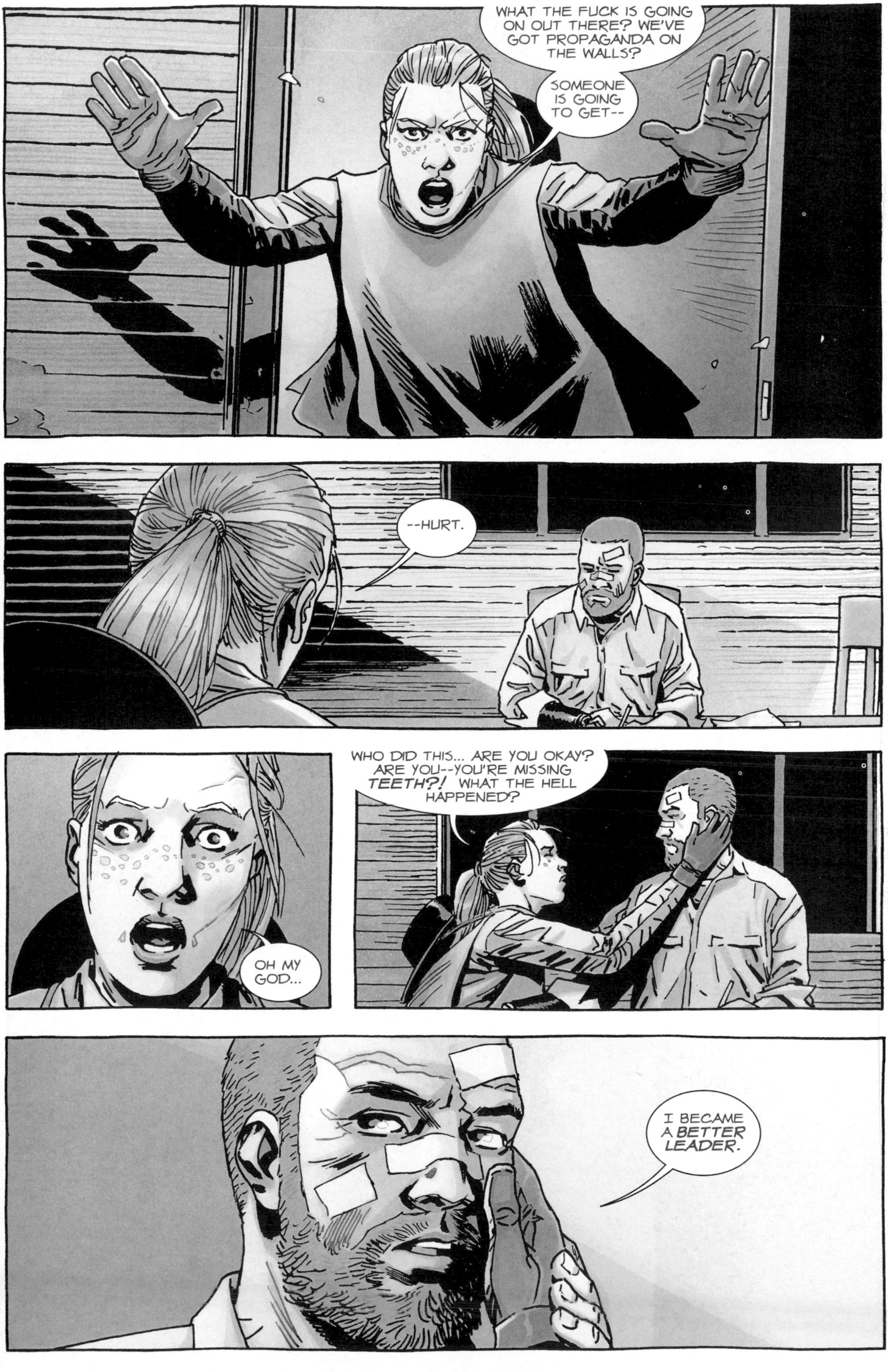
WHAT THE FUCK IS GOING ON OUT THERE? WE'VE GOT PROPAGANDA ON THE WALLS?
SOMEONE IS GOING TO GET--
--HURT.
OH MY GOD...
WHO DID THIS... ARE YOU OKAY? ARE YOU--YOU'RE MISSING *TEETH?!* WHAT THE HELL HAPPENED?
I BECAME A *BETTER LEADER*.

HE'S HANDSOME AS ALL HELL. I CAN ONLY IMAGINE HOW MANY ABS HE HAS HIDING UNDER THOSE LAYERS. THE GUY HAS CORE STRENGTH *FOR DAYS.*

ADD TO THAT HE'S ABOUT THE KINDEST PERSON OUT HERE. REALLY LIVES UP TO THE NICKNAME, Y'KNOW?

I MEAN... *JESUS...* AM I RIGHT?

ALL DUE RESPECT, I'M NOT SURE YOU'RE THE BEST PERSON TO BE GIVING SOMEONE RELATIONSHIP ADVICE.

OUCH. AND FUCK YOU. DON'T TURN THIS AROUND ON ME. YOU'RE JUST DUCKING THE SUBJECT.

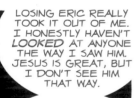

LOSING ERIC REALLY TOOK IT OUT OF ME. I HONESTLY HAVEN'T *LOOKED* AT ANYONE THE WAY I SAW HIM. JESUS IS GREAT, BUT I DON'T SEE HIM THAT WAY.

AND TO BE HONEST... HE'S GOT THAT BOOTY CALL AT THE HILLTOP. ALEX... I THINK HE'S LEADING HIM ON. I DON'T LIKE THAT.

I CAN'T REALLY GET A GRASP OF WHAT'S GOING ON THERE.

I HAVEN'T SPENT ENOUGH TIME AROUND ALEX... BUT WHATEVER IS BETWEEN THEM IS BETWEEN THEM.

I KNOW ENOUGH TO SEE THAT JESUS IS TOYING WITH THAT GUY'S EMOTIONS. I DON'T--

KRIK.

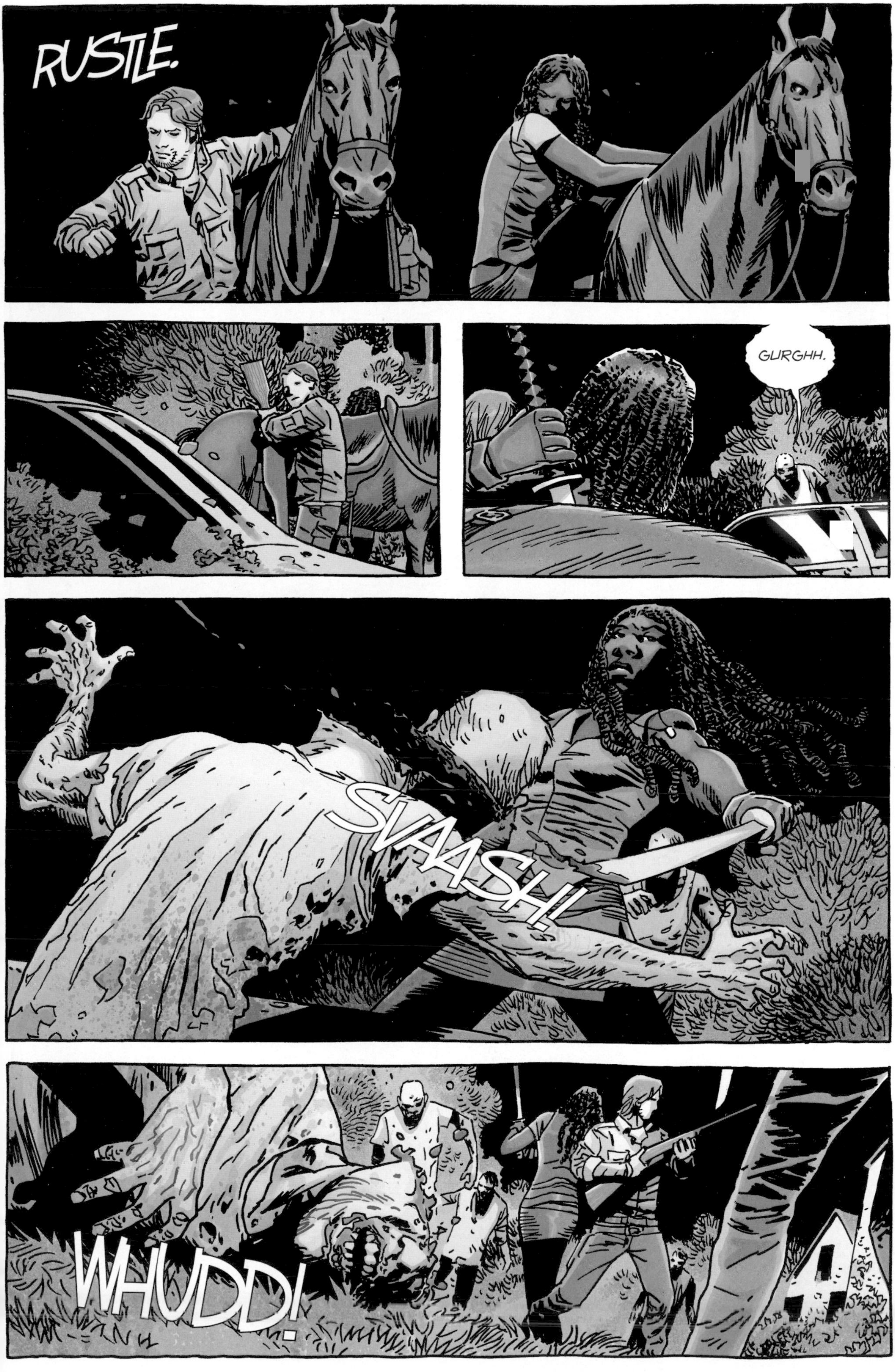
RUSTLE.
GURGHH.
SVAASH!
WHUDD!

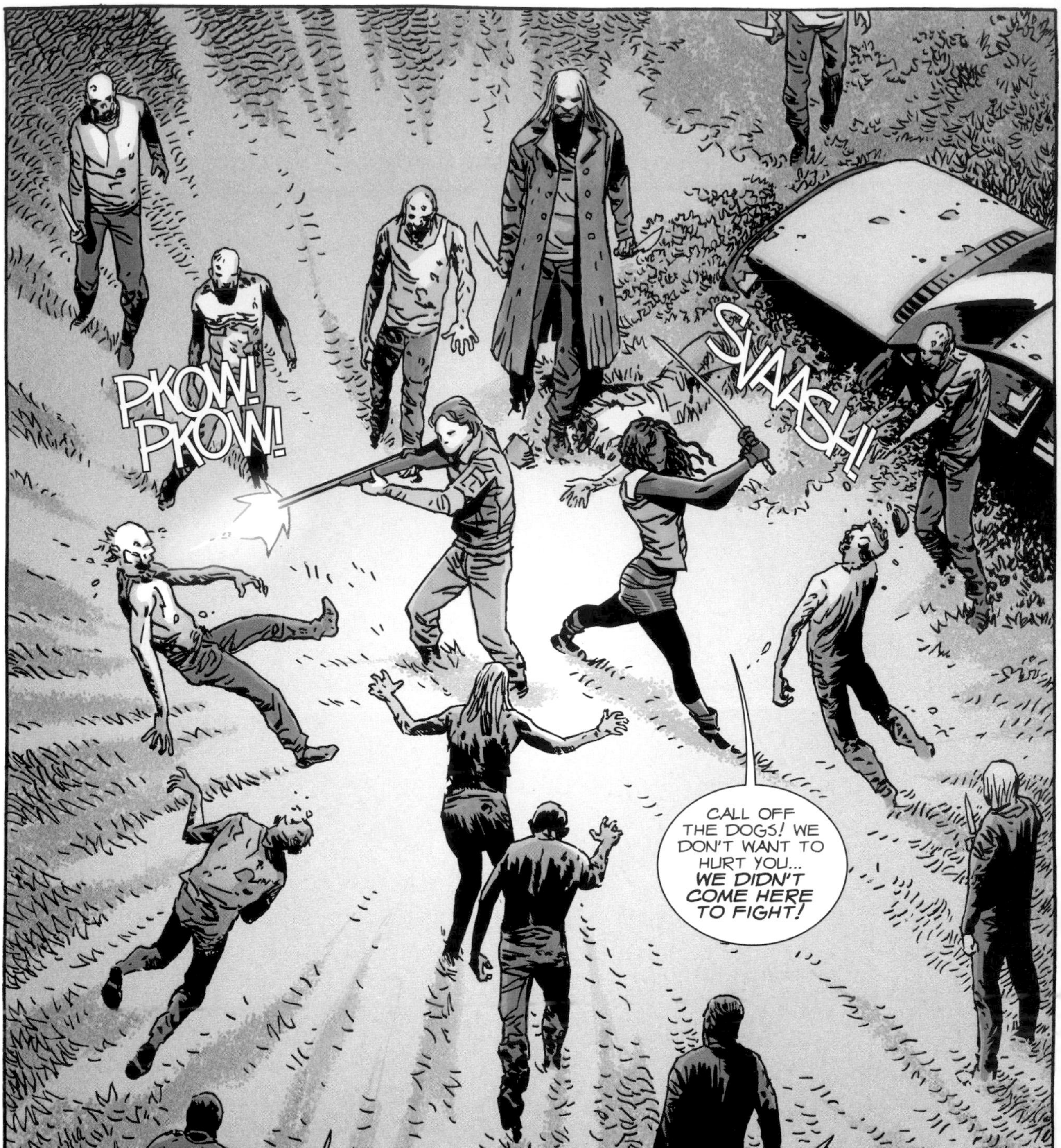
PKOW! PKOW!
SVAASH!
CALL OFF THE DOGS! WE DON'T WANT TO HURT YOU... ***WE DIDN'T COME HERE TO FIGHT!***

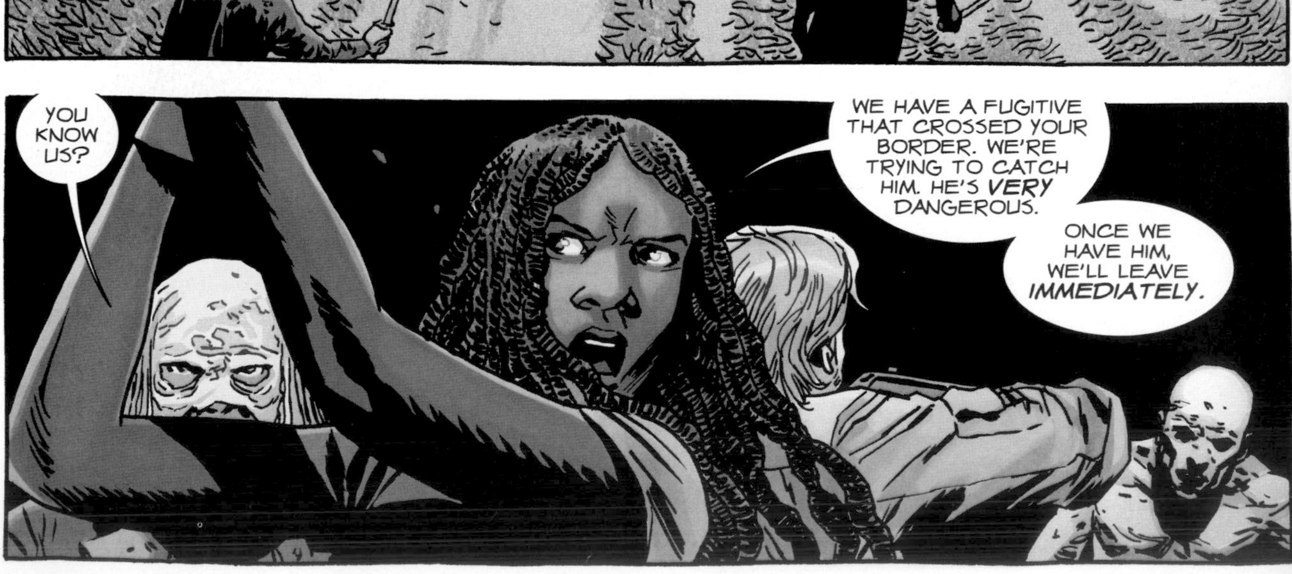
YOU KNOW US?
WE HAVE A FUGITIVE THAT CROSSED YOUR BORDER. WE'RE TRYING TO CATCH HIM. HE'S ***VERY*** DANGEROUS.
ONCE WE HAVE HIM, WE'LL LEAVE ***IMMEDIATELY.***

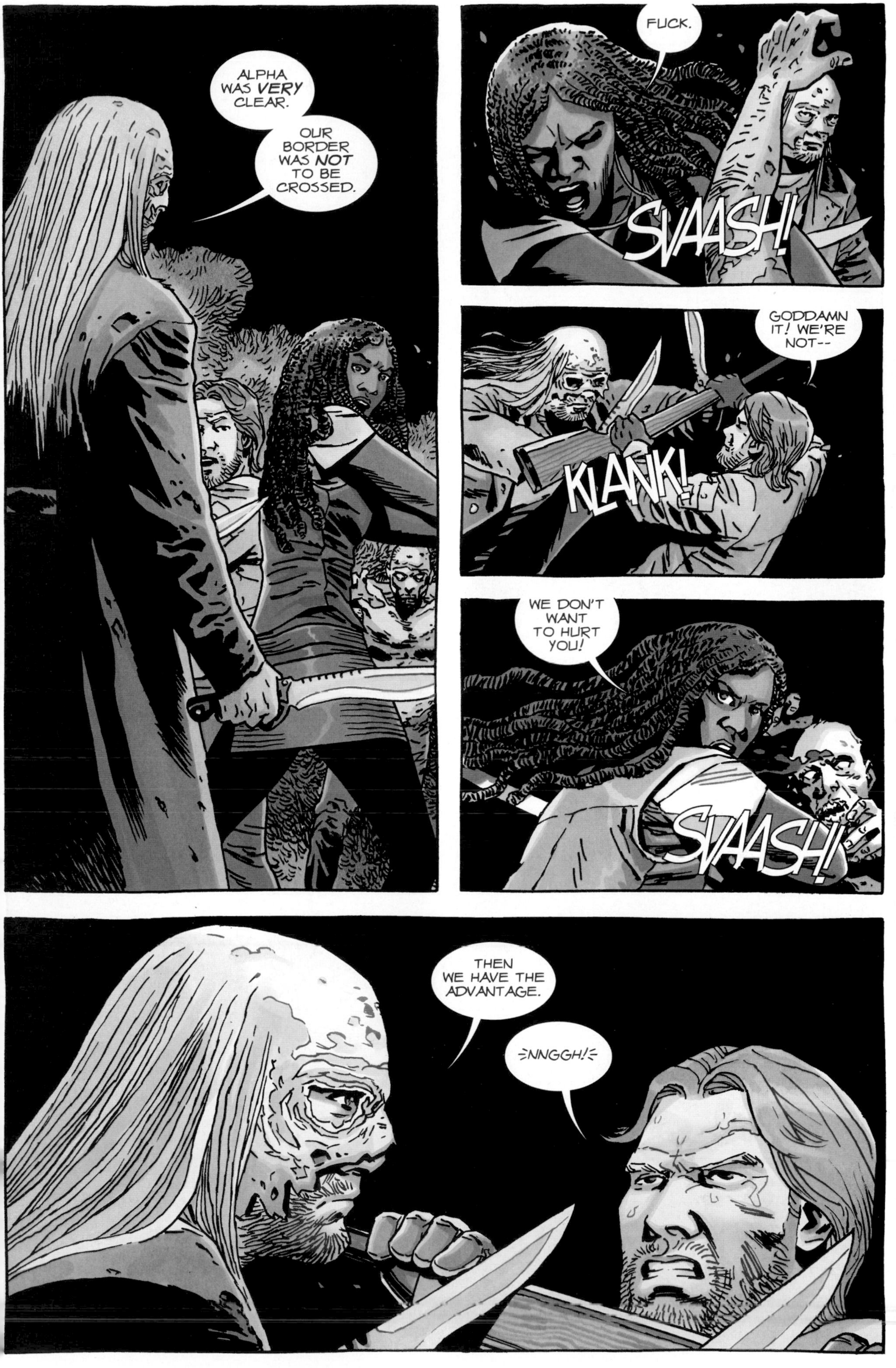
ALPHA WAS VERY CLEAR.
OUR BORDER WAS NOT TO BE CROSSED.
FUCK.
SVAASH!
GODDAMN IT! WE'RE NOT--
KLANK!
WE DON'T WANT TO HURT YOU!
SVAASH!
THEN WE HAVE THE ADVANTAGE.
NNGGH!

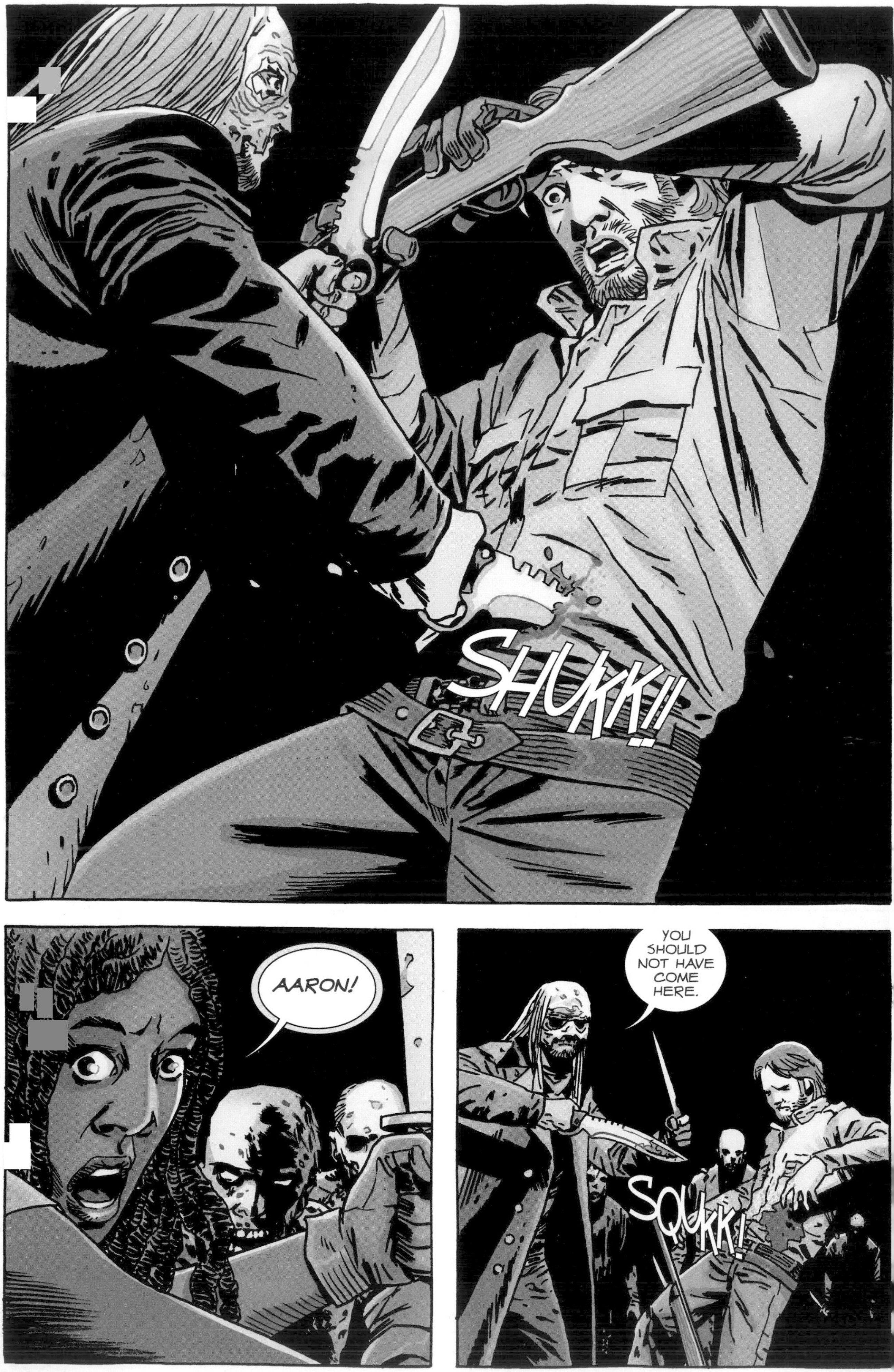
SHUKK!!
AARON!
YOU SHOULD NOT HAVE COME HERE.
SQUKK!

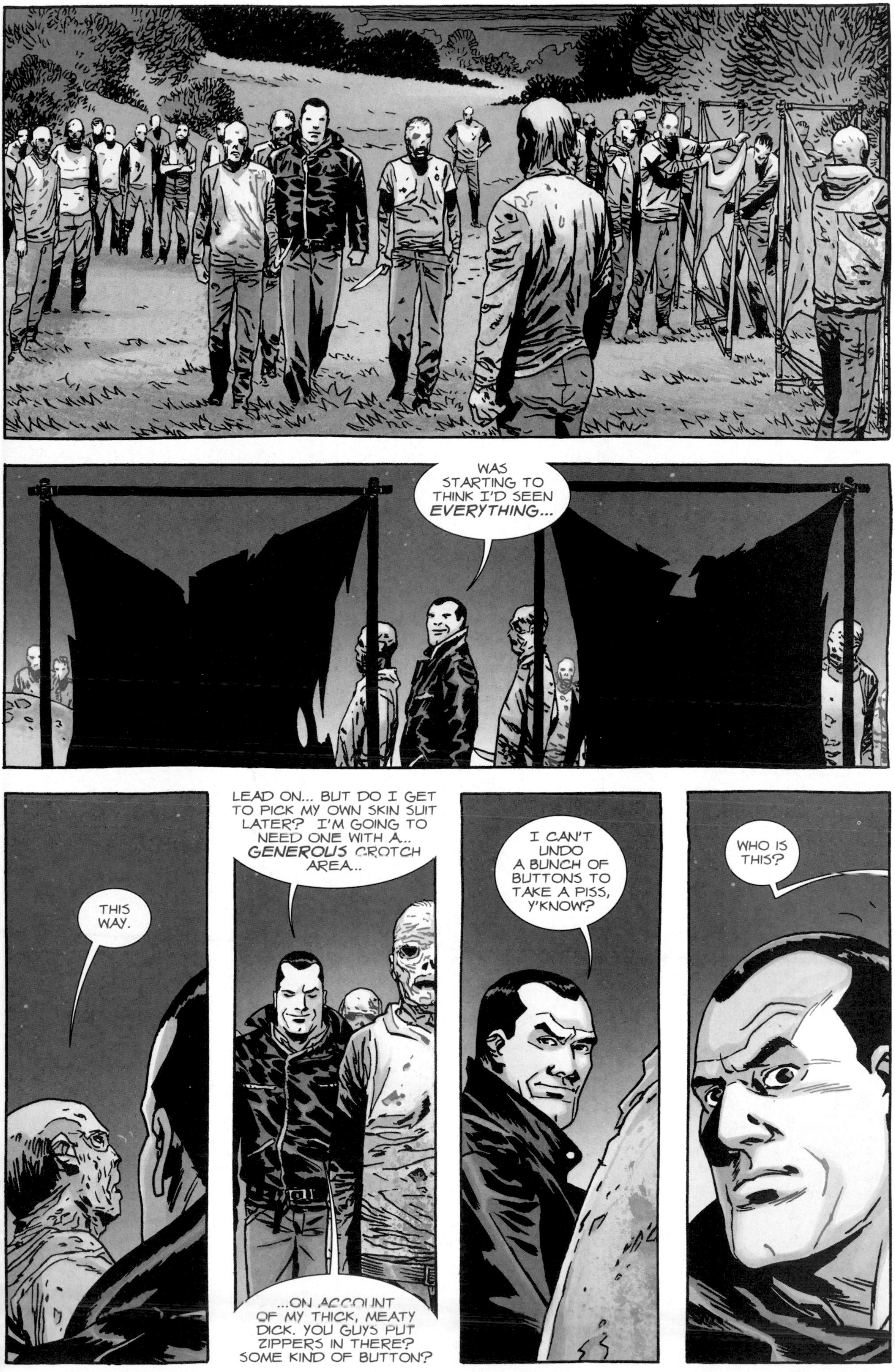

WAS STARTING TO THINK I'D SEEN *EVERYTHING*...
THIS WAY.
LEAD ON... BUT DO I GET TO PICK MY OWN SKIN SUIT LATER? I'M GOING TO NEED ONE WITH A... *GENEROUS* CROTCH AREA...
...ON ACCOUNT OF MY THICK, MEATY DICK. YOU GUYS PUT ZIPPERS IN THERE? SOME KIND OF BUTTON?
I CAN'T UNDO A BUNCH OF BUTTONS TO TAKE A PISS, Y'KNOW?
WHO IS THIS?

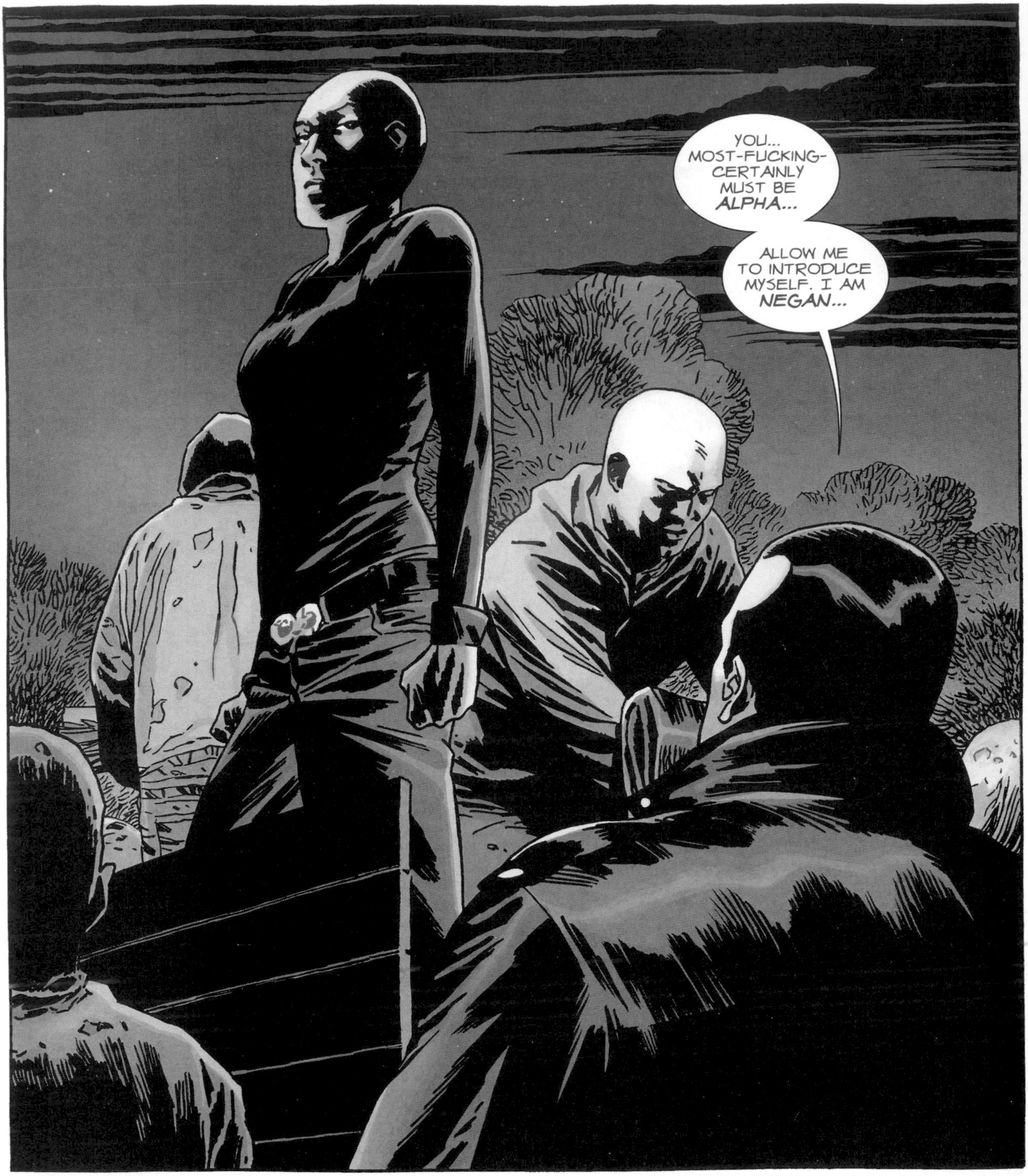
YOU... MOST-FUCKING-CERTAINLY MUST BE ALPHA...
ALLOW ME TO INTRODUCE MYSELF. I AM NEGAN...
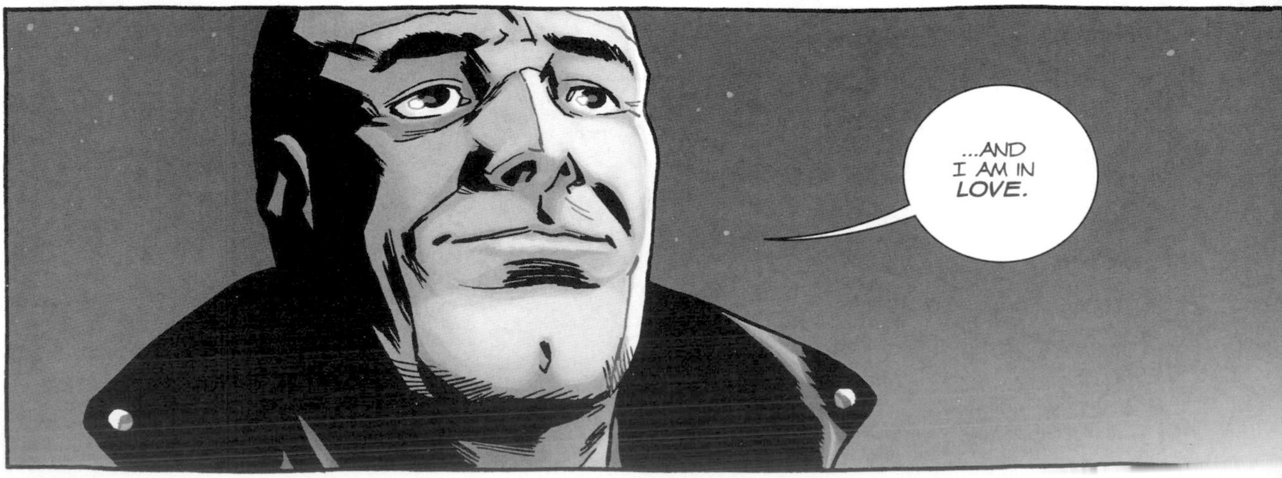
...AND I AM IN LOVE.

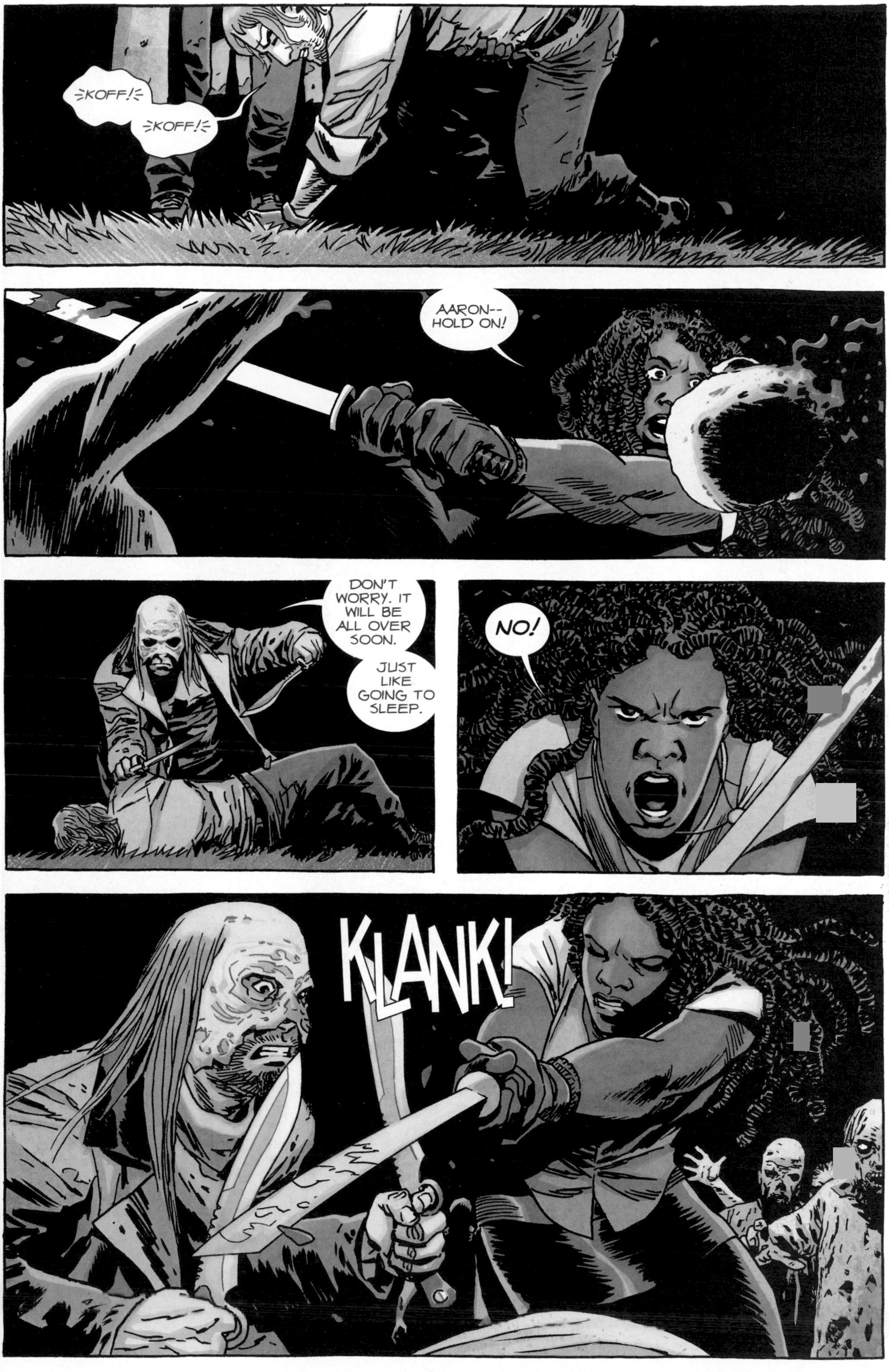

KOFF!
KOFF!
AARON-- HOLD ON!
DON'T WORRY. IT WILL BE ALL OVER SOON.
JUST LIKE GOING TO SLEEP.
NO!
KLANK!

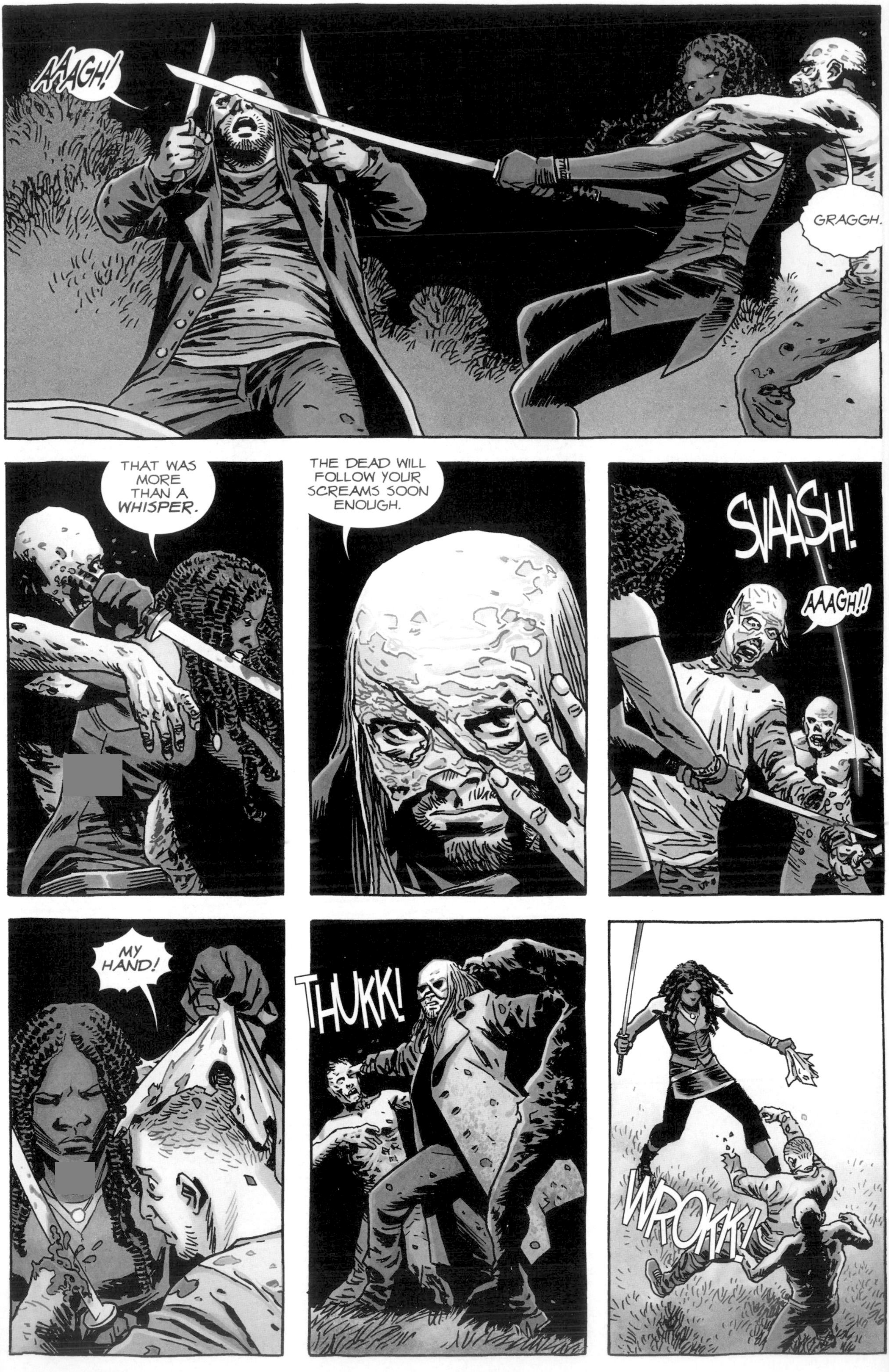
AAAGH!
GRAGGH.
THAT WAS MORE THAN A WHISPER.
THE DEAD WILL FOLLOW YOUR SCREAMS SOON ENOUGH.
SVAASH!
AAAGH!!
MY HAND!
THUKK!
WROKK!

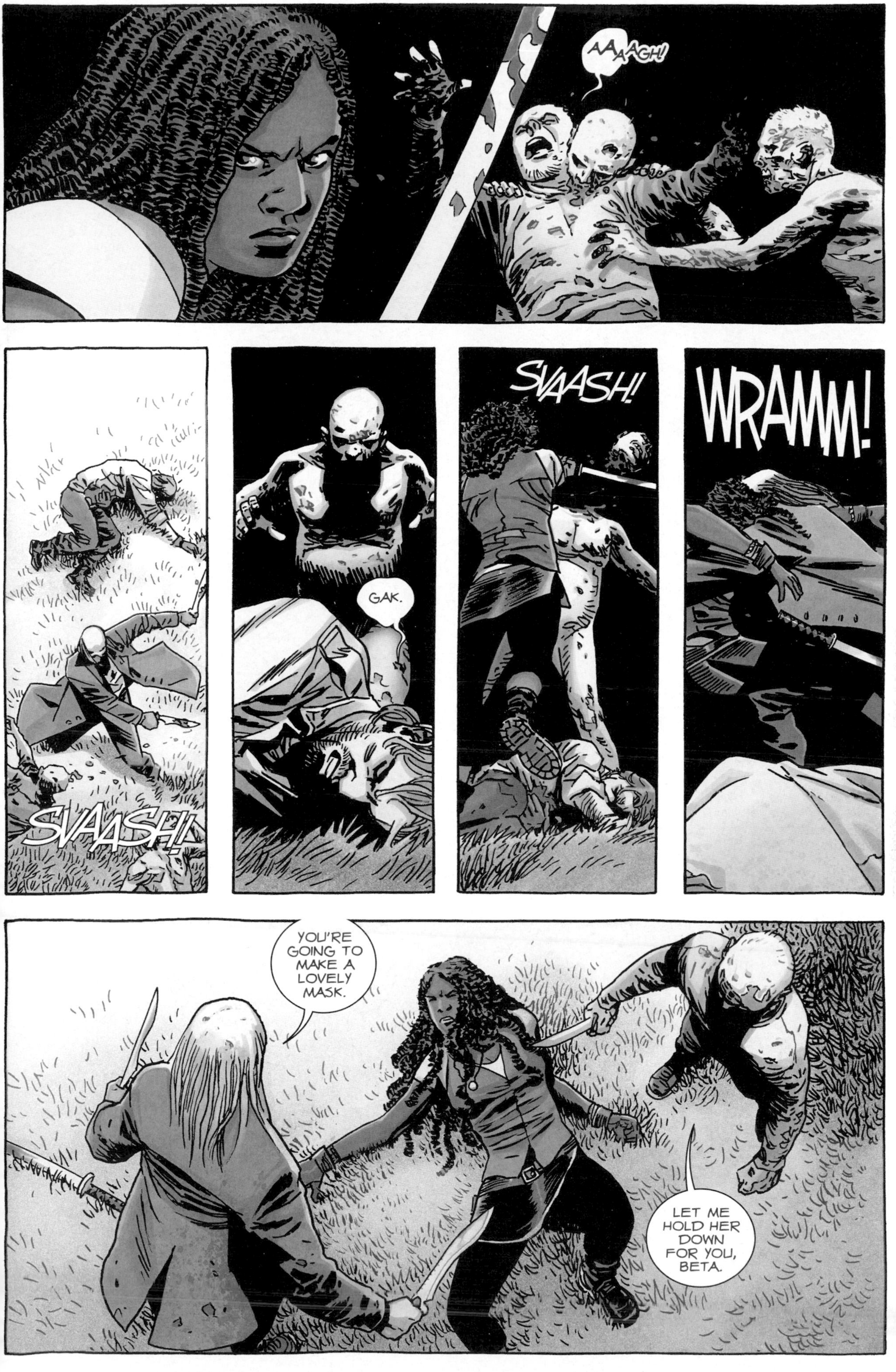
AAAAGH!
SVAASH!
GAK.
SVAASH!
WRAMM!
YOU'RE GOING TO MAKE A LOVELY MASK.
LET ME HOLD HER DOWN FOR YOU, BETA.

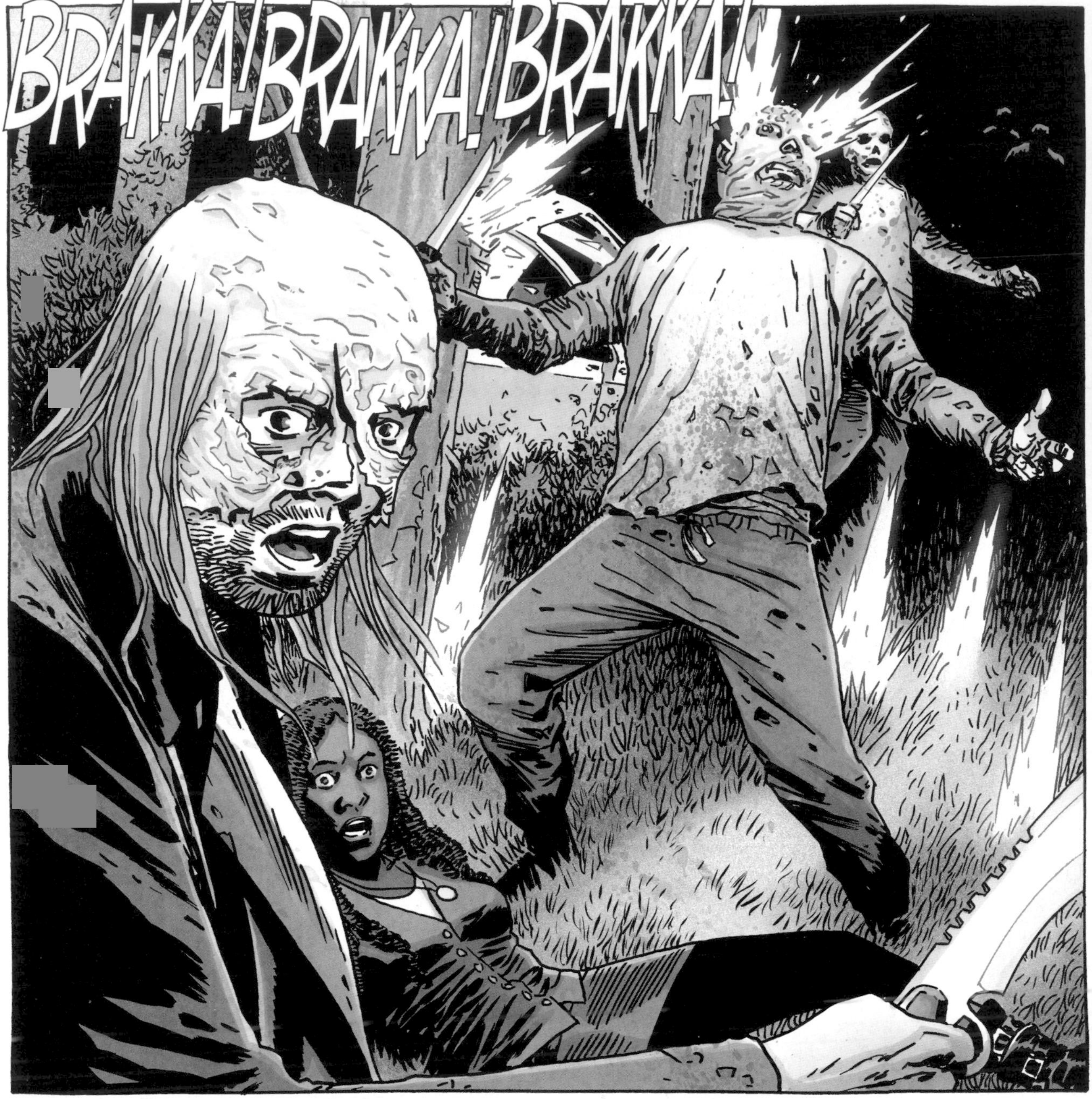
BRAKKA! BRAKKA! BRAKKA!

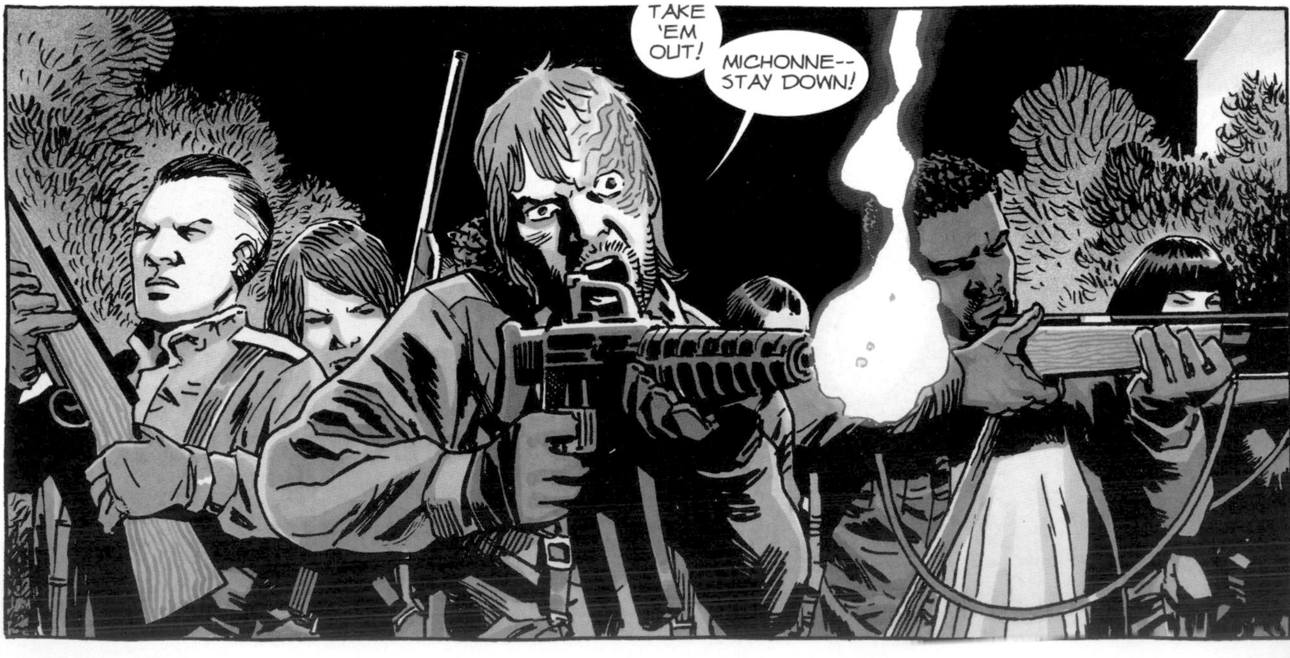
TAKE 'EM OUT!
MICHONNE-- STAY DOWN!

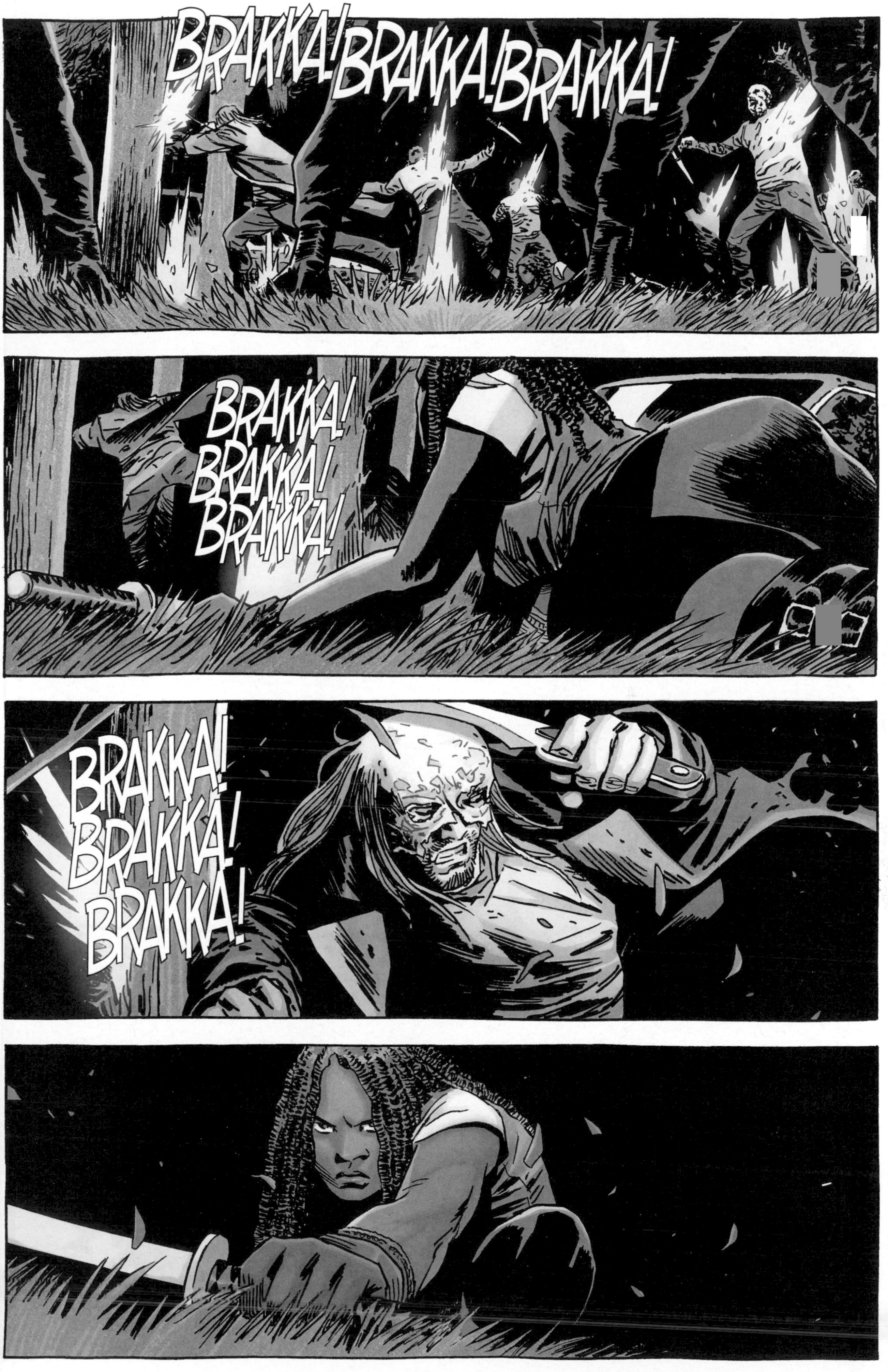
BRAKKA! BRAKKA! BRAKKA!
BRAKKA! BRAKKA! BRAKKA!
BRAKKA! BRAKKA! BRAKKA!

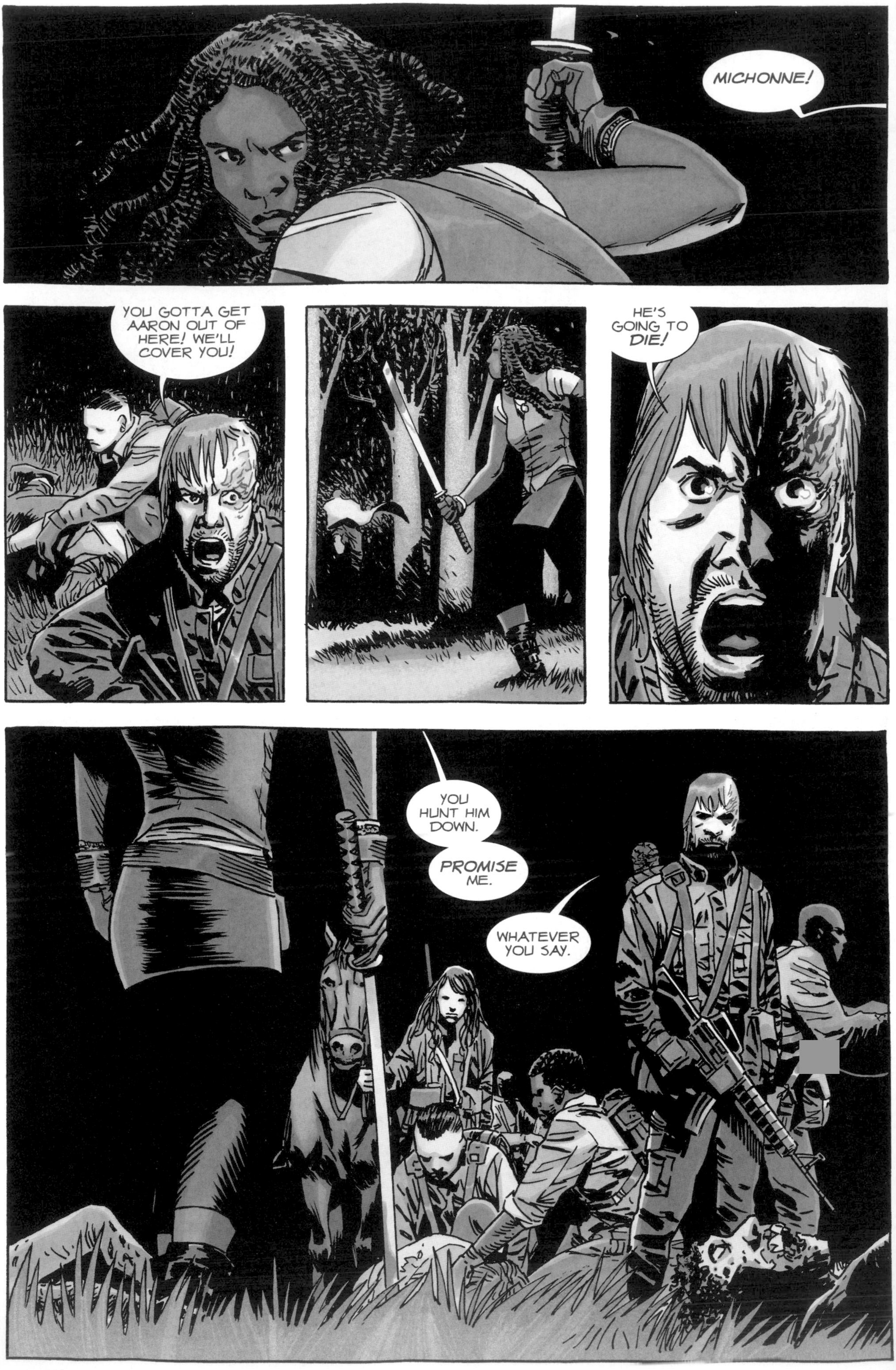
MICHONNE!
YOU GOTTA GET AARON OUT OF HERE! WE'LL COVER YOU!
HE'S GOING TO DIE!
YOU HUNT HIM DOWN.
PROMISE ME.
WHATEVER YOU SAY.

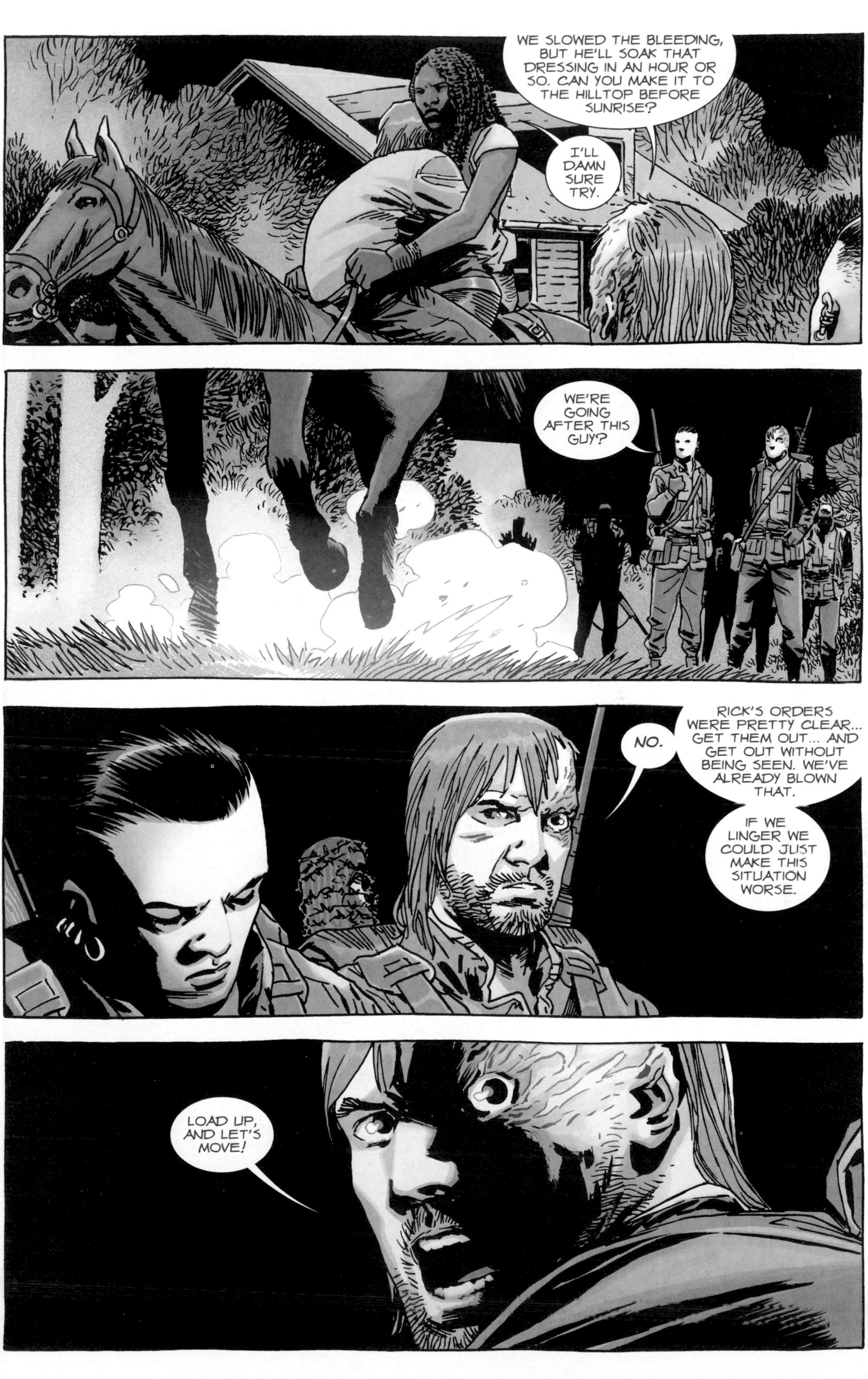
WE SLOWED THE BLEEDING, BUT HE'LL SOAK THAT DRESSING IN AN HOUR OR SO. CAN YOU MAKE IT TO THE HILLTOP BEFORE SUNRISE?
I'LL DAMN SURE TRY.
WE'RE GOING AFTER THIS GUY?
NO.
RICK'S ORDERS WERE PRETTY CLEAR... GET THEM OUT... AND GET OUT WITHOUT BEING SEEN. WE'VE ALREADY BLOWN THAT.
IF WE LINGER WE COULD JUST MAKE THIS SITUATION WORSE.
LOAD UP, AND LET'S MOVE!

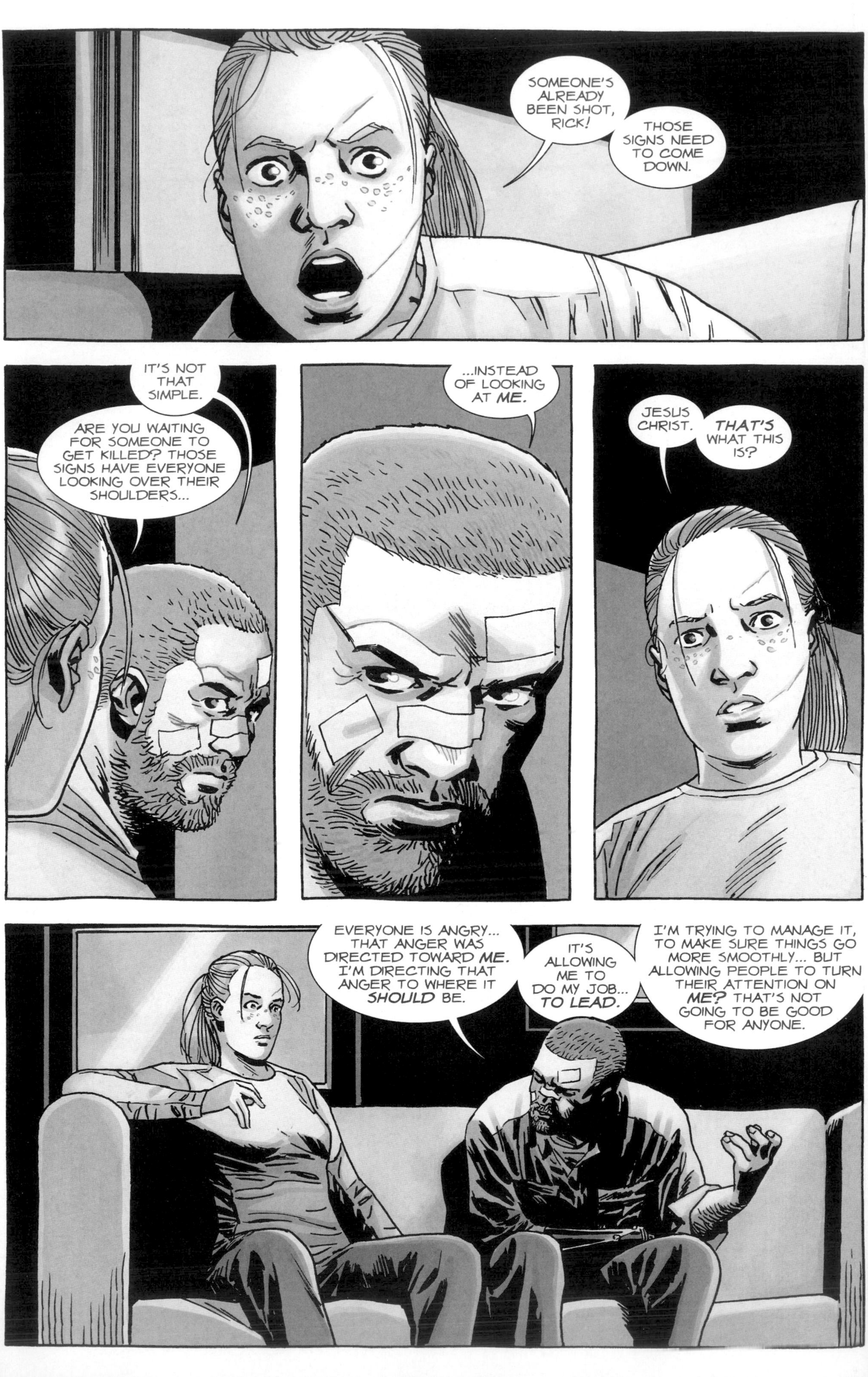
SOMEONE'S ALREADY BEEN SHOT, RICK!
THOSE SIGNS NEED TO COME DOWN.
IT'S NOT THAT SIMPLE.
ARE YOU WAITING FOR SOMEONE TO GET KILLED? THOSE SIGNS HAVE EVERYONE LOOKING OVER THEIR SHOULDERS...
...INSTEAD OF LOOKING AT ME.
JESUS CHRIST.
THAT'S WHAT THIS IS?
EVERYONE IS ANGRY... THAT ANGER WAS DIRECTED TOWARD ME. I'M DIRECTING THAT ANGER TO WHERE IT SHOULD BE.
IT'S ALLOWING ME TO DO MY JOB... TO LEAD.
I'M TRYING TO MANAGE IT, TO MAKE SURE THINGS GO MORE SMOOTHLY... BUT ALLOWING PEOPLE TO TURN THEIR ATTENTION ON ME? THAT'S NOT GOING TO BE GOOD FOR ANYONE.

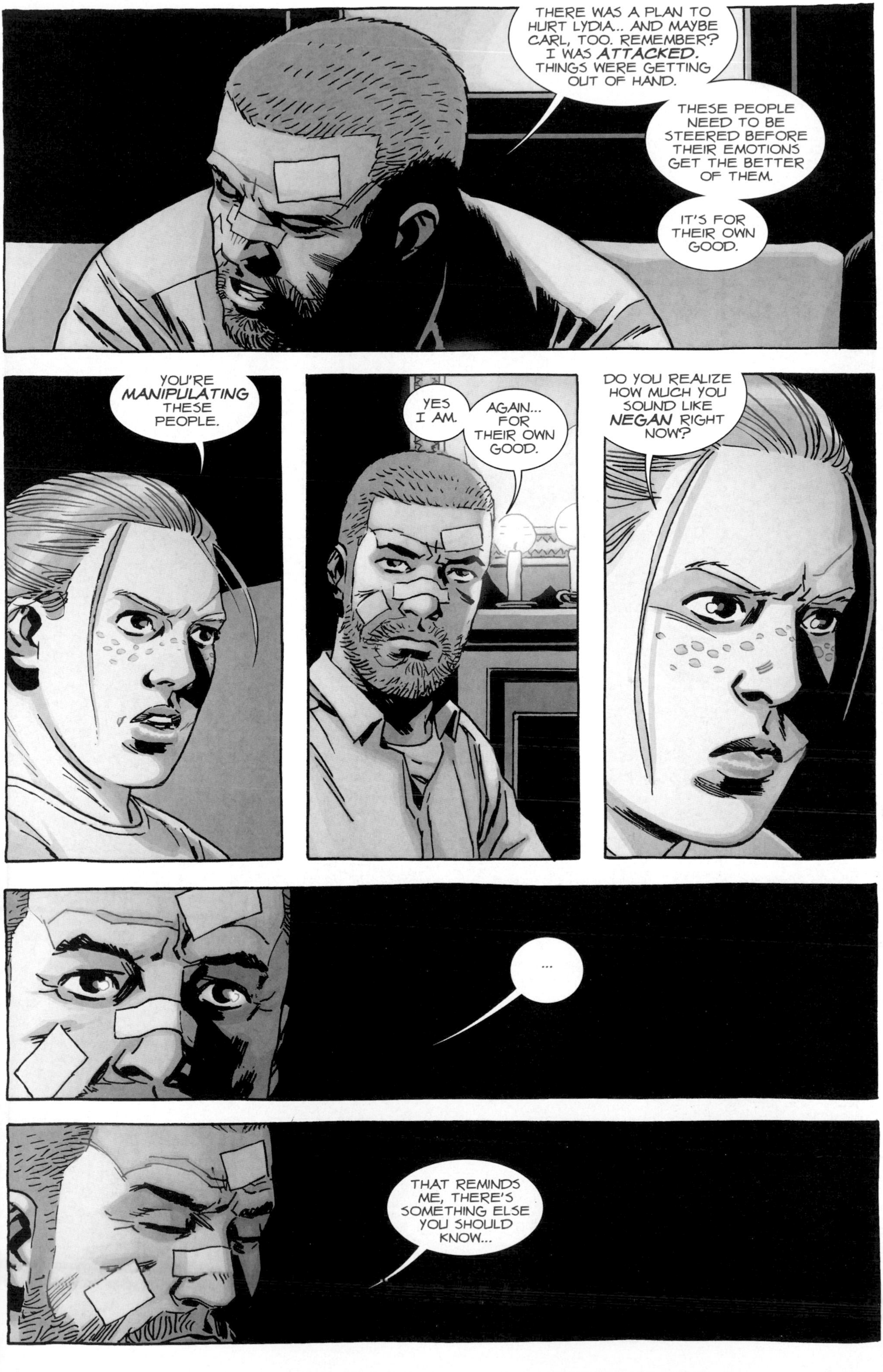
THERE WAS A PLAN TO HURT LYDIA... AND MAYBE CARL, TOO. REMEMBER? I WAS ATTACKED. THINGS WERE GETTING OUT OF HAND.
THESE PEOPLE NEED TO BE STEERED BEFORE THEIR EMOTIONS GET THE BETTER OF THEM.
IT'S FOR THEIR OWN GOOD.
YOU'RE MANIPULATING THESE PEOPLE.
YES I AM.
AGAIN... FOR THEIR OWN GOOD.
DO YOU REALIZE HOW MUCH YOU SOUND LIKE NEGAN RIGHT NOW?
...
THAT REMINDS ME, THERE'S SOMETHING ELSE YOU SHOULD KNOW...

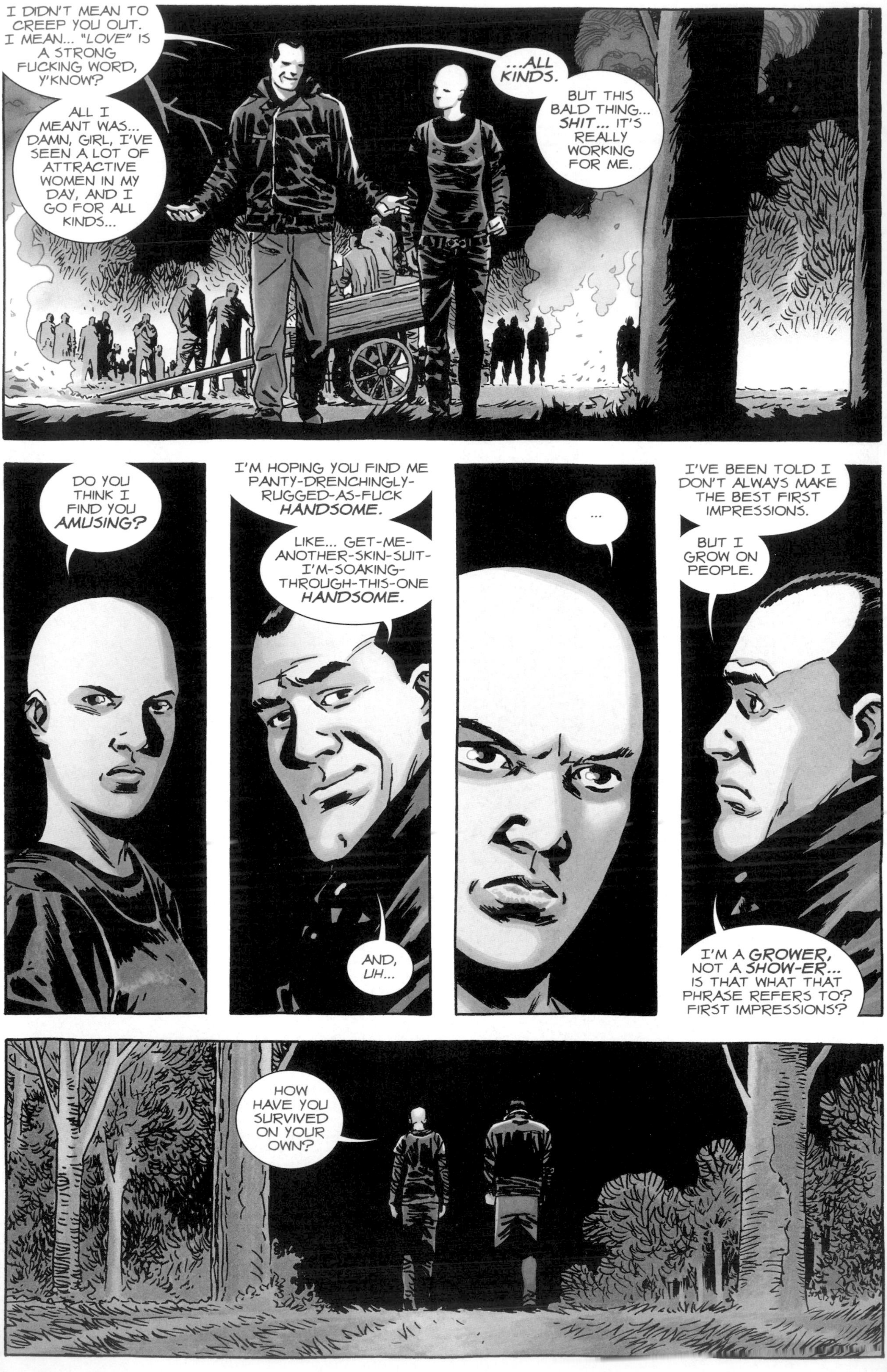
I DIDN'T MEAN TO CREEP YOU OUT. I MEAN... "LOVE" IS A STRONG FUCKING WORD, Y'KNOW?
ALL I MEANT WAS... DAMN, GIRL, I'VE SEEN A LOT OF ATTRACTIVE WOMEN IN MY DAY, AND I GO FOR ALL KINDS...
...ALL KINDS.
BUT THIS BALD THING... SHIT... IT'S REALLY WORKING FOR ME.
DO YOU THINK I FIND YOU AMUSING?
I'M HOPING YOU FIND ME PANTY-DRENCHINGLY-RUGGED-AS-FUCK HANDSOME.
LIKE... GET-ME-ANOTHER-SKIN-SUIT-I'M-SOAKING-THROUGH-THIS-ONE HANDSOME.
AND, UH...
...
I'VE BEEN TOLD I DON'T ALWAYS MAKE THE BEST FIRST IMPRESSIONS.
BUT I GROW ON PEOPLE.
I'M A GROWER, NOT A SHOW-ER... IS THAT WHAT THAT PHRASE REFERS TO? FIRST IMPRESSIONS?
HOW HAVE YOU SURVIVED ON YOUR OWN?

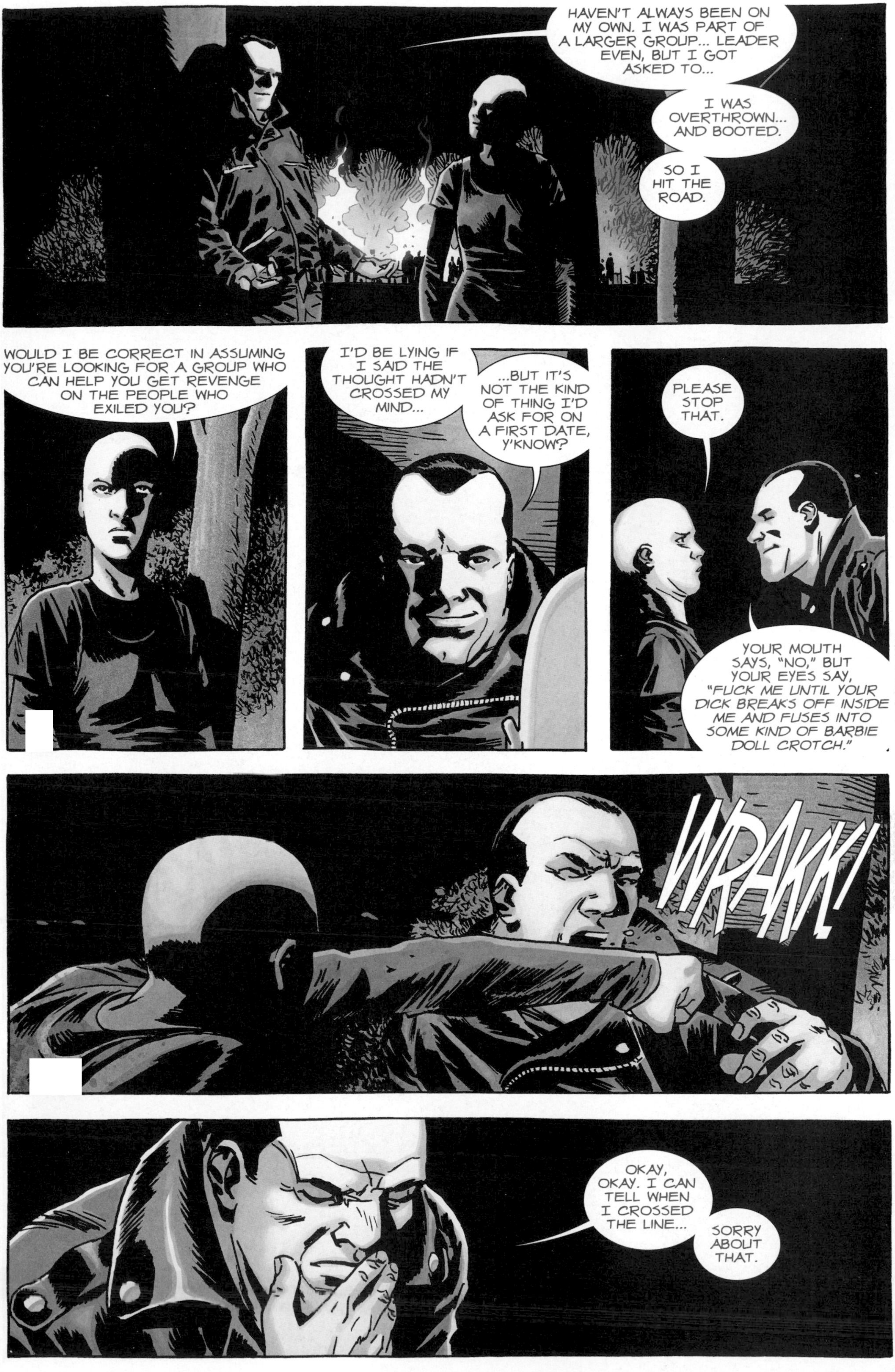
HAVEN'T ALWAYS BEEN ON MY OWN. I WAS PART OF A LARGER GROUP... LEADER EVEN, BUT I GOT ASKED TO...
I WAS OVERTHROWN... AND BOOTED.
SO I HIT THE ROAD.
WOULD I BE CORRECT IN ASSUMING YOU'RE LOOKING FOR A GROUP WHO CAN HELP YOU GET REVENGE ON THE PEOPLE WHO EXILED YOU?
I'D BE LYING IF I SAID THE THOUGHT HADN'T CROSSED MY MIND...
...BUT IT'S NOT THE KIND OF THING I'D ASK FOR ON A FIRST DATE, Y'KNOW?
PLEASE STOP THAT.
YOUR MOUTH SAYS, "NO," BUT YOUR EYES SAY, "FUCK ME UNTIL YOUR DICK BREAKS OFF INSIDE ME AND FUSES INTO SOME KIND OF BARBIE DOLL CROTCH."
WRAKK!
OKAY, OKAY. I CAN TELL WHEN I CROSSED THE LINE...
SORRY ABOUT THAT.

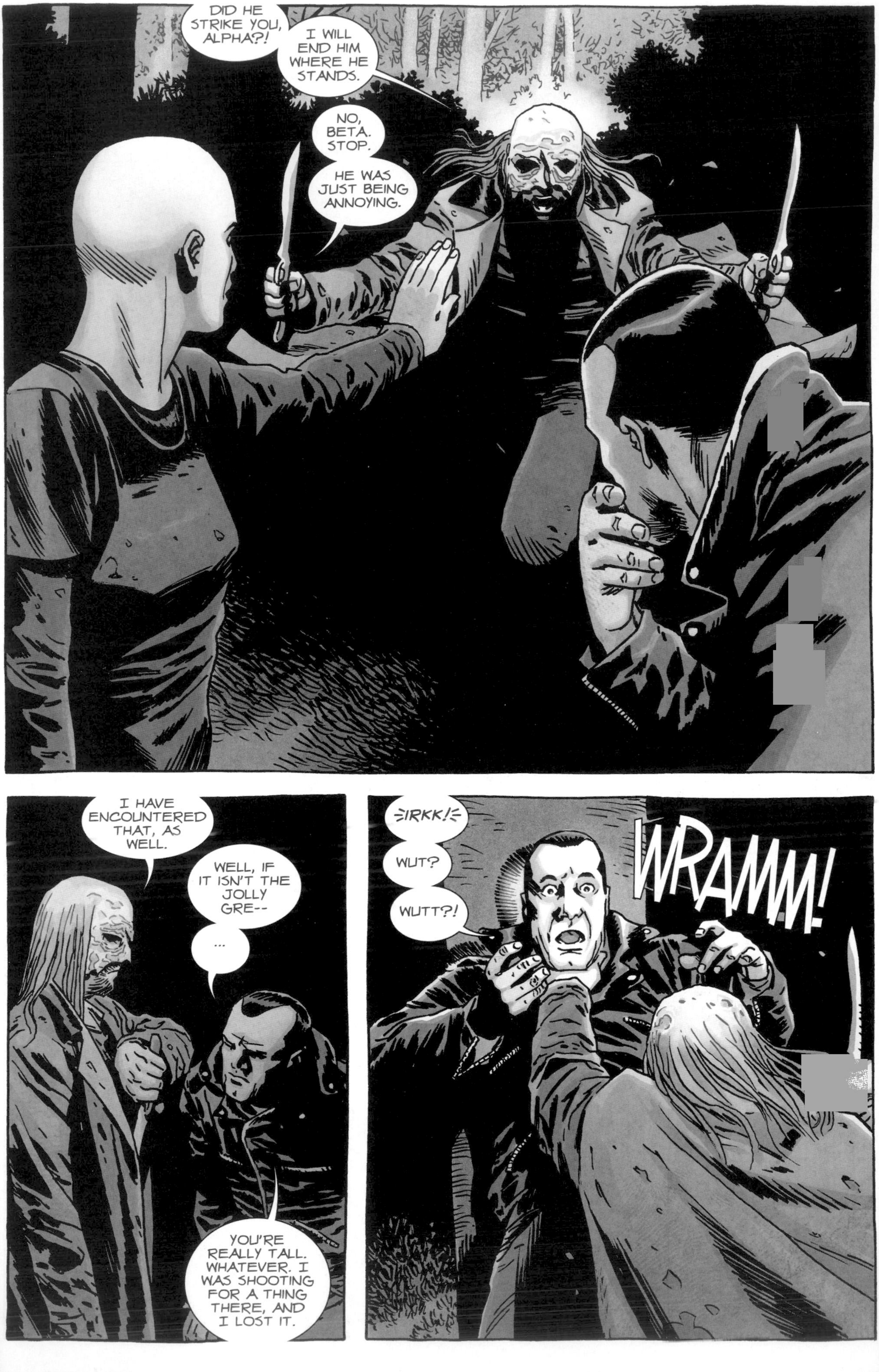
DID HE STRIKE YOU, ALPHA?!
I WILL END HIM WHERE HE STANDS.
NO, BETA. STOP.
HE WAS JUST BEING ANNOYING.
I HAVE ENCOUNTERED THAT, AS WELL.
WELL, IF IT ISN'T THE JOLLY GRE--
...
YOU'RE REALLY TALL. WHATEVER. I WAS SHOOTING FOR A THING THERE, AND I LOST IT.
!IRKK!
WRAMM!
WUT?
WUTT?!

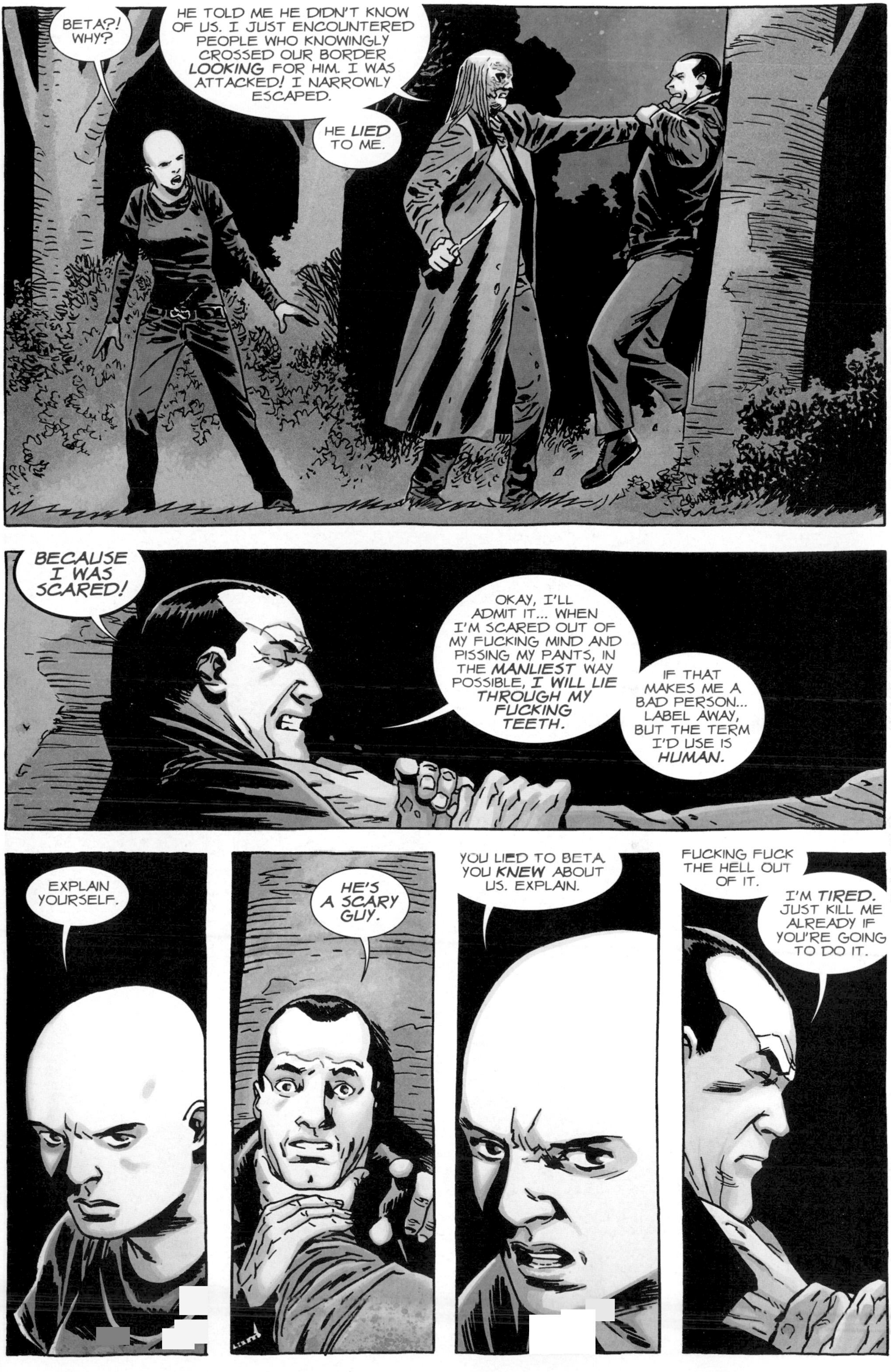
BETA?! WHY?
HE TOLD ME HE DIDN'T KNOW OF US. I JUST ENCOUNTERED PEOPLE WHO KNOWINGLY CROSSED OUR BORDER LOOKING FOR HIM. I WAS ATTACKED! I NARROWLY ESCAPED.
HE LIED TO ME.
BECAUSE I WAS SCARED!
OKAY, I'LL ADMIT IT... WHEN I'M SCARED OUT OF MY FUCKING MIND AND PISSING MY PANTS, IN THE MANLIEST WAY POSSIBLE, I WILL LIE THROUGH MY FUCKING TEETH.
IF THAT MAKES ME A BAD PERSON... LABEL AWAY, BUT THE TERM I'D USE IS HUMAN.
EXPLAIN YOURSELF.
HE'S A SCARY GUY.
YOU LIED TO BETA. YOU KNEW ABOUT US. EXPLAIN.
FUCKING FUCK THE HELL OUT OF IT.
I'M TIRED. JUST KILL ME ALREADY IF YOU'RE GOING TO DO IT.

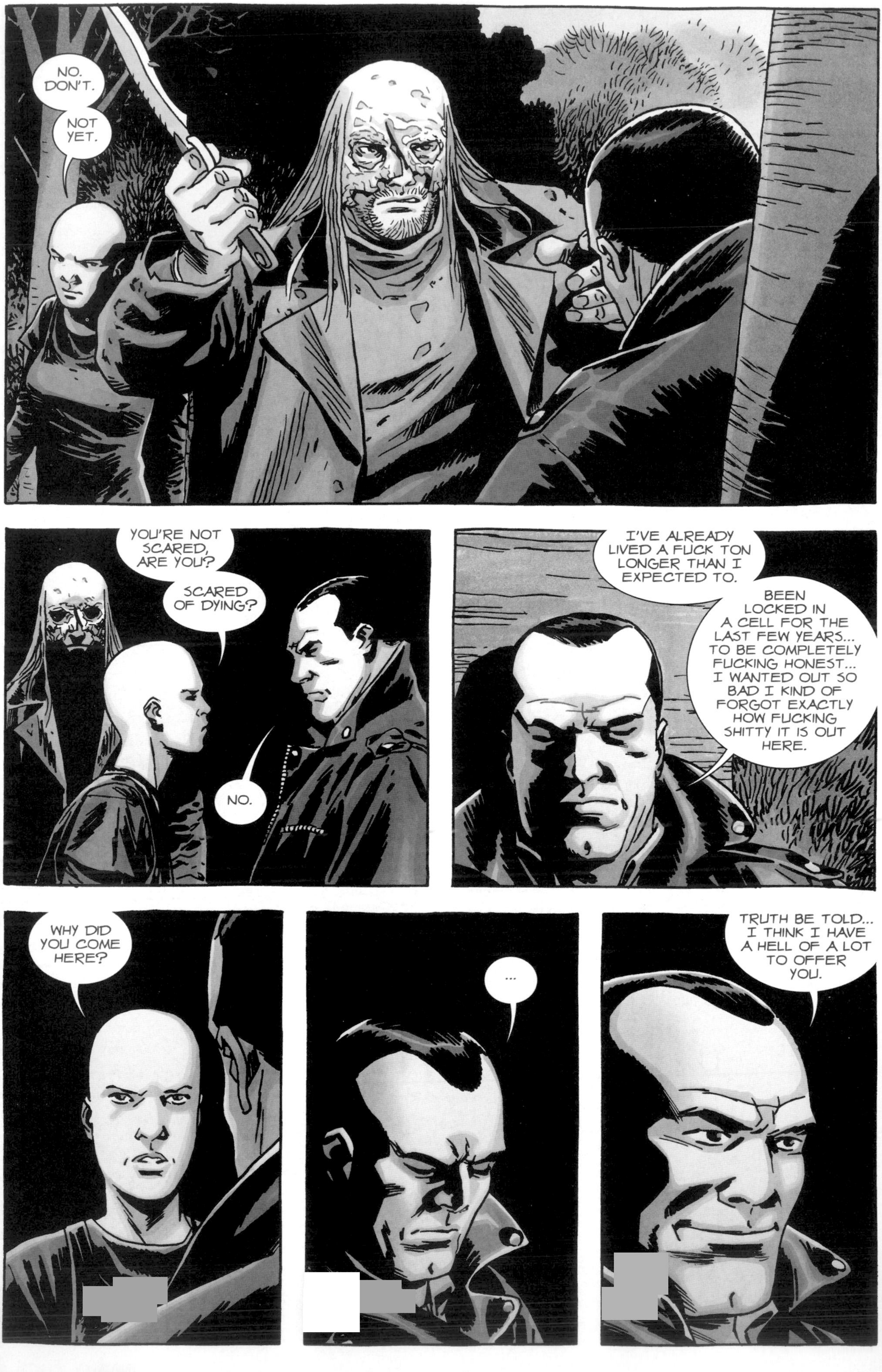
NO. DON'T.
NOT YET.
YOU'RE NOT SCARED, ARE YOU?
SCARED OF DYING?
NO.
I'VE ALREADY LIVED A FUCK TON LONGER THAN I EXPECTED TO.
BEEN LOCKED IN A CELL FOR THE LAST FEW YEARS... TO BE COMPLETELY FUCKING HONEST... I WANTED OUT SO BAD I KIND OF FORGOT EXACTLY HOW FUCKING SHITTY IT IS OUT HERE.
WHY DID YOU COME HERE?
...
TRUTH BE TOLD... I THINK I HAVE A HELL OF A LOT TO OFFER YOU.

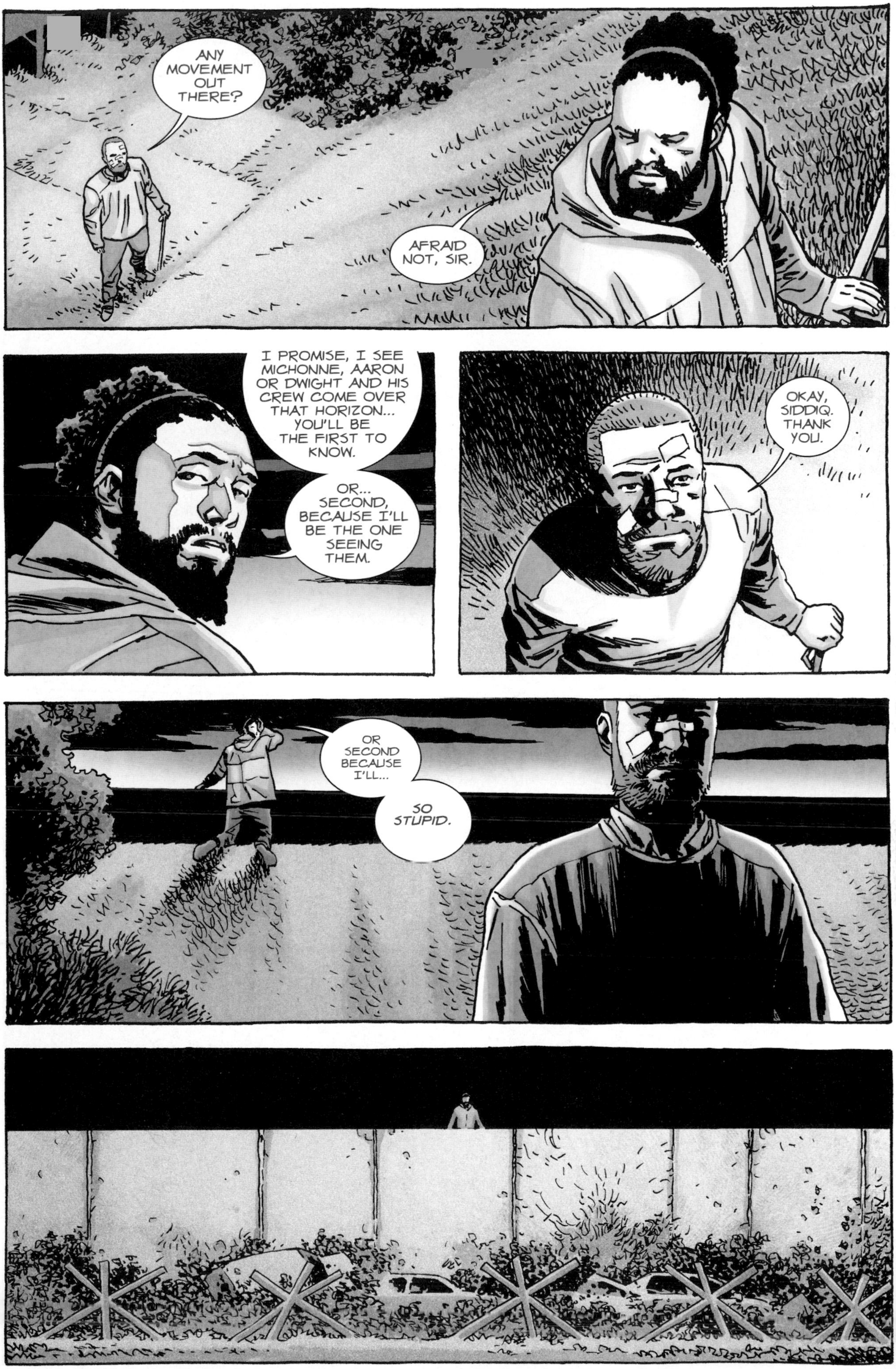
ANY MOVEMENT OUT THERE?
AFRAID NOT, SIR.
I PROMISE, I SEE MICHONNE, AARON OR DWIGHT AND HIS CREW COME OVER THAT HORIZON... YOU'LL BE THE FIRST TO KNOW.
OR... SECOND, BECAUSE I'LL BE THE ONE SEEING THEM.
OKAY, SIDDIQ. THANK YOU.
OR SECOND BECAUSE I'LL...
SO STUPID.

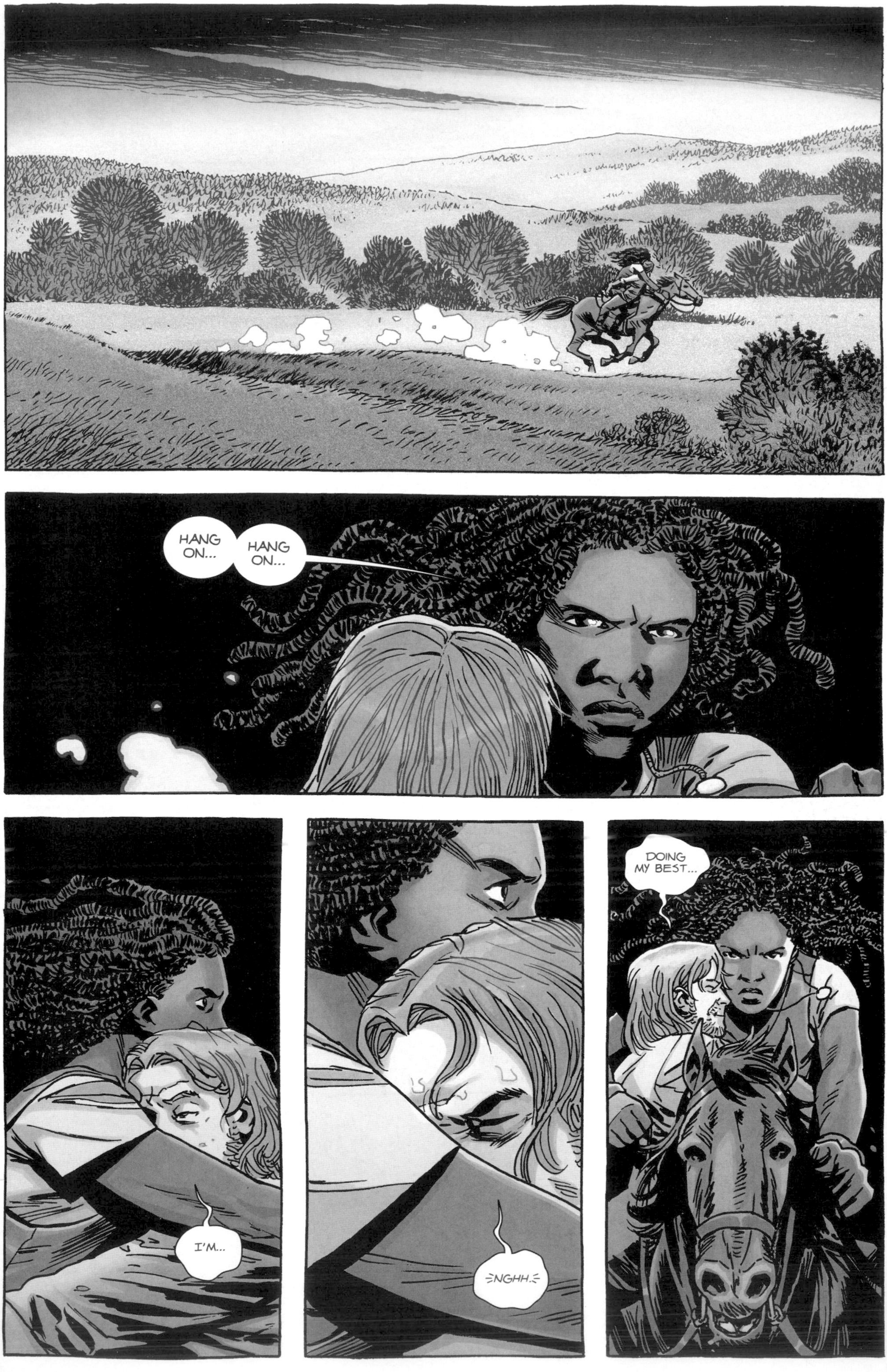
HANG ON...
HANG ON...
I'M...
NGHH.
DOING MY BEST...

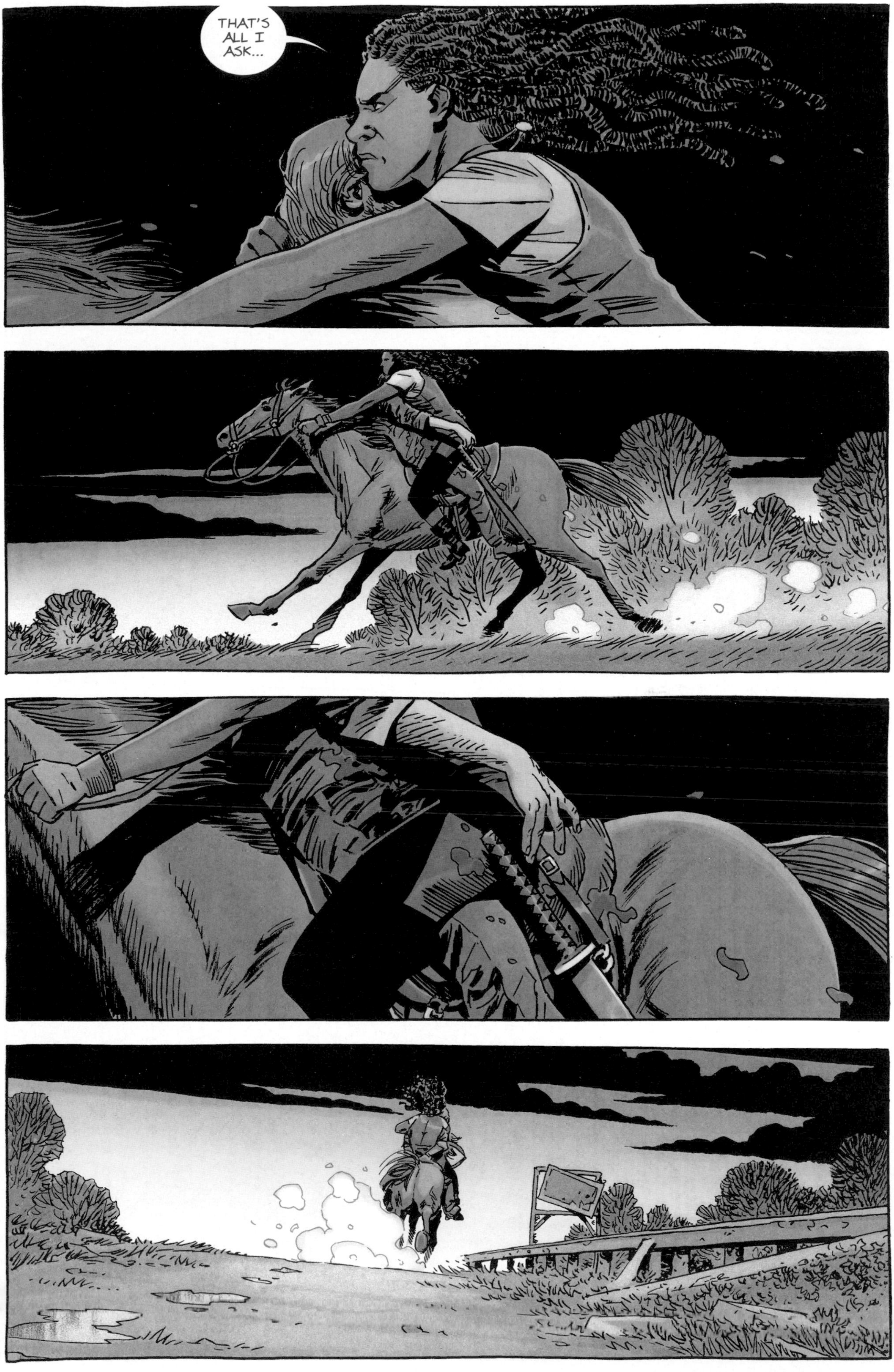
THAT'S ALL I ASK...

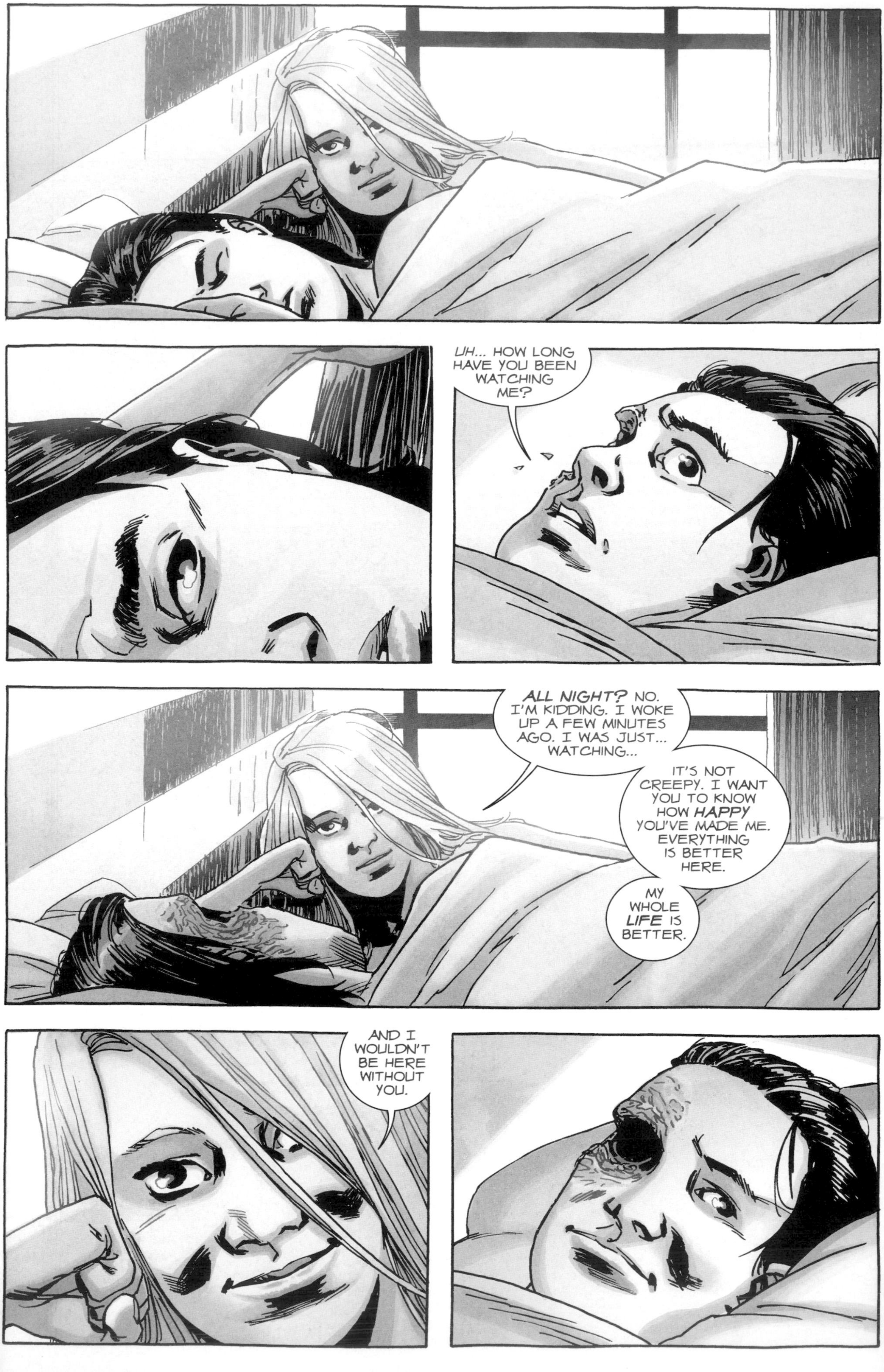
UH... HOW LONG HAVE YOU BEEN WATCHING ME?
ALL NIGHT? NO. I'M KIDDING. I WOKE UP A FEW MINUTES AGO. I WAS JUST... WATCHING...
IT'S NOT CREEPY. I WANT YOU TO KNOW HOW HAPPY YOU'VE MADE ME. EVERYTHING IS BETTER HERE.
MY WHOLE LIFE IS BETTER.
AND I WOULDN'T BE HERE WITHOUT YOU.

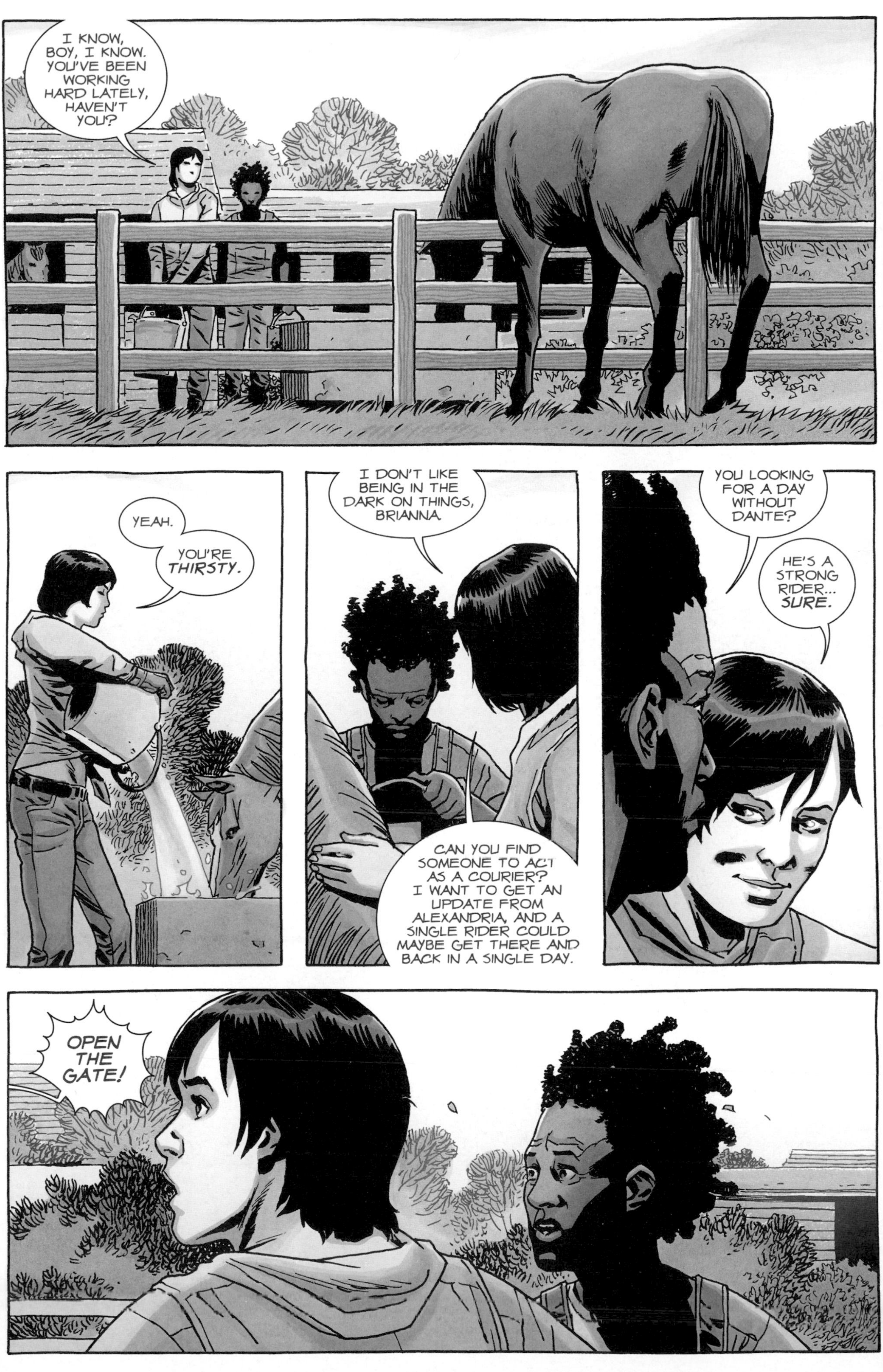

I KNOW, BOY, I KNOW. YOU'VE BEEN WORKING HARD LATELY, HAVEN'T YOU?
YEAH.
YOU'RE THIRSTY.
I DON'T LIKE BEING IN THE DARK ON THINGS, BRIANNA.
CAN YOU FIND SOMEONE TO ACT AS A COURIER? I WANT TO GET AN UPDATE FROM ALEXANDRIA, AND A SINGLE RIDER COULD MAYBE GET THERE AND BACK IN A SINGLE DAY.
YOU LOOKING FOR A DAY WITHOUT DANTE?
HE'S A STRONG RIDER... SURE.
OPEN THE GATE!

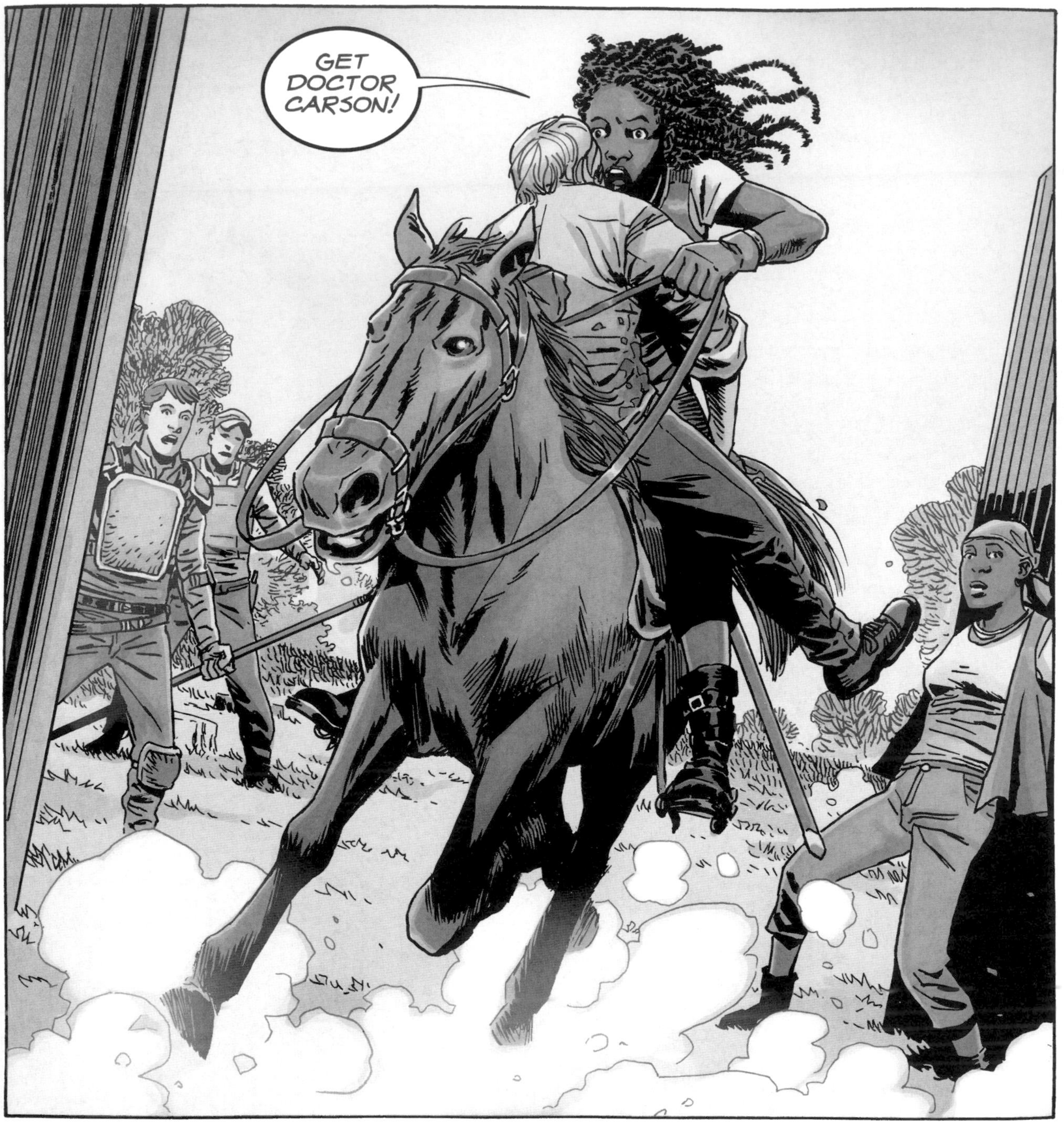
GET DOCTOR CARSON!

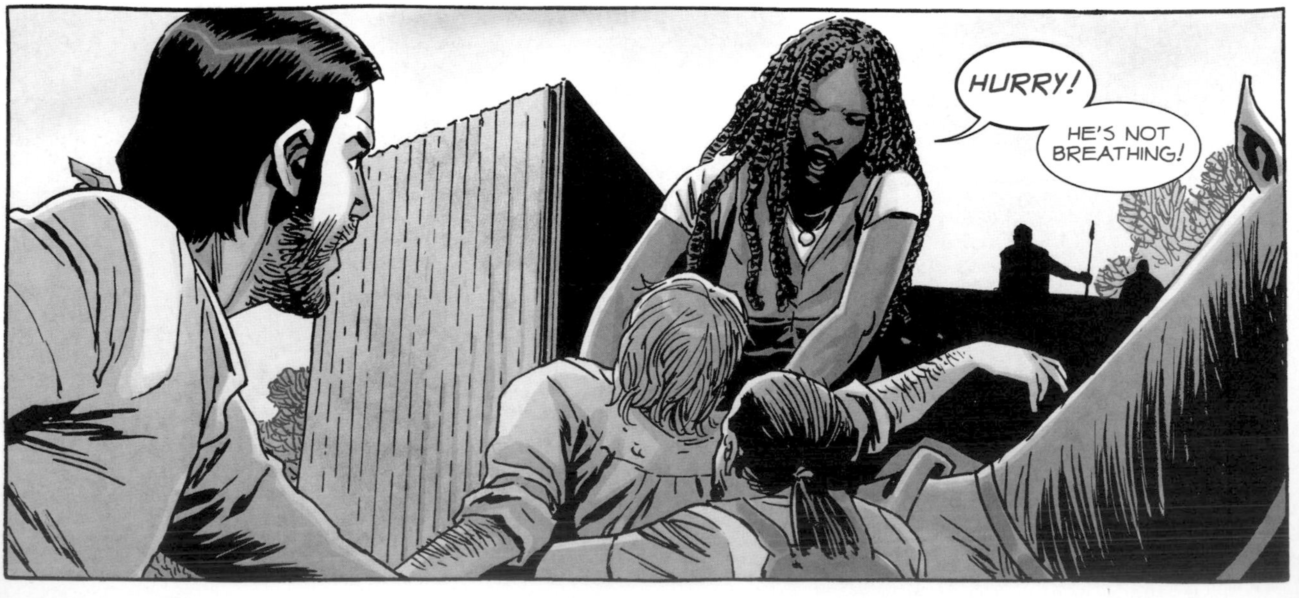
HURRY!
HE'S NOT BREATHING!

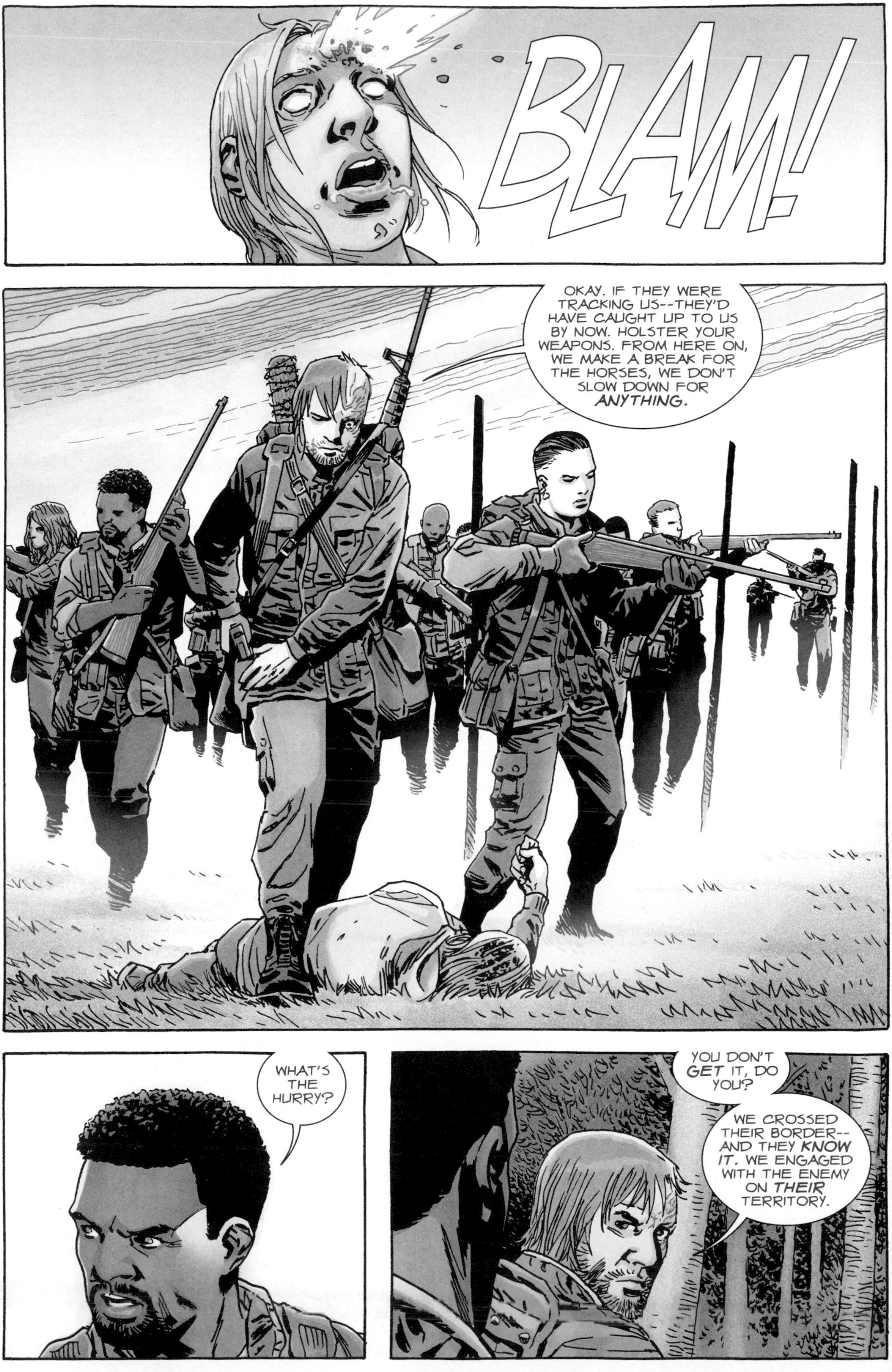
BLAM!
OKAY. IF THEY WERE TRACKING US--THEY'D HAVE CAUGHT UP TO US BY NOW. HOLSTER YOUR WEAPONS. FROM HERE ON, WE MAKE A BREAK FOR THE HORSES, WE DON'T SLOW DOWN FOR ANYTHING.
WHAT'S THE HURRY?
YOU DON'T GET IT, DO YOU?
WE CROSSED THEIR BORDER-- AND THEY KNOW IT. WE ENGAGED WITH THE ENEMY ON THEIR TERRITORY.

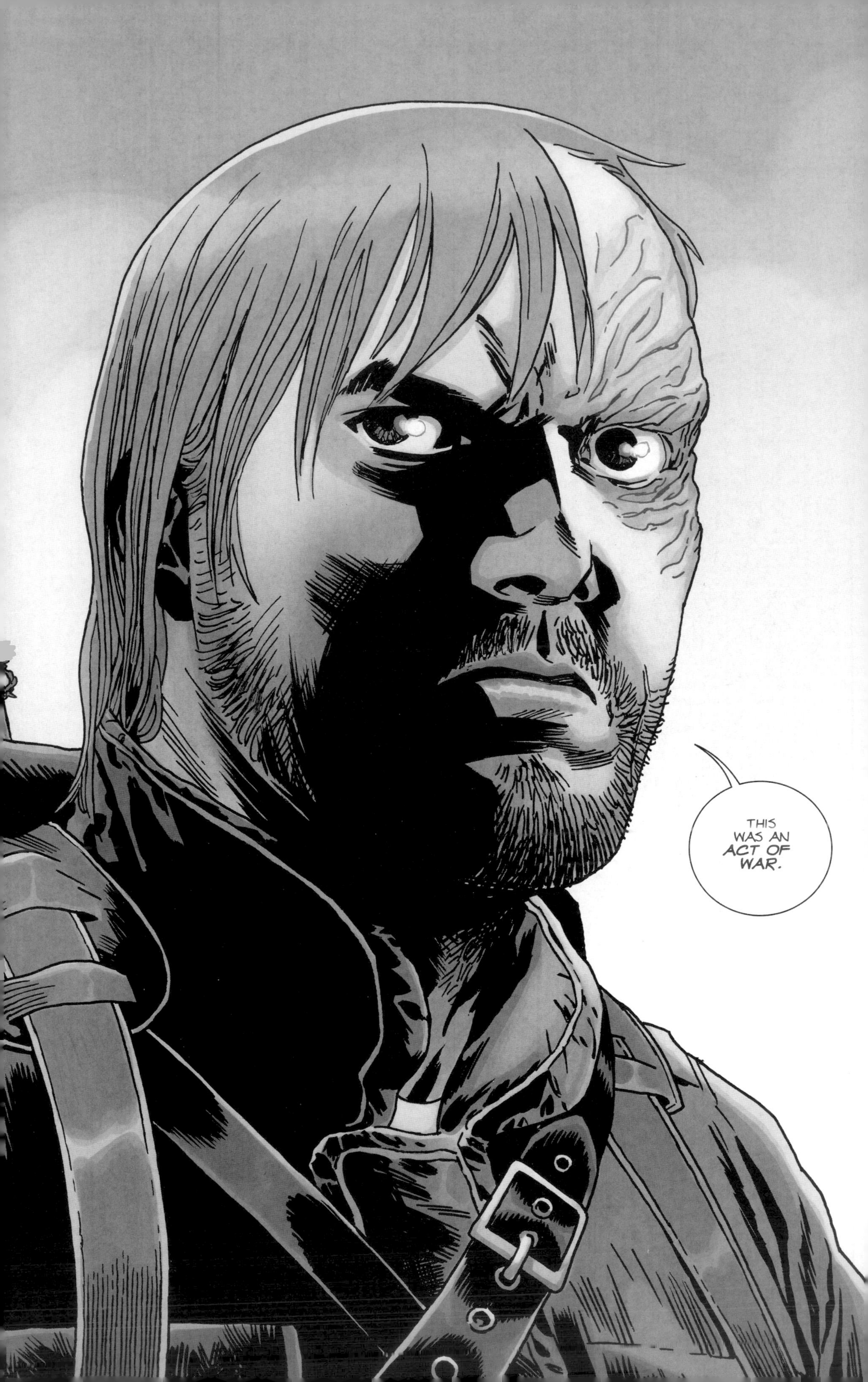
THIS WAS AN *ACT OF WAR.*

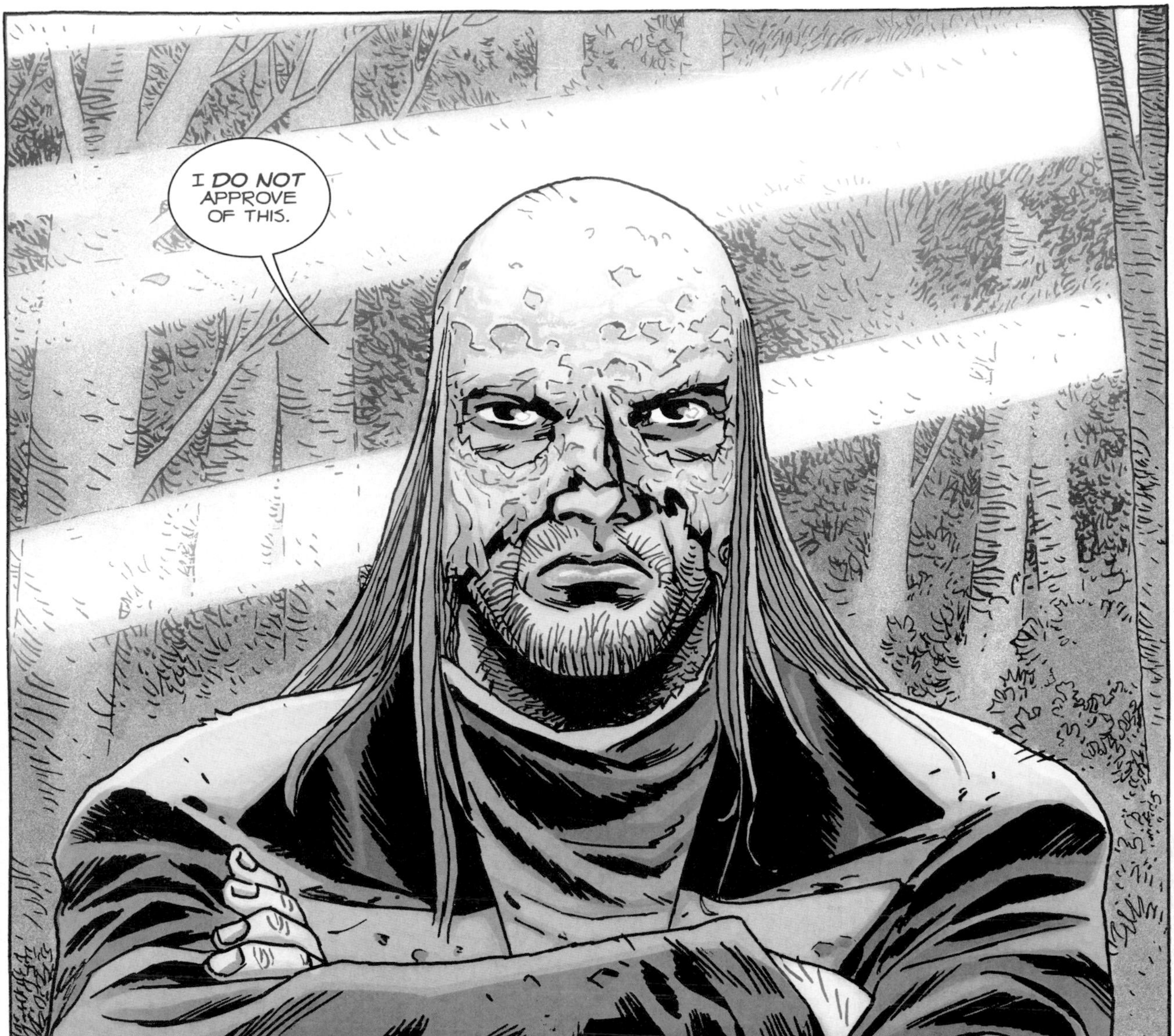
I DO NOT APPROVE OF THIS.

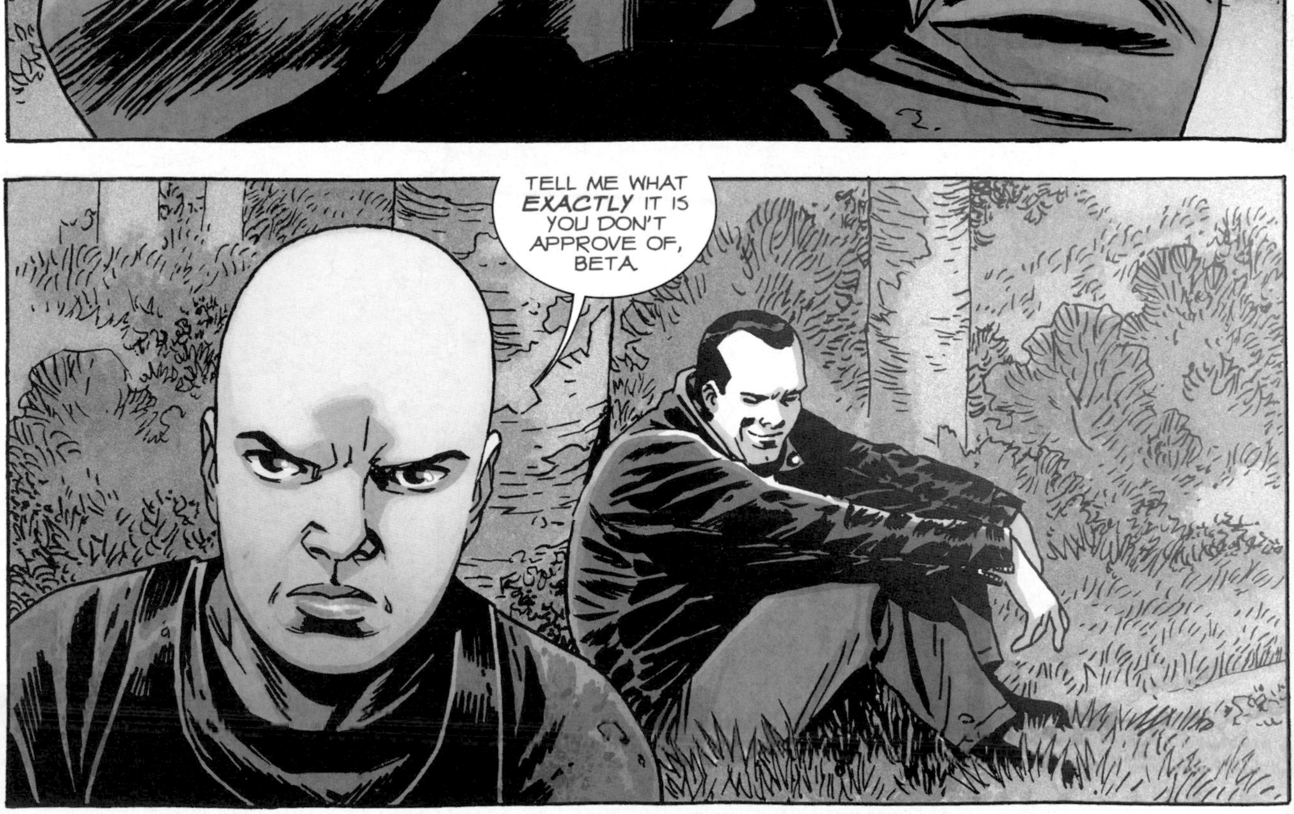
TELL ME WHAT EXACTLY IT IS YOU DON'T APPROVE OF, BETA.

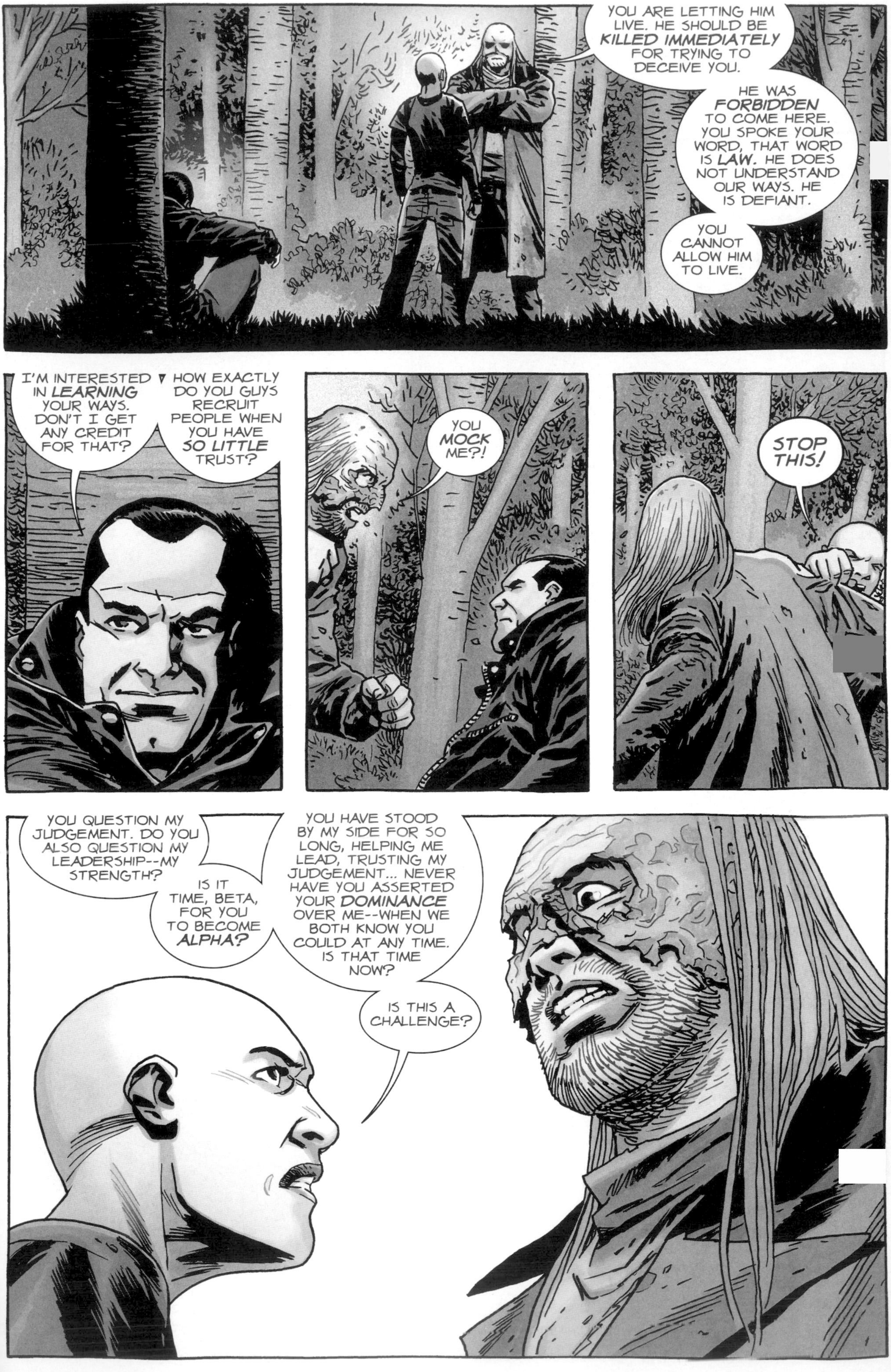
YOU ARE LETTING HIM LIVE. HE SHOULD BE KILLED IMMEDIATELY FOR TRYING TO DECEIVE YOU.
HE WAS FORBIDDEN TO COME HERE. YOU SPOKE YOUR WORD, THAT WORD IS LAW. HE DOES NOT UNDERSTAND OUR WAYS. HE IS DEFIANT.
YOU CANNOT ALLOW HIM TO LIVE.
I'M INTERESTED IN LEARNING YOUR WAYS. DON'T I GET ANY CREDIT FOR THAT?
HOW EXACTLY DO YOU GUYS RECRUIT PEOPLE WHEN YOU HAVE SO LITTLE TRUST?
YOU MOCK ME?!
STOP THIS!
YOU QUESTION MY JUDGEMENT. DO YOU ALSO QUESTION MY LEADERSHIP--MY STRENGTH?
IS IT TIME, BETA, FOR YOU TO BECOME ALPHA?
YOU HAVE STOOD BY MY SIDE FOR SO LONG, HELPING ME LEAD, TRUSTING MY JUDGEMENT... NEVER HAVE YOU ASSERTED YOUR DOMINANCE OVER ME--WHEN WE BOTH KNOW YOU COULD AT ANY TIME. IS THAT TIME NOW?
IS THIS A CHALLENGE?

NO. YOU ARE MY ALPHA.

I HAVE SWORN *NEVER* TO CHALLENGE YOU. I AM SORRY.

PLEASE FORGIVE ME.

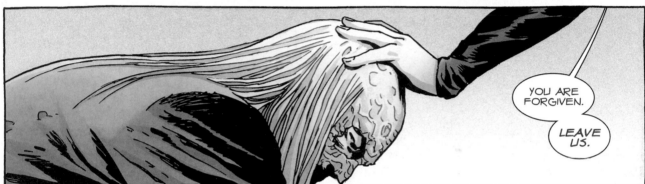

YOU ARE FORGIVEN.

LEAVE US.

WELL... THAT WAS FUCKING AWESOME.

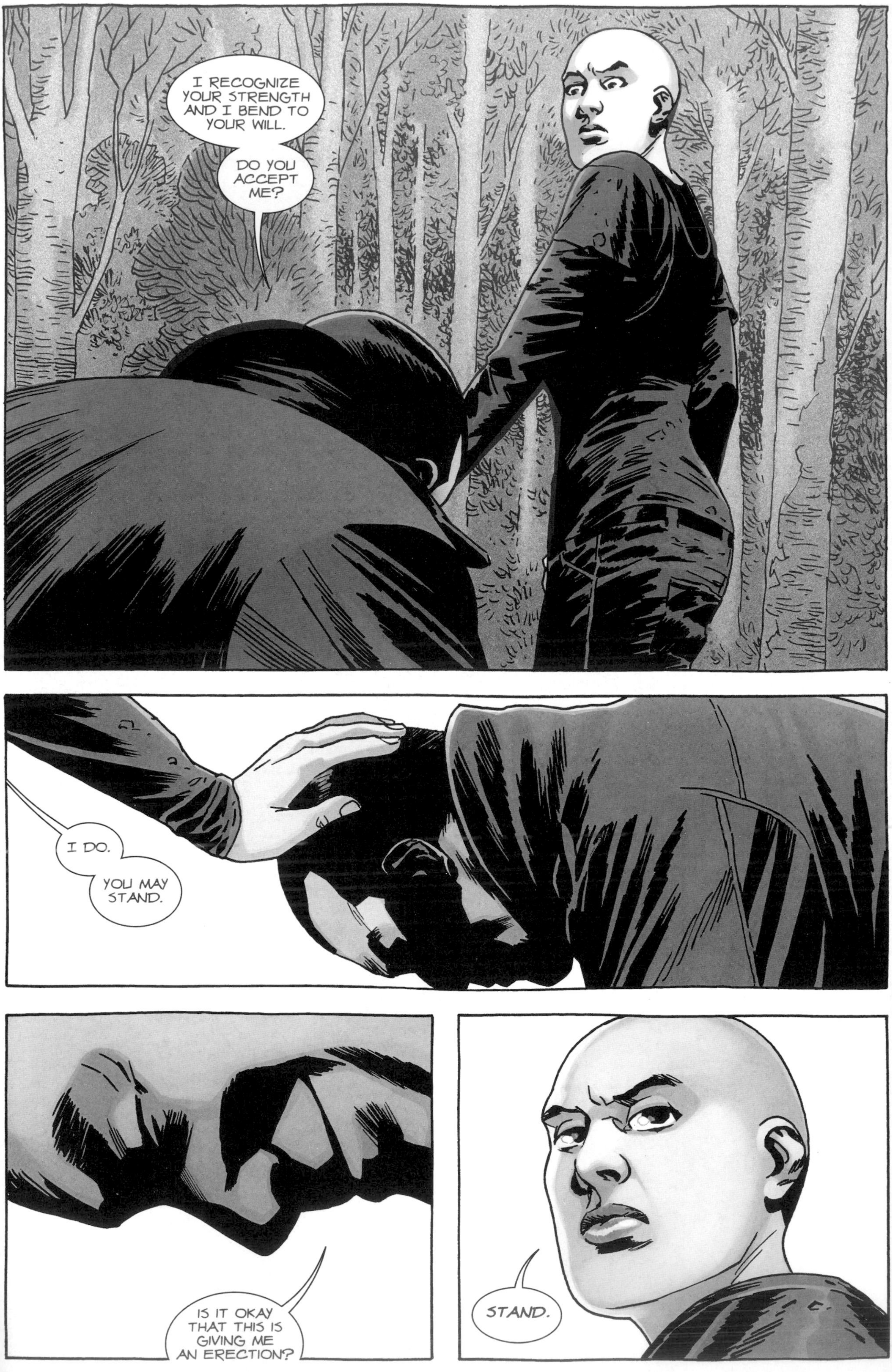
I RECOGNIZE YOUR STRENGTH AND I BEND TO YOUR WILL.
DO YOU ACCEPT ME?
I DO.
YOU MAY STAND.
IS IT OKAY THAT THIS IS GIVING ME AN ERECTION?
STAND.

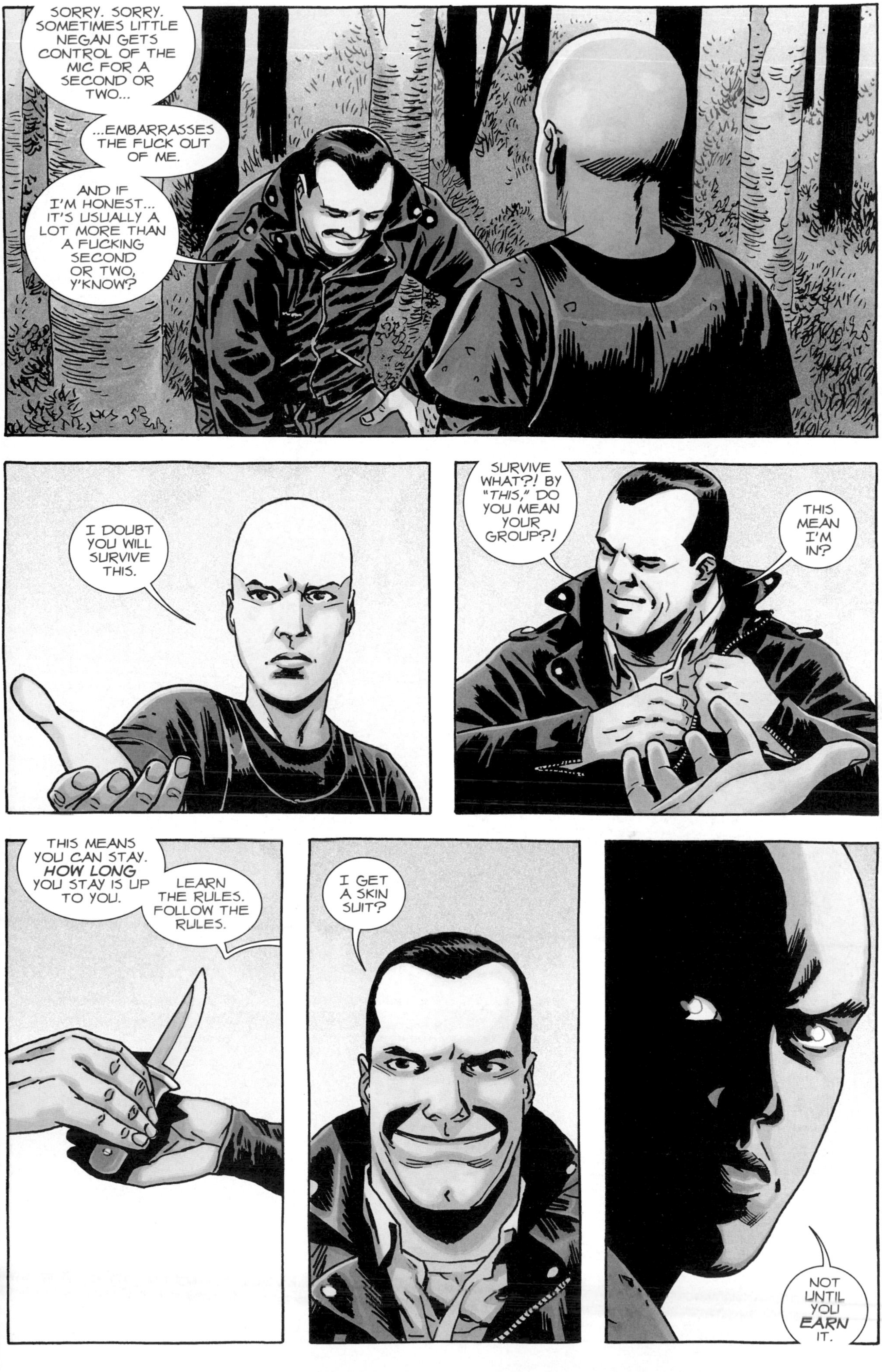
SORRY. SORRY. SOMETIMES LITTLE NEGAN GETS CONTROL OF THE MIC FOR A SECOND OR TWO...
...EMBARRASSES THE FUCK OUT OF ME.
AND IF I'M HONEST... IT'S USUALLY A LOT MORE THAN A FUCKING SECOND OR TWO, Y'KNOW?
I DOUBT YOU WILL SURVIVE THIS.
SURVIVE WHAT?! BY "THIS," DO YOU MEAN YOUR GROUP?!
THIS MEAN I'M IN?
THIS MEANS YOU CAN STAY. HOW LONG YOU STAY IS UP TO YOU.
LEARN THE RULES. FOLLOW THE RULES.
I GET A SKIN SUIT?
NOT UNTIL YOU EARN IT.

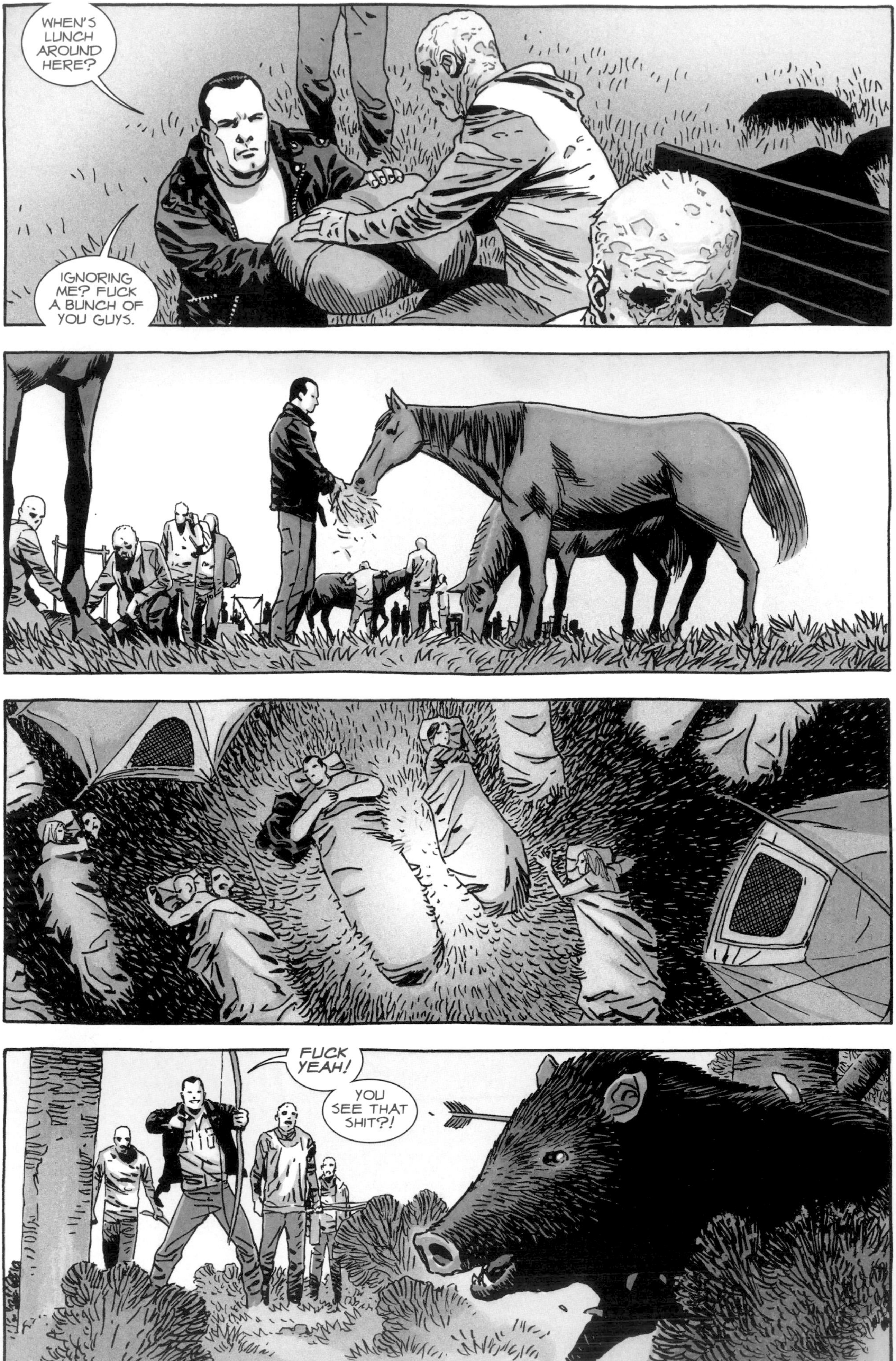

WHEN'S LUNCH AROUND HERE?
IGNORING ME? FUCK A BUNCH OF YOU GUYS.
FUCK YEAH!
YOU SEE THAT SHIT?!

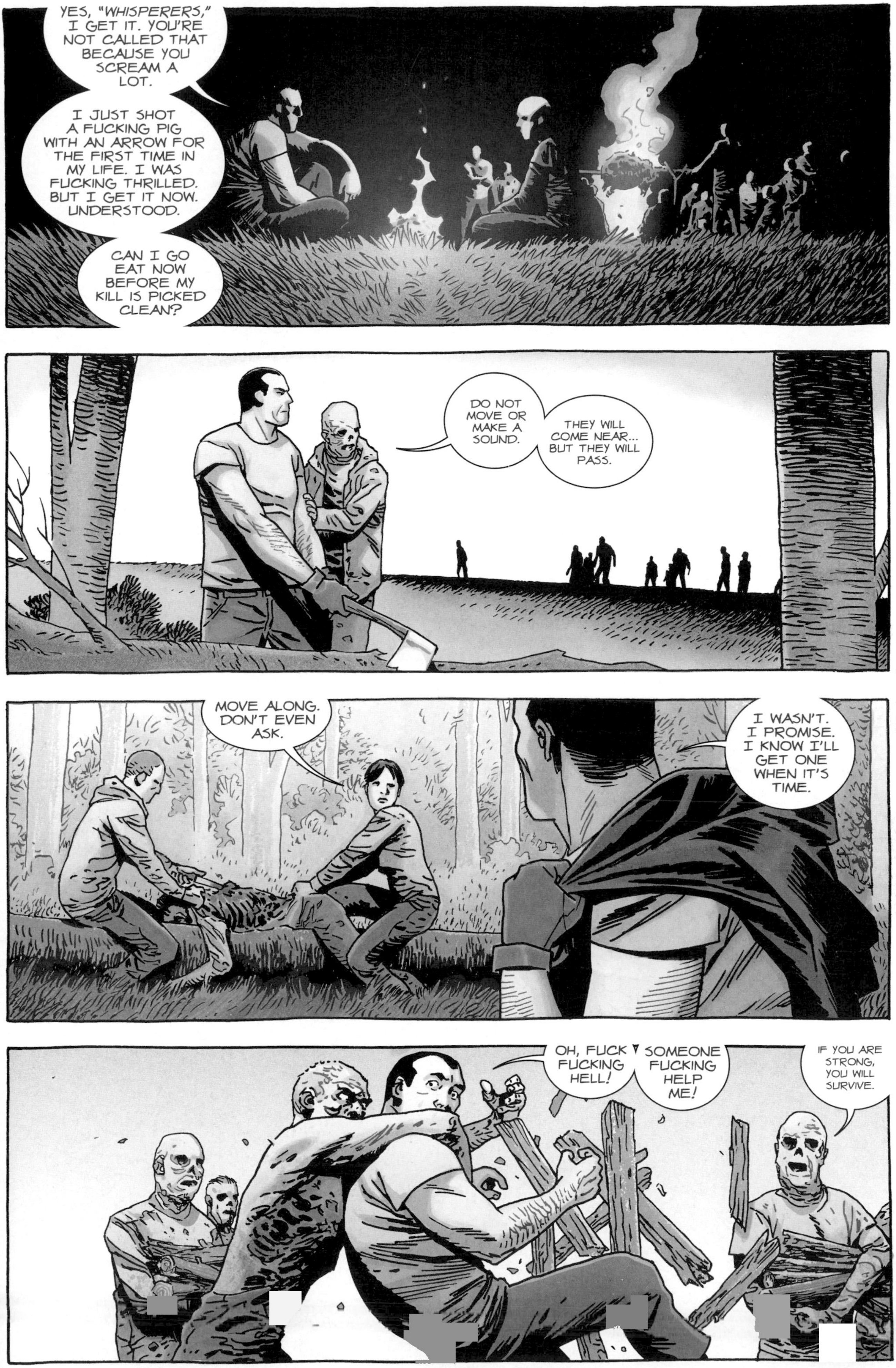
YES, "WHISPERERS," I GET IT. YOU'RE NOT CALLED THAT BECAUSE YOU SCREAM A LOT.
I JUST SHOT A FUCKING PIG WITH AN ARROW FOR THE FIRST TIME IN MY LIFE. I WAS FUCKING THRILLED. BUT I GET IT NOW. UNDERSTOOD.
CAN I GO EAT NOW BEFORE MY KILL IS PICKED CLEAN?
DO NOT MOVE OR MAKE A SOUND.
THEY WILL COME NEAR... BUT THEY WILL PASS.
MOVE ALONG. DON'T EVEN ASK.
I WASN'T. I PROMISE. I KNOW I'LL GET ONE WHEN IT'S TIME.
OH, FUCK FUCKING HELL!
SOMEONE FUCKING HELP ME!
IF YOU ARE STRONG, YOU WILL SURVIVE.

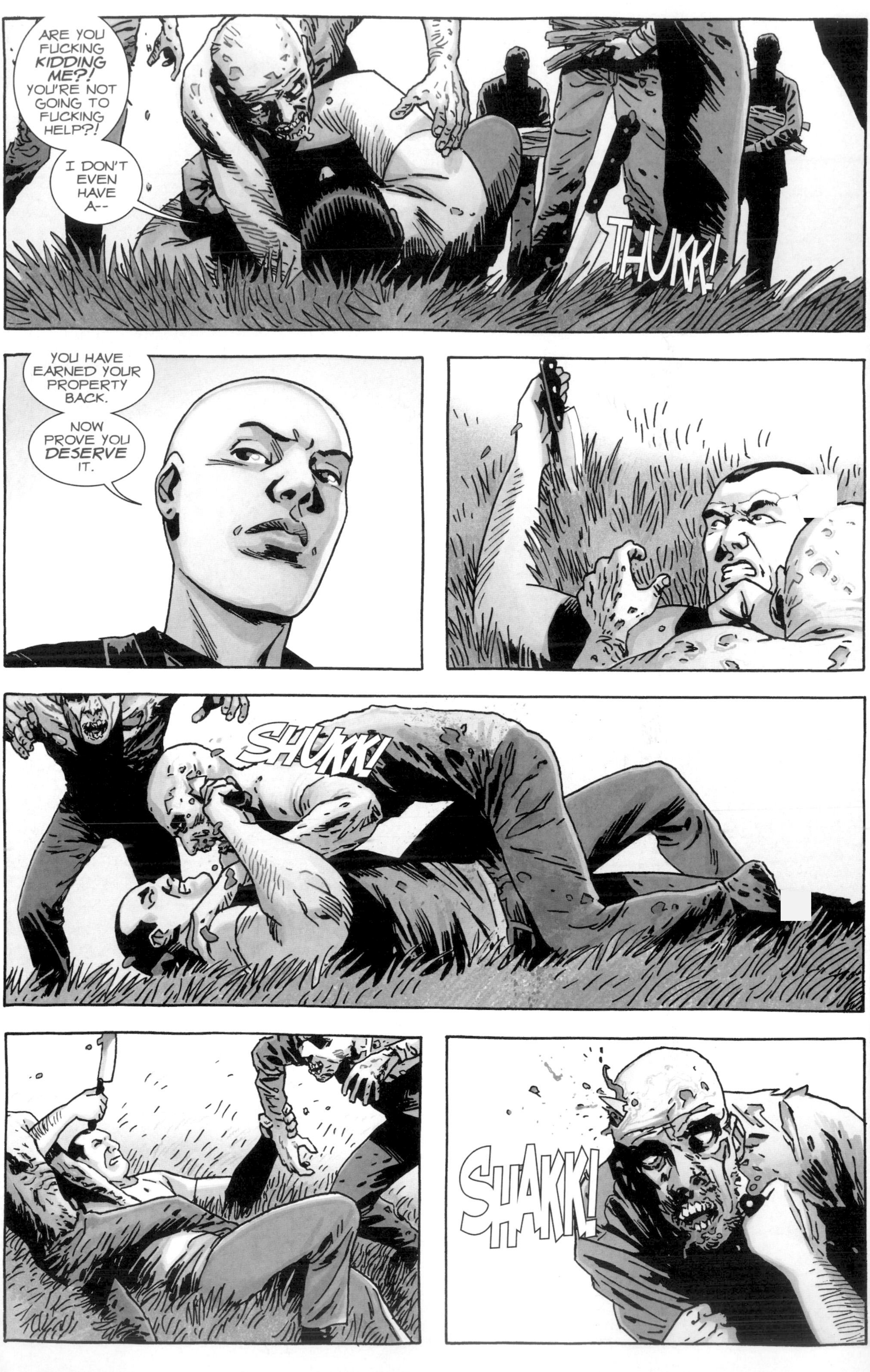
ARE YOU FUCKING KIDDING ME?! YOU'RE NOT GOING TO FUCKING HELP?!
I DON'T EVEN HAVE A--
THUKK!
YOU HAVE EARNED YOUR PROPERTY BACK.
NOW PROVE YOU DESERVE IT.
SHUKK!
SHAKK!

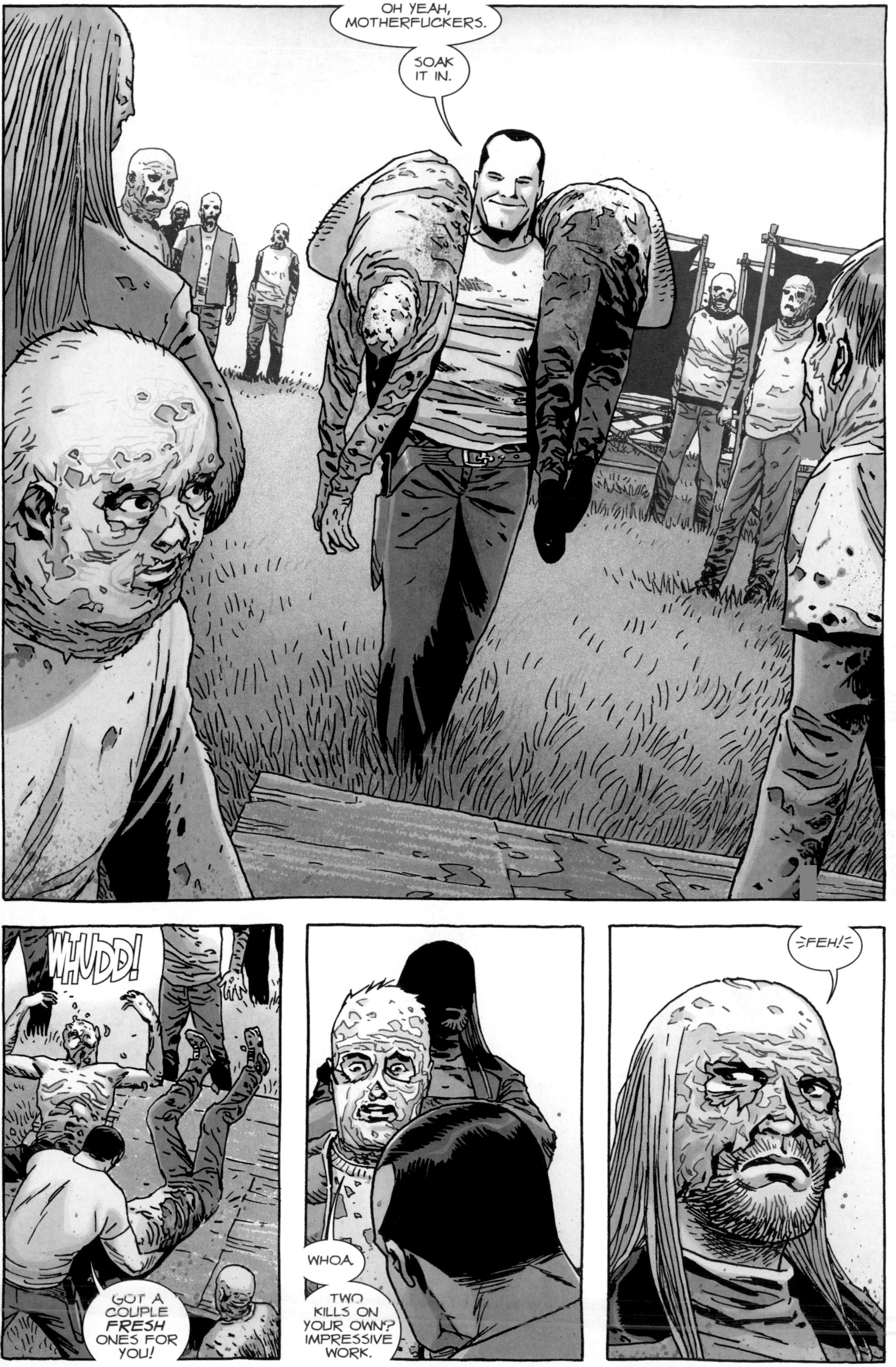
OH YEAH, MOTHERFUCKERS.
SOAK IT IN.
WHUDD!
GOT A COUPLE FRESH ONES FOR YOU!
WHOA.
TWO KILLS ON YOUR OWN? IMPRESSIVE WORK.
FEH!

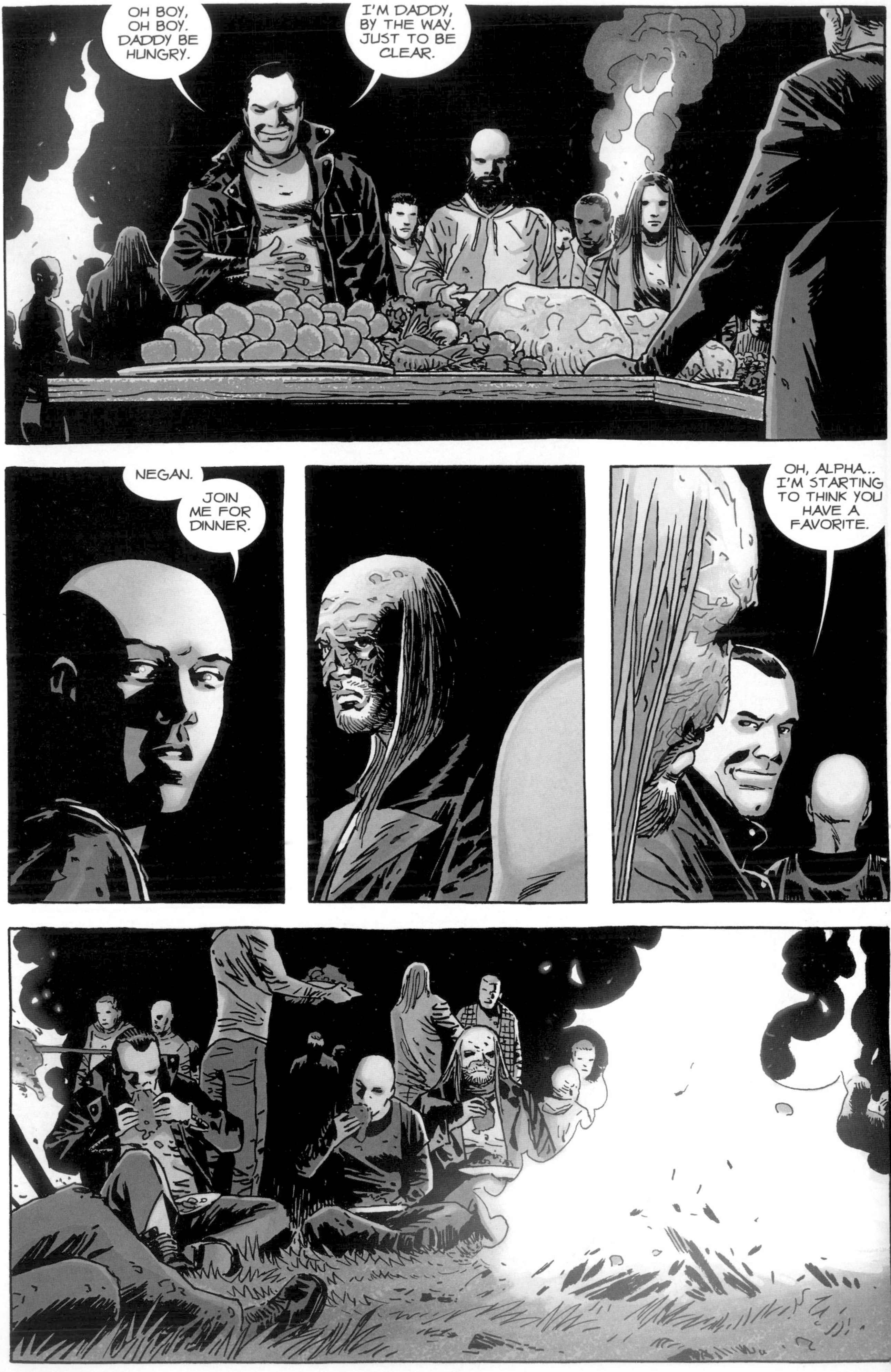
OH BOY, OH BOY. DADDY BE HUNGRY.
I'M DADDY, BY THE WAY. JUST TO BE CLEAR.
NEGAN.
JOIN ME FOR DINNER.
OH, ALPHA... I'M STARTING TO THINK YOU HAVE A FAVORITE.

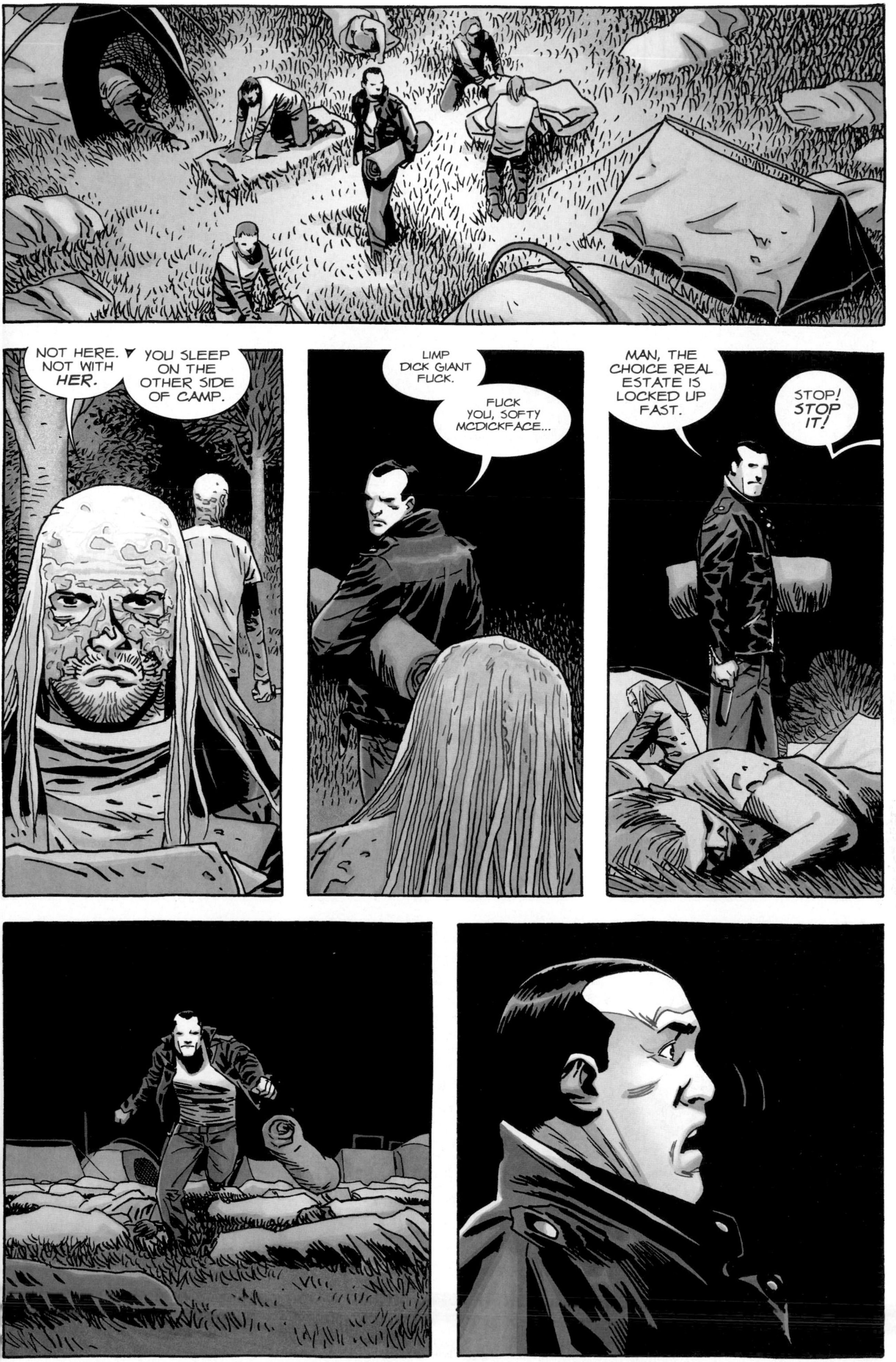
NOT HERE. NOT WITH HER.
YOU SLEEP ON THE OTHER SIDE OF CAMP.
LIMP DICK GIANT FUCK.
FUCK YOU, SOFTY MCDICKFACE...
MAN, THE CHOICE REAL ESTATE IS LOCKED UP FAST.
STOP! STOP IT!

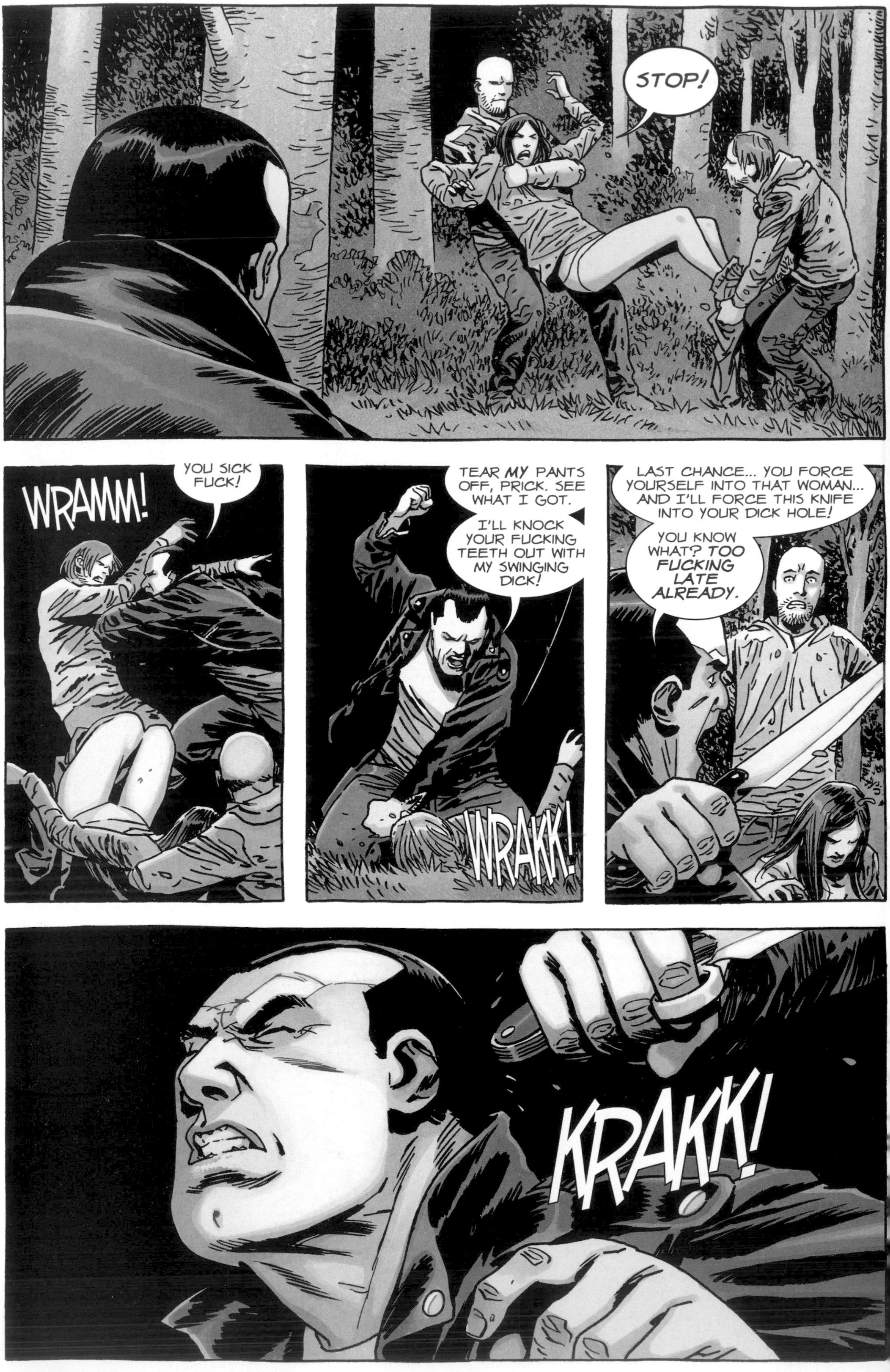
STOP!
WRAMM!
YOU SICK FUCK!
TEAR MY PANTS OFF, PRICK. SEE WHAT I GOT.
I'LL KNOCK YOUR FUCKING TEETH OUT WITH MY SWINGING DICK!
WRAKK!
LAST CHANCE... YOU FORCE YOURSELF INTO THAT WOMAN... AND I'LL FORCE THIS KNIFE INTO YOUR DICK HOLE!
YOU KNOW WHAT? TOO FUCKING LATE ALREADY.
KRAKK!

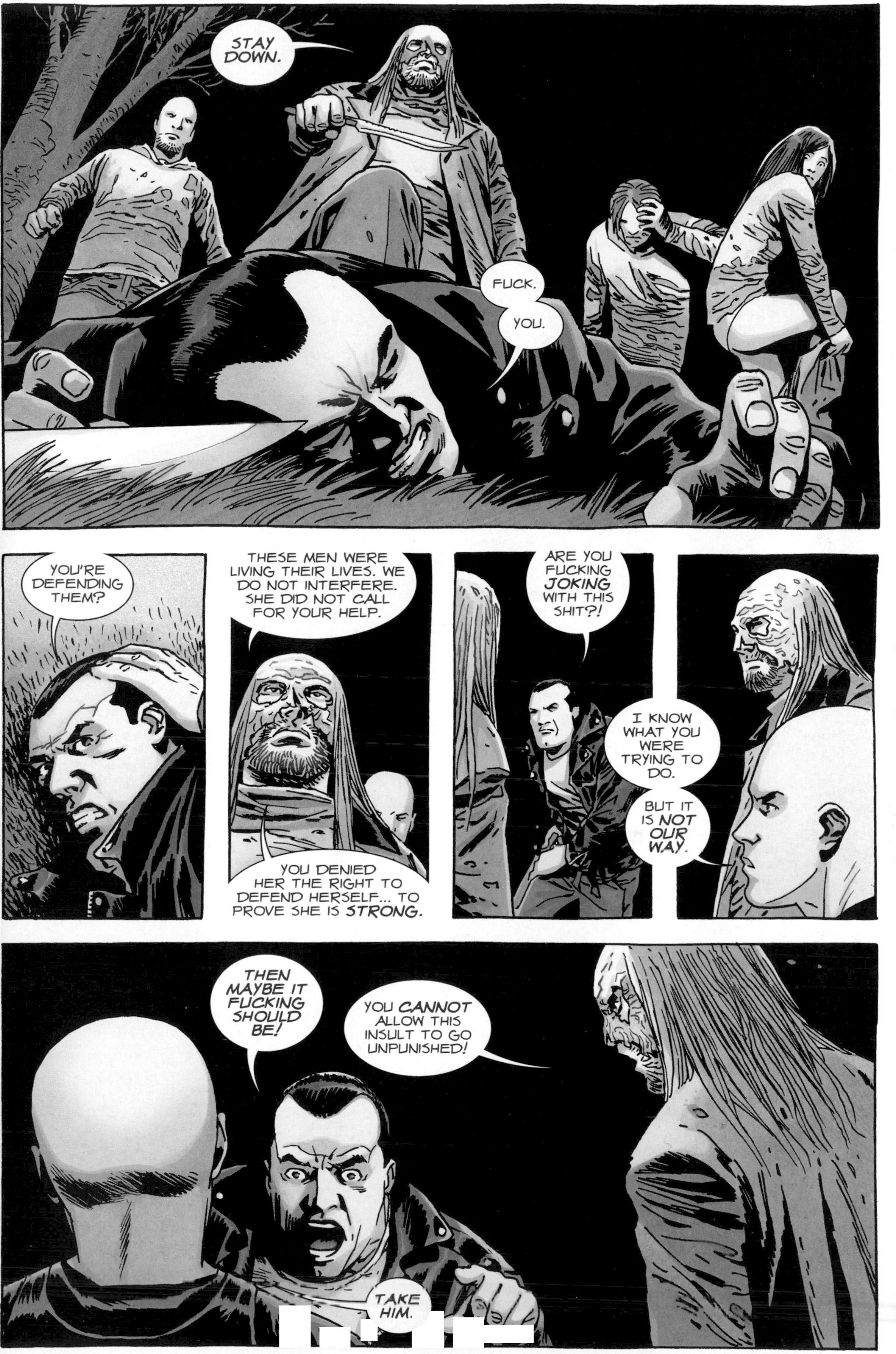
STAY DOWN.
FUCK.
YOU.
YOU'RE DEFENDING THEM?
THESE MEN WERE LIVING THEIR LIVES. WE DO NOT INTERFERE. SHE DID NOT CALL FOR YOUR HELP.
YOU DENIED HER THE RIGHT TO DEFEND HERSELF... TO PROVE SHE IS STRONG.
ARE YOU FUCKING JOKING WITH THIS SHIT?!
I KNOW WHAT YOU WERE TRYING TO DO.
BUT IT IS NOT OUR WAY.
THEN MAYBE IT FUCKING SHOULD BE!
YOU CANNOT ALLOW THIS INSULT TO GO UNPUNISHED!
TAKE HIM.

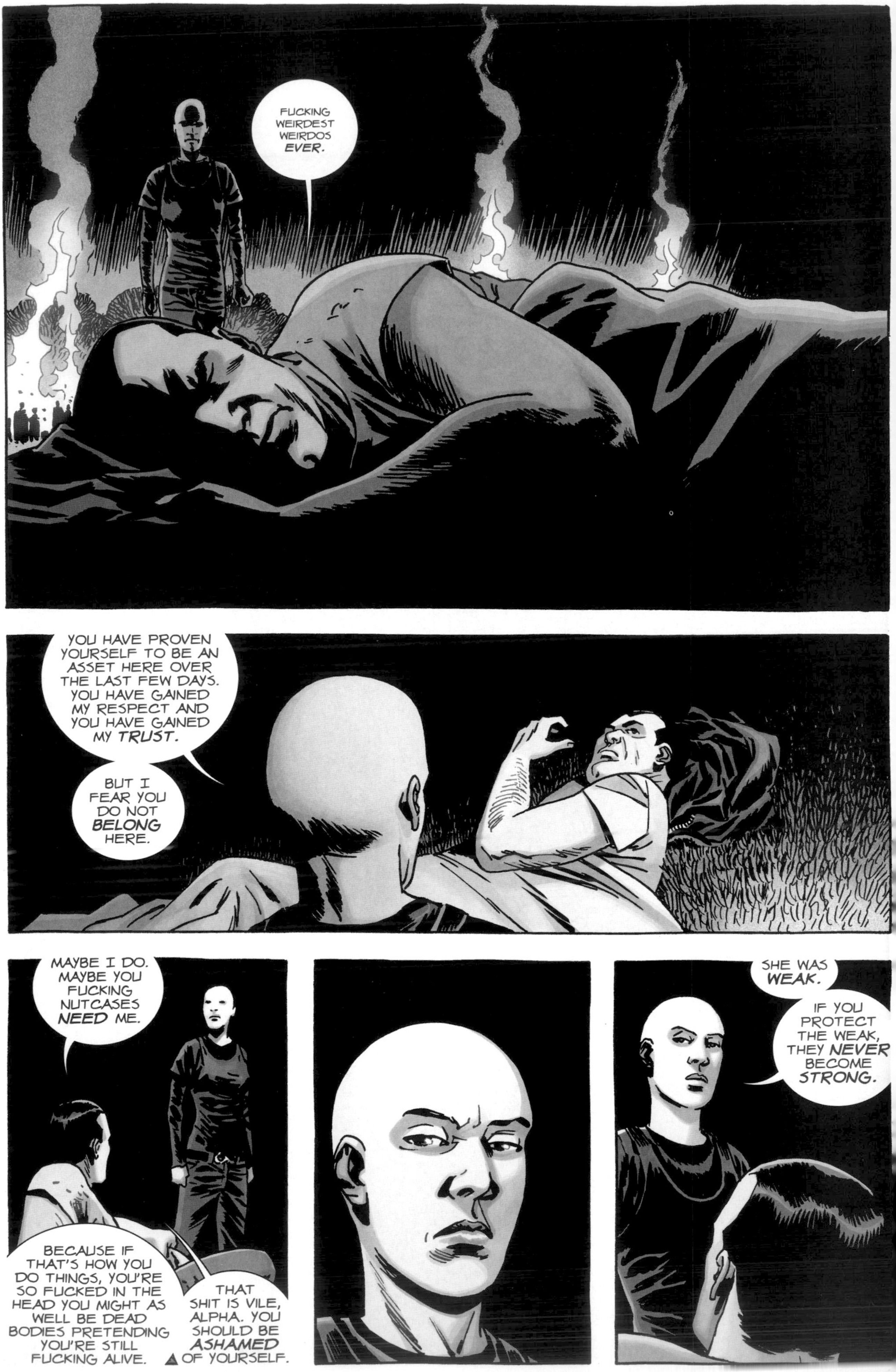
FUCKING WEIRDEST WEIRDOS EVER.
YOU HAVE PROVEN YOURSELF TO BE AN ASSET HERE OVER THE LAST FEW DAYS. YOU HAVE GAINED MY RESPECT AND YOU HAVE GAINED MY TRUST.
BUT I FEAR YOU DO NOT BELONG HERE.
MAYBE I DO. MAYBE YOU FUCKING NUTCASES NEED ME.
BECAUSE IF THAT'S HOW YOU DO THINGS, YOU'RE SO FUCKED IN THE HEAD YOU MIGHT AS WELL BE DEAD BODIES PRETENDING YOU'RE STILL FUCKING ALIVE.
THAT SHIT IS VILE, ALPHA. YOU SHOULD BE ASHAMED OF YOURSELF.
SHE WAS WEAK.
IF YOU PROTECT THE WEAK, THEY NEVER BECOME STRONG.

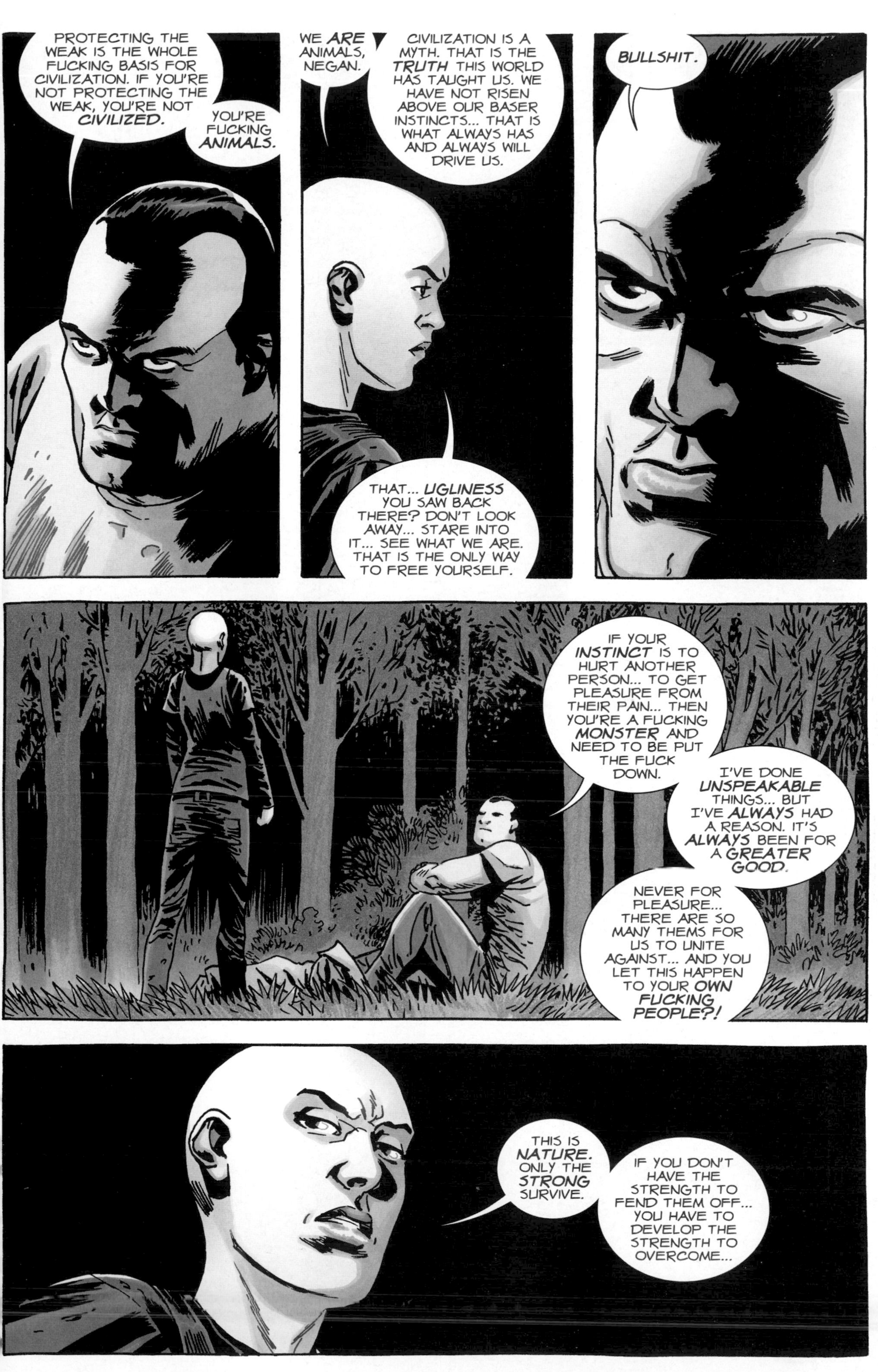
PROTECTING THE WEAK IS THE WHOLE FUCKING BASIS FOR CIVILIZATION. IF YOU'RE NOT PROTECTING THE WEAK, YOU'RE NOT CIVILIZED.
YOU'RE FUCKING ANIMALS.
WE ARE ANIMALS, NEGAN.
CIVILIZATION IS A MYTH. THAT IS THE TRUTH THIS WORLD HAS TAUGHT US. WE HAVE NOT RISEN ABOVE OUR BASER INSTINCTS... THAT IS WHAT ALWAYS HAS AND ALWAYS WILL DRIVE US.
THAT... UGLINESS YOU SAW BACK THERE? DON'T LOOK AWAY... STARE INTO IT... SEE WHAT WE ARE. THAT IS THE ONLY WAY TO FREE YOURSELF.
BULLSHIT.
IF YOUR INSTINCT IS TO HURT ANOTHER PERSON... TO GET PLEASURE FROM THEIR PAIN... THEN YOU'RE A FUCKING MONSTER AND NEED TO BE PUT THE FUCK DOWN.
I'VE DONE UNSPEAKABLE THINGS... BUT I'VE ALWAYS HAD A REASON. IT'S ALWAYS BEEN FOR A GREATER GOOD.
NEVER FOR PLEASURE... THERE ARE SO MANY THEMS FOR US TO UNITE AGAINST... AND YOU LET THIS HAPPEN TO YOUR OWN FUCKING PEOPLE?!
THIS IS NATURE. ONLY THE STRONG SURVIVE.
IF YOU DON'T HAVE THE STRENGTH TO FEND THEM OFF... YOU HAVE TO DEVELOP THE STRENGTH TO OVERCOME...

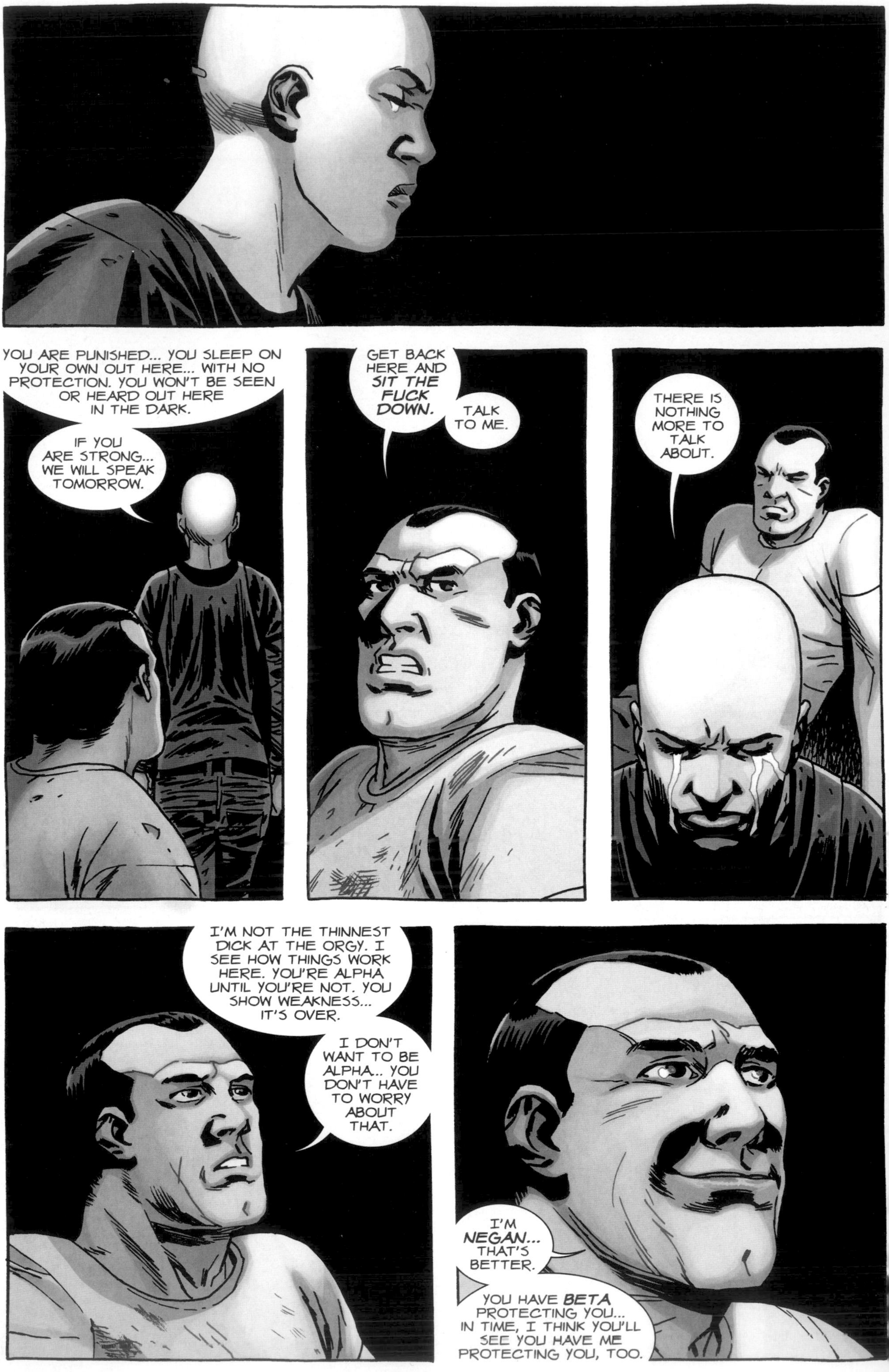
YOU ARE PUNISHED... YOU SLEEP ON YOUR OWN OUT HERE... WITH NO PROTECTION. YOU WON'T BE SEEN OR HEARD OUT HERE IN THE DARK.
IF YOU ARE STRONG... WE WILL SPEAK TOMORROW.
GET BACK HERE AND SIT THE FUCK DOWN.
TALK TO ME.
THERE IS NOTHING MORE TO TALK ABOUT.
I'M NOT THE THINNEST DICK AT THE ORGY. I SEE HOW THINGS WORK HERE. YOU'RE ALPHA UNTIL YOU'RE NOT. YOU SHOW WEAKNESS... IT'S OVER.
I DON'T WANT TO BE ALPHA... YOU DON'T HAVE TO WORRY ABOUT THAT.
I'M NEGAN... THAT'S BETTER.
YOU HAVE BETA PROTECTING YOU... IN TIME, I THINK YOU'LL SEE YOU HAVE ME PROTECTING YOU, TOO.

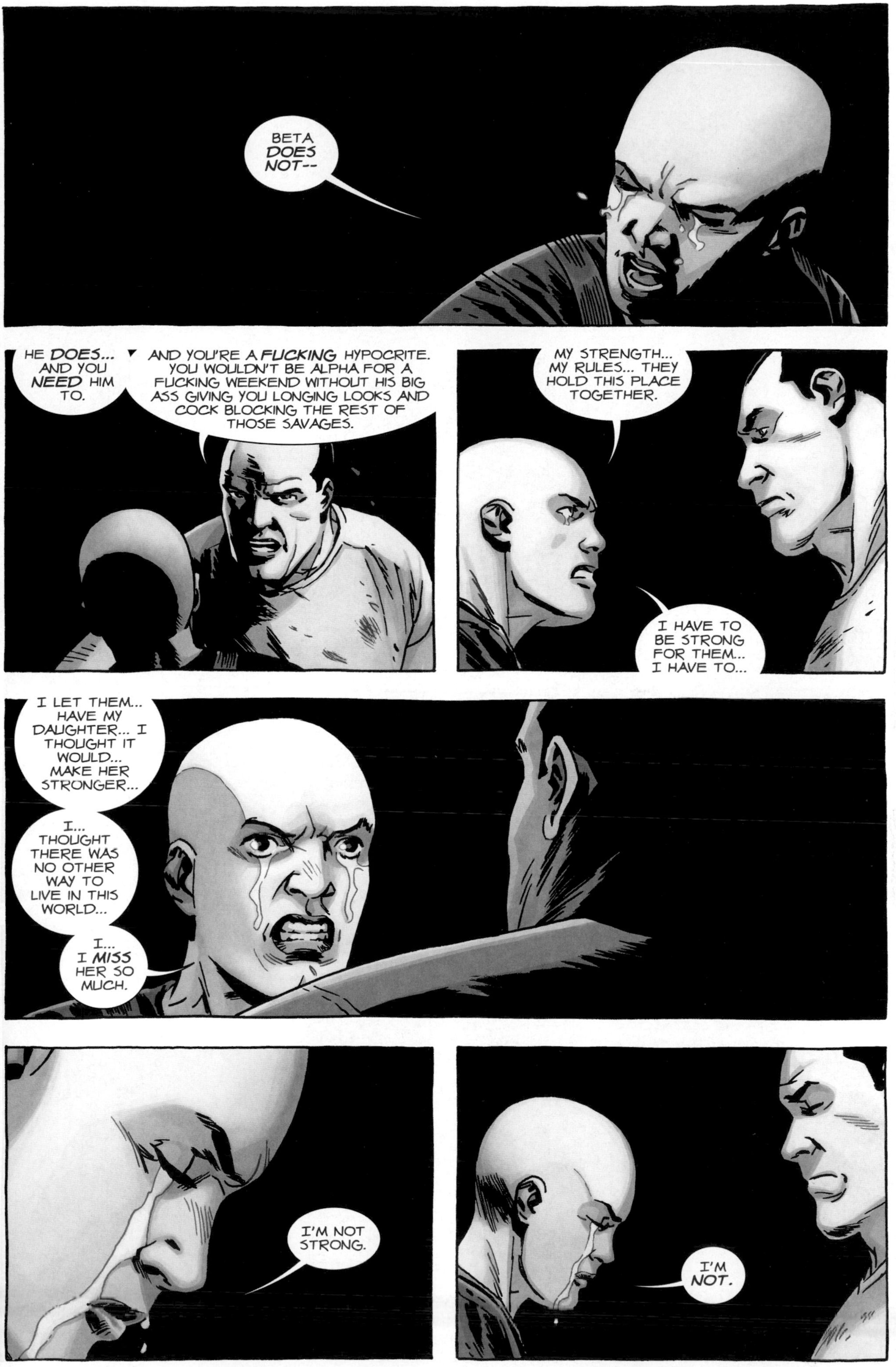

BETA DOES NOT--
HE DOES... AND YOU NEED HIM TO.
AND YOU'RE A FUCKING HYPOCRITE. YOU WOULDN'T BE ALPHA FOR A FUCKING WEEKEND WITHOUT HIS BIG ASS GIVING YOU LONGING LOOKS AND COCK BLOCKING THE REST OF THOSE SAVAGES.
MY STRENGTH... MY RULES... THEY HOLD THIS PLACE TOGETHER.
I HAVE TO BE STRONG FOR THEM... I HAVE TO...
I LET THEM... HAVE MY DAUGHTER... I THOUGHT IT WOULD... MAKE HER STRONGER...
I... THOUGHT THERE WAS NO OTHER WAY TO LIVE IN THIS WORLD...
I... I MISS HER SO MUCH.
I'M NOT STRONG.
I'M NOT.

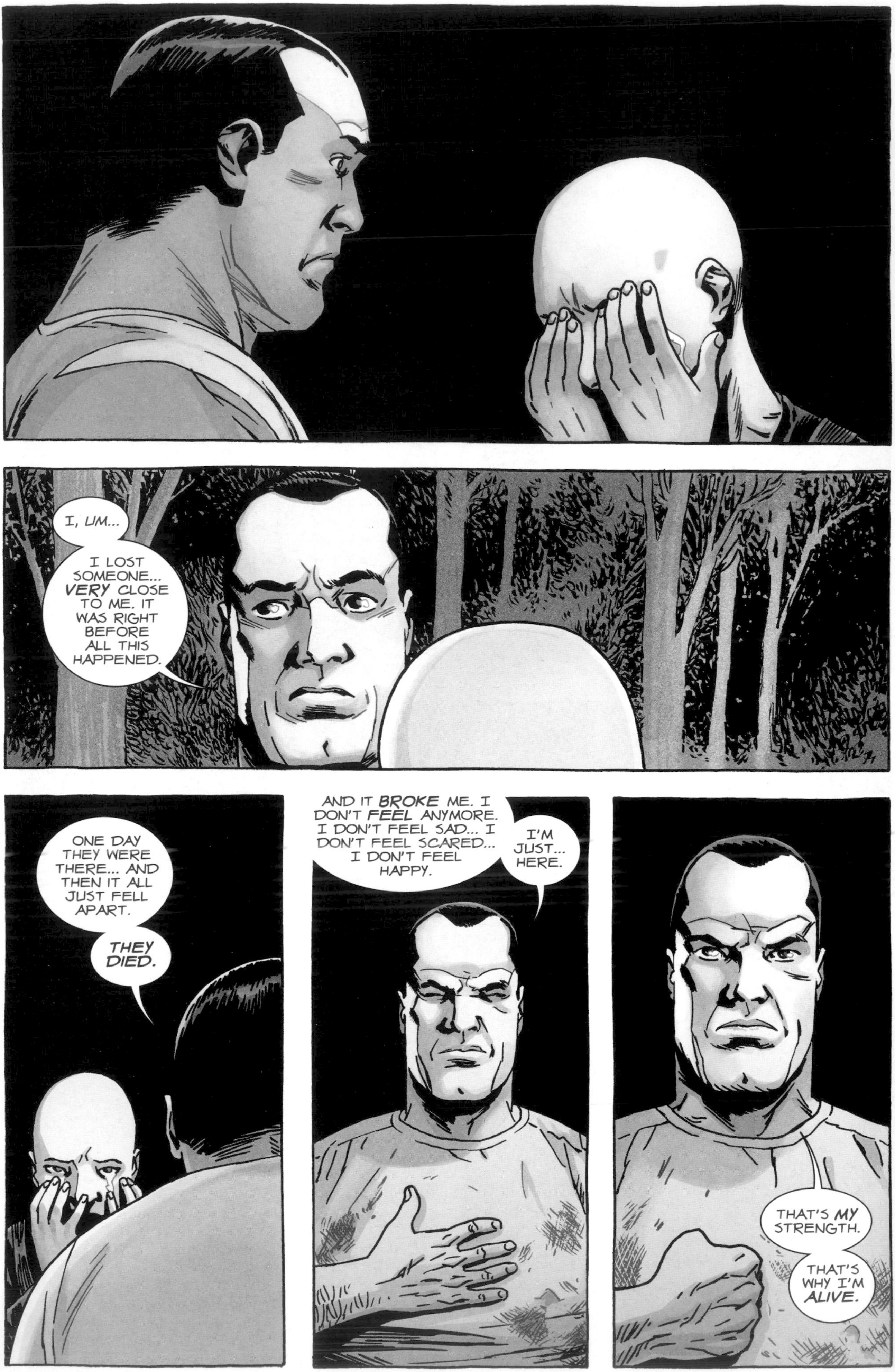
I, UM...
I LOST SOMEONE... VERY CLOSE TO ME. IT WAS RIGHT BEFORE ALL THIS HAPPENED.
ONE DAY THEY WERE THERE... AND THEN IT ALL JUST FELL APART.
THEY DIED.
AND IT BROKE ME. I DON'T FEEL ANYMORE. I DON'T FEEL SAD... I DON'T FEEL SCARED... I DON'T FEEL HAPPY.
I'M JUST... HERE.
THAT'S MY STRENGTH.
THAT'S WHY I'M ALIVE.

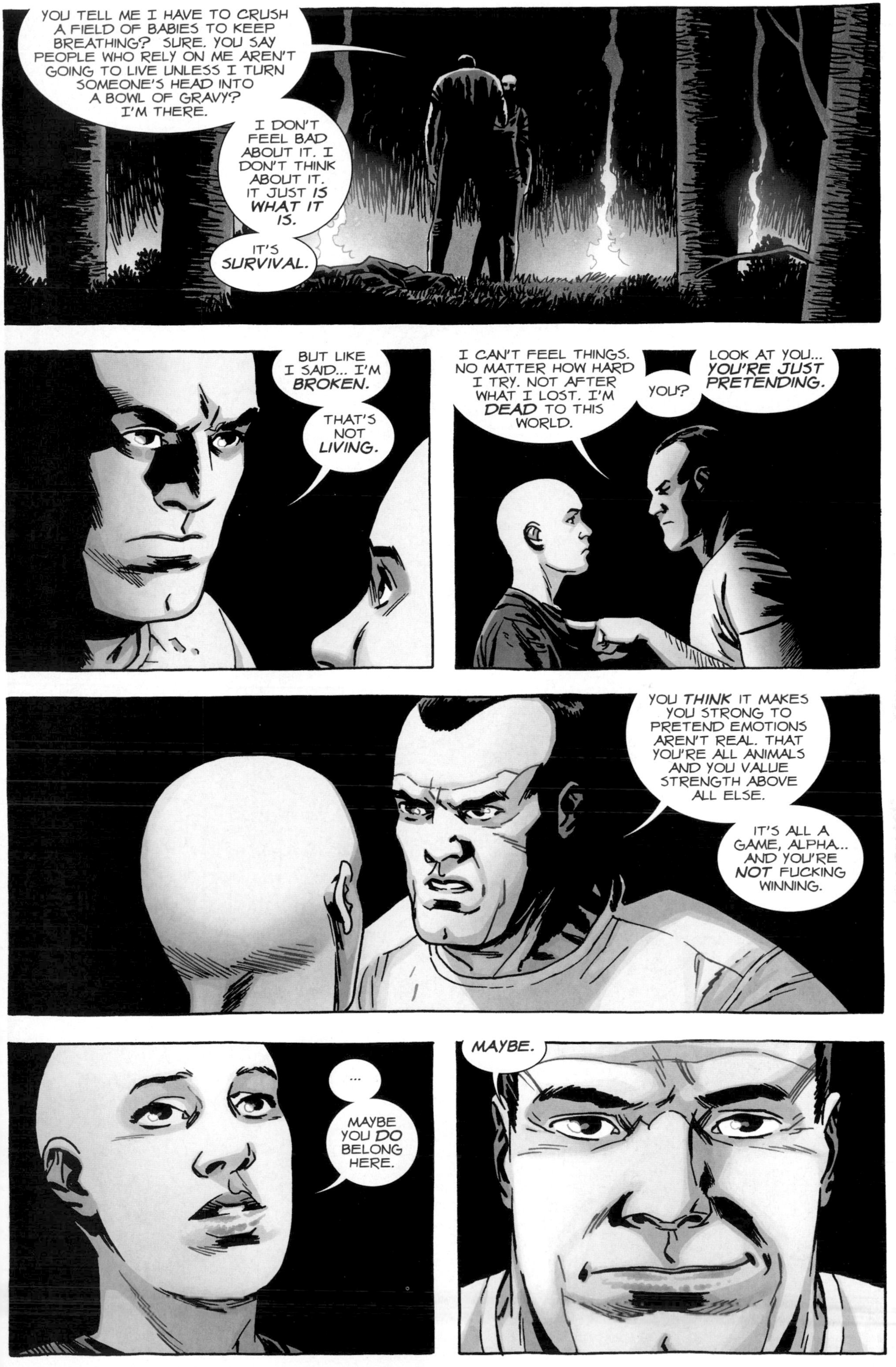
YOU TELL ME I HAVE TO CRUSH A FIELD OF BABIES TO KEEP BREATHING? SURE. YOU SAY PEOPLE WHO RELY ON ME AREN'T GOING TO LIVE UNLESS I TURN SOMEONE'S HEAD INTO A BOWL OF GRAVY? I'M THERE.
I DON'T FEEL BAD ABOUT IT. I DON'T THINK ABOUT IT. IT JUST IS WHAT IT IS.
IT'S SURVIVAL.
BUT LIKE I SAID... I'M BROKEN.
THAT'S NOT LIVING.
I CAN'T FEEL THINGS. NO MATTER HOW HARD I TRY. NOT AFTER WHAT I LOST. I'M DEAD TO THIS WORLD.
YOU?
LOOK AT YOU... YOU'RE JUST PRETENDING.
YOU THINK IT MAKES YOU STRONG TO PRETEND EMOTIONS AREN'T REAL. THAT YOU'RE ALL ANIMALS AND YOU VALUE STRENGTH ABOVE ALL ELSE.
IT'S ALL A GAME, ALPHA... AND YOU'RE NOT FUCKING WINNING.
...
MAYBE YOU DO BELONG HERE.
MAYBE.

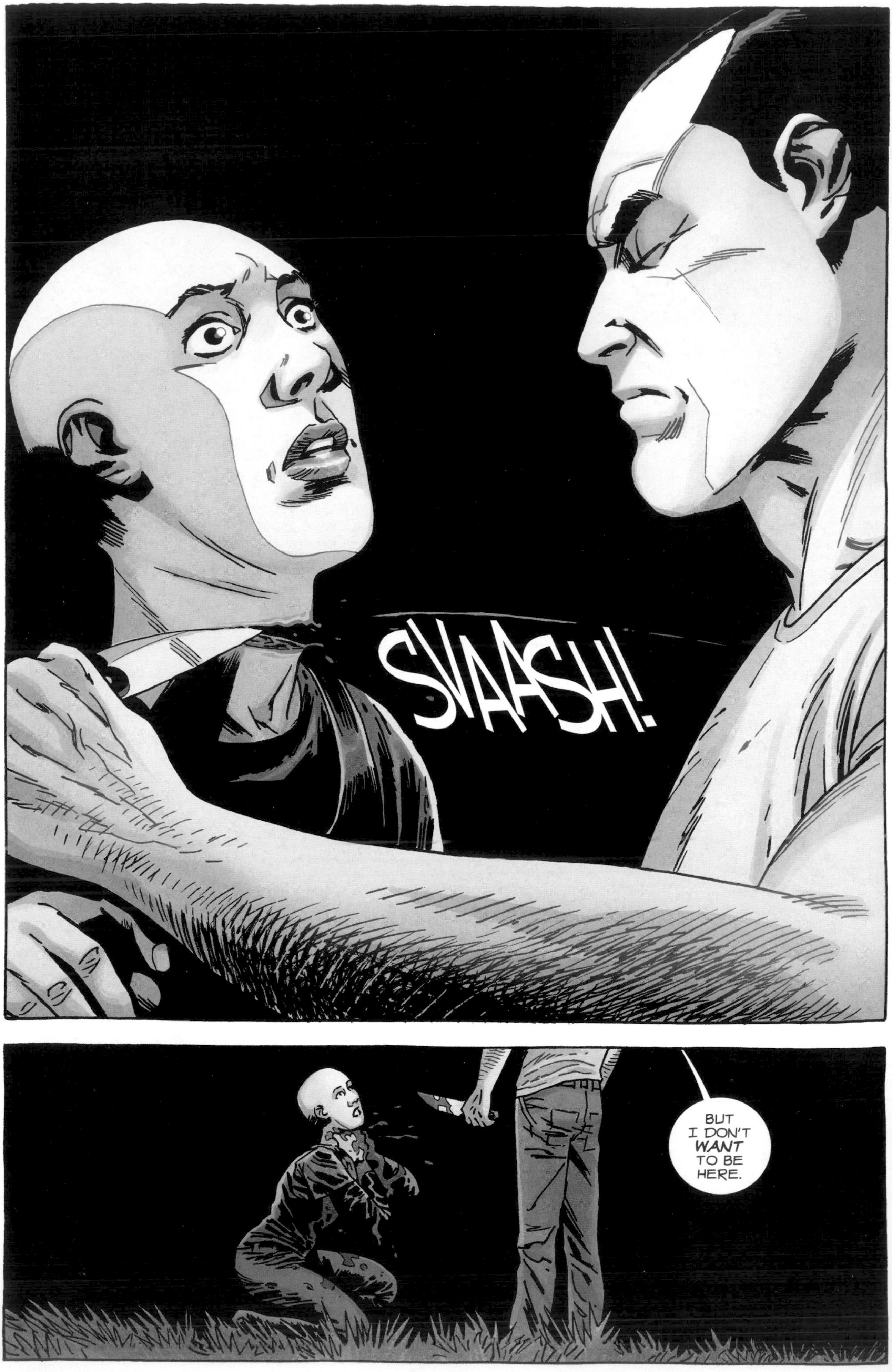
SVAASH!
BUT I DON'T WANT TO BE HERE.

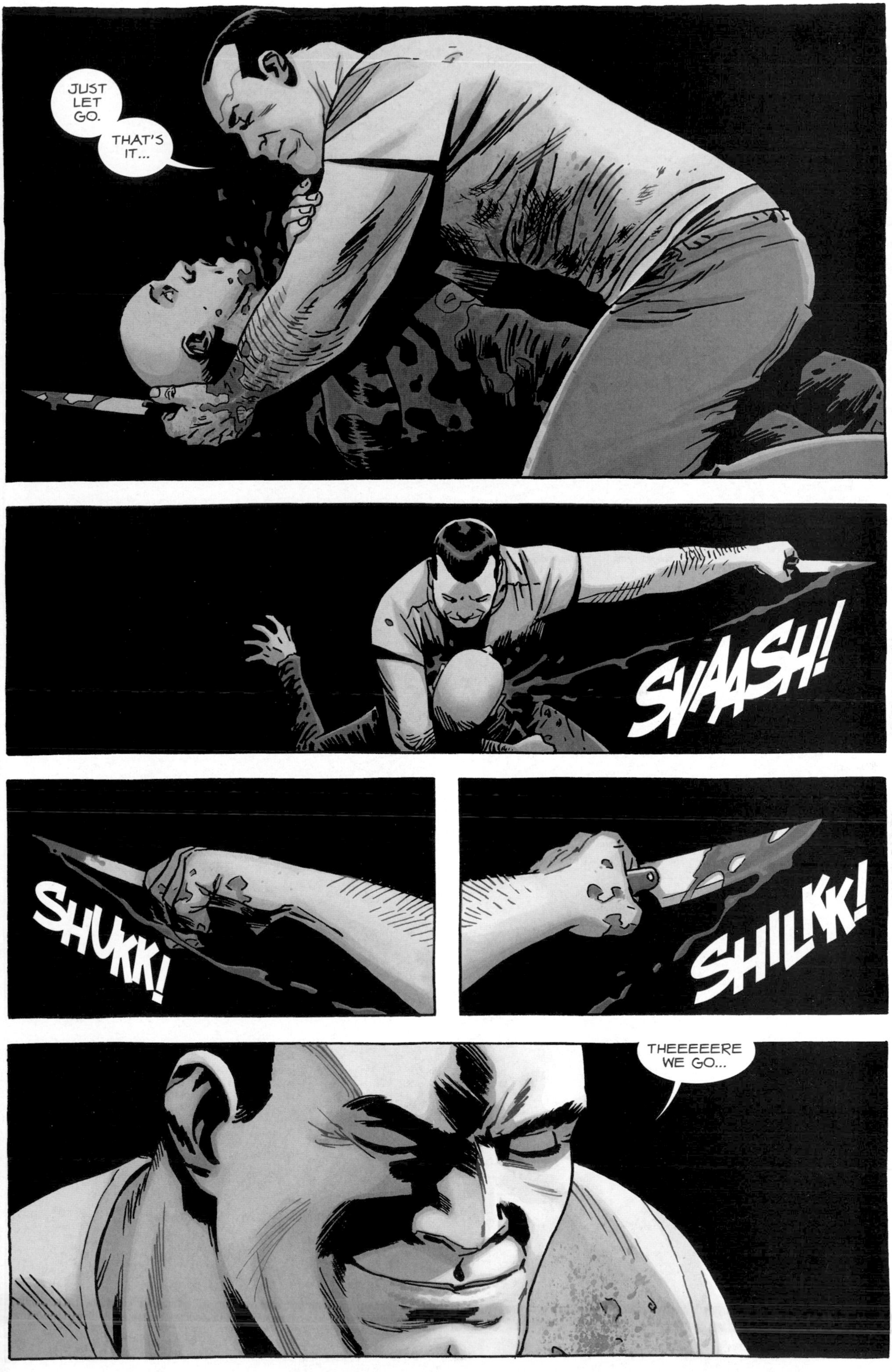
JUST LET GO.
THAT'S IT...
SVAASH!
SHUKK!
SHILKK!
THEEEEERE WE GO...

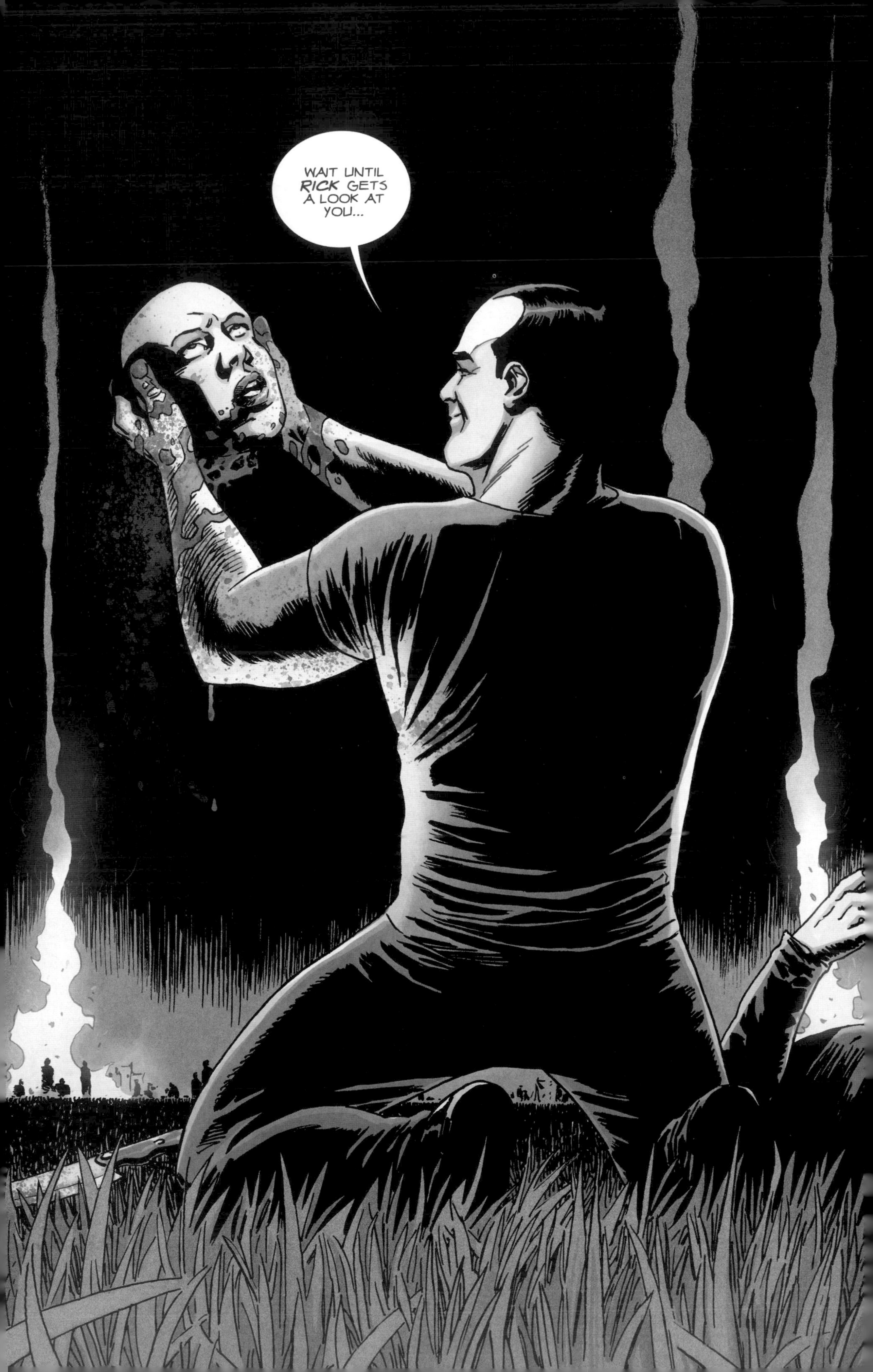
WAIT UNTIL RICK GETS A LOOK AT YOU...

to be continued...

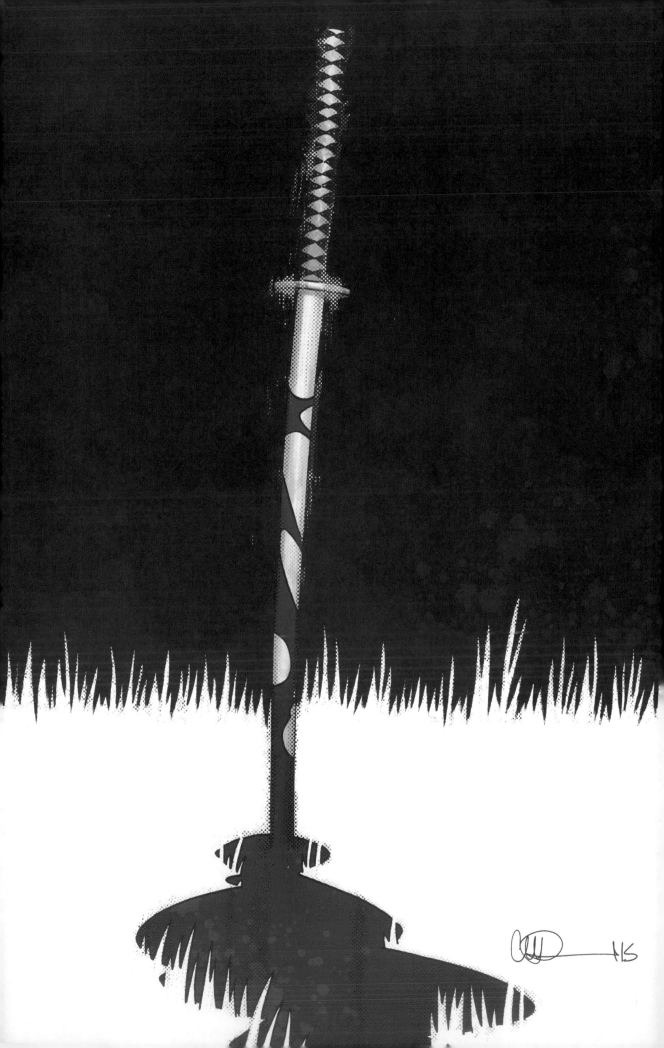

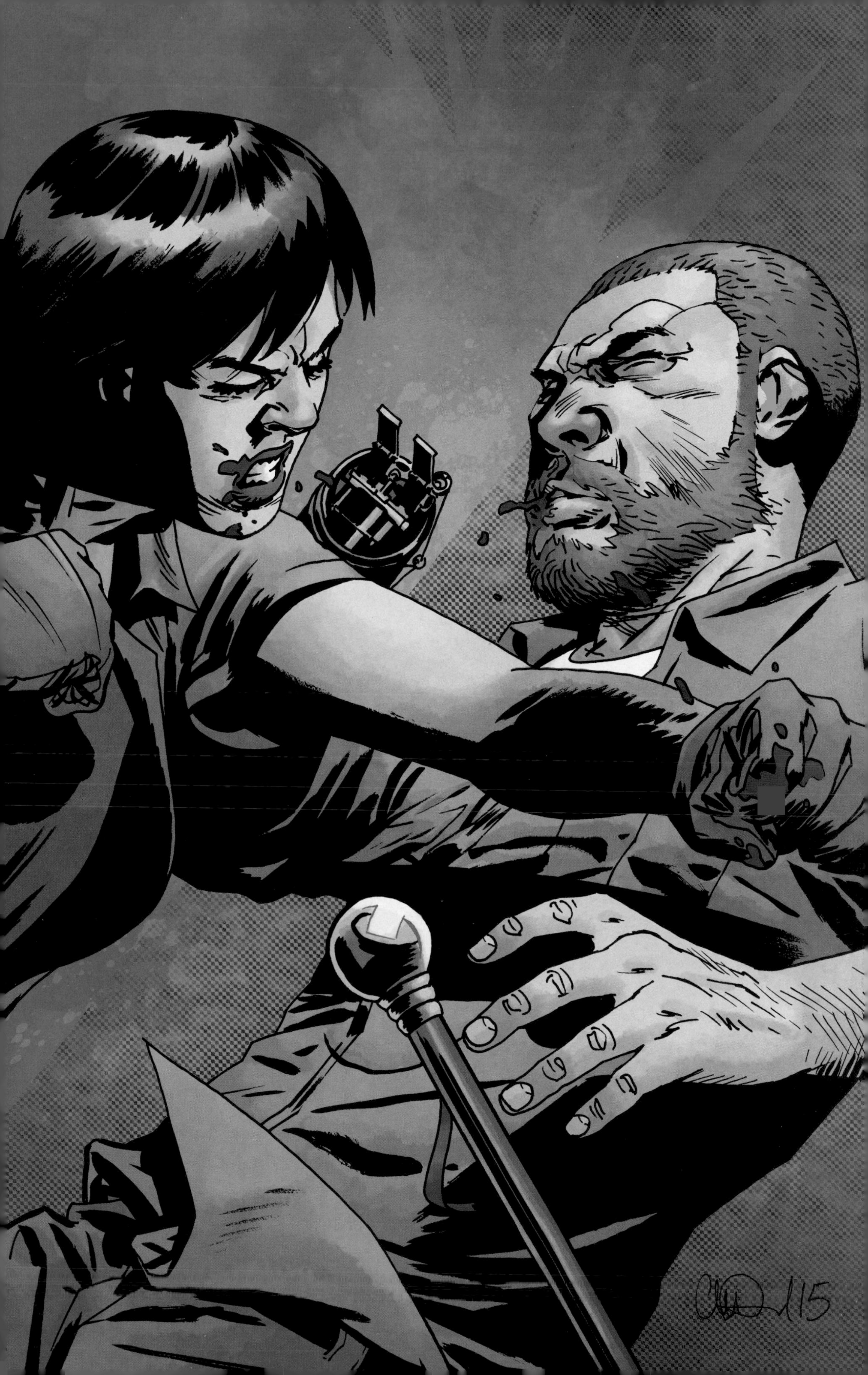

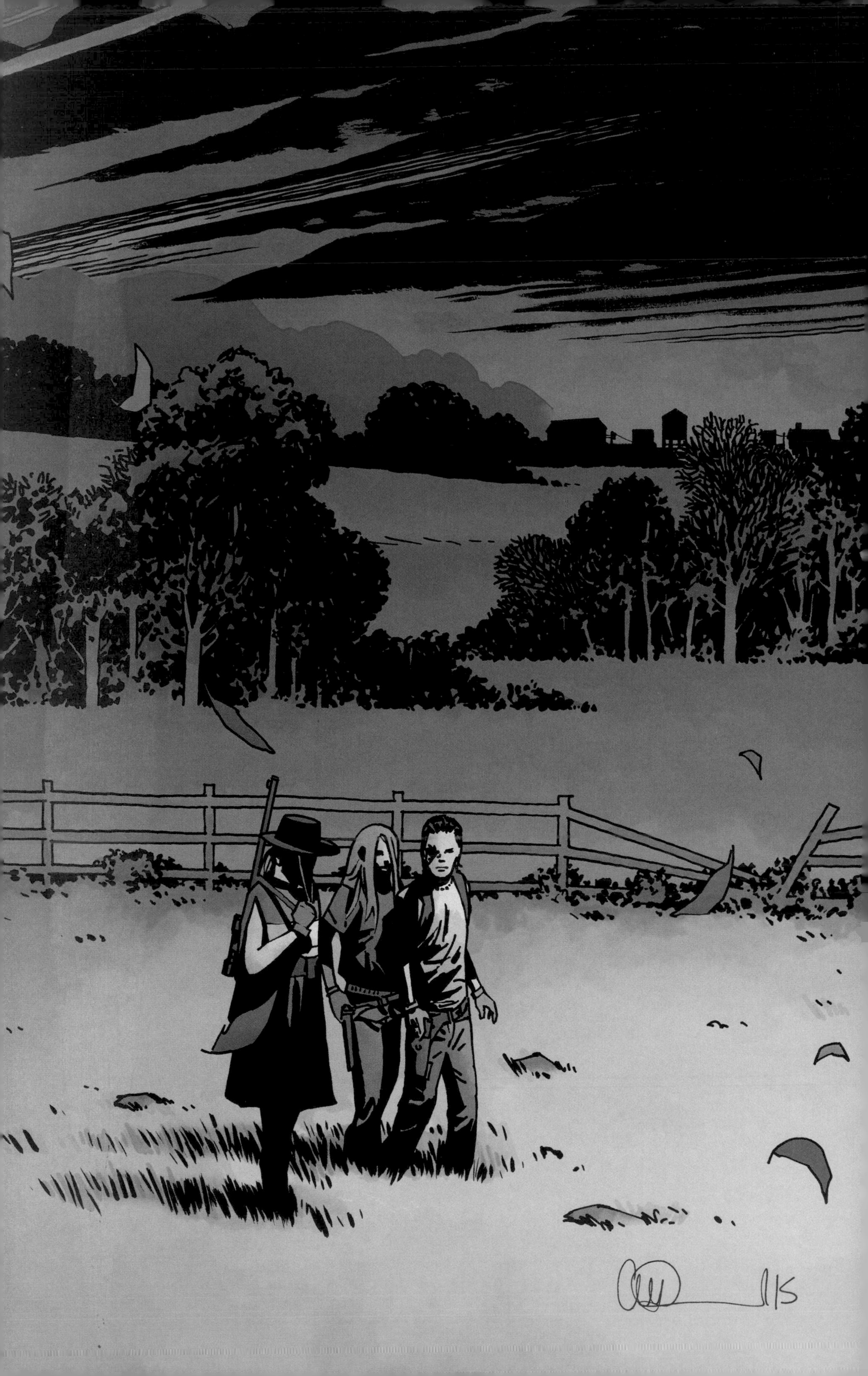

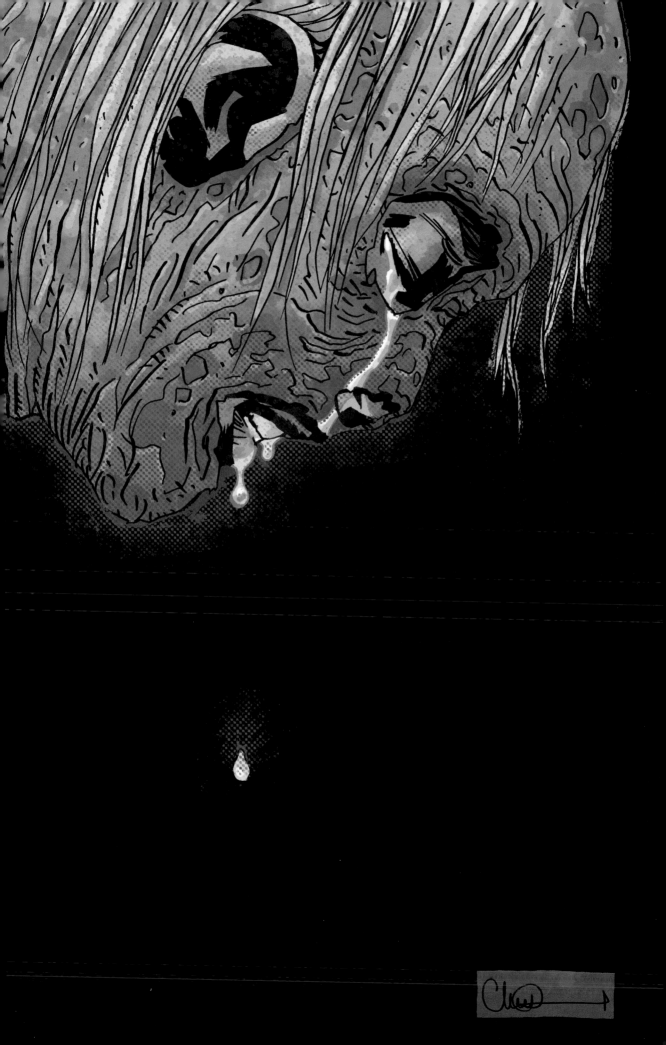

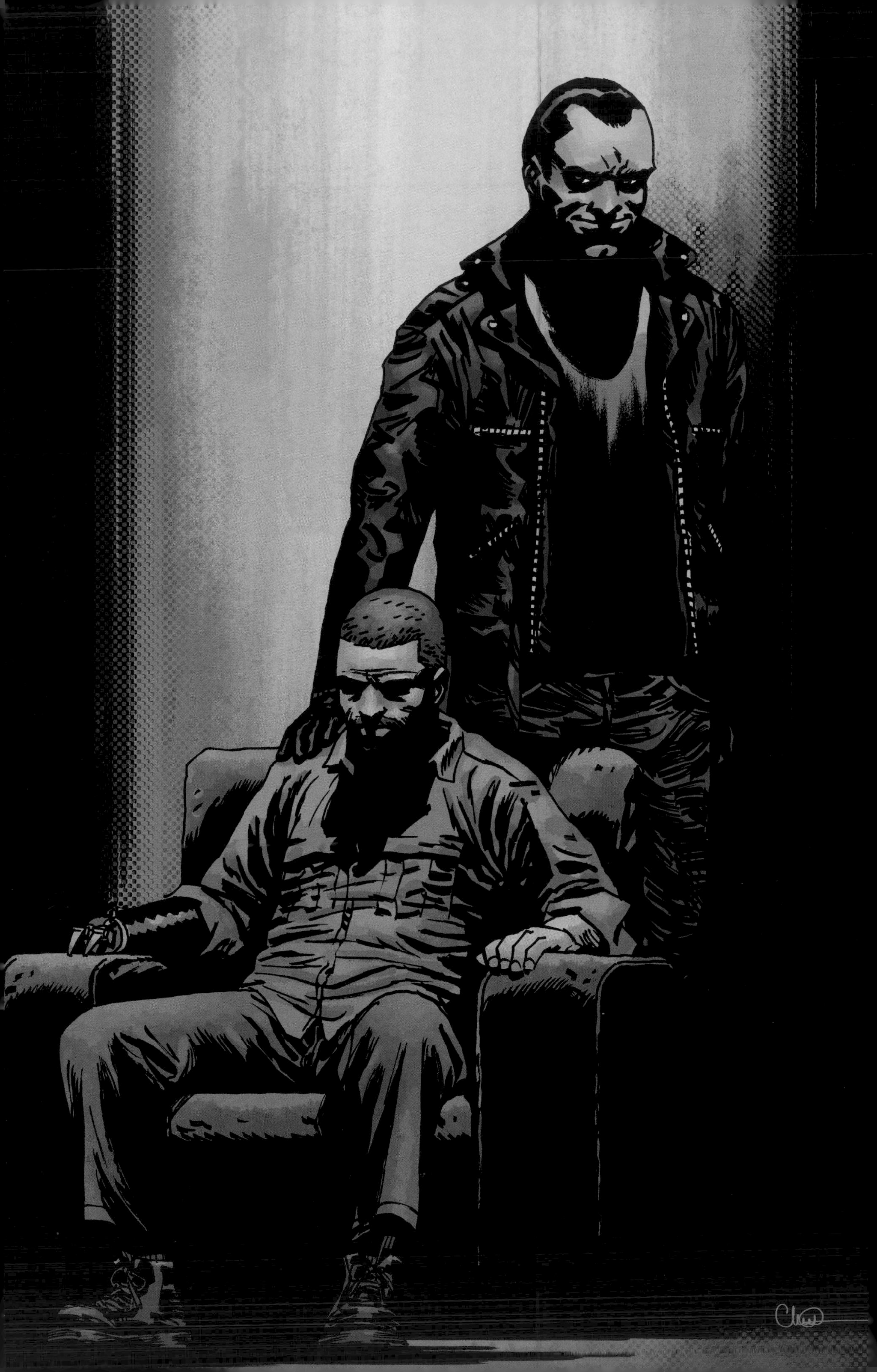

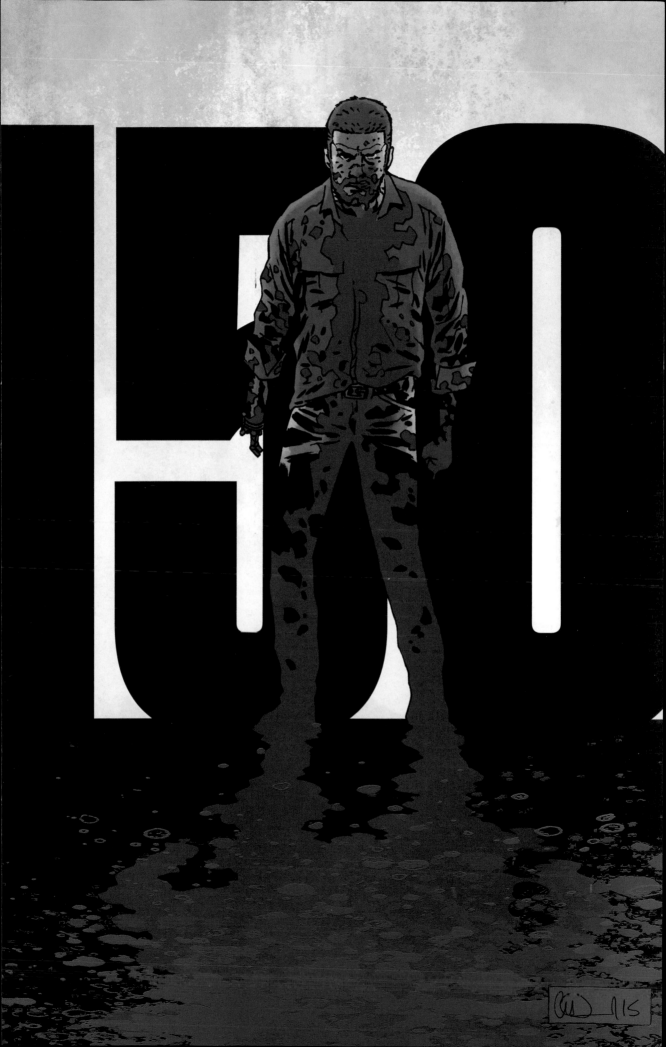

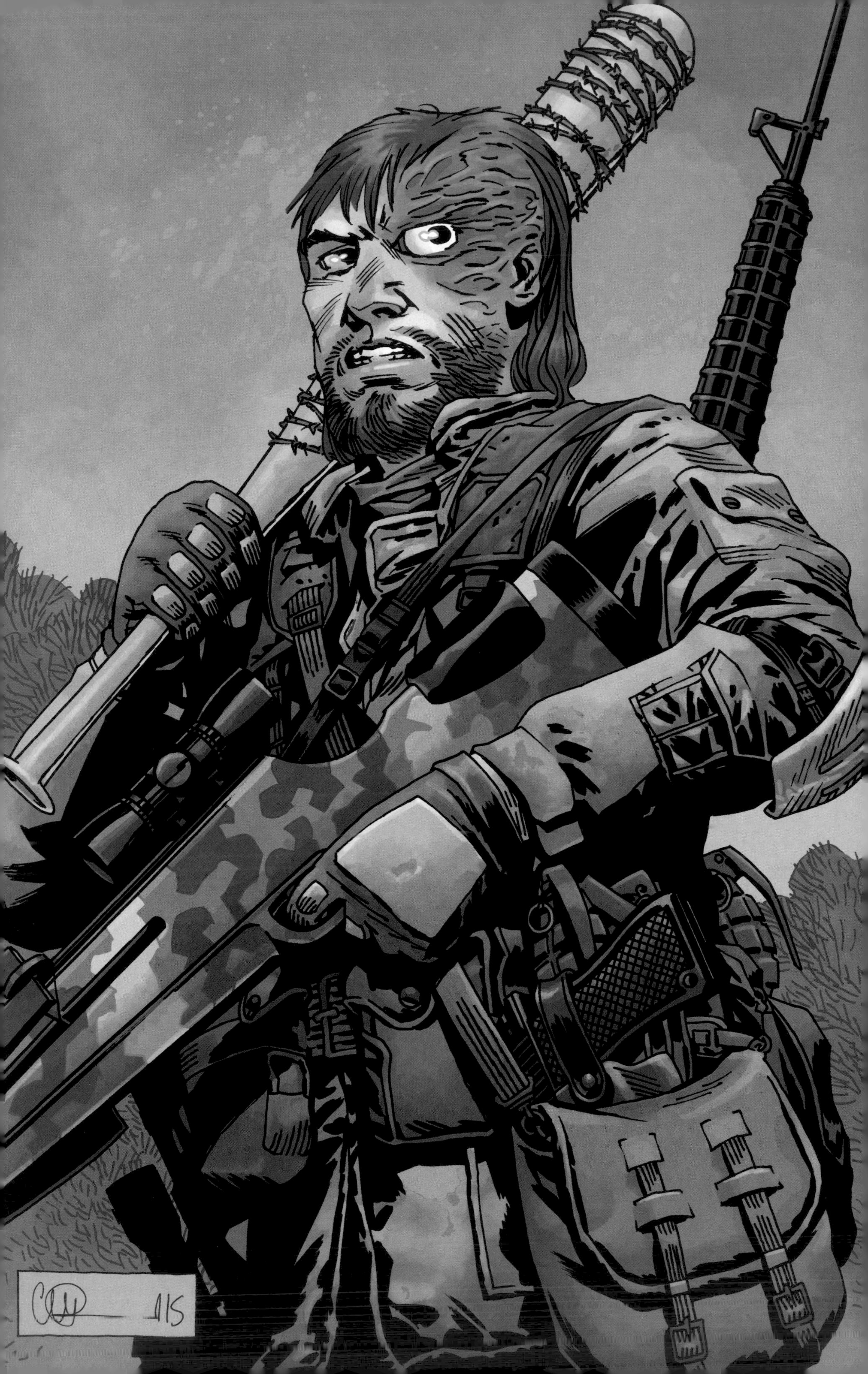

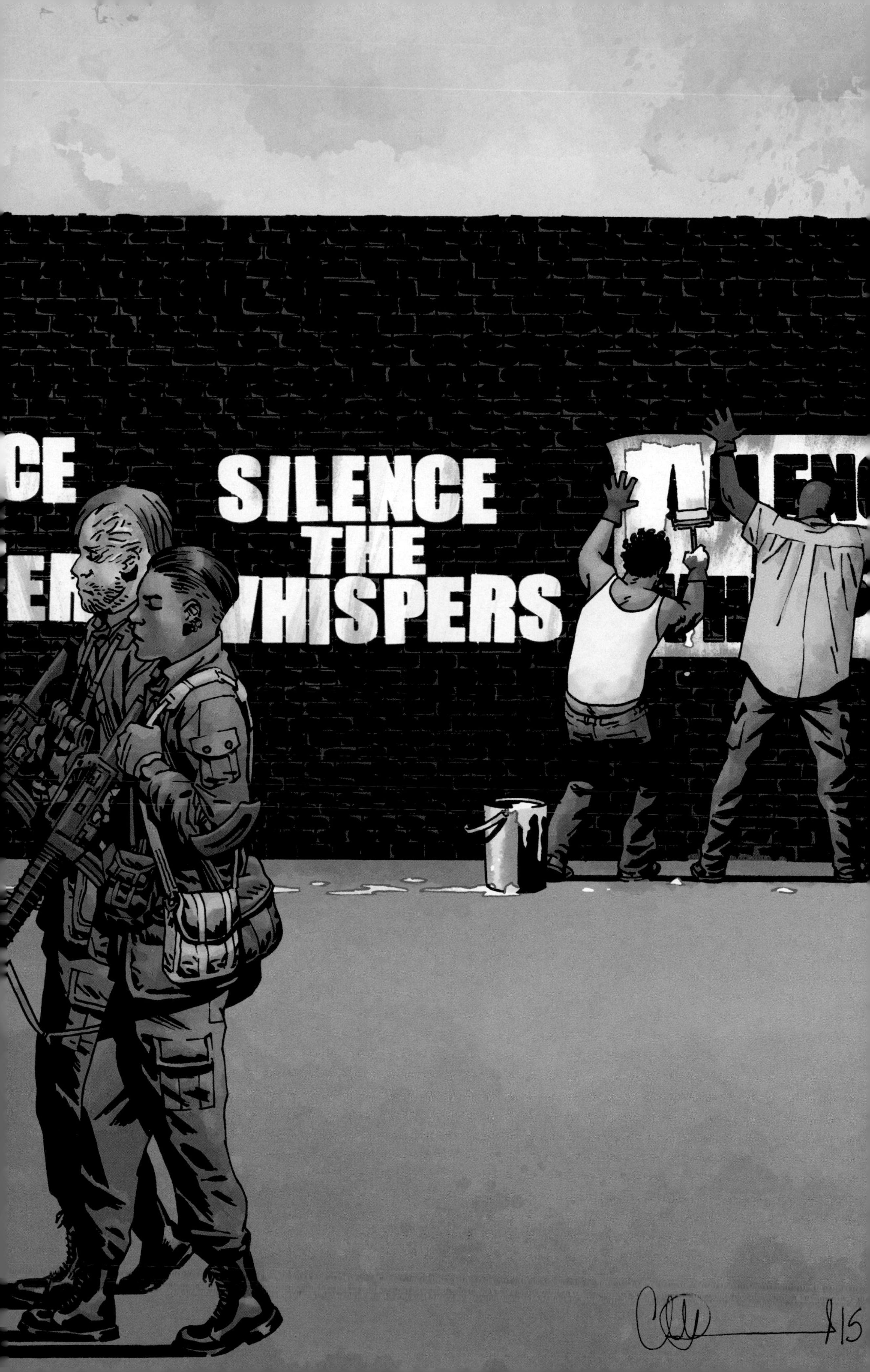
SILENCE
THE
WHISPERS

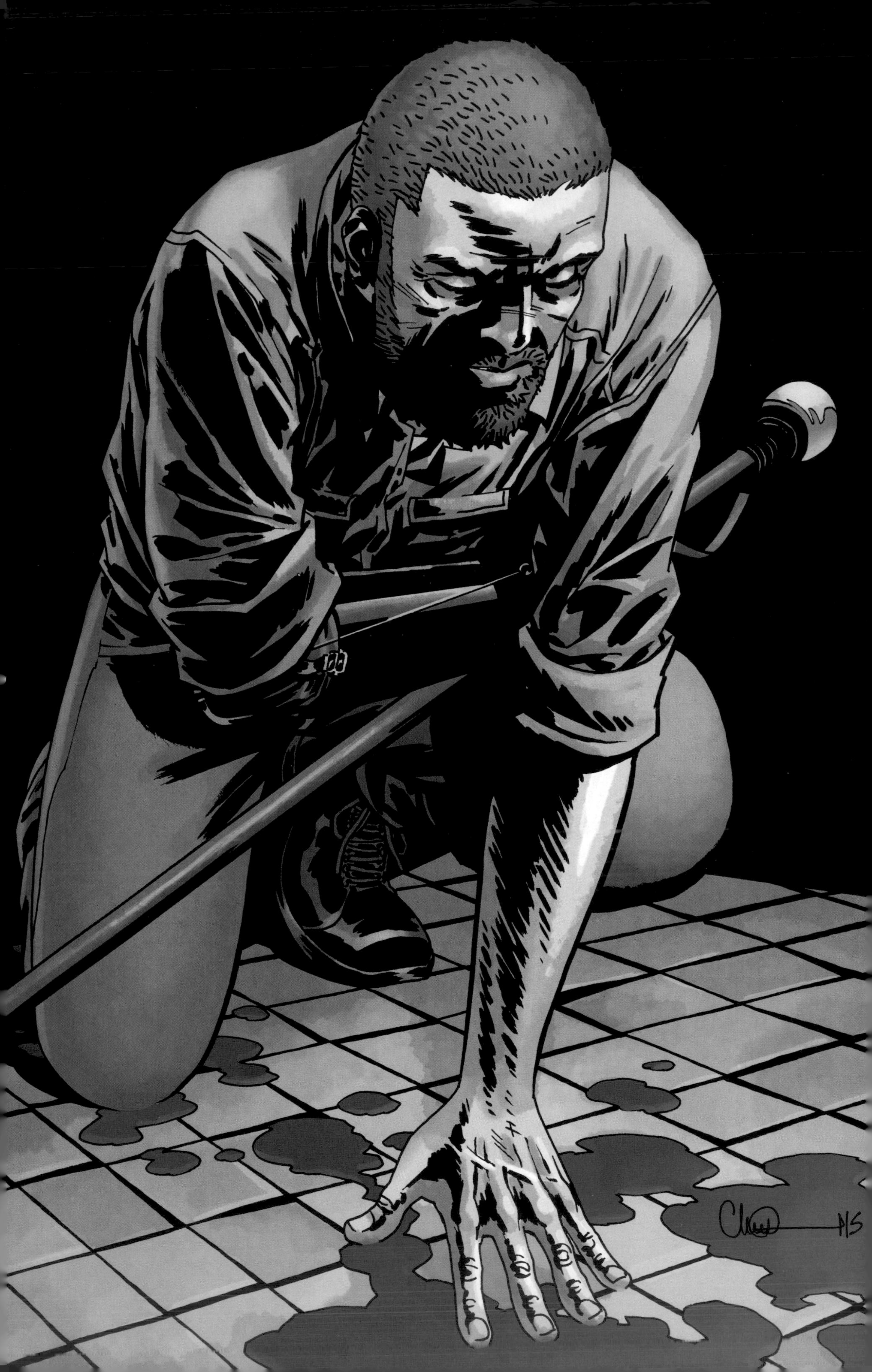

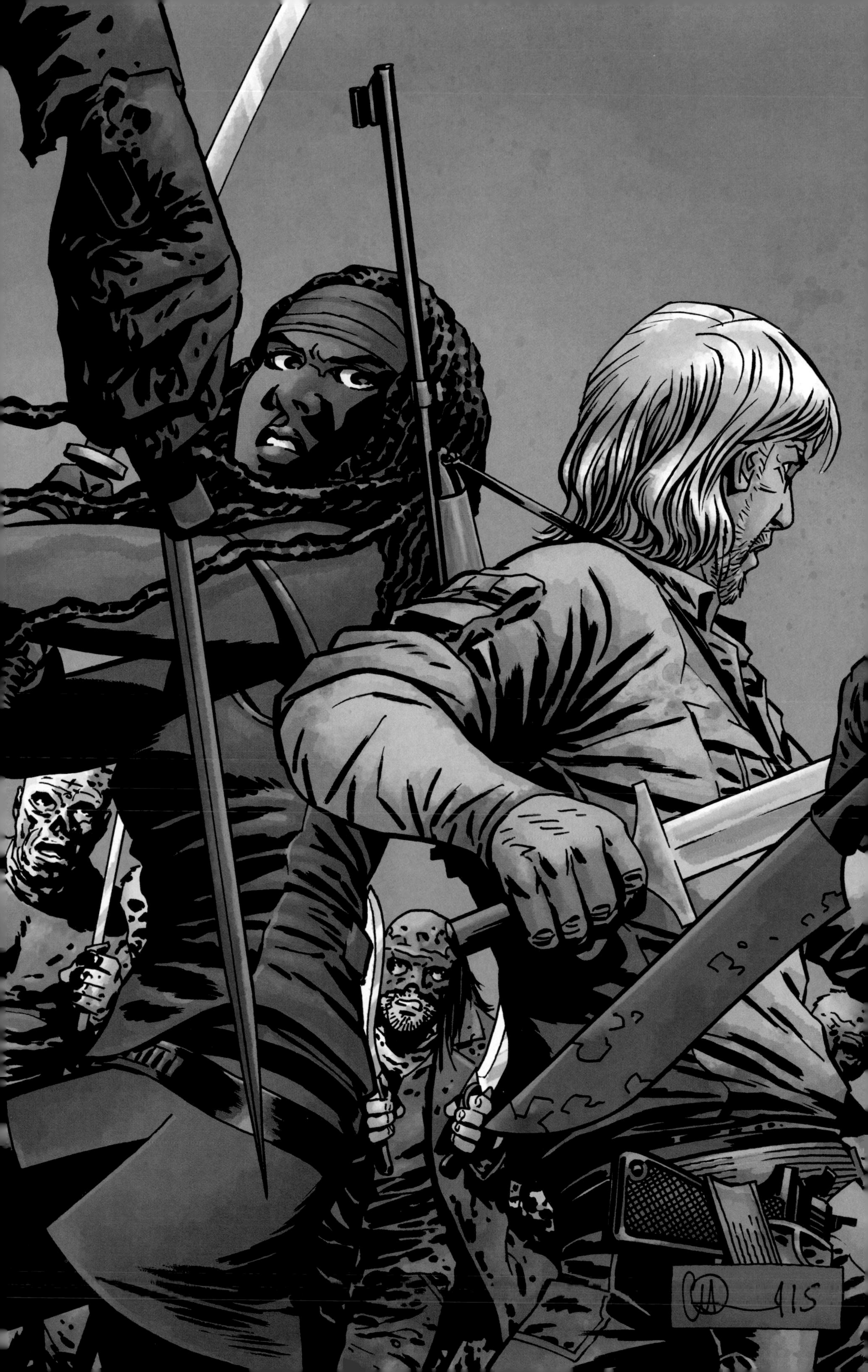

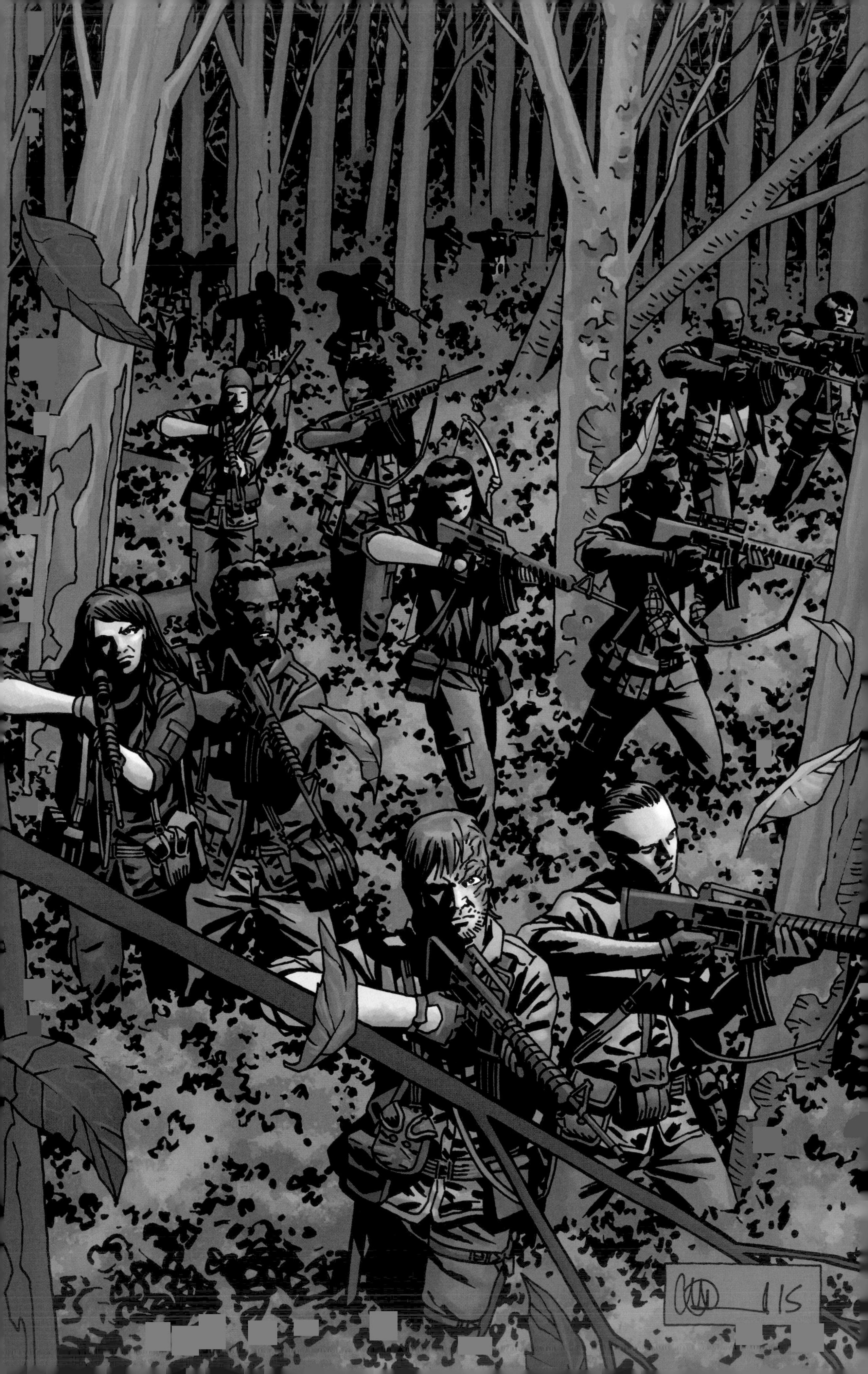

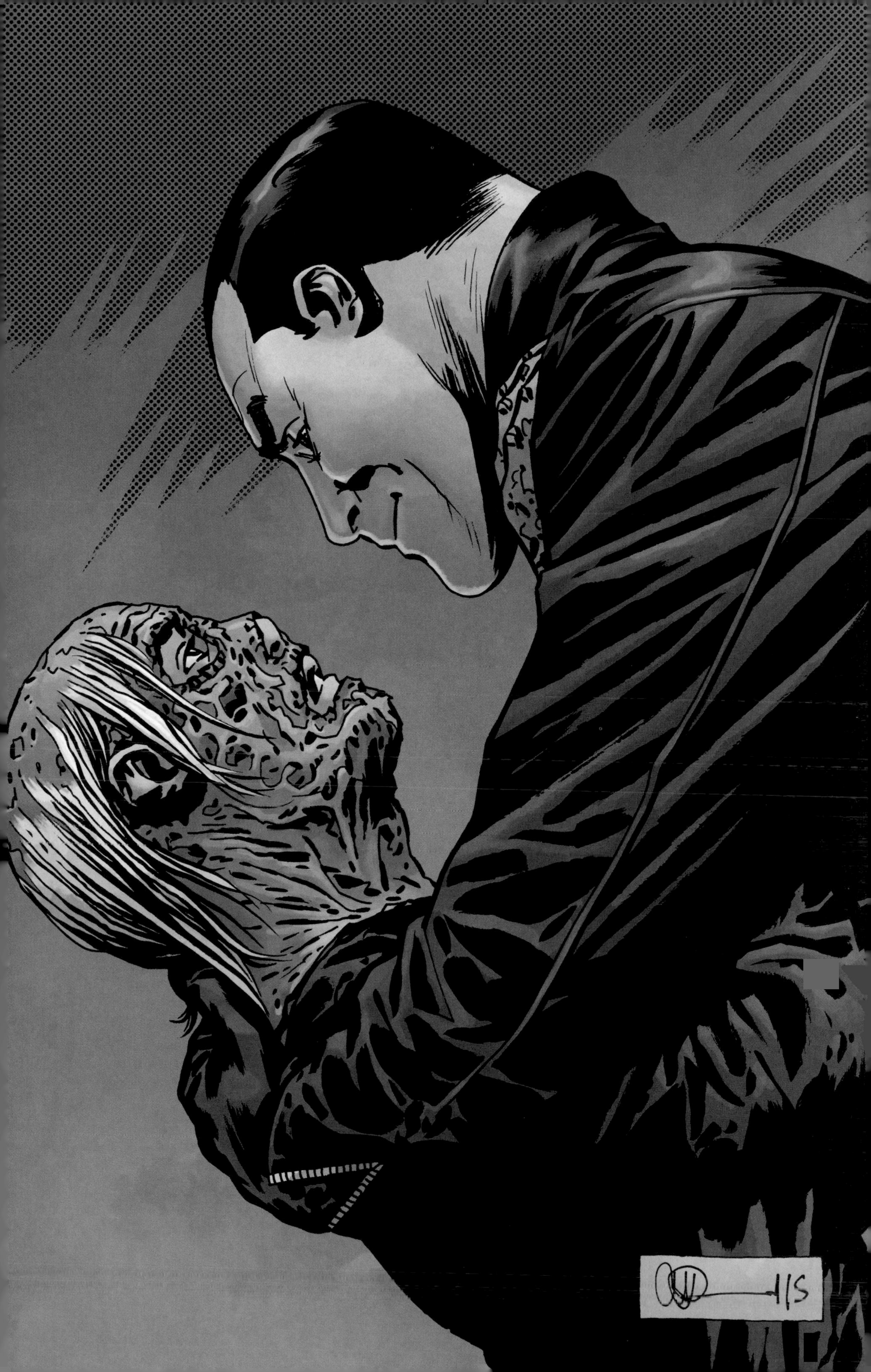
115

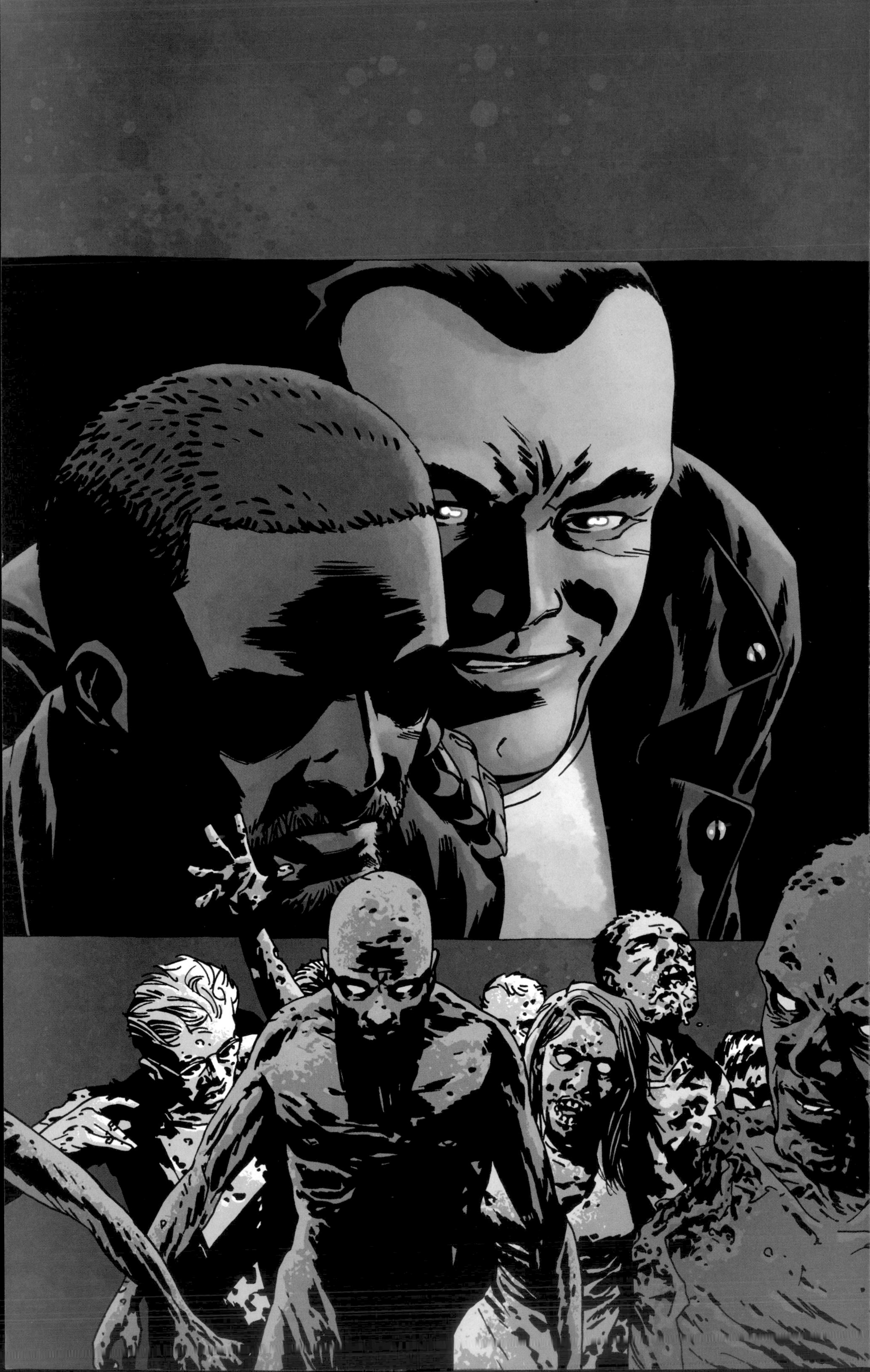

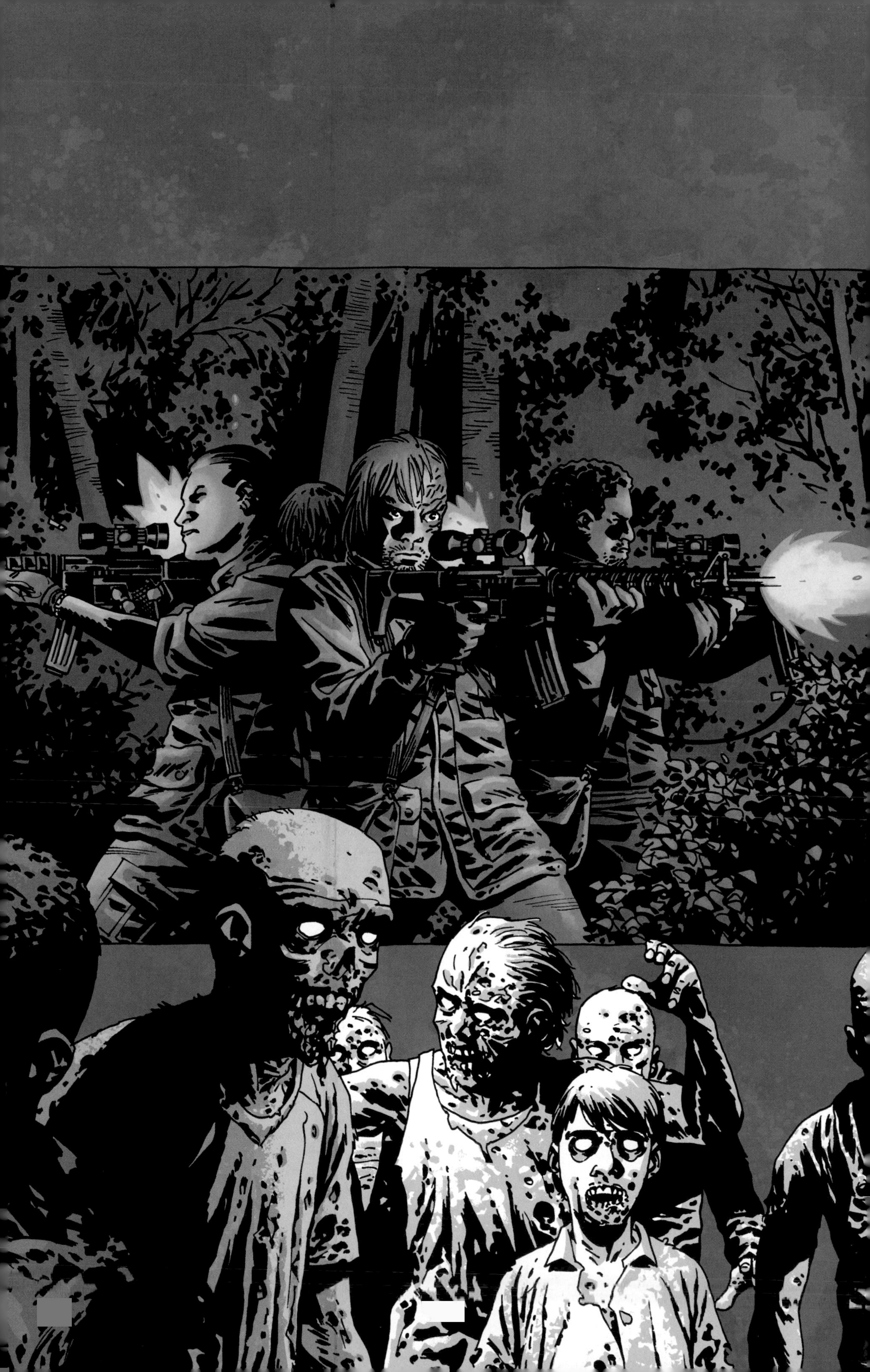

for more tales from ROBERT KIRKMAN and SKYBOUND

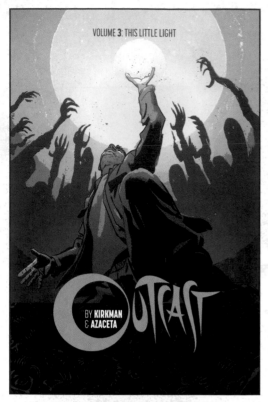

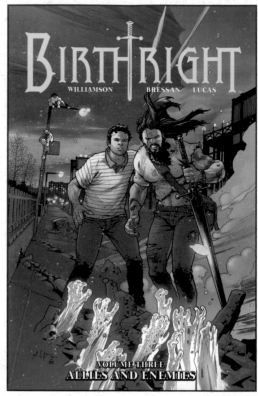

VOL. 1: A DARKNESS SURROUNDS HIM TP
ISBN: 978-1-63215-053-0
$9.99

VOL. 2: A VAST AND UNENDING RUIN TP
ISBN: 978-1-63215-448-4
$14.99

VOL. 3: THIS LITTLE LIGHT TP
ISBN: 978-1-63215-693-8
$14.99

VOL. 1: HOMECOMING TP
ISBN: 978-1-63215-231-2
$9.99

VOL. 2: CALL TO ADVENTURE TP
ISBN: 978-1-63215-446-0
$12.99

VOL. 3: ALLIES AND ENEMIES TP
ISBN: 978-1-63215-683-9
$12.99

VOL. 1: FIRST GENERATION TP
ISBN: 978-1-60706-683-5
$12.99

VOL. 2: SECOND GENERATION TP
ISBN: 978-1-60706-830-3
$12.99

VOL. 3: THIRD GENERATION TP
ISBN: 978-1-60706-939-3
$12.99

VOL. 4: FOURTH GENERATION TP
ISBN: 978-1-63215-036-3
$12.99

VOL. 1: HAUNTED HEIST TP
ISBN: 978-1-60706-836-5
$9.99

VOL. 2: BOOKS OF THE DEAD TP
ISBN: 978-1-63215-046-2
$12.99

VOL. 3: DEATH WISH TP
ISBN: 978-1-63215-051-6
$12.99

VOL. 4: GHOST TOWN TP
ISBN: 978-1-63215-317-3
$12.99

VOL. 1: FLORA & FAUNA TP
ISBN: 978-1-60706-982-9
$9.99

VOL. 2: AMPHIBIA & INSECTA TP
ISBN: 978-1-63215-052-3
$14.99

**VOL. 3: CHIROPTERA &
CARNIFORMAVES TP**
ISBN: 978-1-63215-397-5
$14.99

VOL. 1: "I QUIT."
ISBN: 978-1-60706-592-0
$14.99

VOL. 2: "HELP ME."
ISBN: 978-1-60706-676-7
$14.99

VOL. 3: "VENICE."
ISBN: 978-1-60706-844-0
$14.99

VOL. 4: "THE HIT LIST."
ISBN: 978-1-63215-037-0
$14.99

VOL. 5: "TAKE ME."
ISBN: 978-1-63215-401-9
$14.99

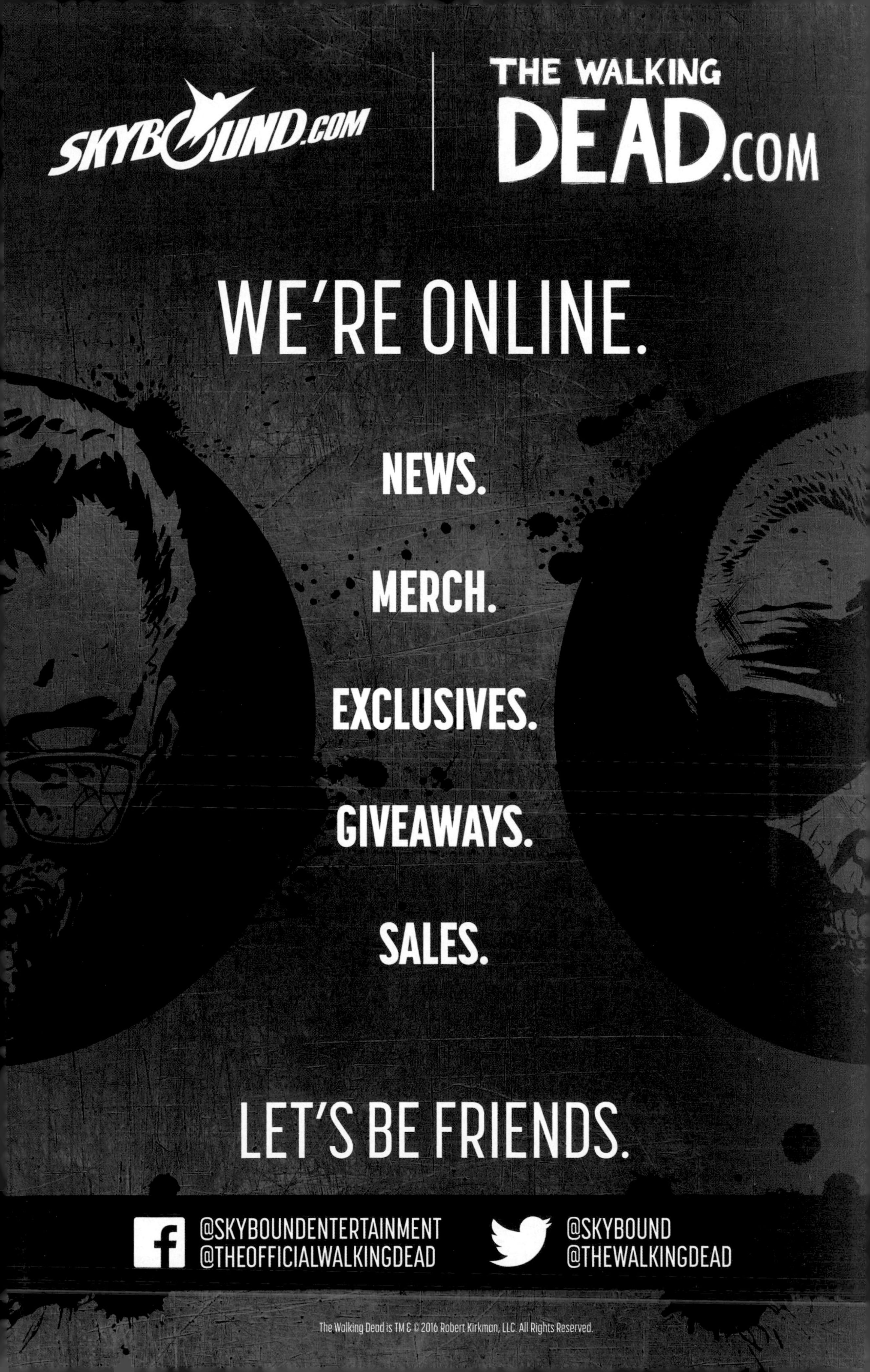
SKYBOUND.COM
THE WALKING DEAD.COM
WE'RE ONLINE.
NEWS.
MERCH.
EXCLUSIVES.
GIVEAWAYS.
SALES.
LET'S BE FRIENDS.
@SKYBOUNDENTERTAINMENT
@THEOFFICIALWALKINGDEAD
@SKYBOUND
@THEWALKINGDEAD
The Walking Dead is TM & © 2016 Robert Kirkman, LLC. All Rights Reserved.

FOR MORE OF THE WALKING DEAD

TRADEPAPERBACKS

ROBERT KIRKMAN TONY MOORE
THE WALKING DEAD
VOLUME 1
DAYS GONE BYE

VOL. 1: DAYS GONE BYE TP
ISBN: 978-1-58240-672-5
$14.99

VOL. 2: MILES BEHIND US TP
ISBN: 978-1-58240-775-3
$14.99

VOL. 3: SAFETY BEHIND BARS TP
ISBN: 978-1-58240-805-7
$14.99

VOL. 4: THE HEART'S DESIRE TP
ISBN: 978-1-58240-530-8
$14.99

VOL. 5: THE BEST DEFENSE TP
ISBN: 978-1-58240-612-1
$14.99

VOL. 6: THIS SORROWFUL LIFE TP
ISBN: 978-1-58240-684-8
$14.99

VOL. 7: THE CALM BEFORE TP
ISBN: 978-1-58240-828-6
$14.99

VOL. 8: MADE TO SUFFER TP
ISBN: 978-1-58240-883-5
$14.99

VOL. 9: HERE WE REMAIN TP
ISBN: 978-1-60706-022-2
$14.99

VOL. 10: WHAT WE BECOME TP
ISBN: 978-1-60706-075-8
$14.99

VOL. 11: FEAR THE HUNTERS TP
ISBN: 978-1-60706-181-6
$14.99

VOL. 12: LIFE AMONG THEM TP
ISBN: 978-1-60706-254-7
$14.99

VOL. 13: TOO FAR GONE TP
ISBN: 978-1-60706-329-2
$14.99

VOL. 14: NO WAY OUT TP
ISBN: 978-1-60706-392-6
$14.99

VOL. 15: WE FIND OURSELVES TP
ISBN: 978-1-60706-440-4
$14.99

VOL. 16: A LARGER WORLD TP
ISBN: 978-1-60706-559-3
$14.99

VOL. 17: SOMETHING TO FEAR TP
ISBN: 978-1-60706-615-6
$14.99

VOL. 18: WHAT COMES AFTER TP
ISBN: 978-1-60706-687-3
$14.99

VOL. 19: MARCH TO WAR TP
ISBN: 978-1-60706-818-1
$14.99

VOL. 20: ALL OUT WAR PART ONE TP
ISBN: 978-1-60706-882-2
$14.99

VOL. 21: ALL OUT WAR PART TWO TP
ISBN: 978-1-63215-030-1
$14.99

VOL. 22: A NEW BEGINNING TP
ISBN: 978-1-63215-041-7
$14.99

VOL. 23: WHISPERS INTO SCREAMS TP
ISBN: 978-1-63215-258-9
$14.99

VOL. 24: LIFE AND DEATH TP
ISBN: 978-1-63215-402-6
$14.99

VOL. 25: NO TURNING BACK TP
ISBN: 978-1-63215-612-9
$14.99

VOL. 26: CALL TO ARMS TP
ISBN: 978-1-63215-917-5
$14.99

VOL. 1: SPANISH EDITION TP
ISBN: 978-1-60706-797-9
$14.99

VOL. 2: SPANISH EDITION TP
ISBN: 978-1-60706-845-7
$14.99

VOL. 3: SPANISH EDITION TP
ISBN: 978-1-60706-883-9
$14.99

VOL. 4: SPANISH EDITION TP
ISBN: 978-1-63215-035-6
$14.99

HARDCOVERS

THE WALKING DEAD
BOOK ONE
a continuing story of survival horror.

BOOK ONE HC
ISBN: 978-1-58240-619-0
$34.99

BOOK TWO HC
ISBN: 978-1-58240-698-5
$34.99

BOOK THREE HC
ISBN: 978-1-58240-825-5
$34.99

BOOK FOUR HC
ISBN: 978-1-60706-000-0
$34.99

BOOK FIVE HC
ISBN: 978-1-60706-171-7
$34.99

BOOK SIX HC
ISBN: 978-1-60706-327-8
$34.99

BOOK SEVEN HC
ISBN: 978-1-60706-439-8
$34.99

BOOK EIGHT HC
ISBN: 978-1-60706-593-7
$34.99

BOOK NINE HC
ISBN: 978-1-60706-798-6
$34.99

BOOK TEN HC
ISBN: 978-1-63215-034-9
$34.99

BOOK ELEVEN HC
ISBN: 978-1-63215-271-8
$34.99

BOOK TWELVE HC
ISBN: 978-1-63215-451-4
$34.99

BOOK THIRTEEN HC
ISBN: 978-1-63215-916-8
$34.99

COMPENDIUMS

The ultimate edition of The New York Times bestseller!
THE WALKING DEAD
COMPENDIUM ONE
Robert Kirkman • Charlie Adlard • Tony Moore • Cliff Rathburn

COMPENDIUM TP, VOL. 1
ISBN: 978-1-60706-076-5
$59.99

COMPENDIUM TP, VOL. 2
ISBN: 978-1-60706-596-8
$59.99

COMPENDIUM TP, VOL. 3
ISBN: 978-1-63215-456-9
$59.99

SPECIALTY BOOKS

THE WALKING DEAD
THE COVERS

THE WALKING DEAD: THE COVERS, VOL. 1 HC
ISBN: 978-1-60706-002-4
$24.99

THE WALKING DEAD: ALL OUT WAR HC
ISBN: 978-1-63215-038-7
$34.99

THE WALKING DEAD COLORING BOOK
ISBN: 978-1-63215-774-4
$14.99

OMNIBUS

THE WALKING DEAD

OMNIBUS, VOL. 1
ISBN: 978-1-60706-503-6
$100.00

OMNIBUS, VOL. 2
ISBN: 978-1-60706-515-9
$100.00

OMNIBUS, VOL. 3
ISBN: 978-1-60706-330-8
$100.00

OMNIBUS, VOL. 4
ISBN: 978-1-60706-616-3
$100.00

OMNIBUS, VOL. 5
ISBN: 978-1-63215-042-4
$100.00

OMNIBUS, VOL. 6
ISBN: 978-1-63215-521-4
$100.00

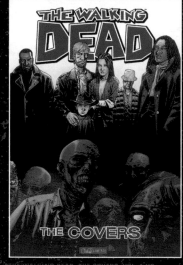

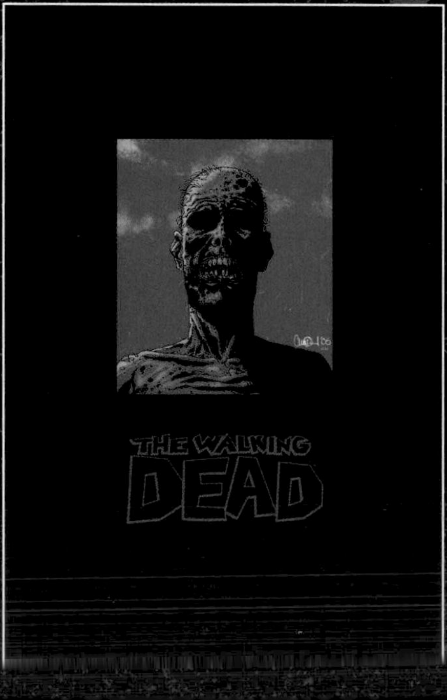